THE
PLAYBOY®
INTERVIEWS

THE
PLAYBOY®
INTERVIEWS

THEY PLAYED THE GAME

EDITED BY STEPHEN RANDALL AND
THE EDITORS OF *PLAYBOY* MAGAZINE

PRESS™
Milwaukie

M Press
10956 SE Main Street
Milwaukie, OR 97222
mpressbooks.com

Portions of this book are reprinted from issues of *Playboy* magazine.
Cover and series design by Tina Alessi and Lia Ribacchi

Library of Congress Cataloging-in-Publication Data

The Playboy interviews : they played the game / edited by Stephen Randall and the editors of Playboy magazine.-- 1st m press ed.
    p. cm. -- (The Playboy interviews)
  Includes index.
  ISBN-13: 978-1-59582-046-4
  ISBN-10: 1-59582-046-9
  1. Athletes--Interviews. I. Randall, Stephen. II. Playboy (Chicago, Ill.) III. Series.
  GV697.A1P553 2005
  796.092'2--dc22

2006002235

ISBN 10: 1-59582-046-9
ISBN 13: 978-1-59582-046-4
First M Press Edition: June 2006

10 9 8 7 6 5 4 3 2 1

Printed in U.S.A.
Distributed by Publishers Group West

CONTENTS

INTRODUCTION

By Stephen Randall
Deputy Editor, Playboy
magazine

These are not your father's sports pages. The names in this volume are familiar and, yes, they are hardly strangers to the public spotlight. They are some of the most famous and influential men and women from the world of sports—and they've lived much of their lives with a TV camera nearby. Yet you're about to enjoy a different, more revealing look at them—unlike anything you've experienced in other media.

In the world of journalism, the *Playboy Interview* is unique. It is the only monthly magazine feature that allows important people from various walks of life to engage in a lengthy, intelligent and unpredictable conversation about a variety of subjects. When athletes are interviewed regularly—almost daily, in some cases—they become media savvy and speak in often banal sound bites that serve as little more than filler for local newscasts. Or, at best, they are the subject of longer profiles that are so skewed by the writer's bias and ego that we learn more about the author than we do the subject. Rarely do sports stars get the opportunity to speak in depth in their own words, answering intelligent questions from an interviewer who—unlike a talk show host or many sports writers—remains in the background, introducing topics and guiding the conversation, but always allowing the person answering the questions to occupy center stage.

That's how Hugh Hefner envisioned the *Playboy Interview* back in 1962. *Playboy* magazine was then eight years old, and Hef was shown a partial manuscript by a young writer named Alex Haley. The manuscript was actually a transcript of an interview Haley had done with jazz great Miles Davis. Hef was struck by two things—Davis' fiery intelligence and the fact that the transcript didn't focus strictly on music, but gave Davis a chance to share his views on race, the government and society. Hef dispatched Haley to continue interviewing Davis, and ran the edited transcript as the first *Playboy Interview*. Monthly interviews followed with some of the most significant figures in the twentieth and twenty-first centuries, from Jimmy Carter, Bill Gates and Saul Bellow, to Fidel Castro, Jack Nicholson and Orson Welles.

Playboy's long love affair with sports has provided some of the most memorable *Playboy Interviews*. Following the lead set by Alex Haley and Miles Davis, these interviews are unlike the sports coverage done by newspapers, other magazines and TV. You will get a sense of the true personalities behind the famous names, as if you, not the interviewer, were sitting in the room having an intense conversation. It's an unusual reading experience. These are people you may think you know well. Get ready to meet them for the first time.

THE
PLAYBOY®
INTERVIEWS

HENRY AARON

A candid conversation with base-ball's record-breaking slugger

Baseball is still mainly an American game, but the whole world knows about the flamboyant Babe Ruth and his supposedly unbreakable home-run record. It took the world long enough to notice him, but by now everybody also knows that Henry Louis "Hank" Aaron, long-time outfielder for the Atlanta Braves, is about to break that record. And everybody knows that Aaron has been functioning lately under incredible pressure. Everything he does, on or off the diamond, makes headlines; camera crews and reporters follow his every move, and when he hits the record-breaking shot—if he hasn't by now—they're going to interrupt whatever program you're watching in order to bring you the news.

During the 1973 season, there was also a lot of publicity given to the hate mail, and threats on his life, that Aaron was receiving from people who, for one reason or another, didn't want anyone—especially a black man—to break Ruth's record. What's been lost, amid all the excitement, is the fact that Aaron didn't just come from nowhere to threaten the Babe. Breaking that record is like carving a statue out of a mountain, and Aaron has been chipping away at it over a 20-year span in the big leagues, during most of which he was both underpubli-cized and underpaid. Along the way, he has amassed some remarkable statistics—including several dozen records—none of which seemed to upset the known universe the way his assault on Ruth's home-run total has. He's gotten more hits than any right-handed batter in history. He's tops in total bases and runs batted in. He was the first man ever to get both 500 home runs and 3000 hits—and only the ninth player in baseball history to reach the latter figure. He's won three Golden Glove awards for his defense work. He's had more at bats than anyone but Ty Cobb. And, despite various injuries, he's had 14 seasons in which he played at least 150 games. Perhaps nothing attests to Aaron's consistency and staying power more than the fact that he's never hit 50 home runs in a season—and, early in his career, wasn't really considered a power hitter.

On the other hand, a 12-and-a-half-pound baby figures to become a power hitter; that's what Aaron weighed when he was born on February 5, 1934 in Mobile, Alabama. His father, Herbert, somehow managed to put three of his eight kids through college, despite his meager salary as a rivet-bucker in a shipyard. Henry, though, just wanted to play ball. They didn't have baseball teams at Central High, nor at Josephine Allen, a private school where he finished his secondary education—so he played football instead. But by the age of 15 he was the shortstop for the Mobile Black Bears, a semipro team. And after completing high school, he accepted a $200 monthly salary to play with the Indianapolis Clowns of the old Negro American League. During that season, he was signed by the then-Boston Braves for $350 a month, finished the season with the Braves' farm club in Eau Claire, Wisconsin and a year later, playing for Jacksonville, won the South Atlantic League's batting championship and Most Valuable Player award.

Then, in 1954, he went up to the Braves' training camp, and when Bobby Thomson broke an ankle, Aaron became a regular outfielder for the team, which had moved to Milwaukee after signing Aaron to a contract. From then on, things were just nightmarish for National League pitchers. One said that trying to get a fast ball by Aaron was like trying to get the sun past a rooster. Another said that trying to fool him was like slapping a rattlesnake. Yet another thought that Aaron deliberately missed pitches he knew he could hit, just so he could get the same pitch later with men on base. And collectively, they tagged him with the nickname Bad Henry (he's also known as Hammerin' Hank or simply The Hammer).

But Aaron's style has always been low-key, his manner calm; he's played in cities that aren't big media centers; he's been in only two world series, in 1957 and 1958; and he's black. So for a long time people didn't pay much attention to him. Though stories used to go around that Aaron fell asleep during pitches, in fact, of course, he's a thinking hitter who keeps a mental book on every pitcher in the league, and whenever he's at the plate, he's trying to psych the pitcher into serving up a particular pitch. His memory is also impressive; at the end of any given season, he can recall just about every pitch he hit for a home run that year—who threw it, the situation at the time, etc. But it wasn't until the mid-sixties that sports magazines started running feature articles about Aaron's remarkable talents; and it wasn't until 1967 that his salary reached the $100,000 mark. After the 1971 season—he hit 44 home runs that year, at the age of 37—the Braves finally signed him to a reported three-year contract at $200,000 a year. And more recently, Aaron has augmented that income by signing several lucrative advertising contracts, one with Magnavox, which will "borrow" the bat and ball with which he breaks the homerun record and display them around the country.

Ironically, as Aaron has come within striking distance of Babe Ruth's lifetime home-run total, the credit—and attention—he had craved for 19 years has finally come his way, with a vengeance. And not all of it has been friendly. Yet, in 1973, while virtually under siege, Aaron had a truly fantastic season, batting over .300 despite a very slow start and hitting 40 home runs even though, as a 39-year-old with the normal aches and pains, he sat out more than a few ball games. By the end of the season, one home run short of Ruth's total of 714, he had become an authentic hero to the black community; last fall, when he got married for the second time—to Billye Williams, who hosts a TV talk show in Atlanta—*Jet* gave it the same kind of coverage that *Life* used to give to coronations.

Since the opening of the new—and record-breaking—season seemed a perfect time to publish an interview with the beleaguered Braves star, *Playboy* sent Associate Editor Carl Snyder (who interviewed former world heavyweight boxing champ Joe Frazier in our March 1973 issue) to Atlanta several weeks before Aaron was due to begin spring training. Here is Snyder's report:

"I arranged to meet Aaron at his office in Atlanta Stadium. Arriving first, I chatted with his secretary, Carla Koplin, and inspected the various awards, clippings and souvenirs in the office, until Aaron arrived—dressed in a leather coat and carrying a book called *The Living Bible Paraphrased*. While signing baseballs and making some decisions about his schedule, he kidded the people around the office—'You should read something like this, it'd be good for you'—with a sense of humor that he's shy about revealing in public; later, he checked to make sure my tape recorder hadn't been running.

"Our sessions, which were spread over three days, took place entirely in his '74 Chevy. He asked out front if we could do the interview in the car, and I said yes. Aaron told me he had turned down a book offer because the writer wanted to 'lock' him in a room. The interview was done in bits and pieces between various stops, including: the YMCA in downtown Atlanta, where he was working out daily; the academy where his sons go to school; the dentist's, where I watched as one of his upper front teeth was polished (he was also in the process of getting a root-canal job); his financial advisor's office; his house, where we made one brief stop (on the way there, he proudly pointed out the home of Atlanta's new black mayor, Maynard Jackson, who'd been sworn in at a public ceremony the night I arrived in town); various gas stations and dry-cleaning places, where he'd invariably use the telephone; and several restaurants, the most noteworthy being Sgt. Wyatt's Country Bar-B-Que, where I had some dynamite ribs while Aaron and Sgt. Wyatt traded stories of hunting expeditions (besides being an avid fisherman, as he says in the interview, Aaron also loves to track elk in British Columbia).

"While Aaron was in one dry-cleaning place—I waited in the car—a bunch of black kids came by and recognized him; but he just frowned at them and wanted to know why they weren't in school. He's very concerned about his own kids—Gaile, Henry, Jr., Lary and Dorinda—and mentions them frequently. At one point, he asked me a few questions about the magazine business; he turned out to be surprisingly up to date on it, perhaps because Gaile, a journalism major at Fisk University in Tennessee, has already done some newspaper work during her summer vacations.

"As far as the interview was concerned, Aaron would think about each question before answering; if he didn't understand a question, or didn't like it, he would say so. I felt as I imagine pitchers must feel when they have to decide what to throw him. He is truly a man of few words, but he became animated whenever the conversation dealt with bigotry or racial discrimination. He didn't respond too much, however, whenever I mentioned Babe Ruth—and he made it clear that he didn't want to talk about any of his outside business interests. He's very conscious of how he appears to people: once he started whistling as we were walking through a parking lot, but when

I glanced at him, he stopped. Aaron holds the world pretty much at arm's length; he moves very deliberately, whether he's driving or on foot; and he dominated every situation in which I saw him, as much by his silence as by his words. The man projects incredible strength and determination, more so in person than through the media. But you don't stay in the big leagues for 21 years, or hit over 700 homers, if you're any kind of softy.

"We've all read or heard that Aaron, unlike Ruth, isn't the stuff that folk heroes are made of; I think that's wrong. He may not come up with the grand gestures that Ruth specialized in, but his laconic style is well suited to this age of overamplification. Despite the remarks of some Atlanta bartenders—who tried to tell me that they were 'letting' Hank break the record—I think that in a few years the name Henry Aaron will have the same kind of legendary aura as John Henry, Paul Bunyan—or Babe Ruth, for that matter."

PLAYBOY: We understand that when the Braves teach hitting to their young players, they don't exactly use you as a model.

AARON: Right. Everything I do is unorthodox—the way you're not supposed to do it. I hit off my front foot. I have a wiggle in my bat and I run on my heels. You wouldn't teach a kid to do any of those things. But it's just like everything else, you know—you can't fight results. Like Stan Musial; they said he'd never hit, standin' way back in the batter's box and crouchin' like he did. So it just proves that you have to do things your natural way. If you can do it better by hittin' a certain way—well, go ahead and do it.

PLAYBOY: What exactly *do* you do when you're batting in a game?

AARON: Well, to be successful at hittin', you have to be able to guess what pitch you're goin' to get. And when you guess right—when you get your pitch—you've got to be able to do somethin' with it. You don't have to hit a home run every time up, but you have to be able to hit the ball hard. That's what I've been able to do for 20 years—to look for a certain pitch in a certain situation and to hit it hard. I feel I can hit just about any pitch out of the ball park if I get the one I'm lookin' for.

PLAYBOY: Do you actually see the bat and the ball make contact?

AARON: Yeah, I can see contact—especially if I'm swingin' the bat right and hittin' the way I'm supposed to, with the bat out in front of me.

PLAYBOY: Do you ever worry about getting hit by a pitch?

AARON: I've never had any fear of bein' thrown at. I get hit sometimes, you know, but it only hurts for a little while, and it makes me more determined to get up and do somethin' the next time. If they frighten you, they can run you out of the league. Of course, I've been hit three or four times in the head. And sometimes they throw at you deliberately. I can remember once when Vernon Law, who didn't have a world of stuff but was noted for his control, hit me in the head with a pitch. Roy Face hit me in the head, too, and Drysdale threw close. But they've never been able to frighten me.

PLAYBOY: Were you discouraged a year ago when you had such a tough time getting base hits?

AARON: No. I was confident, and I knew all along that I'd get things goin' again.

PLAYBOY: What was the reason for your slow start?

AARON: Well, I went to spring trainin' knowin' that I had to work twice as hard as some of the younger players to get in shape. I've had one philosophy about playin' baseball, and that is to take spring trainin' very, very seriously. I know a lot of players go down there, finish their workouts or practice, and by one o'clock they're worried about gettin' to the golf course. But my main job is to do one thing, and that's to get the jump on everybody else, because the earlier I can get in shape, the sooner I can start doin' the things I want to do. If I get some momentum in trainin', it'll carry right on into the season. When we broke camp last year, I thought I was ready. But I wasn't, you know? It took me another three and a half weeks to really get myself in tiptop shape. And I felt awful; the ball club was goin' bad and people were puttin' everything on me. My legs felt weak, and my arm was no longer as strong as it used to be. That was why they moved me from right field to left field; they thought that if I didn't have to make that long throw, or cover all that space, it would benefit me and help the ball club, too—which it did.

But I felt ashamed about it. And people were sayin', "Well, the only thing he's concentratin' on is hittin' home runs." And it seemed that way. It looked that way. Because I had maybe 13 hits—and 10 of 'em was home runs. It seemed at the time like I couldn't do anything else *but* hit home runs. And I didn't want to put Eddie Mathews, our manager, in the position of havin' to say "Henry, we've gotta set you down; you're gettin' too old." I don't ever want anybody comin' up and tellin' me that, and I don't ever want anyone feelin' sorry for me. And at that point I thought maybe a lot of people *were* feelin' sorry for me, in a way—because while I was gettin' my share of home runs, they aren't all that counts. You've got to be able to get your share of base hits—and also to steal bases and things like that. This was also the time that the hate mail started pourin' in, because I was gettin' so close to Babe Ruth's record. It got so my life was bein' threatened just for doin' my job.

PLAYBOY: What did you do about the threats?

AARON: All I *could* do was carry any threats on my life to the police department and to the commissioner's office. That was it. And the commissioner has assured me that anything their office can do, they'll do it.

PLAYBOY: You have security?

AARON: Yeah, in certain areas—but they can't do but so much to help. I still get hate mail every day, but you get used to it after a while. Anyway, I don't really worry about hate too much since Jesse Jackson came to my rescue. And when I say "rescue," I mean that. Before then, I had heard of Jesse and I respected him. But after all of this stuff came out, Jesse met me at the airport one night in Chicago, and he had about 100, 200 kids to meet me. That's kinda late for kids to be out, but they sang songs and everything right there at the airport. After that, I got to know Jesse real well. I had dinner with him, and that whole weekend was dedicated to me. I got to know all his aides. And I came to believe in what he was doin'. I said that if there was anything I could do personally to help in any way, I would. I think we athletes sometimes sit back and as long as things are goin' good for us, we don't want to disturb the applecart. We forget where we came from. You know? If not for baseball, I'd just be an average black for white people to step on. We in sports get lost sometimes, wrapped up in our own little thing, and as long as we got a dollar, we forget about how there's 15,000,000 other blacks in America that's starvin' to death—not only blacks but whites and everybody else.

PLAYBOY: With or without hate mail—to get back to that—you had your share of base hits by the end of the 1973 season.

AARON: Yeah—I hit .301, I think.

PLAYBOY: You also ended the season with 713 homers, one short of the record. Were you disappointed to come so close and not make it?

AARON: No. It didn't bother me at all, to be frank with you. A lot of people said, "Well, what're you gonna do now? You gonna go in a gopher hole and lay there till next season?" Because, you know, I could have an automobile crash or get in an airplane and have it drop. I said, "Listen, whatever will be, will be—I can't change it. I've got to live my life the way I've been livin' for 40 years. I can't be any more careful than I've always been." Actually, if I'd taken full advantage of the situation—if I'd played some of the time in doubleheaders or if I'd played day games after night games—I probably could have hit that home run. But I wouldn't have been fair to my teammates, nor the manager, by doin' that. It's more important to get a winnin' attitude on the ball club. People said, "The ball club's gonna finish in fifth or sixth place anyhow; why not take advantage of it?" But that's kinda selfish—and I've never been a selfish ballplayer. I'm a member of the Atlanta Braves, and whenever I leave here, I'd like for the young players to say, "Henry Aaron was a winnin'-type ballplayer; he wasn't just for himself. He didn't go out there just for the sake of hittin' a home run." Of course, it *is* a disappointment to close out my career with a losin' ball club, but I take into consideration that we're in a rebuildin' stage. We have some good ballplayers; it's just a matter of puttin' everything together. It'll probably be two, three years before we can develop the habits of a championship team.

PLAYBOY: Do any of your teammates resent your success?

AARON: I'm sure that some have been jealous—but I wouldn't be in a position to name them.

PLAYBOY: Was there ever any jealousy between you and Eddie Mathews?

AARON: If there ever was, it was friendly. It was never the kind of thing where he would come up in the ninth innin' and I wouldn't want him to hit the home run that would win the game. It was a friendly type rivalry, and I think this is a healthy situation. Back in the days when Spahn and Burdette were pitchin' on our ball club, they would compete with each other in wins and losses, but after the ball game they would go and drink beer, maybe have dinner together. One record that's very dear to my heart is the record that Mathews and I hold as far as hittin' home runs as teammates. We happened to break the record of Ruth and Gehrig—and I think that the record we set will probably never be broken, because it's so hard to find two teammates who compare so equally in their work, in their skill at the job, and are gonna play together that long. Mays and McCovey might have done it if they had come up at the same time. But you never hear any talk about this record; it's never been played up at all. I don't know whether it's because Eddie and I played together all those years in smaller cities or whether it's because Mathews was basically the same type player I was—not flashy, although he was probably a little bit flashier than I was—or if it's because this particular record happened to be broken by a black player and a white player.

PLAYBOY: In those years, you didn't get much publicity. Wasn't that depressing?

AARON: Well, I've always been one to roll with the punches. I felt all along that one day, if I just stayed healthy, the attention *some* ballplayers were gettin' had to roll *my* way. Because I had the credentials. I wasn't an overnight success: I was able to perform over a period of years, you know, and to really get my thing *down*. When you're number two, you try harder. If I'd been playin' in New York City, I would have been nationally known maybe 10, 15 years ago. But I happened to play in two smaller cities. I've never criticized the newspapers: I felt all along that the media were just hoppin' on whatever they thought, at that time, was a hot item. And I just wasn't a flashy-type ballplayer. Maybe, somewhere down the line, this has hurt me. Years ago somebody said, "Why don't you *be* more flashy?" I don't know what they wanted—maybe for me to pretend I was hurt every time I slid into a base or to have my cap fly off every time I ran.

But I just did the things I knew I could do in the only way I knew I could do them. I'm a very low-key guy—this is just Henry Aaron's style—and I can't change. Today, Willie Stargell is in a situation just about like the one I was in a few years ago. He's had three of the greatest seasons, back to back, that any ballplayer has ever had, and yet he's been slighted as far as the MVP award. If he'd been playin' in a city like New York, he probably would have *been* the Most Valuable Player. But the last three years, I've just tried to maintain the same kind of home-run pace as Willie—or McCovey or Johnny Bench.

PLAYBOY: But your own home-run pace picked up considerably during that time. Are you a better hitter now than you used to be?

AARON: No, I don't think I'm nearly the hitter that I was 10 years ago. I'd have to be kiddin' myself to think that, at age 40, I'm as quick with my bat as I was 15 years ago. There's no way I could be. On given days I am, but if I have to play 10 days in a row or play a day game after a night game, I just can't generate the bat speed that I used to. This is a young man's game, and that's the way it'll always be. However, I think that's one reason why I hit more home runs now than, say, 15 years ago: The older you get, the carefuller you get. When you get to the plate, you don't want to swing at anything unless you know exactly what you're swingin' at. But I would say that 10 years ago, there's no way they could have defensed me the way they have the last three years.

PLAYBOY: You mean—

AARON: By puttin' on the shift. That's another thing that's made me more of a home-run hitter: I have to hit with power to beat the shift. It's completely gotten me away from thinkin' about an average or of just hittin' the ball through the infield to the other side. I have to hit with power and I'm concentratin' so much that when I get my pitch and hit the ball—well, it might be my only hit of the game, but it's a home run.

PLAYBOY: Have you done anything special to get in shape for this season?

AARON: Well, I haven't picked up any baseballs yet, but I've worked out at the Y every mornin' at nine o'clock, swimmin' and playin' a lot of handball. People probably thought I was busy as hell this winter, but I wasn't. I promised after the season was over that I would stay away from the banquet circuit—and I didn't put on but three pounds. I feel like I've been blessed in that respect; I've never had any problem with my weight. And I've been able to come back from my injuries, whether you want to call that fortunate or unfortunate. I had an operation for calcium in my leg, I'm not sure what year, and before that I had a hemorrhoid operation. And I broke my ankle in my first major-league season, but bein' so young, I was able to recuperate with no ill effect.

PLAYBOY: No loss of speed?

AARON: Well, I never was a speed demon. I was always a pretty good base runner, but it was the element of surprise: Nobody ever thought I was gonna steal.

PLAYBOY: What's the hardest part of the game to cope with as you get older?

AARON: That would have to be the travel, because you get so much of it. And the older you get, the more it tires you out—packin' and unpackin', movin' through airports and time zones, goin' in and out of hotels. It really takes a toll on you. And I just don't go out. You know? I stay in my room—in seclusion. Because if I'm recognized, I wind up signin' a bunch of autographs instead of seein' the things I want to see. But lately it's been gettin' so I can't even rest in the hotel, because once the kids find out where I am, they just come to my room and knock on the door, and all day long I have to sign autographs.

PLAYBOY: You don't like that?

AARON: I just hate to get in a crowd where I'm gonna be subject to people stickin' pencils in my face. They might accidentally poke one of my eyes out. You know? So I don't get into that situation. I've always been a loner anyway, I don't know why—and sometimes it's good, sometimes it's bad. Because lately I've had to be alone more than ever. I just couldn't go anyplace. I've had to be isolated, which I'm already accustomed to, but still, you like to have some kind of outlet—to talk to people, or go to the movies, or do something. But it just hasn't been possible, the last few months, and I don't think it's gonna get better.

PLAYBOY: Rumor has it that your recreation usually involves going off by yourself anyway.

AARON: Well, I like to go fishin', you know. I go back to Mobile a lot, and I have my boat there—actually, two boats, a 27-foot cabin cruiser and a 13-footer, which I keep at my mother's house. I go fresh-water fishin', deep-sea fishin' out on the Gulf, and I've gone to Mexico to fish. I love fresh-water fishin' the best, but I'll go anyplace as long as there's fishin'.

PLAYBOY: Is it the challenge of bringing in the catch or the chance to get away?

AARON: Both. But I suppose just gettin' away is the most important thing—not havin' to hear the telephone ring and not bein' able to look at a TV. That is just the greatest thing in the world.

PLAYBOY: Being isolated in the wilderness, obviously, is very different from being isolated in a room where there's nothing but a TV and a telephone. During the season, isn't it hard to stay in your hotel so much?

AARON: Not the way baseball is played today. Practically all the games are night games. So if you're playin' on the West Coast, say, and the game is over at 11:30, it's 12 o'clock or 12:30 by the time you get back in the hotel. And then you sleep till the next day, about 11 or 12—so actually the day is shot again. I think baseball players spend half their lives either ridin' in a plane or in bed sleepin'.

PLAYBOY: Have you read *Ball Four*?

AARON: Yes—part of it.

PLAYBOY: According to Jim Bouton, ballplayers on the road don't always go to bed in order to sleep. The guys in the book seem interested more in boozing and woman chasing than in playing baseball, and they come off as pretty immature characters. Is that accurate?

AARON: I suppose it is. But I'm sure that a lot of doctors and other professional people are just as immature as baseball players. They get drunk, they chase women and everything else. There are also a lot of immature *women*. They chase ballplayers just like the guys chase them. It's not a one-sided story.

PLAYBOY: According to Bouton, a lot of ballplayers also take pep pills in order to play better.

AARON: Well, to be honest with you, I've never seen a ballplayer take anything to stimulate him before a game. Maybe they do, and maybe Bouton has seen it—but I never have. I've taken a mild sedative in order to go to sleep, and I've seen other guys do the same—but I just don't believe you could function if you took somethin' to stimulate you.

PLAYBOY: A lot of fans claim they need stimulants when they try to *watch* baseball. Is the game too slow, out of touch with the times?

AARON: I know a lot of people say baseball is dull, but it's survived wars and everything else that's come along. Football has gained in popularity, but I was glad to see that, because I've always been a great football fan. Back in the Green Bay days, when Vince Lombardi had the old team back there, I used to go out and watch football in Milwaukee—just sit on one seat and stretch my legs out over three other ones. But it hasn't taken anything away from baseball; you can't really compare baseball and football.

PLAYBOY: What do you think of attempts to liven up the game, such as the American League's designated-hitter rule?

AARON: I think it's a fantastic rule. I think it's one of the greatest things that's ever happened to baseball. And talkin' to the American League players and fans, they love it, too—simply because it doesn't leave the game with a dull moment. If you've got a pitcher up there, you're either gonna bunt with him or he's gonna strike out. You do get pitchers that'll hit the ball consistently—your Tom Seavers, your Gibsons, maybe a Rick Wise. But for every one of those guys, they've got 10 other guys that ain't gonna touch the ball. It's gonna be an automatic out. Well, maybe that's a good thing—the fans can go buy popcorn. Seriously, though, I think it's a great rule. And it's helped a lot of ballplayers who probably wouldn't be in the big leagues now. Like Orlando Cepeda, who had a lot of trouble with his knees; it's given him a new lease on life. Or Tony Oliva; he was one of the brightest young stars that ever came into the league, some years ago, and he had knee trouble, too. So that rule's gonna help him an awful lot.

PLAYBOY: What about other changes people keep proposing, such as standardizing the ball parks?

AARON: I think every ball park should be built or fixed for that particular club. If you've got a good pitchin' staff, then make it a large ball park. For example, the Dodgers, ever since they've been in Los Angeles, have concentrated on speed and pitchin'. When they had Koufax and Drysdale, they felt they could beat anyone if you just gave them two runs. If you've got sluggers, make it a park where people can see home runs;

they're not gonna come into the stadium just to see the team lose, lose, lose. But make it a *fair* park. If a pitcher makes a mistake and a guy hits the ball 340 feet, that's supposed to be a home run, regardless of what you think about it. Just like a hitter don't have any business swingin' at bad pitches, a pitcher don't have any business makin' a bad pitch. If he does, then he's supposed to be hurt by it.

PLAYBOY: What about the orange baseball? Would that make it easier for hitters to see what they're swinging at?

AARON: Well, I can't argue with Charley Finley. Much as people might say that his ideas are no good, the fact is that he *has* brought a lot of good ideas into baseball. He brought in the colored uniforms, and before he did, they were just goin' with the same old dull ones. But really, I can't say whether I like *this* idea until I swing at an orange baseball.

PLAYBOY: Do you agree with the people who claim that night baseball is responsible for the decline in .300 hitters?

AARON: No, I don't. In fact, when I was much younger, I would *prefer* playin' night games. It didn't bother me at all. Now that I'm older—and don't ask me the reason for this—I would much rather play day games. It just seems like every time I gotta play a night game, I'm tired—maybe from just lyin' around the hotel. But I've talked to most of the younger players on our club right now, and for some reason, they would much rather play night games.

PLAYBOY: If night baseball isn't the problem, why are batting averages generally lower than they used to be?

AARON: Well, the owners and the management don't concentrate on battin' as much as they do on pitchin'. They're worried about gettin' five, six or seven innin's out of the pitcher, then bringin' in a fresh one. They're not as concerned with the hitter as they used to be.

PLAYBOY: Is the disappearance of the minor leagues part of the difficulty in developing fresh baseball talent?

AARON: Well, it's true that a lot of minor-league cities have been stripped of their teams. Ball clubs used to carry as many as three or four triple-A farm clubs. Major-league players used to go play in the California league after they could no longer play in the big leagues—but now they have to go to Japan. The economic structure of baseball has changed in such a way that the owners can't afford to have triple-A teams. I think the kids comin' up today have had somethin' to do with it. They're smarter, they're better athletes and they demand more money. When I first came to the big leagues, the minimum was $5000—and I don't care if you're talkin' 'bout how a dollar is worth a dollar or 90 cents or 10 cents; $5000 is still just $5000. So I think that in this way, the game has changed along with society and everything else—and it's changed for the good.

A few years ago, they were spreadin' a lot of big bonuses around, and we had four or five big-bonus players on our club. All these kids got about a hundred or so thousand dollars to sign a contract. It took me about 14 years to start makin' that kind of money. People said, "Don't you resent them?" No, they were just a lot smarter, and they had agents to negotiate their contracts for them. Which I didn't; the only somebody I had negotiatin' my contract was Syd Pollack, the owner of the old Indianapolis Clowns. When he sold one of his black players, he would just give you so much money and keep the rest. It was that simple. White ballplayers were comin' out of college, or the Babe Ruth League, and they were givin' 'em big bonuses—but they weren't givin' any to *black* players.

PLAYBOY: When you went to the National League in 1954, did you get hassled for being black, as Jackie Robinson did?

AARON: I went through the thing of segregated housin' in spring trainin'. But when I got to cities like Philadelphia, Chicago and New York, they were integrated, and I never heard any name-callin' there. Jackie went through things every place he went; North and South, he was reminded that they didn't want him to play major-league baseball. Only a handful of us could have taken even a little dab of what he took. But when I came up to the Braves, I *was* under pressure to excel; I knew I wasn't gonna keep a job just because I had a great year in the Sally League. I had to show the Man that I could play major-league ball. So I got off to a good start in spring trainin', and when Bobby Thomson broke his ankle, I was the best ballplayer they had down there to replace him. So I got my chance. And fortunately, I played under a manager—Charlie Grimm—who let me make mistakes and profit by 'em.

PLAYBOY: Was he your best manager?

AARON: No. Ben Geraghty had to be the greatest manager I ever had. I played for Ben in the Sally League, and it was the first year they ever had blacks in the league. There were three of us on the team. I'm also sure it was the first time Ben Geraghty had ever managed blacks—and he was just super. Ben used to sit down and talk and have a bottle of beer with us. And he knew an awful lot about baseball, more than just hittin' the ball—how to play the game itself, how to approach it. But the league was highly segregated, and Jacksonville wasn't one of your liberal cities; the fans didn't want us playing there.

PLAYBOY: How do you account for your ability to perform under the kind of pressure you faced in Jacksonville—or that you faced last season?

AARON: Just by bein' black. I think every black person is prepared to deal with pressure because they're *born* under adversity, and they live under pressure every day of their lives. They know damn well that they've gotta go out there and do better than the average person in order to keep their job.

PLAYBOY: When did you first become aware that to be black meant getting second-class treatment?

AARON: I suppose when I was about 10, not because of anything that happened to me, but just realizin' that we were livin' on the wrong side of the tracks and that my father was barely makin' ends meet. But Mobile has always been a little bit more open than the average Southern city. Spring Hill College, for example, has been integrated for as long as I can remember; there's always been blacks and whites goin' to school there.

PLAYBOY: What kind of future did you look forward to as a kid in Mobile?

AARON: I never thought about anything but playin' baseball. My mother and father wanted me to go on to college after I got out of high school, but I wanted to play major-league ball—and after Jackie broke in, I thought blacks had as good a chance as anybody if they could show they had major-league skills. My mother was a little disappointed that I didn't go on to school, and I would be very disappointed if one of my kids didn't go on to college, regardless of what kind of ability they might have in sports.

PLAYBOY: After you'd played with the Braves in Milwaukee for 11 years, the franchise moved to Atlanta. Were you uptight about returning to the South at that point in your career?

AARON: Well, I didn't want to be labeled a wooden god when I got here in Atlanta—and then have them discover that I can strike out with the bases loaded, too. I just wanted to be a baseball player. As it turned out, movin' here was one of the most fortunate things that ever happened to me in an economic sense, because it's a growin' city, and I got here just in time to be in on that. On the other hand, Milwaukee was a great city to me, to my family. I was born in the South, my ex-wife was born in the South, and we were accustomed to the habits and the happenin's of the South. But the kids were content in Milwaukee, they were happy with their friends, and they had no real contact with segregation.

PLAYBOY: Isn't there segregation in Milwaukee?

AARON: Of course, segregation is everywhere—but they didn't come in contact with it up there, because they were so small. Anyway, I had no animosity about movin' here, but some little things I said were blown out of proportion. People said, "Well, he said he didn't want to move here because he didn't want the Ku Klux Klan knockin' on his door." But I never made those statements. I feel quite comfortable stayin' here.

PLAYBOY: The city looks fairly well integrated. Is that an illusion?

AARON: Well, Atlanta is a metropolitan city and it has its problems, but they're no bigger or more outstandin' than other cities' problems. You're gonna run into people anywhere that don't want their kids to go to school with black kids, don't want to sit next to you at the lunch counter or—out of meanness—just don't want to give you respect as a human bein'. You know? And rather than bein' judged by your character, you're judged by your color. You're gonna find this everyplace. In fact, I have never lived a day in my life that in some way—some small way, somewhere—someone didn't remind me that I'm black.

PLAYBOY: For example?

AARON: For an example, last night. I go to a basketball game where my kid is playin'. And I'm lookin' at the referee *deliberately* callin' fouls on him just because he's the only black kid out there. I'm not askin' 'em to *give* him anything, but it just tears me apart inside. *I* can take it, you know, but I say: how in the hell can a man stand out there, a grown man, and be so hateful and resentful toward a *kid*? But they are; they stand out there callin' these fouls, and the kid can't do *nothin'*. I had to go out and talk to him. But what can you do? What the hell can you do? I get angry; I get so angry I feel like goin' out there and punchin' somebody in the mouth. If it was myself, it would never bother me, because, as a grown person, I would know how to get back at 'em. But he's a kid, and all he's doin' out there is playin' the same type of game that the other nine white boys are playin'. But if he gets any kind of aggressive out there—like they are—they're gonna call fouls on *him*. It's a shame, but that's just the way it is.

PLAYBOY: Do black and white ballplayers socialize together?

AARON: They socialize more now than they used to. Some of the young players, the younger kids that aren't married, they—what you call it?—they date. I've seen white players with black girls and black players with white girls. But when I first came up, you never saw that.

PLAYBOY: In recent years, you've been very outspoken about racial inequities in baseball, but at one time you had a reputation for being quiet. What happened to turn you around?

AARON: I've *always* spoken out. But before, when I said somethin', nobody listened. It's just like a high school student versus a guy with a master's degree. I've got my master's degree now, in baseball, and I paid my dues—and now that I'm closin' in on one of the most prodigious records in the world, every time I say somethin', it's in print. And that's the difference. I've said the same thing over and over again—that I think there's injustice in baseball. As far as my personal wealth is concerned, I owe everything to baseball. But I still say that I've given baseball more than it's given me. And I think the average black player can say the same thing.

PLAYBOY: Why haven't the major leagues ever had a black manager?

AARON: I don't know what the answer is. I don't know what they could be afraid of. My brother Tommie's managin' in Savannah; he took over for Clint Courtney last year and did a good job. But as for a black gettin' a chance to manage a major-league club, I don't know. It's been decades since Jackie Robinson broke into baseball, since the black player proved he's super on the field. Now it's time for the owners to give him a job that's equal to his character. And baseball, as much good as it's done for a lot of people, has dragged its foot on this situation much too long, much longer than any other sport.

I've heard some talk that if baseball ever *fires* a black manager, then how's the black community gonna feel? Hell, black players are fired every day from jobs; how do they feel about them losin' *those* jobs? I realize that if I was the manager of a ball club, that if I wasn't doin' the job, pretty soon somebody would come along and take my job away from me; and they *should*. It's the easiest thing in the world to replace a manager, but it's harder'n hell for you to replace 40 ballplayers. I realize this, you know—I'm not that dumb. So I think that's a stupid thing for them to say.

PLAYBOY: Will this be your last season?

AARON: I hope so. I'm lookin' forward to it bein' my last season.

PLAYBOY: If the National League should go for the designated-hitter rule, would you consider prolonging your career in that capacity?

AARON: Well, they don't have it now, and if they don't have it by the time I retire, I'm not gonna worry about it. I don't think, in any case, that I would consider it until after I break the record, because there's been enough asterisks behind that thing already—you know, people talkin' about how I been to bat so many times more than Babe Ruth, etc.

PLAYBOY: What do you say to people when they bring that up?

AARON: I don't say anything to them, because you can argue with a person the rest of your life about baseball, about what Ruth would have done today compared with what he did 40 years ago. I just walk away, so as not to give 'em the satisfaction of me holdin' a conversation. You know? But I'll give you my thinkin' on that: I'm not out tryin' to destroy Babe Ruth's record. Personally, I don't think any black man *can* destroy a white man's record, because it just ain't gonna happen in this time. The press ain't gonna let it happen: white people in general ain't gonna let it happen, and it just ain't gonna happen.

But I still say that regardless of how you look at it, whether you say Ruth would have hit so many more home runs if he hadn't been a pitcher, I wasn't *responsible* for him bein' a pitcher. You know? If he felt like he wanted to be a pitcher for five years, that was his business. They say, "Well, he didn't go to bat but so many times, so you can't legally say you hit more home runs." Well, you know, I got 3500 or 3600 hits, too, and I can argue the point that maybe Ruth hit all these home runs and had this fantastic battin' average—but he never did get 3000 base hits. You can argue till you're blue in the face about records and how a person would do, so I just don't say anything. I just keep doin' the best I can.

PLAYBOY: Looking back over your 700-plus homers, are there any that you feel were especially important?

AARON: Several. One is the home run I hit off Billy Muffett in '57 that clinched the pennant for the Milwaukee Braves. That's probably the most outstandin' one, simply because it put us in the world series against the Yankees. My 700th home run was also one of the most excitin'—and historical—moments of my career. And then there's the first home run I hit in an All-Star game, which came rather late—in '71. I thought I was never gonna do it.

PLAYBOY: Since you've been within striking distance of the home-run record, have you ever doubted that you were going to make it?

AARON: Yes. Two years ago, during the baseball strike. I felt I had to take advantage of every opportunity, every chance—and I knew I wasn't the youngest player in the league. So if I took off for 11 days like that, I was gonna have to work that much harder to get myself in shape. I thought, that year, if I could have ended up hittin' 40 home runs, then it probably would have been a waltz for me last year. But I didn't hit that many home runs, and that put a lot of pressure on me for the '73 season. I knew that if I had any chance of doin' it, I had to have a great season last year—I mean, a *great* season, I'm not talkin' about one where I hit 25 or 30 home runs, you know. I wanted to go into this season with less than five home runs to go, because it's gonna be awful tough for me to get 20 or 25 more. And I still feel that way. A ballplayer's likely to have a bad season any year, and at my age I have to take that into consideration.

PLAYBOY: After 20 years in the big leagues, do you feel as though you've outlived your time?

AARON: Not really. Stan Musial played till he was about 43 or 44, I guess. Ted Williams played until he was 41 or 42. Willie Mays just retired: and Eddie just retired about five years ago. So if I can finish another year, I feel like I'm still ahead of the game.

PLAYBOY: Do you want to manage after you hang up your spikes?

AARON: No. I wouldn't want to manage—I'm sure of that.

PLAYBOY: What do you want to do?

AARON: Well, I'd like to remain in baseball in some capacity. There haven't been too many real opportunities for blacks after they stop playin', other than coachin' first base. I don't want to be a first-base coach; I think that would be somewhat of a *de*motion rather than a *pro*motion. I wouldn't like to be a "superscout," either. I would like to work in the front office in some way. Like I say, black players haven't put a dent in the front office yet, so it's time to look in that direction—and I think that with the knowledge I've picked up over the years, I would certainly be an asset to some organization. If not—well, I've been fortunate enough to invest in a few deals that have paid off, and if I had to quit the game today or tomorrow I could go on livin'. I don't think I'd have to go out and beg pennies.

PLAYBOY: Are you sorry that your playing career is nearing the end?

AARON: Well, I always knew the day was gonna come; nobody goes on forever. And I've had a great career. I don't have anything to be ashamed of. I worked hard for what I've achieved, and I appreciate everything anybody has ever done for me. But it's not like a doctor's career nor a lawyer's career. They can go on practicin' forever. In sports, there just comes a day when you have to quit; it was a blessin' of the Lord that I was able to play so long.

 June 1986

KAREEM ABDUL-JABBAR

A candid conversation with the greatest basketball player of all time

At the advanced age of 39, Kareem Abdul-Jabbar—a dinosaur by professional basketball standards—continues to act less like a lion in winter than like a stallion in spring. The National Basketball Association's only active player to have graduated from college before the start of the seventies, Abdul-Jabbar, a graceful, 7'2" scoring machine, has virtually rewritten the league's record books. Now nearing the end of his 17th pro season (the only NBA player ever to reach that milestone), Abdul-Jabbar adds to his fistful of career records each time he sets foot on court.

Before the start of the season, he had already become the NBA's all-time leader in scoring, in most field goals attempted and made and in most blocked shots. By the end of the current campaign, his one-man assault on NBA stats will also include most minutes and most games ever played by a pro. Forget such items as his appearance in 15 straight All-Star games and his place as the NBA's all-time scoring leader in post-season play.

Oddly enough, Abdul-Jabbar cares very little about all of the above. He just wants to win, period. As the captain and heart and soul of the Los Angeles Lakers, he led his team last season to its third league championship in the past six years. He's intent on a repeat performance this season and, with Los Angeles having easily won the Pacific Division title, it seems likely that the NBA championship series will again pit the Lakers against their archrivals, the Boston Celtics. Says Milwaukee Bucks coach Don Nelson, "The Celtics and the Lakers are head and shoulders above the rest of us, and we just have to face it."

Nelson and most other NBA coaches have also wondered aloud how Abdul-Jabbar can continue performing without showing any signs of wear and tear. If anything, he has actually improved in recent years. Last season, he averaged 22 points per game—his highest figure since the 1981-1982 season—and his .599 field-goal average was the second highest of his career. Singer Neil Young used to complain that rust never sleeps; he obviously had never met anyone with Abdul-Jabbar's natural undercoating. Time simply refuses to dim his shooting eye. His sky hook, which *Playboy* once described as "the most beautiful basketball shot ever invented," remains as eerily accurate and unstoppable as ever.

Despite his athletic brilliance, however, Abdul-Jabbar has long been one of sport's most enigmatic—and least popular—superstars. For most of his career, he has had a distant relationship with the press and public alike. Much of that can be traced to his troubled adolescence. Born on April 16, 1947, in New York City, Ferdinand Lewis Alcindor was a studious, shy youngster raised by middle-class parents. Unfortunately, he grew up at a time when blacks were still subject to segregation, Jim Crow laws and lynchings, and all that left its mark. His parents wanted their son to get a good Catholic education and sent him to Power Memorial High School in Manhattan. Alcindor excelled at academics and basketball and was close to Jack Donohue, the school's basketball coach. But then, during half time of a sloppy game against a weak opponent, Donohue tried to fire him up by telling him, "You're acting just like a nigger!" Not a bright move. Alcindor went into a shell at that point.

While a student at UCLA, Alcindor renounced Catholicism and became a Muslim. In 1971, he publicly announced that he had changed his name to Kareem Abdul-Jabbar, Arabic for "noble and powerful servant" of Allah. Abdul-Jabbar then avoided the press the way Muslims avoid alcohol and barbecued ribs. It wasn't until after he split up with his personal spiritual advisor that he began opening up to people, a process that accelerated after his house burned down in January 1983. Abdul-Jabbar's fans knew that their man had lost thousands of jazz records in the blaze; when fans from cities around the league began sending him records, Abdul-Jabbar—almost like Sally Field at last year's Academy Awards—suddenly realized, "They like me." Since then, his view of America and the world has become much more sanguine.

To interview the man most experts consider the greatest player in the history of basketball, Playboy sent freelancer Lawrence Linderman to meet with Abdul-Jabbar in Los Angeles. Linderman reports:

"Even though I'd suggested we interview Abdul-Jabbar, I regarded the assignment with more apprehension than I'd felt before any of my 22 previous *Playboy Interviews*. Some years ago, I had interviewed him for a short *Playboy* feature and had come away thinking I'd never met a man so filled with gloom and icy anger. To my great surprise and relief, he no longer had a psychic chip on his shoulder. To his great surprise and relief, he had ended his isolated, alienated existence. In some ways, he's almost like a monk who, having observed a lifelong, self-imposed vow of silence, one day discovers how joyous it can be to get in touch with the world—and with himself as well.

"When we met, Abdul-Jabbar was in the process of moving into a huge stone mansion built on the Bel Air site where his ranch house had burned down three years before. During the couple of weeks we devoted to the interview, workmen were still putting the finishing touches on the outside of the house. Inside, the cavernous place was mostly bare. Although Abdul-Jabbar had bought furniture six months before moving in, a shipping company had misplaced his things; and when I saw him about a month later in New York, his furniture was still somewhere in transit.

"In any case, he had a table and chairs in his kitchen, and that's where we began our conversations. A few months before, he had announced his intention to bow out of basketball after the 1986-1987 season; that provided the opening subject for our interview."

PLAYBOY: Not long after you said that the current season would be your last, the Los Angeles Lakers announced that you'd agreed to play one more year. Do you really intend to play next season, or was that announcement a smoke screen enabling you to duck a yearlong series of "Farewell, Kareem" nights?

JABBAR: Oh, no; barring injury, I'll probably play one more year; but I won't make that decision until the end of the playoffs. If I don't think I can play up to my expectations, then I'll quit. In all probability, though, I'll be out there again next fall.

PLAYBOY: You've come close to retiring during each of the past three years. Why haven't you? Does the game mean more to you than perhaps you suspected?

JABBAR: Well, first of all, it's a great way to make a living; and even though I've probably had enough adrenaline rushes to last three life-times, I still enjoy the competition. I've also enjoyed proving certain people wrong. After the '83 season, the Lakers didn't sign me and I became a free agent—and no one offered me a contract for months. I was out there all alone, and a lot of people just wrote me off. They felt that at 36, I was on my way out; but eventually the Lakers and I got together and, lo and behold, here I am, still hanging around. We won the NBA championship last year, and I had a very successful season, which dispelled all that talk.

PLAYBOY: You'll be 40 before the end of next season. What inroads have the years made on your ability?

JABBAR: I really haven't seen any. In fact, because of my conditioning program, I think I'm probably realizing more of my physical potential than I did ten years ago. I always knew that I had to pay close attention to my cardiovascular condition, strength training and stretching, but I don't think I finally got all three of them straight until a few years ago, and that's what's kept me in the game. Believe me, if you don't have it physically, it doesn't matter whether you want to play or not—it just doesn't happen.

PLAYBOY: Are you saying you don't have to pace yourself differently during games?

JABBAR: I don't, no. I've found that it's better to play as well as I can for as long as I can. After that, the coach can take me out; but I think that if you check, you'll find that I've been playing more minutes than any other player on the team. I'm calling it quits after next season only because I want to spend time with my children, but I really think I could play a few more years at the same level.

PLAYBOY: You're no doubt aware that most sports fans have long considered you enigmatic, if not downright sullen and hostile. How did that come about?

JABBAR: Basically, it was my own fault, because I never tried to communicate with sportswriters; and as a result of all the negative interaction between me and the press, I got a bad image. I was described as distant, cold, etc.—but it didn't matter to me. I knew that if I talked to these guys and decided to court the press systematically, I'd get certain benefits, but I just didn't care. I always had my guard up, and I was unapproachable.

I think I felt that way until a couple of years ago, when I finally got tired of being bum-rapped in the press. I found that when I worked just a little bit at trying to communicate and smooth things over, I got a great result: People seemed to feel a lot differently about me. Their image of me and their support of me have taken on a different tone. It's much more like, "He's one of us." I had to work for that, and I had to learn about that, and I'm glad I finally absorbed those lessons and made them useful in my life. Being liked and having people come up to me and feeling comfortable about it have made the adjustment worth the effort.

PLAYBOY: Why had you decided not to talk to the press in the first place?

JABBAR: Probably because when I was in high school and then at UCLA, sportswriters assumed that the teams I was on would win championships. That idea of foregone success took the thrill out of playing. Because of all the attention and all the great expectations, there was just no sense of discovery, no surprises. They'd already put me at the top; they had said that's where I belonged, and by doing so, they took away the fun of it. Any success I had was going to be taken for granted, and I knew it. And I was right.

PLAYBOY: You mean you got pissed off just because sportswriters correctly assessed your ability?

JABBAR: It didn't piss me off, but it was a downer. In my senior year of high school, there were 60 other players at least seven feet tall who were going on to college, yet it seemed to be a foregone conclusion that I'd lead whatever school I went to to the NCAA championship. That put pressure on me; but fortunately, my coach at UCLA was John Wooden, and his whole thing was, "We'll ignore all that talk and just play basketball."

PLAYBOY: UCLA did, indeed, win national championships during the three years you played there. When you graduated, a lot of sportswriters called you the greatest college ballplayer of all time, and nowadays they're calling you the greatest pro of all time. How do you react to such praise?

JABBAR: It's very flattering and it's nice to be considered in that light, but I don't get too excited about it. I know that I've been very successful and that it's hard to measure success.

PLAYBOY: Modesty aside, have you ever suspected that you might be the best player in the game?

JABBAR: At times, yes, but basketball is a funny game: There are certain things forwards have to do, other things that guards have to do, and centers have something else that they have to do. It's hard for me to measure myself against players like Julius Erving, Dave DeBusschere, Chet Walker, Elgin Baylor, John Havlicek and all of the other great forwards I've competed against. Same thing with guards: I just can't find any basis for comparing myself with players like Oscar Robertson and Magic Johnson.

PLAYBOY: You, Wilt Chamberlain and Bill Russell are overwhelmingly regarded as the three greatest centers of all time. How do you compare yourself with them?

JABBAR: Hard to say, because the game has changed since they left it. Today, NBA teams have to shoot within 24 seconds, and the three-second lane is 16 feet wide. Wilt played a long time with a 12-foot-wide lane, which meant he could get closer to the basket before taking his shots, so it's hard to compare what he did with what I've done. Still, how many players are going to average more than 50 points a game, as he did one season? Bill Russell never had overwhelming individual stats, but he was the key ingredient in the greatest dynasty in the game. Yet I can't compare myself with him, either, because basketball is a team game, not an individual game. When I was in the seventh grade, I started going to Madison Square Garden regularly, and I learned how to win by watching Russell play. Bill played for his teammates. He passed the ball a lot, he rebounded and started the fast break and was always there plugging up the middle on defense—he was content to do that. Russell showed me that if you play for the other guys on the team, you get a lot more out of everybody.

PLAYBOY: What did Chamberlain show you?

JABBAR: Chamberlain played the game the same way Russell did, except he scored so much more. But his teams had to get more points from him. He'd score 45 points and his teams would still lose.

PLAYBOY: One year, Chamberlain led the NBA in assists. Do you think it might have been a reaction—

JABBAR: To everybody's saying that he shot too much? Yes, absolutely. Wilt had to fight people's dissatisfaction that his teams didn't win. There he was, this great dominating player, and his teams didn't win championships. Well, Wilt wasn't playing for the right team. As an individual, he was in a class by himself, but his teammates—they were OK, but not the supporting cast Russell had.

PLAYBOY: Do you think Chamberlain is still frustrated by the way people perceive him and his place in basketball history?

JABBAR: If you want to get Wilt ticked off or bitter, just mention Bill Russell. You will incite him.

PLAYBOY: In 1984, you supplanted Chamberlain as the leading scorer in pro basketball history, mostly on the strength of your hook shot, which your coach, Pat Riley, calls "the ultimate offensive weapon." Most followers of the sport—and players, as well—think your patented sky hook is the most difficult shot in basketball. Do you agree?

JABBAR: Not really, no. I think if you start shooting the hook early enough—and I had the form and release down pat when I was a freshman in high school—it becomes no more difficult than any other shot. And it has one built-in advantage: Because you release the hook from high up and behind your body, nobody can get a hand on it.

PLAYBOY: No one has ever blocked your hook shot?

JABBAR: I think maybe once or twice somebody I hadn't seen came in from behind me and blocked it, but players who've guarded me, no, they couldn't get to it. Nate Thurmond, who played for the Golden State Warriors, was the best in the league as far as playing me one on one went, but even he never blocked the shot. These days, nobody gets to play me one on one anymore. The last time that happened was against Houston; they let Akeem Olajuwon play me one on one for a quarter, and that was it.

PLAYBOY: How do teams defend against you?

JABBAR: Oh, every time I get the ball, at least two and sometimes three guys converge on me. That happens every night, because I'm a target, somebody who has to be taken care of.

PLAYBOY: How do opponents try to take care of you?

JABBAR: Guys do anything they can get away with, such as using their shoulders and forearms—normal play includes just about everything short of throwing blows. Rick Mahorn, now with the Detroit Pistons, has a lot of lower-body strength, and he's one of the players who'll put a knee up under my behind and actually lift my feet off the floor.

PLAYBOY: But they still don't shut you down. If you hadn't been so consistent with your hook, do you think you'd have been able to do more with other shots?

JABBAR: I would have had to, but I never really considered it, because my hook shot is very accurate. And when I sink it, it makes opposing centers mad. They really get angry. It's not like I'm somebody who's doing a physical number on them. I'm more like somebody with a foil who's sticking them every time.

PLAYBOY: How mad have opponents gotten?

JABBAR: To the point of being funny. Mahorn and I really got into it one night. I'd scored a lot of points, but toward the end of the game—a game that the Lakers had no chance of winning—Rick turned to me and said, "No, you can't shoot the hook anymore." Next time the Lakers came down the court, Rick positioned himself way up on my left side—the side I go to when I shoot the hook—so I immediately turned the other way and made a lay-up. Mahorn shouted, "Yeah, that's right, Kareem, but forget the hook—that's out!"

PLAYBOY: Which players are difficult for you to guard?

JABBAR: My defense in the pivot is pretty effective. The toughest guy for me throughout my career was Dan Issel, who's retired now. Dan could hit 20-foot jump shots all night long, so I'd have to get out there with him, which left the middle open for his teammates.

PLAYBOY: You're the NBA's all-time leader in scoring and blocked shots; but in any given year, you're rarely among the league's top ten rebounders. Why not?

JABBAR: Well, I led the NBA in rebounds the first year I played for the Lakers, which was also a year when the team did horribly. Our whole concept now is team rebounding, which is why I don't rebound numerically the way I used to. The idea is that if I get 20 rebounds and the rest of the team gets three, we're going to lose, so everybody on the team has to rebound. My biggest responsibility is to prevent the guy I'm guarding from getting an offensive rebound, because second shots are like nails in your coffin. When my man can't get near the basket, Magic or Maurice Lucas or Kurt Rambis will be there to get the rebound.

PLAYBOY: Who are the league's toughest rebounders?

JABBAR: Oh, Akeem Olajuwon is very good because of his agility. Jeff Ruland and Jack Sikma are great rebounders, too. But if you asked us who's number one in that department, I think we'd all say Moses Malone. He never stops coming at you and he's strong as a bull.

PLAYBOY: In his *Playboy Interview* [March 1984], Malone told us he sometimes feels he should wear boxing gloves on the court. Is that what it's like for all NBA centers?

JABBAR: No, that's just the way Moses plays. He's very physical and very smart. In 1983, the 76ers blew us out of the finals in four straight games, and Moses was just relentless. I had to appraise what I was doing wrong insofar as the way I played him, so I went to Pete Newell, who has a summer camp for teaching pros the fundamentals of whatever it is they're not doing right. Newell's the professor—about 25 years ago, when he coached the University of California, his team won the NCAA championship. Anyway, I took Pete some video tape of our '83 play-off games against the 76ers and asked him to critique my performance against Moses.

PLAYBOY: What were you doing wrong?

JABBAR: Specifically, I was holding my hands at my sides and, just before a rebound, Moses would lean against me and pin one of my arms to my side. He'd knock me off balance for a split second, which was enough to let him get the rebound. Moses makes his living doing things like that. Newell showed me that I had to keep my hands and arms up higher and use my butt to knock people's weight off me so that I didn't get thrown off balance. The next two years—'84 and '85—my rebound average went up.

PLAYBOY: Basketball is supposedly a noncontact sport, yet it's become very physical in the past decade. Why?

JABBAR: Well, the closer you are to the basket, the more physical the game gets. Coaches generally want players to take shots from as close to the basket as possible, because the closer you are, the higher your shooting percentage. What happens is that everybody tries to get as close to the basket as he can. On offense, I'm not allowed anywhere near the basket. That's the book on me: Play me as physically as possible, to the point where you take a few fouls and see what the refs will let you get away with. I'll tell you, by the end of the season, I feel like a piece of chopped meat. The area under the hoop is serious, serious territory, and because centers play closest to the basket, they have the most serious job. There's very little levity under the basket. That's where most people end up bleeding.

PLAYBOY: Don't you think you're confirming what Malone had to say about wearing boxing gloves during games?

JABBAR: Oh, I'm definitely not into fisticuffs.

PLAYBOY: Then why have you been involved in fights on court?

JABBAR: I think you're probably referring to the Kent Benson episode, and if what led up to it happened again, I probably wouldn't react the same way. In 1977, in a game against Milwaukee, I was just standing in the lane, waiting for the ball to come down court, when Benson, who was then a rookie, looked at me, looked up court and then just fired an elbow into my solar plexus. That was one thing I wasn't going to tolerate.

PLAYBOY: You'd never caught an elbow?

JABBAR: I'd never gotten one that was so blatant and that also knocked the wind out of me. I mean, when he hit me, I went down—and when

I jumped up, about seven seconds later, I was outraged. I threw one right hand at him, and I've never decked anyone so badly. When the league finished its investigation, I got fined, and I'll never get over that, because it was as if I were the villain. The film clearly shows that wasn't the case.

PLAYBOY: You once said that before games, you work up a sense of antagonism toward the center who'll be guarding you. Is it really as grim as all that?

JABBAR: If I said antagonism, I didn't really mean it in a personal way against other players. And even though the level of competition is very high, I've gotten friendly with guys like Mahorn and Issel. Dan's a funny man, and he'd always have something ironic to say about what was happening. I've got to appreciate him as a person. His little daughter didn't know anything about basketball, but after she saw me in *Airplane!* and found out I played against her father, she asked Dan to get my autograph; so in his house, I'm a movie star. Bob Lanier, who played for Detroit, was also very funny. Bob wanted the refs to call every play his way, and he also wanted every rebound and didn't want you to run down the court too fast.

PLAYBOY: Would he actually tell you that?

JABBAR: Oh, he'd get mad at me for running down the court too fast. And then he'd yell at his coach, too: "Hey, I'm in here trying to score, trying to rebound—what do you expect, man, everything?" I knew that Bob used to smoke cigarettes at halftime, so I'd make him run a lot, and by the fourth quarter, he'd always be out of it. During games, we got to the point of blows being thrown; but away from the court, Bob and I always got along. Lanier said he loved the Bruce Lee movie I was in, *Game of Death*, because I got killed.

PLAYBOY: How did you happen to be in that movie?

JABBAR: Bruce and I were buddies. I'd studied *aikido* in New York one summer while I was a student at UCLA, and when I returned to Los Angeles in the fall, the editor of *Black Belt* magazine introduced me to Bruce, and we began working out together.

PLAYBOY: How much progress did you make in martial arts?

JABBAR: I did pretty well. Bruce wanted somebody to train with who could give him some problems, and he liked sparring with me because of my height and reach—that gave me enough of an advantage to make him work a little bit. Bruce graduated me a couple of times in his own discipline, which was called *jeet kune do*. Basically, it was boxing and kicking, plus a few blocking techniques.

PLAYBOY: Was his death a shock to you?

JABBAR: It was a terrible shock. I was on my way to see Bruce when he died—a blood vessel burst in his brain. I'd been traveling around the world and was coming home from Pakistan, and I decided to stop and see Bruce in Hong Kong. So I sent him a telegram and told him I was coming in, and three days later, when I got to the airport at Singapore to fly to Hong Kong, his death was reported in all the newspapers there.

PLAYBOY: Did you continue studying martial arts after Lee died?

JABBAR: No, but it wasn't because of Bruce's death, which I took as a personal loss. I'd mastered what he had taught me and wasn't that keen about going any further with it. Once you mature to the point where the prospect of combat doesn't obsess you, it changes you a lot. You don't worry "Can I kick this person's ass?" and you understand that you don't always have to be involved in life-and-death confrontations. The only thing I do now is a form of yoga taught in Los Angeles by Bikram Choudhury, who won the world championship in weightlifting. Bikram's yoga class is designed to enhance muscle elasticity.

PLAYBOY: Let's shift gears. For the past several years, newspapers have reported widespread drug use in the NBA Are such stories accurate?

JABBAR: I can only speak of what I've seen, which is that guys who do a lot of drugs don't last too long in the NBA The physical demands made on a basketball player are so extensive that anything that detracts from your conditioning tells on you real soon. If we're talking about players who keep their heads above water and who fool around a little at an occasional party, yes, I think we've seen only the tip of the iceberg. But if we're talking about guys who get heavily into drugs, they end up having serious problems and are out of the league very quickly.

PLAYBOY: Would you level with us about your own drug use?

JABBAR: Well, I went to school in the sixties and used grass when I went to movies and concerts—the usual profile. I tried LSD a couple of times in college, and that was definitely enough.

PLAYBOY: Did you have bad trips on LSD?

JABBAR: No, I never freaked out. I got a lot of *laughter* out of it—the absurdities of life are not that pronounced until you take a strong psychedelic. But your perception becomes obscured, and I didn't like that, because I wasn't in control. When I realized how easily you could lose your grip on reality, I said, "Whoa! I've had it with *this* stuff."

PLAYBOY: You've admitted that you once tried snorting heroin. What were the circumstances?

JABBAR: I just wanted to try it—that's how bright *I* was. After my junior year at UCLA, I was back in New York for the summer, and I went up with some friends to Saint Nicholas Park in Harlem, which was a safe place for junkies to hang out. I had two or three snorts right around 11 o'clock at night, and after that, when the guys passed the stuff over to me, I pretended to snort more, but I'd had enough. More than enough: For two or three hours, I couldn't focus both of my eyes at the same time.

PLAYBOY: Why did you want to try heroin? Was it a *macho* thing to do?

JABBAR: Yeah, I really wanted to show that I was one of the guys. Along with the other junkies, I sat in that park until four in the morning. I got home at seven and I had to go to work at 7:45.

PLAYBOY: What kind of job did you have?

JABBAR: I was working for the city—my job was to talk to kids about not screwing up their lives. Nice, huh? My friend Julian Dancy, a guy I grew up with and went to high school with, picked me up in his car and immediately knew what I'd been doing. I suppose it was hard for him to miss it: During the drive over to where I was speaking, all of a sudden I said, "I have to throw up now," and I rolled down my window quick. I'll never forget the look on Julian's face: It was a combination of disgust, anger and disappointment. I knew I never wanted to see that look directed at me again.

PLAYBOY: Did a lot of your friends have problems with drugs?

JABBAR: Yeah, and some of them are dead as a result. One guy I grew up with dealt cocaine and died of malnutrition—and when they found him, he had almost $5000 in his pocket. He was eating two or three hot dogs a day, but his main consumption was cocaine.

PLAYBOY: What about your own consumption of cocaine?

JABBAR: That started and really ended right before my rookie year in the NBA. A guy I'd known since we'd both been kids was dealing cocaine, and he had some great stuff. He said, "Hey, Kareem, let's do some hangin' out," and I said, "Right!" So I hung out with him for the better part of a day, and I did too much. I got real wired and, later on, I went for a drive. I wanted to get on whatever expressway it was, and you know how some on ramps begin as two lanes and then merge into one? Well, another driver and I got to the on ramp at the same time, and I just decided I was going to get to the expressway first. I mean, he was not gonna beat me! So I floored it, which was not a bright move: It had been raining and the highway was slippery. My car went into a skid, jumped the curb and then did one and a half turns on wet grass. I remember thinking, I could be wrapped around a tree trunk! Why did I do this? I definitely knew that the stuff had altered my personality. At that point, I realized it was best to leave cocaine to people who really wanted to do it. There were occasions after that when I fooled around with it, but I didn't get pulled in.

PLAYBOY: Did you ever freebase cocaine?

JABBAR: No, although when that started, some people tried to get me hooked on it. That wasn't something I wanted to try even *once*.

PLAYBOY: The majority of NBA team owners and officials would like to have players tested for drug use. What's your position on that?

JABBAR: I understand their sentiments—they want to do something to protect the sport and the business. There's been a public loss of confidence in the NBA because drug use is so pervasive. The real problem is that they're just seeing what everyone else is seeing: Cocaine has hit the whole of American society. The military, the sports and entertainment industries, the legal and medical professions—anywhere you look, the more affluent parts of society are riddled with drug use. But because basketball players have had a lot of esteem, it's more disappointing to people. I think the NBA is simply trying to do what it can to salvage the respect the public has had for its athletes.

PLAYBOY: Would you object to mandatory drug testing of NBA players?

JABBAR: Yes, I would. Aside from the constitutional ramifications, I think it's moving into an area where athletes would be treated like children. Basketball is not the defense industry or something that's absolutely necessary to our society. I'm not totally against mandatory testing, but I think the NBA should find a less heavy-handed way to satisfy its need to monitor players.

PLAYBOY: If you were put in charge of the problem, how would you try to eliminate drug use in the sport?

JABBAR: Jesus, that's tough to answer. I really think a good education program is always the way to go. Most people do not want to kill themselves or harm themselves. And if you can explain that to them in terms they can understand, usually they'll make the switch.

PLAYBOY: Having had your own fling with it, what can you tell people who want to try cocaine or are having their first experiences with it?

JABBAR: I can tell them that cocaine is very attractive. And that it's insidious. You think you're having a nice time, and in reality, you're on the way to the gallows. As in most cases with things like this, you don't see it until it's too late. You don't realize you have a cocaine problem until the blood vessels in your nose burst, or your teeth fall out, or you're dying of malnutrition, or you've lost your job and your family. That's when you find out you have a problem. Ishmael Reed wrote the most ironic—not funny, just ironic—thing I've read on this subject. Reed says cocaine is the Incas' revenge on the Europeans.

PLAYBOY: The subject of religion has come into the conversation tangentially; do you mind talking about what caused you to become a Muslim?

JABBAR: I don't mind at all. That came about after a long search. I always went to Catholic schools, because they were the best schools in New York at the time and my mother wanted me to get the best education possible. I hadn't truly been indoctrinated into the religion until I went to school, and when I learned about Jesus Christ at Power Memorial, well, it was a wonderful and illuminating encounter. But what they ended up teaching had nothing to do with the life of Jesus.

PLAYBOY: What did you think you were being taught instead?

JABBAR: I couldn't verbalize it at the time, but in hindsight, it was more like thought crime, and I put up with it because everybody else did. After all, this was our connection with the eternal and all that, and there were certain things you weren't supposed to think about.

PLAYBOY: Such as?

JABBAR: Sex. But then puberty showed up, and that was it: From that point on, I knew that Catholicism wasn't for me. We were being told that it was a sin to think about sex, and meanwhile, you'd have these hormones racing through your body at five times the speed of light.

PLAYBOY: How did you deal with those attacks of wild male hormones?

JABBAR: At first, I tried telling myself, "Don't even think about sex," but that was impossible; it's called adolescence. And, of course, I didn't know that all my friends who were supposedly getting all these women were lying to me. There I was, envying my friends and at the same time thinking, If it happens, it means I'll have to go to hell.

PLAYBOY: Were you ready to sacrifice your soul?

JABBAR: Oh, yes, but only for Sophia Loren. She never seemed to be around, though, and I didn't lose my virginity until I was 17.

PLAYBOY: Did you feel as if you had come late to the party?

JABBAR: No, because everybody else was dying, too. There were certain girls we'd see and we'd all go, "Ohhhh!" I had plenty of company in those days. When it finally happened, I knew it had to get better. And it did, too—as they say in Paris, "Eventuellement."

PLAYBOY: What went wrong the first time?

JABBAR: Nothing, except for the effect it had on my nervous system: I had the shakes for about five minutes afterward. It was probably more like 30 seconds, but it sure felt like five minutes. You know, I really did have a religious conflict about premarital sex, and it wasn't until later that I found out it was a charade everybody played, but I took it seriously. I was one of those kids. [*Laughs*] I suffered for my idealism.

PLAYBOY: Would it be fair to suggest that you were more naïve than most of your classmates?

JABBAR: Oh, yeah. But at the same time, I was truly curious as to whether or not there really was a Supreme Being and what, if anything, made human beings unique. I wanted to get some rational, in-depth knowledge about the subject, so in my senior year in high school, I started reading just about everything I could get my hands on—Hindu texts, Upanishads, Zen, Hermann Hesse—you name it.

PLAYBOY: What most impressed you?

JABBAR: Hesse's *Siddhartha*. I was then going through the same things that Siddhartha went through in his adolescence, and I identified with his rebellion against established precepts of love and life. Siddhartha becomes an aesthetic man, a wealthy man, a sensuous man—he explores all these different worlds and doesn't find enlightenment in any of them. That was the book's great message to me, so I started to try to develop my own value system as to what was good and what wasn't. And then, in my freshman year at UCLA, I read *The Autobiography of Malcolm X*, and that made more of an impression on me than any book I'd ever read.

PLAYBOY: And that attracted you to the Islamic religion?

JABBAR: It was a combination of Malcolm and my Catholic upbringing, because Muslims are very affirmative about the Old Testament. It's the same basic tradition; the dispute comes as to who was going to be the final prophet that Jews, Christians and Muslims all believed was coming. Basically, Jews, Christians and Muslims all believe in the God of Abraham. That's a common thread.

PLAYBOY: Then how do you explain the deep divisions among the three religions?

JABBAR: That's the baffling thing about it: None of the people who hold up these causes are acting the way Mohammed or Jesus or Moses or David taught people and showed people how to act, with the examples being their own lives. It's a strange thing to observe.

PLAYBOY: Did you consider becoming a Black Muslim?

JABBAR: No, but after my sophomore year at UCLA, I went up to a Black

Muslim rally in Harlem, because Muhammad Ali was the speaker, and I'd always admired him. I was a college all-American by then, and when the rally was over, I was invited to have dinner with Ali at Louis Farrakhan's house in Queens. We didn't really discuss religion that night, but when I started reading about them, the Black Muslims didn't appeal to my sense of what was really true.

PLAYBOY: With what did you find fault?

JABBAR: The Black Muslims were xenophobic. It also seemed to me that the people at the top of the pyramid were doing great, but the people at the bottom were out selling newspapers in the freezing cold. I knew some of those guys, and they had to buy whatever they didn't sell. I didn't see any need for that. But what the Black Muslims talked about as far as black people's helping one another improve our conditions in America went made sense. That was the one thing about the Black Muslims that appealed to me, because Christian churches, for all their strength and ability to organize in the black community, have never seemed to mount anything economic or political that can protect and advance black people's interests.

PLAYBOY: What do you think of Farrakhan's views today?

JABBAR: I think he's misleading. I don't feel it's possible for blacks to have a separate society within America. Black society has existed in America as a different kind of minisociety, but what the Black Muslims are talking about—a kind of independent nation-state—well, I just don't think it can be achieved. I would be overwhelmed with joy if black people could achieve economic and political independence and strength, and I think those are realistic goals. But they won't ever be achieved through Farrakhan's insular, separatist, hostile attitude. I believe that's going to create a polarization that'll take black people back several steps before they can walk past that point again.

PLAYBOY: Many people see Farrakhan as an anti-Semitic demagogue, whipping up racial hatred. Do you agree with anything he stands for?

JABBAR: There are certain things I definitely agree with him on. Black people *do* need to be economically and politically more sophisticated and capable. That's absolutely correct, but the stuff Farrakhan tacks onto that; well, I just can't deal with it. The whole thing about white people as devils—was John Brown the Devil? A lot more like him would have really helped black people in America. I just don't agree with the Black Muslims' racist delineation of who's good and who's evil.

PLAYBOY: What induced you to become a convert to the Islamic faith?

JABBAR: When I started learning about it, I read the Koran and different things Muslim mystics had written, and there was this body of knowledge that perhaps wasn't black, but it wasn't European, either. I think a lot of black people are attracted to Islam in this country because the religion espouses egalitarianism, and the morality is basically the same that you find in Christianity. But the religion itself is a little more realistic. There's no hierarchy of priests that can rip you off.

PLAYBOY: That's a pretty strong statement; why do you feel so hostile toward Catholicism?

JABBAR: When I was a freshman at UCLA, I did a lot of research and learned that Arab Muslims had enslaved black people in East Africa and that Christians had enslaved black people in West Africa, so no one can point a finger. But I also came across a papal bull, written in the 15th or 16th century, that basically said, "It's all right to enslave blacks and make them Christians. Let the slave trade roll." And the Catholic Church received a percentage of the profits. That was really it for me and Catholicism.

PLAYBOY: How did you feel about white people at that point?

JABBAR: I went through a period of angry racism and was affected by it for a little while, but then I realized that it was making me ill. My parents had always subscribed to *Jet* magazine, and well before I had had any personal experiences with whites, I had read about black people's being lynched. I remember when the black church in Birmingham was bombed, and that really got to me for months. When I was 15, my parents sent me down to North Carolina by bus to attend the high school graduation of a family friend's daughter. It was 1962, and I saw Jim Crow signs ["Whites Only"] all the way through Virginia and North Carolina. Black people couldn't drink at the same water fountains, use the same rest rooms or eat at the same restaurants as whites. It was hard to understand it, and the more of it I saw, the less trust I had for white people other than the ones I'd known.

PLAYBOY: The exceptions?

JABBAR: [*Laughs*] Right, the exceptions. I'm very thankful for those exceptions, because when I started to think logically about the subject of race again, I realized there had always been exceptions in my life, so I had to throw that theory out. I got some help with that.

PLAYBOY: From whom?

JABBAR: A man named Hamaas Abdul-Khaalis. My father had known him in the late forties and early fifties, when they were both very active as musicians. He told me that if I wanted to know more about the Muslim religion, I should talk with Hamaas, so I went to see him. Hamaas was then working for a Harlem agency that helped high school dropouts get their equivalency diplomas. He showed me that being anti-white or anti-Semitic was ridiculous and an infection—that's the best word I can use for it. He was a sincere, down-to-earth guy, and he understood how to live as a Muslim in America and still function as an American.

PLAYBOY: Is that difficult to do?

JABBAR: No. The Prophet Mohammed said that the faith can't be a burden on you, so if you have to work and can't make all your prayers, that's not a big deal. There's a lot of pragmatism and flexibility in Islam, but most of the world doesn't know that, because the people who make headlines and support the Islamic cause are coming from a very radical political position.

PLAYBOY: Are you referring to Lebanon and Khomeini's Iran?

JABBAR: Yes, and that situation really saddens me, because there's a lot of senseless slaughter going on there, and I share so much with a lot of those peoples. There's nationalism of all types, political fervor of varying degrees, and none of it is really based in logic.

PLAYBOY: What do you think should be done about the Palestinian problem?

JABBAR: I don't see any solution to it at all. There's just going to be more senseless death and destruction among people who really shouldn't be at odds. The most eloquent explanation of what's going on over there was given to me by a Hasidic Jew from Brooklyn. He quoted David Ben-Gurion as to how the Israeli state should evolve and said that what the Israelis are now doing is a little crazy.

PLAYBOY: In what way?

JABBAR: In essence, he said that Jews had had to forcefully make a place for themselves, but now, having done that, they've become too caught up in the theory that might is right. To keep a people under your heel just because it feels good or it's convenient or whatever—well, it's eventually going to work against Israel. I can see, 30 or 40 years from now, the same type of incidents that led to the uprising in the Warsaw Ghetto happening someplace in the West Bank. And for what? Those people—the Palestinians—are human. They will react to suppression the same way any people do, the same way Jews finally did.

PLAYBOY: Yet organizations such as the PLO still won't recognize Israel's right to exist. What would you have Israel do?

JABBAR: I just think it's time for Israel to lighten up a little; but I'm saying that as someone who lives 7000 miles away from the situation, and I'm not trying to preach a sermon. I do know that the two things needed in the Middle East are tolerance and restraint on the part of all concerned, and those two things just don't exist there. And so there's going to be more tragic loss of life.

PLAYBOY: Soon after you met Hamaas Abdul-Khaalis, you bought a house in Washington, D.C., that he used as an Islamic center. In 1973, a group of Black Muslims—intent on murdering your mentor—invaded that house and killed seven people, including three of Hamaas' children and his grandchild. Why were the Black Muslims after Hamaas—and were they after you, as well?

JABBAR: I don't think I was in any real danger, but they wanted to kill Hamaas because he'd written letters to them and to other Muslims saying that Elijah Muhammad, the Black Muslims' leader, was a sham and a fake. I'm assuming that was an affront that couldn't be tolerated by the Black Muslims. They sent some people to kill him, but he was out of the house when they came, so they killed his family. From that point on, Hamaas just kept building a bigger and thicker wall around himself. Four years later, in 1977, Hamaas and some other people from my house in D.C. took over some buildings, held hostages, and one person died.

PLAYBOY: Why did he do it?

JABBAR: That was Hamaas' way of protesting the opening of a film called *Mohammad, Messenger of God*—it's forbidden to create any likeness of the Prophet or alter the teachings or facts of his life. I went to visit Hamaas in jail before the trial, which was the last time I saw him. It's hard to know what's going on in somebody else's mind, but it seemed he was maintaining his usual demeanor and attitude.

PLAYBOY: Do you think he would have tried that takeover if his family hadn't been murdered?

JABBAR: Hamaas claims that had nothing to do with it, but I don't believe that. It just seems to me that he ended up doing something really destructive—there was loss of life, and all the brothers involved in the takeover with him were separated from their families. I didn't see any logic in what he'd done, only harm. It finally made me realize you can't give your life over to anyone. It's much better to make your own decisions and live with your own mistakes than to allow someone else to make decisions for you.

PLAYBOY: Had you done that with Hamaas?

JABBAR: Yes, I gave up way too much. I'd been seeing two women, both of whom converted to Islam because of me and studied the religion with Hamaas. When I decided to marry one of them in 1971, Hamaas strongly advised me to marry the other one instead—and I did as I was advised, even though I knew I wasn't in love with her. The wedding ceremony was held in the Washington house I'd bought for Hamaas, and it was a personal disaster: Because they weren't Muslims, my mother and father weren't permitted to attend. I knew they were outside in the hallway while the ceremony was going on, but I didn't know how to challenge Hamaas. After the wedding, I split. I went and saw my parents, and my mother was very upset, and that wound didn't heal until recently—I'm talking, like, within the past two years.

PLAYBOY: You left your wife in 1973. Was the marriage itself a disaster?

JABBAR: It wasn't a disaster, no. My ex-wife is a wonderful lady and a sincere Muslim, and after the divorce we still saw a lot of each other. I'm very fortunate in that we've eliminated our differences and we have a very positive relationship and beautiful children. I'm thankful for that. I couldn't ask for more.

PLAYBOY: How many children have you?

JABBAR: Habiba and I had three children, and I have a fourth from my relationship with Cheryl Pistono.

PLAYBOY: Cheryl Pistono has been depicted as the person most responsible for getting rid of your shyness and reluctance to deal with people. Do you think that's true?

JABBAR: Cheryl definitely helped, and she was the right person for that. But it was something I wanted for myself, and if I hadn't wanted it, it wouldn't have happened. We started living together in 1979, and by then I was no longer dealing with the Muslims in Washington, D.C. When I'd go out, Cheryl would go out with me, and there was a reaction in the press that was like, "He's with a woman. We can talk to this woman." And they could talk to Cheryl—she has quite a personality.

PLAYBOY: Was she a social buffer for you?

JABBAR: Yes, she played that role. We stopped living together at the beginning of 1984, when . . . let's just say the relationship ran its course. I'd rather not talk about that in public. I don't want to minimize anything Cheryl did for me, but I remember when people started writing that Cheryl was the reason I was happy, and then other people started writing that Magic Johnson was the reason I was happy. The truth is, I was happy just because the Lakers were winning.

PLAYBOY: Before last year, your team hadn't beaten the Celtics in eight NBA finals, including the 1984 championship series. Did you think the Celtics were some kind of jinx for the Lakers?

JABBAR: No, they're just an excellent team; but I thought we should have beaten them in 1984, and we would have if not for two critical mistakes. We lost two games to them in the '84 series because we threw the ball away at crucial times. We really beat ourselves and knew it, and we wanted another shot at them last year, because we had a lot to prove.

PLAYBOY: The Lakers and the Celtics seem to be in a league by themselves. How do the Celtics try to beat you?

JABBAR: The same way they beat everybody else. The Celtics play tough defense and they rebound well. They pride themselves on being a tougher team than we are; at least, they did last year.

PLAYBOY: Tougher in what sense?

JABBAR: That they were more physical and could outrebound us. They thought they had an advantage there, and so did a lot of sportswriters, who'd portrayed the Lakers as quiche eaters. But we knew that if we limited McHale's post-up baskets and played tough defense on Bird and didn't give him any second shots, we could beat them, and that's what happened. It's very rare for a team to win two championships in a row, and it's very important to me that we do it again this year.

PLAYBOY: If the Lakers get to the finals this season, do you think Boston will be there waiting for you again?

JABBAR: It wouldn't surprise me.

PLAYBOY: The Celtics have a team that's two-thirds white in a league that's 70 percent black. Does that strike you as odd?

JABBAR: [*Laughs*] We're not supposed to talk about these things. That's a really loaded question.

PLAYBOY: It's not loaded at all; we're being straightforward here. Do you think that Boston's management has a policy of keeping the team predominantly white?

JABBAR: Well, some teams do seem to relish the prospect of having a star player who's white. The Celtics certainly have a couple of star players who are white, and they're great basketball players. If I were a coach or a general manager, I'd want them on my team no matter what their color was. I'm not trying to put racial overtones on this, but as far as what Boston's policy *really* is, we'll never know.

PLAYBOY: Still, basketball fans often debate whether or not the racial makeup of an NBA team affects its popularity. What do you think?

JABBAR: If race were so important, the NBA wouldn't have set new attendance records the past two seasons. But there's something else to remember here: Whenever you have a winning team, people seem to forget about race very quickly. We get very tribal, but when push comes to shove and the heat gets turned on, we're all about the same basic things and our humanity overcomes all that other crap. A book I read called *Bloods*, about black soldiers, really brought that point home to me. A black guy who'd never really dealt with white people and resented them got put together in Vietnam with a white guy from the Deep South who considered himself Klan material. When they found themselves out there fighting Charley, they suddenly didn't care who the other guy was—they were on the same side, and screw all that other stuff. Vietnam changed everybody's thinking about who's OK and who isn't. You know how they say there are no atheists in foxholes? I don't believe there are a whole lot of racists in foxholes, either.

PLAYBOY: What about in the rest of American society?

JABBAR: I think it's changing and for the better. For example, a teammate of mine for several years on the Lakers was a guy named Norman Nixon. Norman grew up in Macon, Georgia, and is eight or 10 years younger than I am—and he attended an integrated high school and never saw a "Whites Only" sign. That, to me, is a monumental change, especially in view of what I told you about my trip down to North Carolina when I was in high school. Certain things have definitely changed for the better. The racist structures that were supported by law have pretty much been struck down, and any that remain are very vulnerable to attack when spotted. As far as the battle for men's hearts and minds is concerned, that continues. But that always will continue.

PLAYBOY: Are you optimistic about the eventual outcome of that battle?

JABBAR: Yeah, I am. People are starting to understand what it means to have a free and open society that respects the rights and appreciates the contributions of all its citizens. Our democracy has never been perfect, and it was hard for Americans to admit that in respect to blacks. Maybe that was understandable, given the fact that blacks weren't brought here to become presidents of corporations. We were brought here to tote that barge and lift that bale. We were brought here to be a convenience. Our men did manual labor and our women slept in their masters' beds. George Washington had something like 18 children with women who were his slaves. You know how people are always wondering. "Why are they all named Washington?" [*Laughs*] Well, it's legitimate. Jefferson also had a lot of black kids with his slaves. We are, within our population, the children of American presidents. [Historians have concluded that Washington had no such children.]

PLAYBOY: Did you change your name from Lew Alcindor as a stricture of your religion or was it a conscious decision to rid yourself of a slave master's name?

JABBAR: It was a combination of both. As far as I was concerned, I was latching on to something that was part of my heritage, because many of the slaves who were brought here were Muslims. My family was brought to America by a French planter named Alcindor, who came here from Trinidad in the 18th Century. My people were Yoruba, and their culture survived slavery—there are still traces of it in New Orleans and throughout the West Indies Cuba, Puerto Rico and French-speaking islands like Trinidad. My father found out about that when I was a kid, and it gave me all I needed to know that, hey, I was somebody, even if nobody else knew about it. When I was a kid, no one would believe anything positive that you could say about black people. And that's a terrible burden on black people, because they don't have an accurate idea of their history, which has been either suppressed or distorted. And I'm speaking from experience.

PLAYBOY: You weren't taught black history in school?

JABBAR: The history books I read throughout grade school and high school contained absolutely nothing about what black people did for this country. The only thing I learned was that black people were slaves and that Lincoln freed the slaves and then black people got dumped on during the Reconstruction. I was almost an adult before I found out that Crispus Attucks, a black, had been the first American to die in the Boston Massacre. And it wasn't until I was playing in the NBA that I found out that the Battle of Bunker Hill wasn't decided until Peter Salem, a black guy, shot Major John Pitcairn. Thousands of black people fought hard for America in the Revolutionary War. You know how the cavalry always shows up on time in the movies to save the settlers? Those were really black troops of the Ninth and Tenth cavalries, the buffalo soldiers. They chased Geronimo, they fought Pancho Villa along the borders, and during the Spanish-American War, they fought under General John J. Pershing at San Juan Hill. When you find out things like that, your attitude changes. When I understood what blacks had done here, it was like, "Hey, we've always been involved in meaningful things in America, but nobody's aware of it." Black kids need to know that; they need to know they belong here and have something to offer. Right now, it seems to me that black people only get credit for urban crime and welfare fraud, with a little rhythm-and-blues thrown in. I think that if our contributions to America became better known, it would give young blacks the incentive to do something. It would also give whites an appreciation of what we've contributed, and they would stop looking down on us as baggage.

PLAYBOY: Why haven't the educational systems in predominantly black cities been able to do that job?

JABBAR: No city's educational system is capable of dealing with what black kids have to overcome in order to get an education. The black family structure is a mess, and because there's no supervision outside the school, whatever the kids are taught is rarely reinforced at home. It's a vicious cycle, with child pregnancies being one of the biggest problems. Kids are great at producing babies, but when they see that raising them is an 18-year job, they say, "Screw that." So then we have more kids with no supervision, kids who end up being just like their parents. Until that can be overcome, blacks are not going to be very well educated.

PLAYBOY: Have you tried to do anything about that?

JABBAR: Yes, I worked with Arthur Ashe when he tried to start a literacy program, which consisted of having prominent blacks go around the country to promote literacy. We tried to do whatever we could to make kids deal with books and have some vision of what they'd like to do with their lives. It's proved to be more of a task than Arthur or I or anybody else could overcome.

PLAYBOY: Is it fair to say you're one of the nation's leading role models for black kids?

JABBAR: Yes, but for the wrong reasons. Black kids all want to go out and play basketball or football, and they should be thinking that there's an easier way to make a living. They should be thinking about going to school and having a career that lasts as long as they want it to last. They should be thinking about careers in law, in medicine, in accounting, in various technologies. Unfortunately, you have kids hoping for careers that hinge on their physical abilities, and that's not going to make it. You know how many jobs there are in pro basketball? About 275. And the average pro's career lasts about four years. It's so redundant and depressing. It's the only thing these kids talk about. It's part of the vicious cycle much of the black community has lived with.

PLAYBOY: Do you feel that that kind of thinking may be changing in the black community?

JABBAR: In terms of black people's moving to help themselves, it's a slow process. And understandably so, because until about 20 years ago, the political and economic development of black communities had been stymied by Jim Crow laws and *de facto* racism and a long history of suppressing black voting rights. It's changing, but it's like we're going from A to B, and the rest of the country has been around the alphabet twice. Blacks still don't have too much faith in the political process, and that's hurting us now.

PLAYBOY: How?

JABBAR: We're not using the political process as effectively as we could to improve our position. A lot of people were surprised when Harold Washington—another one of George's descendants—got elected mayor of Chicago and Wilson Goode got elected mayor of Philadelphia. It's an important new phenomenon, and an encouraging one, and we're going to have to understand what political power means on a local basis and then project it nationally. But because of all the mistrust, I don't know how quickly the black community will exploit its political power. I remember that when I was at UCLA, one of the things we used to say was that if we had James Brown and The Temptations down at the Coliseum, you couldn't keep black people out of there. But if we went down and said, "Look, we're gonna get together and organize to liberate black people," nobody would show up. That used to be a tirade we'd go on for days. But, again, black people don't trust the political process, because we've been zapped by it too many times.

PLAYBOY: Among contemporary politicians, who do you think has been most helpful to black Americans?

JABBAR: President Jimmy Carter, primarily because of his fantastic effort to establish Federal guidelines for hiring minorities. Unfortunately, the current administration is trying to eliminate all that.

PLAYBOY: How do you feel about Ronald Reagan?

JABBAR: I see a lot of indifference there. I think his attitude is that since the Constitution is such a great document, we don't have to force anybody to do anything, because the Constitution will protect everyone. But if that were true, there would have been no need for the Voting Rights Act, because all the rights blacks were supposed to have were clearly defined in the Constitution. Yet we couldn't exercise those rights, which is why the Voting Rights Act was necessary. I just think Reagan is out of touch. He doesn't know what reality is for a black person, and maybe that explains his indifference.

PLAYBOY: You have a lot of credibility with the public, so you may very well be asked to lend your name to various politicians' campaigns. Do you plan to become more active in politics?

JABBAR: Well, I'd like to keep that credibility, which will make it real hard for me to get involved. But there are certain politicians I respect, such as Mayor Tom Bradley of Los Angeles and Senator Bill Bradley of New Jersey. I don't know that much about Bill's politics, but I know he's honest, which is why I sent him money for his first Senatorial campaign. There are several politicians from California whom I like, and I also respect a guy from Brooklyn named Al Vann, who's done very well organizing black political groups in order to get access to the reins of political power in New York. I think that's what the black community really needs—people who can organize them and show them there's some blood to be gotten out of the turnip. It takes patience and a lot of demonstration before some people understand it, but when they do, it makes for meaningful change.

PLAYBOY: Is there a place for you in that process?

JABBAR: Not at present, but in the future, maybe.

PLAYBOY: When athletes retire, there's a vacuum in their lives that has to be filled. Will you miss the challenges, competition and life of a basketball player?

JABBAR: Sure I will. Fortunately, I still have the friends I made, so that'll take the edge off it; but the life—moving around the country like we do and knowing the people we know—yeah, I'll miss it.

PLAYBOY: In the world of sports, is it important to you how people perceive what you've accomplished?

JABBAR: No, because I've already gotten enough recognition to the point where I know I've impressed a few people. More than a few people. So there's no need for me to go on and on and on. I've played professional basketball longer than anyone else, and it's been great fun just fighting off the inevitable for as long as I have. I've achieved enough to back off without any regrets. I just hope that in remembering me, people will acknowledge my professionalism and consistency.

PLAYBOY: If you're able to control the next 20 years of your life the way you have the past 20 years, what would you like to accomplish?

JABBAR: Well, first I'd like to continue to have a positive relationship with the people who are important in my life, especially my kids. And I want to be able to maintain my business and financial entities. Beyond that, it's hard to say what I'd like to achieve. You're talking about the larger scheme of things, and that's still a big question mark. That's the adjustment I'm going to have to make—finding a direction and being able to move. Right now, I don't know where to direct my social thoughts, religious thoughts, political thoughts and thoughts about uplifting my people. I'm just one person, and at this point, all I know is that I'll play basketball for one more season, and then I'm going to rest for as long as it takes to rid my system of those 5:30 A.M. wake-up calls—the ones you get so that you can catch that next plane to that next game.

LANCE ARMSTRONG

A candid conversation with one of the world's greatest athletes about those drug rumors, the 40 million yellow bracelets and his life with Sheryl Crow

The most dominant athlete on earth has survived a mess of bike-race crashes, the kind that have killed a few racers. Half a dozen times he has collided with a car and escaped with scratches—except for the time he broke his neck. And then there was the cancer in his testicle, his lungs and his brain. Lance Armstrong survived that, too, and went on to win the 1999 Tour de France, the first of his record six straight victories in cycling's Super Bowl.

It's an oft-told story but worth recapping: In 1996 Armstrong's right testicle ached and swelled. He coughed blood. Tests showed cancer had spread throughout his 25-year-old body. After the testicle was removed he had brain surgery, then months of chemo so aggressive he got burns on his skin—from the inside. His racing team dumped him. He nearly quit cycling but then rebuilt his body and career. His 1999 Tour de France—he was the second American ever to win—was hailed as a once-in-a-millennium Cinderella story, a heartwarming fluke. Then the cussedly fierce Texan, who is slightly more intense than nuclear fusion, reeled off five more Tours in a row, a feat that may never be matched.

Today Armstrong, 33, is one of the two or three top jocks in the world, known and admired by millions, if not billions. He is also reviled by a vocal minority who call him a dope-abusing slimeball. Never mind that he has taken hundreds of drug tests and passed every one. His critics' reasoning goes like this: Cycling is famous for blood-doping scandals, and Armstrong rules cycling, so how could he be clean? His answer: "Test me!" It's hard to imagine any athlete who has given more pee and blood to prove his innocence. In fact, he invites the U.S. Anti-Doping Agency to test him 24/365. On the day we met him at the Hollywood Hills home of his girlfriend, rocker Sheryl Crow, he had given the USADA Crow's address in case the testers wanted to drop by.

Next month Armstrong goes for his seventh straight Tour de France win. The race is the most grueling challenge in sports: more than 2,000 miles over almost a month at speeds up to 70 miles an hour, up and down mountains in all weather. But he expects to win. Armstrong is coming off an epic year—his yellow LiveStrong bracelets are on wrists all over the world, and he bounced from a recent divorce into Crow's shapely arms. Betting against him is a loser's move.

We sent Kevin Cook to meet Armstrong. "I was impressed," says Cook, "and not just by Crow's imposing house and grounds. Armstrong is impressive: smart, funny and tastily profane. He oozes confidence without conceit. It's more like courage. He and Crow are clearly more than an item—they're a couple. They are renovating her house together, very much like husband and wife. Crow said hey and chatted a minute when I arrived. She and her beau may be famous, but they see themselves as a Missouri girl and a Texan who just happen to be hanging in this Hollywood Hills palace.

"Armstrong and I talked while his masseur worked on his legs— female readers should know Lance was bottomless under a towel—and then poolside, overlooking L.A. as the sun went down over Santa Monica Boulevard."

PLAYBOY: Were the LiveStrong bracelets your idea?

ARMSTRONG: All my idea. No, I'm kidding—I had nothing to do with them. It was Nike. They'd made millions of rubber bracelets in different colors for basketball players and called them "ballers." So I'm sitting around one day, and someone says, "Let's take a baller, color it yellow and put Lance's LiveStrong on there." Kind of ironic, a baller—

PLAYBOY: After your testicle was removed, your buddy Robin Williams called you the Uniballer.

ARMSTRONG: They said, "We'll sell them for a dollar and donate the proceeds to the Lance Armstrong Foundation." I thought they were crazy.

When they said Nike would make 5 million of them, I'm thinking, Right, sure. But they did, and they made a million-dollar donation, too.

PLAYBOY: When did you know those bracelets were taking over the world?

ARMSTRONG: Sheryl took one on the *Today* show—she was the first to do media with one. Then I went to Europe, and the Tour hit. You saw a lot of them then because they were sold as part of our Tour caravan. But it was at the Olympics when I thought, This thing is going off. Athletes from all countries and all sports were wearing them. Justin Gatlin won the 100-meter dash with one on. Then Morocco's Hicham El Guerrouj won the 1500 with his on. Here's the greatest middle-distance runner of all time, a Muslim who had never won Olympic gold. He crosses the finish line, goes down on the ground, praying to Allah, and all you see is this yellow band. Oh my God, that might be the coolest thing I've ever seen.

PLAYBOY: Tens of millions of people wore the bracelets. Did all that support offset the criticism from people who say you must be a doper?

ARMSTRONG: Yeah. There are stories saying, "He's doped" or "What he does is not possible." There's a disgruntled ex-employee saying she found kryptonite or something.

PLAYBOY: You mean the allegations in *L.A. Confidential*, a book published in France that, with no evidence, calls you a blood doper.

ARMSTRONG: Yeah. That's out there. But there are also 40 million yellow bands in the world. That outweighs the negative publicity. As far as the negative stuff goes, all I can say is thank God we're tested. When baseball players were charged with using steroids, what was their defense? Nothing. Saying "It's not true." Whereas my defense is hundreds of drug controls, at races and everywhere else. The testers could roll up here right this minute. They knocked on my door in Austin last week. In a way it's the ultimate in Big Brother, having to declare where you are 365 days a year so they can find you and test you. But those tests are my best defense.

PLAYBOY: What are you expecting at this year's Tour de France?

ARMSTRONG: The course is different. There will be fewer uphill finishes and fewer time trials. Those are the two ways you win. If you ask, "How did Lance win six Tours?" the answer is "He put time on 'em in the mountains, and he put time on 'em in the trials." So if those get reduced, it's not working for me.

PLAYBOY: Are Tour organizers trying to Lance-proof the course to give other guys a better chance?

ARMSTRONG: Doesn't matter. The three uphill finishes we'll have are superdemanding. The final time trial is really hard. So there's no excuse for not winning. I can't roll into Paris and say the course was too easy. I'll have my opportunities to kick ass.

PLAYBOY: But it'll be tougher this year?

ARMSTRONG: Only in the sense that I'm getting older. Gray hair, aches and pains.

PLAYBOY: Who's your prime competition?

ARMSTRONG: Same old, same old. Jan Ullrich, of course. Ivan Basso will be good.

PLAYBOY: Ullrich has finished second five times. He's Joe Frazier to your Ali.

ARMSTRONG: His T-Mobile team is strong. Ullrich, Andréas Klöden and Alexander Vinokourov—those three on one team are a force. But if you look at our Discovery Channel team, with me, José Azevedo and Yaroslav Popovych, we have a triple threat too.

PLAYBOY: How much significance would seven wins have?

ARMSTRONG: None.

PLAYBOY: You're grinning. But six was the record breaker. Nobody had won more than five Tours, not even the great Eddy Merckx or Miguel Indurain.

ARMSTRONG: Six was huge. I tried to downplay it publicly, but it was heavy. It was history. I got superstitious and wouldn't talk about it. There's something about that record—so much can happen. A crazy spectator could run out and punch you.

PLAYBOY: That's what happened to Merckx in 1975, when he was going for his sixth.

ARMSTRONG: Exactly. Thank God we live in a time when every second is filmed and photographed. At least nobody thinks he could get away with doing that.

PLAYBOY: Merckx would have won six if not for that sucker punch. But he didn't win the next year, in 1976. If you win your seventh, you'll top even the six he deserved to have.

ARMSTRONG: Right. Because it's fair to say he would have won six. It's also fair to say he was the greatest of all time, not me.

PLAYBOY: Americans know the Tour de France, but we don't follow other races. You're also in the Tour de Flanders.

ARMSTRONG: Yeah. There will be a million Flemish people on the side of the road.

PLAYBOY: Do we overemphasize the Tour de France?

ARMSTRONG: The sport does. They've done an amazing job building that franchise into a 500-pound gorilla leveraged with global TV and global sponsorships. It's the one race the riders have no say on. For other races we can dictate how long the time trials will be or how nice the hotels are. With the Tour they say, "If you don't like it, screw you."

PLAYBOY: If you win another Tour or three, will you retire, sit around on the couch and get fat?

ARMSTRONG: I'll be a fitness junkie forever, not out of shape like some guys. But I'm not naming names . . . *achoo-lemond!*

PLAYBOY: During that sneeze one side of your mouth mentioned Greg LeMond, your boyhood hero, who won three Tours but now rips you. He suspects you're a doper. What's your relationship with LeMond?

ARMSTRONG: None. What he did in 1989 and 1990 was phenomenal. But Greg's not even worth talking about today. And I don't need to hear from him—he'd only shove his foot farther down his mouth.

PLAYBOY: Why are great athletes motivated by grudges? Tiger Woods never forgets a slight. Michael Jordan carried a grudge against *Sports Illustrated* over a cover line—"Bag It, Michael"—that suggested he should quit playing baseball. He wouldn't talk to that magazine even after a later cover line read "Don't Bag It, Michael."

ARMSTRONG: It's good that somebody's got *SI* by the balls.

PLAYBOY: You're like that too, aren't you? Twelve million people say, "What a grand performance," but then one guy—

ARMSTRONG: Yeah, one prick says, "He's not so hot," and that's fuel. That's motivation. Whenever I come across that stuff I hit "Save" and store it on the hard drive.

PLAYBOY: Were you always that way?

ARMSTRONG: No. Not at 10, 20 or even 25. Through my illness I learned rejection. I was written off. That was the moment I thought, OK, game on. No prisoners. Everybody's going down.

PLAYBOY: In one of the worst corporate moves ever, your sponsor, the French company Cofidis, dropped you when you were sick.

ARMSTRONG: And they'd been there when I announced the diagnosis. They said, "We're going to stand by Lance, support him, nurse him back to health and see to it that he wins the Tour de France." So you take those words literally. You say, "That's great—I've got support." And then—*boom.*

PLAYBOY: Later, after you won a stage on your way to a Tour title, you cruised past the Cofidis team's director and said something.

ARMSTRONG: I said, "That was for you."

PLAYBOY: How has Cofidis been doing since then?

ARMSTRONG: [*Smiling*] They haven't done much.

PLAYBOY: Would you have won six Tours if you hadn't gotten cancer?

ARMSTRONG: I would have won zero.

PLAYBOY: You've beaten all the other guys, but what would happen if the 1999 Lance Armstrong rode against you? Who would win?

ARMSTRONG: If I'm in race shape, I think today's Lance wins. More experience, better tactics, more calmness in the race. And a team that's 10 times stronger.

PLAYBOY: It's a team sport. There are time trials in which the whole team's time counts, not just yours. And in the racing pack, the peloton, your teammates protect and pace you, often riding just ahead so you can draft behind them.

ARMSTRONG: Our 1999 team was the Bad News Bears, but in 2004 we were stacked, just unbeatable.

PLAYBOY: Do you have a favorite Tour de France?

ARMSTRONG: My most aggressive race was in 2001. That was the one I wanted most, and it was probably the most fun. The fake-out on Alpe d'Huez—

PLAYBOY: You faked exhaustion. Ullrich and his Deutsche Telekom team thought you were toast and zipped ahead. One reporter said they were "hammering like the hounds of hell." Then you took off.

ARMSTRONG: And made up two minutes on Ullrich. That was my best day on the bike, hands down.

PLAYBOY: But now you're less aggressive, more methodical.

ARMSTRONG: More selective. Last year, for example, I couldn't get rid of Basso on the climbs. But we had an individual time trial ahead, and I knew he'd give back time there.

PLAYBOY: He's better at climbs than sprints. And you're more patient than the Armstrong of 1999.

ARMSTRONG: The riskiest thing you can do is get greedy. You learn that your tank is only so big, and if you just keep burning you'll run out of fuel. In 2000 I cracked and lost a lot of time, could have lost the Tour. I'm more respectful of that possibility now. Over time you develop a feel for when you're going into the red. There are times you have to do that, but not always. What's best is when you're going faster than anybody else but you're not killing yourself, not subtracting from what you can do the next day. Like last year—not once was I ever totally in the red zone.

PLAYBOY: It sounds like you're ready to win again.

ARMSTRONG: It's hard to know in advance. In 2003 it was all red, all suffering.

PLAYBOY: You've said you like suffering.

ARMSTRONG: There are different kinds. There's the kind you get when your tank is empty and you look up and see 100 guys in front of you. That's devastating. That's just rusty pain. But when you're hurting and you hear on the radio that you've got 10 seconds on your biggest rival, and now it's 20 seconds, or in 2001 two minutes on Ullrich—that's a true sporting high. You're numb to pain. You can't feel the lactate in your muscles, and you just go faster and faster, which is not what I felt today.

PLAYBOY: You had a training run, Hollywood to Pasadena.

ARMSTRONG: I'm not in shape yet. I go out to suffer—my pain threshold is low and my body weight is high, which makes for a nasty mix of suffering and heaviness. And I know how it feels to ride fast. Today is one of those "Damn, why do I do this?" days.

PLAYBOY: The leader in the Tour gets a yellow jersey. What happens to the jersey after you ride? Do you wash it?

ARMSTRONG: You get a new one every day, but I like to keep wearing the first one. It feels better once you break it in, like a favorite old T-shirt you've worn a thousand times. On the last day I'll take it off and save it. All six of my last-day jerseys are up on my wall. If they weren't glassed in, they'd be stinky.

PLAYBOY: Can you ask for extras?

ARMSTRONG: Yep. They know you'll give a few away. Maybe I shouldn't say, but I've got about 400 of them.

PLAYBOY: There's an interesting etiquette in pro cycling. The whole peloton slows down and waits if a rider stops to pee. And when you were struggling in 2000, two riders from the Vini Caldirola team let you draft off them. Weren't they hurting their own chances?

ARMSTRONG: Their team wasn't going to win, so they had no real skin in the game. They just had a certain respect and empathy for me. That's part of our sport. It happens in NASCAR, mostly between teammates. Who's to say it doesn't happen in the NFL? Every year there's some goofy scenario—some bullshit team trying to get a wild card beats a team that has a spot in the playoffs locked up.

PLAYBOY: Is cycling etiquette dying? Tour stars often let lesser guys win stages if they're no threat in the overall standings, but last year you went all out. Your approach was *pas de cadeaux*, no gifts.

ARMSTRONG: Last year was unique. The run-up to the Tour was stressful. I'd been written off 30 different times, my obituary written every day. That just built up in the hard drive until I was thinking, All right, dudes, let's go!

PLAYBOY: Grudges again.

ARMSTRONG: I was excited. And there were so many sprint finishes. For me a four- or five-man sprint finish is just too intense to pass up.

PLAYBOY: Let's talk about crashing. On one training ride in France you zoomed into a blind corner and hit a truck coming the other way.

ARMSTRONG: Hit it head-on. The bike split in three pieces. My helmet just melted. And the driver got belligerent. French guy. He was mad that I'd bent his little piece-of-junk truck, and I'm lying there with a cracked C7 vertebra, a broken neck. What's really scary is crashing in a race. The first week of the Tour is the worst. You've got 200 guys who want to be at the front, and it's aggressive and gnarly and windy. I look straight ahead, just waiting for some kook in front of me to crash. Then the race goes on, and you add rain or cobblestones. Last year on the cobbles I was so scared I felt like a child, just terrified.

PLAYBOY: People think you're immune to fear.

ARMSTRONG: Two things scare me. The first is getting hurt. But that's not nearly as scary as the second, which is losing. If you're caught behind a crash in a windy section with 50 guys in a pile in front of you—game over.

PLAYBOY: Don't they give you some leeway? You're a six-time champ.

ARMSTRONG: If you're in the middle of 50 guys, they don't care who you are. They don't care if you've won the Tour once or six times. Everybody's desperate. We're all killers to some degree. It's easy to get quacked—that's what we call it when a guy comes into you without looking.

PLAYBOY: Worse than getting quacked is getting flicked.

ARMSTRONG: That's when it's intentional. Direct from the German *flicken*. It means you got fucked.

PLAYBOY: The sport is more colorful than people think. When French fans booed and whistled at you and your U.S. Postal teammates, you responded by booing each other. You had team jingles, too—chants you'd repeat before a stage, like "Somebody's going to be my bitch today, bitch today, bitch today."

ARMSTRONG: There's less of that now that our team has gotten more and more international.

PLAYBOY: That would be hard to put into Esperanto.

ARMSTRONG: Yes, it's tough to tell a Portuguese guy what you mean by "Who's going to be my bitch today?" I might have only one other American with me this year, George Hincapie. I'll have to talk smack with George.

PLAYBOY: You're even more famous in Europe than you are here. Do you like being a celebrity?

ARMSTRONG: *Celebrity* and *fame*, those words make me uncomfortable. Some athletes are addicted to fame, but that's not what gets me off.

PLAYBOY: Aren't you courting it by being with Crow?

ARMSTRONG: She's no stranger to the public eye. But I don't live with Sheryl Crow, rock star. OK, she lives in Los Angeles, and she's arguably the queen of rock and roll. But I live with Sheryl Crow from Kennett, Missouri, who still talks to her mother and father every day, a girl who's funny, likable, smart and athletic. She's not out getting trashed every night like some people in her profession.

PLAYBOY: You're also buddies with Bono of U2 and Lyle Lovett. Whose music is better, Crow's or theirs?

ARMSTRONG: Ha. It's different. I will say I like her music, and I'm not saying that just because she pays me to.

PLAYBOY: You and she kissed after you won a Tour stage last year. One reporter described it as "fiery, impetuous and nearly unending." Was that your best career kiss?

ARMSTRONG: I don't remember that one. We have a lot of long, juicy kisses. Kissing's good for relationships.

PLAYBOY: Are you two very much alike, or are you opposites?

ARMSTRONG: Similar. We're type A people who can't sit still. Sheryl couldn't sit here and talk to you for an hour. She'd be shaking her foot the whole time. Sometimes I'll be talking to her and say, "Calm it with the foot!"

PLAYBOY: What was the first thing you and she said to each other?

ARMSTRONG: We talked about trading guitar lessons for bike-riding lessons. But to be honest, I wasn't much concerned about the guitar lessons.

PLAYBOY: Lovett married and broke up with Julia Roberts. Did he give you any advice on celebrity romance?

ARMSTRONG: Lyle's about as down-home as they get. He still lives on the ranch he grew up on, and he's trying to reconstruct it. He never left Texas. He did spend time in L.A. and New York with Julia, but I think that was tough on him. To some degree it's like that for me. I miss Austin. I miss my three kids, who live there with their mother.

PLAYBOY: You have a cat named Chemo—

ARMSTRONG: Not anymore. I lost the cat in the divorce. What's up with that? It was my cat!

PLAYBOY: Do you still have a house just a couple doors down from Kristin, your ex?

ARMSTRONG: No, that wasn't a good thing. Too close. I'm building a new house about a mile away. I'm trying to spend more time in Austin, and that'll happen soon enough. When cycling is over, my main commitments will be to my kids and to Sheryl. I'm still learning how to live in a relationship. I wasn't successful the first time.

PLAYBOY: Crow took you to the Grammys last winter. Melissa Etheridge was there—she'd lost her hair after chemo for breast cancer. Did you talk to her about that?

ARMSTRONG: We sat together in the front row. She's done with treatments now. She's in that phase when you wait to see what the next scans show, what the next set of blood work reveals. Melissa looked great. I thought she was mighty courageous, rolling out with no hair, performing onstage and just killing. I was nearly crying.

PLAYBOY: Not too many bike racers get front-row seats at the Grammys.

ARMSTRONG: Someone behind me yelled "Lance, Lance!" I turn around and it's James Brown, and the Godfather of Soul has a yellow band around his wrist. That was wild. It's a three-hour show, and I was dying, just jonesing for a cold beer, when this lady walks out and hands me one. In the whole Staples Center, I'm the only one with a beer. Sheryl says, "Who gave you that?" Then Melissa sings, comes back and says, "Did you get your beer?" She'd heard me groaning, "God, I need a beer," so she had someone find me one. Sweet lady.

PLAYBOY: When you were sick you got involved in every medical decision. Now you tell other patients to be the same way.

ARMSTRONG: You've got to ask questions, get second and third opinions. That can be tricky because people feel loyal to their doctors. A cancer diagnosis is devastating news, and they develop a bond with the doctor who tells them. But you've got to act in your own interest. Do some politicking, not just with doctors but with nurses, administrators, the hospital pharmacist. Tell the pharmacist, "Dude, give me the good batch, the fresh stuff." Ask the nurse how she's doing: "How'd you sleep last night? Did you have a good breakfast? Oh, and make sure my dose is right." I was highly aware of their importance. That's where I learned to build a team.

PLAYBOY: In the hospital?

ARMSTRONG: Right. Saying, "Craig and Larry, you're my head doctors. LaTrice, you're my head nurse." It's critical to know the nurses. They're working for you 90 percent of the time, while the doctors are there 10 percent of the time.

PLAYBOY: It's been more than eight years since your diagnosis. The chemo damaged your kidneys, didn't it?

ARMSTRONG: Some. I was on 24-hour hydration because they changed the drug protocols at the last minute. The first one I'd been on was tougher on the lungs. If I was ever going to race again, I needed something different. Now I'm supposedly in the clear. I still get nervous about relapsing, but everything seems normal.

PLAYBOY: Any other lasting effects?

ARMSTRONG: Sterility.

PLAYBOY: Is that permanent?

ARMSTRONG: It's about 50-50. I might get it back.

PLAYBOY: What if you and Crow want to have a child?

ARMSTRONG: That's possible. We've talked about it.

PLAYBOY: You had a sperm sample frozen in 1996. Does it have a particular shelf life?

ARMSTRONG: It's tougher to use sperm that's been frozen for eight years. I don't know how many there are in the sample. Ten million, maybe. That sounds like a lot, but it's not.

PLAYBOY: Have you been tested lately?

ARMSTRONG: No. Going to the lab for that test is not the most glamorous thing in the world. Going into that little room in 1996, that was no fun. And I'd just had surgery to remove the bad testicle. That's a big cut—I could barely walk.

PLAYBOY: You had the testicle cut out before donating the sperm?

ARMSTRONG: Two days before. Painful? Dude, it was terrible. But I had to do it if I was ever going to have kids.

PLAYBOY: How did you get in the mood to . . . donate?

ARMSTRONG: No choice. I didn't have a wife yet or anybody to have kids with. Sure, it was awful, but now I have three healthy little miracle children. I'm glad I limped down to that lab in San Antonio.

PLAYBOY: They give a guy some ammo for that. Magazines.

ARMSTRONG: I don't think it was *Playboy*. For that kind of ammo *Playboy* is sort of a slingshot. You can read it. That's why we're talking. But there are some shoulder rockets in that field—if *Playboy* were one of those weapons of mass destruction, I wouldn't be doing this interview.

PLAYBOY: After you lose a testicle, does the other one stay where it was or does it move to the middle?

ARMSTRONG: It stays. Mine stayed left. You also produce less testosterone. The one that remains picks up a bit of the slack for his buddy who's gone, but not all of it. Since 1996 I've had chronically low testosterone, and I can't do anything about it.

PLAYBOY: It's a banned substance. You couldn't race if you replaced the testosterone you lost.

ARMSTRONG: I have to wait until I retire. It's not a question of being manly or being a sexual god, but I worry about osteoporosis. Chronically low testosterone leads to brittle bones.

PLAYBOY: Does it affect your sex drive?

ARMSTRONG: [*Smiling*] Not yet.

PLAYBOY: What do you think of drug testing in other sports?

ARMSTRONG: Baseball is the hot topic. Look at Jason Giambi and the Yankees. They need to test for steroids. In the future I think franchises and sponsors are going to hold the athletes responsible. If they're not clean, sponsors and teams will go after their money—not just to stop paying salaries but to get back previous payments. And that's serious because we all spend our money when we get it. If you're a baseball player who tests positive and your team wants your salary back from last year, can you get it back and repay them?

PLAYBOY: You mentioned Giambi. How about Barry Bonds?

ARMSTRONG: I'm not one of those cynics who think there are 10 different undetectable compounds. I'm not going to say Barry Bonds has something under the table. But then BALCO was all about making something undetectable.

PLAYBOY: Do drug scandals in other sports hurt your cause?

ARMSTRONG: No. My first line of defense is that I've been competing for a long time, and my body looks the same. I won the world championship when I was 21, the youngest ever. It's been a steady progression from there. The drug spotlight has been shining on me since 1999, and my performances have not diminished. But when that light hits some athletes they disappear.

PLAYBOY: Suddenly the guy goes from 44 home runs back to 15.

ARMSTRONG: Or he doesn't run as fast. My second line of defense is that while some sports haven't had testing, I've been tested for years, in and out of competition. And third, I've always pushed the International Olympic Committee and the Tour de France to increase testing. What other athlete do you know who has donated money to his sport's governing body to pay for drug controls?

PLAYBOY: How many pro cyclists use performance-enhancing drugs?

ARMSTRONG: I don't know. I like to think the sport is cleaner than its reputation. The head medical inspector for the Tour de France tells our team, "Guys, you're so dominant, I'm suspicious too. But I'm the one screening the blood and urine samples, and they are pure as driven snow." If we can do it, why can't everybody else? But you'll always find athletes looking for shortcuts. It's ironic that cycling has done more than any other endurance sport to test them, and when you test you're going to catch some guys. But every time you do, some fucker is sure to write, "Look how dirty the sport is!" That's the risk of testing.

PLAYBOY: Is your Discovery Channel team the only clean one?

ARMSTRONG: The whole roster is 28 guys. Someone could be at home doing something that's not clean, but I don't think so. We screen our guys and pick the ones with integrity and talent. When you've got those two things, you don't need to take risks, and cheating would be a huge risk. It would jeopardize the entire program, our $15 million-a-year baby. If one of us gets popped, we all go home. Nobody wants that.

PLAYBOY: How many drug tests have you taken?

ARMSTRONG: Maybe 200 in the past six or seven years. Not as many before that because I wasn't as successful. Maybe 100. So the total is around 300.

PLAYBOY: For the record, how many of those tests were positive?

ARMSTRONG: Zero.

PLAYBOY: Do you worry about sabotage? Could somebody spike your blood or urine?

ARMSTRONG: I worry about that every day. They could spike your food or the water you drink.

PLAYBOY: Some cyclists train by sleeping in an "altitude tent" with thin air that helps thicken the blood. It's a legal way to make your blood more efficient. Have you got one?

ARMSTRONG: A tent's not big enough. I've got an altitude cubicle.

PLAYBOY: You sit in there and work on a computer?

ARMSTRONG: No, you sleep in it. We sleep in it. We can get Sheryl's whole bed in there.

PLAYBOY: So in a virtual sense you've joined the mile-high club.

ARMSTRONG: Oh, I've joined that club in a literal sense.

PLAYBOY: Boxers avoid sex before a fight. But the Tour de France lasts almost a month. What happens?

ARMSTRONG: It's safe to say there's very little sex going on during the Tour de France, if any. Coaches and team directors would prefer you didn't have sex all year.

PLAYBOY: Your coach, Chris Carmichael, has said you're not unique as a physical specimen but that you're pretty special. Isn't your heart 30 percent bigger than normal?

ARMSTRONG: It's bigger. And my muscles supposedly produce less lactic acid. But you know what's interesting? There's a big artery that runs from the middle of your body to your lower half, down to your legs. I had some scans done, and the doctors couldn't believe it: My artery is three times the size of a normal person's.

PLAYBOY: You used to play a lot of golf, but then you quit. Why?

ARMSTRONG: Why? Because I suck.

PLAYBOY: You alluded earlier to your divorce. Do you see it as a failure in your life?

ARMSTRONG: Yes.

PLAYBOY: The biggest one?

ARMSTRONG: Yes and no. Our marriage and divorce wasn't a total failure, because we wanted children, had children and love them deeply. Kristin and I aren't husband and wife, but we'll always be mom and dad, and we work on that.

PLAYBOY: She's a devout Catholic, and you're not religious. You also differ in that respect with President Bush, a man you've known since he was governor of Texas.

ARMSTRONG: I have to be careful here. I like the president. He is a deeply spiritual man. And I don't know if that spirituality has any place in the highest office. Having said that, I think the majority of the country disagrees with me on this.

PLAYBOY: Doesn't every leader say he's got God on his side?

ARMSTRONG: Exactly the point. The beliefs of the president and of mainstream America are not necessarily shared by people around the world. We can't force our beliefs and our freedoms on others. I mean, there are a billion Muslims in the world. There are Muslims, Jews, Buddhists, hundreds of forms of religion, and none of us is right or wrong. I think we need a serious line between church and state.

PLAYBOY: Do you and Crow discuss getting married?

ARMSTRONG: Do people discuss that? I thought the guy just asked the girl.

PLAYBOY: That's the old-fashioned way.

ARMSTRONG: Sometimes the girl puts on a little pressure. The other day I heard about a girl who asked the guy to marry her. How do you like that?

PLAYBOY: What would you say?

ARMSTRONG: We actually talked about that. Sheryl said, "Don't worry. I won't ask you to get married."

PLAYBOY: Your father took off before you ever knew him, and you've said you don't want to know him. You dismiss him as "the DNA donor." But what if he gave you your physical attributes?

ARMSTRONG: I don't think he's athletic. All I needed was my mom, who got pregnant at 17 and never quit on her baby—me. My mom was against quitting anything. She was stronger than most mothers and fathers together. I thought of her during my first pro cycling event, when I finished 111th out of 111 finishers. But about 200 guys started, so there were 80 or more quitters. At least I didn't quit.

PLAYBOY: Growing up without a dad around must have been tough. Did you have the birds-and-bees talk with your mom?

ARMSTRONG: Never had one.

PLAYBOY: Did you feel cheated? Did that slow your development?

ARMSTRONG: Probably. You know when you're 11 or 12 and kids play truth or dare or spin the bottle? You have to kiss a girl and then French kiss a girl, and man, you don't want to mess up your first time. That's pressure. I really wasn't up to speed in those games. But the way things turned out, I can't complain.

BARRY BONDS

A candid conversation with base-ball's highest-paid player about jumping like Michael Jordan, talking like Richard Pryor and crying like Diana Ross

It is said that a great baseball player can do five things well. He can run, throw, field, hit for average and hit for power. Barry Bonds is five for five, which is why in the next six years he will earn $42 million more than the president of the United States. But to many fans, Bonds also exemplifies other qualities: greed, arrogance and the bombast that makes today's jocks seem less heroic than those of the past.

Sure, he may be a great ballplayer, as even his detractors admit. Yes, he is a hunk—*People* magazine called him one of the 50 most beautiful people in the world. He's also a devoted family man who speeds home from the park to spend time with his wife, Sun, and two toddlers, Nikolai and Shikari. Still, Barry Bonds pisses people off.

Maybe it's the contract. After leading the Pittsburgh Pirates to three straight divisional titles, he spurned the Pirates' offer of $5 million to sign with the San Francisco Giants last winter. San Francisco agreed to pay him $43.75 million over six years—$7.3 million per year. Even that wasn't quite enough. Bonds also demanded a private hotel suite on road trips, a perk the club dutifully added to the richest contract the game has ever seen.

Maybe it's the jewelry. A diamond cross hangs from his left ear and a mammoth diamond ring adorns his left hand. Under his Adam's apple hangs a pendant that reads "Barry Bonds 30/50" in diamonds and gold, a none-too-subtle reminder of his 30-homer, 50-steal feat of 1990.

Maybe it's his celebrated attitude. Bonds is not shy. On the field he is among the most graceful of athletes, but he is also a showoff.

He taps his glove to his chest or his hip before fancily shagging fly balls, employs a quick-wristed "snap catch" that adds further style to the putout and poses after hitting home runs: Standing frozen at the plate, he watches the ball soar into the cheap seats, relishing his moment of triumph. Off the field he speaks his mind, insisting that he is worth almost $44 million if anyone is, though he sometimes turns frosty and refuses to speak to reporters, fans or even teammates.

Of course, for Bonds, both attitude and ability are family traits. His father is Bobby Bonds, who played in the big leagues from 1968 to 1981. The elder Bonds batted .268 with 332 career home runs and 461 stolen bases. He almost won a most-valuable-player award in 1973, when he hit 39 homers, drove in 96 runs and stole 43 bases for the Giants. But Bobby Bonds—who as a minor leaguer had waited outside while teammates ate in whites-only restaurants—was thought to be moody if not militant. In those days before free agency, he was shuttled from team to team seven times in 14 years. During that time he provided his wife, Pat, and their children with a comfortable sub-urban life, complete with the advantages Barry needed to become an even better ballplayer than Bobby was.

After batting .467 for Serra High School in San Mateo, California, Barry Bonds hit .347 with 45 home runs in an all-American career at Arizona State University, tying an NCAA record with seven consecutive hits in the College World Series. Drafted by the Pirates in 1985, he reached the big leagues after only 115 minor-league games. In 1986 he led National League rookies in home runs, RBIs and stolen bases. Four years later he was an All-Star, the first player ever to bat .300 or better with 30 or more homers, 100 or more RBIs and 50 or more steals in a single season. He was the league's most valuable player that year, finished a close second in 1991 and won his second MVP award last season, when he batted .311, hit 34 home runs, drove in 103 and won a third straight Gold Glove award for his fielding.

At the age of 29, Bonds owns one more MVP trophy than Babe Ruth. If he can claim another he joins Mickey Mantle, Jimmie Foxx, Yogi Berra, Stan Musial, Roy Campanella, Joe DiMaggio and Mike Schmidt as one of eight men to win the award three times. No one has ever won four times. Bonds says he wants to be the first.

Bobby Bonds and Barry Bonds have hit more home runs than any other father-son duo in the game's history. Only five players have ever had multiple 30-homer, 30-steal seasons, and two of those men are named Bonds. Now that Bobby is back from a five-year absence from the game, both of them are San Francisco Giants. Bobby is the Giants' new batting coach. Bobby's friend Willie Mays—the Hall of Famer who is Barry's godfather—is also with the Giants. Barry, of course, is the club's superstar.

Contributing Editor Kevin Cook spent parts of the past winter and spring with Bonds. Cook reports:

"I knew of Bonds's reputation for being aloof or even surly. I found him difficult to pin down—he often postponed our meetings for a day or two—but each time we met he was engaging, thoughtful and funny.

"We began at the Beverly Hills offices of his agent. I noticed his tendency to look blankly past people. It could have been aloofness or a defense against being rushed by half a dozen people calling his name. Once we sat down in a corner office, he was pleasant and animated, stopping only to call 'my man Arsenio,' who couldn't come to the phone. Bonds took a break to peruse a sheaf of papers that turned out to be the latest revision of his contract, which he signed with a multimillion-dollar scribble.

"We also chatted at Bear Creek, the Nicklaus-designed golf course close to his new 12,000-square-foot house near San Diego. An avid golfer with a 10 handicap, he is a wizard at escaping sand traps and a gleeful competitor—laughing when his opponent's ball bounces off the green and into a trap. When he hits a drive just right—one of his infrequent 300-yarders—he finishes the swing exactly the way he does after hitting a home run, and says, 'Damn, look at that one.'

"At Scottsdale, Arizona, the Giants' spring-training home, I found Barry's father sitting in the locker room at Scottsdale Stadium smoking a cigarette. Bobby Bonds spoke softly, with evident pleasure, of Barry's youth. He remembered worrying because his first son seemed to be left-handed, an attribute that would limit the positions he could play on a baseball team. Wanting Barry to be right-handed, Bobby 'wouldn't let him take his baby bottle with his left hand. I'd pull it away and get him to take it with his right. But then he'd just switch it over, so I lost that one.'

"On the practice field at Scottsdale, Barry shagged flies and took batting practice. Still rusty after four months without facing live pitching, he spent a few frustrating minutes tapping ground balls and hitting pop-ups. When he finally sent a ball over the fence and down the street beyond, his face lit up. 'They'll never find that one,' he said."

PLAYBOY: How does it feel when you hit a home run?

BONDS: Like one perfect boom. You're in a zone all by yourself. No matter where the ball is, no matter what the pitcher does, you know exactly what's going to happen. Everything is perfect in that one particular second. It's in slow motion. You don't hear anything, you don't even feel it hit your bat. That's the zone—it's strange, it's fun, but it's only temporary.

PLAYBOY: After hitting one, you often stand frozen at the plate, admiring your work. Aren't you showboating?

BONDS: The way I see it, out of 162 games, 600 at bats, you may hit 20 to 30 home runs. Enjoy 'em. The pitchers enjoy it when they strike you out. Relievers enjoy themselves when they get that last out and save the game. Let me enjoy my time. I mean no harm. I worked my butt off to get where I am. All the hard work I did, in this one split second, paid off.

PLAYBOY: Are you a hot dog?

BONDS: Sure. I can be very arrogant and cocky on the field, but that's what makes Barry tick. That's my comfort zone. I'm doing my job, giving the people what they paid for. Entertainment. Like when I tap my glove on my chest before I catch a fly ball. People like that. But there's a point to it, too. It lets my teammates and the fans know everything's under control. You can yell, "Mine, I got it," but sometimes the crowd is so loud, the other outfielder can't hear you. When I'm tapping to say it's mine, you can't miss my gesture. It's like I'm moonwalking across the field.

PLAYBOY: Did anyone ever tell you to cut it out?

BONDS: Guys will say, "I get tired of you catching the ball like that every time I hit it." I say, "If you have a problem, don't hit it to me."

PLAYBOY: You're not shy out there.

BONDS: It's like I become a Hollywood star on the field, like Michael Jackson. I can't dance like him or excite people like he does, but I can hit my glove on my chest and people like it. It's a move no one's seen before. When I jump over the wall for a ball, I feel like Michael Jordan flying in air. When I crash into the wall, I'm Rambo, this invincible man. You know the movie *Predator*? The dude who knows where you are and can see you, but you can't see him? When I hit my game-winning home run off Lee Smith, I was the Predator. I knew what was going to happen. It was incredible. I can see you, but you can't see me, and something good is going to happen.

PLAYBOY: How many people do you have in your uniform?

BONDS: [*Laughs*] You get a lot of characters out of me. I can be radical, subtle or mean. When I run my mouth, I'm Richard Pryor. I can feel smart and want everybody to listen to me, like Bill Cosby. After I signed with the Giants and everyone asked how it felt to come home, to be with my idol Willie Mays—he's my godfather—and with my father, I got all sensitive. Choking up, crying at a press conference. And I thought, yes, now I'm Diana Ross.

PLAYBOY: You said you could be mean.

BONDS: Some days I'm like the deaf girl in the movie *Children of a Lesser God*, the one who had such an attitude all the time. I won't talk to anybody. My teammates, coaches, nobody. Stay out of my face, because I don't hear anybody and I'm not talking.

PLAYBOY: Why?

BONDS: That's how I feel that day. I'm not always the best person to be around. I can be a butt.

PLAYBOY: Does that bug your teammates and coaches?

BONDS: [*With his fingers in his ears*] Sorry, I can't *hear* you!

PLAYBOY: Sounds like the time to bring up a touchy subject. How can a ballplayer be worth $44 million?

BONDS: It's entertainment and entertainers get paid a lot. But I'm not going out buying everything I see. It's for my kids more than anything else. I wanted a house big enough so that my kids didn't have to share a room. When I was a kid I always had to give up my room when my grandparents came to visit. I didn't want my kids ever to have to give up their rooms, and now they sure don't.

PLAYBOY: How did you hear about the biggest contract ever signed in baseball history?

BONDS: The owner, Peter Magowan, called me. He said, "How would you like to play for San Francisco?" The first thing out of my mouth was, "Oh, I get to go home." So I said yes and that was it. Next thing I know my agent calls and it's "Barry Bonds, this is your contract!" My head blew up like a balloon. I freaking wanted to go to the Empire State Building and jump, since I could fly at that point. Then I got nervous. Scared. I didn't want it to happen. I thought, "Nah, maybe $4.7 million is fine for me." That's what I was making before. No one cares about that. Now that everyone's breaking $4 million, it's "just" $4.7 million. When I was in the minor leagues I had four roommates and slept in a lounge chair for two months because I couldn't afford a bed, and I was happy. I could take $4 million and be happy, but at the same time, I couldn't. You're not going to turn down what a man wants to pay you.

I think of it like this: The San Francisco Giants, my bosses, are paying me forty-whatever to do a job, and I want them to get their money's worth. I think, God, I have to thank them for what they've done for me and my family. I've got to be the best of the best. People say, "Don't add all that pressure on to you," but what can you do? You think about it. You don't want to make your boss look like an idiot. You don't want to make yourself look like an idiot. I know there'll be days when I get pissed off or when I go home and cry because I'm not living up to expectations, but I still have to think, This man is paying me to do a job. Give him his money's worth. Throw away the fans, throw away the media, throw away everything and go to work for the man who gave you the money.

PLAYBOY: Forty-four million creates a lot of expectations.

BONDS: I hope I don't let them all down. You can't focus on the money too much, though. You'll catch yourself trying to prove too much. I have to not be nervous about it.

PLAYBOY: How does that much money affect the people around you?

BONDS: It causes problems. I just wrecked one of my Mercedes-Benzes. We had a lot of rain and flooding around my house. The street gave way and washed the car down the street, with me and my wife in it. We had to climb out the window. It messed up the car. So pretty soon I'm calling up the place where they're fixing it and they say, "Barry, we're having a little problem with the insurance company. There might be a $10,000 difference here. You just signed that big contract, so why don't you write us a check?" I got pissed. It hurt my feelings to be treated like that. I said, "I'm sorry to disappoint you, but it's none of your damn business what my salary is. Would you treat me that way if I were the average Joe Schmo?" I just thought it wasn't right. It's not fair—I worked for that money just like anybody else. It's important to me.

On the other hand, with people I like, with my family, it can be fun. I can show them my tax form. I say, "Look at this—that's what I paid in federal income tax." My aunt says, "I could live a lifetime on that." I can help my family. And there's my looks. Being in *People* magazine, one of the beautiful people, that was a trip. It's so funny. Somebody once said that when you don't have money you're ugly. When you have a little bit of money you're cute and when you get rich you're fine as hell. I don't think I'm very good-looking, but some people now are telling me, "Oh, you are so fine." I'm like, "Give me a break. I was just cute when I didn't have any money."

PLAYBOY: What do you think made you such a fine ballplayer?

BONDS: Some of it is genetics. Black people in general have the genetics for sports. My dad was a hell of a player, too, so I was gifted with a lot of athletic ability. Everything was easy for me, all sports, when I was a kid. I'd work half as hard as other kids did and I was better. Why work when I had so much ability? I'd outhit and outthrow and outrun everybody. Some other kids were jealous. They'd say, "You get everything you want because Bobby Bonds is your dad. You get to start on the team because Bobby Bonds is your dad." It hurt, hearing that, but since I was hitting nearly .500, I guess they were wrong. I was the best one in high school. College, too. I took it for granted that, damn, baseball was easy. That's a great feeling, just being strong and natural, but it can destroy you. You think you're bigger than the game, so you never learn anything. In the minors, number-one draft pick, you shoot right past people who have a lot more heart than you do. Then you're in the majors. All of a sudden you get some of the limelight, there are women after you, you're staying out all night. You love it, but you forget your job. I was in the major leagues four years before I woke up.

PLAYBOY: Still, you led National League rookies in homers, RBIs and steals in 1986. In the four years you claim you were dozing, you had 84 homers and more than 100 steals. You were one of the best outfielders.

BONDS: I was doing fine. I was good. But not good for me. I was just average for me. Then I went to get a haircut. This was in the off-season, in 1989, at Fred Tate's barbershop in Pittsburgh. Ninety percent of the black athletes get their hair cut there. I'm getting my hair cut, they have the radio on, and a guy on the radio says what a great athlete Randall Cunningham is, but what a great quarterback Joe Montana is. I weighed the two and thought, I'm so bored with having great ability, having the potential of being a great player. I want to be a great player like Joe Montana. So that haircut was my inspiration. I realized that what I'd been doing—walking off the field thinking I could have done better, cutting myself short—was wrong. Wrong to me, my team and even the game. I just wanted to try harder, so I could leave the game with nothing left undone. That's when I thought, I'm going to work my tail end off before it becomes too late.

PLAYBOY: Did you talk to your dad about any of this?

BONDS: My dad and Willie. They both said the same thing. They said

I wasn't the player I should be. "If you want the Hall of Fame, if you want to leave the game with nothing left undone, you have to dedicate yourself, not sit on your butt." They were right, but I had to see it for myself. So that winter, I stayed in Pittsburgh and trained hard—hitting, running, working with weights. Since then, every off-season I take three weeks off. The rest of the time is for work.

PLAYBOY: Through 1989 your career batting average was .253. In the three years since then, you've batted .301 with an average of 31 homers, 111 RBIs and 45 steals. You've won three Gold Gloves. The one time you weren't voted the National League's MVP, you were the runner-up. Are you satisfied now?

BONDS: No. I want two more MVPs. Nobody's ever done that. But I'm happy. Now when I walk off the field each year, knowing I did what I could, I feel refreshed.

PLAYBOY: Does competition with your dad motivate you?

BONDS: No, we're friends now. But it used to bother me early in my career when people kept calling me Bobby. I think that had a lot to do with my success, because I was determined to have my own name.

PLAYBOY: What else have you learned in the big leagues?

BONDS: Other things to practice. Playing racquetball because it's quick, to make me a little better and quicker defensively. Playing golf in the off-season. That helps mentally—it's all concentration—and it's good that it's a smaller ball. I'll take a bunch of golf balls, throw them up and hit them with a baseball bat. Hitting smaller objects is good practice. Tennis balls, too—I put numbers on them, have somebody pitch them to me and I try to see the numbers. And you learn about things you can't control. Guys like Will Clark and me, we're like a golden trophy, a big golden egg everybody wants to see day in and day out. We have to produce. That's why we work extra hard in the off-season, and just as hard in the season. But we're more dependent on the other players than anybody thinks. We're more dependent on them than they are on us. They'll say, "Barry Bonds, we can't win without him." They seem to forget that I need Royce Clayton on base for me to produce, I need freaking Robby Thompson on base. We are the average Joe Blow good athletes without those little guys around us. They're the ones who put the puzzle together. If I have Robby Thompson and Willie McGee hitting .190 ahead of me, I'm not driving in a lot of runs. That's why I admire the little guys, the smaller athletes who have to work three times as hard to do their job. I really look up to a guy like [former Pirates catcher] Mike LaValliere. When you think about what he has to go through to keep himself in shape and be an outstanding catcher in the major leagues—am I going to sit back, take it easy and not work as hard as he does? I couldn't live with myself.

PLAYBOY: What other active players do you admire?

BONDS: Guys who were playing when I was a kid. Ozzie Smith, Dave Winfield. Nolan Ryan is the biggest of all. I faced him in spring training. He struck me out three times in a row. Three pitches every time. One-two-three. One-two-three. One-two-three. I was in awe. Nolan Ryan played with my dad on the Angels. Now I'm on the field with him. My dad said, "Don't think about it. Just play like you played in high school." I was like, "Are you kidding? This is Nolan Ryan." But you get used to it. If you can see the ball, you can hit it. Time and experience help, too. You see things faster. You can tell a fastball or a slider by the way it spins. Or if the ball starts way up high it has to come down—obviously that's a curveball. As soon as it leaves the pitcher's hand I'm thinking curveball. You can go through 1000 thoughts in that split second, but what it comes down to is to see it and hit it. I'm arrogant enough to do that.

PLAYBOY: What does arrogance have to do with it?

BONDS: Arrogance is why I'm a butt on the field at times. That field is my home and I don't want anybody invading my home. When I go to the ballpark, leave me alone! This is my castle. You don't have any right to interfere with me here. And that's how it is with pitchers, too. The mound is yours, but this batter's box and home plate are mine. I won't invade your space. Don't invade mine. If you put that pitch in the way of my progress, I'm going to knock the hell out of it.

PLAYBOY: You've been knocked pretty hard in the press. Do you feel you deserve it?

BONDS: Some of it. Some of it might be jealousy, or prejudice. Sometimes my mouth gets me in trouble. But I look at it like this: Everybody watches everything I do. It's like Richard Pryor says: "When I fart, everybody hears it." Some other guy farts and it's no big deal. Somebody hits a home run and says, "Damn, I crushed that ball." If I say that, it's bragging. Why can't I feel good like he did? Sometimes you can't win, though. I've signed 1000 autographs in a day. You could sign 2000 but it's not enough. I say thank you to them. Thank you, thank you. Then it's "Thanks, but I've signed enough," and I walk to my car but they still come. They hound you till you say, "Leave me alone, please." If I've been polite, shouldn't I get the common courtesy of being able to go home? No, they say, "Oh, you're too good now. You make so damn much money, this is how you treat people?" Plus, I see the same faces all the time. They're getting your autograph to sell it, and they mess it up for everybody else.

PLAYBOY: Now that you've made a name for yourself, you're sick of writing it over and over, at least for the same people.

BONDS: People I barely knew in school expect things. We never hung out before, when I had nothing, but we're supposed to now? They want an autograph, too. They'll say, "You don't want to sign this? You're too good for us?" I say, "No, I'm not, but I didn't come home to sign your piece of paper. I came home to be with my friends and family."

PLAYBOY: Quite a few sportswriters demonized you, particularly after you turned down the Pirates' offer of $25 million for five years. You were called obnoxious, a spoiled brat, "a symbol of baseball's creeping greed and selfishness, complete with diamond earring." You were a detriment to the club even with 33 homers and 114 RBIs.

BONDS: Hey, if the press paid me, I'd be giving interviews all day. They don't. They come around all the time before a game, when I have to prepare. I have to stretch, think about the game, get ready to do my job. So a lot of times I won't talk. Maybe they get mad, so they write that way.

PLAYBOY: How do you fight back?

BONDS: When people who wish they could play baseball get down on me because I'm not perfect, I say, "I bet I could do better at your job than you could do at mine." I could go back to school and study and become a lawyer, but could a lawyer become a good athlete? Probably not. I could learn how to press Record on a tape recorder and write for a newspaper or a magazine. But could you ever be good in baseball? Probably not. So don't degrade what I do, because I could put you to zero.

PLAYBOY: What's the most unfair thing writers say about ballplayers?

BONDS: That we don't try. I don't think any major-league player doesn't try. It's embarrassing to drop a fly ball. It's embarrassing to strike out. You're just not going to go out in front of 30,000 people and embarrass yourself.

PLAYBOY: Do you get really angry about bad press?

BONDS: Words don't affect me. You can't bother me verbally. Sometimes you can on a personal level, maybe, but not professionally. Professionally, I couldn't care less what people think. Applaud, enjoy the show. I don't need your sympathy.

PLAYBOY: On a personal level, though, you're a pretty emotional guy. You cried when you were placed on the disabled list last year.

BONDS: It's been a big pride thing for me that I never went on the DL. When it happened, man, I never cried more in my life. I had spankings from my dad and my mom, a freaking chipped bone in my knee. But nothing was more painful than going on the disabled list. I'd rather be out there stumbling around with people booing and screaming than be helpless like that. But I just couldn't swing. I had torn a muscle in my side. I kept saying I didn't want to go on the list, but I couldn't even pick up a bat. Kent Biggerstaff, the Pirates' trainer, told me they were disabling me. I went berserk. Throwing everything out of my locker, turning the locker room upside down. Tears, hurt. Then I was down on my hands and knees, helpless. The guys were on the field. I couldn't even go out on the field. I wasn't dressed. And not being in uniform for the first time in my whole career, I was thinking, Oh, this ain't right.

I watched the game on TV in the locker room, yelling and screaming: "Don't swing, dude!" Or "How could he take that pitch?" I thought, Dang, put me in the stands and I'd be as bad as everybody else. But you become a fan. I was just tripping out: "Andy, what are you doing?" "Jose, swing the bat!" I was like that for three weeks, the whole time I was disabled. I wanted them to win so bad I couldn't believe it. And they kept winning, which made me think maybe I wasn't as important as I thought.

PLAYBOY: You came off the DL on the Fourth of July against the Reds' Greg Swindell. Were you nervous?

BONDS: The first at bat, I was scared. I knew that if I tore it again I was out for the season. But I had to get that first swing out of the way. So I swung as hard as I could. I literally closed my eyes and swung. Missed it by a mile.

PLAYBOY: You've mentioned fear a few times already. Is there really so much to be afraid of?

BONDS: There's a lot. I get afraid on the field all the time. You fail in baseball. Go three for 10, .300, that's seven other times you screwed up. If you have some success against Lee Smith, it might give you some added courage the next time. But it still was only that one time. You can also be afraid of the baseball, getting hit by the ball, but I've never been afraid of pain. Not baseball pain.

PLAYBOY: What kind of pain, then?

BONDS: Emotional. I'm afraid of myself, I guess. You're always worried about others in the game—coming up after you, wanting your job or more money or fame, even guys on your own team—but mostly it's myself, being afraid of when baseball might end. A lot of things can happen. An injury, or just time passing. Maybe I'll get bored one day and not want to play anymore. Or just get older and lose it. Not be good anymore. I get tired faster than I used to. I think I'm smarter now, smarter and better, but sometimes when I run I feel a little slower. I'm going to miss it when it's over. I'm not the old-timers' game type.

PLAYBOY: So what you're telling us is that you're basically a terrified, melancholy bundle of nerves on the field.

BONDS: Not so much on the field. That's where I'm comfortable. I've had some serious problems, but not out there in my castle. There was a time when I thought my wife and my family wanted to hurt my career, just because they wanted my time. I'd say, "There's no way I'm giving up my career for you." They never asked me to, but I was always reminding them. "If you think I'm going to do that, forget it."

PLAYBOY: Why did you remind them?

BONDS: I think it was just stupidity on my part. I am more loyal to my wife and kids and parents than to the game, but I'm married to the game, too. There are things I have to accomplish. I want that World Series ring. Of course, to do that I'll have to stop stinking in the playoffs.

PLAYBOY: Your dad never went to the Series, either.

BONDS: We're hoping we can go together this year.

PLAYBOY: What do you remember about your father's playing days?

BONDS: Going to games with him when he was with the Giants. Running around on the field. I remember my dad and Willie going up against the fence, making catches. I wasn't much of a fan. My friends knew more about his stats than I did. I was playing little baseball games in the clubhouse with the other guys' children. Tito Fuentes' kids, Gloria and little Tito. Gaylord Perry and Juan Marichal had all girls, but they would play. Later, when my dad was with the Yankees, Sandy Alomar Jr. We'd use those little bats they gave away on Bat Day. We'd step on beer cups, mush them all together to make baseballs and knock them all over the place.

In the summer, when school was out, my mom would take us to wherever my dad was playing to see his games. But a lot of the time he wasn't around. I learned most of my baseball from playing with friends. I had some good school coaches, too.

PLAYBOY: When you were nine years old your dad hit 39 homers for the Giants. He was an All-Star.

BONDS: It's hard on you when you have a famous father. Everybody thinks he does everything for you. Your friends are always reminding you. I hit almost .500 in high school. What bat did he swing for me? You get tired of hearing, "Oh, it's because of your dad." It's nobody's fault, it's just life—we're best friends now—but when you're a kid you get tired of hearing about your father all the time. I really remember more about my mom. She did everything for us. She always took me to baseball or football practice. She always wrote "from Dad" on the Christmas presents. My mom was at all the school events. My dad never went. He was playing baseball.

PLAYBOY: He must have instilled some competitive drive in his sons. When he was home, he'd play games with you—pool, mostly—and the loser had to do push-ups.

BONDS: Yeah, a lot of push-ups. You had to do them. But if you won, you got to pick your favorite candy bar.

PLAYBOY: And watch your dad do his push-ups for you. That must have been almost as good as the candy.

BONDS: I didn't like my dad that much. We didn't become close until I was in college. I resented him when I was a kid. Not that he was abusive. There's a fine line between abuse and discipline. I don't like people who turned out good saying, "I was abused." I can't say that. I can say he whupped my butt plenty of times, and sometimes I didn't feel I deserved it. Most of the time he would give you the benefit of the doubt, but sometimes he'd hit you with his hand. Smack your leg. "Don't lie to me!" When I was 10 or 11 years old it stopped—you'd just get grounded after that—but before that, we got our share of spankings. It would hurt your feelings more than anything else. But if you didn't cry, it was like you were showing him up. And don't cry too much, either. He knew it didn't hurt that bad. So you just cried and apologized, and he was cool.

PLAYBOY: You had to cry correctly?

BONDS: You had to know how to cry.

PLAYBOY: What did you do to earn a spanking or a leg slap?

BONDS: Disobey. Hit a ball through a window after he told us not to play in the backyard. You couldn't lie. You'd just tell the truth and he'd let you go. He was very direct. "Why" doesn't fit in his vocabulary. If you let a ground ball go through your legs and you tried, fine. Just don't come in with an excuse. Say, "I screwed up." If you jump off the roof, don't say your brother pushed you. Say, "I felt like jumping, Dad. I could have hurt myself, you're right, but I just felt like it." He'd say, "Well, don't do it again." He'd never punish you for telling the truth. You could stop a lot of spankings that way.

PLAYBOY: Other than playing pool for push-ups, what kinds of things did you do with him when you were little?

BONDS: He took me out on a boat fishing with him all the time. I hated it. I got seasick. He'd say, "You're my son. Let's go." But I was a mama's boy. I'd rather watch my mom put her makeup on. Or put on a wig and dance with her; we would both pretend we were Janet Jackson. She'd say, "Go with your father." We always bitched that we never got to see him, but when he wanted to do something I'd be whining, "Mom, I'm not going."

I wouldn't play golf with him because I'd end up being his caddy. He tried to make it fun, though. He'd get an extra cart for me and my brother to drive, but we'd just sit in the cart. You know how kids are—nothing their parents do can ever be right. I think I devalued a lot of the good things he tried to do. He was just being Big Dad. People who complain about their parents, I really hate that. If you think you turned out pretty good, be happy with your parents. They drove you to be what you are.

PLAYBOY: Were you rebellious as a teenager?

BONDS: No more than anybody else. I'd cut school, get in a little trouble, to see what I could get away with. But I told my parents. I told my dad I smoked a joint. I told him I smoked cigarettes. Smoking joints—I stopped that stuff right away on my own. With the cigarettes, he and Mom made me smoke a whole pack right in front of them. Cigarette after cigarette. It worked pretty well. I got sick and didn't touch those things for a long time.

PLAYBOY: Did he talk to you about sex?

BONDS: No, he knew I wasn't going to say what he wanted to hear. He would never say, "How are you doing with the girls? You getting laid?" Yeah, sure, Dad. Like I'm going to tell you voluntarily. He would say one thing: "I have no control over what you do outside this house, but if I'm a grandfather before I want to be, I'll break your neck." He was laughing, so you knew he was cool about it. My parents were always open with us. My mom and dad were naked all the time. Nobody cared about nudity. I shared a room with my sister. I knew about tampons when I was 10. I think you grow up healthier that way. My own family is like that now. My wife is from Sweden, man. Nudity's all they do.

PLAYBOY: Ballplayers do it, too, they say, especially on the road. Before you were married in 1988, you were a young star making $100,000. How was life as a big-league bachelor?

BONDS: It was great. You swallow it up too much at first, but I think you deserve it. It's a big deal, being in the big leagues. Suddenly you have girls, groupies, money, pulling you in each and every direction. Anyone who doesn't like that isn't human. It's exciting. I was 21 years old, ripping and running the streets. Fame, girls, everything. You have one girl late one night. You're up until four in the morning with this person or that. It was one big party. But you outgrow it. You have to, because it wears you down. You never sleep. It can mess up your career, so you outgrow it.

PLAYBOY: Was there a particular Baseball Annie in every port for every Pirate?

BONDS: The groupie girls, most of them were taken anyway, so you don't really get into them. I may have had two girlfriends at a time; it was hard enough to entertain one, let alone two. People think athletes are always with those same publicized groupies, but you're afraid of them more than anything else.

PLAYBOY: Are ballplayers worried about AIDS?

BONDS: I think you know who you're messing around with. If you're messing around with somebody who's messing around with everybody, then you know what you're getting into. Just don't make excuses. Magic Johnson accommodated a lot of people, which was probably his own fault. You cannot fault the man for spreading the disease because he did not know, and he doesn't blame anyone but himself. Now he tells people to practice safe sex. That's the key, safe sex.

PLAYBOY: Did you practice safe sex?

BONDS: I can't say I did. Not all the time. I can just tell you that I was lucky. Very, very lucky.

PLAYBOY: Is AIDS changing athletes' lives?

BONDS: Oh yeah. Times are changing. If you're gonna do what you have to do, you better make sure it's safe. But the life is more family-oriented now. It's not so much running the streets chasing women. Guys are spending time with their families.

PLAYBOY: Let's talk about yours. You married Sun in 1988, a little over a year before you matured into an MVP. She's petite, you're a big guy. She's quiet, you can be loud. She's white, you're black. How did you get together?

BONDS: We met at a nightclub in Montreal in 1987. Sun was a bartender. I wound up going to another club and she went to the same place with a girlfriend. We danced, talked, had some fun. I wouldn't say it was love at first sight because I don't believe in that, but it was chemistry. We met each other's needs. We fit together. [*Laughs*] When you have a hole and a screw, and the screw fits, it makes everything tight and you stay put.

PLAYBOY: What were your needs?

BONDS: I had to settle down. I was running the streets too much, losing my desire to play baseball. She gave me something to shoot for, someone to play for. If it weren't for Sun I wouldn't have two MVP trophies. She's probably the most intelligent woman I ever met. Being from Sweden, where they don't have much television, she reads all the time and she's a quick learner. She'd never lived in the States, but she got her high school equivalency diploma without studying. I gave her the driver's license manual, she read it and passed the test the next day, perfect score. And she is a great mother. Sun has more patience than toilet paper. I tell her, "Toilet paper just sits there and waits. It sits there and waits, just like you."

PLAYBOY: She must think that's awfully flattering.

BONDS: No, but I like to kid her.

PLAYBOY: What was it that you provided for her?

BONDS: Stability, I guess. I had a job. I had my own condominium. I was making $100,000, which was a lot when I was single. It started to run out a little after that, but that's part of the price. We have two lovely kids, and there's something else I like: Our families are great together. They accepted one another from day one. You see, in Sweden there's no color barrier. "You love my daughter, and that's all that matters." It was the same with my parents: "You love our son, then it's fine." There's no jealousy, no prejudice, no color involved. That's how people should be.

PLAYBOY: Was Sun a baseball fan?

BONDS: Sun couldn't care less. She didn't know what a scoreboard was. I think that's what made us click. It wasn't about money or anything like that. She just thought I was a handsome guy. She came to a game in Montreal while we were dating. She sat down and she sat so tall. My wife's only five-three, but to me she was the biggest, prettiest woman in the place. I didn't wave or anything—I'm very professional on the field—but I knew she was there. I'll never forget the black dress she had on. And a black jacket. And I'm out there thinking, Man, I'm marrying this girl!

PLAYBOY: When you were on Arsenio Hall's show, he seemed surprised that you took Sun along one night to go clubbing with him.

BONDS: He likes it that I go out with my wife and she can handle it, knowing that women will be all over me. She doesn't trip out. She just sits while I do my duty: "Hi, how about a hug?" It's hard on her. Sun likes her privacy. But she knew exactly what she was getting when she married me. It's a package deal; she married public property.

PLAYBOY: You have a son, Nikolai, who is three, and a daughter, Shikari, who's two. What have you learned about being a dad?

BONDS: I didn't know what a full-time job it would be. We could have all the nannies we wanted, but we want to take care of our own children. You wouldn't trade it for anything, but it's a job. Sometimes you wish it were easier. And you think back to how you were raised and all the times your parents said, "Wait till you have kids of your own." All the things you said you'd never do—you'd never spank your kids, or yell at them. You'd let them do what they wanted. Yeah, right. It's fun because you know you were sticking your foot in your mouth when you were little. That's what having kids is, putting your foot in your mouth. You start giving your own parents the benefit of the doubt.

PLAYBOY: What do Nikolai and Shikari think about baseball?

BONDS: My son goes to the batting cage with me. He's three and he's already hitting. He knows what I do, but my daughter doesn't comprehend it. Whatever her brother says, she says. When he says, "Daddy hit a home run," she says, "Home run," so I have a two-home-run day.

PLAYBOY: You've never had a two-homer day at Candlestick Park, your new home. In fact, you have hit only four of your 176 career homers there. You once said you'd never play for the Giants "because it's cold and they need a new stadium." Other than $43.75 million, what changed your mind?

BONDS: The thought that I won't be on the visiting team. One thing I really hated about Candlestick Park was the accommodations for the other team. There are heaters and bathrooms in the home dugout, but not in the visitors' dugout. For the visitors there's no bathroom, no heat, no nothing. It's windy and cold. If you have to go to the bathroom, you have to run across the field in front of all those people, all the way back to the clubhouse. But the home team has bathrooms. The home team has heaters. I'm the home team now, so I hope they don't change it. Let them stay miserable on the visiting side.

PLAYBOY: What happens on and around the field that the fans don't see?

BONDS: The reality. The fact that it's not as easy as it looks. But there's other stuff, crazy things. Deion Sanders has a pair of lucky underwear shorts he's been wearing since college. [Former Pirates infielder] Chico Lind had real knives in his locker, big Rambo knives; he would take a fake knife and stab you, give you a heart attack. There's crud done to rookies. You send a rookie to baggage claim so he misses the bus to the hotel, or tape him up and throw food on him so the birds will fly down and peck the food—but I never did that much. I'd rather be with my friends. Bobby Bonilla is my best friend and always will be. We came up together, played A-ball together. One time we were playing down in the minors and I struck out three straight times. Bobby had the whole team throw their hats on the field for my hat trick. Bobby Bo and I are close. We're going to open a Harley store together. We love that motorcycle. I have two Fatboys. Bobby has one, too. His is black and it's beautiful—the tank and all the trim are 24-karat gold.

PLAYBOY: Did you really call your buddy Gary Sheffield last year to say you were going to pass him in home runs?

BONDS: I was kidding. There was no way. My heart said I could do it, but my brain said, You're crazy. Right after I said it, that night, he hit two and had 30 already. I was almost 10 behind. It was September and I'd had a bad August, but I told [hitting coach] Milt May, "Something tells me I can do it." I went for it. Beat him 34 to 33.

PLAYBOY: After that, you lost a heartbreaker in the National League play-offs. Did you watch the World Series on TV? It's hard to imagine whom you would root for.

BONDS: Toronto. I liked Atlanta because I know those guys, but I was for the underdog.

PLAYBOY: What do you think of the baseball skills of some of the celebrities you've seen?

BONDS: Michael Jordan came to Pittsburgh and took batting practice. He can hit. But then he threw to me in the batting cage and almost hit me. And a couple years ago in spring training, a guy in a Tigers uniform was talking to me about hitting, asking a lot of questions. It was weird because ballplayers don't do that to other players. So I tell him, "Hey, see the ball, hit the ball." He says, "Man, the ball jumps off your bat," and I'm like, yeah, thanks. Then I look and the back of his jersey says "Selleck" on it. I'm thinking this dude looks familiar, but I still haven't put two and two together when somebody asks me how it was talking to Tom Selleck. I was so embarrassed. "There's no freaking way I was standing right next to him and didn't know it." My wife thinks he's gorgeous. He can hit, too. He's huge, six-four or something—he's not too keen on forkballs and stuff, but throw it straight and he'll hit it.

PLAYBOY: You're also friends with Magic Johnson.

BONDS: I went to his Super Bowl party. He's always friendly, always lovable, just a super man. I love him to death. It was crushing, what happened to him, but he took it like a man. I was proud of him for standing up and facing his problem. When people tried to label him, to say he was gay—that's a bunch of crud. So when I see him I always hug him. I kiss him on the cheek. He's one of my idols.

PLAYBOY: Lately, there seems to be a lot more mingling of sports stars and entertainers, sort of a bicoastal hot tub full of people who have been on the covers of *People* and *Sports Illustrated*. Is the line between jocks and other celebs dissolving?

BONDS: We're all entertainers. Acting, singing, sports, we're all entertainers and we all make millions. What's cool is that they love you as much as you love them. I'm in awe of all of them, but a lot of actors, for instance, are sports fans, so they can be in awe of me, too. Although there are some with their noses up. Like when I did the NAACP Image Awards. I don't want to name names and hurt people, but some of those stars wouldn't even say hello. I thought, Come on. If you make a million more than me, that's only one extra boat you can buy, so who gives a damn? Look at Michael Jackson. He's the greatest entertainer in the world, but ever since he was a kid, he probably just wanted to go outside and play baseball with the guys. That's why I said on Arsenio, "Michael, you're invited to come play ball with me and my friends any time you want. We'll close down the stadium and play with you. Of course, if you really can't play, you'll have to sit on the bench. You can't moonwalk on the field." I haven't heard from him. I still like him, though. And you know what pisses me off? The way he gets treated. He has never said anything derogatory about anyone. He's never been a drunk driver. You don't hear he's used drugs. Yet people downgrade him because he wants to do his own thing. But if you were in his shoes, with his money and his fame and his life, you would, too. So tip your hat to him. Tip your hat to goodness, that's what I say. There's enough crap in the world.

PLAYBOY: One reason he's talked about is his appearance—and the way it keeps changing.

BONDS: So what? Go to Hollywood, see all the women with breast jobs and face-lifts. He was right when he said Beverly Hills would not exist without all that. Go to Roxbury or one of those other nightclubs and you walk into a big—excuse my French—titty farm. Boobs and faces lifted all over. Why does he get criticized? All he does is donate $50 million to charity. What is he supposed to give, hundreds of millions? To me he's a black hero, and we don't have many. It's always the same: It's "Oh, how great Elvis was." But Elvis Presley was on drugs. The Rolling Stones, too. Michael Jackson has never done anything wrong, so give him a break.

PLAYBOY: Done. Meanwhile, you've gone a little Hollywood yourself. You did a cameo in a film called *Rookie of the Year* and just finished a new TV movie, *Jane's House*, with James Woods and Anne Archer.

BONDS: Anne Archer is so fine. I was in heat the whole time. I'll tell you another thing I liked: One day we were shooting in a mall. People kept asking for my autograph. The producer said, "Funny—we have one of the top actors in the country and one of the top actresses, and everybody wants your autograph." I said, "You know why? We're in a sporting goods store, boy. You're on my turf now."

PLAYBOY: Who do you play in *Rookie of the Year* and *Jane's House*?

BONDS: Myself. It's pretty easy to do. I want to play someone else. I want to act. James Woods and Anne Archer gave me a great compliment. They said I should think seriously about acting, since I was pretty good for never having done it before. But I'm not a natural. I know that the only way for me to get better is to work at it.

PLAYBOY: You've said you aren't troubled by nudity at home. How about the workplace? Some players don't want women in the locker room.

BONDS: That doesn't bother me at all. Women reporters are professionals, too. A hundred percent of the women in men's locker rooms are professional. It's not like they're sitting there looking and slobbering.

PLAYBOY: Why do you think it has been such an issue for so many pro athletes?

BONDS: Male ego. That's all it is. Do you think a woman reporter never saw a naked man or heard the word "shit"? She knows what comes with the territory, and she's not stealing anything from you, so get off your high horse. What's so important about a locker room anyway? It's a stinky place where you take a shower and then leave.

PLAYBOY: There's no shortage of male bonding in sports, where guys stick together. Who were your mentors?

BONDS: Dave Stephens, my high school coach, took me under his wing. My dad was always gone, so I'd be over at Dave's house. I was like his second son. My dad and I finally became friends when I was in college. He and Willie and I talk a lot about hitting, and they were the ones telling me to start dedicating myself a few years ago, saying I couldn't just sit on my butt in the off-season if I wanted to be in the Hall of Fame. Dusty Baker, my new manager, grew up with my dad. I've known him since I was a baby. He's a man I respect. But I will never forget Jim

Leyland. That man is the best. More than the strategy he brings to the game, what makes him a great manager is the way he relates to you. Leyland deals with you head to head, man to man. He knows you're not in boot camp. You get as much leeway as you want as long as you play by the rules, and he really has only one rule. Be on time. He doesn't care how you get to work, he doesn't care what you wear. Just be on time and give him three hours of your time. I'm going to miss him.

PLAYBOY: And yet you had that celebrated shouting match with him at spring training in 1991. You started yelling and he was heard to say, "I've kissed your butt for three years. No one player is going to ruin this camp. If you don't like it, you can go home."

BONDS: Why do you bring that up? It's bad.

PLAYBOY: It happened. You had lost your arbitration case against the Pirates and had to settle for a $2.3 million salary instead of the $3.3 million you wanted. Then you had a personal photographer, a friend, taking pictures of you at camp and you told other photographers to get out of your face. You even shoved one of them. Coach Bill Virdon and the Pirates' PR man objected. You hollered at them, and Leyland came after you.

BONDS: The press keeps bringing that up.

PLAYBOY: Your dad told us he thinks the Pirates arranged the incident because they wanted to make you look bad, maybe to alienate your Pittsburgh fans—to keep the fans on the club's side in your battles over money. That's why there happened to be a TV camera and microphone nearby.

BONDS: It wasn't an accident. They set me up.

PLAYBOY: Do you really think that?

BONDS: Why would a microphone and TV crew be right there at that time? Just to stir up shit. The funny thing is, my dad told me before I went to spring training, "They're going to set you up when you get there." He was right. After that, for the first time in my life, I didn't want to play. I started out 17 for a 100, .170. I felt raped, almost. I knew how a woman who was raped felt. I couldn't hit, couldn't play until I got that off my back.

PLAYBOY: How did you get it off your back?

BONDS: Leyland did it. He called a press conference. He said, "Leave him alone. With all that Barry Bonds has brought to this city, it's time to get off his back." I'll never forget that, not as long as I live. My whole season turned around. And later in the season, even after the season, we talked. He said, "Barry, I wish you well. You deserve every penny you get. You're the best baseball player, you deserve to be paid the best. For three years you worked harder than any athlete I've ever seen, and I'm damn proud of you." You can't forget a man like that.

PLAYBOY: How will you remember him?

BONDS: He made me better. I could say anything I wanted to him. If I didn't like him that day I'd say, "You know, I don't like you, you little midget. You're not even an athlete. You can't hit. You never even played in the big leagues."

PLAYBOY: What did he say to that?

BONDS: Oh, he rode my butt. "Hey, Barry, if I tell you I like you, you'll just want me not to like you. That's what you thrive on. If I give you any sense that I like you, you're thinking, No, don't. You want me to like you but you're just not sure."

PLAYBOY: Was he right?

BONDS: Probably.

PLAYBOY: All this sounds Freudian enough to justify a question out of left field. When you dream at night, is it baseball?

BONDS: All the time. I dream I'm at the ballpark. I hit a home run, run the bases. Then I hit another one. I hit three. I hit four. Now I have a chance to hit five and break the all-time record. All of a sudden I'm at a zoo, or up on top of the Empire State Building, trying to get back to Shea Stadium to play the Mets. I can see they're trying to find me. But they go, "Wait a minute, he's gone," and they send up a pinch hitter.

PLAYBOY: Does he hit the fifth home run?

BONDS: I don't know. That's when I wake up.

PLAYBOY: In your dream are you still wearing a Pirates uniform, or are you a Giant?

BONDS: It's just a baseball uniform, just baseball.

PLAYBOY: When we were talking about Michael Jackson you implied that the reason he gets more criticism than Elvis or the Rolling Stones is simple racism. Baseball isn't exactly free of it. Cincinnati Reds owner Marge Schott was suspended for racism: keeping a swastika on her desk, allegedly referring to some black players as "million-dollar niggers." Would you be willing to play on Schott's team?

BONDS: As long as she gave me my check every two weeks. What she said was degrading, but I doubt that we've all said only nice things about people all our lives. What she did was wrong, just like it would be wrong to go out of the privacy of your home and call Marge a white piece of trash. She got caught, now she's being punished. Prejudice is childish and stupid. Someone else's culture, their history, should be amazing to people, not a burden. But there's prejudice everywhere. My wife is half Swedish and half Portuguese. I'm Afro-American. So if you're like some prejudiced people you might want to say something to me about what I am doing married to her. But the thing is, why would you care? Are you jealous because she's married to me? Are you jealous because I'm married to her? Even if I weren't married to her, I ain't going to marry you, so what's the difference? I mean, if I were single, I wouldn't even date you.

PLAYBOY: Early in his career, your dad wasn't allowed in whites-only hotels and restaurants in the South. Life was even harder for his father, a black man living in prewar America.

BONDS: My grandfather grew up in a time when black people used to have to walk on the other side of the street, and he was never angry about it. That seemed weird to me. When he would tell about some guy calling him boy or nigger, treating him like dirt, I'd say, "Man, I would have killed him. Ain't nobody going to degrade me like that." But my grandfather said, "If you were born at that time, that was how it was. No, I would not put up with it now, but that was the way we had to live then."

PLAYBOY: Did you feel outrage for him?

BONDS: I felt happy, because of the way he turned out. My grandfather had a lot of reasons to be bitter and hateful but he wasn't. He didn't have a stitch of prejudice in him.

PLAYBOY: How do you think you would react to the bigotry he had to put up with?

BONDS: I couldn't deal with it now. But if I'd been born back then I guess I would put up with it, because I would have to. You could be killed if you didn't. I don't have to deal with anything like that, which is a good thing about society today. Life is easier for me than it was for him.

PLAYBOY: But society isn't color-blind yet.

BONDS: No, it's not. Look at Mike Tyson in jail. The Clarence Thomas situation with Anita Hill, that's a big deal. Steve Howe got suspended for drugs eighty thousand times and he's back in baseball. Is that discrimination? I don't know, but it's upsetting. Where does it come from? What are people afraid of? Everybody fights together when there's a war. The whole country comes together, then the war is over and everybody's separate again. I wish there weren't any black and white, but there is. We can't change that, so let's try to enjoy the show together.

PLAYBOY: Your father in his day was considered one of the more militant black ballplayers. That may be one reason he was traded seven times. You seem to be more philosophical.

BONDS: I just think it's sad, the way things are even today. There are only so many black celebrities. Let us enjoy them. There's just a handful of us. All we can do is say, "Please, let us have ours." If it's me or Willie Mays or Jackie Robinson, do you have to say, "Jackie Robinson was a drug addict"? How can you criticize him when he couldn't stay at your hotel? Do you know how Mandela felt in prison? How can you make any kind of judgment when you never walked down the street with Martin Luther King? We have only a few heroes. Let us cherish our own, the little that we have. That's not asking too much.

PLAYBOY: How do you want to be remembered?

BONDS: I'm going to be forgotten, probably. I may never make the Hall of Fame. I haven't done anything yet to make it. But I want to go to the Hall of Fame, partly because of my father. Not for the status or anything. I just want my photo or my glove or my bat there, to say that this is my family and I was part of it and a part of baseball.

JIM BROWN

A candid conversation with the football superstar turned actor and civil rights activist

Among professional-football fullbacks, Jim Brown remains the legendary standard by which all others are measured. At six feet two and 230 pounds, Brown was the most powerful and elusive running back ever to play the game. With a massive neck, steely arms and thighs thicker than most men's waists, he could drag tacklers with him as he ran, send them flying with a straight-arm, sidestep them with his misdirective footwork and out-distance them with his flashing speed. During nine seasons with the Cleveland Browns, this gut strength and incredible agility—combined with a juggernaut determination to win—netted him 15 NFL records that most sportswriters agree won't be topped easily or soon. Before a budding alternate career as a movie actor and militant involvement in the race struggle provoked his abrupt resignation from pro ball in 1966, Brown had crashed his way to a record lifetime total of 126 touchdowns and led the league in yards gained for eight of his nine seasons, piling up a whopping 12,312 yards in the process—also an all-time record.

Because repeated and jarring contact with bone-crushing opposing linemen is one of the position's occupational hazards, injuries have sidelined every other notable running back in pro-football history. But Brown's superb physical condition and playing ability made him a unique exception to that rule—despite many a lineman's rapacious attempts to put him on the bench, if not in the hospital; and he gave them plenty of opportunity to try, by carrying the ball in roughly 60 percent of all offensive plays. An adept ball carrier off the field, too, he led the 1962 revolt of Cleveland players that successfully brought about the ouster of their brilliant but inflexible head coach, Paul Brown. The following year, as if to vindicate the uprising, Jim Brown became football's sole runner to pass the mile mark in a single season—a feat veteran sportswriter Myron Cope called "perhaps the most incredible sports statistic of our time."

Brown's phenomenal prowess led the editor of *Sport* magazine to label him the "Babe Ruth of football," who "sits alone, indestructible, superhuman." It also gave him the additional—and more tangible— honor of taking home the biggest paycheck in pro ball, an estimated $65,000 a year. But the crown didn't rest easily on Brown's head. Despite lavish kudos from the press and considerable nationwide attention, his natural reserve remained undented; to the public and most teammates alike, he remained icily aloof. The first rumblings of his eventual abdication came as early as 1964, with the publication of his autobiography, *Off My Chest*. In it, Brown demonstrated that his hard-driving, no-nonsense brand of football was a graphic metaphor for his lifestyle: He appraised various football personalities with a brutal candor that left many bruised and angry; and he revealed an attitude of racial militance—further explored here—that added a facet of passionate social commitment to his already complex image. Unwillingly and briefly, Brown adopted yet another persona in 1965. In the period of a few months, two girls accused him of molesting them. One refused to press charges, but the other took her case to court. After Brown was acquitted, she tried again with a paternity suit—and lost that, too.

Not surprisingly, today's controversial Jim Brown is the product of a diverse and paradoxical background. Born on an island off the Georgia coast, he spent his first years in the care of a great-grandmother. At the age of seven, he moved north to Long Island to live with his divorced mother, a domestic worker. Always big and strong for his age, Brown applied his talents more in the street than in school and soon fought his way to "warlord" status in the Gaylords, a teenage gang. If local officials hadn't quickly recognized his rare athletic abilities, the Jim Brown story might have been another *Rebel Without a Cause*; but they turned him on to sports, and by Brown's senior year, athletic events at Manhasset High School were drawing overflow crowds who came to see him in action—in football, basketball, baseball, track and lacrosse. Shattering records in nearly every sport he tried, Brown was graduated with full-scholarship bids from 42 colleges. Ironically, he selected Syracuse, where Brown claims he wasn't really wanted—for reasons that had more to do with race than with football. Still on the fifth-string team after his freshman season, he crashed the varsity ranks as a sophomore, went on to become a Syracuse legend—and began to be called the greatest all-round athlete since Jim Thorpe. Then, turning pro with the Cleveland Browns, he set—even in his rookie year—new professional records.

During the off seasons, Brown began to dabble in the myriad pursuits that finally lured him away from football. He tackled show business, first as host of a modest daily radio show in Cleveland, then as a Negro cavalry trooper in *Rio Conchos*, a movie Western. He broke into the business world by traveling and interning as a marketing executive for the Pepsi-Cola company. And in a move coinciding with occasional outings as a commentator on closed-circuit theater telecasts of boxing matches, he allied himself with Main Bout, Inc., a sports-promotion agency. Main Bout eventually handled the fights of the controversial and racially militant Muhammad (Cassius Clay) Ali, and Brown's association with the firm gave further flower to his own growing image as a hard-line racial activist: Some of his colleagues at Main Bout were Black Muslims. Brown disclaimed membership in the sect but said that he felt its views voiced the true feelings of most Negroes.

Amid the national controversy in 1966 that saw a Muhammad Ali fight blocked out of arenas across the country, Brown quietly signed to play a role in his second motion picture, *The Dirty Dozen*, to be filmed in England that summer. He planned to return in time for fall football practice; but in England, heavy rains kept delaying the filming. Soon the Cleveland Browns were at practice—without their star fullback. Pressed by sportswriters, team owner Art Modell announced a daily fine until Brown returned; but Brown finally flanked the penalty with the bombshell announcement that he was quitting the game. Fans refused to believe it, thinking he would join up again once the film was finished. Though Brown did come back to Cleveland after completing the movie, it was only to reaffirm his retirement and announce that he intended to spend his time helping his race—by heading the National Negro Industrial and Economic Union, an organization he had founded. More motion-picture offers were in the works as well, he added. Jim Brown was done with football for good—but not with the limelight.

In the following months, he enlisted nearly 100 famous Negro sports figures to help him with his fledgling NNIEU and opened offices in several cities across the country. When *The Dirty Dozen* opened and Negroes in unprecedented numbers flocked to see him—aptly cast as a racially militant soldier—it became clear that Brown's burgeoning screen fame showed every promise of rivaling his legend on the gridiron. At this point in his new career, we sent Alex Haley to interview the many-sided athlete-actor. "When I met him in Cleveland," reports Haley about the first of their many encounters, stretching over several weeks, "I soon discovered that his life now is probably more strenuous than when he was playing football. Between movies, he hustles through a 16-hour day that includes time at home, in his NNIEU office, at public appearances and on the golf course—where he chafes if his scores reach the upper 70s. To keep up the pace, he burns a tremendous amount of fuel: I saw him consume two pounds of barbecued ribs as an appetizer while a four-pound T-bone broiled. Dessert was a quart of ice cream topped by a can of peaches.

"Brown tried to concentrate on my questions, but his Cleveland schedule—and his characteristic initial wariness—made it impossible. We agreed to meet again later in California, where he would be filming his third picture, the $8 million Cinerama production *Ice Station Zebra*, in which he co-stars with Rock Hudson. During our meetings in his dressing room, he proved appreciably warmer and more candid. Returning from camera calls, he relaxed as easily as he once did upon leaving the field after a game. Dropping his well-known mask of impassivity, he became amiable and animated, especially when he was talking about football. When racial matters came up, however, he turned dead serious and often punctuated his pungent remarks with a baleful glare and a meaty forefinger jabbed in my direction.

"Despite the long shooting days, Brown rarely went out at night, choosing instead to stay in his room and study his script. On weekends, though, he roamed, visiting friends like Lee Marvin and Bill Cosby, going into Los Angeles ghetto areas to talk to the kids there and putting in as much time as possible at his Los Angeles NNIEU office. One day we got to the office and found a small crowd there being regaled by Muhammad Ali. Ali playfully made a lightning feint as Brown entered; in mock seriousness, Brown—who had once turned down an offer of $150,000 to become a fighter—invited him out back. Muttering dire warnings, Ali followed Brown outside, where they touched fingertips and whirled into a flashing, furious, open-handed bout. Head down, Brown would probe for an opening, while Ali danced, dodged and swatted back. Then they stopped as suddenly as they had begun, both sweat-soaked and laughing. In spite of the schoolyard levity they maintained throughout, I couldn't help feeling they were testing each other, secretly wondering what might happen in a ring."

The interview ended when Brown left for San Diego to do scenes parachuting from a plane to rendezvous with an atomic submarine for his role in *Ice Station Zebra*. He would fly next to Bombay to film *The Year of the Cricket*. Beyond that lay a three-year contract with MGM that involved several more motion pictures. In one of them, *Dark of the Sun*, which premieres next month, Brown co-stars with Rod Taylor as a black mercenary involved in the Congolese uprising. No other athlete in history had ever managed such a successful transition to show business. We began by asking him about it.

PLAYBOY: What's your reaction to Lee Marvin's observation about your performance in *The Dirty Dozen*: "Well, Brown's a better actor than Sir Laurence Olivier would be as a member of the Cleveland Browns"?

BROWN: That's great! I never heard that one before. Lee's wild! I love him! But about what he said: Look, my parts so far haven't really demanded too much of me as an actor; I know that and I'm not trying to rush myself. What I feel I'm not ready for, I stay away from. At this point I'm relying upon my presence; I'm concentrating on acting *natural*; and I'm soaking up every technique I can handle from the pros. I think everyone I work with can see that I'm trying to apply myself, and they go out of their way to teach me new things. So you might call it on-the-job training. Of course, I've always tried to be good at anything I get involved in. That's another way of saying that eventually I hope to be regarded as a good professional actor—I mean by other actors. They're the best critics.

PLAYBOY: As a longtime pro in another field, how did you feel about being the rookie of the cast in *The Dirty Dozen*?

BROWN: I felt that was to my advantage. Everybody knew I had everything to learn, and they knocked themselves out helping me; so I probably learned faster than most rookies in films. The role I played helped me, too. I was Robert Jefferson, a college-trained soldier condemned to death for murdering a white racist who had brutally assaulted me. I strongly identified with Jefferson. I could feel and understand why he did what he did. I just made myself Robert Jefferson in my mind. And Bob Aldrich, the director, gave me every break he could. He rarely talked with me, but when he saw me getting uptight, he would say things that were constructive and calming. Even so, the pressure would build in me—you know, the doubts about whether I was really good enough to be there with them. But when Kenny Hyman, our producer, brought me a script for another movie, offering me a part, that was a sign of approval that meant a lot.

PLAYBOY: While the picture was being made, a rumor circulated that you weren't getting along with several members of the cast. Was there any truth to that?

BROWN: None. I got on with that cast as well as I ever have with any group in my whole life. Went out socially with most of them; never any arguments at all. That story must have been manufactured by press agents. I'm beginning to find out that press agents are an occupational hazard in this business—their imaginations. This particular story got started in Leonard Lyons's column, that Lee Marvin and I left a party at Sidney Lumet's and that we had a bloody fight to the finish outside. It was completely fabricated! In fact, Lee and I had a beautiful relationship.

PLAYBOY: Marvin has said there is an acting void that you can fill, especially among Negroes: "He's seemingly more believable to the average Negro than guys like Poitier." And director Robert Aldrich has said, "There isn't another Negro actor around quite like Brown. Poitier, Belafonte or Ossie Davis aren't Brown's style." Do you think they're right?

BROWN: I don't know; maybe I *am* shaping a new movie personality. I'm just being myself; that's all I know how to do. I'm sure not taking anything away from any of those you named—and others like James Earl Jones. But there's a crying need for more Negro actors, because for so long, ever since the silent screen, in fact, the whole world has been exposed to Negroes in stereotype roles. Have you ever been to any Negro theater with a movie going, with a Negro in it? Well, you can just *feel* the tension of that audience, pulling for this guy to do something good, something that will give them a little pride. That's why I feel so good that Negroes are finally starting to play roles that other Negroes, watching, will feel proud of, and respond to, and identify with, and feel *real* about, instead of being crushed by some Uncle Tom on the screen making a fool of himself. You're not going to find any of us playing Uncle Toms anymore. In my first picture, *Rio Conchos*, I played a cowboy who fought not only Indians but white guys, too. And I played a realistic Negro in *The Dirty Dozen*. And in this picture I'm shooting now, *Ice Station Zebra*, I play a Marine captain on an atomic submarine. It's not a part written for a Negro, or for any race in particular; it's a part with no racial overtones whatever. That's why I can say, before this picture is even released, that a lot of Negroes are going to come to see it.

PLAYBOY: How did you get the part?

BROWN: Robert O'Brien, MGM's president, was very happy with my *Dirty Dozen* performance and he discovered that unprecedented Negro audiences were attending. He said, "Hell, this is beautiful all around!" He called me about five one morning and said if there was a part I could play in *Ice Station Zebra*, he'd have me in Hollywood the next day. A white actor had been tentatively slated for this part, but he wasn't signed, because he was still negotiating for something else; and the next day I was in wardrobe. In fact, they went over the whole script to be certain that no racial overtones would occur because a black man was in the role. I dug the part not only for that reason but because, again, I could personally identify. Marine Captain Anders is my kind of officer—a *man*, self-sufficient as hell, bad, uptight, ready to do a hell of a job. He doesn't care who likes him or who doesn't, so he doesn't try to be liked. He's a terrific soldier, very tough on his men, but fair, and anything he asks them to do, he can do better.

PLAYBOY: Have you gained any more confidence in yourself as an actor since *Dirty Dozen*?

BROWN: I think so. It's just like football: I had to get that first play under my belt before I'd stop trembling. I still get keyed up, but I keep it under control. And when I'm called to go before the cameras, like I used to do before a game, I just cut off my emotions and go act out whatever the script calls for me to do. The only difference is that in football, we didn't have a specific script; the other side wouldn't have followed it, anyway.

PLAYBOY: What made you decide to quit football so abruptly at the height of your career? Was it the movie offers?

BROWN: Look—I loved playing football. It did a lot for me; it changed my life. Otherwise, I could have been some kind of gangster today; I led a gang when I was kid, you know. But, taking a realistic look at my life and my ambitions, at the things I wanted to achieve, it was time for a change, see? I find this new career just as satisfying, and even more rewarding financially, and something I can keep at far longer than I could have lasted in football. Besides that, my other activities are benefited, especially working to increase Negro participation in the country's economic life. That's very important to me. Sure, sometimes when the weather's crisp outside and I'm watching a game on television, it's hard not to be out there with the ball. But still, leaving the game when I did is probably as lucky as anything that ever happened to me. Of course, I had some concerns about giving up football's certainties for the movies' *un*certainties. But the hard fact is that I feel I quit just in time. I go out still in my prime and without any injuries. I got out before I ever had to do like I've seen so many guys—sitting hunched over on the bench, all scarred and banged up, watching some hot young kid out there in their place; and, worse than that, just wondering if they'd slowed down so badly they'd never be called to go into the game anymore. You see, I believe a man grows up. He discovers there are other worlds. Basically, I'm a guy who has to progress or I feel I'm stagnating—I don't mean just materially, but as a person. My interests have expanded in various areas—in racial relations, my various investments and, of course, my new movie career, but most of all in my sense of responsibility to my people. For the rest of my life I am committed to taking part in the black struggle that's going on in this country.

PLAYBOY: Another of the factors involved in your decision to retire, according to reports, was a contractual dispute with Browns owner Art Modell. Four years before, he had supported you in yet another dispute—against Cleveland coach Paul Brown. Acceding to an ultimatum from you and several other players, Modell finally fired Brown at the end of the 1962 season. Why did you insist on his dismissal?

BROWN: Well, first of all, it wasn't any *vendetta*, at least no personal kind of thing against Brown. At one stage in his career, Paul Brown was a genius; he set new trends in the game. But the man's ego was such that when other coaches openly stole his ideas, and added new twists, Paul Brown simply could not, or would not, change and adapt to the new styles of playing. And we players increasingly saw this. Our professional lives, our careers, were involved. We happened not to be the brainless automatons he wanted his players to act like. So we did what we had to do—in what we saw as the best interests of the players, the owner and the fans. And later events proved us right. That's really all there was to it.

PLAYBOY: What were some of the adjustments you felt Paul Brown should have made but didn't?

BROWN: Well, the major thing, we felt, was that Paul immensely favored a ground game, with intricately devised through-the-line plays. And in passing, he liked only short passes. That's just two major areas where his refusal to change cost us games we could have won. The game had accelerated very fast, see, until any coach not utilizing long passes or frequent touchdown-run threats was bound to become obsolete. Paul would only very rarely approve our trying the long-bomb pass, which other teams used often. And I was the Browns' main runner. Man, I *loved* to run—especially on those outside sweeps; that was my major touchdown potential. But Paul refused to give me enough wide-running sweep plays. When we saw ourselves continually losing when we knew we could have won, it just took the heart out of us. We lost that burning desire to win that a team has to have if it's *going* to win. How do you think we felt coming off a field beaten, and all of us there in the locker room knowing that the tremendous power we represented simply wasn't being used to its capacity? I don't like to knock the man, but truth is truth, that's all. If he had just been willing to compromise, to adjust only a little, he could have remained the top coach in pro ball. Anyway, some other players and I finally told Art Modell that unless the coaching methods changed, we'd either insist on being traded or quit. Well, any owner of a team is first and foremost a businessman. That next January—this was 1963—Art announced that Blanton Collier was replacing Paul Brown as head coach. We went into the new season a thinking, working team again. I had my best year and we took second place in the Eastern Conference. Then, in 1964, we won the league championship.

PLAYBOY: And you won the Hickok belt as the year's best professional athlete. In your entire pro career, you accumulated 126 touchdowns among your 15 all-time NFL records. Do you think anyone ever will equal or better those records?

BROWN: I think every record I've ever made will get wiped out, ultimately. Once people declared that my Syracuse records would never be broken; then Ernie Davis—the late Ernie Davis—broke all but three of them; and then Floyd Little broke all but one of Ernie's records. Records are made to be broken. You remember the four-minute mile? The 10-second dash? The seven-foot high jump? Always, you're going to have young guys coming along and improving. That's great, the way it needs to be, because that's progress, that's advancement. My personal records were never that important to me, anyway. As a matter of fact, I almost hated to break a record when I was playing, because I always felt I was becoming more and more a statistic in people's minds than a human being. But I never dwell on what I did; it's history now. I have a lot of pleasant memories of a game that was a good part of my life.

PLAYBOY: Among the records you set, none seems likely to last longer than the 12,312 yards you gained in nine pro seasons—a large proportion of which you amassed in the spectacular sweep runs you made famous. Was the sweep your favorite play?

BROWN: Well, like I said, I loved those long sweeps—but any play that gained yardage was a good play as far as I was concerned. Most plays, you understand, aren't for long runs; they're just after a crucial few yards, maybe one yard, maybe even *inches*, for a first down. That's your power plays, which can be just as important as some flashy run. But you say I made the sweep runs famous; that's very flattering, but the fact is that I never would have been able to make them without a lot of company—without guys like John Wooten and Gene Hickerson, the Browns' guards, to clear a path for me. Once they did, once I was through the hole and into the other team's secondary, that's when I was on my own. Then I had a man-to-man situation going—me against them: that's when I'd go into my bag of stuff. They're in trouble now—I'm in their territory; 55 things are happening at once; I'm moving, evaluating their possible moves, trying to outthink and outmaneuver them, using my speed, quickness and balance. I've always had very good balance. I'm ready to use a straight-arm, high knee-action or shoulder-dipping. There's the full or half straight-arm, or just the forearm, then the shoulder. In the leg maneuvers, I'd "limber-leg," offering one leg, then jerking it away when somebody grabbed. Or high-stepping would keep a pair of tacklers from getting both legs at once. In that secondary, it was just a step-by-step thing, using brainwork and instinct; but sometimes it got down to just out-and-out strength and brute force.

PLAYBOY: The great linebacker Sam Huff was once asked how to stop you. He said: "All you can do is grab hold, hang on and wait for help." Detroit's tackle Alex Karras was even more graphic about it: "Give each guy in the line an ax." Why did they have so much trouble tackling you?

BROWN: I'm the one that had trouble getting past *them*. You just don't run over guys like them; I had to try and fake them some way, like maybe drop a shoulder and struggle to get by. Some guys, of course, if they were small enough, I'd just run over them. When we hit, I'd dip a shoulder, hitting his pads, and cross either with a straight-arm to the helmet or a clubbing forearm.

PLAYBOY: Speaking of that forearm, Matt Hazeltine of the Forty-Niners has said: "Brown really shivers you. I wonder how many KOs he would have scored when there were no face masks." Did opposing players ever try to retaliate for all the clubbings you dealt out on the field?

BROWN: Oh, sure. If you're a successful, aggressive back, a scoring danger, roughings are a routine part of the game. But it still got pretty hairy sometimes. The biggest thing I resented was guys going after my face—fingers under my mask, after my eyes. That's the only thing that ever brought me close to turning chicken. I would get up, not dizzy, but I still couldn't get my eyes clear. You know how you blink and your eyes still won't clear? One time I remember, a Philadelphia Eagles defense man jammed his hand up under my face mask; I felt him clawing for my eyes and I got my teeth in that hand. Man, I tried to eat it up! I'll bet it hasn't run under any more masks since then. Later, there was a protest about my biting him. I said, "Look, I can't bite anybody *through* a mask, can I? Any hand under there was under there for some purpose, right?" There was no fine.

PLAYBOY: On two occasions, you became involved in fights on the field. What made you blow your usual cool?

BROWN: Well, once was when the Giants' Tom Scott and I punched it out that time in Cleveland Stadium; the reason, again, was my eyes. In a Giants game two weeks before, I'd been hit and gouged in the eye seven or eight times, until I was half blinded for the next couple of weeks. I went to the eye doctor and got drops and stuff, and I made up my mind that if anybody ever again came deliberately close to my eyes, I would retaliate in spades. So when I felt Scott's fingers grabbing for me, I just swung on him and we had that little scuffle. It really wasn't much of a fight, but we both were put out of the game. The only other time I swung on anybody was with Joe Robb of the Cardinals. He hit me twice. I didn't mind being hit; that's part of the game—but he hit me for no reason, no reason at all, and that I *did* mind. So I hit him back. But generally, I felt that my best retaliation on some guy was to run over him on the next play and make him look bad. That could hurt him worse than a punch. Most things didn't upset me too much, though. It's natural for the players to get emotional and fired up in a game. In fact, sometimes funny things happened.

PLAYBOY: Like what?

BROWN: Well, like sometimes guys would get all excited and call somebody a name. Once in 1963, we were playing a preseason exhibition game against the Pittsburgh Steelers. On a third-down play, I fell pretty heavily on Lou Michaels, who's now with Baltimore. He was real mad about it, and when I got up, I was moving off and I heard him holler, "Why don't you go back to the *Mafia*, Brown?" I stopped and hollered back, "Mafia? You're mixed up, you dumb chump!" Lou was all flustered for something to say, and he finally stuttered, "I mean the *niggers*!" Man, it was so funny, it cracked me up!

PLAYBOY: In the course of your entire football career, despite all the fights and roughings, you were never sidelined by a major injury. Most sportswriters consider this almost miraculous. Did you really manage to avoid getting hurt or did you just avoid showing it?

BROWN: A little bit of both—plus a lot of pure luck. It's true that I was never hurt badly enough to miss a game, but I did get a lot of what you might call small injuries at different times—cuts, bruises, sprains, and so forth. That's part of the game. Look at my hands; see those scars? I still can't shake hands with much grip: can't even get an ordinary grip on a doorknob. I got hit on a nerve once. And though most people never knew it, during the 1962 season I played all the way through with a badly sprained right wrist. It was tough for me to shift the ball from hand to hand in open field, as I liked to do when running. Of all the blows I got, though, there's one I'll never forget. It was either 1958 or 1959, against the Giants. I had to hit the line, just one yard, for a touchdown. The Giants did a lot of submarining; and whenever I met submarining lines, if the gain was vital, I'd try leaping over their line—which can get you hurt. Well, we *had* to have this touchdown, so I went up to the line, expecting to jump, but then I saw just this little sliver of daylight and I decided to go against all my principles of caution and just drop my head and take a chance of getting a hell of a headache and go through somebody's stomach. Well, I stuck my head in there, and *Vrooom!* It was like I'd been caught in a vise between their tackle and end; then a Mack truck crashed against my helmet. Sam Huff! I had made the touchdown, all right—but, man! Bells ringing, afraid somebody was going to have to help me up and all that. I finally got myself up, slow, the way I always did. But it was like, *Jesus!* I was addled, you know? Nobody's used to blows like that. I played it cool, though, walking off like I was all right, because I didn't want anybody to know. But I guess the worst one-game injury was later that same year, also against the

Giants. I drove into a charging line and in the pile-up, I got kicked in the head. My memory was knocked out; I stayed in the game, but I couldn't remember anything—even having come into the stadium to play the game. Our quarterback, Milt Plum, explained my assignments in the huddle and I carried the ball by instinct. That was in the first half; but even in the second half, I was still dreamy. Nobody knew it, though, but my teammates. Every tackle, whether I'd just had a brush block or I'd really been clobbered—like this time—I always reacted the same way. I got up slowly and I went back to the huddle slowly, without expression. It kept people from knowing if I was hurt, because I never acted any different, see? Even if my head was ringing, I could make that slow rise and walk. That's the main reason I had that no-hurt reputation.

PLAYBOY: Didn't your physical condition have anything to do with it? Dr. W. Montague Cobb, a Howard University anatomist, has said, "Jim Brown's bone structure must resemble forged vanadium steel—the hinging of ankles, knees, elbows; the 'crawl' of muscles, the dynamism of effort easily tapped are all in immediate evidence."

BROWN: He's looking at the wrong part of my anatomy. I've always made it a practice to use my *head* before I use my body. I looked upon playing football like a businessman might: The game was my business; my body and my mind were my assets, and injuries were liabilities. The *first* basic was to be in absolutely top-notch physical condition—even more than any coach would ask you to be in. I always tried to train harder than anybody else. I even developed my own set of extra calisthenics, things I could do in a hotel room if I had to. And over the years, I made for myself a careful study of what things usually cause injuries and, as much as I could, I avoided doing those things. For example, you'll see backs constantly jumping into the air, over a line; they think it looks so dramatic. Well, it *can* work—in fact, I did it myself, as I mentioned earlier, whenever I felt there was no other alternative—but sooner or later, somebody's bound to catch you up there in midair and break you in half. Another invitation to disaster is to use your head as a battering ram. If you do, pretty soon you're going to get it unhinged, like I did with Sam Huff. You'll also see some backs trying those fancy crossover step maneuvers—the left-leg-over-the-right-leg bit; I used to do that kind of thing at Syracuse; I was a regular fancy Dan. By pro-ball time, though—playing against guys who outweighed me by 60 or 70 pounds—I had learned better. I learned that if I was going to make it with the pros, I was going to have to develop something extra, something more than sheer muscle and flashy footwork. I was going to have to *outthink* the opposition. I would say that I credit 80 percent of the success I enjoyed to the fact that I played a *mental* game. The purely physical part—keeping in condition, running, passing, stuff like that—I'd credit with no more than 20 percent. It's just common sense: Physically, many guys in pro football are more than my equals—big, strong, fast son of a guns. But some simply don't get as much out of themselves as others. Why? Their mental game doesn't match their physical capacity. My game pivoted on having planned ahead of time every move I intended to make on the field. The nine years I was in pro ball, I never quit trying to make my mind an encyclopedia of every possible detail—about my teammates, about players on other teams, about the plays we used, about plays I knew *they* used and about both our and other teams' collective and individual tendencies.

I know you've heard that I was supposed to have a reputation for being distant, aloof and hard to get along with, especially in football seasons, most especially close to gametime. Well, maybe I was. Maybe I was rude to people and had very little to say to anybody. The reason is that I was focused mentally on that coming game. I was concentrating, visualizing things that I knew could happen and what I would do if it went this way or that way. I knew I had it working right when I started seeing plays in my mind almost like I was watching television. I'd see my own line in front of me, the guards, the halfbacks, the quarterbacks and then the other team over there—especially big Roger Brown and Alex Karras, two of the best tackles in football. Both of them are quick, agile, smart, fast and big, and they like to hit *hard*. Notice I don't just say they hit hard, but they *like* to hit hard—that's mental; that's positive thinking, see? I'd walk around in the locker room, seeing Roger Brown in my mind—for some reason, not his face or hands or shoulders, but those thighs of his. Massive thighs, like some huge frog. I always envision Roger hopping up in the air, jumping over blocks—all 300 pounds of him. And Alex Karras—in pro football, he's just a little cat, just 250 pounds, but he's built like a stump, with a boxer's sneering mouth. I hear him growling; he actually growls when he's charging. Positive thinking again, see? Anyway, I'd be watching them mentally across the line and sizing up the moves they might make against me. I'd see plays running and things happening—see myself starting a run and having to make spur-of-the-moment changes of strategy and direction. Every play I ever ran, I had already run a thousand in my mind. Right now, I can see a sweep run. I'm starting—my first three steps are very fast. Then I'm drifting, to let my guard in front of me get into position. There he is; now others are throwing their blocks; my guard is blocking their halfback to the outside. Now I accelerate and I shoot through the gap. That outside linebacker is my greatest danger now. I can see the order in which the tacklers are going to come. I'm looking for that end first, or maybe that outside linebacker, since no one could get to him right away. I see myself making all kinds of instantaneous adjustments, step by step, through their secondary—and then into the clear and all the way for a TD. Do you see what I mean? You get a jump on the game when you visualize beforehand not only the regular plays you run but also the hundred and one other things that might happen unexpectedly. So when you're in the actual game, whatever happens, you've already seen it in your mind and plotted your countermoves—instantly and instinctively.

PLAYBOY: You've been talking only about plays on which you were the ball carrier. One of the few things for which you were criticized as a ballplayer was your alleged refusal to block for your teammates when someone else was carrying the ball. How do you—0

BROWN: Who said that about me?

PLAYBOY: Washington Redskins coach Otto Graham, among others. He has also said that the Browns would have been a better team without you.

BROWN: Well, I never saw that quote, but I'll assume it's true, because Otto has made a lot of other comments disparaging my playing ability. I think maybe it's time I reveal something I haven't before that might cast a light on his real reason. See, Otto and I had always been good friends, and we were playing in a pro-am golf tournament at Beechmont Country Club in Cleveland, when Otto had a bad break. He drove a ball off the second tee and hit a man in the nose. Maybe two years later, this guy decided to sue Otto. I was busy practicing for a game when Otto's attorney came on the field asking me a lot of questions about the event. I told him I remembered the man was about 25 or 30 yards away when the golf ball hit him, and I didn't really remember too many other details. Evidently, the lawyer reported to Otto that I didn't wish to be cooperative. Well, shortly after that, I read the sports headline that Otto Graham said I couldn't or wouldn't block and the Browns would maybe do better without me. I've always refused to fire back at him, feeling that he said it in the mistaken belief that I didn't want to testify in his behalf.

PLAYBOY: But many others—coaches, players and fans alike—have made the same charge about you.

BROWN: Look, in the Browns' system, I simply wasn't cast to do blocking; our offense was geared for me to run. I think I had only five or six blocking assignments in our whole repertoire of plays. I'd have been the league's best blocker if the Browns had another guy doing the major running. But there are many, many great blockers in pro football and relatively few very good runners. If I had started blocking like the best guard out there and doing less running, we'd probably have won considerably less and my salary would have gone down by around $25,000. In fact, since the team depended on me running, I could even have lost my position. I always tried to satisfy the coach I worked for, and running was what they always asked of me—even in college. I always took Glen Kelly's point of view: He said he wouldn't hitch a racehorse to a milk truck.

PLAYBOY: Throughout your first year at Syracuse, the coaches didn't even want you as a starting player on the freshman team, let alone as its star fullback. Until your sophomore season was well under way, in fact, you were relegated to the fourth or fifth string on the varsity team. Why?

BROWN: I was black, that's why. You see, before I went to Syracuse, a Negro named Avatus Stone had been a great ballplayer there—a quarterback, a great punter. They wanted him to play end, but he refused and finally left and went to Canada. But the *real* rub was that Stone had been very popular among white coeds—which made him very *unpopular* with white males. So when I arrived, the only black man on the team, the coaches had nothing to say to me except, "Don't be like Avatus Stone!" My whole freshman year, I heard so many sermons about what I should be like, I got so many hang-ups, that my attitude became as bad as theirs. In practice, I was snubbed and ignored until I got to where I'd just sprawl out on my back during drills and nobody said a word to me. I was as sullen as they were, and the freshman season ended and the sophomore season began with me on the fifth string. But I hustled like mad when sophomore training season opened; and when the games began, they had moved me up to second string. I got in a few games, but nothing spectacular happened until, finally, in the fourth game, against Illinois, we had a lot of injuries on the team and I started. We got badly beaten, but I carried 13 times, averaging five yards, and the fans caught that. When I was on the bench, they started hollering, "We want Brown! Brown! Brown!" Man, that made me feel 10 feet tall! Then came my really big break—against Cornell. We lost 14 to 6, but I made a long touchdown run, over 50 yards, as I remember; and altogether I gained about 150 yards. Then, in the next game, against Colgate, I made two touchdowns. That did it; overnight, the fans made me a campus celebrity and, man, did I love it! In my junior year, I opened thinking I had it made and Pittsburgh bottled me up for 28 yards in 12 carries and the coaches demoted me to second team. That made me so mad I saw fire; and in the next practice scrimmage, I left first-string tacklers lying out all over the field and ran four touchdowns in five plays. After that, they left me on the first string. That's how I got accepted, you know? I mean accepted as Jim Brown, not Avatus Stone. And I'm saying nothing against Stone, because he's a beautiful cat. I'm just saying my personality was my own and I didn't happen to feel that white coeds had any monopoly on desirability for me. Anyway, once the coaches made up their minds, they were men enough to realize they had been wrong and they became fair in dealing with me, and then I gave them all I had. I think maybe having to fight my way up the way I did taught *me* more about being a man, too.

PLAYBOY: Did you have to contend with race prejudice in pro ball as well?

BROWN: Of course! *Every* Negro in this country, I don't care *who* he is, is affected by racial prejudice in some of its various forms. Athletes probably enjoy as much freedom as any black men in this country—but they're by no means exempt from discrimination. The relationship with white players *is* much better now; they respect whoever can help them win that championship bonus check. And the fan reaction is greatly improved, because so many Negroes are starring and there are now even black team captains. The problems arise *off* the playing field—and I'd say that the major problem area is related, in some way, to white women. It's a major factor why black and white players don't socialize, because sooner or later they are going to be in some situation involving women. The black athlete who is desirable to white women is going to run into all kinds of trouble. If he gets anywhere around white men with her, fellow athletes or not, pretty soon that black man is going to get reminded that he is not free, that he's still black in white men's eyes, star on the field or not. It's one of the reasons black athletes no longer particularly try to socialize with, or even get along with, white teammates. When the game is over, the whites go their way and the blacks go theirs, with very few exceptions.

PLAYBOY: According to the Cleveland press, that separatism didn't apply to white women, at least in your case.

BROWN: I see I've got to remind you I'm married—married to a *black* woman. I think I'm no different from the vast majority of black men:

I'm not dying to have a white woman. Stokely Carmichael uses a good statement in this area when that subject comes up. He says, "The white woman can be *made*! OK, we've got that settled—so let's go on to something important!" When I was in college, I dated both black and white coeds. It didn't matter to me. I've never seen any difference in white or black women. It's a question of individual characteristics, personality, habits and tastes. All that mattered to me was *pretty* girls. I always went after the finest-looking, the real *foxes*! I have a nickname, "Hawk," which comes from having very good eyesight. Visually, I appreciate anything that I consider beautiful—if it's a car, if it's a suit, a painting, a woman or what have you. And the woman I appreciate most is my wife, Sue, who seems to be happy and very much in love with me. I have never denied her and I have never denied those three big babies we have at home in Cleveland. So I'm sure that I'm doing no big damage by looking.

PLAYBOY: Speaking of babies, you were once the defendant in a paternity suit filed by an 18-year-old Cleveland girl. Though you were subsequently exonerated, it didn't exactly enhance your public image. What were the details of the case?

BROWN: Actually, I was sued for assault and battery. Then the same party sued me for paternity. I figured, hell, I'm strong enough to fight it out publicly, and that's what I did. I sat a week in that hot courtroom, missing a number of important commitments. It never would have gone to court if I had been guilty; I would have dealt with it the way a man *should* deal with a thing of that nature. Anybody who doubts that doesn't know me.

PLAYBOY: Quite apart from paternity suits, it's fairly common knowledge that you've long been the target of demonstrative admiration by many female football fans. Is it just coincidence that most of them happen to be white?

BROWN: You're just tipping around the edges of the big question at the bottom of the mind of every white man in this country: "What about you blacks and white women?" Right? Well, OK, let's talk straight about that. I'll tell you the very first thing that always knocks me out about that question. Why is there always the implication that the white woman is just mesmerized, just helpless, if she's with a black man? Everybody knows the smart, hip, twentieth century white woman is in complete control of herself and does exactly what she damn well wants to do and nothing else. So what's the reason the white man has her pictured in his mind as hypnotized and helpless with a black man? The other thing that bugs me about that question is the assumption by the average white man that any black man he sees with any white woman has got to be sleeping with her. To me, that instant assumption tells me a lot more about that white man than it does about the black man—or the white woman. Let's assume he's right that a lot of white women are either openly or secretly attracted to black men. It happens to be true—but let's ask ourselves why. Well, the answer is that the white man himself has *made* his woman this attracted to us.

PLAYBOY: How?

BROWN: For generations, he has painted the black man as such an animal that it's not only natural but inevitable that the white woman's mind occupies itself with this big, exciting *taboo*. And, yeah, a lot of them do more than *think* about it; they decide to find out. And when they do, they find that the black man isn't the gorilla the white man has painted; that he may be as much of a gentleman as any man she has known and may even pay her more respect than her own kind. You can't blame her for responding—and you can't blame him for responding to *her*, because he's the same man who for 300 years couldn't open his mouth or he would *die*, while he saw the white man having sex as he pleased with the black woman. Let me tell you something interesting to do. Every time you see a Negro from now on, just take note of his complexion. See how few are jet black and reflect how *all* the Africans brought over here were jet black. It might help you to do some thinking about who genetically changed the color of a whole *race* of people, diluted them from black Africans not into black *Americans* but into *Negroes*; even the word is a white man's creation, a stigma, a kind of proper form for "nigger." Historically, there's been about a thousand times more sex between white men and black women than between black men and white women—and a thousand times more black man-white woman sex goes on in white men's *minds* than ever does in fact. And I'm not in the least criticizing where it *is* fact. I believe that whatever any two consenting adults—black or white—do in their own privacy, without causing harm to any other party, is entirely their own business. The white man may consider it *his* business; in fact, most do; but I don't feel that it's *mine*!

I know, and I accept, that certain exposures to white women will likely encourage and develop friendships. I use the expression "friendships" because I don't want to be guilty of doing the same thing that I accuse people of doing to me—just see me *talking* with some white woman and instantly they assume, "There goes sex." I can't tell you how many times that has made me sick in this country. I can't remember once when someone wasn't waiting to see me outside the stadium after a game—different friends, some of them from college days, some of them white women. Half the time, their husbands and children would be standing off to one side and they would run up and hug me. It was a very warm thing between the two of us; after all, we hadn't seen each other in years—at least it *should* have been warm. But I can't remember one single time when, before I got through the crowd, I didn't catch some white faces giving me that frowned-up, dirty look that was saying, "Him and white women again!" Something beautiful and completely platonic disrupted by somebody who didn't even *know* us. Hell, it didn't even have to be a *grown* white woman! I've known it to happen with little girls! The autograph crowd is around, say, everybody excited and happy—and all of a sudden there's this little girl, under 10, say, whose parent tells her, "Go tell Jim Brown hello." OK, I bend over and the little girl, with instinctive affection, starts to reach up to hug my neck and kiss my cheek. You know? But I've been that route before. I anticipate the impulsive intent of a sweet, innocent little child—and I have to maneuver somehow to prevent her acting natural. Because too many times before, see, I had straightened up from a child's embrace and caught the disapproving white facial expressions. Finally, I began to feel that I'd just rather not see my old friends in that kind of situation. Which meant that *I* was becoming prejudiced. Many a time since then, I have walked on through a crowd, not speaking to anybody, and it helped to build my "mean and evil" reputation. But this kind of bitter experience isn't unique with me, or even with black athletes; it happens to every black man and woman in America.

PLAYBOY: Though you've certainly experienced many of the injustices familiar to all Negroes, isn't it also true that you enjoy, as a celebrity, certain privileges that are denied to the average Negro?

BROWN: Well, I do have some of what you might call "back-door advantages." Numerous doors and opportunities have opened for me personally, for the individual me. I've got a few dollars in the bank, and a home, and my family eats and dresses well and I drive a good car. When I consider that my forebears were slaves, I know I'm lucky to be where I am and have what I do. But to me, these are always a reminder of the fact that the same doors are not open for *all* black people. Although I appreciate the advantages for selfish reasons, this constant awareness of inequity makes them mean less to me. And there's something else a lot of people don't realize—that the more successful a black person is, the harder it is for him to live with the things that still go with being black. Let me give you an example, just one of the common examples. You've earned the money to buy yourself a better home in a better residential area, and you haven't even signed the papers before the word leaks out and white people start *running* before they'd live near you. The poor, ignorant type? No! Your better-class white people. The people who in another setting would smile to see their kids rushing you for autographs. How is one supposed to feel about that? I never will forget being bluntly refused an apartment in Cleveland soon after I moved there. The landlady looked me in the face and said. "We only take whites." I wound up buying the home we have now, in a nice, modest, predominantly Negro neighborhood. At the other place, I hadn't been eager to live around white people; I had just wanted a place near the field where the Browns practiced, which would be more convenient for me. It wasn't integration I was after; I just was bitter about being *segregated*, you understand?

PLAYBOY: Have you encountered any other kind of overt discrimination since you became well-known?

BROWN: Are you kidding? I don't even like to think about it. But I'll give you just one example. There was nothing really uncommon about the incident itself in the average Negro's experience, particularly in the South. But it had me choked up and bitter for a long time after it happened. It was in 1957 and I was in Army training down in Alabama. Three buddies of mine and I were in my convertible, with the top down, driving to Tuskegee. We had just gone through this little town, enjoying ourselves, when all of a sudden this police car roared up behind and barreled past us, cut us off and stopped; and, baby, I'm looking at this cop getting out with a drawn gun. "Get out, niggers!" We got out. "What are you making dust all over white people for?" Just about then, another car pulled up and stopped and another white guy got out. The cop was saying, "You hear me, nigger?" Well, my emotions were such that I hardly trusted myself to speak. "I don't know what a nigger is!" I said. Then he jammed the pistol right in my stomach. "Nigger, don't you know how to talk to white folks?" One of the guys with me said, "He's not from down here; he's from up North." The cop said, "Nigger, I don't care where you're from. I'll blow you apart! Where did you get this car, anyway?" I said, "It was given to me." He said, "*Given* to you! Who gave you a *car?*" I said, "It was given to me at school." "*What* school?" I said, "Syracuse University." Just about then, the other white man came over closer and he said, "That's right. I recognize this boy. He plays football up there." That was my reprieve. The cop took the gun out of my belly and said, "I'm going to let you go, but you better drive slow and you better learn how to act down here, nigger!" So we got back in the car and drove on. I don't know why I even told you that; it's not good to dredge that stuff up in your mind again. But you see, you don't forget a thing like that, not if somebody handed you every trophy in football and 15 Academy Awards. That's why a black man, if he's got any sense at all, will never get swept away with special treatment if he happens to be famous, because he knows that the minute he isn't where somebody *recognizes* who he is, then he's just another *nigger*. That's what the Negro struggle is all about; that's why we black people have to keep fighting for freedom in this country. We demand only to live—and let live—like any ordinary American. We don't want to have to be somebody *special* to be treated with respect. I can't understand why white people find it so hard to understand that.

PLAYBOY: If you feel as strongly as you say about winning equal rights for Negroes, why didn't you ever join the Negro celebrities who participated with Dr. King in such nonviolent demonstrations as the Selma march?

BROWN: I felt I could do more by giving my time to my own organization—the National Negro Industrial and Economic Union—than by flying to Alabama and marching three days, another celebrity in the pack, almost a picnic atmosphere, and then flying back home a so-called hero because I'd been so "brave." I'm not knocking those who did; I'm just saying I felt differently about it. That kind of demonstration served its purpose well; but it finally outlived its usefulness.

PLAYBOY: In what way?

BROWN: I'd compare Dr. King's methods with Paul Brown's brand of football. Like King, Brown was a genius in his time, but he refused to change and finally he became outdated. I think the sit-ins, walk-ins, wade-ins, pray-ins and all those other -ins advanced the movement tremendously by awakening the nation's conscience—making millions of white people aware of and sympathetic to the wrongs suffered by black people. When the white population was at that point, I think the movement's direction should have been altered toward economic programming for Negro self-help, with white assistance. Think what could have been accomplished if the nation's black leaders, at that time, had actively mobilized the goodwill of all the millions of white people who were willing, even anxious, to help the Negro help himself. We could have had millions, white and black, working toward that goal, with tremendous results. That was what I felt and what I tried to do, in forming my National Negro Industrial and Economic Union. But no one listened—not in the movement and not in Washington. What happened, instead, was that the marching went on and on, getting more and more militant, until a lot of white people began to resent it—and to feel threatened. Whenever any human being feels threatened—it doesn't matter if he's right or wrong—he starts reacting defensively, negatively. We lost the white sympathy and support we'd fought so hard to win: badly needed new civil rights legislation began to die on the vine; existing laws were loopholed, modified or ignored; poverty funds dried up. On the threshold of real progress, the door simply closed in our faces. The inevitable consequences of that frustration set fire to Watts, Detroit, Newark and two dozen other cities.

PLAYBOY: Police authorities in several cities have claimed that the riots were fomented not by frustration but by "Communist agitators." Do you think there's any truth to that charge?

BROWN: If by "fomented" they mean planned, like some kind of revolutionary battle strategy, they just don't understand the explosive state of every ghetto in this country. The average ghetto Negro is so pent up and fed up with white lies, hostility, hypocrisy and neglect that riots don't *need* planning. All they need is a spark to set them off, and the cops usually provide that without any help from the Communists. Once a riot gets started, of course, the Communists, along with a lot of others, will be out there fanning the flames. Communist money and people are working in every ghetto, especially the major ones. It's no big secret that the Communists' main objective in this country is to attract a large following of Negroes. You'll hear black kids standing around on corners talking defiantly about "feudalism" and "capitalism" and "man's exploitation of man" and all that stuff; they don't even know what the words mean, but it sounds hip to them, you know? If there's anything the vast majority of Negroes in this country have proved, however, it's that they aren't Communist-inclined. They don't *need* Communist indoctrination to tell them that they're second-class citizens, and they don't need Communist help to become *first*-class citizens. They can—and will—do it on their own, no matter what it costs. Black people are demonstrating that they're willing to die for total freedom. There's not going to be any turning back now. It's going to be either total freedom or the concentration camps I hear they're getting ready for us. If there's anything the black man has learned thoroughly in his history in this country, it's that begging, appeasing, urging and imploring has gotten him nowhere. He just kept on getting slapped around, and only when he started to slap back did he begin to get any kind of respect.

PLAYBOY: Are you an advocate of Negro violence?

BROWN: Don't talk to me about *Negro* violence. The greatest violence this country has ever known has been on behalf of the various vested interests of white people, demanding whatever they were convinced were their rights. You could start with the American Revolution. Then the Indian wars—outright criminal violence, depicted in the history books and on television as heroic! Then the Civil War, in which the black man wasn't really the true issue; he was nothing but the excuse. And on down the line to the labor movement. Heads got split open, people shot down, property destroyed all over the country. If you want to talk about race riots, the Irish, not black people, fought the bloodiest riot ever seen in America; in the late 1800s, they went looting and burning and killing down Lexington Avenue, which was then the richest, most fashionable part of New York City. There's no point in dragging this out forever, if you see my point.

PLAYBOY: You've strayed from our original question: are you an advocate of black violence?

BROWN: I am a 100-percent advocate that if a man slaps you, you should slap him back. I know that if a man hits me, I'm going to try to hit him twice—harder—because I want him to do a lot of thinking before he ever hits me again. I am an advocate of freedom for everybody, freedom that isn't something handed out at one group's discretion and taken away if someone makes that group angry. The law is the law; that's what I believe, and I believe right is right. We're all supposed to abide by this country's so-called laws—not only the laws against civil disorder but the laws *for* civil *rights*. There's a very simply stated way to eliminate the race problem: just enforce the same laws and the same standards for everybody, black and white alike. That's the only thing the black people are after. Am I personally an advocate of black violence? I'm an advocate of *stopping* black violence before it *starts*—by facing the facts, by curing the *reasons* black people engage in violence. I've gotten frantic calls from high places when riots were in progress, begging me to "do something," and my reaction has been, "Later for you! When I was trying to tell what our NNIEU could do to *prevent* riots, you didn't want to listen. Well, now you've waited too late!" Whatever I think, or any other black personality thinks, isn't going to make any difference once riots get started.

PLAYBOY: Can they be stopped, or do you think they'll escalate, as some predict, into a race war?

BROWN: If nothing is done to *prevent* riots—and I don't mean with more tanks—race war is a very real and immediate probability. Too many black people who have been kept methodically at the bottom of the ladder for centuries don't really care what happens. They figure, what have they got to lose? The building up of police forces, the various thinly veiled threats, like concentration camps, have no deterrent effect whatever. All it does is make the blacks madder, and that will send them out in the streets quicker than anything else. As of right now, only a very small percentage of Negroes have actually rioted, or even have thought about physically participating in rioting. But the number grows with every threat. And there's one thing in particular that I'd think about a long, long time if I were any city's police chief or mayor or a state governor—and that's the curfews that get slapped down whenever there's trouble. After the Watts trouble, which involved only a few of the Negroes in Los Angeles, suddenly a "riot area" curfew was declared that went far beyond the locale of the rioting—all the way to the borders of the total black community in Los Angeles, excepting only the handful of so-called upper-middle-class blacks who happened to be living in so-called integrated high-income areas. With that single act, hundreds of thousands of Negroes—be they criminals, hoodlums, preachers, doctors, lawyers, nurses, schoolteachers, firemen, policemen or politicians—discovered that it made no difference, that what really was being put down was *black people!* Nobody caught in that curfew net ever will think the same again. It was very obvious to them what was being said.

PLAYBOY: You said the riots may escalate if nothing is done to prevent them. What do you think *can* be done?

BROWN: First of all, these mayors' and governors' offices have got to drop this implied revenge attitude I was talking about—building up police forces and beefing up the National Guard. That's just working toward the concentration camps. There's got to be, somehow, some truly sincere understanding achieved between Negro leaders and the concerned state and city administrations. And by Negro leaders, I don't mean the Martin Luther Kings and the Whitney Youngs; I mean the people who have followings in the ghettos. They've got to be listened to, and worked with, and given respect, and urged to help with programming where money and other aid will actually filter down to the lowest level of the ghetto, where you find the people most prone to riot—those who are most bitter and alienated and frustrated and suspicious. So much has been done *to* them, it's a pins-and-needles job to make them believe anybody actually will do anything *for* them. But if the city governments are willing to listen to and work with these *real* Negro leaders, I think there is a tremendous chance of quieting racial disorders. I say this because I head up an organization—the NNIEU—that offers, free, some of the greatest black talent in this country, most of it never used before. I can call upon 50 or 60 of the top black athletes in this country to run summer programs and work directly in communities with these young kids. But when I can't get the Vice President's committee to fund such a summer program, I think something is radically wrong.

PLAYBOY: Considering the mood of Congress in the wake of the riots, isn't it unrealistic to expect the federal government to allocate funds for a program implemented by ghetto gang leaders who many whites feel were instrumental in starting the riots?

BROWN: It was unrealistic, it seems to me, to expect that the people sealed up in these ghettos would remain quiet in them forever. If you're trying to stop riots, I call any man qualified, street hoodlum or not, if he controls the people who riot. I know what I'm talking about; I've seen what can happen with these people. You've got to persuade the black men who are respected in their area to go in and crack the door, crack the ice. I've been able to do this myself a few times in a few places. The ghetto people know I'm straight, that I speak up and stand up and I wouldn't betray them. I've gone into ghettos and talked with the toughest cats. I've told them, "Now, look, I think you know I'm my own man. Now, here's what seems to me a hell of a program, but it needs your help to get wide community support behind it." In most cases, these guys will give 100-percent support. Give the toughest cats a certain respect, because *they* have respect from the people you're trying to reach with help, and they'll work with you. Sure, they're hostile and suspicious, but they'll talk sincerely with you if they figure you're *with* them. You find their greatest disappointment and bitterness come from promises, promises that proved later to be some political sham or that just weren't followed up. Whatever program there is has to be followed up, day to day. And the best people to monitor that is these tough guys: give them jobs doing it. All they want is decent salaries; they have to eat, to live, just like anyone else. But I find that city administrations don't like this idea. They're still after political points. They want to dictate the terms, and the ghetto people resent anybody bringing them any program with white strings, so naturally it gets nowhere. And that's why we're likely to have more black uprisings, which lead to more white "revenge" talk, and threats, and the vicious cycle continues. I hope that black freedom can be won peaceably. That's my *hope*. But things I keep seeing make me skeptical. Historically, great battles for freedom have seldom been won peaceably.

PLAYBOY: Have you read the polls that show that a large majority of Negroes think the whites would lose in a race war?

BROWN: Yes, I have. That's emotionalism. Because, without a doubt, black people couldn't win any mass encounter. How could they? Outnumbered 10 to one? With a handful of guns, some homemade Molotov cocktails, sticks, rocks and switchblades? Against the white man's jets, tanks, chemical warfare and H-bombs? That's just plain silly. I think anybody who doesn't realize this simply isn't being a realist. But this is just one of many facts of life about which black people, especially the extremists, aren't being realistic.

PLAYBOY: You were affiliated, as an official of Main Bout, with the Black Muslims who ran the organization. Do you feel that the Muslims' extremist philosophy of separatism is realistic?

BROWN: No, I don't. Like many, many Negroes—maybe 90 percent of us privately—I agree with much of what they say, but I don't personally accept their separatist philosophy, and I'm not a member. My business relationship in Main Bout with Herbert Muhammad and John Ali was a very pleasant and compatible one, however, and I respect the organization for instilling black people with pride in their race and for teaching black people to pull themselves up by their own bootstraps and take care of their own. I also respect the Muslims' right to practice their own religion—a right legally recognized by the government, if not by the white press, which I feel has grossly misrepresented them. The main reason they're so disliked by whites is that so much of what they say about the black condition is the truth, and white America doesn't like to hear the truth about its own bigotry and oppression.

PLAYBOY: Do you feel the same way about such black-power firebrands as Stokely Carmichael and Rap Brown?

BROWN: I feel there is a need for them. Unfortunately, the average white seems to need a good scare from the Carmichaels and Rap Browns before he'll listen to less dramatic requests. Speaking for myself, I think it's too easy to just go out and threaten Whitey. What is that doing to help black people? At the same time, I've been turned down by so many administration officials, seeking money and support for our self-help program—and not just turned down but suspected of being "subversive"—that I've been tempted to take the easy way, too, and start hollering against Whitey myself. As long as administrations refuse to sponsor programs that give black people constructive alternatives to violence, I can't really blame these guys for their extremism. I think they symbolize a lot of those their age who are sick of passive resistance, who are really fighting for freedom—young Negroes with great pride in themselves and their race. They are not trying to be assimilated; but they believe there should be, and must be, equality. Like them or not, they are what the white man is going to have to deal with more and more. They're brash and fearless and they're going to fight in any and every way they feel necessary to be respected and to win their freedom in this country. Where I disagree with guys like Stokely and Rap is that it was a mistake for them to get identified with merely defining and defending black power. It has deflected their energies from effective programming into sloganeering.

PLAYBOY: How would *you* define black power?

BROWN: First and foremost, I'd define it as a creation of the white press. From the moment Stokely Carmichael used the expression in a speech two years ago—though he quickly explained that he meant it in the sense of political and economic power—the press, and millions of white people, instantly interpreted those two words as an ominous threat of black mass uprising. It says more to me about the interpreters than about the two words. To me it says white fear, white guilt seeking a justification, a target. It was whites, not blacks, who turned it into a hate thing and used it to label exponents of black power as advocates of racial violence.

PLAYBOY: Would you call yourself an exponent of black power?

BROWN: I'm for black power the same way I'm for Irish power, Jewish power, labor power, doctor power, farmer power, Catholic power, Protestant power. I'm for all the special vested-interest groups using their economic and political strength to demand that others pay them respect and grant them equality. Only I call it *green* power. That's my idea of what needs to become the black people's special interest. I want to see black people pooling their monies, their skills, their brains and their political power to better themselves, to participate more fully in the mainstream of American life. And that requires white support. The black people simply don't have the money to support the programs needed to train them in what they can do for themselves.

PLAYBOY: When you say you need white *financial* support to help Negroes help themselves, does that mean you share the deepening cynicism of such militant Negro groups as CORE and SNCC about the direct personal involvement of white volunteers, however sincere and committed, in the civil rights movement?

BROWN: Speaking for my own organization, the one I've founded—which is the only one I can really speak for—we know that there are many, many sincere and truly committed white people, and one of our major efforts is to get more and more of them to help us. But we no longer want or need the same kind of help they've offered in the past: we don't want them to march with us anymore, because marches are a thing of the past; and we don't want them to work with us in the ghetto anymore. We want their moral and financial support—as long as there are no strings attached to either—but we want them to work with their own kind and leave us alone to work with ours.

PLAYBOY: Why?

BROWN: Simply because the people in the ghetto just don't trust whites, no matter how sincere or well intentioned they are; hell, they don't even trust the average so-called accepted black leaders—which is to say, the black leaders approved of by the white establishment. The suspicions and hostilities, born of 300 years of white bigotry and betrayal, run too deep. But that's where we can use all the help we can get from concerned whites: in uprooting racial prejudice where it originates—in the hearts of *other* whites.

What it comes down to is: who can work best where? For the same reason a white man would last about five minutes preaching brotherhood on a Harlem street corner, black people can't run around in white communities trying to change white attitudes; they'd get arrested for "disturbing the peace." Sincere white people have got to go to work upstairs, downstairs, next door, down the block—talking, teaching, reasoning, organizing, whittling away at white prejudice wherever they find it; and they'll find it everywhere. Our job, the job of sincere and committed blacks such as the athletes in my NNIEU—who may be the only kind of guys the toughest street cats will accept and listen to—is to work inside the ghetto to eliminate the *effects* of racial prejudice and discrimination by helping black people acquire the green power they need to make life, liberty and the pursuit of happiness a tangible reality rather than an empty catchphrase.

PLAYBOY: How did you evolve this strategy of liberation through economic self-help?

BROWN: Well, when I was with the Cleveland Browns, as you know, for some time I had a summer-season job with Pepsi-Cola. I had access to much of their internal operational program, and they had me do a lot of traveling to various places, as a representative. In the process, I began to get a pretty good understanding, better than any I had before, of how economics is the very foundation of this country. When I say white people have got to face some hard truths, I also believe that black people have got to face some hard truths; and the most basic of these truths is that, for all the crimes committed against him, the black man in America still has not begun properly to take advantage of even the limited opportunities that he *has* had. We have become a consuming people and we have produced almost nothing. Therefore, automatically, what few dollars we make don't circulate among us, to help *us*; they go into other pockets instead. We've wasted too much time hollering and complaining that we don't have this, we can't do that, and so forth—all because of Whitey. We've squandered energies that should have been spent focusing upon what we *could* have and *could* do with what we *do* have! As a race, we suffer from a terrible mistrust not only of the white man but of each other. That's why we've never really been able to get together, why we haven't had more cooperative business ventures. For another thing, we're just not economically oriented by nature; we're too impulsive, impractical, unpragmatic and emotional about money. It's the sad truth that we continue to drink the best imported Scotch, to wear the finest shoes, to drive the biggest Cadillacs, and we don't own one single distillery, shoe factory or Cadillac agency—at least not to my knowledge we don't. Right now, for instance, there are thousands of jobs going begging that industries are offering to black youth. The message in that fact for black people, I think, is loud and clear: get off the streets and into the schoolrooms and the colleges and the libraries.

Now, in saying all this, by no means am I letting the white man off the hook. He has sinned; he has held the black man down for centuries. I'm just saying that the black man, in hard fact, hasn't done enough to help himself. We've used our being a minority as a crutch. We're said to be 10 percent of the population; but the Jews are only about three percent, fewer than six million, and they came here with far less than black people now have in resources and they met all kinds of prejudices. But they worked together; they used their brains and the law and money and business acumen, and by now you can't find any ethnic group in America commanding more respect. *Commanding* it! Do you know that once Jews weren't wanted in Miami? So they bought it. Same with the Catskills. I rarely give a speech today without suggesting the Jews as a model of what black people need to do with themselves economically.

Anyway, this was the trend of the private thinking I had been doing for a long time—about how the black people could truly become a part of American society and share in its good things. Well, the Pepsi-Cola experience gave me the insights and the know-how I needed to put that thinking into action—by getting others who feel as I do to help me form an organization to help black people help themselves economically. The first thing I needed was a staff to whom black people would listen, from whom they would take advice and guidance. And I knew of one ideal group—black athletes. It may sound immodest, but it's a fact that we tend to be heroes among black people, especially black youth. Something that's haunted me for years is that look I have seen so many times in some of those black teenagers' eyes looking at me up close: for just an instant, that animal hipness and suspicion leaves the face and you see a look in the eyes that seems to say, "For God's sake, for just a minute, will *somebody* care?" It gets to me, because I was that kid once, see? So it's one of those "There but for the grace of God" things with me—and it's the same for all the other athletes I know. So among my own teammates, and wherever we played, I filtered the idea around. And that's where I got my first major encouragement. They just snapped it up! It was funny, man! On the field, cats were trying to run over each other, break each other in half; then the evening after the game, we're all huddled together excitedly discussing this new project. Guys like John Wooten and Walter Beach of the Browns, Bernie Casey of the Atlanta Falcons,

Brady Keys of the Pittsburgh Steelers, Bobby Mitchell of the Redskins, Leroy Kelly, Bill Russell, Curtis McClinton, Timmy Brown, lots of others. We mapped out an organization that would sell memberships to anybody and everybody for from $2 to $100, to raise money to finance good ideas for small black businesses, because so many good black ideas can't obtain financing. And we decided to make use of black professional people—these "middle-class Negroes" we hear so much talk about—to draw them in with us, to lend their talents to young Negroes in all the various ways they could. And we decided to use the image value of black athletes in personal-contact programs with black youth, especially in the ghettos.

We all put in some of our own money to get it started. I personally donated more than $50,000. Then we hired a secretary and rented an office in the ghetto area of Cleveland, where people wouldn't feel uncomfortable coming to see us. Well, we've been almost two years now working, researching, recruiting, opening another office in Los Angeles and operating limited programs in four other cities. With more financing, I think we have the potential of being one of the most meaningful and effective programs anywhere in this country.

PLAYBOY: How many Negro athletes are involved now?

BROWN: About 100, at least, from stars to rookies, from old-timers like me down to young kids like Lew Alcindor. He works for us like a Trojan in his off time. Quite a few *white* athletes have come in with us, too, as investors in black business ideas. And you wouldn't *believe* some of the *non*athletes who have volunteered to come and work with us for nothing but subsistence! People like Spencer Jourdain, a Harvard graduate, who quit a great job at Corning Glass to work full time for us, just for subsidy, because he's so committed to our idea.

PLAYBOY: With so little city, state or federal support, financial or otherwise, how much have you been able to achieve?

BROWN: Well, aside from a couple dozen new black businesses now in operation, I think we could rightly claim some major credit for the fact that last year, Cleveland didn't prove to be the nation's number-one riot area, as had been predicted by the so-called experts. We got together with the city administration and with the Greater Cleveland Foundation and persuaded them to cooperate, through the NNIEU, with those who were truly in control of the ghetto—the kind of people who really control every ghetto, people your average sociologists couldn't even *talk* to, because they don't know their language, even. The really tough cats, you know? The kind who are the most dangerous people in any society. Like this young man called Ahmad, who has a very sizable following and influence in Cleveland's ghetto. We got together with him and we got him to agree to serve on a committee to discuss ghetto needs, to offer plans, and we saw in Ahmad a very changed attitude—because suddenly this guy was given some *respect*, see? Now *he* works to do constructive things for the area. We were also able to get the Greater Cleveland Foundation to fund a youth center for us. One of the first things we did was establish courses in black history, business administration, economics and many other such self-help subjects. We offer entertainment, too—dancing, theater, talent night; the kids love it. And we've developed a job-procurement program. We involved everybody we could get our hands on, with special emphasis on redirecting into constructive channels the energy of special groups who were capable of starting trouble. One young fellow, who had been viewed generally as a prime troublemaker, we were able to turn into a crackerjack director of our youth center; we have six Cleveland Browns athletes doing volunteer work *under* him. We're headed into the 1968 summer now. The popularity of our youth center has so overflowed it that we're asking the Greater Cleveland Foundation to fund five more of them for us. I truly think that if we can expand, we're capable of conducting special programs simultaneously in at least six major cities. We want to open formal offices also in Washington, New York, Boston and Chicago. Given more city-administration aid and cooperation, I know we can prove what we can do. If anybody else wants to help us, or just find out more about us, would you be good enough to print that our NNIEU headquarters address is 105-15 Euclid Avenue, Cleveland, Ohio 44106?

PLAYBOY: Gladly. On another front, how do you feel about the election of your former NNIEU legal counsel, Carl Stokes, as mayor of Cleveland—and about the victories of several other Negro candidates for high city office throughout the country?

BROWN: Cleveland—and the country—will benefit. Carl won not because of—or despite—his being a Negro, but because he's a takeover guy who's going to produce a positive, dynamic administration for black and white alike. As for other Negro mayors and city officials in the North, like Hatcher in Gary, it simply had to happen, because otherwise, with the big Northern cities becoming more and more Negro-populated as white people rush to the suburbs, we wouldn't have representative city government. But the most heartening sign to me is the fact that Negroes are competing with—and winning against—white candidates on the basis of personal qualifications rather than skin color, and winning with white support.

PLAYBOY: You seem to be much more optimistic about the racial situation than you were a few years ago—and much less cynical about the prospects of white cooperation. Why?

BROWN: The only change is that once I dealt with the negative aspects; now I deal with what I see as positives. I'm working now trying to do something about what ails us black people. Now I have an organization. I have responsibilities toward the people who believe in me. We've talked, talked, talked about discrimination for years. Now I'm trying to help get rid of it.

PLAYBOY: With the kind of movie schedule you've been keeping, do you feel you're giving all the help you should?

BROWN: Not nearly as much as I'd like. But the other athletes carry on full time when I'm away, as their schedules permit. And whatever success I earn in the movies is going to be invested in building and promoting the NNIEU; so I don't feel like I'm neglecting my duty. What bothers me more is that I haven't been able to be at home with Sue and the kids more than a few weeks at a time for about 18 months now. I don't think the kids will suffer too much because of it, thanks to the great job Sue is doing in keeping them well adjusted; but I'd like to be there more, all the same. I'm getting older, you know, and I want my family ties to be as strong as the ties to my people. The best way I can see to strengthen both of them, in the long run, is by doing what I'm doing: trying to become a good actor. I may not make myself any more popular by saying some of the things I've said to you today, but I'd lose respect for myself if I told anybody just what I felt they *wanted* to hear. Just about whenever I've stood up and spoken my mind about situations that bothered me as a black man, somebody I thought I trusted, somebody I thought knew and understood me, has advised and urged and all but begged me—with the best of intentions—not to express my objections publicly. "Jim," they tell me, "it'll hurt your image. It'll alienate the goodwill of your public"—meaning the *white* public. Well, I don't need that kind of concern for my welfare. I'm not going to be anybody's little boy. I'm a *man*, a *black* man, in a culture where black manhood has been kicked around and threatened for generations. So that's why I don't feel I need to take too much advice about how I'm supposed to think and act. And that's why I have to tell the truth like I see it. Maybe some people will holler; maybe they'll hate me for it. But I'll just stick it out, walk tall and wait for the truth to be vindicated.

PLAYBOY: How long do you think that will take?

BROWN: I can't say how long; I can't worry about that. That doesn't even matter to me. All that matters is to see more and more black people mobilized and working toward constructive self-help goals. I want more black people to realize the hard fact that unless we do this, all the other gains aren't going to make any difference. If in my lifetime I can see that this idea really has taken hold, then I will have the satisfaction of knowing that true freedom—as black men and as black *Americans*—will finally be within our grasp.

DALE EARNHARDT JR.

A candid conversation with the son of the Intimidator about life with Dale Sr., Nascar drivers who cheat, racing's worst track and how fame changes everything

How tough is Dale Earnhardt Jr.? How tightly wound is Nascar's favorite son, the speed-burning scion of the great Intimidator himself? Well, hell, he'll be happy to tell you—once he wakes up.

Earnhardt Jr., often called Little E or just Junior, wears his fame as casually as his T-shirt and jeans. He loves his sleep, too, and after a night of partying he'll snooze through lunchtime, or nod off on his couch at the drop of a Budweiser baseball cap. Days of Thunder? More like days of slumber.

But strap Earnhardt into a 780-horsepower, quarter-million-dollar race car and he morphs into a different guy—a feared competitor who will run over you at 200 miles per hour. With the hair-trigger reflexes and brass balls he inherited from his dad, the seven-time Winston Cup champ, Earnhardt Jr. won two Winston Cup races in 2000 and earned more than $2 million. This year he's among the sport's leaders in winnings and Winston Cup points. At 26 he is a crossover star, the first stock car hero to score with the MTV crowd. That means wealth, women and song for an ultraeligible bachelor who built a little party nook in his basement—a full-scale nightclub with a smoke machine, nuclear sound system and dance-floor space for 225 revelers.

Yes, it is definitely a blast to be Junior. But it is also a damn heavy load. It always was, and then it became infinitely more complicated on February 18, 2001, when his father died in a crash on the last turn during the last lap of the Daytona 500. Since that day, Little E has done a lot of growing up. He has defended Sterling Marlin, the driver who bumped the Intimidator's famed black number three car moments before the crash. Dale Jr. has also taken on a larger role at Dale Earnhardt Inc., his father's multimillion-dollar company. And of course he has raced harder than ever, starting only eight days after Dale Sr.'s death, when he drove in the Dura Lube 400 and crashed on the first lap.

His surprising views on that wreck—and on topics that include speed, honor, fear and contraception—make this an extraordinary sports interview. But, then, Dale Earnhardt Jr. has never lived an ordinary life.

He was born on October 10, 1974, four and a half years before his dad's Winston Cup debut. In those days the elder Earnhardt wasn't the Intimidator to anybody but his family. Young Dale, whose parents divorced when he was three, grew up idolizing his father, a stern, even chilly figure who responded to Junior's boyhood mischief by sending him to military school.

Dale Sr. wasn't a full-time dad. He was busy building his legend—winning Rookie of the Year and Winston Cup titles back-to-back, winning two Driver of the Year awards, winning 34 times at Daytona International Speedway, winning more than $41 million for driving like a madman. How tough was the man in black? Once, when a crash sent another car flying and the 3000-pound vehicle landed on the Intimidator's car, he carried it piggyback to the finish line and won by a split second. As the Earnhardt legend grew, so did the Earnhardt fortune. Dale Sr. became a motor-sports mogul whose private fleet included a helicopter, a Learjet and another plane; his reported earnings in 1999 were $26.5 million.

Dale Jr. took up stock car racing when he was 17, hoping to win a couple hundred bucks. He raced at dusty ovals all over the Carolinas, winning only three times in more than 100 tries. Then came 1996, when the Intimidator gave his 21-year-old son a car to drive in Nascar's Busch Series, the sport's top minor-league circuit. That's where Junior became a star. Zooming to Busch Series crowns in 1998 and 1999 (fans called him the Dominator), he earned a ride in the big show, the Winston Cup series, where the kid in the Bud-red number eight car won two races in his rookie year. Despite cooling off and finishing second in Rookie of the Year voting to Matt Kenseth, Junior was Nascar's biggest new star since Jeff Gordon.

Then came the 2001 Daytona 500, the race that took his father's life and changed Junior's life forever. Young Dale has shown skill and courage at death-defying speeds ever since that cataclysmic day at Daytona.

We sent sportswriter Kevin Cook to North Carolina to see how the young man who has been called "the future of Nascar" is dealing with his past, present and future. Cook reports:

"From the Charlotte airport you take the Billy Graham Park and I-77 to Mooresville, North Carolina, where Main Street dozes in the shadow of a grain silo. Just down the road is the headquarters of Dale Earnhardt Inc., a sleek 108,000-square-foot complex that racing folks call the Garage Mahal. Across the road is a smaller palace: a little blue house with a swimming pool and a brown brick garage out back. This is Junior's house, a celebrity hangout nicknamed Junior's Place—the only North Carolina 'nightclub' worthy of an MTV special.

"Small and wiry, with a wispy red mustache and goatee, Dale Jr. yawned a lot at first. I think the guy needs more sleep. But when something sparks his interest or pisses him off, his eyes narrow and you feel the sharp focus he brings to his dangerous job. I suspect he loves to race but is starting to hate the complexities that fame—not just success, but being his father's son—adds to his life. He still seems a little overwhelmed at the thought of being the only living Dale Earnhardt."

PLAYBOY: Let's start fast. How does it feel when you hit a wall at 190 miles per hour?

EARNHARDT: It hurts! I blew a tire at California this year and thought, I am going to hit the wall. In that spot you're not in charge of the car. You're just sliding. You turn the wheel all the way left and nothing happens. You can't help tensing up, but at the moment you smack the wall, you have to go limp, relax all your muscles. If you put your arm out straight, you'll get a compound fracture in your forearm.

PLAYBOY: Is that instinct, or did you learn how to crash?

EARNHARDT: I'm ashamed to say that I've wrecked 10 or 15 times, enough to really know how.

PLAYBOY: How about after the crash?

EARNHARDT: You've done 15 to 50 feet of sliding, then smack! It stuns you for a second. You come off the wall and you're still moving, but you can't steer or slow down. Will you hit something else? Are you in oncoming traffic, with cars going 200 miles an hour? Once you get the car stopped, you're like this [*touching his arms and legs*]. Any sharp pains? If not, pull your window net down—that's the signal you're OK.

PLAYBOY: After your tire blew in this year's NAPA Auto Parts 500, was your radio still working?

EARNHARDT: I could hear my crew asking about the backup car. I ain't even stopped! Next thing I heard was, "Get the backup car out there, damn it!"

PLAYBOY: We have to talk about your father's crash. Late in this year's Daytona 500, your team was running one-two-three. It was Michael Waltrip, you and then your father in third. But Sterling Marlin was gaining. It was your dad's job to get in Marlin's way. Here's how one newspaper put it: "It appeared that Earnhardt was willing to wreck his own car to keep Marlin behind him." Is that true?

EARNHARDT: He didn't decide to wreck. Michael was leading the race. I was in second, so I was in the same situation as my father. You want to win, but it's your teammate up there. If you hold your position and he wins, the team wins.

PLAYBOY: In that spot, you take one for the team.

EARNHARDT: Right. That's what he was doing.

PLAYBOY: What were you thinking during that last lap?

EARNHARDT: That I want to win the Daytona 500. But if I try to pass Michael and then for some reason I don't win, I'd never hear the end of it from my father. "You fucked up," he'd say. "You should have stayed in line!"

PLAYBOY: After the race, with Marlin getting death threats from some Earnhardt fans, you said that blaming Marlin for your father's death "is ridiculous and I will not tolerate that."

EARNHARDT: Sterling did nothing wrong.

PLAYBOY: But he bumped the number three car.

EARNHARDT: That's not wrong. For a second, there was room for him to go under my father. My father moved down to close that hole, and Sterling wasn't of a mind to get out of the way, that's all. I spoke to him after. I said I will always be his friend. One day he may feel some guilt, I don't know. If he ever wants to talk to me, I'll talk.

PLAYBOY: Could you see the crash?

EARNHARDT: [*Nodding*] You're doing quick glances at the mirror—I saw smoke and cars at the wrong angles, cars crashing. Then the race ends and I'm excited. "Man, I finished second in the Daytona 500!" Even though he crashed, my father was going to be happy about that. I went looking for him, but he wasn't at the care center. Some cops took me to the hospital. I was about five minutes behind him. Never saw him. I'm sure I could have if I'd wanted to, but I didn't, not after I knew.

PLAYBOY: A week later you raced again, and crashed.

EARNHARDT: A guy just plowed into me. Zipped me right into the wall. Everyone talked about how it looked just like my dad's wreck. That was embarrassing.

PLAYBOY: What did you do wrong?

EARNHARDT: Nothing. I got put into the wall.

PLAYBOY: Then why be embarrassed? Just because the crashes looked alike?

EARNHARDT: Yes. I was ashamed that I mocked my father.

PLAYBOY: At a press conference in May, you said you knew what really happened when your father crashed. "I know what the facts are," you said, but "I'm not going to tell." What is it that you know?

EARNHARDT: I know my father's seat belt broke.

PLAYBOY: That's what Nascar has been saying, but there was an emergency medical technician who claimed the belt was intact. How do you know he was wrong?

EARNHARDT: By my father's injuries. He had impact with the steering wheel. That means the belt had broken, or he couldn't have been that far forward. That's a long way—you could hit your chin on the wheel, maybe, but not your chest. He had broken ribs from the wheel, and that has to mean a broken belt.

PLAYBOY: Some people think you have some information that Nascar hasn't released.

EARNHARDT: No, it's from looking at the car and knowing what his injuries were—those things tell me what happened.

PLAYBOY: How has his death changed you?

EARNHARDT: It brings death closer. In this job your instinct is to block it out. Now it's always there. But you know what? I'm more determined to succeed. Before, I wanted to be a champion. Now I'm going to be a champion, I have to be a champion.

PLAYBOY: How much of your skill is inherited? Do you have better genes than other drivers?

EARNHARDT: Some of it's reaction time and peripheral vision. People say that my dad had eyes in the back of his head, and I'm good that way, too. My pulse rate's slower than average, like his was. But there's confidence, too. Just being around him, seeing him win all those races, gives me an edge over a guy whose father wasn't a driver. I'll go up against that guy, thinking I'm going to beat him because it's in my blood. Even if I didn't inherit my father's ability, that helps.

PLAYBOY: Your dad won the IROC, the International Race of Champions, last year. There was a funny moment before the race: His car was directly behind yours in the grid, and he bumped you a couple of times.

EARNHARDT: He was fucking with me. Like saying, "Hi, kid." I would have bumped him, but I qualified higher.

PLAYBOY: You crashed in that race. He went on to win, bumping Mark Martin and slipping past Martin on the last lap. Do you relish moments like that? Was that a classic?

EARNHARDT: Well, no. What he did that day—passing in the last corner—it's very brilliant, awesome and exciting. But there's nothing special about the move itself. It's a move that happened 150 times in the race. But he waited, and saved it for that last moment, and got a win out of it.

PLAYBOY: Your dad was the sport's most famous tough guy. Was he tough at home, too?

EARNHARDT: When I was about seven, he went out one day to cut down a tree. Climbed up with a chain saw to cut the limbs off. He's up there in a denim shirt, with gloves and boots and his sunglasses, sawing away. After about 15 minutes he comes down and his glove is torn. There's jagged skin on the back of his hand, and I can see down to the bone. He says, "Damn it." I'm like, "Daddy, you're cut bad. You need stitches." But he says it's OK. "Cut it when I first got up the tree, but I was already up there, so I stayed."

PLAYBOY: You were three years old when your parents divorced. At first you lived with your mother, Brenda, who was his second wife.

EARNHARDT: Until I was six. Then one morning I wake up and the kitchen's on fire. Something in the wiring. That house burned down, and I went to live with my dad.

PLAYBOY: Had he wanted custody before that?

EARNHARDT: No.

PLAYBOY: You lived with your father and Teresa, his third wife. They hired nannies to look after you.

EARNHARDT: That was weird, because a nanny is a stranger. They weren't bad, but they were strict. Nannies want to make a good impression on their employers, so they're tough on the kids.

PLAYBOY: Did you watch your father's races on TV?

EARNHARDT: I loved that. I would race my Matchbox cars on the floor while he was racing on TV. I didn't really miss him on those days. I did on the weekdays, though. I felt like when the race was over, he'd come home. But he was always working on his cars.

PLAYBOY: Where was your mother?

EARNHARDT: She married a fireman and moved to Virginia. We only saw her twice a year, so it was hard to keep a connection. Now she's down here again—my sister Kelley just had a baby, so our mama's back here to help.

PLAYBOY: It's hard to picture the Intimidator sitting you down for a talk about the birds and the bees.

EARNHARDT: We were on the way to a racetrack somewhere. I was 12, and I'd learned about sex in school, but he had some things to tell me. "Use a rubber," he said. He was adamant about that: "Wear a rubber and don't get some girl pregnant. Don't get in that situation when you're just starting out in life." See, that's the trap he fell into. My brother Kerry, too.

PLAYBOY: They both got girlfriends pregnant and married young?

EARNHARDT: Yes. "So if you think you won't get a girl pregnant because you pull out in time," my father says, "well, one time you'll make a mistake." I was a little embarrassed, really. I didn't want to hear that from my daddy.

PLAYBOY: A lot of boys at that age think, I wish I had that problem.

EARNHARDT: That's exactly how I felt. You're 12, you and your buddies are stealing *Playboys*, wondering if you'll ever get lucky enough to be with a girl.

PLAYBOY: How long did it take you?

EARNHARDT: About six years. The girl I lost my virginity to, I knew her all through high school. She was the second-best-looking girl in my class, and she flirted with me. We did that high school date deal, where you hold hands in the hall and go out for a couple of weeks, and then you break up over the telephone. She basically ruined me by dumping me, because I just wanted her more. Finally, after we're out of high school, I asked her out again. By then I was 18.

PLAYBOY: Still a virgin at 18?

EARNHARDT: Yes. And she tore me up in my trailer.

PLAYBOY: Did you follow your father's advice?

EARNHARDT: About the rubber? Yes, I did. We went at it again and again. It lasted 30 or 40 minutes. I thought I did pretty good. I'm still an endurance type, and if I fail the endurance test, I'm quick to get going again.

PLAYBOY: They call that a man's refractory period.

EARNHARDT: Mine's about three or four minutes. Got to use it while you can.

PLAYBOY: Here's the Wilt Chamberlain question: How many partners, career total?

EARNHARDT: Not so many. Fifteen to 20.

PLAYBOY: Would they call you a gentle lover or a rambunctious one?

EARNHARDT: In the middle, but more toward rambunctious. I'm careful who I'm with. A couple years ago, when I started seeing what a little success can do, I thought, Man, this could get to where girls are knocking on my door—and I'm gonna let 'em all in! But it doesn't work that way. I am real fucking scared of contracting a disease, for one thing. Or just making a mistake, like my dad talked about. I don't want a kid running around right now, because he wouldn't turn out right. He would be spoiled and ruined. He'd be a troublemaker.

PLAYBOY: Are you in a relationship now?

EARNHARDT: Just got out of one. It's a hard thing—with the attention I've been getting, it's harder to know if somebody loves you for you. But the relationship thing is largely my fault. When I start dating someone it's awesome, but after a while I start resisting it. Two things I really enjoy are being with the guys and being by myself, but now there's less of both. When I race on weekends, the girl can't understand why I don't want her there. I could afford to take her, right? So if I don't, she resents me and I feel like a bastard.

PLAYBOY: Other than your birds-and-bees talk, did your dad give you advice about girls?

EARNHARDT: Not too much. This one girl was hot as hell, and I brought her around to meet him. Next day he says, "That girl smokes pot." I knew it was true, but I said, "No, she don't." He says, "I know she does, and I know where she gets it."

PLAYBOY: She wasn't the only one.

EARNHARDT: I tried this and that, just like everybody else in the fucking world. Smoking weed at a party. Trying mushrooms. It was fun.

PLAYBOY: What's Nascar's drug policy?

EARNHARDT: Nascar doesn't have a drug policy. If they find out that you're doing something—and they will find out—they have a fatherly way of handling it. Me, I figured out what was cool to do, and what wasn't cool, before I started driving in the big time.

PLAYBOY: What did you get the Intimidator for Father's Day?

EARNHARDT: A card, something like that. There wasn't that much going on between us.

PLAYBOY: He wasn't the world's warmest dad.

EARNHARDT: But he was busting his ass and putting food on the table. I missed him bad sometimes, but when he was around it was great. We'd always have a big time at Christmas. We knew he loved us. And, looking back, I think that if he had not been so adamant about his career, the Earnhardts wouldn't be as fortunate as we are now.

PLAYBOY: He packed you off to military school, though.

EARNHARDT: Well, I got kicked out of Christian school. Not for anything serious—a couple of fights, talking in class, sleeping in class—but it got me dismissed. So he and Teresa sent me to Oak Ridge Military Academy, here in North Carolina. Had to get up every morning at six when they blew the bugle. Shoes had to be gleaming, the buckles and buttons on your uniform, too. After school it was study from seven to nine, then run to brush your teeth and lights out.

PLAYBOY: Did you go home on weekends?

EARNHARDT: If you got too many demerits, you couldn't. And my dad was racing, so sometimes I wouldn't go home because he wasn't there. But I'm not complaining. Once it was over, I knew more than the guy up the street who hadn't been to military school. I was more like an adult.

PLAYBOY: From there you went to Mooresville Senior High. You were Little E, son of the town's biggest hero—

EARNHARDT: But for some reason that worked against me. It wasn't cool to be Dale Earnhardt's son. I wasn't one of the preps or the fucking jocks. I was too small for football, so I played soccer my freshman year. Our soccer team went to the nationals every year, so the soccer guys were popular. But even when I was on the team, I wasn't one of them, couldn't be. Looking at them walking around in their polo shirts with their collars buttoned up—I thought they were a bunch of idiots.

PLAYBOY: What did you do after school?

EARNHARDT: Shoveled shit. That was my job—get home from school, go straight to the horse barn and shovel it out. It's hard work, and you don't even want to think about the smell.

PLAYBOY: The Earnhardts still own horses, don't they?

EARNHARDT: We've got eight horses. One is a Clydesdale that Budweiser sent me, a badass big horse.

PLAYBOY: After high school you worked at your dad's auto dealership.

EARNHARDT: I did a lot of oil changes. Made $16,000 a year. That was a job I liked—working with friends in the shop. We'd go to the same place for lunch every day and party at night. This went on a few years. I'd have parties in the double-wide trailer I lived in, and we'd get so damn rowdy we'd break the doors off. You would tackle a guy and push him through a door for the hell of it. I'd have to go buy new hinges and put my doors back on. It was a normal life, as opposed to this. Now my life changes all the time. People come and go, and you worry about trust and loyalty.

PLAYBOY: Success doesn't simplify things, it complicates them.

EARNHARDT: That it does.

PLAYBOY: Is it worth it?

EARNHARDT: The racing is great. Drivers like to downplay the sheer speed of it. They always say, "Aw, it's just like driving around town." But it's really cool! It's like water-skiing—the first time you water-ski you're yelling, "Slow down!" Then you get to liking it and you're hauling ass, cutting cones and yelling, "Faster!" I remember my first time driving at Talladega, the fastest big-ass track we run on. I'm 18 years old, going down the back straightaway. I ain't quite up to full speed, but I'm going fast enough to doubt I can make it around the corner without hitting the wall.

PLAYBOY: How fast?

EARNHARDT: Getting toward 195. So I'm looking at the corner way down there ahead of me, thinking, No way can I turn that corner. But they say you go around Talladega wide open. You just hold her down and go. So I did, and turned that corner, and damn—it was great. The car sticks to the ground better than you'd think. It feels like a huge hand is pushing down on you. The faster you go, the more air you have pushing down, and the better the car sticks.

PLAYBOY: You'll use another car's draft to pull you along, too.

EARNHARDT: The air changes lots of things. My car might be turning great when I'm by myself, taking the corners fast, but if I get up behind somebody, I won't have that direct air on the nose of my car. I'm sharing part of his air, and now my front wheels want to slide. So I'll try to poke a headlight out, to get a little air on the nose. Then I can turn better.

PLAYBOY: When you're stalking another car, looking to pass, what are you looking at?

EARNHARDT: You're searching for flaws—mistakes that are repetitive. Maybe he's overdriving a corner, every corner, and you're handling better than him when you exit the corner.

PLAYBOY: Are you watching his tires? His bumper?

EARNHARDT: A lot of drivers do that, but I look at the left front tire. If he goes into a corner and he's turning it excessively, I know his car is tight. If he's turning that wheel more than I'm turning mine, he's tight. So if I push him—if I force the issue—I can make him move up the bank in a corner, out of my way.

PLAYBOY: Tight means what?

EARNHARDT: It means his front won't turn the way he wants. He's fighting it in the corners, and I can take advantage of that.

PLAYBOY: When do you make your move?

EARNHARDT: Soon. Maybe the next turn. Most tracks we run on, the corners are the same at both ends, so if he's doing that at one end, he'll do it at the other. That gives me four chances. Sooner or later, I'm gonna get by him.

PLAYBOY: You can't do it all by yourself. Nascar drivers often succeed by cooperating—at least for a few laps. How do you tell another driver, "Let's work together and pass these guys"?

EARNHARDT: You might put out a straight hand: "Let's go this way." It doesn't matter who the guy is. It's whoever the hell is in front of you or behind you.

PLAYBOY: How do you dissolve that relationship? There comes a point where you and he are running first and second, and now you're enemies.

EARNHARDT: That's right.

PLAYBOY: How do you signal, "OK, we're not working together anymore"—

EARNHARDT: You don't.

PLAYBOY: —and bump and pass the guy you've been working with?

EARNHARDT: When you're ready.

PLAYBOY: And he's not.

EARNHARDT: [Grinning] That is what it's all about.

PLAYBOY: Do you ever get bored, bombing around racetracks?

EARNHARDT: Actually, that can happen at Talladega. I've run two or three 500-mile Winston Cup races there, and three or four Busch races, and it's just so big you can entirely drop your guard—the whole back straightaway you're just holding the wheel straight for 15 or 20 seconds. Forever. So to go out there and race around by myself is boring as hell.

PLAYBOY: You'd rather be in traffic.

EARNHARDT: It's not boring. It's when there's almost a wreck, or when somebody gets up close in back of you and you almost lose control—that's when you remember how fast you're going.

PLAYBOY: A big track like Talladega poses other problems, too.

EARNHARDT: It sure does. After that long straight, if you don't go into the corner exactly right—if you miss by the slightest bit—you know you're screwed. You just messed up a lap that was an entire minute long, and now you've got to run another whole lap trying to make that time up.

PLAYBOY: How much of winning is driving talent, and how much is having a good car?

EARNHARDT: Depends on the track. At a small racetrack like Richmond, where handling is everything, it's almost all car. The guy who wins is no better than the guy in fifth place. He'll be pulling away and you say, "Damn, his car turns better than mine." You never say, "He's a better driver than me." Five or six years ago it was more about the driver. Nowadays the cars are so close technology-wise, so competitive, that you can't take an illhandling car and force it into contention. Right now I'd say it's 75 percent car, 25 percent driver.

PLAYBOY: Do Nascar drivers and their crews cheat?

EARNHARDT: The cheating in Nascar is so good that a guy got caught during qualifying at Daytona, and I'm not sure what he did.

PLAYBOY: You're talking about Jerry Nadeau.

EARNHARDT: Guys will cut a little piece of a car in half, hollow it out and weld it back together. Other stuff is so technical it'd take a scientist to explain it.

PLAYBOY: The drivers and crews who get caught aren't punished much. They are fined, but that's it.

EARNHARDT: Yeah, it's bullshit. If a guy's caught cheating after he wins a race, I'd take the win away.

PLAYBOY: Have you ever been fined for cheating?

EARNHARDT: No, just fighting. One day Tony Stewart and I were banging around on the track—no more than what you see every week. So the message comes down: "Come to the Nascar trailer." It's like the principal's office. So me and Tony Eury, my crew chief, go up there, and here comes Stewart and his crew chief. Stewart and I were laughing, but his crew chief starts running his mouth. "You're a daddy's boy," he says. "You got everything handed to you." I just flew off the damn handle and started swinging. And Nascar fined me $5000. I think they called it "conduct unbecoming a driver."

PLAYBOY: You tangled with Jeff Burton at the 1999 NAPA 300.

EARNHARDT: That's the time I was passing the pit exit at 195 miles an hour, and guys were pulling off the racetrack going 100 less than me. So here I come, and the force of my car moving past another car pushes me into a third car and we all crash. It was a hell of a wreck, just awesome.

PLAYBOY: Awesome?

EARNHARDT: Like bowling. The ball goes down there and, *boom*, the pins go flying. It's a huge strike! But those guys were pissed, coming into my garage, saying, "What the hell were you thinking?" I said, "Dude, stay the hell away from me."

PLAYBOY: How close were you to fighting?

EARNHARDT: Oh, not very. I don't know if drivers really get that angry. I mean, when Rusty Wallace and Jeff Gordon got hot at each other recently, were they really going to punch each other? Not even close. I think national TV and the corporate involvement in Nascar have shined the thing up to where drivers are businesslike. They'll shake their fist and go, "What the fuck were you doing? Shit!" Then it's "OK, I gotta go home now—see ya!"

PLAYBOY: Does that hurt the sport?

EARNHARDT: No, because when you're strapped in that car, it's a heated fight. It's not "My sponsor's better than your sponsor," or "Me and my fans against you and your fans." It's a one-on-one battle—a series of one-on-one battles with the guys you need to pass, through the entire race. But when the fight's over, a guy won't swing his fist at that other driver like he swung at him with his race car. He gets out of the car and he sees the crowd, the cameras. He's back to civilization again.

PLAYBOY: Can you hear the crowd?

EARNHARDT: Sometimes, and it charges me up. I want them to like me. Standing there for driver introductions before a race, I'll watch the other drivers walk across the stage, and listen to the fans' reactions. There will be 10,000 fans, and some guys only get a couple of claps. Here's a guy competing at this level, risking everything, and nobody claps. And you know what? He doesn't care! He's just like, "Which way to my car?" Jeff Gordon will walk across and there's a mix of cheers and boos. I'm thinking, Man, that would make me feel bad. I never want to get booed.

PLAYBOY: This year, many Nascar races have started with tributes to your father. Does that mess with your mind?

EARNHARDT: It's odd as hell. I'm glad people think that much of him, but right at that moment I'm ready to race. The crowd's hollering. I'm pumped. "And now, a moment of silence." And I might have a little memory, like time we went deer hunting. Next thing it's "Gentlemen, start your engines," and I'm like, "Oh, shit."

PLAYBOY: Does a race wear you out more mentally or physically?

EARNHARDT: It wears out my neck. There's a headrest in the car, but when you're driving hard you are not laying your head back. You're right up on the wheel, leaning into the corner. It's like leaning into a strong wind all day. After a race my neck hurts, mostly on the left side.

PLAYBOY: What's your pain reliever?

EARNHARDT: Beer. If I'm sore after a race, I'll drink four or five beers and get in a good mood.

PLAYBOY: You earned $515,000 for winning last year's Winston All-Star race. How much of that do you get to keep?

EARNHARDT: It's based on incentives. The higher I finish, the more I keep. If I win a race, I get 45 percent. For anything outside the top 10, it goes down to 30 percent.

PLAYBOY: You've crashed quite a bit on racetracks. Any adventures as a civilian driver?

EARNHARDT: I had four speeding tickets by the time I was 18, but none since. Got those four tickets from four different officers, and each one told me he gave my daddy his first speeding ticket. It's their claim to fame, but they can't all be right. I also had a 1991 S-10 extended-cab pickup that I wrecked a bunch. Just kept flipping it over. I'd come to a 90-degree corner out in the country. There'd be signs with arrows pointing to the turn, and I'd take out three of those signs. Once I hit some ice and rolled that truck into a ditch.

PLAYBOY: Did you feel safe, crashing at only 50 or 60 miles an hour?

EARNHARDT: You're safer in a race car, which will mash like an accordion from the nose all the way to the fire wall. A street vehicle doesn't have so many crush zones. The front will mash back only so far, then it stops and forces you to take the rest of the blow.

PLAYBOY: What did your dad say when you flipped your truck?

EARNHARDT: I thought he'd be mad, but he laughed.

PLAYBOY: He has only been gone for a few months. Do you find yourself talking to him, wondering what he'd say?

EARNHARDT: Not out loud, but I'll think those things. For instance, I wanted a big old air compressor for the shop in my backyard. He said no, get a small one. Now, with him gone, I'll make that decision. That's a petty thing, but I still wonder if I could have talked him into it. Maybe I'll go through my whole life wondering stuff like that. It might get harder, too. Right now I can recall his demeanor, I can see him. Ten years from now it will be harder to know what he'd want us to do.

PLAYBOY: What about the Earnhardt empire? Your stepmother, Teresa, has taken over much of the decision making. You told one reporter that you trust her even more than you trusted your father.

EARNHARDT: Financially, yes. He always joked that before he met Teresa, he owed the bank money. Afterward, the bank owed him.

PLAYBOY: A lot of rich families fight over what they inherit.

EARNHARDT: The way I see it, Teresa is almost as responsible for what we have as Dad was. I sure didn't build it. They created it, and if she wants it, it's hers.

PLAYBOY: Let's talk about how you got started in racing. You raced go-carts first.

EARNHARDT: I was only 12, and after about 10 races my dad said, "It's not safe. You're not doing that anymore." So I waited four years and then sold my go-cart for $500. Took the money to a junkyard over in Kannapolis.

PLAYBOY: Kannapolis, birthplace of both Dale Earnhardts.

EARNHARDT: Bought a 1978 Monte Carlo for $200. I spent the rest on parts and started building a race car.

PLAYBOY: Why a Monte Carlo?

EARNHARDT: Price. I'm looking at 10 acres of junk cars, and that's the cheapest one there. Remember, I'm 16 and don't know what the fuck I'm doing. I say, "Hey, what can I get for $200? That one? All right, I'll make it work."

PLAYBOY: Where did you work on it?

EARNHARDT: Here in Mooresville, in my dad's garage. My half brother Kerry and me found a roll cage, fixed it up and put it on there.

PLAYBOY: You're a mechanic and a welder, too?

EARNHARDT: That was the hard part. We cut a hole in the floor of the car and mounted the cage to the chassis. The cage had to be wide enough to sit in and drive, but not so wide that we couldn't get the door back on. Then the seat goes in, and you have to mount it so it won't fly out if you run into something. Painted it, put a big number eight on it. That was hard work, but I learned to work on a car. My sister Kelley raced cars, too. I wound up building two cars for her, from the ground up, and one for my brother.

PLAYBOY: How fast was that Monte Carlo?

EARNHARDT: Somewhere around 140 on the flat, about 90 for a lap around the little tracks we ran on.

PLAYBOY: In 1994 you were the new kid on Nascar's Late Model Stock Car circuit, racing around little ovals from Concord, North Carolina, to

Myrtle Beach and Florence, South Carolina, to Nashville, and you won only three races in 119 tries. What happened?

EARNHARDT: At each of those tracks there was one guy who dominated. He was the track champion, and he won every race. His car had the biggest motor. His carburetor was bigger. Maybe his tires were greased up, and maybe the track's head inspector worked for the people who sponsored the guy. I mean, the cheating was blatant.

PLAYBOY: You must have been furious.

EARNHARDT: No, I loved the racing. I was having a blast.

PLAYBOY: Once you got the right ride, you dominated the Busch Series, then last year you won in Texas as a Winston Cup rookie. How did you react to that first victory?

EARNHARDT: It took a second to sink in, then I realized it. I sat there in the car and said, "Holy shit!"

PLAYBOY: You have mixed feelings about fame, don't you?

EARNHARDT: It's mostly cool. The Charlotte Hornets asked me to come to a playoff game, and they had a number eight jersey for me with my name on it. I talked in an interview about being a big Elvis Presley fan, and I started getting Elvis stuff in the mail. A police officer in New Hampshire sent me an Elvis autograph, just to be nice. My sponsor sends me cases and cases of free Budweiser—more than I can drink. I'm doing the *Playboy* interview—this is cool shit a lot of drivers don't get, and I recognize that. A lot of circumstances had to fall into place for all this to happen. I mean, three years ago nobody knew or cared who I was. Now people drive past my house just to look at it. Some of them knock on the door, too.

PLAYBOY: Half of North Carolina knows where you live. Your house isn't exactly bristling with security.

EARNHARDT: I'm putting up a gate. And there's security across the road, at the company headquarters. They have a camera on my house, and they'll talk back and forth by radio: "There's a white female coming up the driveway." Another time I was watching TV and a couple of girls walked in my door and asked me out on a date, just like that.

PLAYBOY: Your groupies seem to travel in pairs.

EARNHARDT: They ain't supermodels, though. It's never the supermodel types who do that.

PLAYBOY: Do your friends get jealous?

EARNHARDT: Not about that. It's more that they'll think I'm becoming an asshole. They'll say, "Let's go out with this guy." I'll say I don't know the guy, so I'm not riding with him. Because I have to be afraid. If something gets messed up, it's not his name they'll put in the paper, it's mine. So some guys may say, "He thinks he's too good for us," but it isn't that.

PLAYBOY: Bet you never thought you'd be image conscious.

EARNHARDT: Me and my friends used to party all the time, and my dad would get mad and say, "Quit that!" As I get older, I start to think about how I'm perceived. People come out of the woodwork, and they may not have the best intentions. I'm just trying to keep watch.

PLAYBOY: You mentioned playing computer games. You're a pretty big gamer, aren't you?

EARNHARDT: I am. I play for fun, but one time it helped me on the track. I had never raced at Watkins Glen, but then I drove it in a computer game and it was like having a map to a maze. The game was accurate down to the shift points on the track—the places where you shift gears—within about 25 feet. So when I pulled out on the racetrack, it was like déjà vu. "Ooh, this is weird. I can do this!" I came out of turn one in second gear and shifted into third just before the next bend, exactly like the game. A fast lap on that track is a minute and 13 seconds. Without the game it would have taken me hours of practice laps to run under 1:20, but my first lap was under 1:20. Within two hours I got down to 1:16. That game cut my learning curve in half.

PLAYBOY: Have other drivers tried that?

EARNHARDT: It's not common practice. Don't tell them.

PLAYBOY: What other video games do you play? Tomb Raider?

EARNHARDT: No, not that crap! Fictional games don't appeal to me. I like what's real. If it's a war game, it needs to be a battle that really happened.

PLAYBOY: Do you shop on the Web?

EARNHARDT: I saw an ad at AutoTrader.com and bought a 1969 Corvette. I sent a buddy to Miami to look at it, and this 'Vette was a badass ride. It had everything I wanted except side exhaust, and we put that on.

PLAYBOY: Did you get a discount when the seller found out who wanted his car?

EARNHARDT: No, he pushed the price up. I paid about $40,000.

PLAYBOY: What else is out there in your driveway?

EARNHARDT: I've got that Corvette, a new Camaro, two more 'Vettes on the way, and a 1971 Corvette that's being worked on. But all I really drive is my big old red pickup with the rattles and dings. Don't have to worry about that one. If something happens, I don't even fix it.

PLAYBOY: Suppose somebody wants to soup up his car. What's one thing he can do under the hood to make the car go faster?

EARNHARDT: Almost every car built today has a computer, and every one of those computers has a chip in it that keeps the horsepower down. Change it and you'll run faster.

PLAYBOY: Where do I get a new chip?

EARNHARDT: At the dealership. People with Corvettes, Camaros even pickup trucks are always talking about their hop-up kits: "Hey, I just got a chip for my 'Vette." Pop that chip in, it's instant horsepower.

PLAYBOY: Do you tinker with computers at home?

EARNHARDT: I can install modems, memory and graphic cards—anything but the motherboard. When we put a big sound system in the basement, I bought a computer and rigged it so we can mix and play songs through the computer.

PLAYBOY: Guys all over the country figure you're partying every night in Junior's Place, probably with two or three Nascar groupies at a time.

EARNHARDT: That'd be cool, but I haven't been that fortunate. About all I can say along those lines is that I once had a time in my race car trailer. This was when I was running late-model cars, and we had a gooseneck trailer to haul my car around the Carolinas. Well, this girl was about to move away, and we wouldn't have many more chances, so one night when I was out there working on my car, she stopped by. I had a buddy with me. We gave him a case of beer and told him to keep watch. But not on us.

PLAYBOY: Let's do some quick question and answer. Which drivers do you hate to see in your rearview on the last lap?

EARNHARDT: Jeff Gordon, Rusty Wallace, Bobby Labonte.

PLAYBOY: How about the next generation? Ten years from now, who'll be winning the Nascar races that you don't win?

EARNHARDT: Matt Kenseth is going to be good. He has serious talent. Elliot Sadler, too. And the guy who has been driving my father's car this year, Kevin Harvick, is very good. He's brash; I like that.

PLAYBOY: What's Nascar's worst track?

EARNHARDT: Darlington. It's old. It's eggshaped. It's full of seashells. They use crushed rock and seashells in the asphalt mix. It's so coarse you get an awesome grip for four or five laps, but then your tires wear off and you're just sliding around, trying not to hit something. Go out on that track and rub your hand on it—it'll actually cut you.

PLAYBOY: Which is more fun to drive, a Busch Series car or a Winston Cup car?

EARNHARDT: The Busch car is lighter, with a little shorter wheelbase, so it handles better. It's easier to drive when it handles good, and you can still get it in and out of the turns on the days when you're wrestling it. When a Winston Cup car isn't handling, you'll slam on the brakes in a corner and it doesn't want to turn. It just wants to roll over.

PLAYBOY: Is there any vehicle that you wouldn't drive?

EARNHARDT: A monster truck. They intimidate me. I know somebody who drove one of those things and wound up with a broken back.

PLAYBOY: Last year *Sports Illustrated* asked Nascar insiders to name the dirtiest driver. Your father won in a landslide. "He'd wreck his own mom," one crew member said. But would he have wrecked his son?

EARNHARDT: No, he wouldn't. He might move me out of the way, but I'd keep running and finish second.

PLAYBOY: People call you Dale, Dale Jr., Junior and Little E. What do you prefer?

EARNHARDT: Call me Junior.

PLAYBOY: You've been doing some writing for Nascar.com. Is this your contemplative side coming out?

EARNHARDT: Come on. I sit at home and pull something out of my ass once a month, and if it sucks no one'll tell me it sucks.

PLAYBOY: You wrote a column about your dad. He didn't think it sucked.

EARNHARDT: Well, I loved him, didn't I? Since he died, people have tried to make it sound more theatrical, but we were pretty much like any other father and son. He was hard to talk to, but that was just him. I wrote that thing and thought he should hear it first. He was sitting upstairs in his office. "I've been writing this online column for Nascar," I said, and I read it to him. I'm halfway through, and he gets out of his chair and walks over to me. I thought he was mad. But he says, "Man, I knew how you felt, but that really puts it in perspective." And since he died, that's something I think about a lot. He knew how I felt. He knew how I loved him.

PLAYBOY: Nascar doesn't retire numbers. Should that policy change? Should your father's number three be retired?

EARNHARDT: No. I might want it one day, or my son might.

PLAYBOY: Your son?

EARNHARDT: Yes, I want a son.

PLAYBOY: Dale Earnhardt III?

EARNHARDT: I think I may call him Ralph Lee Earnhardt.

PLAYBOY: Ralph Earnhardt was your grandfather. He was a stock car champ in the fifties, the first Nascar star in the family.

EARNHARDT: Now all I have to do is find his mom.

PLAYBOY: Suppose you do, and in four years you're 30 with a wife and a toddler. Will that change your view of your job? Will you worry more? Drivers always say they're aware of the risks, but nobody ever quits racing because the risks are too high.

EARNHARDT: Are you sure about that? I mean, I don't want to start talking out of my ass, but I think that's a big factor when drivers hang it up. They're probably thinking, I've got a wife, I've got kids, I've had a good career. I should quit before—

PLAYBOY: Do you wish your father had thought that way?

EARNHARDT: No, because he was still winning. Most drivers retire because they're at the bottom of the barrel. They're just hanging on, making fools of themselves.

PLAYBOY: Daytona 500—February 2020. You're 45 years old. Are you still out there racing?

EARNHARDT: Only if I can still win.

PLAYBOY: So you won't be one of those guys who hangs on too long?

EARNHARDT: No way. Not me. Of course, all of them probably used to say that, didn't they?

BRETT FAVRE

A candid conversation with Green Bay's MVP about his cajun image, his troubled family, his battle with pills and the art of well-timed flatulence

The National Football League's most valuable player is a freckle-faced prankster. "Just a regular-type guy who can throw a ball," he calls himself. No golden boy like the Cowboys' Troy Aikman or the Broncos' John Elway, Brett Favre (rhymes with carve) is a scrambling improv artist. Last year he was the league's most valuable player for the second straight year. He led the Green Bay Packers to victory in Super Bowl XXXI and celebrated with pranks like putting red-hot ointment in teammates' jockstraps.

Favre, 28, is a throwback to the days when pro football was 22 men beating up one another with 500 people in the stands. From tiny Kiln, Mississippi, this son of a high school football coach would fit right in with Bronko Nagurski and Ray Nitschke. He wrestles teammates and plays practical jokes like the rowdy country boy he is.

Excusing himself to go to the bathroom, he announces, "'Scuse me—gotta go drain the old pipe."

After the Packers' Super Bowl win, Favre went to the White House to meet President Clinton. He wrote a book (*Favre: For the Record* was published by Doubleday in October) and opened a restaurant. He signed a seven-year, $47 million contract with a $12 million signing bonus. But he spent most days relaxing, enjoying a round of golf and a beer with friends back home in Mississippi. Still, he calls it "the worst time ever."

Before the 1996 season Favre announced he was addicted to Vicodin, a potent painkiller used by many NFL players. The league's MVP spent 46 days at the Menninger Clinic in Topeka, Kansas, and the NFL put him on probation for drugs and alcohol. Next came news that Brett's sister, Brandi, a Mississippi beauty queen, had been involved in a drive-by shooting. She was sentenced to a year's probation. Soon their older brother, Scott, was in trouble, convicted of felony DUI. Scott Favre had driven into a railroad crossing; a train killed his passenger, a family friend. Scott was placed under house arrest. As the result of some bureaucratic confusion, Scott was picked up earlier this year for probation violation and served 67 days in jail. "Trouble never seems to be far away," Brett says.

Despite all this, he never appears to lose his humor. Outwardly, at least, Favre is still the cocky rifleman from Hancock North Central High School. In 1987 he chose the University of Southern Mississippi because it was the only Division 1A school to offer him a scholarship—as a defensive back. As the Golden Eagles' seventh-string quarterback, he played defense and even tried punting. No one considered him a top talent. But soon he was starting, pulling off upsets of Alabama and Auburn and, in 1989, top-ranked Florida State. Then came his own car crash. Driving home one night he flipped his vehicle and suffered a concussion, deep cuts and a "mildly" broken back. Five weeks later he pulled off a 27-24 stunner over Alabama.

Drafted by the Atlanta Falcons in 1991, Favre was a backup QB again, a clipboard jockey. "Hated it," he says. But he liked Atlanta. Suddenly rich beyond his dreams, a 22-year-old making $660,000 a year, he spent his nights partying and soon wore out his welcome with the Falcons' coaching staff. In 1992 Atlanta traded him to Green Bay for a draft choice.

Packer general manager Ron Wolf and coach Mike Holmgren loved Favre's raw talent. They wanted to bring him along slowly, to ease his transition to Green Bay's complex offense, which forces a quarterback to make dozens of snap judgments on every play. When starter Don Majkowski got hurt in 1992, Favre trotted in and led the Pack to a 24-23 win. He completed a club record 64.1 percent of his passes that year. At 23, he was the youngest QB ever selected for the Pro Bowl.

His unpredictability drove fans wild, but nothing worried Favre. "My game is getting flipped at the line of scrimmage—running the ball, getting up limping and throwing the next pass for a touchdown," he says.

In 1995 he passed for 38 touchdowns, the third-best total of all time. Last season he topped himself, passing for 39 touchdowns while leading the Packers to their Super Bowl win. It was Green Bay's first title since Super Bowl II in 1967.

We sent Contributing Editor Kevin Cook to huddle with Favre. Cook reports:

"We met at a golf course in New Jersey. I also spoke with him at a private airport, a hotel and at his humongous new home in Green Bay. Favre lives like a jet-setter, but he's still as down-home as it gets. One night I bought him an Amstel Light and he almost threw his arm out wrestling with the bottle cap. For all his fame and money, he remains a twist-top kind of guy.

"During football season he lives in a mansion by a creek in southwest Green Bay, where Brittany Favre, nine, answered the door and ran away. I also met Brett's wife, Deanna, who is as petite and angular as he is big and meaty.

"We sat in his den and talked for hours. His big-screen TV was blank, but there were reminders of NFL action all around: game balls, player-of-the-week citations, a big photo of a Favre touchdown pass to his buddy Mark Chmura, the Packers tight end.

"His keen eye for detail surprised me until I remembered his history. Favre was nobody until he learned to read NFL defenses, to read the future in the twitch of a cornerback's leg. It is a task he often performs with 280-pound Lions and Bears in his face. How tuned to detail is Favre? He says that he sometimes sees a play unfold in the instant between the snap and his receivers' first steps.

"Favre isn't as famous as he probably should be. Green Bay, population 96,000, is the league's smallest media market. His family's legal problems haven't helped his image, and his own rehab stint surely cost him endorsements. With so much to celebrate and regret, he is a sadder but wiser young man these days.

"Of course, he'll still spray you with shaving cream.

"Shortly before his triumphal visit to the White House, Brett told me he planned to give Bill Clinton 'a few choice words' about taxes. That's where we picked up the next time we met."

PLAYBOY: Did you straighten out the president on taxes?

FAVRE: Aw, what do I know? I let it go. And whoever's in the president's seat, Republican or Democrat, it works out the same. The more you make, the more they take. I know I wouldn't want Bill Clinton's job. Us athletes think we don't have any privacy—that man can't pee without 30 people watching.

PLAYBOY: What did you think of the White House?

FAVRE: Awesome security. It's like an airport; it takes 20 minutes to get the team through the metal detectors. We're getting checked over by security while a crowd of Packers fans is cheering us.

PLAYBOY: Cheeseheads in D.C.?

FAVRE: They're everywhere now. I'll go to New Jersey and see more Packers fans than Giants fans. I try to enjoy it because it could all be out the window next year. When a guy says, "You're my favorite quarterback," sometimes I want to say, "Yeah, right. Where were you two years ago?"

PLAYBOY: Did you hang out with President Clinton?

FAVRE: The team waited around for an hour. Then the handlers showed me and Reggie White, Mike Holmgren and our team president, Bob Harlan, what to do when Clinton came in. Where to stand, how to present him with a Packers jacket. That's when I saw him on the putting green. I looked through the trees and saw the president out there in his suit and tie, with his security guys all around, putting. I'd never seen a man play golf in a suit.

PLAYBOY: Had you met him before?

FAVRE: Last season he gave a talk in Green Bay, then came to Lambeau Field to see us. We had a little take-your-guard-down moment. He called me off to the side and said, "I've kept up with you. I know what you've been through." I'd had some troubles: my brother going to jail, me going to rehab. He said he wished me well. So it was nice going to the White House as Super Bowl winners. I said, "Good seeing you again." He said, "You had a great year, Brett. I was pulling for you."

PLAYBOY: Packers tight end Mark Chmura, a rabid conservative, boycotted the White House trip.

FAVRE: Mark was pissing into the wind. We all got on him for it. We all said, "Right, Chmura, like the White House gives a shit. The president is losing sleep because he won't get to meet Mark Chmura." I think Mark missed something good. We got to see where the president works and putts.

PLAYBOY: What other perks do you get for two MVP awards and a Super Bowl?

FAVRE: Getting treated better by guys I look up to. Now when I meet guys like Dan Marino and Jim Kelly, they treat me like one of them. If I'm in a restaurant with my wife, they'll come over and sit by me. We'll have a drink together. Three years ago those guys probably wouldn't have talked to me. Before 1995 no one really gave a shit. Now it's, "Brett, great year, good to see you."

PLAYBOY: Are they phonies?

FAVRE: That's just how the league works. To have a guy like Marino or John Elway or Steve Young or Joe Montana talk to you, you have to earn it. Now I've done it. It's nice to fit in.

PLAYBOY: Who do you think is the next great quarterback?

FAVRE: I hope I am for a while. I would say that the best young quarterback is still in college: Peyton Manning. In the pros, Drew Bledsoe can be a great one. Mark Brunell, too. Trent Dilfer is a good quarterback. And Ty Detmer—he's my sleeper.

PLAYBOY: Last year's Super Bowl clinched your status. Were you nervous before the game?

FAVRE: I was sick. I caught the flu on Thursday, three days before the game. That night was the worst. Had the hotel room up to 80 degrees, but I was freezing under the covers. Finally the fever broke, though I was still weak on Friday. But I said, "Shit, I am not going to let this flu kill me." Took my brother Scott and some friends to Bourbon Street. We ate oysters and shrimp, drank a few beers and had a big time. It was what I needed. Got up the next day ready to play football.

PLAYBOY: It would have made news if people had seen you with a beer. You were reportedly not allowed to drink as a condition of your rehab.

FAVRE: We had a private room. It cost a few thousand dollars, but it was cheap for the fun I had. Those are the times you realize how much the spotlight takes away from you. You'll pay $5000 for a room where you can be yourself for a while.

PLAYBOY: What was your pulse rate an hour before the Super Bowl?

FAVRE: My heart was going a mile a minute. Then [backup quarterback] Jim McMahon said, "I've got an idea." McMahon had already won his Super Bowl with the Bears and he knows how to stay loose. People say Jim is a dick, but we're similar; we're both who-gives-a-shit guys. I had his poster on my wall when I was little. Before the Super Bowl McMahon starts throwing footballs at the nameplates on the lockers, knocking guys' names off. Pretty soon we're all doing it. Me, McMahon and a bunch of other guys. Balls are flying all over the room. Holmgren comes in and says, "What the hell is this?"

PLAYBOY: When did you know you'd won Super Bowl XXXI?

FAVRE: Second play of the game. After that touchdown pass, I threw the way I wanted all day. The strange thing was how it wasn't as vivid as I expected. No disrespect to New England, but I knew we were better and would win. So the Super Bowl was anticlimactic. I tried to work up some emotion, but I guess I'd let it all out during the season. Now it was just phew!—relief.

PLAYBOY: Did you dream about Super Bowls as a kid?

FAVRE: My brothers and I did. Sundays we'd watch pro football on TV, then go out and pretend we were Archie Manning or Roger Staubach. My dad was the high school football and baseball coach. We'd go see his teams play, and those guys were my heroes. I saw the catcher adjusting his cup, so I'd reach down and play with my balls, too. I tried chewing tobacco, since Dad and all his players did it. I got sicker than dog shit. My little brother, though—that son of a bitch could chew and spit when he was three years old.

PLAYBOY: Did your dad punish you for it?

FAVRE: He's a tough guy, Irvin Favre. He looks like Sergeant Carter on *Gomer Pyle*. But he let us sow our wild oats a little. When I dipped tobacco and threw up he said, "That'll teach you."

PLAYBOY: Is it true you never cried when he spanked you?

FAVRE: My dad would whip my ass with anything from a yardstick to a black rubber hose. I deserved it. Once I shot one of my brothers with a BB gun. Then I hit him on the head with a brick. I hit the other brother with a baseball bat. It hurt, getting whipped, but I wasn't a crier. I faked it. I didn't want more spanking, so I would fake crying when my dad tore up my ass. Then he'd go away and I would laugh.

PLAYBOY: Were you always good at sports?

FAVRE: I could always throw. Even as a kid I could break a window from 50 yards. My brothers and I slept in the same room. This was way down on the river in Mississippi. It got so dark you couldn't see the brother next to you. We'd lie there and talk about the home run we were going to hit or the football game we were going to have. There was a little weight set by the bed, and I would pump weights in the dark. Scott and Jeff laughed at me.

PLAYBOY: Your bayou background made people see you as a hillbilly. Deion Sanders called you Country Time.

FAVRE: I brought some of that on myself. Coming from college at little old Southern Mississippi, I wanted to get noticed. Even if I wasn't from Alabama or Notre Dame, I felt I was the best quarterback in college football. But, then, who doesn't think that?

PLAYBOY: Actually, it's unusual.

FAVRE: I thought I needed something to get me over the top. That's why I told reporters I wrestled alligators. But it wasn't true and it made me look like a goofy redneck. I was like Terry Bradshaw when he came out of college, supposedly this dumb hillbilly. Bradshaw had to win four Super Bowls before people finally figured out that he was a bright guy.

PLAYBOY: How smart are you?

FAVRE: Probably brighter than a lot of people think. I am smart and hard-nosed and hardworking enough to play the game. I think I'm a hell of a football player. It's getting to where guys on other teams say, "Shoot, you're not so dumb after all."

PLAYBOY: You always had the arm for the job.

FAVRE: In high school I used to bet the other guys five dollars they couldn't catch a ball I threw. They went to the far end of the hallway, I threw my hardest and they couldn't catch it. That really got my rocks off.

PLAYBOY: Did you play other sports?

FAVRE: My first thought as a kid was to be a major-league pitcher. I threw hard, in the low 90s, but nobody knew where it was going. I played basketball and was awful. Couldn't shoot at all. Couldn't dribble without watching the ball. But with football I found my calling. It's a good game for someone who will go out and knock himself silly to get a win.

PLAYBOY: Take us back to your youth in Kiln, Mississippi. You didn't really wrestle alligators—

FAVRE: They were around, though. We had four dogs eaten by alligators. We lost a Labrador just last year. Lucky was his name. A 13-footer got him.

PLAYBOY: One big chomp and Lucky was gone?

FAVRE: Alligators don't eat a dog right away. First they roll it around and let it writhe awhile before they take it down. Our family was always familiar with alligators. One time three of them were in the backyard. My brother Scott and I got a pack of Oreo cookies. We threw it in the river and watched them tear it up. After that they'd be there when we came home from school. If we didn't have Oreos we'd throw hot dogs and bread. Then one day Daddy comes home and the alligators are up on the bank by the house, waiting for their cookies. My dad went berserk. He shot all three of them.

PLAYBOY: You fatten them up, and he kills them.

FAVRE: I doubt that he killed them. It's hard as hell to kill an alligator with two or three shots. But they did go back in the water.

PLAYBOY: You definitely have an unusual family history.

FAVRE: One of my grandfathers was a full-blooded Indian. The other grandfather, Benny French, was 27 years older than his second wife. In fact she went to the school prom with old Benny's son, but she ended up marrying Benny.

PLAYBOY: Making her the stepmother of your uncle, her prom date. Did it make for tense family reunions?

FAVRE: Oh, no. Everyone gets along great.

PLAYBOY: You and your wife, Deanna, were childhood sweethearts.

FAVRE: Deanna and I went to catechism together when we were seven. We started dating when I was an eighth grader. She was my prom date all three years in high school.

PLAYBOY: Few fans know how bumpy your road to stardom was. You've had family troubles of one sort or another since you were a teenager.

FAVRE: I was 18 and Deanna was 19 when she got pregnant. People say, "You damn ass, making her look bad. Why didn't you marry her?" But we weren't ready for that. We never would have made it. Five years later we'd be like 90 percent of the people who get married for that reason—divorced and hating each other.

PLAYBOY: How did you handle being teen parents?

FAVRE: We agreed to love our daughter and take care of her without getting married. When I was at Southern Miss I went out partying with the guys, then drove all night to see Deanna and Brittany. Here I was, 20 years old, changing diapers in the middle of the night and playing football the next day. When I got to the Falcons I would drive down the old back roads after midnight to see Deanna and Brittany, then drive back and play on Sunday. Sometimes Deanna and I couldn't stand each other. We dated other people. We didn't get married till last year, after Brittany, who's now nine, kept asking us to do it.

PLAYBOY: Are you a fun dad?

FAVRE: I let Brittany wear my Pro Bowl jersey. It hangs down to her ankles like a dress. She also rides on my back when I do pushups. Try doing 30 or 40 of those with 80 pounds on your back. It will get you in shape.

PLAYBOY: How worried will you be when she starts dating?

FAVRE: I have thought about that. I know my daughter could get pregnant someday. I just don't want it to happen until . . . well, ever! [Laughs]

PLAYBOY: At the age of 28, you have already suffered almost half a dozen concussions. You have had numerous surgeries in addition to the usual aches and pains.

FAVRE: My pain threshold is pretty high.

PLAYBOY: NFL players are supposed to ignore pain.

FAVRE: Football demands that more than any other sport. It's so violent it is unbelievable. But we choose to play, so I don't bitch and complain if I wake up sore the next day. It pisses me off when guys sue the NFL after their careers are over, saying it's the league's fault they got hurt. It's a risky game. If you can't accept that, don't play.

PLAYBOY: Some blame NFL doctors for handing out pain pills like candy.

FAVRE: I don't blame football one bit. My trouble with painkillers was my own problem.

PLAYBOY: How did you become addicted to Vicodin?

FAVRE: You want to play. You don't want to give the other quarterback a shot at your job. I also have a streak going. I have played 80-some games in a row, the most in the league. The record is 118 and I plan on breaking it. I never took painkillers on game day. People think I was playing on them. I would like to see anyone take a couple Vicodin and try to play football. Shoot, you can't walk a straight line.

PLAYBOY: What do they do?

FAVRE: Numb you. Plus they made me a little goofy. I took a fancy to them. There were times when I wasn't hurting but I took them anyway. And got them from other guys on the team. That's when I realized it was getting out of hand. I was taking them because I liked them.

PLAYBOY: Last year you were recovering from ankle surgery when you had a seizure. Brittany said, "Is Daddy dying?" What happened?

FAVRE: Now, people have seizures all the time. By then I was off the Vicodin. The team doctors knew I'd taken a fancy to those. They gave me Demerol for the ankle. The Demerol kept me from sleeping. I wouldn't sleep all night, and finally the lack of sleep caused a seizure.

PLAYBOY: In any case the league sent you to a rehab center in Topeka, Kansas after you admitted your Vicodin addiction.

FAVRE: That was not my idea. I thought I could stop on my own.

PLAYBOY: Did you go to meetings? Did you say, "My name is Brett and I'm a pill popper"?

FAVRE: I sat there and never talked. But I did meet some good people in rehab. Bank presidents, CEOs. I learned that a lot of people who have trouble with drugs are bright. They have money and intelligence. Other people might put them on a pedestal, and they want a way to get down. To get lost. Me, maybe I wanted to hide from celebrity status. I still wasn't used to it. Maybe that's why I took pain pills and sat up all night watching TV, escaping everything. I don't know. They had a gym at the rehab center. I had nothing to do but work out, so I got in the best shape of my career.

PLAYBOY: You were strong enough to knock a hole in a wall.

FAVRE: I thought they should have let me out sooner.

PLAYBOY: After 46 days your Vicodin addiction was supposedly under control. Yet the NFL announced that you could no longer drink alcohol. Do you know why?

FAVRE: League policy. They think drinking will make you want painkillers again.

PLAYBOY: True?

FAVRE: Maybe for some people, but not me. I could drink ten beers with you and I still wouldn't want a pain pill. Trust me, I've had enough of them.

PLAYBOY: Was it galling to be put through urine tests? Were you tempted to sneak a beer?

FAVRE: Sure, it pissed me off. And every once in a while I did have a beer. I knew how the test worked. Drugs stay in your system forever, but not beer. If you drink a beer tonight, it won't show up on the test at nine tomorrow morning.

PLAYBOY: Any other rehab war stories?

FAVRE: They couldn't believe how much gas I had. I have been known to fart, and with the good fruit diet we got in Topeka I was fully loaded. I was killing them. They tried to stop me. They gave me some Beano, but it didn't work. They had to give up and open the windows.

PLAYBOY: Suppose you jam your shoulder this year. Do you take aspirin?

FAVRE: Motrin. Three or four Motrin.

PLAYBOY: Long-term plans?

FAVRE: I wonder how many more years I should play. It might take only one hit to mess you up. I want to be able to run around and toss a baseball with my kids when I'm 40.

PLAYBOY: How does a concussion feel?

FAVRE: It doesn't hurt. You just don't know who you are for a minute. I have had three or four concussions, and maybe a couple more I don't know about. Sometimes you get hit and knocked silly, but it might not be a concussion. I might be concerned if I had three or four more. Or if they started happening easier. But that hasn't been the case so far. Every concussion I've had, I really got the shit knocked out of me. So I'm not worried.

PLAYBOY: Your first major injury happened off the field. In 1990 you nearly died in a car crash.

FAVRE: I had my seat belt on but still wound up in the backseat. My brother Scott was in the car behind me. He said it looked like a plane wreck, glass and pieces of trees all around. Scott had his golf clubs with him. He got out his putter and broke the car window to get to me. I had one of those concussions where you don't know who or where you are, but I was talking. I kept asking him if I could ever play football again.

PLAYBOY: Your injuries soon got worse.

FAVRE: After a week in the hospital I had terrible stomach pains. They did emergency surgery. The doctor went in and found 30 inches of my intestine had died. They took it out and sewed me up. I played five weeks later.

PLAYBOY: By then you were 30 pounds underweight, yet you led the Southern Mississippi Golden Eagles to a last-minute upset of Alabama. The Alabama coach called it "a miracle" and you an instant "legend." Since then you've made a habit of pulling off miracle plays, yet you often poor-mouth yourself.

FAVRE: I'm scared people will think I have a big head. Sure, I claim I don't give a shit what anybody says, but I actually hope they'll say I'm still just a good old guy like I was in high school. It's the truth.

PLAYBOY: Ever find yourself scratching your butt just to prove it?

FAVRE: [*Laughs*] No, that comes natural. If I'm on a golf outing with Marino and Kelly and they're getting ready to hit, I'll rip a big fart. They say, "That's awful!" But why? Everybody does it. Just because you're a professional athlete or a politician doesn't mean you stop taking dumps and scratching your ass. Of course, there's a time and place for humor like that. I don't go to corporate events, where everyone is in a suit and tie, and start cutting farts. Not loud ones, anyway.

PLAYBOY: You were once the only NFL star who still lived with his parents.

FAVRE: That was my first two years in the league. I remember my dad and I wore the same kind of underwear: BVDs. We called them grippers because they grip your balls real good. So to keep from getting them mixed up I would write "BF" or my number, four, on mine, and Irvin wrote "DAD" on his. Then one day I'm in the locker room when somebody sees the word "DAD" written on my briefs. Picked up the wrong ones at home. It's bad enough to fit into your dad's underwear; you don't want the whole team to see it.

PLAYBOY: When Atlanta drafted you in 1991, the Jets were poised to take you on the next pick. Would you have liked being Broadway Brett?

FAVRE: I didn't want to be. You can own New York if you do great, but if you screw up the media and fans will disown you. Atlanta was closer to home. I was relieved to hear, "Atlanta takes Favre with the 33rd pick."

PLAYBOY: How did you spend your bonus?

FAVRE: I put about 70 percent of it in stocks and bonds, conservative stuff, and bought a $30,000 maroon Acura. I'm pretty tight with money. Today I have a small house in Hattiesburg, Mississippi, near where I grew up, plus a house in Green Bay and some land back home. Deanna drives a Lexus and I drive a truck. I wasn't so conservative off the field. I was immature. Being third string was no fun, so I said what the hell and went partying. Which I don't regret. It probably helped get me out of Atlanta, where they weren't going to play me.

PLAYBOY: Did you fail in Atlanta?

FAVRE: No. They didn't give me that chance. If I had had the chance, would I have done the job for the Falcons? I don't know. I still didn't know how to read defenses, how to drop back and look around and see the defense unfold.

PLAYBOY: Did the Falcons veterans put you through the usual rookie hazing?

FAVRE: I fought it. I was the only rookie that year who didn't get his head shaved. They got me back by putting all my clothes in the shower. On rookie day you had to stand up and sing your school song. Southern Miss didn't have a school song, so I sang a country song. The whole team was yelling Yee-ha! at me. It was embarrassing.

PLAYBOY: Yet you bravely fought them off even when they tried to shave your head.

FAVRE: I hid in my room.

PLAYBOY: How do the Packers haze their rookies?

FAVRE: We don't. Mike's policy is, we're one team from the first day you get here.

PLAYBOY: What was your quarterback rating as a rookie?

FAVRE: Zero. That year I was 0-5, with two interceptions. Want to know how bad that is? Today I am the third- or fourth-highest rated passer in history. I'd be one spot better without those five passes.

PLAYBOY: How do you read a defense?

FAVRE: It takes years to learn. First you need to keep thinking while Bruce Smith or Charles Haley or Leon Lett or Kevin Greene chases you all over the field. You don't see defensive players so much as feel their presence. All I'm looking at is the receiver coming across. We have a three-step drop, a five-step and a seven-step. With a seven-step drop you can really sit back and read what's happening out there, wait for it all to unfold. With a shorter drop, you have to think faster. But now, after five years in our offense, I can tell if a receiver's going to be open even before he makes his move.

PLAYBOY: What makes a great scrambler?

FAVRE: Take someone off the street and throw him out there with the pocket breaking down, and he would be scared to death. That's when I feel comfortable. It's a seventh sense—you feel someone coming behind you and you dodge him. Awesome, isn't it? I love watching those plays on film. "Damn, how'd I do that?" It makes you kind of ejaculate on yourself.

PLAYBOY: Like your shovel pass against Carolina—

FAVRE: Kevin Greene had me tackled. He was bringing me down with my arms pinned, but I shoveled it out for a touchdown. And Greene says, "Wow." That meant a lot to me, hearing that from him.

PLAYBOY: Do you have any other tricks up your sleeve?

FAVRE: Throwing a touchdown left-handed. I'm waiting for the right moment.

PLAYBOY: You are also a noted clubhouse prankster.

FAVRE: I pull guys' pants down in front of everyone. I'll put Heet ointment in your jock. Shaving cream in your helmet. If a guy's taking a dump, I like to go over the top of the stall and pour a five-gallon bucket of ice water on him. Oh, that's miserable. I got my buddy Frank Winters that way. He was halfway through a good dump when I poured the ice. Stopped him cold. He said he couldn't finish.

PLAYBOY: Do your victims ever manage to exact any revenge?

FAVRE: They ain't sneaky enough. There was one time: We're sitting in a meeting when I feel my balls start to burn. They got me with Heet in the jock. But I wouldn't react. Imagine that burning, man—20 minutes of it, but I never let on. Meeting ended and I ran for a wet towel.

PLAYBOY: In the NFL grown men not only play pranks, they room together. That was once an economy move, now it's just tradition. Why not room by yourself? You can afford it.

FAVRE: Winters and me, we've roomed on the road for six years now. He's my center. We're like brothers. Some guys room alone, but I need people around me. Guys, mostly. My wife gets mad because I can't go off on a business trip without asking four or five buddies along.

PLAYBOY: Are men more pack oriented?

FAVRE: Women don't understand us. When guys play golf we'll sit in the clubhouse afterward for hours. Have some beers, go over our scores, laugh and joke. Nobody wants to go home. It's like that with a football team on the road. Frank and I are typical roomies. We watch movies in the hotel room, talk about the game, fart and burp and throw our clothes on the floor. I have just started to think about retiring someday. When football is over I'll probably miss the jokes and locker room bullshit more than the games.

PLAYBOY: You and center Winters have an odd partnership.

FAVRE: I have to put my hand on his ass a hundred times a day. And he'll fart, too. I can't do anything about it. You can't call a time-out. You have to go through with the play.

PLAYBOY: Do Green Bay's cold winters bother you?

FAVRE: It gets so cold it's funny. One game, Mike Holmgren called a time-out. He was yelling instructions, but I burst out laughing. Mike had a big snot bubble frozen to his mustache.

PLAYBOY: Ever meet your fellow Southerner and Green Bay hero Bart Starr?

FAVRE: Bart is a friend. I would take any advice I could get from him, but that's not his way. All he has said about football is, "Brett, you brought back the Packers tradition."

PLAYBOY: A big part of that tradition is Reggie White. You helped to persuade him to sign with the Packers in 1993.

FAVRE: Shit, I was tired of him chasing my ass.

PLAYBOY: In his Philadelphia Eagles days White once slammed you to the turf, separating your shoulder. He was trying to hurt you, wasn't he? To knock you out of the game—

FAVRE: That's his job. I tried to get loose, but there was no way. Yes, he did it on purpose. He'll tell you that. But it's perfectly legal. In football you try to win.

PLAYBOY: What if he had gouged your eye?

FAVRE: Now, when you start poking eyeballs and ripping people's teeth out, that's pushing it a little.

PLAYBOY: How did you woo Reggie White?

FAVRE: All I said was, "Reggie, this is small-town America. There's no better place to play football. Come play with us and you'll see." Every team wanted Reggie, but we got him. We got the best defensive player ever, by far.

PLAYBOY: Better than Lawrence Taylor?

FAVRE: Oh yeah. Maybe the best player, period. Certainly in the top five. I was blown away when Reggie came to Green Bay and said we would win the Super Bowl. That helped me believe it. And now when Saturday rolls around and we all jump on the team plane, I feel like we could take on Iran or Russia and win. We're the Green Bay Packers! Want to hear something weird? When I fly commercial by myself, I get scared. But I feel safe on the team plane. Like we could all rescue one another if the plane went down.

PLAYBOY: What does the Reverend Reggie White think of your club-house pranks?

FAVRE: He likes them. I curse and drink beer around him. You can tell Reggie a dirty joke, too, as long as it's not about him. He told me he'd drive me home if I ever went out and drank too much.

PLAYBOY: Can you win another Super Bowl?

FAVRE: We've built something good here in Green Bay. We've kept getting better and better, and now we are on a plateau where we can't get any better. Now we have to maintain. If I can maintain my performance we'll win again. One day I might be seen as the best quarterback ever.

PLAYBOY: Do you worry about your health?

FAVRE: If we were to win three Super Bowls I might think about retiring. Going out on top. The older I get, the less elusive I'll be. I have to think about Deanna and our little girl.

PLAYBOY: Is that why you finally got married last year?

FAVRE: I couldn't keep Deanna and Brittany waiting forever. Little Brittany kept asking why mommy and daddy weren't married. I said I didn't know if I was ready. Finally I was at the rehab center with 46 days to think, and I realized something. I was always waiting to wake up someday and be grown up. That was never going to happen.

PLAYBOY: Has marriage changed your life?

FAVRE: It's better, but there are surprises. Living in a house full of women I can't walk around like an old slob. I thought Deanna and I would do everything together once we got married. I would come home and find dinner cooked, everything rosy. But we hardly do anything together. Before you live with someone you're always trying to get together. After, you're always going different directions. She goes to work out, I go play golf. So when guys say they can't wait to be married, I tell them it's not what they think. You might be all over each other the first year, but there will be times when you can't stand each other, and more times when you go your separate ways. And this is a marriage I love. Wearing this ring . . . it makes me feel like I've arrived a little bit as a man. I'm more of a grown man now.

PLAYBOY: Do you want more kids? Are you thinking of raising a little QB of your own?

FAVRE: I want to have a couple of boys. We've been trying, but Deanna got sick and the doctor said that if we want more children we'd better have them fast. She may have to have surgery, have her ovaries out. That was a blow to us, hearing that. Brittany wants a little brother. She wrote us a note the other day. "I want a baby brother." With a picture of her holding the baby. "I will take care of it," she wrote. And your heart just [he touches his chest]. I told her, "Brittany, we're working on it."

PLAYBOY: Have you told your daughter where babies come from?

FAVRE: No way. I couldn't. Of course Deanna says, "I'm not telling her, you tell her."

PLAYBOY: Back in Mississippi, your family had a terrible time last year. Your sister, Brandi, a former Miss Teen Mississippi, was involved in a drive-by shooting.

FAVRE: She was giving another girl and the girl's boyfriend a ride home. The boyfriend had had an argument with another guy at a party, and the boyfriend shot at him from the car. Brandi told the truth and she was fine.

PLAYBOY: Your older brother, Scott, had more serious trouble.

FAVRE: Scott and Mark Haverty, my best friend, were in the same car. Scott was driving. They stopped on a train track.

PLAYBOY: A train hit them. Mark Haverty died. Your brother recovered from his injuries, but the police said he was driving drunk. He was convicted and sentenced for causing Mark's death.

FAVRE: But Mark's family testified on Scott's behalf. That's unusual in a vehicular manslaughter case. They felt Scott had suffered enough. It could have happened to a lot of guys. So Scott was sentenced to 15 years, with 14 of it suspended. He got a year of house arrest. He had to wear an ankle bracelet that told the cops where he was.

PLAYBOY: Should Scott have arranged for a designated driver?

FAVRE: This was a mistake between two buddies. I mean, there's nothing good about drinking and driving, but who hasn't done it? They were unlucky. It could just as easily have been Scott who was killed. If I had been home that night it could have been me.

PLAYBOY: Then, last May, Scott was arrested again. He was charged with violating his probation. What happened?

FAVRE: Hell, Scott didn't do anything wrong. It was Memorial Day. His probation officer said he could visit the family. He was going over there to help my dad fix the fishing boat. It's only two and a half miles, but there was a roadblock. Now, whoever heard of a roadblock at 7:30 in the morning? But there it was. The police told him he was driving with a suspended license. He had been notified by mail, like they said, but we get so much mail at my parents' house, and most of it's for me. My mom got the letter but didn't open it. So that morning they arrested Scott. Handcuffed him. He called me in Green Bay. Said they were sending him to prison. He was crying on the phone. He said he wanted to kill himself. I said, "Bullshit. It's a misunderstanding." But the next afternoon, my brother was gone. The judge says he's going to prison for 13 years. Thirteen years! That's like death. We're hoping the judge will hear our side. There's a glimmer of hope he'll give Scott a lesser sentence. I can imagine what he's thinking in a prison cell right now. He's thinking about Mark. If they'd taken a different turn that night, everything would be OK. Our mom's doing bad. Seeing your son go to prison, that's hard to take.

PLAYBOY: She had one son in prison and one in the Super Bowl.

FAVRE: I feel guilty about that. Maybe I should just sit instead of playing, show more remorse and compassion. But that won't help Scott. So I occupy myself. I played golf most days until training camp started. Now here I am in my fairy-tale world playing football while Scott sits in prison, and I have done more bad things than he's ever dreamed of. I just wish I had my brother back. I wish I had my best friend Mark back, too. When I'm thinking about that and people talk about the Super Bowl, I want to slap them. I would give up my ring in a heartbeat to trade places with my brother. [*In early August Scott Favre was released from the Hancock County jail after a hearing determined he had been wrongfully jailed.*]

PLAYBOY: Was it difficult for Scott, being your older brother?

FAVRE: We never talked about it. Back when he was the high school quarterback, I wanted to be just like him. I wanted to be him. Later on, maybe it was the other way. I'm sure we all wish we could be a Super Bowl quarterback. Sometimes I felt bad when people asked him how it felt to be my brother, like it was some honor. He told them that he beat me at golf.

PLAYBOY: How have you managed to win two MVPs and a Super Bowl with so much on your mind?

FAVRE: Sometimes when I'm alone in my truck I ask myself that question. I think I have had to grow up more than most 28-year-olds. I'm still cheerful and happy in the locker room or when Deanna and I have guests over. But sometimes it feels like I'm faking it. At our team meeting today I looked around at the guys laughing. That was me a few years ago, when the worst thing that could happen was an interception. The games are still great. Playing football on Sunday, I'm gone. That might be why I perform so well. It's so good to get lost in the game for three hours.

PLAYBOY: Football is your escape?

FAVRE: Maybe that's how I got in trouble with pain pills. When the game ends you have to go back to thinking about all the damn things in your life. The pills help you not think.

PLAYBOY: Do you have phobias?

FAVRE: I'm a little scared of the dark. It was so pitch black at night where I grew up, I like a little light on when I sleep.

PLAYBOY: The two-time MVP sleeps with a night light?

FAVRE: I'll leave the TV on. I usually watch TV until it watches me.

PLAYBOY: Anything funny about being a football hero?

FAVRE: People send you strange things. My second year in Green Bay I started getting hate mail and love mail. I really felt I'd arrived when girls started sending naked pictures. One was wearing nothing but a cowboy hat.

PLAYBOY: No nude cheeseheads?

FAVRE: Actors are funny, too. Charlie Sheen and David Spade are friends of mine. Darius Rucker from Hootie & the Blowfish, too. The athletes all wish they could sing and dance, and the singers and actors wish they could play sports.

PLAYBOY: Can you dance?

FAVRE: I can moonwalk a bit. I watch MTV and dance to the videos. It's pretty awful.

PLAYBOY: Your childhood home is now a tourist attraction.

FAVRE: Things are changing. My mom redid the room my brothers and I grew up in. She took down all our sports posters, even my poster of McMahon and Walter Payton. At least she didn't throw it away. She got all our old stuff laminated. Fans drive up and down our little road nonstop. We finally paved it. I never thought we'd have a real road.

The county wouldn't do it, so we paid for it: half a mile of paved road for $40,000.

PLAYBOY: What do you and Irv talk about? He must have popped his lid when you won the Super Bowl.

FAVRE: He never said so. My dad and I were never big talkers. He never gave me the birds-and-the-bees talk.

PLAYBOY: Mom did that?

FAVRE: No, I got by on hearsay.

PLAYBOY: Do you and your dad talk only about football?

FAVRE: We're both hardheaded. Not very sentimental. My father and I have never sat down and had a long talk like you and I are doing. But we get along. It's a great relationship. Last year after we won the NFC championship game—we're going to the Super Bowl!—Irv came to the locker room. He was crying. I was still on a high from the game, laughing and hollering, but he had tears in his eyes and I remember he hit me. Kind of punched me and said, "Good job, good job."

PLAYBOY: How was he after the Super Bowl?

FAVRE: Back to form. He told me, "Next year you've got to be even better."

PLAYBOY: Whom did you root for in the Super Bowls you didn't make?

FAVRE: I haven't watched one since I got to the NFL. If I'm not playing, I don't want to see it.

PLAYBOY: You called Reggie White one of the top five players ever. Who are the other four?

FAVRE: Joe Montana and Jerry Rice. Bart Starr, Dick Butkus, Ray Nitschke.

PLAYBOY: That's five. Want to keep going?

FAVRE: Deion Sanders. Lynn Swann, Roger Staubach, Archie Manning, Mike Singletary. Ray Guy, the great punter. Let's see, who else? Johnny Unitas, George Blanda, Deacon Jones, L. C. Greenwood, Walter Payton.

PLAYBOY: Does Deion belong in that group?

FAVRE: Yes. I don't attack Deion's ass when we play. He's too good. Is he a showboat? No, because it isn't showboating when you can get the job done. It's style. Deion has style and he'll do anything for a teammate. He bought clothes for me in Atlanta. I was a complete unknown. Deion takes one look at my clothes and says, "I'll show you how to dress." He bought me two tailored suits.

PLAYBOY: Turning you into the clothes-horse you are today.

FAVRE: I prefer walking around in my underwear, but I can wear a tuxedo. And I still have those two tailored suits.

PLAYBOY: Do you have any good memories of the rehab center?

FAVRE: I learned to play piano. Started off with one hand, then put them together. Just trying to do it makes you look at real musicians with amazement. Football is easy, that shit is hard.

PLAYBOY: What did you play?

FAVRE: I learned to play "Ode to Joy."

PLAYBOY: How much more can you achieve in the NFL?

FAVRE: Winning another Super Bowl. Going into the Hall of Fame. I expect to be in the Hall of Fame. But mostly I hope that in 20 or 30 years people will say, "That goddamn Favre, you had to watch yourself around him. He'd throw ice or put something in your jock, but on Sunday that son of a bitch was ready to play."

WAYNE GRETZKY

A candid conversation about life on and off the ice with the young hockey superstar considered by many to be the world's best athlete

In keeping with the *Playboy* tradition of interviewing heads of state, we bring you Wayne Douglas Gretzky of Canada. For those who don't follow the puck, he is Jim Thorpe on skates, Jesse Owens with a stick, Babe Ruth in hockey shorts. Going by statistics alone, Wayne Gretzky is the greatest athlete of the 20th Century. Going by the polls, he is more famous than everyone else in Canada combined.

Gretzky doesn't have the flash of Bobby Hull or Bobby Orr; he can't skate like Gilbert Perreault or Guy Lafleur; he can't muscle like Phil Esposito or Bryan Trottier; he's not a pure shooter, like Mike Bossy. Still, barring injury, Gretzky will score more goals than anyone else who has ever played hockey. Gordie Howe holds the all-time scoring record, with 1850 points. It took him 26 years to score them. Gretzky has earned more than 1000 points in fewer than six full seasons. If he keeps up his present pace, he'll pass Howe in 10 years. At the age of 24, he already holds more records in hockey than any other athlete in any sport, period.

What the Great Gretzky has is a sixth sense—an ice sense, like Larry Bird's or Magic Johnson's court sense. He knows where everybody on the ice is, and he knows where the puck is going. He generally gets there first.

When a hockey player scores, which isn't often (hockey scores read like baseball scores), the last player to touch the puck gets credit for the goal. Usually, the two players on his team who touch it before him each receive assists. Goals and assists are worth a point apiece in a player's stats. The reason they have equal value is that the players who passed the puck are often as important to the goal as the scorer, if not more so.

Until recently, 50 goals was a magic number in hockey. Any 50-goal scorer was an instant superstar. With expansion and longer schedules, 100 points (goals and assists, remember) became the household-name plateau. At first, only Esposito and Orr were doing it. Then a few more—Marcel Dionne, Lafleur, Bossy and Trottier—joined them at the summit. Now there are a number of 100-point men. And then there's Gretzky, who year after year finishes 40, 50, even 60 points ahead of everyone else. According to his stats, Gretzky is 33 1/3 percent better than the second-best player in hockey. It's unlikely that anyone else in any sport is, or has ever been, that much better than his "peers."

Wayne Douglas Gretzky was born in Brantford, Ontario, on January 26, 1961. He's been famous ever since. His father, Walter, taught him to skate when he was two years old. By the time Wayne was five, he was playing on an all-star team with 10- and 11-year-olds. At the age of 10, he was averaging six goals a game. At 14, he left home to play Junior "B" hockey in Toronto, against 19- and 20-year-olds. Three years later, he was a pro, starring for the Indianapolis Racers of the old World Hockey Association. After only eight games, he was sold to the Edmonton Oilers. The Indianapolis Racers promptly folded. Wayne signed a 21-year personal-service contract with Oilers owner Peter Pocklington, making him—at 17—the highest-paid player in hockey.

That summer of 1979, four teams from the WHA, including Edmonton, merged with the National Hockey League. The scouting report on Gretzky was that at 5'11" and 170 pounds, he was too small and slow to compete in the bruiser-dominated NHL All he did was tie for the 1979-1980 scoring title with 137 points. The next year, he totaled 164, breaking a decade-old NHL record by 12 points.

Gretzky's third season was astonishing. He had 92 goals (the previous record was 76). With 212 total points, he broke his own scoring record by 48. Mike Bossy of the New York Islanders had a great season, scoring 147 points—only 65 fewer than Gretzky.

Last season, Gretzky led the league with 87 goals and 205 points. Double-teamed at every turn, he still led the Oilers into the Stanley Cup finals against the Islanders, winners of four straight Stanley Cups. Gretzky and company won. The aurora borealis came out over Alberta. As his sixth season began last fall, Gretzky held or shared at least 34 NHL records. He has the longest scoring streak in history—51 consecutive games (in one of them, his only point, a goal, came with two seconds left in the game). He has set the standards for most goals and most total points in a season. He has even shattered hockey's most sacred record—tantamount to a baseball player's breaking Joe DiMaggio's 56-game hitting streak: Maurice "Rocket" Richard once scored 50 goals in the first 50 games of a season; Gretzky broke that one in 39 games.

He makes about $1,000,000 a year playing hockey, plus $2,000,000 or so for endorsements. In Canada, he is as popular as the maple leaf; and thanks to his squeaky-clean image, he's a marketer's dream. There are a Gretzky doll, a breakfast cereal, a watch, a lunch box, a bedspread, wallpaper and TV commercials. How many jocks have their own wallpaper? The hockey stick he endorses went from 12th place to first in sales in 18 months. In addition to the penthouse in which he lives, he owns interests in office buildings and shopping centers in Edmonton and a high-rise in Calgary and hefty amounts of gold bullion and securities. He and his managers run the Gretzky empire from lavish offices, appointed in oak, marble and brass, in two landmark buildings in Edmonton. Their empire is multinational: The 3000 letters Gretzky receives each month come from everywhere, some of them simply addressed Wayne Gretzky, Canada.

To find out what makes the Great One so great, we sent freelance writer Scott Cohen to Edmonton to speak with him before and after the Oilers' Stanley Cup victory last season. Cohen's report:

"Wayne Gretzky is unspectacular off the ice. He looks more like a surfer than a hockey player. The attribute that stands out most is his genuineness—fame hasn't gone to his head. He doesn't wear his money; he wears a sweatshirt and jeans. He owns a sports car but doesn't speed. He is loyal to his family and calls home three times a week. When he's not playing or doing endorsements, he's appearing at a banquet or a benefit or hosting a golf or tennis tournament on behalf of one of his many charities. Any girl in the country would be glad to break the ice with him; he has one girlfriend. His modesty is exasperating at times. I had thought I might be interviewing the most boring person on earth, but I, like a lot of people, had underestimated his intelligence and clarity of purpose.

"Gretzky's penthouse is tasteful, comfortable, low-key. The decor is modern and masculine. His only possession that even hints at hype is a portrait of himself by Andy Warhol. The interview, which took place in Wayne's living room and at a restaurant over lunch, began with the topic of his pervasive presence in Canada."

PLAYBOY: Your face is on billboards, posters, cereal boxes, dolls and magazine covers all over Canada. Outside Canada, you're fast becoming a household word. You hear your name a thousand times a day. You sign hundreds of autographs. Don't you get tired of being Wayne Gretzky?

GRETZKY: No. I drive to the rink, see a billboard, look at it—and I can stand it. [*Grins*] You hear Michael Jackson everywhere, too, but he's still great to dance to.

PLAYBOY: Don't you get tired of signing all those autographs, or do you accept that as part of the job?

GRETZKY: It really isn't part of the job. You don't have to sign autographs. Nobody is going to throw you in jail for not signing. I believe it goes with being a professional athlete.

PLAYBOY: At what point would fame become a liability?

GRETZKY: I don't think it will ever become a liability. How can I ever become more famous than Reggie Jackson? It's impossible, just because of numbers. There are almost as many people living in New York State as there are in all of Canada. If I ever became too well known, I could move to Houston, where nobody would know me. I don't think you can become too famous as a hockey player.

PLAYBOY: Your fame is based, of course, on your being considered by many the most talented athlete in the world. How do *you* account for your gift?

GRETZKY: I think the success I have comes from believing in myself as a person and as a hockey player, utilizing all my teammates properly and having respect for the other player, that he's as good as I am. Those are the three major reasons.

PLAYBOY: That's a little vague. Any good player could say that.

GRETZKY: Well, I also got a head start by playing at the age of two. By the time I was five, I was playing against 11-year-olds.

PLAYBOY: Still, you must have had something special, something you were born with, to be able to play with kids twice your age.

GRETZKY: I had natural ability—plus, there was no other league for me to play in at that time. Either I played with older kids or I didn't play. At that time, kids didn't learn to play hockey until they were six or seven. I had been skating as long as most 10-year-olds.

You know, when I was two years old, I was doing the drills—taught to me by my father—that I saw eight years later, in 1972, when the Russians came over. People were saying, "Look at those drills; look at what they're doing," but I had been doing those things for eight or nine years, and they were nothing to me. My father is a very intelligent man, and to him, everything in life is fundamentals and basics.

PLAYBOY: You were pushed to work pretty hard at it, weren't you?

GRETZKY: I worked hard, but there are a lot of others who worked hard at a young age, too. A lot of it has to do with being gifted. But there are a lot of people who are gifted. Whether it's in business, schooling or sports, you have to utilize your gifts. I also believe there are players who aren't doing as well as I am who are more talented than I.

PLAYBOY: Who do you think is the best player?

GRETZKY: I don't know who the best is, but I can tell you whom I respect most: Denis Potvin, Mike Bossy and Bryan Trottier.

PLAYBOY: Who else would be on your all-star team?

GRETZKY: Gilbert Perreault and Paul Coffey. The goal tender has to be Billy Smith. He's won four Stanley Cups.

PLAYBOY: What have you learned from those players?

GRETZKY: I can't *do* what other players do, so I really haven't learned much. I can't hit people like Trottier can. I can't shoot as quickly as Bossy. I can't deke like Guy Lafleur. I'm not strong, like Potvin. I have to be Wayne Gretzky.

PLAYBOY: Yet each year, you outscore those players by a very wide margin. Let's see if we can't pin down the way you assess your abilities, starting with the most obvious—passing and scoring.

GRETZKY: My feeling is, let the puck do all the work. That's why Bossy and Trottier and Jari Kurri and I have success. People think that to be a good hockey player you have to pick the puck up, deke around everybody and take a shot, which is not true. Nobody can skate as fast as that little black thing. We move the puck, give and get it back, give and get it back.

PLAYBOY: What about your shooting?

GRETZKY: You don't have to have a hard shot. You just have to be quick and bang it in there as fast as possible. Bossy can shoot that puck quicker than anyone else. Bang, it's in the net. As simple as that. Then there are guys with a hard shot, but I can't do that.

PLAYBOY: One reason you do score as much as you do is your knack of being in the right place at the right time. How do you explain your ability to anticipate plays?

GRETZKY: I developed that just by being a smaller hockey player than everyone else. I had to be ahead of everybody else or I wouldn't have survived. If I weren't thinking, I could have been seriously injured. My dad always argues that instinct can be taught. Some guys are smart enough to learn it, but there are other guys in the league who are not smart enough and can't learn.

PLAYBOY: How about your stamina? You play longer and harder than most players in the league, and you seem to be strongest at the end of the game, when others are the most tired.

GRETZKY: I used to do track and field as a kid. I was in a track club when I was six and seven, and I used to run three-, four-mile races. As I got older, the races got longer. The fact that I grew up running built up my endurance to a high level.

PLAYBOY: Have you been tested by medical experts to see if there is something special about you?

GRETZKY: Yes. Our team doctors tested my endurance, strength, reflexes and flexibility with machines, bicycles and drills. They tested every guy on the team and I did *bad* in all the tests—except endurance.

PLAYBOY: What do you think that demonstrated?

GRETZKY: You can't measure a guy's enthusiasm or intensity by having him sit on a bike or push on a machine. If you test a dull guy, you're going to get an accurate reading; but if you test an emotional guy, you won't.

PLAYBOY: Sportswriters have said you seem to be able to see everything that's going on on the ice. Do you have exceptional peripheral vision?

GRETZKY: They call it peripheral vision; I call it fear. *You* would be able to get out of the way, too, if Potvin were going to hit you. He's a big, strong boy. And, again, growing up, I was always the small guy. When I was five and playing against 11-year-olds, who were bigger, stronger, faster, I just had to figure out a way to play with them. When I was 14, I played against 20-year-olds, and when I was 17, I played with men. Basically,

I had to play the same style all the way through. I couldn't beat people with my strength; I don't have a hard shot; I'm not the quickest skater in the league, though at times I can be as fast as anybody. My eyes and my mind have to do most of the work.

PLAYBOY: But are you able to see the entire game in a way others can't?

GRETZKY: I try to but, of course, I can't see everybody on the ice. I try my best to know where everybody is. So do all the good players in the league. I think that when I'm on the ice and teams see I have the puck, they send two or three players at me. That leaves openings for other players. I think that's why I get a lot of assists.

PLAYBOY: Do you see other players or do you *sense* them?

GRETZKY: I sense them more than I actually see them. I get a *feeling* about where a teammate is going to be. A lot of times, I can turn and pass without even looking. Somebody will say, "Gosh, he didn't look but knew exactly where Jari Kurri was." True but not true. We've worked together for four years and have been to countless practices, and he knows I'm going to throw the puck there and I know he's going to be there. That's why it's important to know the other players and play together.

PLAYBOY: When you're skating up ice with the puck, are you aware of who the defense man is on that side of the ice?

GRETZKY: All the time. When I'm on the ice, I know who else is on the ice, and when I go into our zone, I can even tell when somebody new has come onto the ice. A perfect example is when I play against the Rangers. It's no secret that if Barry Beck hit me, he would kill me. It's not as if he would intentionally hurt me. He's a big, strong man, and if I got myself into a position where I got hit by him, forget it. He could seriously hurt me. So when I'm on the ice, I try to go to the side opposite from where he is. The same with Potvin. I don't think there's any question that Potvin is the best defense man in the league. I think he's one of the reasons the Islanders won four Stanley Cups in a row.

PLAYBOY: How would *you* stop Wayne Gretzky?

GRETZKY: I can't tell you that. If I tell you, then I'm in trouble. I know the best way to *defend* against Wayne Gretzky, the way that bothers him the most. Obviously, the Islanders know. They're killing me. Steve Kasper of Boston knows.

PLAYBOY: What do they do that other teams don't?

GRETZKY: They play a lot more intelligently. First of all, they have more talent than other teams. Obviously, that's going to make it harder right off the bat. And then, if I'm fortunate enough to get by their players, both teams have great goal tenders.

PLAYBOY: If a guy covers you too closely and keeps getting in your way, will you pretend you were tripped or hooked to draw a penalty?

GRETZKY: Would I take a dive? Sure I would. I'll tell you why. A lot of times, when you're hooked, the penalty isn't called, which is fine; but if fighters—not necessarily Kasper—know they can get away with hooking players, they will do it all night. But if you start diving when a guy's hooking you and he gets a penalty here and there, he's going to give you room. He's going to think that if he does that again, he'll get a penalty. That's the only reason I dive. If a guy is really sticking close to me throughout the hockey game, again, I can't knock him over, I can't stop and drill him in a fight, so I have to figure out ways to shake him.

PLAYBOY: Is it getting increasingly difficult for you to avoid drawing penalties?

GRETZKY: I think more people are trying to check me now than ever before, and I have to take a stand at some point. My stand may not be very forceful, but I have to let them know they can't just elbow, slash or push me around and expect me to take it with a smile. But looking back on my penalties, I see that most have been for tripping, all accidental. Bossy gets four, five penalties a year, and three of them are for accidental tripping. I'm amazed that some guys go an entire year without a penalty. How do they do that? A lot of times, you get a tripping penalty because you're tired at the end of a shift or you're lazy on a play. It depends on how disciplined you are.

PLAYBOY: In the past, the NHL placed a lot of emphasis on physical strength. Given your size and build, do you think you would have been the player you are today?

GRETZKY: I might never have played 20 years ago. There's no question that I might not have made it. I remember people saying to me 10 years ago that I might not make it, because I was too small. No, 20 years ago, I definitely would not have been able to play in the NHL.

PLAYBOY: Even though there were a lot of small players who made it?

GRETZKY: But those guys had something special. They were fabulous skaters. Maurice Richard, Yvan Cournoyer—they were flamboyant skaters. I was never a smooth skater. The game in the sixties was a lot rougher and a lot more defensive-minded. Today it's a lot quicker, the puck is moved more, the training is better, the travel is better, there are more players from the U.S., Europe and maybe Russia, there is more technique. I just can't imagine that every professional group in the world—from writers to doctors to lawyers to football players—has improved and hockey is the only one that has gotten worse. I don't buy that.

PLAYBOY: Let's talk about the most prominent topic in the game: Is violence necessary in hockey?

GRETZKY: First of all, I don't think there's any question that hockey was violent back in the late sixties, early seventies, with bench-clearing brawls and that type of thing; but since then, the league has done a tremendous job of cleaning up the violence. That's evident by the fact that a person of my size, 5'11", 170 pounds, can play the game without being seriously injured. I think the European influence is also a big factor in changing the emphasis of the game from being able to fight to being able to skate.

PLAYBOY: Don't fans *want* to see violence?

GRETZKY: Teams used to think that violence brought people into the building. Sure it does, but we have to appeal to a bigger market than just the 15,000 people it may bring to a particular rink. The NHL realized that and cleaned it up.

PLAYBOY: Nevertheless, don't players fight because fans want them to, even if they may not feel like it themselves?

GRETZKY: No. Rod Gilbert said it best: "People used to ask me if fights in hockey were fixed. If they were, I would have been in more of them." They're real. You don't fight just to please the fans. You fight for reasons of temper, frustration. I don't think you take a punch in the face for the fans.

PLAYBOY: You say the NHL has cleaned up its act, but you can't deny that hockey still seems more violent than other sports.

GRETZKY: That's only because there *is* fighting. In other sports, I believe, if you fight, you're automatically ejected from the game. In hockey, you're not, the reason being that you're carrying around a hockey stick, which is a lethal weapon. I'd rather take a punch in the face than a stick over the head. That's why refs let the fighting go on for a long time. If the referees break up a fight that has just started, chances are, those guys are going to fight their next time on the ice anyway. If it's an even fight, the referees let the players fight, and if it's unfair, they break it up.

But I don't think hockey is any more violent than other sports. I'd be more scared standing in front of the plate with the pitcher throwing a ball 100 mph at my head. Nobody's ever been really hurt in hockey fights. The worst that can happen is a guy breaks a nose, I guess, but there are only a few guys in the league who fight, anyway—12 out of 20 guys on a team don't fight. You don't see a fighter fighting a nonfighter. That's just the way it is. It's an unwritten rule that fighters fight and guys who don't want to fight don't. A fighter knows that if he drops his gloves off with me, I'm not going to fight, so he doesn't waste his time.

PLAYBOY: Who are regarded as the best fighters in the NHL?

GRETZKY: I guess Dave Semenko, Clark Gillies, Behn Wilson and Barry Beck. Those four are the guys I would name, anyway. I don't think I've forgotten anybody. I hope I haven't. I don't want anybody to be upset with me.

PLAYBOY: When a fight breaks out on the ice and players from opposing teams pair off, whom do you look for as an opponent?

GRETZKY: I always look for Pierre Larouche, Thomas Gradin, Neal Broten—all the *little* guys I can grab [*laughs*].

PLAYBOY: What do you talk about while you're grabbing each other?

GRETZKY: Well, the guys who don't want to fight might talk about whether or not we're going to each other's charity golf tournament, how's business, how's the wife and family. You meet a lot of people around the league and you become friends.

PLAYBOY: What *would* provoke you to fight?

GRETZKY: Frustration, temper, like anybody else.

PLAYBOY: Would you throw the first punch?

GRETZKY: Yeah. I was in a fight where I threw the first punch. A player did something I thought wasn't called for. He slashed me pretty hard a couple of times, and I felt I was being taken advantage of. It was silly and stupid of me to fight. I mean, I'm not going to hurt anyone. Fortunately for me, he was a good enough guy, because he could have grabbed me and broken me in half. Instead, he held on to me.

PLAYBOY: Will an opposing player try to draw you into a fight so that you get a penalty and have to sit out part of the game?

GRETZKY: That happens a lot, but that's where it comes back to common sense and brains. A player having a good game must realize that getting into a fight does neither him nor the team any good. That's why people on a hockey team have different roles, and without naming names or pointing a finger at a guy, people on our team know when to step in and fight another player.

PLAYBOY: Every team has its fighters. On your team, isn't it Semenko's job to protect you?

GRETZKY: I would be wrong to say that it wasn't, but he's a policeman for the entire team, not just for Wayne Gretzky. He knows his responsibilities. He's not there to just take care of me. Coach Glen Sather doesn't say, "David, go out on the ice and *get* that guy." But situations on the ice do occur, and if David doesn't do his job, he's spoken to. You get into a physical game and that's where guys on the team like David and Mark Messier come through.

PLAYBOY: You say no one has really gotten hurt from fights. But what about such tactics as elbowing and high sticking?

GRETZKY: I guess those are the things most players get injured from. It's tough, but it's no different from a football game when players are kicking other players and stepping on guys' fingers. It's all part of winning. You can't blame a person for doing what he can to win a hockey game.

PLAYBOY: Who are the dirtiest players in hockey?

GRETZKY: I'd rather not say. There are some guys I would say I purposely stay away from because I don't trust them, but you'll find them in every sport. The toughest guys in the league, not necessarily the dirtiest, without doubt, are Beck, the Sutter brothers—all of them—Rob Ramage of St. Louis, Glen Cochrane of Philadelphia; and, when he wants to be, I think Potvin is the toughest.

PLAYBOY: How have you avoided getting hurt? You've been injured only twice.

GRETZKY: I've been lucky, I guess. The style that I play makes for few chances of injury. If you're moving around and see what's coming, you have a better chance.

PLAYBOY: Some say the reason you don't get hit hard is that you don't go into the corners, where most of the hard hits—elbows and high sticks—occur.

GRETZKY: No. That's where I get the most points, from the corners. The real reason I don't get hit so much is that I played lacrosse. In lacrosse, there's always cross-checking. You learn to roll with the checks and never get hit straight on. I don't put myself in a position where anyone can hit me straight on. That's the biggest thing. I learned when I was a kid that it's tougher to hit a moving target than a target that's standing still.

PLAYBOY: Let's talk a bit about the way you prepare for a game. What is the day of a game like for a professional hockey player?

GRETZKY: The night before a game, I'm always in bed before 10:30, 11 o'clock, religiously. I'm up around 8:30 in the morning, have a cup of tea and something light to eat, like a piece of toast, and read the newspaper. I'll go to the rink where we'll practice at 10:30, and after practice, at about 12:30, I eat. Then I spend the rest of the afternoon watching the soap operas. I go down to the rink at about four or five. When I get to the rink, I'll play Ping-Pong with a couple of the guys. Most of the guys show up about 5:30, except for about six of us. Ping-Pong loosens me up, relaxes me and takes my mind off what's going to happen.

PLAYBOY: When do you start thinking about the game itself?

GRETZKY: I don't actually sit down and think about what I will have to do in a game. I know whom I'm playing against. In the back of my mind, I know that I'm playing, say, the New York Islanders. I worry about getting myself ready, thinking about the way I'm feeling that day, if I'm feeling more energetic than the previous day or, if I have a nagging injury that day, wondering if it's going to bother me. Basically, I worry about myself and don't think about the other team.

PLAYBOY: Are you as superstitious as most hockey players?

GRETZKY: Oh, yeah, about my sweater's always being tucked into my pants. I'm superstitious in that I follow the same routines: how I get dressed, being the first on the ice at the start of the game and each period.

PLAYBOY: Every team in the NHL has at least one player who is superstitious about being the first on the ice. What happens when two of you have that superstition?

GRETZKY: It goes by seniority. I've been here for six years, and it would be pretty tough to knock me out of that spot. The other players may not admit to it, but it's even part of their superstition that I go out first. I don't know how that came about. I started doing it in the other league and kept doing it.

PLAYBOY: Where did the superstition about tucking your sweater into your pants come from?

GRETZKY: From the fact that I was five years old and playing with 10-year-olds; the team bought sweaters for 10-year-old kids and mine came down to my knees, so my dad tucked it in for me. I kept doing it.

PLAYBOY: Are you superstitious about your number—99?

GRETZKY: Yes. That came about because I had worn number nine as a kid, and when I got drafted in Junior "A," there was already somebody with a number nine, so the coach said I should wear two nines. When I went to Edmonton, Bill Goldsworthy wore nine, so I kept 99. One night, my sweater was stolen—I think it was in Pittsburgh—and the trainer was wondering what I was going to wear. He was ready to get on the telephone and have my dad fly down with a sweater from a previous year, because I wouldn't wear another number. But they found it.

PLAYBOY: What about black tape on the blade of your hockey stick? Is that because it makes it harder for the goalie to see the black puck or is it another superstition?

GRETZKY: Any goalie who can't see the puck because of black tape is in the wrong sport. Gordie Howe scored a lot of his 800 goals using white tape. I use black tape that has white baby powder on it. I find that when the puck is spinning, the black tape seems to catch it and stop it from spinning. As far as the baby powder goes, I use it because the stick will collect snow along the bottom and the baby powder stops it from sticking. I use it for that reason [*smiles*]—and also because it's a superstition.

PLAYBOY: You're the guy goalies fear most, but which goalies do *you* respect most?

GRETZKY: I respect the goalies on the bad teams, because they handle more shots. Who do I think is the best? Well, I guess the guy who's had the most success against us is Billy Smith of the Islanders. He's had a lot of success against other teams, too. There's no question that he's the best money goalie; but then again, he has a very good team in front of him. He won't get shots that other goalies will, because his defense men are better and smarter than those on a lot of other teams.

PLAYBOY: Great scorers have often claimed that they shoot without aiming. Do you aim or just shoot?

GRETZKY: Most shots I aim. *Most* shots. There are a lot of shots that you're basically hoping will go in. The thing that I remember is that 100 percent of the shots you *don't* take *don't* go in. A lot of times, you are in situations where you can aim the shot. I mean, you can put it in a general direction: top left corner, between the goalie's pads.

PLAYBOY: Is it more satisfying to put it between the goalie's legs?

GRETZKY: Nope. They don't ask you how at the end of the year; they ask how many.

PLAYBOY: How many of your hundreds of NHL goals do you remember?

GRETZKY: Pretty much all of them. I can tell you almost everything that happened in my most recent hockey game.

PLAYBOY: Can most players do that?

GRETZKY: A lot of the guys can. My father can tell you what happened from the first minute to the last. I'm not kidding. He has a photographic memory.

PLAYBOY: Could your father have been a professional hockey player?

GRETZKY: He was an average hockey player. He was too small to be a professional, but he understood the mechanics.

PLAYBOY: Could he have been a professional coach?

GRETZKY: First of all, I think you have to aspire to be one, and he never did. I believe he could have been a good hockey coach, but he would have been a better teacher for kids. We forget to teach the kids step one before we teach them step two. An example is coaches teaching 10-year-olds how to slap the puck when they should be teaching them how to wrist the puck. It's senseless. You never see a 10-year-old Russian slap the puck. For years, I played minor hockey, and the coaches used to holler, "Dump it in, dump it in!" What is that going to teach kids? Let them carry the puck and pass it around, then go in and score. That's a game. It's fun for kids. There's no money involved. Sure, I like to win, but you also have to do it properly. Ten-year-olds dumping it in will do nothing for them when they're 16. In order for us to be the best, we have to come together as a united country. We need a system that teaches everybody the same thing: how to stick-handle, how to shoot, the proper way to skate. Forget hitting and everything. When I was 10, the coach used to yell, "Take his head off!" But no one was going to hit me at that age. Other kids couldn't skate as well as I could.

PLAYBOY: Do you think two-year-olds should go to hockey school, as you did?

GRETZKY: I wouldn't want to send my two-year-old son to hockey school. But when I skated seven hours a day, I never considered it practice. It was fun. I never once said, "I'm going to skate for seven hours and practice as hard as I can." I guess that's why I have been successful. When I was four, five, six, I used to skate for seven hours or eight hours a day, easily. I used to be out there sometimes from eight in the morning until lunch hour, sleep for a couple of hours, then skate from four to six and then go back with my dad after dinner for a couple more hours. That's what I enjoyed doing. I had no desire to go to the movies or watch TV.

Even when I got older and other things came along, like dating, nothing except hockey ever entered my mind.

PLAYBOY: Did you practice in your backyard?

GRETZKY: Yeah. My dad would flood it with a garden hose, make a rink with two-by-fours along the sides and put up boards at the ends so when I shot the puck, it wouldn't go into the neighbor's yard. There were two nets and two night lights, one at each end.

PLAYBOY: What did you have in your backyard during the summer?

GRETZKY: A pitcher's mound. We lived about five houses from the corner, and when I was nine years old, there was a lot of dirt down there, and I would take a wheelbarrow, fill it up with dirt and build a pitcher's mound.

PLAYBOY: Whom did you pitch to?

GRETZKY: My father.

PLAYBOY: Your father spent a lot of time with you on athletics; didn't he have to work?

GRETZKY: Oh, yeah. He worked for the telephone company from eight to five Monday through Friday. But he didn't do anything else; he was devoted to his children. At that time, there were only my sister and myself. My little brother had just been born.

PLAYBOY: How did your dad devote himself to your sister?

GRETZKY: My sister was quite athletic, too, and that made it a lot easier for my father. There could have been a lot of problems between my sister and myself and my father and my mother. But she was involved in figure skating and track and field, so it worked out very well. I moved away from home when I was 14 and my brother Keith was seven years old, so my father had plenty of time for him. Now he's working with my youngest brother, who's 12.

PLAYBOY: How talented are your brothers?

GRETZKY: I have three brothers and, quite honestly, I think two of them will be professional hockey players.

PLAYBOY: Are they as good as you were at their ages?

GRETZKY: One is, the youngest.

PLAYBOY: Do you think it's hard to be a sibling of Wayne Gretzky's?

GRETZKY: Very hard, but as hard as it is, it still has some fringe benefits. I'd like to be a 16-year-old and have a brother who wins a car and gives it to me. I'm sure Keith is going through a lot of pressure being my brother as far as hockey goes for being compared with me; but then again, he may get that extra chance because he *is* my brother.

PLAYBOY: Getting back to the pitcher's mound, could you have been a major-league pitcher?

GRETZKY: I don't think so; but then again, I always had confidence that if I pursued it properly, I would have had a chance. I did well where I did play—in Ontario, which has the top leagues in Canada—but it's so hard to compare Canadian talent with American. I was offered a tryout by the Toronto Blue Jays when I was 17, but I didn't take it. I was playing what they call Junior Ball, which is what you play from the age of 16 to 20, and I'm glad I decided not to go.

PLAYBOY: Did you ever doubt that you would become a professional hockey player?

GRETZKY: Until the day I signed, I doubted I would be one. I was in high school, plugging away, getting my education. I was in the 11th grade when I was offered a contract with the Birmingham Bulls in the WHA I was 17; that was the first contract offer I had had. Then the New England Whalers offered me a contract. But when the Whalers found out that they had a chance of getting into the NHL, they phoned and said they couldn't sign me, because I was underage and it would ruin their chances. So Nelson Skalbania, who owned the Indianapolis Racers, signed me. After eight games, he sold me, Eddie Mio and Peter Driscoll for about $350,000, plus another $500,000 . . . oh, I can't remember. I do remember getting on an airplane and not knowing whether we were going to Edmonton or Winnipeg. The three of us were taking off in a private jet. We got into the air and somebody said, "The deal is done; we're going to Edmonton." But somebody hadn't paid the bill for the flight, and we were told that if it weren't paid, we wouldn't land. So Mio pulled out his Visa card and paid for the flight. He had a $600 limit and the guy took it.

PLAYBOY: What would you be doing now if you hadn't been signed?

GRETZKY: I have no idea. I was hoping to go to the university. That was my only goal.

PLAYBOY: Were you a good student?

GRETZKY: I had acceptable grades. I wasn't a brilliant student. I missed a lot of school because of hockey, but I still got by.

PLAYBOY: Did you ever fantasize about playing hockey in the Olympics?

GRETZKY: I think the Olympics are great and they're a good learning experience for some people and they promote peace in the world—but they're not the biggest thing in the world. More emphasis is put on the

Olympics in the U.S. than in Canada. Americans are brought up believing that if you win a gold medal in the Olympics, you'll be a national hero. In Canada, if you win an Olympic gold, it's nice, but you still have to raise your own money and pay for your travel and training. You're not going to make $200,000 to $300,000 a year, the way a guy from the U.S. who wins a gold medal will.

PLAYBOY: You were locally famous by the time you were 11. How did that affect you at school?

GRETZKY: I would get embarrassed. When I was 11 and 12, there would be a picture of me in a magazine and the teacher would hang it on the wall.

PLAYBOY: Were you very popular?

GRETZKY: No. I had friends, though. I knew all the girls, but I didn't socialize except on the athletic teams.

PLAYBOY: You said you moved away from home when you were 14. Are you sorry you left home when you were so young?

GRETZKY: It's the only thing I do regret. I would have loved to grow up with my family and my brothers. I missed a lot of years. That's why I feel so bitter when people tell me they want to send *their* kid away from home at the age of 12. Parents are thinking of themselves and not their kid. In my case, I didn't move away because of hockey. Everyone thought that's why I moved. Sure, I was going to play against tougher competition, but the reason I moved was so I could be just another person in a big city, where nobody would know who I was. I wanted to get away from the pressure of having to perform at a certain level every day. My parents felt that the pressure might get to me. As it turned out, it was the best thing that could have happened to my career.

PLAYBOY: Did your parents want you to finish high school and go on to college?

GRETZKY: When I turned pro at 17, they had to sign a contract to make it legal, and they made me promise that I'd live with a family and go to high school. I did that until I was sold to Edmonton.

PLAYBOY: Will you ever finish school?

GRETZKY: Four years ago, I would have said yeah. Now I don't think I need it. The only reason for me to go back to school would be to be able to say that I'd gotten my diploma.

PLAYBOY: Wouldn't you like to take some business courses?

GRETZKY: I would like to know more about business, but I feel I'm learning about it firsthand. In the past, the majority of players had to work at jobs in the off-season. Now they're making big money and they have to take care of their finances. That is your job in the summer. Players now have to take the time to learn about business. The category "dump jock" has been tossed out the window. Some guys, as in every profession, are more intelligent than others. Randy Gregg, on our team, is a doctor. I don't know if he's the most intelligent player in hockey, but he's doing well apart from hockey. I don't know a whole lot about business and I'll never say I am a businessman, but I am studying hard. I have some of my own stocks now that I follow.

PLAYBOY: What do you do with the money that you don't invest? Is it available to your family?

GRETZKY: All of it is. If my brothers want to go to college, I'd love to pay for them. I have X amount of dollars in the bank, and if my family asked for it, I'd give it to them.

PLAYBOY: Have they asked?

GRETZKY: No. I bought them a few acres of land two miles from where they live to build a house. They said they'd build one, but when I went away on a holiday and came back, they had already started building an addition to *their* house. I knew then that they would never build. Maybe I'll build a house there someday.

PLAYBOY: If you're in a waiting room and there's a choice between *Sports Illustrated* and *Business Week*—

GRETZKY: I'll pick up *Business Week*. I won't hesitate to do that. The biggest change in my life is my interest in business.

PLAYBOY: By the time you were 18, you were a millionaire. How were you prepared to deal with it?

GRETZKY: I guess the big thing, whether or not you have money when you're growing up, is to have to answer to only one person, yourself. As far as the money goes, I make tremendous money. I guess you don't know how much you make unless you spend the time counting it. Basically, it goes into the bank. I live not on a budget by any means but with guidelines. I'm fortunate in the sense that I have a nice car, a beautiful place, I can travel; but if I stop doing my job, I'll lose it all.

PLAYBOY: How much money per month do you live on?

GRETZKY: I live on about $1500 to $2000 pocket money, not counting bills. My condominium is paid off; I bought it for cash. Now, if I want to go out and buy a leather coat, I can do it. The great thing about the money that I have is that I've earned it myself; it's mine. I get advice from everybody, parents included, but there are times when I say, "Hey, I earned this money."

PLAYBOY: When you received your first big paycheck, what was the most expensive thing you bought?

GRETZKY: A 1979 silver Trans Am with a T roof, C.B., stereo. I bought it in the States when I was with Indianapolis, and when I got sold to Edmonton, I sold it, because I couldn't take it across the border.

PLAYBOY: How much money do you have in your pocket right now?

GRETZKY: I don't have a cent. I carry one credit card. I never carry cash. I just hate going to the bank. I hate lines and waiting. I'm patient in a lot of ways, but I'm impatient in a lot of other ways, such as standing around in airports, standing in line at the bank.

PLAYBOY: There are many people who work at harder, more meaningful jobs than playing hockey. Do you feel guilty because they earn a fraction of what you do?

GRETZKY: I think the greatest thing about living in North America is our freedom to do what we want to, and we all grow up having the same choices. What these people do is tremendous work. It's not rewarded the same way that ours is rewarded, yet their work is more important than our work. The only difference is that they don't get 18,000 people paying $20 a head to *see* them work.

I do my job to the best of my ability. I'm making good money and I'm entertaining. Then I look at somebody making $40,000,000 a year singing and entertaining people. How do you justify making that much? It's unfortunate that those people doing something more beneficial aren't making more money than entertainers. To the hockey players, it's work, a job and a responsibility to win the Stanley Cup, but to the fan watching the game, it's entertainment. People in Moose Jaw, Saskatchewan, don't care who wins the Stanley Cup as long as they're watching good hockey.

PLAYBOY: Do you feel you've paid your dues?

GRETZKY: Not like a lot of other people. There are a lot of players who work harder than Wayne Gretzky, who may be more dedicated than Gretzky, who haven't made it, who may still be on two-way contracts. But that doesn't mean that I didn't work hard and that I'm not dedicated. I've just been a little more fortunate. I feel I made pro on my own, all by myself, and I worked to get there.

PLAYBOY: Do athletes pay dues at all in the larger sense?

GRETZKY: Looking at it realistically, you play hockey from the age of 20 to 28, and that's it. The average hockey player today plays five years. Let's say you play eight. Let's say you make $100,000 a year. After eight years, you've made $800,000. Out of that, you pay your agent five percent, the government 40 to 50 percent, so over eight years, you've made only about $350,000. People say, "How can you not have any money left?" You've got to live. You have to have a car. You may have a family to support; you may have to buy a house. You've got to work after you retire from hockey. What is a hockey player going to do? A lot of guys have nothing to fall back on.

PLAYBOY: The classic example of that is Derek Sanderson, who during the late sixties, early seventies had the potential to be a huge hockey superstar but ended up blowing $2,000,000, alcoholic and with the aid of crutches, hardly able to work. Do you keep him in mind to keep yourself honest?

GRETZKY: He's been through a lot of bad times, and we don't like to use him as an example. We don't like to keep bringing his name up publicly. I'm sure he's depressed enough over what has happened. Sanderson is used as an example by every hockey coach. I've never been around other hockey teams or their dressing rooms, but I'll bet he is used all the time by other managers: "Don't do drugs! You'll end up like Derek Sanderson!" I feel sorry for Sanderson, but I don't feel sorry for him. There are more than enough people who went out of their way to help him—teammates, coaches, friends. I know a lot of the people who tried to help.

PLAYBOY: You said earlier that you couldn't blame a player for doing what he had to do to win a game. What if a player took an undetectable drug that helped him play better?

GRETZKY: That could be the best question I've ever been asked. [*Pause*] I think that in the long run, it's not going to help the team. The proven history of drugs is that they affect you in a way that is negative, not positive. . . .

PLAYBOY: That's over the long run. What about the short run— one game?

GRETZKY: I don't know. It's a tough question. The individual will be hurt in the long run. Personally, I would be opposed to it, but what are you going to say to a guy who does a drug and scores two goals? The big thing, I guess, is that drugs are illegal.

PLAYBOY: Do fans offer you drugs?

GRETZKY: Not fans but people. "Hey, Gretzky, you want to buy drugs?" I've heard that since I was 12. It's everywhere, not just in sports. One good thing about hockey is that they've cracked the whip on it. But I don't think there's any hockey player doing drugs while he plays. One thing we have that no other sport has is the art of skating. I have a hard enough time skating. I can't *imagine* how a guy could skate when he's doing drugs.

PLAYBOY: You've been exposed to a lot of temptations since you were a kid; have you ever wished you could be less disciplined, live a more carefree life?

GRETZKY: Not at all. I don't stop doing the things I want to do because I'm in the public eye. I'm Wayne Gretzky, the individual, the one person I have to answer to when I get up in the morning, when I go to practice, go to dinner. The question is whether or not I did the right thing, and all I have to say to myself is yes.

PLAYBOY: How does your image of yourself differ from the media's?

GRETZKY: I don't think there's much difference. The biggest problem was last season, after we beat New Jersey 13 to 4 and I said that thing about New Jersey's being a Mickey Mouse operation. That was a mistake, to criticize another organization. There's a difference between what Wayne Gretzky thinks and what he says. Ordinarily, I would have said what I did only to friends. Two years ago, I wouldn't have said it to the media; last year, I did.

PLAYBOY: What do you do to bust loose?

GRETZKY: I go to Las Vegas for a couple of days. I'm not a big gambler, but I go down once a year with a thousand dollars and say, "If I lose it, I lose it." I've been lucky. The most I've ever won is $1000. It's nice for me to sit at the table, which I do from eight at night to four or five in the morning. Then I go to sleep, get up, lie by the pool, eat and do the same thing, and I love it. It's one of the few places you can go and nobody cares. The dealer may know who you are, but everybody else is gambling.

PLAYBOY: We know what you can do. What *can't* you do?

GRETZKY: I can't sing and I can't dance. I am the worst dancer you'll ever meet. I have no musical intelligence, no feel for it.

PLAYBOY: What was the last record you bought?

GRETZKY: The last record I bought, which must have been three years ago, was by Jack Green, on the suggestion of a friend. I also bought a Cliff Richard record. But I really can't spend a lot of time listening to music.

PLAYBOY: What else can't you do?

GRETZKY: Fly; I'm not comfortable in planes. A couple of years ago, I went to a hypnotist. It worked for five or six months, and then I started getting progressively worse. I guess my big fear is of putting my entire life in the hands of pilots. I like to be in control all the time.

Speed also bothers me. I've owned a Ferrari for four years, and I've never had a speeding ticket in my life. Everyone I lend the car to gets a speeding ticket. People get the feeling that they have to go fast in this car. I keep it in second gear and chug along. I have to lend it to friends to have them clean the carbon out.

PLAYBOY: Don't you have *any* vices?

GRETZKY: Oh, yeah, I'm human. I do have a bad habit of swearing on the ice. I forget that there are people around the rink. It's a problem. I hope I'm heading in a direction where I can correct it, but I don't know if I will be able to.

PLAYBOY: Who are you cursing out—yourself? The refs?

GRETZKY: Everybody. Everybody but my teammates.

PLAYBOY: Since all you've ever done in life is play hockey, do you wish you were more well rounded?

GRETZKY: I think I've learned a lot of things through hockey—about the people I've met and the different fields they're in, the places I've been, the cities I've seen, the parties I've been to. I think I *am* a more well-rounded person because of hockey.

PLAYBOY: You said you watch soap operas to relax before a game. Do you know what's going on in all the soap operas to date?

GRETZKY: Oh, yeah. I watch *All My Children, One Life to Live, General Hospital, The Young and the Restless*. I can tell you what's going on in all of them.

PLAYBOY: Haven't you appeared on *The Young and the Restless*?

GRETZKY: Yes. I was in Las Vegas last summer at an awards ceremony, and a lady there who was part of the ceremony asked me if I would like to be on and I said, "Sure." I played a bad guy.

PLAYBOY: How did you prepare for your role?

GRETZKY: I talked with Ed Marinaro [of *Hill Street Blues*]. I had only five lines. I had no problem remembering them, but it was a difficult experience for me. I was shaken, to be honest. It was the first time I had ever acted. I just knew that people's expectations would be so high and that whether I did a good job or a bad one, I was going to be criticized. But I also knew that if I had read the papers, they would have said that I would never be a pro hockey player, that I was too small. I knew I would be criticized, but you can't believe everything you read.

PLAYBOY: Would you like to act seriously?

GRETZKY: No. I have a curiosity about acting, you might say, but I don't lie in bed at night thinking that I will be an actor or that I want to be an actor. On the other hand, it would be nice if there were something for me to step into when I was done with hockey.

PLAYBOY: You say you know what's going on in the soaps; do you know what's going on in Beirut?

GRETZKY: Yep.

PLAYBOY: Nicaragua?

GRETZKY: No, not so much Central America. I know that the stock market's falling out. I know exactly where we're at on nuclear power, and that scares me. I watch the news every night that I can. I know what's going on in Poland, of course.

PLAYBOY: Your ancestry is Polish; how Polish do you feel?

GRETZKY: Very. I understand Polish. My grandmother has relatives who are still there.

PLAYBOY: Do you follow fashion?

GRETZKY: Yes. I love clothes. I read the fashion sections in *Playboy*; all the guys do. That's basic reading around here.

PLAYBOY: What kind of clothes do you like?

GRETZKY: I'm flexible. If something looks nice, I'll wear it, whether it's jeans or leather pants, sweaters or sweatshirts.

PLAYBOY: Do you like loose- or tight-fitting clothes?

GRETZKY: Very loose stuff. When I travel, I like to feel comfortable.

PLAYBOY: Do you notice what other guys wear?

GRETZKY: Oh, yeah. I used to watch Tony Geary in *General Hospital*. He's the same height and has the same kind of build and has blond hair, like me. I had never worn green before I watched that show. I used to hate green.

PLAYBOY: Since we're talking about light topics, here's a light exercise: How do you think your hockey skills would translate to other fields? With your skills, what sort of statesman—or soldier or lover—do you think Wayne Gretzky would make?

GRETZKY: I think that as a statesman, I'd be offensive. As a soldier, I'd be more defensive; I'd be worried about my life and I'd be watching every minute. And as a lover . . . I'd probably be defensive. I'm a very defensive person as far as letting people into my life.

PLAYBOY: Are the women who are able to break through your defenses the ones you end up with?

GRETZKY: No, definitely not. I like to be the one who opens the conversation. I'm defensive when girls come up and get too pushy with me.

PLAYBOY: Is that what happens when you go to parties?

GRETZKY: One of the things that enable me to live the way that I have is that I'm not a very private person. Privacy is not a big thing on my list. If I went to a party with 40 people and I knew 10 or 12 people there, I'd get right into the middle. The only time I like to be alone is in the afternoon before a game. That's when I watch the soaps.

PLAYBOY: So no ambitions toward being a sex symbol in the Joe Namath tradition?

GRETZKY: That's not a void I need to fill. There are a lot of guys around who would do better at being a sex symbol than Wayne Gretzky.

PLAYBOY: How many women have been in your life?

GRETZKY: Vickie Moss was my first girlfriend. I never dated anyone else.

PLAYBOY: How did you meet?

GRETZKY: [Teammate] Kevin Lowe and I were at a nightclub in Edmonton, and she was singing. I was 18 years old. A friend of mine whom she knew introduced us between one of her sets. I asked her if she'd like to have a drink. She sat down and hasn't left since. The thing about her that clicked in my mind was that she knew *nothing* about hockey. My defenses went right down. She does, however, have nine brothers who are big sports fans. She told them she was dating some hockey player. Then, one day, I showed up on their doorstep and they all panicked. [*Laughs*] So we weren't exactly high school sweethearts but the closest thing to it.

PLAYBOY: Wouldn't it be difficult being Mrs. Wayne Gretzky?

GRETZKY: It would be harder than being Wayne Gretzky. It's tougher for her to get her own identity. She does have her own identity with the people who know her, but most people are asking her, "How's Wayne's shoulder?" "Isn't it great that he set a record?" "That was a great goal he got last night!" Being Mrs. Wayne Gretzky is a lot tougher.

PLAYBOY: Will you be getting married?

GRETZKY: I don't know. I've thought about it. If I get married, I'm going to start a family. She's just starting her career, traveling down South and going to Japan to cut an album, and I wouldn't want to interfere.

PLAYBOY: Do you live together?

GRETZKY: No. She does a lot of traveling in her career, and I'm gone an awful lot, so we don't. We do manage to see a lot of each other. She gives me room for my career and I give her room for her career, and that's why we have a great relationship. It's as simple as that.

PLAYBOY: All right, out there on the ice: Besides career goals and assists, what records are left for you to break that aren't your own?

GRETZKY: Mike Bossy can say, "This year I want to get 50 goals in 50 games"—and do it. I can't. I have doubts about myself, and if I don't accomplish the feat I set for myself, it might really disappoint me. Bossy is a strong enough person that he said it and did it and that was it. I admire him for that. I admire guys like Trottier, Potvin, Bossy, guys who've played six, seven years and maintain the same level each year. That's the only goal I set for myself, to be a *consistent* athlete. That separates the superstars from the stars.

ALLEN IVERSON

*A candid conversation with the
NBA's dervish MVP about life in
the hood, his tattoo addiction, his
battles with the press and learning to love Larry Brown*

When Allen Iverson was named most valuable player of the National
Basketball Association last season and subsequently led the Philadelphia 76ers to the NBA Finals against the mighty Los Angeles Lakers,
his turbulent career suddenly took on an air of redemption. Five years
earlier, the six-foot guard had exploded onto the NBA scene, just
three years removed from a jail sentence on a "maiming by mob"
charge that would later be overturned. He was viewed as a threat
to the establishment—an establishment that had embraced the non-
threatening image of Michael Jordan.

Iverson was the anti-Jordan. He quickly sparked two in-your-
face style trends that transcended the insular world of professional
sports: He began to adorn himself with tattoos, and he wore his hair
in cornrows, one of the first athletes to adopt a style already fashionable among rappers. While a prodigy on the basketball court, his
breathtakingly quick game was overshadowed by a series of off-court
controversies. There were his friends from back home who were arrested for drug dealing while driving his car. There was the night in
1997 when he was charged with carrying a concealed weapon and
possession of marijuana. There were the rebellious run-ins with his
traditionalist coach, Larry Brown, and a controversy sparked by the
promotion of a rap CD he'd cut. His lyrics offended gay and women's
groups, and he subsequently shelved the CD's release.

After the CD imbroglio in the fall of 2000, a Philadelphia colum-
nist went so far as to call Iverson "nothing but a thug with money."
But then something happened. His tempestuous relationship with

Brown achieved a sort of détente, and his team jumped out to a 10–0 start and went on to post the best record in the NBA's Eastern Conference. Suddenly, Iverson was being seen for what he was on the court: the littlest player with the biggest heart, a fiery competitor who willed a perpetually undermanned team to victory after victory. Those who had criticized him embraced him and began to see past the macho pose and swaggering street persona. For his part, Iverson didn't view his story as one of redemption so much as vindication of his hip-hop-inspired creed to "keep it real."

Iverson was born on June 7, 1975 in Hampton, Virginia to his single 15-year-old mother, Ann. His biological father, with whom he has no contact, is in jail. The man who raised him, Michael Freeman, has spent much of the past 10 years in and out of correctional facilities. These days, Ann can be seen courtside at Sixers games, wearing an Iverson jersey and holding aloft a sign that reads "That's My Boy!" Growing up, Iverson says, Ann was his one and only role model, someone who "did what she had to do to put food on the table."

It was on the playgrounds of Hampton that Iverson's famed crossover dribble had its roots. The basketball court and football field (Iverson was an all-state high school quarterback) were escapes from a perilous world where chalk outlines and yellow police tape were a common sight, and from a home that often would have no plumbing or electricity. As a senior in high school, Iverson was charged with taking part in a racially motivated brawl. Despite having no record, he was tried as an adult and sentenced to five years in jail. Former Virginia governor Douglas Wilder granted him clemency and the conviction was later overturned for lack of evidence, but Iverson still feels the effects of four months of incarceration. "It made him harder," says his mother. It was she who approached then Georgetown coach John Thompson and implored him to help her son.

Once Iverson was released, he starred for two seasons under Thompson, who was demanding off the court and indulgent on it. Thompson was known for a predictable and heavily choreographed offense, but he let Iverson run wild. "Think about what's happened in that child's life," Thompson said at the time, in response to those who were surprised by his tolerance of Iverson's freewheeling style of play. "The last thing he needs is structure. He needs to be free as a bird. He needs to fly."

In two seasons under Thompson, Iverson averaged more than

20 points per game and started to develop his crossover dribble, an in-your-face move that has done for ballhandling what Jordan and Julius Erving did for the slam dunk: turn it into a weapon of intimidation. Iverson led Georgetown to within a game of the Final Four as a sophomore, just before making himself eligible for the 1996 NBA draft. The 76ers chose him with the first overall pick, and Iverson went on to average over 23 points per game and earned Rookie of the Year honors.

But Iverson's entry into the pro ranks was stormy. On the court, his selflessness was questioned after he scored an NBA record 40 or more points in five consecutive games—and his team lost each and every one. Off the court, his friends were widely dismissed as his "posse," and he seemed to become sullen and uncommunicative. Even today, Iverson is distrustful of those outside his inner circle, and he rarely grants in-depth interviews.

Playboy sent Larry Platt, editor-at-large at *Philadelphia* Magazine and the author of 1999's *Keepin' It Real: A Turbulent Season at the Crossroads With the NBA,* on the road with Iverson for a series of conversations. He found a defiant yet introspective superstar still intent on remaining true to those who have been true to him. Platt reports: "People don't live their lives by moral codes anymore—but Iverson does. He has his code branded on his neck, where he wears a tattoo of the Chinese symbol for loyalty.

"I found a newly wedded Iverson still grieving over the October murder of one of his best friends. Rashan "Rah" Langeford died after being shot seven times following an argument in his hometown of Newport News, Virginia. Iverson, who has seen more than his share of death on the streets of his youth, kept returning to the subject of the lost friend, getting choked up at one point. Our conversation began with Iverson's decision to emblazon on his skin his form of self-definition."

PLAYBOY: People are curious about you, maybe because you've been so inaccessible to the media. When we're asked what you're like, what should we tell them?

IVERSON: Tell them not to believe what they read or hear. Tell them to read my body. I wear my story every day, man.

PLAYBOY: What do your tattoos mean?

IVERSON: I got 21 of them. I got "Cru Thik" in four places—that's my crew, that's what we call ourselves, me and the guys I grew up with, the guys I'm loyal to. I got my kids' names, Tiaura and Deuce [Allen II], 'cause they're everything to me. They make me want to make better decisions every day. I got my wife's name, Tawanna, on my stomach. A set of praying hands between my grandma's initials—she died when I was real young—and my mom's initials, Ethel Ann Iverson. I put shit on my body that means something to me. Here, on my left shoulder, I got a cross of daggers knitted together that says "Only The Strong Survive," because that's the one true thing I've learned in this life. On the other arm, I got a soldier's head. I feel like my life has been a war and I'm a soldier in it. Here, on my left forearm, it says "NBN"—for "Newport Bad News." That's what we call our hometown of Newport News, Virginia, because a lot of bad shit happens there. On the other arm, I got the Chinese symbol for respect, because I feel that where I come from deserves respect—being from there, surviving from there and staying true to everybody back there. I got one that says "Fear No One," a screaming skull with a red line through it—'cause you'll never catch me looking scared. This one here, on my right forearm, used to be a grim reaper holding a basketball, 'cause that's who I am to other guards in this league. But I changed it to a panther after my friends teased me and said it looked like a damned flying monkey.

PLAYBOY: When you first came into the NBA, you had only two tattoos, "The Answer," your nickname, and a rendering of a bulldog, the Georgetown mascot. Then, during your rookie year, you got more tattoos and started braiding your hair. Was that in response to all the negative publicity you got that year, all the speculation that you were a thug and a hood?

IVERSON: Once I got my first tattoo I was addicted. It was stuff I really meant and really felt, and I just put it on my body. And then the NBA airbrushed my tattoos off the cover of some magazine, and that upset me. I have my mom's name on my body, my kids', my grandmother's who passed away. Things that mean something to me. And for that to happen, it was kind of tough. But they didn't look at the meaning of my tattoos—they just saw that they were tattoos, and they airbrushed them off. But they're a part of me.

PLAYBOY: Was that the kind of thing you were talking about at your MVP press conference last season, when you looked right at your boys standing in the back and said, "I did this my way." Did you mean you resisted the advice to, as you see it, sell out by consciously trying to "cross over"?

IVERSON: Exactly. People used to always tell me to wear a suit, look this way, look that way, cut my hair, stuff like that. But those things don't make you the person you are—the person inside does. I've never been any bad type of person—it's just that people didn't want to even try to understand me. They looked at the tattoos, the baggy clothes and the jewelry and judged me on all that. But, I mean, I was 20, 21, 22 years old, going through a phase in my life. I wanted to grow as a person, but having this talent, they expected me to act like I was 30 or 35 years old. I was in this learning process, and they were rushing me. I had to grow up fast, and when I made mistakes people acted like it was such a big thing. But I was young and I made mistakes. I still make mistakes. When I said I did it my way, I meant I was just being real to myself. I hadn't changed the type of person I am, I just got smarter. I made smarter decisions and tried to do what was right for Allen Iverson and his family.

PLAYBOY: The media take on you by the end of last season, though, was that you'd changed, you'd matured—

IVERSON: Nah, I'm just getting older. I mean, when you're 26 you're not the same as when you were 21. People find that hard to believe, and I don't know why. It happens automatically. You were probably in college at 21 and then five years later you're working at your newspaper and going to bed earlier.

PLAYBOY: Hell, we were frantically trying to stay in school so we'd have an excuse to still be immature—

IVERSON: [Laughs] Bet nobody was writing about how immature you were. It's funny, no one's saying they were wrong about me back then. They're saying I've changed. I ain't no saint all of a sudden. The saddest part is that it took winning for those people to even try to understand who I am.

PLAYBOY: So the next storyline is "He's changed, he's grown up"?

IVERSON: Yeah, yeah. It's like, "Let's write about that so we can sell some more papers," even though they don't know if I've changed, because they never tried to understand me five years ago.

PLAYBOY: Another example of that took place at the beginning of last season, with the promotional release of a single from your rap CD, which you've now decided not to release. On the first day of training camp, you told reporters you wouldn't talk about it, because you knew they weren't there to honestly try to understand rap music.

IVERSON: Man, they were there to judge me. I've gone through it with the media since I was 17, when I got thrown in jail. I'll never be able to understand the media, but I think I can put up with them, I can deal with them, I can accept anything they say about me or write about me, because they've said so many things. I've just got used to it and I try not to give them anything negative to write about me.

PLAYBOY: In last season's playoff series against Toronto, you dropped the first game at home and were in a tight game two. The whole season was basically on the line, and you came up with 54 points, including your team's final 19 points in the game's last eight minutes. Afterward you were asked where such a performance came from and you said just two words: "Life. Poverty." Can you elaborate on that?

IVERSON: It came from struggle. I struggled all my life. Even when things were good, they weren't that good. That all made me harder. And now I look at this as just a game. That's what it is, just a game. There are a lot more serious things going on in the world than basketball. But basketball has always been a time when I can get my mind off everything that's going on around me and concentrate for two hours on just this.

PLAYBOY: So basketball is actually a release for you?

IVERSON: Exactly. You just put that in perspective and know it's just a game. Win or lose, it's a game. Yeah, you want and try to win, but if you lose, you know when you look in the mirror that you gave the effort.

PLAYBOY: Was basketball always an escape for you?

IVERSON: Growing up was hard, man. We had busted plumbing, so there was sewage shit floating around our floors. Sometimes we had no lights, because it was a question of food or the light bill, and my mom wasn't about to let us go hungry. So I'd hit the playground morning, noon and night.

PLAYBOY: What about now? Your friend Rah was murdered in October, just after you had elbow surgery. Did not being able to play make that tougher to deal with?

IVERSON: That was the hardest thing. I couldn't even get on the court to try to take my mind off it for a couple of hours. It just stayed on my mind, and it still does, except when I'm on the court. I think about the good times we had, the things we went through. Most of all, I keep telling myself that he did his job with helping somebody—me. He helped me so much just by being a real friend and always telling me when he thought I was wrong. When he thought I was right, he stuck up for me. And I needed that in a friend, instead of a bunch of people telling me everything I want to hear. That's not going to help. But losing Rah has helped me realize a lot of other things that I wouldn't have paid attention to, so I use that as a positive.

PLAYBOY: What other things?

IVERSON: A lot of things dealing with my life and how I live. How I go through life. The responsibility. Rah had three kids, you know? And now I have to take care of those kids. So when I leave this place and God calls me, I want my wife and my kids and my mother and my sisters to be taken care of. I want there to be enough there for all those kids to go to college and do something with their lives. That's what I'm concentrating on every day. How to be the best father, best husband, best teammate, best son, best cousin, best brother I can.

PLAYBOY: You really looked up to Rah as a rapper, didn't you?

IVERSON: Him and E [Iverson's friend Eric Jackson], they were the best I ever heard. Now it's important for E to do his rap thing, because we know Rah would have wanted him to go ahead. It was hard for me not to do the rap thing, because I know how much Rah wanted it. We used to talk about it when we were younger, how if one of us got the opportunity to get enough money, we'd start our own record company. So once I could do it for them, I didn't want them going out there in the music world and getting jerked around. I was like, "Let's do this ourselves." But once I had a deal and everything went down, the controversy was just too much. People took it the wrong way. It's like when you see Bruce Willis or Samuel L. Jackson in a movie and they got guns and they're shooting people. It's just an art form. I'm not that guy rapping. I'm just talking smack. It's like a movie. You know Bruce Willis don't do the things he do in the movies, right? It's just a movie. Everyone took it all out of proportion and I got so much flack about it, and I don't think I would have if I wasn't a basketball player.

PLAYBOY: Your raps were tame compared with, say, Eminem's.

IVERSON: I don't knock Eminem. I mean, he's trying to feed himself and his family and he's expressing himself. You don't know what that guy's been through in his life, and that's a talent he was given. God gave him that talent. And he's just using it to the best of his ability. I don't think he's out there shooting anybody or provoking violence or anything like that. He's trying to sell records. My hat's off to anybody trying to do something positive with their life instead of being out there getting in trouble. But it was tough not being able to do that rap thing.

PLAYBOY: You can revisit it at some point, though, right?

IVERSON: Nah, I want to leave that chapter in my life because the people in the media took the fun out of it. It used to be fun. I remember doing it when I was in high school, elementary school, just standing on the corner, rapping. Talking trash, you know. I just wanted to give my friends the opportunity to realize their dream. But it didn't fit right with people—all these people were getting a negative vibe from it—so then it didn't fit right with me. I didn't want people drilling into kids' heads that I was some negative bad guy who walks around looking for trouble. So rather than paint that picture of me, I'll leave it alone and won't do it again. I never wanted to do it for money, I just wanted to do it because it was special to me.

PLAYBOY: Actually, your aborted rap CD would not have been the first time you laid down some tracks. You appeared on Mase's "Pay Per View." By the way, Mase gave up the rap game to become a preacher. Is that conversion for real?

IVERSON: [*Smiling*] Must be, he don't go to titty bars no more.

PLAYBOY: Mase was quite a high school ballplayer in New York, too.

IVERSON: Yeah, he talked that shit. I played against him one time. He was just running his mouth a whole lot. I played him one-on-one for $10,000. I told him we were going to play to 20, I'd give him 19 and the ball five times in a row. Then I was gonna score 20 unanswered. So we started playing, and once I stopped him five times in a row, he started beating me up, fouling me every time. I tied it at 19 and he knew he was in trouble, because I shot a jumper and missed and he grabbed the rebound and put it back in. He didn't take it back or nothing. And then he ran off the court, jumping around like he won. Hell if I was about to pay him [*laughing*].

PLAYBOY: Rappers like Master P, Dr. Dre and Puffy are not only the product, they're also the entrepreneur behind the product. A couple of years ago you fired David Falk as your agent, saying you "felt like the prey." Was that act influenced by the examples of hip-hoppers who were calling the shots in their own careers?

IVERSON: Definitely—I just wanted to be in charge of my own shit. I didn't need an agent anymore, with the new NBA rules and everything. I felt all I needed was a lawyer. I would never say anything bad about David Falk, I would never assassinate his character. Anything we went through was because I put myself in that predicament. I was young and came out of college early into a world of hyenas. I didn't know as much about the business as I know now, or as much as I will know, but I'm learning. I always played like a professional on the basketball court, but I didn't handle myself like a professional. And I'm not going to be tough on myself and feel like I should have been able to do that. I was so young. I had to learn, and I'm happy with my progress and where I'm at right now as a person.

PLAYBOY: We were talking earlier about your struggles growing up. Is it true that when you were 16, eight of your friends were murdered?

IVERSON: Yeah, that was the summer I met Rah. I mean, they were guys in the neighborhood. I call them friends, because I saw them every day. I had dealings with them, at the playground, whatever. It was wild, that summer. Tony Clark was one of them. He was my best friend. He was a real cool guy, about six years older than me, who looked out for me on the streets. He taught me a lot of things about how to survive. And his girlfriend killed him. Stabbed him. There were a lot of other guys dying that summer in the neighborhood. So my mom said once the school season started, she didn't want me back out in that part of Newport News. My father was living out there. So that's why I was out there, staying with him. She got herself back on her feet and I went and stayed with Gary Moore, who was my football coach when I was a kid. Now he's my personal assistant.

PLAYBOY: Were you scared growing up in that environment?

IVERSON: It was just life, man. You didn't have time to be scared. It's hard to think when you're scared. I'd rather be smart. I've never been scared of anything, being where I'm from, the things I've seen and been through.

PLAYBOY: So that's why there's no pressure in a basketball game?

IVERSON: After all the shit I've seen, you think I'll feel pressure from a game? Seeing how life can end at any second makes me play so hard. I know to play every play like it's my last. Who knows if you'll be around for the next play—you know what I'm saying?

PLAYBOY: You once said God was with you in that jail cell and that you always had faith you'd get out and get back on the road to realizing your hoops dream. Where did you get that faith?

IVERSON: It comes from my grandmom and my mom. They were church-going people. Even now, before games, my mom sprinkles holy water on my face and blesses me. They helped me realize it was all because of God that anything positive was happening to me. And the negative things as well. But I never thought He'd put anything on me I couldn't handle. I always just trust in Him and believe in Him. I know there's somebody that wakes me up every morning, I know there's somebody that gave me this talent. A lot of guys around here play basketball, but none of them play it at this level and none of them get a chance to see what I've seen in my life. That's what makes me feel good about the friendship I had with Rah. He saw things he might have never seen, he been to places and he experienced things. I know he had fun, because he was a happy-go-lucky guy. And in one night, all that ended. But I know I'll see him again. We'll have fun like we always had. I just miss laughing with him. I even miss arguing with him, and me and him used to argue damn near every day. That's because we cared about each other.

PLAYBOY: Michael Jordan was cut from his high school team. Julius Erving once said that the first time he picked up a basketball he "couldn't play worth a lick." Was it the same for you, or were you a prodigy from day one?

IVERSON: I remember coming home one day when I was eight years old, and my mom said, "Get ready, you going to basketball practice." And I said, "What? Basketball?" I was crying, saying, "I don't want to play basketball. Basketball's for punks. I don't play basketball, I'm a football player." And she was like, "Well, you're getting out of here and you're going to practice." Man, I cried all the way out the door. And then when I got there, I seen so many people from my football team. I caught on fast, just watching other guys. I seen what a layup was, what a jumper was. And, man, ever since that day, I've been playing basketball. I fell in love with it. Every team I played on, I was the best player, from that day on.

PLAYBOY: How do you explain that?

IVERSON: That's God, man—there's no question about it. And I was strictly a football player before that day. I thought basketball was soft.

PLAYBOY: Do you still think that?

IVERSON: Hell, no! [*Laughs*] Hell, no. Look at me, man [*pointing to bulky wrap around his surgically repaired elbow*].

PLAYBOY: Jordan is like a craftsman, known for his work ethic. But your talent seems more creatively inspired. Do you consider yourself more of an artist than a laborer?

IVERSON: Yeah, I'm always creating something. If I'm not creating on the court, I'm coming up with lyrics or I'm drawing cartoons. I'm a caricaturist. I draw and draw and draw, so when my basketball career is over I'll have all this artwork and I'll do something with it. I spend a lot of my time drawing caricatures of my teammates and my family. See, when I play my last game, that's it, I'm done. There will be no comebacks for me. If my daughter or son want to play the game, I'll help them out. After I leave the game, that's when I'm going to concentrate on developing myself as an artist.

PLAYBOY: What's life like at the Iverson household these days?

IVERSON: Man, I got the greatest household. I got the greatest wife, Tawanna. I love her. She's helped me so much, more than you can imagine. Just helping me become the person I am—and the player. Being there for me all the time. She's a great mother, she's a great wife. Words can't even explain how I feel about her. I've been with her 10 years. I met her in high school, 10th grade.

PLAYBOY: What's a typical night like?

IVERSON: Just watching VCR movies.

PLAYBOY: Kids climbing all over you?

IVERSON: Nah, it's, "Y'all gotta get out of here. Go in your own room, we're watching a movie right now." I ain't going to lie to you, there's a whole lot of noise in my house. All these kids do is run around, make noise, tear up the house. Tiaura puts Tawanna through hell when I'm not around. I don't even have to say nothing to her. I just look at her—she knows the look I give her, the "you better calm your ass down" look. But that's the best part of this life, my wife and kids. Like right now, I'm on a long road trip, eight days. To go back home to my family makes me feel good, regardless. If we're playing out in Los Angeles and lose, we have to take that long flight back to Philly, but once you get there, it's all over. You don't even think about the game no more. The game is secondary.

PLAYBOY: As recently as the summer of 2000, it looked like you and coach Larry Brown couldn't co-exist. Your team tried to trade you. In fact, they did, but your then-teammate Matt Geiger nixed the deal by refusing to waive some contract provisions. How did that affect you?

IVERSON: That was a tough learning experience. It showed that people on teams always talk about being family, but this is really a business and they can give up on you. I been through hell in this organization, coming from winning only 22 games, then 31 games, and the way the media treated me and my friends at first. And then gradually I became better and better, and we started to win. I felt, after all that, this was how I was going to be treated? You gonna send me to a worse situation than this one? I'm winning now, and now you're sending me to a loser? I felt bad about that, but I had to look at myself, too. That was the maturing I had done, understanding that many of the things that were going on I had a lot of control over. And I wasn't doing my part.

PLAYBOY: What do you mean?

IVERSON: I had to make some changes, but that didn't mean I had to sell out who I am—basically, I just had to get to practice on time. That was the big problem. You never could question anything about my basketball skills. But Coach and myself, we just didn't communicate. We would have a meeting and we would talk and it would be like, "OK, all right, cool." And then the shit would keep on happening. We didn't try to understand each other.

I knew he wanted to win and I knew he knew I wanted to win, but we didn't try to build that best-player-and-best-coach-in-the-world relationship, like Magic had with Pat Riley and Michael had with Phil Jackson. Now I tell him that's the kind of relationship I want with him. Now I look at him and I know he's the best coach in the world. I watch things other coaches do and I've been in wars with this guy and this guy's taken us from the bottom to the top. I know what type of guy he is.

PLAYBOY: Growing up, did you think you'd ever get so close to a 61-year-old Jewish white man?

IVERSON: Aw, man, you kidding? I understand him so much now. I know who he is and vice versa. I don't have nothing to hide from him and he don't have nothing to hide from me. We can talk to each other now. Before, it was like he'd talk to me and I could just tell that he thought I was like, "Man, get out of my face," when I was really paying attention to him. He'd be like, "Why are you looking like that?" I'd be like, "What are you talking about? I'm listening to you. I'm right here with you. I don't want to fight you today." We just had to get to know each other on a better level. Once that happened, the sky was the limit. Honestly, I got a lot of respect for the guy. I love that guy. I love who he is and what he stands for. I can't believe we used to bump heads like we did, but if it got us to where we're at right now, I'm glad we went through all of it.

PLAYBOY: We want to ask you about your game. How do you do it?

IVERSON: [*Pounds chest*] This is all I got. All heart.

PLAYBOY: How do you not get your shot blocked? You're barely six feet tall.

IVERSON: I know how short I am. And I know when I go up against a guy, I have to put it up higher than a regular-sized guy. But I try not to think about what I do out there. I just do it, you know what I'm saying?

PLAYBOY: After all you've been through, do you have a tough time trusting people?

IVERSON: It's hard, man. I don't trust too many people. Just from experience, from going through different things. Just from getting my heart broken. Like different reporters. I'm looking at you and I'm thinking, Here's the coolest reporter in the world. Because you seem that way. You're not talking about the same thing, you've got different questions. It's interesting to me. And then the next day, the article comes out and it's a bunch of bullshit. I just look at it like everybody's trying to make some money, everybody has to try and sell—and negativity sells. It was tough, seeing that a guy would sit down and talk to me and we'd have a great talk, and then the article would be terrible.

And you know, guys come around because they want to hang out with me and just be around me, or they got their eye out for whatever being around me can bring. It's tough. I'd rather just be around the people I know love me and I care about and try and keep it like that. As far as everybody else, wassup, wassup—you know?

PLAYBOY: Do you sense that a lot of the people who say they care about you wouldn't if you weren't a ballplayer?

IVERSON: That's just real life, man. This lifestyle is so unbelievably hard. People think it's all peaches and cream, but it's not. It's not fair when you can't go to a restaurant with your kids and eat without being bothered. It's not right for people to chase your car down, trying to get an autograph.

PLAYBOY: And unlike a lot of other guys, you don't seem that into the whole celebrity thing. You don't do a lot of endorsements, for example. Is it just that you'd rather play ball, hang out with your friends and be left alone?

IVERSON: Yeah, that's all I ever wanted to do, just hang out. But that part of my life has disappeared, because you see where it's headed. A lot of times, I'll go out, and at the end of the night somebody will be fighting, somebody can get shot.

PLAYBOY: Is this what you meant when you said you've learned some things from Rah's death? That going out can get dangerous?

IVERSON: Yeah, and I'm not even talking about myself getting in fights, or whatever. I'm talking about just being around my peers. It's getting old, going out and all that. I'd rather be in a room with my teammates, playing cards. Or at home with my wife, watching a movie. This life is so hard, and I never knew it was going to be. Everybody is watching every move you make. As soon as you make that one mistake, *boom!* People look at you like you ain't even human, like you need to be caged up or something. In actuality it's a mistake you've probably made a dozen times, or someone in your family has probably made. But you don't hear about those people making mistakes. You just hear about us. The media talk so good about us, and then once they get a chance to talk bad about us, that's when they take those shots.

I always think God is going to look out for me, but I also think he's going to look out for the people who throw dirt. I don't wish nothing bad on anybody at all. I ain't never been a guy to assassinate anybody's character. How can I feel bad about somebody doing it to me if I run around doing the same thing? I'd rather die the way I am, like this, being true to people. I don't want to go around assassinating people's character, because then I'm the media.

PLAYBOY: For your MVP press conference, you wore a black T-shirt that said "Newport News Hood Check" and listed on the back the toughest neighborhoods from back home. You said you wanted the guys back there to see you were thinking of them. How important is it to you to represent your hometown?

IVERSON: It's everything, man. I like paying props to where I come from. I ain't going to forget where I came from. I dress like the people of my time. I'm a skinny guy, so I like baggy clothes. And I like Timberlands. I like jewelry. That's what helps kids, where I'm from and from all over the world. They see that I'm older than them, but I'm just like them. I come from where they come from. I'm living proof that you can do something positive with your life. Whatever you want to be, anything. You want to be a doctor? A lawyer? An athlete? You can do anything you want to do. But it's gonna take something. You have to give something to get something.

People always used to tell Gary Moore, "Man, AI's got it easy." And he always used to tell them, "Do you know that guy has to wake up every morning and run up and down that court for three hours? You think that's easy?" Yeah, I love to play basketball, but I don't like getting up every morning and running around and going to this place and that place. I mean, I don't want to do that all the time. But I do have a job. My job is hard because I have to be focused and play as hard as I can, with the whole world watching me.

PLAYBOY: That reminds us: You've been walking around singing that Tupac Shakur song, "All Eyez on Me."

IVERSON: Yeah, it's always like that, all eyes on me. But I accept it and I know who I am and I know God put me on this earth to do something special—and I'm not talking about playing basketball. I'm going to do something special that will help a lot of people. I want to build a hospital.

I told my mom when I was little, that's what I wanted to do. A hospital for my people. If not that, I'll do something to help young inner-city kids—and that's besides the softball charity game I do back home. I want to do something to help other people not as fortunate as I am.

PLAYBOY: Yet, whenever you have done something charitable, you've always insisted it not be publicized. Why?

IVERSON: I'm not shouting, trying to show people I do things with kids. I'd be happy if every time I went to a hospital to visit the kids, there'd be no media there. It makes it look like the only reason I'm doing this is for the media. Me and my teammates care about kids, seeing sick kids who will probably never be able to come to a ball game. But I don't need media attention for that. I don't think it's fair to go see a sick kid and then the kid has to look into the cameras and have that whole circus around him.

PLAYBOY: You are always telling kids, "Be strong." What message are you trying to get across to them?

IVERSON: To fight, man. This life is hard, and you just have to fight for everything. That's what I did. I even got incarcerated. Then I got out of jail and kept fighting. I was able to get back to where I wanted to be. And I was incarcerated for something I didn't do. I could have easily been bitter and stayed out of Hampton and never did anything for that community. But I didn't. I was the bigger man in that situation, and it meant something to me to do that. For what y'all did to me, I'm coming right back to the same place and I'm going to raise some money for the boys' and girls' clubs. I'm going to do something for these kids and this community, whether you like it or not.

PLAYBOY: [Former Georgetown] Coach John Thompson said that he never once heard you complain about your time in prison. By all accounts, you were a victim. How was it that you didn't act like one, that you didn't complain?

IVERSON: Complain for what? The minister at Rah's funeral said to look at your life as a book and stop wasting pages complaining, worrying and gossiping. That's some deep shit right there.

PLAYBOY: But you knew this at 17?

IVERSON: Man, I knew how to survive, that's it. I had a whole lot of faults, and I did some things wrong, but I tried to never make the same mistake twice. And I just tried to get better. Man, I'm human. That's what makes me feel good about myself. I realize that I'm not any better than you. It's hard enough, man. There are people flying into buildings.

That right there shows you how hard it is in this life. Them innocent people that died. I'm not going to complain about anything.

PLAYBOY: Where were you on the morning of September 11?

IVERSON: I was in bed, in my house in Philly. And my wife came in and said, "I cannot believe what just happened." We turned the TV on and I got up and went, "Oh, my God." I just had this empty feeling, man. It was a bad feeling. For something like that to happen, that means anything can happen. All those innocent people who woke up that morning just like me and went to work like any other day, for them to just die like that? I didn't know anybody in there, but it hurt so bad thinking about those people's families. After I seen both buildings go down, I couldn't watch it anymore. It was so sad, man. And now that this has happened with my man Rah, I really know how those families feel. You know, because it's just like that [*snaps fingers*], and you never see him again. It's crazy, man. I cherish life, I'm just glad to be alive. I don't want no negative pictures painted about me, because my kids are getting to the age where they hear stuff like that. So I'm thrilled about the way people look at me now. I just wish they would have looked at me like that all along.

It's because of the winning, but all you have to do is listen to somebody. If you're a smart person, you can tell if somebody is sincere. I just let my actions do the talking. Watch me on the court, and you tell me if that guy is good or bad. I think you can tell who I am. I think you can tell I'm trying to get better as a person, that I'm trying to be better as a person than I am as a basketball player. Believe that. Because I want to go to heaven. When I die, I want to go see Rah, man. I know he's in heaven, and before I die I want to know that's where I'm going. I don't want to have to guess. I want to know that's where I'm going.

DEREK JETER

A candid conversation with the Yankees star about coping with George, teaming with A-Rod and why he reads the gossip page before the sports page

In a sport oddly denuded of household names and true superstars, Derek Jeter stands tall. The New York Yankee is more than just one of the game's best players; for years he's been a media darling in the world's most fickle city. The 29-year-old shortstop turns up in gossip columns almost as frequently as he does in the sports pages. He has been linked to scores of beautiful and high-profile women. The *New York Post* recently ranked Jeter number one on its year-end list of the city's 34 most eligible guys. For denizens of the Big Apple, Jeter has been Mr. Baseball, pure and simple. Life's been good.

And then A-Rod came into town. In February, when the Yankees signed Alex Rodriguez, widely touted as the game's best player, sportswriters wondered what it would mean—to Jeter. Complicating the issue, the former Texas Ranger is a shortstop with two Gold Gloves (Jeter has none) who had to move to third base when he signed with the Yankees. More drama? The two men had once been the closest of friends, but they had a falling-out three years ago. For gossip-crazed New Yorkers, theirs has become one of the most closely watched relationships in town.

While A-Rod was voted last year's American League Most Valuable Player, Jeter is no slouch. Now in the fourth year of a 10-year, $189 million contract, Jeter owns a .317 career batting average. He has played in the postseason in every one of his eight seasons and often saves his best for October. In 2000, when the Yankees beat the crosstown Mets in the World Series in five games, he was named series MVP. And although the Anaheim Angels wiped out the Yanks in the first round of the 2002 postseason, Jeter hit .500. Last spring Yankees owner George Steinbrenner named him team captain, only the 11th in franchise history.

Off the field Jeter is also a player, known for his dalliances with Mariah Carey, a former Miss Universe and a bevy of models and actresses. As Yankees broadcaster Charley Steiner put it, "If the Yankees are the Beatles, Derek's the cute one."

The son of a racially mixed couple, Jeter grew up in Kalamazoo, Michigan and put on his first Yankees uniform when he was six. In 1992 he was named high school player of the year and was chosen sixth by the Yankees in the June free agent baseball draft. He was voted the American League Rookie of the Year in 1996, his first full season in the majors, and quickly established himself as one of baseball's best all-around players. Jeter's seasonal averages of 207 hits and 124 runs are extraordinary. Long considered the Yankees' leader, he also has a knack for elevating the play of his teammates.

While he's one of baseball's most accessible players, he's one of the most private as well. Like a seasoned politician, Jeter carefully crafts his courteous statements—and sticks to them. Rarely does he lose his composure. "He's kind of vanilla," notes his agent, Casey Close. Conscious of commanding center stage, Jeter admits that he rarely lets down his guard.

We sent journalist Diane K. Shah to Jeter's winter home in Tampa, Florida, where she had to get past the guards posted at his gated community before tackling the more formidable guards in his head.

PLAYBOY: A lot has been made of your relationship with Alex Rodriguez. Until 2001 you referred to him as your best friend. Then, after he signed his $252 million deal with Texas, he said some unflattering things about you through the media—that you never had to serve as a leader and that since you bat second, teams don't worry that you'll beat them. When reporters informed you of this, you said you'd call Alex and talk to him. What happened?

JETER: It was spring training, and he actually came over here the night that came out. Just came by. We talked about it, and that was basically the end of it.

PLAYBOY: We heard that he drove 95 miles from the Rangers' spring-training camp to your house and left phone messages you didn't return. Is that true?

JETER: No. When that stuff went public, I guess it was in the afternoon when I found out about it. We had a game that night, and he drove over while we were playing. So I didn't get the messages that he was at my house until after the game.

PLAYBOY: He was chilling in your driveway?

JETER: He was in the area, but he wasn't in the driveway.

PLAYBOY: Still, you were hurt.

JETER: Sure, it hurts anytime someone you're close to says something you question. But Alex was coming from Seattle and had signed this megadeal. He was on a platform that maybe he'd never been on before. I think he found himself having to defend the reason he got paid so much. Or he was asked, "If you get this, what's Derek going to get?" So he was comparing us, which I told him shouldn't even be an issue. I said, "You didn't pay yourself. You shouldn't have to answer that question. Let them ask the owner." I think he was saying things that maybe other people had said to him.

PLAYBOY: After that it appeared you two weren't close.

JETER: We weren't as close as we had been. We were still friends. The younger you are, the more time you have when the season is over. Now it seems you do more in the off-season than you do during the season.

PLAYBOY: How did you hear about the trade?

JETER: A couple of people in the organization called me.

PLAYBOY: What were you doing when you got the word?

JETER: No idea. Probably watching TV.

PLAYBOY: The last time you'd seen Alex, when you two were making a commercial, did you talk about the possibility of his becoming a Yankee?

JETER: No, because that was before Aaron Boone tore his ACL. It was right around the time when everything was happening with the potential trade to Boston, and he basically didn't know what was going on.

PLAYBOY: Once A-Rod signed on did anybody ask if you were willing to move to second or third?

JETER: That was never an issue. They approached him about playing third base.

PLAYBOY: Isn't it easier to move from shortstop to second than to third?

JETER: Nah, I wouldn't say that. Turning a double play is totally different from second base than from shortstop. Your back is to first. So I would assume it would be easier to go to third base.

PLAYBOY: How did your teammates react to the news?

JETER: Everyone's pretty excited. You're adding one of the best all-around players in the game to your lineup, so it's only going to make us a better team.

PLAYBOY: Is it true George Steinbrenner ordered you to go to Alex's news conference in New York?

JETER: No, he called me and asked if I wanted to go.

PLAYBOY: Some news accounts reported that he demanded you go.

JETER: See, you can't believe everything you read.

PLAYBOY: To what degree are you amused or bothered by the speculation that you and Alex can't get along?

JETER: Neither of us has had problems getting along with teammates before, so I don't see why we'd have problems now. It gives the media something to write about, though. I think it will eventually die down.

PLAYBOY: You've said you're very competitive. What kinds of things will you be competitive about with Alex?

JETER: Well, we're on the same team, so we really don't have anything to compete for. We're playing a team sport, right?

PLAYBOY: How about your batting average versus his?

JETER: No. I don't go into a season saying I want to bat higher than any one of my teammates. That's not a goal. The goal is to win.

PLAYBOY: Who's funnier?

JETER: I think we're funny in different ways. I'm not sure you can rate us. You'd have to be around both of us to make that decision.

PLAYBOY: We noticed a book on the table in your entryway, *Patton on Leadership: Strategic Lessons for Corporate Warfare*, by Alan Axelrod. Any particular reason you own that?

JETER: Mr. Steinbrenner gave it to me after the 1998 season.

PLAYBOY: Was it meant to teach you, or was it meant to explain him?

JETER: I think both. A lot of what's in there are things he says: "If you're going to lead, you've got to sit in the saddle." "You've got to be willing to go out and do the things you ask of the people you're leading." It's pretty interesting.

PLAYBOY: He inscribed it, "To Derek. Read and study. He was a great leader just as you are and will be a great leader. Hopefully of the men in pinstripes." How would you describe your relationship with Big George?

JETER: It's always boss-employee. He's the boss. But I think we have a really good relationship. I don't know how it could be any better in terms of playing for him.

PLAYBOY: But last year, after he questioned your dedication and your late-night hours, you were pissed off. Was that the first time he publicly criticized you?

JETER: No, he mentioned my name, among other players, when the team was struggling a few years ago. He said some guys needed to start stepping it up. He meant me. But the whole thing last year was blown out of proportion. He mentioned a birthday party. How many birthday parties do you have a year?

PLAYBOY: So Steinbrenner was referring to just one party? Your birthday is in June; he's bringing it up six months later?

JETER: It was my birthday party before a day off. The next thing you knew, I'd been turned into a big party animal. Now you read that all the time—I'm the party animal.

PLAYBOY: Steinbrenner said more than that. He said you "always give 100 percent. I need 110 percent." And he said, "If I'm paying a guy $16 million, I want him to listen."

JETER: The whole thing was made larger than life. That was the point of those Visa commercials. We got a chance to make light of the situation and put it behind us.

PLAYBOY: Does he expect you to work for him 24-7, 365 days a year?

JETER: Probably. Rightfully so. When you're a Yankee you represent the Yankees at all times. You don't have days off. If I were to get into trouble today, the first thing you'd see is my name associated with the team. So I don't think you have 20 or 30 days off a year from being a Yankee. You're always a Yankee.

PLAYBOY: How about during the off-season? What if you wanted to go out and enjoy somebody's company until three or four in the morning?

JETER: Oh, I'd be out. I'm a grown man. In the off-season I can do whatever I want, whenever I want to do it. He wouldn't call me if he read I was out until such and such an hour in January. He wouldn't say, "You need to be home."

PLAYBOY: How often do you see Steinbrenner?

JETER: He hasn't been around as much as he used to be. Last season I saw him probably two or three times before the postseason.

PLAYBOY: You both spend your winters in Tampa. Does he ever call you and say, "Let's get lunch"?

JETER: It's happened maybe once or twice. We usually bet a dinner on the Ohio State–Michigan football game.

PLAYBOY: When you get together, does he have a message for you?

JETER: He always has messages. "Make sure you focus this year. I need you focused." Or he'll see me working out and say, "Don't get too big, because we need you to have agility."

PLAYBOY: In the first Visa commercial, in which Steinbrenner chastises you for being out carousing every night, was it your idea that he participate in the conga line?

JETER: No, but I was the one who had to persuade him to do it. It wasn't easy. He did it a couple of times, and then he called it quits. Fortunately they got a good take.

PLAYBOY: Is it ever fun seeing your name in the gossip columns?

JETER: Some of the stories are funny. Some of them amaze me. Like one time they said I was renting an island—some island I'd never heard of—for $23,000 a day and that I was bringing one of three girls I'd never heard of for a birthday party. The thing is, people believe it when they read it. I was talking to Wayne Gretzky the other day about his time in New York. He said they made up things about him constantly. He used to get the newspapers and turn to the gossip pages, and when he'd read something about someone else he'd say, "Really? They did this?" But when he read about himself it was, "Where do they come up with this stuff?" I thought that was funny, because I do the same thing.

PLAYBOY: So you do read the gossip pages?

JETER: Even before the sports section. To make sure I'm not in them.

PLAYBOY: You seem to need to be a perfectionist on the field. Why is that?

JETER: Competition-wise I always want to be perfect. I can't stand losing in anything. If you tell me you want to race down the street right now, I'm going to try to beat you.

PLAYBOY: We're pretty sure you'd win.

JETER: I'll still do everything in my power to beat you, and that started when I was a kid. My dad used to beat me at everything. We'd play checkers, and he would beat me. He would never let me win. Never. We used to watch *The Price Is Right*, and we'd play the showcase showdown. I didn't know how much a refrigerator or a new car cost—I was six years old. We'd sit there and he'd beat me, and then I'd walk to school.

PLAYBOY: Do you ever wish your dad had let you win?

JETER: No—I think my dad was teaching me lessons. Things don't come easily. People aren't just going to let you get your way. I mean, people aren't going to say, "Here, you can have this." You have to work for it.

PLAYBOY: You wrote in your book, *The Life You Imagine*, that you always try to envision something before you do it. Is that because you're conscious of being a role model, or is that just you?

JETER: I think it's me no matter what. When I was younger, before I'd do things I'd imagine what my parents would think. It's the same philosophy I apply today. But now it's more than my parents. Lots of people are watching.

PLAYBOY: It sounds as if you're always watching yourself, like in an out-of-body experience.

JETER: Yes, and I'm pretty much used to it now. I'm always aware that people are watching. There are a lot of things I'd like to do that I can't—or that I choose not to. Say I'm out with some friends and I want to dance on top of a table. I know I can't do that.

PLAYBOY: Doesn't it get tiring, always watching yourself?

JETER: Yes, but I don't think it's a bad thing. When you let that guard down, that's when you get in trouble.

PLAYBOY: Last season was a strange one for you, full of highs and lows. Among the lows: In game six of the World Series you went 0 for 4, struck out twice and made an error that led to a Marlins insurance run. Series over. And you suffered three injuries, including a dislocated shoulder on opening day. Was that the most serious injury you've ever had?

JETER: It was the only serious injury I've had. I was out for six weeks.

PLAYBOY: You were heading to third; the catcher, Ken Huckaby, ran over to cover the base, and you slid into his shin guard. What was your first thought?

JETER: I thought maybe I had broken my collarbone, because I felt a pop.

PLAYBOY: Was there instant pain?

JETER: It didn't feel good. I wouldn't recommend it. I was kind of afraid to look at it, because I thought I'd see it coming out.

PLAYBOY: Did they just push it back in?

JETER: They tried initially, on the field, but that didn't work. I just wanted to get off the field, because you have 50,000 people looking at you. It took a while for them to get the golf cart out there. Then finally we went inside and they popped it back in.

PLAYBOY: There was a bit of controversy, because it was reported that Huckaby tried to phone you to apologize but couldn't reach you. Then a day or two later he walked into your locker room to apologize, and you gave him an icy stare.

JETER: Not true. First, I never expected him to apologize, because I didn't think he purposely tried to dislocate my shoulder. Before the second game he told the media he'd tried to call me on my cell phone, I didn't answer and he left a message. That wasn't true. He doesn't have my cell number. If he wanted to get ahold of me, it's only a couple hundred feet from one clubhouse to the other. Or he could have called the trainers' room, because obviously that's where I was. It was all made up. What bothered me was how the thing was portrayed.

PLAYBOY: Late in the season, against Boston, you pulled a rib-cage muscle. How did that happen?

JETER: Swinging. We were facing a knuckleball pitcher, Tim Wakefield. I think I swung a little too hard.

PLAYBOY: Did you finish the at bat?

JETER: Yes. Then I had another at bat and got a hit. I was on first base, and they took me out. I think I missed a week.

PLAYBOY: Then there you were in the first game of the American League Championship Series, Boston again.

JETER: I think it was the second or third inning. I dove for a ball and my hand rolled over, and I tore a ligament in my thumb.

PLAYBOY: Your left thumb.

JETER: It was a bad year for my left side. It takes three or four months for that to heal. They gave me shots before the games against Boston, but I couldn't feel my thumb. So in the World Series I just played with it. They put a little mold thing—a little cast—inside my glove to stop my thumb from moving around.

PLAYBOY: The rivalry between the Yankees and the Red Sox has reached epic proportions, especially with A-Rod now in pinstripes. It isn't just the fans, is it?

JETER: The rivalry has gotten more intense each year I've been in the major leagues. You have respect for the other team, I think, but it's gotten to the point where in the postseason you've got guys throwing at each other's heads and charging the mound. It's almost like the old days, when they used to fight all the time.

PLAYBOY: Some said that in last year's playoffs, the Yankees used up everything against the Red Sox—seven games, the last one going extra innings—and you had nothing left for the Marlins.

JETER: The series with the Red Sox was emotionally draining because all seven games were intense. But I don't think that's why we lost. We lost because Florida played better than we did.

PLAYBOY: Did it take long to get over losing the World Series?

JETER: Yes, I hate to lose. For a while I didn't like to be out and around a lot of people. I pretty much kept to myself. But you never forget it. I still think about us losing. You want to remember what it feels like, because you don't want to have that feeling again. That's what drives you to try to be better.

PLAYBOY: So not only have the Yankees gone three years without a championship, but to add insult to injury, several days after the series you were waiting to go into a movie theater and got heckled by a fan. "If you hadn't made that error, Jeter, you'd still be playing," she apparently said.

JETER: She was a young girl, and she was yelling about the error I made in game six. And then she said, real sarcastically, "Better luck next year." She seemed to enjoy it. She was probably a Mets fan.

PLAYBOY: How often do you have to put up with that stuff outside the ballpark?

JETER: In Boston, all the time. That's a whole other world. I actually think I'm public enemy number one there.

PLAYBOY: Considering that the Red Sox nearly signed A-Rod, do you think you'll have to fight him for that title?

JETER: Maybe he can share the load with me. That's what I'm hoping for.

PLAYBOY: Is it difficult for you to go out alone?

JETER: I don't go anywhere by myself, period. You never know when you're going to run into someone who's been drinking and is acting foolish. You like to know that someone is always watching your back.

PLAYBOY: Women recognize you on the street and they squeal. Do you like it?

JETER: It's flattering. It's embarrassing, too. But anytime you get recognized, it means you're being appreciated for some of the things you've done. I don't mind it.

PLAYBOY: How many of your teammates get squealed at?

JETER: They're all married.

PLAYBOY: Let's see, you've dated a Miss Universe, a Victoria's Secret underwear model and an MTV hostess. According to the *New York Post*, you demand perfection, at least visually, in your dates. Is that true?

JETER: She has to be a beautiful person. She has to be fun. I like to have fun. I'm always smiling. She has to have a sense of humor, because you've got to enjoy life. Intelligent. But I don't sit down and make a blueprint of how someone must look. I guess you just know.

The more you get to know someone, you understand if you have things in common.

PLAYBOY: You were once linked with Mariah Carey.

JETER: I was a fan of her music, and then we ran into each other a couple of times in New York.

PLAYBOY: The papers said she stalked you.

JETER: I don't know where they would get that from.

PLAYBOY: The papers also had you practically engaged. Was it that serious?

JETER: We didn't date for as long as people think. I've heard all kinds of things. But it was really just a few months.

PLAYBOY: After it ended you said you realized you couldn't make a relationship work if the other person is famous too. Is that an ego thing?

JETER: Not at all. It's just tough when both people are in the public eye. I'm not saying it can't work, but there are a lot of rumors, a lot of gossip, different schedules.

PLAYBOY: You say you're eager to get married, but do you think you need to finish baseball first?

JETER: Not necessarily. I have to admit I'm at a selfish point in my life in terms of what I'm trying to accomplish. But there are times when you wish you had someone to share it with.

PLAYBOY: How do you ask a woman out?

JETER: Initially it'll be as part of a group. Like someone will bring their friends, and I'll have my friends. It's easier that way. Because when you do the one-on-one thing, that's when the media get so involved.

PLAYBOY: Have you ever had to explain to a date what you do for a living?

JETER: I say I have a night job.

PLAYBOY: That's it?

JETER: And that I'm in the entertainment business. [*Smiles*]

PLAYBOY: Do you ever get rejected?

JETER: Everyone gets rejected.

PLAYBOY: Are you involved with anybody right now?

JETER: I'm seeing someone in New York.

PLAYBOY: You're in the fourth year of a 10-year contract worth $189 million. You'll be paid $19 million this year. What are your greatest extravagances?

JETER: I get things for other people. But for myself I have a Hummer, a Ferrari and a Mercedes 600. I got this house six, seven years ago, and I'm not planning on leaving. I have a nice apartment in New York.

PLAYBOY: The Hummer has a satellite dish on the roof.

JETER: I just had DirecTV put in. Only now it won't fit in my garage. I've got to build a bigger garage.

PLAYBOY: Did we spot a motorcycle in there?

JETER: A scooter. It was a Christmas gift from Gerald Williams. He used to play for the Yankees. Now he's with the Marlins, and he lives three doors down. He bought one for each of us, but when we tried to ride them in, the guard stopped us at the gate. You can't drive two-wheeled vehicles here. So we had to load them on a truck and bring them in that way. We ride them at night.

PLAYBOY: You're sure it's not a motorcycle?

JETER: [*Laughs*] It's a scooter. I'm not allowed to ride a motorcycle. It's in my contract. Actually, it's not even my scooter. It's a friend's.

PLAYBOY: Right. What else do you spend money on? Clothes?

JETER: I have a lot of suits. I have a tailor in Chicago. He's Michael Jordan's guy, too. But really, I'm not a huge spender.

PLAYBOY: What music do you like?

JETER: All I listen to is hip-hop and R&B—Jay-Z, 50 Cent, Beyoncé, R. Kelly. That's pretty much it.

PLAYBOY: Two full seasons have passed, but people are still talking about that miraculous play against Oakland in the 2001 division series. Some say it's the infield equivalent of Willie Mays's catch in the 1954 World Series. The Yankees were down two games to none. If you lost game three, your season would be over. The Yankees were ahead one to nothing. Can you run us through it?

JETER: Jeremy Giambi was on first, there were two outs, and Terrence Long hit a long fly to right that fell in for a double. The second baseman, Alfonso Soriano, was the first cutoff man, and the first baseman, Tino Martinez, was the second cutoff man. But when Shane Spencer picked up the ball in right, he threw it over both their heads.

PLAYBOY: So you had Soriano down the right-field line and Tino near first base. Giambi was steaming for home, right? And you were at short.

JETER: I could see that the throw was going over their heads. And I saw the runner wasn't home yet, so I thought if I could get to the ball and get rid of it quickly, we'd have a chance to get him.

PLAYBOY: From out of nowhere you suddenly materialized at first.

JETER: I fielded the ball between first and home and flipped it as soon as I got it.

PLAYBOY: You flipped it sideways to Jorge Posada at the plate—a perfect throw. Giambi was so shocked to see the ball coming that he didn't even slide. When you saw the highlight film, did the play look different to you than in your mind as you were performing it?

JETER: In my mind everything happened in slow motion. When I watched it later I just looked at it really as what I was supposed to do. We'd practiced that play in spring training.

PLAYBOY: But nobody recalls ever seeing such a play before. Is there a name for it?

JETER: They just call it the Play.

PLAYBOY: Two games later the same guy, Terrence Long, hit a pop-up into foul territory at Yankee Stadium. And you did a belly flop into the seats behind third base and came up with the ball. Was that the second most exciting play you've made?

JETER: I think it was exciting to watch. I don't think it was exciting to do it, because it hurt.

PLAYBOY: What's been your most embarrassing moment on the field?

JETER: We were playing in Minnesota. I'm on third with less than two outs. Someone hits a deep fly ball that bounces over the fence. It's a ground-rule double, so you get two bases, and I automatically score. But I'm still standing on third, tagging up in case the ball is caught. When it bounces over the fence, I turn to go, trip over my shoelaces and fall flat on my face. Then they show it over and over on the Jumbotron.

PLAYBOY: You and Alex are among the most famous baseball players today. Probably fewer than 10 are easily recognizable nationwide, whereas the NBA and the NFL have many more. Why is that?

JETER: They market their sports a lot better. I filmed a commercial with Alex and the Marlins' Josh Beckett for Major League Baseball. It's the first time baseball has done that. It's lagging behind the other sports, but I think now it's putting forth an effort.

PLAYBOY: Baseball also lags behind other sports when it comes to drug testing, especially for steroids. This season you'll be randomly tested. Should performance-enhancing drugs be banned?

JETER: Yes, without question, because they put everyone else at a disadvantage. There's also the public's perception. If someone comes back a little smaller or a little bigger, the first thing people wonder is, Did he take steroids before and isn't taking them now? Or is he using steroids now? I think the whole debate is putting a lot of questions in people's heads.

PLAYBOY: You grew up in Kalamazoo, Michigan. Your dad is black; your mom is white. How did they prepare you for your mixed ethnicity?

JETER: For me it was a normal situation. It was all I knew. We'd get funny looks from people. My parents tried to educate my sister and me about why people would stare. They would say it was because people were seeing something they hadn't seen before.

PLAYBOY: Kids can be mean. Did you have problems?

JETER: Not many, because I played baseball, which was primarily white. Then I played basketball, which was primarily black. So I had a lot of friends. But I remember going back home after my first year in baseball. I had just bought a Mitsubishi 3000. That was the greatest car in the world. So I was back home, and I was eating out with a friend. We went back to the car and were about to leave when some kids drove by. Someone shouted, "Bring that car back to your dad" and yelled some racial things. I was so proud to come home, and then you have to hear those kinds of things.

PLAYBOY: Do you feel closer to one race than the other?

JETER: No. My best friend is a white guy I've known since fourth grade. My trainer is Puerto Rican. The catcher on our team, Jorge Posada, is Puerto Rican. I was the best man at his wedding. Sean Twitty, a friend from the minors, is Jamaican.

PLAYBOY: You grew up rooting for the Yankees. Didn't you like the Tigers?

JETER: I was born in Jersey, and I used to spend the summers there because my mom had 13 brothers and sisters, and I had all kinds of cousins. My grandmother was a huge Yankees fan, and she turned me on to the team. Also, my dad liked the Tigers. Since we competed in everything, I couldn't root for the same team he did.

PLAYBOY: You've said you always wanted to play baseball because your dad played.

JETER: He played at Fisk University in Tennessee. Growing up I would watch him play in a softball league.

PLAYBOY: And because he was a shortstop, you had to be a shortstop. Apparently you were clocked throwing 93 mph in high school. Didn't you ever want to be a pitcher?

JETER: I pitched a couple of times in high school, but my arm used to hurt afterward. Plus, I liked to hit. And the shortstop is involved in everything. Shortstop is like quarterback.

PLAYBOY: How much pressure did your dad put on you to excel?

JETER: He never put pressure on me. He always said, "If you want A, B or C to happen in your life, you have to do certain things. He was tough on us in school. We had to sit down and do our homework for an hour every night. Even if we didn't have homework, we had to sit down and do something school-related for an hour. Obviously it worked. I got good grades.

PLAYBOY: And baseball?

JETER: My mom and dad never pushed me into baseball. For me it was fun. I used to drag them out of the house to help me out. If my dad wasn't home, my mom would throw Wiffle balls in the backyard. The high school was over the back fence, so we'd go to the baseball field. The only thing they said was, "If you're going to do this, you're going to have to work, and if we don't see you working at it, then it's going to be time for you to find something else to do."

PLAYBOY: You were picked sixth in the 1992 draft. You dreamed of being a Yankee, but wasn't it a long shot that you'd become one?

JETER: It was luck. I mean, the draft is a crapshoot. I thought I'd be selected by Houston or Cincinnati.

PLAYBOY: Speaking of Cincinnati, do you think Pete Rose should be eligible for the Hall of Fame?

JETER: Pete Rose is a Hall of Fame player no matter how you look at it. What he did on the field—there's no question about it. It's just basically how you view what he did off the field. I wouldn't want to be the one to make that decision.

PLAYBOY: After four full seasons with the Yankees you had 795 hits, more than Pete Rose, Ty Cobb, Hank Aaron and Stan Musial had in their first four seasons. Yet unlike most hitters, you don't pay attention to what pitchers are throwing. You just check the radar gun.

JETER: Basically you go on instinct. I just want to know how hard a guy is throwing. Then you have to recognize what kind of pitch it is so you can know if it's going to end up in the strike zone.

PLAYBOY: You have less than a second to do that.

JETER: You can tell from the rotation of the ball. If it's a slider, it's spinning a little differently than a fastball. If it's a twoseamer, you'll see two seams.

PLAYBOY: Which indicates if it's going to be low and outside or over the plate.

JETER: That's the plan. Of course, it doesn't always work.

PLAYBOY: Your father once said, "Derek has more inner arrogance than anybody I've ever met." And during games you look pretty sure of yourself. Is that how you really feel?

JETER: Yeah, I'm confident. I don't like cocky people. Confidence is how you feel. Cockiness is how you act. I'm always confident. There are times when you struggle, like I could be 0 for 100, but if a big game is on the line, I expect to do well.

PLAYBOY: Other than Pedro Martinez, which pitcher has given you the most trouble? Someone we might not think of?

JETER: Roy Halladay of Toronto. He had a great year last season, winning the Cy Young Award. But he's always been tough for me. He throws a real hard sinker. Also, Derek Lowe of the Red Sox.

PLAYBOY: How did you do against Roger Clemens when he pitched for Toronto?

JETER: He hit me a lot. We'd joke about it. He said I leaned over the plate and he was just brushing me back. Rocket is the type you hate to play against but love to have as a teammate.

PLAYBOY: Were you surprised that he signed with Houston three months after supposedly retiring or that Andy Pettitte signed with Houston too?

JETER: I thought Andy would be back. I wasn't completely caught off guard when he signed with Houston, because I knew it was in the back of his mind that one day he'd get an opportunity to pitch at home. We didn't expect Rocket to come back. But who's to tell you when you should stop doing what you love to do?

PLAYBOY: What's a typical day for you during the season?

JETER: I get up around 10, eat breakfast and go to the gym to lift weights for an hour. No treadmill, because we run too much during the season. Then I'll return home, maybe go back to sleep and get to the ballpark around 3:30.

PLAYBOY: Do you have a personal trainer?

JETER: Year-round. He goes where I go. He travels with me to East Coast cities.

PLAYBOY: You're one of those guys who consider their kitchen no-man's-land. Do you live on snack food? Or fast food?

JETER: I can't cook; that's the bad thing. I go to the grocery store and stock up on cereal, oatmeal, Eggos and stuff, and then when it goes bad I'll go back and get more. Otherwise I eat out. My agent got me a chef as a Christmas gift a couple of years ago. He'd have something waiting for me, and I would warm it up. I think I might have to have him come again.

PLAYBOY: You've got a golf course out back. Why haven't you played more?

JETER: My shoulder injury. I messed up my AC joint, so I had to stop playing golf.

PLAYBOY: Is that why you keep grabbing your shoulder? You've been rubbing it the whole time.

JETER: Really?

PLAYBOY: Does it hurt?

JETER: No. It could be a habit, because it used to hurt all the time. Or it could be old age.

PLAYBOY: Have you given any thought to what you might do after your time in baseball?

JETER: I would love to own a team.

PLAYBOY: Like Michael Jordan? Purchase a percentage of a team?

JETER: No, I'd have to be a majority owner. I'd have to make the decisions.

PLAYBOY: You'd probably need to get your hands on a lot more money.

JETER: Probably.

PLAYBOY: How are you going to do that?

JETER: [*Smiles*] I haven't thought about it yet. But I will.

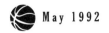 May 1992

MICHAEL
JORDAN

*A candid conversation with
the NBA's in-flight demigod
on life after Magic, basketball's
ego wars and his guarantee for
Olympic gold*

At the age of 29, Michael Jeffrey Jordan is almost certainly more popular
than Jesus. What's more, he has better endorsement deals. Of course,
Jordan, unlike John Lennon, would never say anything so imprudent.
It's not in his nature. Then, too, the estimated $21,000,000 he'll earn
in 1992 from product endorsements is dependent on his image as the
quintessential gentleman, consummate sportsman, clean-living family man and modest, down-to-earth levitating demigod. He maintains
that image effortlessly, perhaps because it's not an image.

It's hard to resist calling Jordan the greatest basketball player the
world has ever seen, but he does have his detractors. Over the past
year, his greatest achievements—leading the Chicago Bulls to their
first NBA championship and being named to the United State's first
pro Olympic basketball team—were counterbalanced by the first
widely publicized criticisms of Jordan, superstar and citizen.

They began when Jordan waffled over whether or not he would
play in the 1992 summer Olympics. First he said he didn't think he
would because he needed to rest in the off-season; then he said he
hadn't made up his mind. A rumor began to circulate that the real
reason for his indecision was his likely Olympic teammate, Detroit
Pistons guard Isiah Thomas, who is probably the nearest thing to an
enemy Jordan has in the NBA. Although Jordan denied wielding the
power of his immense popularity to blackball Thomas, not everyone
believed him. In the end, and for whatever reasons, Thomas was
not initially extended an invitation to be a member of the team and
Jordan, of course, was. He accepted graciously. But it was about that

time that he began to sense, as sportswriter Jack McCallum put it, "a backlash against his fame, a subtle dissatisfaction with the whole idea of Michael Jordan."

It didn't help that Jordan elected not to join the rest of the Bulls at the White House to meet President Bush (for which he received a mild rebuke from Bulls teammate Horace Grant), or that NFL Hall-of-Famer Jim Brown slammed him for not doing enough to help black youth. But the unkindest cut of all came from the best-selling book *The Jordan Rules,* in which *Chicago Tribune* sportswriter Sam Smith depicted Jordan as a sometimes tyrannical and fractious presence among his teammates as they made their championship drive.

Despite these cracks in his image, Jordan's mystique and popularity have remained intact. The pleasure, delight and sheer wonderment he has brought to millions of basketball fans (as well as to patrons of all the products he so engagingly endorses) far outweigh any criticisms thus far leveled against him. Most of us would rather remember the thrills (and cool sneakers) he's given us.

A collection of great Jordan moments would have to begin with the 1982 NCAA championship game, when his jump shot at the buzzer lifted the North Carolina Tar Heels to a one-point victory over the Georgetown Hoyas. Then came his stellar performance at the 1984 Olympics in Los Angeles. And since being drafted by the Bulls after his junior year (he later went back to earn his degree), Jordan's career has been one long highlight film. Most fans will never forget the 1986 playoffs in which he utterly befuddled the Boston Celtics with 49- and 63-point games; or the 1986-87 season, when he led the league in scoring with 37.1 points per game, had more 50-point games than any other player except Wilt Chamberlain and became the second player in NBA history—after Chamberlain—to score 3000 points in a season. In the process, he was transforming a franchise worth less than $20,000,000 in his rookie season into one with a current estimated worth of $150,000,000.

That estimate, of course, factors in last season's drive to the championship, in which Jordan proved once and for all that, contrary to his image as a selfish shooter, he's probably the most complete player in the game today, capable of providing his team with the best shooting, passing and defense in the league, as well as those intangibles of leadership and inspiration. And it is from last year that we retain perhaps the most unforgettable moment: Jordan on the floor of the Bull's locker room, tears streaming from his eyes, as he pressed the NBA championship trophy against his cheek. As long as videotape continues to spin in VCRs, Jordan will have a lasting memorial to his play.

Jordan's private side, of course, is not usually that accessible. After nearly being trampled by 5000 autograph seekers, Jordan has become cautious about being seen anywhere but on the basketball court. He lives his off days by special appointment: eating at restaurants after they've closed, getting what's left of his hair cut after the barbershop has locked up for the evening, shopping in stores after usual business hours. It is ironic that 30 years after the end of segregation in public places, one of the most famous black Americans often has to use the back entrance.

Even if the private Mike has been fast-breaking out of the public eye, the public Jordan plays a commanding in-your-face game. He once told NBC's Maria Shriver, "Even my mistakes have been perfect," and that seems to be the case. Take the Jordan backlash, for instance. Nearly all the newspaper columnists who questioned his hesitation to go to the Olympics also mentioned how Isiah Thomas led his humiliated Detroit Pistons teammates off the floor in last year's Eastern Conference play-offs without shaking hands with the victorious Bulls. For many sports fans, such unsportsmanlike conduct was reason enough for Thomas to be excluded from the Olympic team, whether or not Jordan liked him. When Jim Brown accused Jordan of not doing enough for black youth, the press came to Jordan's defense, emphasizing the work of the Michael Jordan Foundation (which raises money for 25 youth-oriented charities) along with his efforts to fulfill the 75 requests per week he receives from sick children who want to sit beside him on the Bulls bench. (Some children receive the shoes Jordan wore during the game; one boy who died of leukemia was buried in his.)

Although his White House no-show wasn't popular in the major media, it received plaudits in the black press, which interpreted it as Jordan's way of protesting Bush's stands on civil rights issues. Then, finally, there was *The Jordan Rules*, which was supposed to play havoc with the Bulls' team chemistry this season. On the contrary, it seemed to make the team tougher and more cohesive. Meanwhile, America continues to admire Michael Jordan.

"Going to a Bulls game is like going to a temple," says Arthur Droge, associate professor of New Testament at the University of

Chicago's Divinity School. "There's definitely a religious component about it and Jordan is the demigod of the moment." Or, as Larry Bird put it in 1986, "He is God disguised as Michael Jordan."

To track down Jordan, we enlisted sportswriter Mark Vancil, whose rookie season covering the Bulls for the *Chicago Sun-Times* coincided with Michael Jordan's first year in the NBA. As a press-section veteran of innumerable games and championship seasons, Vancil has seen a lot of winners. None, in his opinion, matches Michael Jordan.

"Faster than most of us, Michael seems to have realized that money buys things, but it can't buy time. The Bulls' public-relations department usually dismisses interview requests out of hand. Although Jordan will answer anything inside the walls of a locker room before or after a game, his time, particularly in Chicago, is generally off-limits to everyone but family, friends and contractual obligations.

"With that in mind, I suggested we talk on the road. He agreed and we arranged to meet during an extended early-season road trip that started in Oakland and moved through Seattle, Denver, Los Angeles, Portland and Sacramento. The first session was on Thanksgiving in Portland.

"He talked for almost 90 minutes, and another session was scheduled for game day the following afternoon. The Bulls had won three straight on the trip and 10 in a row overall, but Portland would be a test. With the game less than six hours away, Jordan seemed anxious. He talked about the Smith book, citing specifics that other writers had asked him about. I should go to Sacramento, he said. 'I don't know anybody there. We'll be able to finish up in my room.'

"After a grueling double-overtime victory over Portland, Jordan didn't appear capable of getting to his room. Back spasms left him sprawled on a table, the pain so intense that Jordan, still in uniform more than 40 minutes after the game, had to be helped to the team bus while his clothes were packed.

"He called at four P.M. the next day. 'Come on up,' he said. 'I've got about thirty minutes.' Once I reached his suite, a huge pregame meal arrived: a steak, potato skins, a pitcher of orange juice, water and a salad. Jordan was moving without hesitation. As evidenced by his appearance in 234 straight games, he has always been able to fight through pain. A full day of therapy had eliminated the back spasms, and in an apparently effortless performance that night, Jordan scored 30 points. The Bulls coasted through the final paces of a perfect road trip. An hour after the game, Jordan called and agreed to one last session.

"We began our conversation with a topic much on the minds of the basketball world: Magic Johnson."

PLAYBOY: How did you get the news about Magic?

JORDAN: His agent, Lon Rosen, left me a message at practice and he said it's an emergency, he's got to talk to me. When I called him back, he told me, "Magic's having a press conference today. He's going to retire. He tested positive for HIV."

PLAYBOY: Where were you when he told you?

JORDAN: I was driving home. I almost drove off the road. I said, "This has to be some kind of sick joke." He said, "Well, Earvin wants to talk to you." So he gave me Earvin's number and I called him at home. He was as calm as you and I. I said to him, "Damn, you're calmer than I am. I'm about to drive off the road." He said, "I just want you to continue on with your life. I'm going to be fine, my baby's going to be fine, my wife is fine."

PLAYBOY: Before Magic's announcement, did players talk very much about AIDS?

JORDAN: We were aware of it, but most guys never thought of it happening to heterosexuals. It was always gays, drug users and people who got it from transfusions. But it slapped me right in the face. From all angles, it slapped me.

PLAYBOY: Have you been tested?

JORDAN: I've been tested for the last two years.

PLAYBOY: Why?

JORDAN: Because I've had insurance policies that demanded it.

PLAYBOY: Would it surprise you if there were other sports figures who tested positive?

JORDAN: No.

PLAYBOY: Would it have surprised you before Magic's announcement?

JORDAN: One of your prime personalities has gone public and said he got it through promiscuity. He wasn't the only promiscuous athlete. I'm pretty sure he won't be the last.

PLAYBOY: Tell us about life on the road in the NBA.

JORDAN: There are a lot of things being said about the opportunities you have on the road. Sure, you have opportunities, you have opportunities everywhere. After the game, you see different women. Players have always been knowledgeable about that, to say who's who and what's what. If you don't listen, then you're putting yourself at risk.

PLAYBOY: And there are guys who don't think or listen.

JORDAN: Magic said it himself: You never think it can happen to you. Next thing you know, you're stung by a bee.

PLAYBOY: Are guys really going to learn this lesson, or is it just a passing concern?

JORDAN: It's going to cut down some of the playing around. But I also think it's going to allow for both men and women to be more open-minded about safe sex. I think Magic is going to make players say, Hey, don't be afraid to ask this person. Now it's a given: You have to talk about it.

PLAYBOY: It used to be that a player's primary concern was not getting someone pregnant—

JORDAN: Or getting VD or herpes. Now you pray for that.

PLAYBOY: What was your relationship with Magic early on in your career?

JORDAN: I liked him when I was in high school. They used to call me Magic Jordan. My first car had a license plate with Magic Jordan on it. It was a 1976 Grand Prix.

PLAYBOY: Things were pretty strained between you when you first got into the league, weren't they?

JORDAN: There was a little bit of envy because of the way I came into the league. Magic came in with even more flair and even more success. And he should have been even bigger than I was in terms of endorsements and business opportunities. But he wasn't marketed that way. And I was fortunate to have good people. So there was some envy.

PLAYBOY: How did the two of you get over it?

JORDAN: During my third year, he invited me out to play in his summer charity game. We ironed out our differences in private in the locker room and we began a relationship.

PLAYBOY: There are some differences you haven't ironed out. What's the story with you and Isiah Thomas and the alleged Jordan freeze-out at the 1985 NBA All-Star game? Do you think they were really denying you the ball?

JORDAN: If you go back and look at the film, you can see that Isiah was actually doing that. Once it started getting around that he was freezing me out, that's when the ill feelings started to grow between us.

PLAYBOY: There were some problems even before the game, weren't there?

JORDAN: That was my first All-Star game. I stayed in my room most of the time because I didn't know what to do. None of my teammates were there. I didn't want to be out in a situation that I wasn't comfortable with. The one time I did go out, I got on an elevator with Isiah Thomas to go downstairs for a league meeting. That was the first time I met him. And I said, "Hello, how ya doin'?" That's all I said. I was really intimidated because I didn't know him and I didn't want to get on his nerves. I didn't want to seem like a rookie. You know, to just be so stupid. So I was quiet. I stayed in the corner. When I went down in the room for the meeting, I still didn't say anything. After the weekend was over, it got back to me that I was arrogant and cocky and I wouldn't even speak to Isiah on the elevator, that I gave him the cold shoulder. And I'm saying Isiah Thomas initiated it all.

PLAYBOY: How did that make you feel?

JORDAN: I was really disappointed and upset because I never wanted to step on anybody's toes. When I came into the league, I considered myself the lowest on the totem pole. I'm a rookie, now let me work my way up. When I started with the Bulls, they wanted me to be a vocal leader, but I told coach Kevin Loughery that I didn't feel comfortable doing that. We had all these guys with six or seven years in the league and I was in my first year. How could I tell these guys this and that? The best way I could do it was just to go out and play hard. And that's the way I've always treated it. They took that as disrespect and misinterpreted that whole weekend.

PLAYBOY: The next game after the All-Star break was at home against Detroit. How did you react?

JORDAN: Normally, I would smile and enjoy myself, but I was serious the whole game. It was a grudge game from my standpoint. And the next day, the headlines read "Jordan Gets His Revenge, Scores 49." That's all Isiah needed to see. It was a competition from that point. I always tried to respect him and be kind, but I always would hear talk that he was saying things about me behind my back. I just said, Well, I'm gonna stop trying to be nice. Screw it. Just play basketball. We don't have to be best of friends.

PLAYBOY: Was that experience ultimately good for you?

JORDAN: Well, it taught me about the jealousy that you deal with on this level. But at the same time, this is a business. I'm going to take advantage of all the opportunities. If they were in my shoes, they would do the exact same thing.

PLAYBOY: Other players were jealous of your success in endorsements and business dealings?

JORDAN: Right. But why must I squander my opportunities because those guys never got that opportunity? They don't want me to have it and they're going to be pissed at me if I do it? Screw that. And some people may view that as wrong. I see people writing letters to the editor: "I'm tired of seeing Michael Jordan's face everywhere." Who are you? Because if you were where I am, you'd be doing the same thing. I'm not going to let that bother me. This is a business. I want to take advantage of my opportunities and walk away from the game financially set. I'm not doing anything that anybody else in my position wouldn't do.

PLAYBOY: When did you adjust to being a celebrity?

JORDAN: My fourth year.

PLAYBOY: Not until then?

JORDAN: I was really liking it up until about my fourth year. But that's when you start getting tired. Your moods start to change. People start taking advantage of your niceness. And you want more time for yourself. You change your whole attitude. I'm starting to be more open about everything. Before I was hesitant about saying how I feel.

PLAYBOY: What do you mean?

JORDAN: I'll tell you if I don't like something. Before I would just keep it to myself. Now I'm becoming a little more opinionated because people have become more opinionated about me.

PLAYBOY: Let's talk a little about your public image. Why didn't you go to the White House when President Bush invited the team?

JORDAN: I didn't want to go. I had something else to do. Before I would have said, "Well, I had my reasons." I'd do it in a very respectful way. But that's none of your business. The Bulls knew I wasn't going, so why must I tell you? Go ask them why I didn't go. They knew. I make my stand now because it's easy for people to take advantage of me and become more opinionated about things that I choose to do. I may not be in agreement with what people want me to do. Who gives a damn? They don't live the life that I try to live. Do I ask them why they go to the bathroom?

PLAYBOY: They don't have to deal with what you deal with.

JORDAN: Right, they don't. People say they wish they were Michael Jordan. OK, do it for a year. Do it for two years. Do it for five years.

When you get past the fun part, then go do the part where you get into cities at three A.M. and you have 15 people waiting for autographs when you're as tired as hell. Your knees are sore, back's sore, your body's sore, and yet you have to sign 15 autographs at three in the morning.

PLAYBOY: What happens if you don't?

JORDAN: Somebody will take a shot, saying, "Oh, look at him." On one road trip, we got into Denver at three in the morning and there were people sitting in the hotel lobby. I was tired. I said, "I'm sorry, please, I'm tired." Then I heard, "I guess that's the Jordan rules." I just kept on walking. One of these days I'm going to say, "Go screw yourself." Maybe when I'm walking out of the league.

PLAYBOY: Tell us about your championship season. Was it as turbulent as it was described in *The Jordan Rules*?

JORDAN: I haven't read it.

PLAYBOY: In the book, Sam Smith remarked on all the tickets you got to a sold-out game in last year's finals. The implication was that you were being afforded preferential treatment. Are your Bulls tickets free?

JORDAN: I buy every damn ticket. Ain't nobody giving me tickets. I pay for all those $50 box-seat tickets I give to little kids. For all the loose tickets that I may have after a game that I do not use and I give to [Bulls forward] Scottie Pippen, give to [Bulls forward] Horace Grant, give to people, I pay for them all. I don't ask them to pay me back. I spent $100,000 on tickets last year that I didn't get back. That's money that I paid the Bulls and other teams. So don't bitch at me about all the tickets I spread around.

PLAYBOY: Another anecdote, which presumably shows you as a selfish scorer, had Bulls center Bill Cartwright talking about a game against New Jersey. According to Cartwright, you were complaining that coach Phil Jackson took you out of the game to keep you from scoring more.

JORDAN: Sam Smith says Cartwright said I was bitching about not getting 50 points and that everyone could have scored 20 instead. That's the biggest lie in America. The whole offense is set for Cartwright to score as many points as he can. If he can't score, that's his damn problem. All I can do is throw him the ball. I can't make him move.

PLAYBOY: What about the charge that you want only to score?

JORDAN: I don't go out and just try to score. I score because there is an opportunity to score. It doesn't matter who scores. If you have an opportunity to score, you score. And we win. Smith made it seem like I was selfish in that sense, that all I thought about was getting my points when actually I wasn't worried about that. I was worried about winning. Who cares what happens with the points?

PLAYBOY: The scoring title doesn't mean anything to you?

JORDAN: It doesn't even faze me anymore. If I win the scoring title this year, I win it. If I don't, I don't. I know I could win it if I wanted to. But I just don't try to chase it anymore. I let whatever happens happen.

PLAYBOY: What was your contact with the author?

JORDAN: [Bulls vice president of operations Jerry] Krause and I are the most criticized people in the book, but we're the only two that didn't go to lunch with this dude. It's like he was planning to kill us anyway, so why take us to lunch?

PLAYBOY: Did you expect that this sort of thing would happen to you one day?

JORDAN: I knew people were going to start taking shots at me. You get to a point where people are going to get tired of seeing you on a pedestal, all clean and polished. They say, Let's see if there's any dirt around this person. But I never expected it to come from inside. Sam tried to make it seem like he was a friend of the family for eight months. But the family talked about all this hatred they have for me. I mean, if they had so much hatred for me, how could they play with me? Why didn't they go to [Bulls owner] Jerry Reinsdorf and ask him to trade me? I don't know *how* we won if there was so much hatred among all of us. It looked like we all got along so well.

PLAYBOY: Do you look at your teammates and wonder to yourself if they really said that stuff?

JORDAN: I can imagine some of the things being said from anger or jealousy or disappointment. But I could see Sam Smith actually manipulating, putting words in their mouths, to get his meaning from the situation. Let's say Horace Grant was upset for one game about not getting enough shots and maybe I had a lot more shots than anybody else. Sam can sense that anger, get over there and ask him all kinds of questions. In the book, Sam makes it appear to be a problem all season long. Actually, it's just one game.

PLAYBOY: Anything else bug you about it?

JORDAN: He really exploits certain things. I've heard there was a story about how Pippen, Grant and I were talking about our sons' penises. He said we spent thirty minutes debating whose son had the biggest penis. What's the purpose of that being in the book? You know it's kidding, so what?

PLAYBOY: Let's get back to the championship drive. You seem to feel that it wasn't enough to win the NBA title, you had to do it the right way.

JORDAN: When we were beating Philly in the playoffs last year and Detroit was going against Boston, everyone was saying, "I hope Boston wins." I said, No way. If we're going to go, we have to go the hardest route, or else as a team, we're going to get criticized for it. First of all, Scottie Pippen would never redeem himself from having those three headaches, or whatever he had, in the final 1990 conference championship game against the Pistons. As a team we would never live it down because we always faltered under Detroit's pressure. No one really gained respect from Detroit players.

PLAYBOY: It would have reflected badly on you, too.

JORDAN: All of that would have been right on my shoulders. Yeah, you won a championship, people would have said, but you didn't go through Detroit to do it. I didn't want that crap to happen. I wanted to go the hardest route.

PLAYBOY: There was also the matter of how you compared to Magic and Larry Bird.

JORDAN: When it came to comparisons, this is what always knocked me out of the top two players: People would always say, "All these great plays and he's never taken his team to a championship." So I wanted to go through one of those two. It worked out perfect.

PLAYBOY: Magic made his teammates better. That's something you've been accused of failing to do.

JORDAN: The championship was my opportunity to show I'm not just a scorer. That was the challenge when everyone tried to make it a one-on-one situation, Magic versus Michael. I realized that. But you know, I told people that if we got to the Finals, we were going to win, if I have anything to do with it. I might never get this opportunity again. And when I got to the Finals, all I tried to do was plug holes—scoring, passing, rebounding, whatever—just as they had portrayed Magic as doing.

PLAYBOY: Was there a particular moment in the year when you thought, Maybe we can go all the way?

JORDAN: When we beat Detroit before the All-Star game.

PLAYBOY: The early?

JORDAN: We beat them in Detroit. We hadn't beaten them in Detroit for about 10 games, and once we did, it gave us confidence. We needed to know that we could beat them on their court. In the conference championship series the year before, we had defended our home court well. But we went up there and got stomped in game seven.

PLAYBOY: Let's talk about the Detroit series in last year's playoffs. You blew through New York and Philadelphia, and then came the Pistons.

JORDAN: We were waiting for this. We had the home-court advantage. And we defended our home court the last six or seven times. The first game was a key because you knew they were going to throw shit at us. Pippen knew what Dennis Rodman was going to do. He couldn't let him get into his head. Just play, turn your face and keep going. We won both games in Chicago, so we went up to Detroit and said, Let's sweep them.

PLAYBOY: Could you see the fear in their eyes?

JORDAN: Yeah. They couldn't rattle us. They tried everything to rattle our confidence.

PLAYBOY: Such as?

JORDAN: Throwing punches, throwing guys at you, talking shit. So I'm saying, Well, these guys talk trash all the damn time to everybody. Let's see if they can handle some trash-talking back to them. So I started talking it to 'em. With Mark Aguirre, I said, "This is not your home. You're not in Chicago anymore. You live in Detroit. This is our home." "Rodman," I said, "Rodman, best defensive player? Jump your ass over here if you think you're the best defensive player in the league." And that irritated the hell out of him. Every time he'd go past me, boom, knee me in the corner, knee me in the back. He was trying to frustrate me. And I was trying to do exactly what he would do. I'm trying to knock the hell out of Rodman. I'm telling Scottie to bring him off the screen—boom, I knock him. Rodman got pissed off because we were doing the same shit that he would do. I knew I was getting to him.

PLAYBOY: How about Isiah?

JORDAN: He was really passive. I think that he was so confident that they had something on us that, in a sense, he wasn't needed to win. He was just going to be the director instead of being the aggressor. Once he tried to be aggressive, it was too late.

PLAYBOY: Have Pistons players tried to hurt you?

JORDAN: Laimbeer has. The first time it happened, I thought it was just an initiation into the league. And then the crap started happening every time on the break, he and I angling off at the break. He doesn't even try to block the shot. His whole body is coming at me. And I'm going up in the air, I can lose control, anything can happen. I'm irritated by it but I handle it. I'm waiting for my last year.

PLAYBOY: Is Laimbeer worse than the rest of them, even Rodman?

JORDAN: No, I think Rodman and Laimbeer are just alike. They try to live up to their image of being assholes.

PLAYBOY: The Detroit series was a remarkably thorough beating.

JORDAN: That's why they walked off the court. We embarrassed them. To sweep them four-zip, it was embarrassing. Defending champions, embarrassing. It was like good overriding evil.

PLAYBOY: What do you mean by "evil"?

JORDAN: It was their style of basketball. If you knock a person down on a hard foul, you pick that man up and say, "Are you all right?" The Pistons will knock you down, then, if possible, kick you. They try to use that crap as an intimidator. The evil came out of their attitude, the unsportsmanlike actions. That bad-boy image brought them some gold, but it also brought them a lot of shame.

PLAYBOY: It drives Detroit nuts to hear you say things like that. They feel you don't give them any respect.

JORDAN: Respect for what?

PLAYBOY: All their success.

JORDAN: It's true. Everybody knows it. They were smart enough to utilize their image and win. They didn't win just off brute force. They had talent enough to win. But they could still have that talent without the brutality.

PLAYBOY: Did it surprise you during the last game when they walked off the floor before time had expired?

JORDAN: Yeah, it really did. Isiah Thomas is the president of our players association and yet he is going to orchestrate that unsportsmanlike conduct? Three years in a row, I pushed myself to shake their hands and wish them luck and told them to bring the championship back to the Eastern Conference.

PLAYBOY: That had to be hard to swallow.

JORDAN: Hard to swallow, but out of sportsmanship, this is what you're supposed to do.

PLAYBOY: When did you realize that the NBA title was within your grasp?

JORDAN: In the first game against the Lakers. They played their asses off, we played terrible, but we still had a chance to win down the stretch. That's all we needed from that point on. That gave us our confidence. It was a moral victory for us in the first game. Then in the second game, we went right back and pounded them. Gave us that confidence back that we lost.

PLAYBOY: Most people looked at it from the standpoint that the Lakers got a game in Chicago.

JORDAN: Yeah, but the momentum changed. It's not like it just changed hands, we grabbed it.

PLAYBOY: What were the emotions like before game five against the Lakers?

JORDAN: We were just determined.

PLAYBOY: Were you scared?

JORDAN: Nope, I wasn't scared. We had three chances to win one, right? I wasn't nervous. We went in there relaxed.

PLAYBOY: When did it hit you that the championship was yours?

JORDAN: When [guard] John Paxson started knocking down shots. He was measuring them, boom, he was just knocking them down. I missed some of the excitement by not doing it in Chicago. If we had done it in Chicago, we probably wouldn't have lived, because the fans would have killed us. But it was nearly as bad in L.A.

PLAYBOY: What happened in the locker room after the final game? It looked like you were overwhelmed with emotion.

JORDAN: I tried to fight it, but I couldn't. I suppressed a lot of disappointment over the years. When we won it all, I became more emotional than I have ever been. I don't regret it. It was something I had to let out.

PLAYBOY: Is there going to be any challenge to the Olympics?

JORDAN: You know, it's one of those situations where the challenge is going to be playing together as a team. When you look at the talent and the teams we're supposed to play against, it's a massacre. It should never be close. We taught them the game of basketball. We've got people who have the ability and the height. We're talking about the greatest players that play the game now and the team is the best team that's ever been put together. Who's going to beat us? The Japanese? The Chinese? They can't match up to the athleticism we're going to have on this team. Not to mention the mental advantage we're going to have here with Magic, or whoever's gonna play the point. You have Stockton, Barkley, me, Robinson, Bird . . . come on. These are the people that the Europeans look up to, so how can they beat us? If any game is even close, it will be a moral victory for Europe.

PLAYBOY: What will you do if Bill Laimbeer or Isiah Thomas makes the Olympic team?

JORDAN: I would respect them as teammates and we would play as a team.

PLAYBOY: You still would do it?

JORDAN: If I walk off now, you think there's not going to be a controversy? I would do it to avoid all the publicity and feelings between us. Americans shouldn't be that way when they're representing the country. You just have to do it.

PLAYBOY: Why do you think Magic wants to play in the Olympics? What does it matter, given what he's accomplished?

JORDAN: He has accomplished everything possible in terms of basketball except for one thing: He's never played in an Olympic game. Never had that gold medal. And that can be eating at him. He probably would take that risk knowing that he might give up a day or two of his life. You know what? If I were in his position, I probably would do it, too. I'm going to be in his corner all the way. It adds something to your life when you win a gold medal. You hear the whole world cheering for you. That's far greater than any other cheering you're going to hear in basketball.

PLAYBOY: Even greater than the NBA title?

JORDAN: Yeah. The title is for Chicago and the Bulls fans around the United States, but the Olympics are for everybody in the United States and then some.

PLAYBOY: For all the credit, respect, celebrity and money that have come to you in your career, you remain a black man in a country dominated by white corporate structures. Recently, you have even taken shots from black writers who suggest you're not black enough.

JORDAN: I realize that I'm black, but I like to be viewed as a person, and that's everybody's wish. That's what Martin Luther King fought for, that everybody could be treated equal and be viewed as a person. In some ways I can't understand it, because here we are striving for equality and yet people are going to say I'm not black enough? At a time when actually I thought I was trying to be equal? I try to be a role model for black kids, white kids, yellow kids, green kids. This is what I felt was good about my personality. Don't knock me off the pedestal that you wanted me to get onto. I get criticized about not giving back to the community—well, that's not true. I do. I just don't go out and try to seek publicity from it. I could hold a press conference on everything that I do for the black community. But I don't choose to do that, so people are not aware of it.

PLAYBOY: Does the accusation sting?

JORDAN: Yeah, it's really unfair. Because they ask for more black role models, yet they're stabbing me when I'm up here trying to be a very positive black role model.

PLAYBOY: You don't seem like a very political person.

JORDAN: I always keep my political views to myself.

PLAYBOY: But there are others who want you to be more up-front.

JORDAN: Look at what happened in North Carolina. I got criticized for not endorsing Harvey Gantt, the black guy who was running for the Senate against Jesse Helms in North Carolina. I chose not to because I didn't know of his achievements, I didn't know if he had some negative things against him. Before I put myself on the line, at least I wanted to know who this guy was. And I didn't, but I knew of Jesse Helms and I wasn't in favor of him. So I sent Gantt some money as a contribution. But that was never publicized. It was just that I didn't come out publicly and do an endorsement.

PLAYBOY: How do you handle pressure from Jesse Jackson and other activists?

JORDAN: I never bow to that pressure because I always keep my opinions to myself. I avoid those types of endorsements from a political standpoint. That's just me. That's my prerogative to do so. If you don't like it, lump it.

PLAYBOY: How did you react when Operation PUSH called for a boycott of Nike?

JORDAN: It was a valid point. But if you're going to take that stand about having blacks in more controlling or executive positions, do it with every shoe company. Don't pick the one on top and say, Hey, there aren't enough blacks involved. Because you're targeting Nike while Reebok and all these others are going to gain from us being attacked. That's not fair. Say the whole shoe industry does not have enough blacks in powerful executive positions. OK, I'm with you. Maybe we have to change that. I'm saying, come to the black people involved and ask us, Well, are blacks being promoted in higher positions? We could have said yes. John Thompson is on the Nike board of directors. I hope I can be put on the advisory board, and we're starting to move up. Naturally, you still want to have more. I think PUSH helped get more blacks involved in the business side. But they approached it from a bad angle.

PLAYBOY: You like to play golf, but there's no sport with a richer history of exclusion. Do you think that has irritated some in the black community, that you play at exclusive clubs in spite of their policies?

JORDAN: I think I'm opening the door for blacks to be involved. I was getting more opportunities to go to these clubs. Sam Smith wrote in his book that I would have been declined membership at a Jewish golf course, but that's not true. I never applied. The only golf courses that I applied to, I got accepted. He had me saying that if I won the lottery, I'd go out and buy a golf course and keep out all the Jews. Well, why would I have to win the lottery? I could go buy one now.

PLAYBOY: Where are you a member?

JORDAN: I'm a member in Chicago at Wynstone, at Wexford in Hilton Head, and in Rancho Sante Fe at a place called the Farms. I'm a member at the Governor's Club in Chapel Hill.

PLAYBOY: Do you pay the regular members' dues and fees?

JORDAN: Yeah, I pay. I went through the normal procedures of getting in. I never want it to be a privilege. I don't want to be a token.

PLAYBOY: When was the first time you ever had to deal with racism?

JORDAN: When I threw a soda at a girl for calling me a nigger. It was when *Roots* was on television.

PLAYBOY: How old were you?

JORDAN: I was 15. It was a very tough year. I was really rebelling. I considered myself a racist at that time. Basically, I was against all white people.

PLAYBOY: Why?

JORDAN: It was hundreds of years of pain that they put us through, and for the first time, I saw it from watching *Roots*. I was very ignorant about it initially, but I really opened my eyes about my ancestors and the things that they had to deal with.

PLAYBOY: How long did it take you to get over that?

JORDAN: A whole year. The education came from my parents. You have to be able to say, OK, that happened back then. Now let's take it from here and see what happens. It would be very easy to hate people for the rest of your life, and some people have done that. You've got to deal with what's happening now and try to make things better.

PLAYBOY: What did you think you'd be when you grew up?

JORDAN: A professional athlete.

PLAYBOY: How early did you begin thinking that?

JORDAN: I *always* thought I would be a professional athlete. I always loved sports. I knew one thing I didn't want was a job. Me and working were never best friends. I enjoyed playing.

PLAYBOY: Your dad once said that you were the laziest kid he had.

JORDAN: He doesn't lie. He tried to change me, but it never worked. He couldn't keep me from playing sports. I think my first job was in the 11th grade and I quit after a week.

PLAYBOY: What was it?

JORDAN: I was a hotel maintenance man. I was cleaning out pools, painting rails, changing air-conditioner filters and sweeping out the back room. I said, never again. I may be a wino first, but I will not have a nine-to-five job.

PLAYBOY: You had a bad experience with swimming when you were a kid, didn't you?

JORDAN: I went swimming with a close friend one day, and we were out wading and riding the waves coming in. The current was so strong it took him under and he locked up on me. It's called the death lock, when they know they're in trouble and about to die. I almost had to break his hand. He was gonna take me with him.

PLAYBOY: Did you save him?

JORDAN: No, he died. I don't go into the water anymore.

PLAYBOY: How old were you?

JORDAN: I was really young. About seven or eight years old. Now I ain't going near the water. I can't swim and I ain't messing with the water.

PLAYBOY: Even when you go on a boat?

JORDAN: Not without a life jacket, I won't. Not a little boat, either. It has to be a big boat for me.

PLAYBOY: It doesn't bother you to say that, does it?

JORDAN: No. I don't give a damn. Everybody's got a phobia for something. I do not mess with water.

PLAYBOY: Were you always a star in sports?

JORDAN: No, but I had ambitions of being one. All I wanted to do was play all the time. I used to give up whatever allowance I had to my brothers, for them to wash dishes for me and clean the house.

PLAYBOY: Did it bother your father?

JORDAN: My father is a mechanical person. He always tried to save money by working on everybody's cars. And my older brothers would go out and work with him. He would tell them to hand him a nine-sixteenths wrench and they'd do it. I'd get out there and he'd say give me a nine-sixteenths wrench and I didn't know what the hell he was talking about. He used to get irritated with me and say, "You don't know what the hell you're doing, go on in there with the women."

PLAYBOY: Were you popular with girls in high school?

JORDAN: I always thought I would be a bachelor. I couldn't get a date.

PLAYBOY: Come on.

JORDAN: I kidded around too much. I always used to play around with women. I was a clown. I picked at people a lot. That was my way of breaking the ice with people who were very serious. I was good in school. I'd get A's and B's in my classes but I'd get N's and U's in conduct because I was kidding around, talking all the time.

PLAYBOY: We've heard you did some serious preparation for bachelor life.

JORDAN: I took home economics from seventh through ninth grade. They were easy classes, we got to eat and I was always a greedy person with food. And you got to do things. I always thought I'd be doing my own sewing and cooking and cleaning.

PLAYBOY: What can you do?

JORDAN: Oh, I can sew shirts, I can make clothes.

PLAYBOY: Still?

JORDAN: I could hem pants right now. I can cook and clean and all that stuff. But do I do it? No. I don't want to. But I could if I had to.

PLAYBOY: Did you watch basketball much as a kid?

JORDAN: I used to watch a little ACC college basketball because we never got professional basketball on TV where I lived. I didn't know anybody in the NBA I only knew David Thompson, Walter Davis, guys from my area.

PLAYBOY: When you were a high school senior, did North Carolina recruit you?

JORDAN: They were recruiting me when I was in the 11th grade. My high school coach wrote to them, so they sent a scout down. I went to North Carolina with the Five-Star camp, even though Dean Smith didn't want me to go.

PLAYBOY: Why not?

JORDAN: He tried to keep me hidden. If I was at Five-Star, they would open up the doors of the schools and everybody would notice. I won about 10 trophies in two weeks. I was an all-star and the MVP for two weeks in a row and my team won the championship both weeks. I was racking it up. Then everybody started recruiting me.

PLAYBOY: Was North Carolina your first choice?

JORDAN: I always wanted to go to UCLA. That was my dream school.

PLAYBOY: Why?

JORDAN: Because when I was growing up, they were a great team. Kareem Abdul-Jabbar, Bill Walton, John Wooden. But I never got recruited by UCLA.

PLAYBOY: Even after your success in the Five-Star camp?

JORDAN: By the time they wanted to recruit me, they had heard that I was going to stay close to home, which was not necessarily true. I also wanted to go to Virginia because I wanted to play with Ralph Sampson for his last two years there. He was going into his junior year. I wrote to Virginia, but they just sent me back an admission form. No one came and watched me. Then I visited North Carolina and I was happy with the atmosphere, so I committed early.

PLAYBOY: Weren't you planning to play baseball in college, too?

JORDAN: I wanted to, but I got talked out of it. I still want to play baseball. I may play Triple-A ball this summer. I keep trying to talk to the people in Charlotte. You know George Shinn, the guy who owns the Charlotte Hornets? [Hornets players] Muggsy Bogues and Dell Curry played for his minor-league baseball team last summer. I told them I want to go play baseball. They don't believe me. I'm serious. I may think about football, too. I ain't going across the middle, though. I'll do down and out.

PLAYBOY: If you made a run at baseball, what position would you play?

JORDAN: Well, I used to be a pitcher. But I'd probably throw my arm out just learning all the different things. I'd much rather try to start out in the outfield or first base. I'm going to do it. But I would never want just to step right into the majors. Players would get pissed at me. I don't want that animosity. I want to start off low and work my way up.

PLAYBOY: You have had four pro coaches. Whom did you like to play for the most?

JORDAN: Who was best for me? Kevin Loughery.

PLAYBOY: Why?

JORDAN: He gave me the confidence to play on his level. My first year, he threw me the ball and said, "Hey, kid, I know you can play. Go play." I don't think that would have been the case going through another coach's system. Look what Loughery's doing right now with Miami. He's doing exactly what he did to me. He's giving those guys so much confidence, he's giving them an opportunity to create their own identity as players. With other coaches, you have to fit into their systems.

PLAYBOY: Even Doug Collins?

JORDAN: No, I just felt Doug would have tried to manipulate me. For that sense of control, power. I saw that with the way he dealt with Pippen and Grant. I would have been able to deal with it because I respect all my coaches. But Loughery never tried to do that. I could relate with him as a friend.

PLAYBOY: What about Phil Jackson as a coach?

JORDAN: Phil's a good coach. He has some Dean Smith credentials out there. He's relaxed, he's knowledgeable. He's a philosopher about everything. He believes in sharing the wealth among everyone, yet he believes in not trying to overshadow his team.

PLAYBOY: The Portland Trail Blazers had a shot at drafting you. How would that have changed your life?

JORDAN: I wouldn't have had all this opportunity from a business and financial standpoint.

PLAYBOY: Would your life have been any easier?

JORDAN: No, this has gone exactly the way I wanted it to. Portland already had Clyde Drexler, so it would have been dumb for me to go there.

PLAYBOY: Did your success with Nike surprise you?

JORDAN: Yeah, that was something. First I thought it was a fad. But it's far greater now than it used to be. The numbers are just outrageous.

PLAYBOY: When did you really start getting into the business end of it?

JORDAN: Four years ago.

PLAYBOY: Not until then?

JORDAN: In my first four years, I just loved playing basketball and didn't worry about the money part of it. But I was being tutored and educated by ProServ.

PLAYBOY: What do you mean tutored?

JORDAN: Tutored about financial things, you know, monthly ledgers, where your money comes from and where it goes. My parents did a good job, too. They, as well as ProServ, helped educate me when I really didn't have the interest in it. But it's getting closer to the point where I will step away from the game, so I better have a good handle on it.

PLAYBOY: Do you want to have a certain number of millions in the bank when you retire?

JORDAN: I've provided for when I walk away from the game, from Nike and all the other outlets.

PLAYBOY: I heard about a Canadian company that wanted to pay you a ridiculous amount of money to fly up for one day.

JORDAN: Yeah, they wanted me to sign autographs for a quarter of a million dollars. The autograph stuff drives me crazy. People are dangerous.

PLAYBOY: Didn't you almost get stampeded in Houston once?

JORDAN: There were four or five security guards, 5000 people had me circled, and I was only supposed to be signing for one hour. We got to 10 minutes before I had to leave, and people were wanting more autographs, so they started closing in on me. The tables were breaking and little kids were getting pressed up front because the bigger people were pushing from behind. The security guards couldn't do anything. I finally got the security guards around me and started pushing my way through the crowd. I almost got killed getting out of there. I haven't done any autograph sessions since. Never again.

PLAYBOY: Do you have other limits about what you will and won't do for money?

JORDAN: My time is very important to me, as well as being credible about what I endorse. If I endorse McDonald's, I go to McDonald's. If I endorse Wheaties, I eat Wheaties. If I endorse Gatorade, I drink Gatorade. I have cases of Gatorade, I love drinking Gatorade. I don't endorse anything that I don't actually use.

PLAYBOY: What have you turned down?

JORDAN: Two or three years ago Quaker Oats came to me to endorse Van Kamp's pork and beans—Beanee Weenees, I think it was called. You ever heard of Beanee Weenees pork and beans? It was close to a million bucks a year. I'm saying, Beanee Weenees? How can I stand in front of a camera and say I'll eat Beanee Weenees? If I wanted to be a hardnosed businessman, I could have been in a lot of deals, like the one with Johnson Products. I had a deal with them for their hair-care products. I had two or three more years on that deal when I started losing my hair. So I forfeited the deal. But if I had wanted to be greedy, I could've said, Screw you, you didn't know my hair was falling out so you owe me money. But I didn't.

PLAYBOY: Your Gatorade ad raises a question—what do you like to be called?

JORDAN: They used to call me Mike in grammar school, in high school. When I got to college, everyone called me Michael. It was like a maturity thing. When you're a little kid, they call you Mike. Mike quit this, Mike quit that. As you get older, it's Michael this and Michael that. Now in the pros, it's Air this, Air that. Things change.

PLAYBOY: Once and for all, which is it: Mike or Michael?

JORDAN: Mike.

PLAYBOY: Which individual games stand out in your memory?

JORDAN: The 69-point game against Cleveland stands out. The 63-point game at Boston stands out.

PLAYBOY: Do you ever watch any of them on tape?

JORDAN: Not anymore. I used to. I really don't watch myself play as much. I used to about three or four years ago, just for motivation. When I'd get home and I didn't have anything to do, I'd watch a game, get myself ready and sometimes even watch one before a game. If we're gonna play Detroit, I'll watch a Detroit game. One we won. I don't want to watch a game we lost.

PLAYBOY: Did you watch that Boston game a lot?

JORDAN: The 63-point game? No, I didn't. Because I always knew we'd lose. Every time I'd watch it, we'd lose. We should win. I don't watch that one.

PLAYBOY: When you get in the zone, like you do in those games where you get 50 or 60, do you feel it coming on that day, in the locker room, on the bench?

JORDAN: No, I feel it when the game starts. You just start getting on a roll. Everything that you do is working. You get steals, your offensive game is working. You just take control of it. You're in tune with everything that's going on. You control the tempo, you control everything. It's like you can do anything, you can take your time, you say anything to people, you seem to be just like you're on a playground all by yourself.

PLAYBOY: Can you dictate it now? Can you get yourself in the zone?

JORDAN: I get into it in pressure situations. Somehow you feel the pressure. Either you do it now or you don't do it at all and it starts to kick in. But to explain it you'd have to be a psychologist.

PLAYBOY: Is basketball a refuge for you?

JORDAN: When I step onto the court, I don't have to think about anything. If I have a problem off the court, I find that after I play, my mind is clearer and I can come up with a better solution. It's like therapy. It relaxes me and allows me to solve problems.

PLAYBOY: One constant in your career is that when you are sick or hurt, you often unload on somebody. Why?

JORDAN: I have an uncanny way of focusing when I get hurt. I concentrate on playing and not worrying about the injury. I don't try to be aggressive or to let the injury take me out of my game. I relax and let the game come to me.

PLAYBOY: Do you have any superstitions?

JORDAN: I go through the same routine before every game. I lace up my shoes in a certain way. I wear my Carolina shorts all the time. I wear new socks every game, new shoes every game. And I always notice where my wife or my parents are so I don't have to worry if they got in an accident or didn't get the tickets or whatever.

PLAYBOY: Where do you think you fit in the game? Are you the best?

JORDAN: I can't ever say that I'm the best. I think I play both ends and do more than people perceive. I'm not just an offensive player. I play both ends. I can pass, I think I can play defensively as well as offensively. I don't think most stars can say that they try to do that. You can't say that I'm a one-dimensional player or a two-dimensional player.

PLAYBOY: If you had to put a team around you, what's the one quality you'd want?

JORDAN: Heart. That would be the biggest thing. I think heart means a lot. It separates the great from the good players.

PLAYBOY: Aside from the shots, what else do the great players have?

JORDAN: Mental toughness. When you need a basket, you have to have the confidence in yourself to go out there and hit three great shots. You know you have to do it. That drives me.

PLAYBOY: What's your all-time starting five?

JORDAN: Me and Magic, Bird, Worthy, McHale or Malone, David Robinson or Abdul-Jabbar.

PLAYBOY: And you can beat anyone ever?

JORDAN: I did this with Jerry Krause once. He chose Oscar Robertson, Bill Russell, Jerry West. At small forward he had Dr. J. The power forward was Gus Johnson. I told him I'd kill him. Of all players, the all-time greats, he left off Magic and he left off Bird. He was excluding me. He put West at two [shooting] guard.

PLAYBOY: What if you couldn't pick yourself?

JORDAN: I would put West at two, too.

PLAYBOY: You've never been the highest paid basketball player and probably never will be. Do you resent that?

JORDAN: Since I came into the league, I've never griped about my contracts. I've signed them and I've honored them every year. If anybody stepped up and wanted to give me a raise, I'd accept it. But I'm not going to bitch about it, because I signed the contract. When Patrick Ewing renegotiated his contract last year, he had leverage. He had an option to get out of his contract. And he was going to get the money no matter what. If I play out my contract, I won't be able to get another contract until five years down the road. Who knew this was going to happen three years ago when we did my deal? No one could tell that salaries were going to jump out of the deck. Hot Rod Williams created a whole salary outburst. When I signed my deal for three-and-a-quarter million or whatever I make this year, I was in the top three. Now three years later, you have rookies coming out making two-and-a-half or three million, so they're pushing the salaries up. How can I get a new deal? Do I start bitching? Do I go and gripe to the press saying I deserve more? Everybody knows I deserve more money, but I actually signed the contract. If my boss decides to give me a raise, great. But bitching is not fair. I've always considered myself a fair person. You guys in the press can put the pressure on him. I won't. I hope Reinsdorf is thinking about it. If it happens, great. If it doesn't, then I was screwed again. Am I upset about it? No.

PLAYBOY: Is there anything you do on the basketball court that still surprises you?

JORDAN: I basically expect anything. Isn't that wild? I used to surprise myself a lot: certain moves, how I'd get out of trouble. But at some point, you accept the talent that you have, you accept your creativity.

PLAYBOY: Are you going to need some other creative outlet when you retire?

JORDAN: Golf could do that for me. Because you've got to create shots in certain situations. And the competition is always going to be there. I think it's even greater in golf because you know your opponent is always consistent: You know the course is going to shoot par every day. You always wonder, especially in my profession, what it would be like if I had to play against myself in a one-on-one game. Well, golf is that way because you compete against yourself in a mental way. That's the challenge.

PLAYBOY: How close are you to the end of your basketball career?

JORDAN: I'd say four years. If I make it, I make it. If I get tired of basketball sooner, I won't make it. All this negative crap that has happened. Who needs it?

PLAYBOY: What if Reinsdorf wanted to make it worth your while to play longer to keep the stadium full?

JORDAN: I would never play an extra year for money. I play the game because I love it. I just so happen to get paid. If I don't feel I still enjoy the game, I can care less what a year is worth. I'm not going to play the game just because of money.

PLAYBOY: Somehow, it's hard to imagine you just walking away.

JORDAN: People keep saying, Well, you're never going to be able to walk away, you're always going to want that spotlight. All these old boxers come back, but not me. Once I walk away, I'm walking away. I'm not going to embarrass myself coming back, like I really need that roar of the crowd to live. It was good while it lasted. I've got memories of it. I don't need it again to continue to live. That's what my family is for.

PLAYBOY: What's it like to be a married superstar? Does it take pressure off, or put more on?

JORDAN: It's great.

PLAYBOY: Why?

JORDAN: It was a well-timed decision to settle down and get married. And it's been a more laid-back environment for me with a wife and two kids. If I were seeing a person, I might be more nervous about infection than I am now. It would have been magnified even more for me if I were single. But I made a choice to get married and to have kids and to settle down with the family, and I'm glad I made it.

PLAYBOY: You grew up in a pretty stable family environment. Did it seem natural to get married?

JORDAN: It was like walking into another unknown situation. But I was ready to learn what marriage was all about. Every day you learn something. To live with another person for the rest of your life, that's something you have to work at. You're going to have some good times, some bad times. As a couple, as a unit, as a family, you gotta fight your way through it. But having kids always overrides any problems. And you know, it's sad to say, but especially considering Magic Johnson's situation, I look at my kids and think, I'm very fortunate.

PLAYBOY: Do you want a bunch more?

JORDAN: Not a bunch more. Maybe a couple more.

PLAYBOY: How does Juanita feel about that?

JORDAN: She's with me. But she wants all boys; I want two girls. I had two brothers and two sisters, so I want a combination of both.

PLAYBOY: Are you worried about your boys, in terms of being Michael Jordan's sons?

JORDAN: No. I just want them to have their own lives. I'm not going to try to guide them anywhere. I just want to teach them right from wrong, then let them make their own decisions. I know Jeffrey loves basketball. He has a basketball hoop in every room.

PLAYBOY: Does he understand the game?

JORDAN: Yeah. He travels a lot. He knows how to shoot a free throw. I tell him to shoot a free throw, and he backs up, dribbles, concentrates, boom. When he goes in for a dunk, he holds his form. And when he's really excited about things, he starts shooting and saying Yes! He's a showoff, man.

PLAYBOY: Whom do you look to for guidance?

JORDAN: Most of my guidance has come from my parents. My mom told me to deal with life as it comes, enjoy it as it comes, and that's what I've been doing. Good, bad or ugly. Whatever good that happens, I'm grateful.

I give all my respect and tribute to whoever has a hand in it. But when all the bad stuff comes, I try to deal with it in a positive manner.

PLAYBOY: Are you looking at other players to see how they handled the transition from the NBA back to private life?

JORDAN: Julius Erving is doing exactly what I want to do. Do you ever see Julius? Do you ever hear from Julius? But I know Julius is doing something he wants to do, and he's kind of taken a step back from public life. That's exactly what I want to do. When his time was up and he walked away from the game, he walked away proud, respected. Exactly what I want to do. When I feel that I've reached my peak and I can feel my skills diminishing, or if other players that I used to dominate have caught up with me and are on the same level, I want to step away.

PLAYBOY: You know there's going to be a long line of guys eager to take you apart, too.

JORDAN: And there'd be a long line of articles saying so-and-so killed Jordan tonight. I'd rather step away from the game before I subject myself to that, without a doubt.

PLAYBOY: Very few people have ever been able to walk away.

JORDAN: You know what I think? Very few people play because they love the game. Most of them play because they make good money. They keep playing because of the money. I could care less about it. In five years, I would probably stand to make six to seven million dollars, maybe even more than that. But if I don't love the game, no check is going to keep me playing.

PLAYBOY: Would you ever consider going to play in Europe after you retire from the NBA?

JORDAN: Yeah, I've thought about it. I would love to go to Europe to play for one year. I could play once a week. It would be like a field trip.

PLAYBOY: What won't you miss when you quit the game?

JORDAN: I won't miss the glare, I won't miss the aggravations of people waiting for autographs at all times of the night. The hotels, I won't miss all that.

PLAYBOY: What about the screams?

JORDAN: I won't miss that, either. Screaming for another human being is sort of a waste. What's the purpose of screaming? You're not hurt, are you? I don't need the screams and the cheers and I'm not going to wake up in the middle of the night and say, "Why did the screaming stop?" Because I really didn't need it to keep me going, anyway. It was that inner determination to prove to people that, hey, whatever you think

I can't do, I can do. Even last year after we won it all—and I showed people that I could pass, I showed people I can play defense, I showed people I could shoot—they said, Let's see him do it a whole year.

PLAYBOY: What's left? What's the challenge now?

JORDAN: The challenge is to keep winning and get more rings. People don't consider you great until you have three, four, maybe five rings. They consider you the greatest if your team is winning. I want to continue to win and make sure I'm an important factor in winning.

PLAYBOY: What do you think you'll miss the most about basketball when you retire?

JORDAN: The competition, the pre-season. I get a kick out of that, coming back for the next year and going through training camp and seeing all the new players. You go at them and challenge them every day. When someone asks, "What's Michael Jordan like to play with?" I want them to say he busts his ass at practice. He plays at practice like he plays in the game. When I play against someone that's new in the league, I make him respect me. They may have heard about me, but now you get to see me actually in front of you. That drives me. Like playing out west. They don't get to see us that much. I want to come in and say, This is what you're missing.

BILLIE JEAN KING

A candid conversation with the contentious superstar of women's tennis

If, in these days of raised female consciousness, someone were to write a liberated version of the old "hard-working boy makes good" stories, he could find a ready-made model in the sports world's first genuine woman superstar. Billie Jean King is a living testimonial to the tradition that anyone of modest background who has talent, wants something badly enough and is willing to work his or her ass off can be successful. She's the best-known woman tennis player in the world—and the richest; she's becoming a dynamic sports promoter; and she's even launching a new career in television.

Billie Jean was born November 22, 1943, in Long Beach, California. She was a perfect child, "just a little angel," says her mother, Betty Moffitt. But she hated doing the accepted little-girl things, preferring instead to spend her time in the back yard, playing catch with her father, Bill, now a 31-year veteran with the Long Beach Fire Department. To make ends meet, Moffitt moonlighted at nights in a plastics factory and Betty rang neighborhood doorbells as an Avon lady and was a Tupperware saleswoman. When Billie Jean was four, her father, who couldn't afford to buy her a baseball bat, scrounged up a piece of wood and carved one.

Billie Jean developed fast, and for several years was the biggest kid in her class in school. By the time she was 10, she was a real tomboy—though that's a word she'd like to see stricken from our vocabulary. She loved to play football in front of the family home, especially if she could carry the ball. She never lost a race at the firemen's picnic, beating all comers—boys and girls alike. She played basketball and was shortstop on a girls' softball team, on which she was the youngest player. Even today, she recalls with pride one game in which she made a shoestring catch off a looping line drive, spun and threw to third to double off a runner—saving the game in the final inning. She was mobbed when she came off the field. It was her first taste of public adulation—and she loved it. She still does.

But the Moffitts weren't keen on raising a halfback or a shortstop. One day her mother abruptly ended Billie Jean's football career—on the ground that it wasn't ladylike. Billie Jean asked her father what sport a girl *could* enter. Moffitt thought for a while, and finally suggested swimming—or tennis.

"What's tennis?" asked Billie Jean.

"Well, you run a lot and hit a ball," her father said. "I think you'll like it."

Billie Jean liked it. She did odd jobs for neighbors, raising a quarter here, 50 cents there; her parents chipped in and she bought a nice new racket with maroon nylon strings and a maroon handle, for eight dollars. From the day of her first tennis lesson, in the Long Beach public parks, tennis has been her whole life—almost to the exclusion of everything else.

"A few days after her first tennis game," her mother recalls, "Sister"—that's the family name for Billie Jean—"came home to tell her father and me, 'I am going to be the best woman tennis player in the world.' We took her at her word. She was and is the kind of girl who means what she says."

Every moment she was not in school Billie Jean spent on the courts or in the backyard, banging a tennis ball against an old wooden fence. Finally, she literally demolished it, so her father built a new one for her out of concrete blocks—and set up a spotlight to allow her to keep on practicing after dark.

When she was 15, Billie Jean—or Jillie Bean, as the sportswriters called her—won her first big tennis tournament. Three years later, she became the youngest person ever to win a doubles championship at Wimbledon, the shrine of world tennis—and the place where she would go on to take 18 titles in singles, doubles and mixed doubles.

While attending Los Angeles State College, Billie Jean met Larry King, a handsome blond prelaw student one year her junior. After a two-year courtship, interrupted constantly by the demands of her burgeoning tennis career, Larry proposed in a Long Beach coffee shop—at two A.M. the night before Billie Jean left for an expense-paid three-month trip to Australia, where she was to take private lessons from former Davis Cup player Mervyn Rose. Rose taught her a new forehand, a new service and a bold new strategic outlook on the game.

Billie Jean and Larry were married on September 17, 1965. The newlyweds moved into a little apartment not far from campus and Billie Jean stayed home that first fall and winter—because she thought it important to be a good wife, in the old-fashioned sense. But she was unhappy. She still wanted to be number one. And Larry gave her his full support.

The rest is tennis history. By 1971, Billie Jean had become the first woman athlete to have earned $100,000 in a year. As the most influential figure in the popularization of the game in the past decade, she helped engineer the most talked-about coup in tennis when, in 1973, she defeated 55-year-old Bobby Riggs in a $100,000 winner-take-all "Battle of the Sexes" in Houston's Astrodome. Now 31, and despite two operations on her knees, Billie Jean still plays a man's power game—rushing the net and glowering over it like an angry bear, serving and volleying with machinelike efficiency, relentlessly over-powering her opponents with a combination of strategy and speed. She runs down balls other players wouldn't even attempt to reach. Billie Jean King has reached the top by following a formidable daily training regimen. Every day she rises early, and after several cups of coffee—if there's time, bacon and eggs—she is out on the court, any court, working out with other players. Drilling forehand, backhand, cross court, down the line, for hours. At night, even while watching TV, she flails her legs around with 11-and-a-half-pound lead weights attached to her ankles, which she claims are her weakest point.

Today, Billie Jean and Larry King are partners in King Enterprises, a multimillion-dollar business built around Billie Jean's ability with a tennis racket. She endorses products ranging from tennis shoes to suntan lotion; publishes a magazine, *WomenSports;* recently signed a six-figure, two-year contract with ABC-TV to do tennis commentary, a women's sports special and other projects; and is launching a new syndicated TV series, *The Billie Jean King Show.* The Kings are also among the founders of World Team Tennis, the intercity tennis league that made its debut last year. As player-coach for the Philadelphia Freedoms, she became the first woman coach in any major sport in the U.S.

Billie Jean's open pursuit of money and fame has drawn criticism from tennis purists. She answers: "They love you when you're coming up. But they don't like winners. And they especially don't like me, because I talk about money all the time."

Actually, money is not the only subject Billie Jean talks about—outspokenly. In interviews, in editorials in her magazine, she's spearheading a revolution in women's sports. Her platform is that they should be separate but equal in every way to men's sports. Billie Jean sometimes operates like a thirties labor organizer, taking on all comers from the Amateur Athletic Union and the United States Lawn Tennis Association to male chauvinists everywhere.

To find out what is really going on in the mind of the most colorful and controversial woman athlete in sports today, *Playboy* sent freelancer Joe Hyams to interview Billie Jean. A tennis buff himself, Hyams recently collaborated on a book with Ms. King: *Billie Jean King's Secrets of Winning Tennis*. His report:

"Our first interview was scheduled for 1:30 P.M. at the Hilton Inn near the Spectrum in Philadelphia, where the Freedoms were playing. I met Billie Jean by the newsstand; she was wearing a simple white blouse, faded and baggy blue jeans and a disgusted look on her face. 'I defy you to find a copy of *WomenSports* here,' she said, reaching behind some interviews on the rack's lowest shelf and extricating the current issue of her new publication—which she carefully placed on top.

"In the hotel coffee shop, she ordered breakfast: a cheese omelet, no toast and 'lots of coffee.' I was aware, as always, of how much prettier Billie Jean King is in person than on television or in photographs. Off court she is soft, feminine, sexy—despite the glasses, a broad beam and a flat chest. Every time I see her, I'm reminded of Grace Kelly, who had equally unimpressive vital statistics but was all woman—no question about it.

"During the first of what were to be several candid interviews, we were interrupted half a dozen times by fans, mostly male, who asked for her autograph. Later, we drove in her rented rust-colored Ambassador sedan, which she calls the 'taco wagon,' to the Spectrum for a workout with some of the Freedoms players, and that night I watched as she and the Freedoms won their match against Denver, before a partisan audience of 7583.

"Another day, after a tennis session at the Merrion Country Club, we drove in the taco wagon through a blinding rainstorm across the rolling green Pennsylvania countryside, en route to New York. We paused at a McDonald's, where she ordered a Big Mac and a vanilla shake. 'I used to live on 90 dollars a month,' she recalled, 'working as a park playground director and also standing in a cage at the college athletic department, giving out towels and equipment for women's gym classes. It was a big deal in those days for Larry and me to have a sundae. It cost 25 cents, had two large scoops of vanilla ice cream and was great. As the Virginia Slims people would say, "I've come a long way." The real question, though, is where am I going?' We began our last interview, in New York, on that note."

PLAYBOY: This will be the first year that Billie Jean King has not played the entire Women's Tennis Association circuit. Why did you decide to cut down so drastically at what would appear to be the peak of your career?

KING: I'm not *quitting* tennis. I'll be playing in World Team Tennis. I'm just not playing the WTA circuit this year. I would have liked to have left two years ago, because I was so tired. It's just not worth it to work, work, work, work all the time, as I have for the past 20 years.

PLAYBOY: If you wanted to leave two years ago, why didn't you?

KING: I didn't feel the association was at the stage where I could. But there are a lot of good women tennis players around today. Maybe the first year it was true, as people keep saying, that I was the one who made it go; but not after five years. I want to have some time for myself now, as a person. And I need time to devote to some of my new interests. I'd like to spend more time on *WomenSports*, the magazine I started with my husband, Larry. I'm doing a syndicated TV series, *The Billie Jean King Show*. And I'm going to be giving tennis clinics at Cape Eleuthera in the Bahamas. And, of course, I'd like to see WTT make it in a big way.

PLAYBOY: But isn't WTT in trouble? Aren't there a couple of franchises on the verge of bankruptcy?

KING: I think the future of WTT looks better than it did a year ago. WTT is here to stay; five years from now, it'll be unbelievable. One or two franchises may be in trouble, but out of 15 teams, with the economy the way it is, I think that's good. And it looks as if Colgate is going to get involved, putting up a Colgate Cup that we'd play for, like the Stanley Cup in hockey. They'd also help us sponsor a junior program in the cities where we have tennis teams and they'd help us pay for TV time. With television, we have more credibility, as well as more exposure. Sometimes we have trouble getting press coverage for team tennis. That's why I pulled that stunt of trying to draft Bobby Riggs for the Philadelphia Freedoms. At least it made the papers.

PLAYBOY: It was just a publicity stunt?

KING: Sure. I just couldn't resist it. I also drafted Elton John, just for fun. I met him last September at a party; I have all his records at home. He's promised to write the Freedoms a song and he may even become a part owner. You know, it's funny; a lot of musicians are frustrated athletes, just like many athletes are frustrated musicians. So I drafted Elton, to make him laugh. Which he did.

PLAYBOY: How do you feel about being a hustler for tennis?

KING: I don't know if I'd use that word. You mean a promoter? I've always been that way, I think. I think tennis is a great thing to sell to people, whether they're participants or spectators. I'm hustling for something I believe in.

PLAYBOY: Doesn't all that hustling somehow affect the purity of the game?

KING: No. It makes it more pure.

PLAYBOY: Why?

KING: Because professional tennis, the kind we're promoting, is honest. It didn't used to be honest, in the so-called amateur days, when they called it a pure sport. It was very impure. Now everyone knows where he or she stands. It's a lot easier; it's healthier; it's aboveboard.

PLAYBOY: As tennis has gone from an amateur game to a big-money business, it's become possible for the players to get rich, as film stars, or rock-and-roll performers, do. But, like them, you are beginning to be manipulated by wheeler-dealers; in other words, isn't big money starting to pull the strings in tennis?

KING: To a certain extent. There's a lot of pressure, people wanting you to play here and there, saying, "I'll give you this deal or that deal." For myself, I don't let myself be manipulated as much as I used to. If I don't want to do something, I'm not going to do it anymore. Everything for the game and everything for everybody else but yourself: That's not healthy.

You know, it's hard to have so many choices. I'm lucky in that I *have* so many, but . . . when I was 11 or 12, you know, I had tunnel vision. All I wanted was to be the world's greatest tennis player. I may have thought it was tough when I was younger if I didn't have enough money to buy the kind of dinner I wanted. But that problem was simple, although it might not seem so to the average family trying to make ends meet. Now I don't know which way to go. I have so many opportunities they drive me *crazy*.

PLAYBOY: You've already mentioned some of those opportunities that you've decided to embrace. Your television show, for instance. Tell us something about it.

KING: I'm really excited about it. I've just finished making the pilot, but we'll probably have 12 one-hour shows—specials—on women who participate in sports. I'd like to see other women athletes who excel in their fields be appreciated, the way men athletes are. We'll have a lot of music in the show, too, because I want it to be fun as well as informative.

PLAYBOY: You're the hostess, the interviewer on the show?

KING: Yes. We'll have some guest reporters, too. Donna DeVarona, the Olympic swimmer—she won a couple of gold medals—was a guest reporter on the first show. We featured women drag-boat racers, volleyball players. And I'm going to interview Karen Magnussen. She's a skater, was an Olympic silver medalist; she works with the Ice Capades now.

PLAYBOY: Will you feature only women on your show?

KING: No, I'll do some interviews with men, too. It's supposed to be fun for *people*, not just women's lib. Although it's primarily about women, just as our magazine, *WomenSports*, is.

PLAYBOY: With the publishing business as difficult to get into as it is, what prompted you to start your own magazine?

KING: I think the seed for the idea probably goes back to when I was nine years old and for the first time watched a professional baseball game with my father. I loved to play baseball, football, run track races with the neighborhood boys. But what struck me like a thunderbolt that day was that there were no women on that baseball diamond. My ambition to become a professional baseball player was shattered. Throughout my adolescence, in fact, I found a subtle social pressure against being an athlete. I decided on tennis because it was, and still is, more socially acceptable as a sport for girls.

Over my years of playing tennis, I noticed that women's events received very little coverage in the newspapers and magazines. I used to complain that the sports magazines never gave women a fair shake. The people who published them said, "Well, what can we write about? Women aren't doing that much." That's like putting the cart before the horse or the chicken before the egg. There had to be some way of letting young women know there *was* a way to make a living playing sports, that their desire to compete and excel wasn't abnormal. There had to be some vehicle for women who were interested in athletics to find out what was happening for women in all sports. So one day, Larry and I were driving down the Bayshore Freeway and I was complaining again, and Larry says, "Let's start our own magazine." I said, "Oh, Larry. Of all the businesses to go into, that's got to be the most risky." Especially since we didn't have much capital. But we felt it was the right time to do it, so we did.

PLAYBOY: And how is the magazine doing?

KING: It's small—our circulation's around 200,000. But that's a start.

PLAYBOY: A good start.

KING: Pretty good for a *girl*, huh? Ha.

PLAYBOY: Don't you find some conflict between your role as a publisher and your role as a successful athlete, much in demand for endorsements, and so forth? The first issue of *WomenSports* seemed to feature Billie Jean King on every page, in the ads as well as in the editorial matter.

KING: The first issue was ridiculous. But I'm trying to stay out of it now. I'm proud of being identified with the magazine, though. I've had men come up to me after a match, with *WomenSports* in their hands, and ask me to autograph their copies. Then they start telling me about their daughters who are having trouble in their sports fields and how much the magazine means to them. I want a very low profile on the magazine; it's not just for me. It's for everyone. People on my staff say, "Look, Billie Jean, you're going to have to write something, more than just the publisher's letter." The past two or three months, people have written in: "Where's Billie Jean?"

PLAYBOY: Is it possible that you have become, to many of your readers, the personification of *WomenSports*' lifestyle, as Hugh Hefner is considered by some to be the personification of the *Playboy* lifestyle?

KING: Well, I don't know. I certainly don't live like he does. First of all, I don't have the money he has. And high living doesn't turn me on.

PLAYBOY: You have to get to bed early, watch your diet?

KING: I have to watch my diet. As far as getting to bed early, I don't know. . . . You know what else he has that I don't? Time. But I don't think I'd ever want to live the way he does. It's super for him, if that's where he's at.

PLAYBOY: Lately, some of the sportswriters have started to refer to you in print as sexy. How does that make you feel?

KING: I don't understand it, but right on!

PLAYBOY: Dan Wakefield, writing in *Esquire*, observed that most of his male friends now have their favorite woman tennis player, just as they used to have their favorite movie actress. Do you think it's possible that women athletes are replacing film stars as popular idols? Does a guy put up Billie Jean King's picture in his room today, where a generation ago he might have put up Elizabeth Taylor's?

KING: That's happening to a certain degree. I think people want realism, and sports provide that. You can be a superstar celebrity on television, in movies, but people are sophisticated enough now to know that what they see onscreen, or on TV, is rehearsed, edited, cut. They see me going out and hitting a ball, sweating my guts out, missing the ball and getting angry; that's real. You can't fake it.

PLAYBOY: And when Billie Jean King gets mad, she shows it. What sort of things are you yelling out there on the court?

KING: Very bad words. Four-letter words, some of them. I think coaching this year made me worse; it really put me under. I've been just terrible. I try not to use those words when I'm around young people—although, actually, I think the young people say worse words than I do.

PLAYBOY: You once told a reporter that one of your mother's pet sayings was "Always be a lady." Are you still a lady, Billie Jean?

KING: I still don't know what that word means. I used to ask her, "Mother, what does that mean?" And she'd say, "Well, you know." But I never did. I guess she means "don't swear, and be gorgeous all the time." I'm not into that. That's not the way I am.

PLAYBOY: You're first and foremost a tennis player?

KING: Now I think I'm beyond tennis and into sports in general, and into speaking to women and fighting for their rights. Women depend on me and need me, and there's a lot to be done. I mean, if you look at the budgets for girls in school sports, for example, and compare them with the budgets for boys' sports, they're ridiculous—especially at the high school and college levels. I think it's time we changed the psyche of the country, and not just where women are concerned. I don't want to see women pressured by society to become housewives and mothers, but I also have empathy for the little boy who doesn't want to be a superjock and his father says, "You're going to play in the little league." I don't go for that, either. Let the boy do what he wants to do.

PLAYBOY: As you know, many people feel the feminist movement has created a kind of reverse pressure—to make women feel they *ought* to have a career, that they owe it to themselves and their sisters. What's your feeling about that?

KING: If that were the core of the women's movement, I wouldn't be interested in it and I don't think most women would be involved with it. If a woman wants to have a career, I say fine, don't put her down for it. But if she wants to be a housewife, right on; if she wants to be a mother, that's beautiful. I want every woman to be able to be whatever she *wants* to be. That's what the women's movement is all about. All we want is for every woman to be able to pursue whatever career or personal lifestyle she chooses as a full and equal member of the society, without fear of sexual discrimination. That's a pretty basic and simple statement, but it's hard sometimes to get people to accept it—or even to understand it. And because of the way other people think, it can be even harder to reach the point in your own life where you can live by it.

PLAYBOY: Somewhere along the line, Billie Jean King, champion tennis player, has become Billie Jean King, champion of women's lib. Can you trace that evolution for us?

KING: I think the turning point was around 1966 or 1967, when I started realizing that as a woman athlete I had very few opportunities—and that society really didn't accept women athletes as human beings. It had such negative connotations. And I thought, that's so stupid, because sports are so much fun, and a lot of women had missed out because it wasn't acceptable for them to be athletes. And I used to rant and rave about it to Larry, and he'd say, "Well, that's wonderful. What are you going to do?" And he was the one who said, "Women, first of all, are second-class citizens." And I said, "Whaddaya mean, whaddaya mean?" And he said because people keep women subservient, by opening doors for them and things.

PLAYBOY: You don't like to have doors opened for you?

KING: There's nothing wrong with it, except that it keeps you down in a way. You're not assertive enough. Which is true; women do tend to wait for someone else to make a decision. Not so much anymore, but they did.

Anyway, that all gave me something to think about, and then I started trying to see how I could make things change. Starting with sports. Because there were definitely very few, if any, opportunities for a woman to make a career as an athlete, unless she came from a wealthy family or somebody wanted to sponsor her. There again, you're dependent on somebody else. I didn't want that; I wanted to help create a vehicle that would work for anyone—rich, poor, any color. I started out working very hard for open tennis, until I found out women's tennis would suffer very greatly from that, because the men were going to leave us out. So then I channeled my interest into women's tennis and helped create the women's circuit. And the way it's worked out has been tremendous.

PLAYBOY: So you had sports, not women's liberation, in mind when you started the circuit?

KING: Women's liberation was part of it, in that I was trying to create more opportunities, to make us equal. In practice, I was a women's libber whether I labeled myself that or not. Margaret Court says she's not a women's libber, but she definitely is. She's making her second comeback after two babies and her husband's going to go on the circuit with her and take care of the babies.

PLAYBOY: That's women's lib?

KING: To me it is. Maybe to somebody else it isn't. I think it's great, because they're happy and for them it's right.

PLAYBOY: There was a period during the development of the women's movement when lesbianism was considered to be a badge of honor. Did—

KING: WHAT?!

PLAYBOY: Some elements of the women's movement considered lesbianism a badge of honor.

KING: Oh, God. That's a bunch of bull. I never heard that one.

PLAYBOY: Then you never felt any psychological pressure to try lesbianism as a way to demonstrate support for women's liberation?

KING: No. Gay women turn on to me sometimes, gay women's lib people. I get a lot of letters from them, but they're OK when I meet them. They don't make passes at all. They say, "Thank you for what you're doing to help people be free and to accept each other for what they are." I think that's a healthy thing.

PLAYBOY: Grace Lichtenstein, in her book *A Long Way, Baby*, about women's pro tennis, claims there is a split on the circuit between lesbian and heterosexual players. Is that true?

KING: That's not true. I don't understand parts of that book at all. I think Grace just wanted to sell a lot of books and make a lot of money. She was around only about a month and a half. Maybe a little longer. The book is just her personal opinion.

PLAYBOY: Well, there is another persistent rumor—this one about you in particular. That is that some time ago you told an interviewer that you were bisexual, but that the article was killed when your sponsor, Virginia Slims cigarettes, heard about it and threatened to withdraw support from World Team Tennis.

KING: That's the first time I've heard of that rumor, and it's definitely not true. Although there's some lesbianism among women athletes—just as there is homosexuality among males—it's rarely an issue. It isn't nearly as prevalent as some people seem to think. That's a misconception people have grown up with—that for a woman to excel in sports she must be more male than female. That's nonsense. This kind of thinking puts off many young girls who might want to get into sports. Anyway, I don't think the sex life of athletes is an important issue.

PLAYBOY: You're not a lesbian yourself, then?

KING: My sex life is no one's business, but if I don't answer your question, people will think I have something to hide, so I'm in a bind. I'm damned if I answer your question and damned if I don't, but I'll give you the answer: No, I'm not a lesbian. That's not even in the ballpark for me. But even though that scene isn't in my bag, I think people should be free to do whatever they want to do and get their pleasure any way they can as long as it doesn't hurt somebody else. I'm for liberation at all levels, be it gay liberation or whatever.

PLAYBOY: How do you feel about the fairly common view that as women become more emancipated they tend to become tougher, more masculine?

KING: Society today forces women to stand up for what they believe is right, and a woman who stands up for herself is always accused of being masculine. Speaking personally, I've found that I have to stand up for myself or else I'll come out a loser. When I find I'm getting a little hard, I try to catch myself and say, "Billie, you're getting bitchy," and cool it.

In my opinion, though, masculine and feminine are words that should be eliminated from our vocabularies. Like having a baby doesn't make a woman more feminine, anymore than it makes the father more masculine. If a man is gentle, it doesn't mean he's less of a man. I think he's *more* of a man, and more of a person, yet most people think gentleness is a feminine quality. I don't think we should get hung up on role playing.

PLAYBOY: Do you deal much with other recognized spokeswomen for the liberation movement? Gloria Steinem, Betty Friedan, Germaine Greer?

KING: I know Gloria the best of those three. I think she's a tremendous person, because she has the conviction to try to do what she believes in. Like having enough guts to start Ms. magazine. I really admire her for that. She's into different things than I am, like politics. She's never really been into sports. She thinks they're too violent. I asked her, "Gloria, what are you talking about? Most sports are not violent, they're just fun." She said, "Well, I don't picture it that way, because I grew up in a very poor neighborhood and when I used to walk down the street, I'd see even the bowling-league teams trying to knock each other on the head after the games. I just didn't want to be around that part of life." Now, I grew up in Long Beach and I went to the public parks to play softball, play tennis, so that was my experience as a youngster. I grew up thinking sports are fun and games. Gloria's experience was different, and that's why to this day I can't really get her into sports.

You know, another person I really admire who doesn't get the publicity Gloria gets is Pat Carbine, an editor of Ms. I think she's a tremendous human being; she has a lot of humor. She helped Larry a lot with getting our magazine started.

PLAYBOY: Speaking of Ms., how do you feel about being a Mrs.? In your autobiography, you said you were sorry you were married.

KING: Well, marriage can be bunk, except that it makes it easier to be together. Society leaves you alone more if you're married. But I think the reason I said that in my book was that people had been driving me nuts. They just didn't understand our relationship at all and they were asking the same questions they'd asked for eight years: Where is your husband? Doesn't he travel with you? When are you going to retire? Don't you want kids? And so on. They were always chipping away at me, always expecting me to live up to their own expectations rather than to mine. I think that's a lot of rubbish, but when you hear it day in and day out, it gets a little heavy and tends to weigh you down. If I were single again, I felt, a lot of those questions would stop, or at least my answers would make more sense to people.

I've thought about all that, and I've decided that the reason I was getting such heavy pressure from people is that most everybody likes to be reinforced. A housewife would like me to quit and settle down and have babies, because it reinforces her lifestyle, and some men don't like career women because if their wives went out to work, it might upset the balance of their relationship. Well, that's their opinion and they're entitled to it, but it's not right for me. I believe we should learn to accept people who aren't into our particular roles. For instance, if I meet a family that loves being together 24 hours a day, then I'm happy for them, although it's opposite to the kind of life I lead. But in return, I think they should say to me, "Billie Jean, whatever's right for you is fine with us. You're OK, I'm OK. Do whatever you choose to do." If we could just learn to be more tolerant of others, even though they're not reinforcing our lifestyle, it would be a better world.

PLAYBOY: There's been talk for quite a while that you and Larry are planning a divorce. Is there any truth to it?

KING: The rumors got started when we first got married. People said we wouldn't make it, especially because I was involved in trying to change things. They figured that a woman who's deeply into women's lib has to be domineering. But our personalities have never had anything to do with our marriage difficulties. Our difficulties stem from the demands of our careers. When we were married, we were both so young and idealistic that neither of us had any idea what strange and different directions our lives would take because of tennis. I didn't feel then that I'd be playing too much longer, maybe only three or four years. Then I figured I'd retire and have my kids and settle down as the wife of a successful lawyer. I didn't really know then that tennis was on the verge of a series of revolutions that would change the game forever, and neither of us had any idea what impact all of that would have on our own lives.

PLAYBOY: What were the worst years for your marriage?

KING: I think our worst time together was in 1969, right after Larry finished law school. He wanted to live in Hawaii and I said fine, but right away I was miserable. That made my plane trip to the East Coast—where most of the tournaments were held—11 hours. And in the islands, they couldn't care less about tennis; there just wasn't anything for me to do there. So I'd hop into Honolulu for a week, and it was great when Larry had time off; but he was just starting to practice law and didn't *have* much time off. And when he did, he liked to go swimming. I didn't, but I'd go lie on the beach and get a suntan. At night we'd usually go out with other lawyers and their wives, but that was another problem. I just couldn't handle the social scene. I felt lost whenever I was there and for the first time I thought that perhaps Larry and I were on different levels. During the next four years, I thought about divorce a lot, and by the end of 1973, we were both talking about it. But we decided to hang in and now I'm glad we did.

PLAYBOY: What made you both decide against a divorce?

KING: I'm not sure, except that we both stopped talking about it. Part of the reason was that during the winter of 1973 and 1974 I was caught up in the aftermath of my match with Bobby Riggs and I was trying to get *WomenSports* off the ground. I was also getting into shape for the 1974 Virginia Slims tour. And Larry was tied up almost daily with World

Team Tennis. Even if we had finally decided to go ahead with it, I think neither of us would have had the time to file the papers.

More important, I think we've come to a pretty solid understanding about where our relationship is. He's got his career and I've got mine and they're like two big intersecting circles. At those points where they meet, everything's great. Where they don't meet, what can I say except that we can both handle it because we know that's just the way things are going to be for a few more years. If we had divorced, it wouldn't have been a traditional split at all, because I'm pretty sure we would have kept on living together. Considering the amount of traveling we both did and the time we were already apart, even a divorce wouldn't have changed our relationship very much at all.

Actually, Larry and I are very blessed because we have something most couples don't have, and that is the same type of goals. It sounds cold to me when I hear myself saying that, but our goals are mutual. He works his bahoola off with all the administrative and technical details and I'm out there on the court working my bahoola off, but we're both working for the same thing: to improve tennis and other sports in this country and to give all people—men *and* women—an equal opportunity to achieve whatever goals they set for themselves.

PLAYBOY: Apart from your common goals, how do you and Larry feel about each other now?

KING: I still love him and I know I always will. And I know he loves me. But we disagree on the meaning of love. To him, it's liking someone the most, and I feel love is something special and far different from liking. I understand what he's saying, however. He's just not as emotional as I am. I'm more old-fashioned, and to me love is really indescribable. It's something extra, something special.

On the other hand, I don't feel loving each other means Larry and I have to be together 24 hours a day. I don't think that's where it's at, at least not for me. You can't measure love in time spent together, and too many men get a sense of power from insisting that their wives be with them when they want them. The important thing is *wanting* to be with someone; then, when you're together, you really appreciate each other more. You remember the times apart and make more of the time you have together, which I don't think most people do. But Larry and I are into that now. We really enjoy the time we have together, because it's precious.

PLAYBOY: What kind of guy is Larry?

KING: Very busy. His mind is always going. He's very stubborn. Very intelligent. A lot of us are book smart, but he's more: He's book smart as well as being able to fit together the pieces of a problem and make it work.

PLAYBOY: What's he like as a husband? Is he jealous?

KING: No. He's very proud, we're both proud of what the other has done.

PLAYBOY: Are you jealous?

KING: Of what? Of Larry? No. I think it's great. I like to see him get more recognition for what he's done.

PLAYBOY: We mean jealous maybe of Larry and other women. Does that ever occur to you?

KING: Oh, yeah, it occurs to me. I would probably be jealous. That's a good question. I think I'd have to have a pretty good reason before I'd get uptight.

PLAYBOY: But he's not really jealous in that sense?

KING: I don't know if he is or not. He keeps his emotions in. He's not like me in that sense; I'm much more out front.

PLAYBOY: How important is tennis to him?

KING: He loves it. He's working at it, of course, from an administrative point of view. And he goes out and plays every moment he gets. I'm sure I'm the one who got him into it as deeply as he is, but he played tennis before I met him. At least three or four years before I met him.

PLAYBOY: Well, does he have reason to be jealous? Joyce McGonnigal of Johns Hopkins University was quoted in a recent issue of *Sports Illustrated* as saying that the audience for women's sports these days usually consists of "boyfriends, lovers and other strangers." Do you find men turning on to you, following you around?

KING: Well, the Virginia Slims circuit has its own groupies, fellows who hang around our tournaments. It doesn't always give me a very good feeling, because I don't know if they like me as a person or because I'm a celebrity. I have a hunch if I weren't Billie Jean King, they wouldn't be interested in me, so I don't pay much attention to them. Besides, I'm married, so that gives me a little protection. I *think.* I don't know.

PLAYBOY: Have you ever thought of trying an open marriage?

KING: Larry and I talked about it after reading the book *Open Marriage* and, although it sounds good in theory, I think it would be pretty tough to put into practice. It really depends on the couple. Speaking for myself, I don't think I could handle it, and I'm not willing to experiment with it, because it might destroy what we already have.

PLAYBOY: You've been married for nearly 10 years; by that time, most couples have had at least one child. But in 1972 you made headlines when you admitted to having had an abortion. What were the factors that dictated your decision?

KING: I got pregnant in late February 1971. I took the usual tests and when they came out positive, there was absolutely no question about what I would do. Larry and I agreed on an abortion from the beginning. There was very little discussion about morality involved in our decision; we just both agreed that it was absolutely the wrong time for us to bring a child into the world. Even though we had been married for five and a half years, our marriage was not on as secure a footing then as it is now. We needed more time together by ourselves to see where our relationship was headed. And I was entering a period of great change in my life, personally and professionally, and under the circumstances, I felt it just wasn't proper to start a family. Additionally, I didn't want to become a mother unless I could devote myself fully to motherhood and I knew that was something I couldn't do, wasn't prepared to do, at the time. So I decided to go ahead with the abortion.

PLAYBOY: What was it like?

KING: It was the simplest operation I've ever had. I went to a hospital in California, was knocked out, had the abortion, spent two hours in the recovery room and later the same day, Larry took me home. There was no pain, no trauma.

PLAYBOY: The news didn't get out till more than a year after that. Why didn't you talk about it?

KING: I didn't think it was anybody's business. But I signed a petition for *Ms.* magazine indicating that I was in favor of legalized abortion. Then Mark Asher, the tennis writer for *The Washington Post*, asked me directly in an interview whether I'd had an abortion. I hedged the answer, because, although I'd told some close friends about it, I had never told my parents, because I was certain they wouldn't understand. Asher's story was headlined "Abortion Made Possible Mrs. King's Top Year." Although Asher hadn't quoted me as saying I'd had an abortion, he'd put two and two together and the story was out on the wire services and got big play. My parents found out about my abortion from the papers, not from me. Meanwhile, Larry and I went to Hawaii and when we returned to San Francisco for Mother's Day with my parents, my mom told me she had cried for three days when she read about it. She just didn't understand. I tried to explain it as well as I could: that Larry and I love kids and want children, but the timing was wrong. Mainly, I was sorry I hadn't had the guts to tell her myself.

PLAYBOY: What was the public reaction to news of your abortion?

KING: Hate mail started to come in, most of it unsigned and most of it vicious. But, overall, a lot of good came from it. Several women have told me that just knowing I'd had an abortion made it easier for them to have theirs, and that was really a big plus. Even now, I don't expect everybody to accept what I did, but it was our choice—Larry's and mine—and that's the way I think things like that have to be decided. I certainly don't want to put my own standards on other people and I don't want them putting their standards on me.

PLAYBOY: Do you think, in retrospect, that you did the right thing?

KING: It was the right thing for me at that time, and it was right in the sense that I've been able to help other women who may want an abortion but are afraid of censure from friends, family or society. I don't think every woman is meant to be a mother. A lot of women have children because of social pressures on them, especially from their peer group. Like, when a high school class graduates and some of the girls get married, two years later everybody is supposed to have a baby. That's just reinforcement of each other's roles again. That's got to be changed. I'm not saying, "Don't have babies." What I'm saying is, "Make sure you're doing what you want to do when you bring a child into the world."

PLAYBOY: Would you like to have children someday?

KING: Yes, definitely. Larry and I talk about it a lot. I think children are super and I want to have kids by the time I'm 35 just for bodily reasons. But it wouldn't make any difference to me if I had them in or out of marriage. I know that'll blow everybody's mind, but when I have kids, they'll be Larry's, whether we're still married or not.

PLAYBOY: If you weren't married to Larry and were free to choose, would you marry a tennis player?

KING: You marry the person you love and not the person's profession. Many people have a hang-up about marrying someone in the same profession, because if the woman outshines the guy, then all hell breaks loose. But I think that if two people are in the same profession, they should be able to help each other and be more understanding instead of being competitive.

PLAYBOY: What do you think of the romance between Chris Evert and Jimmy Connors?

KING: I have mixed feelings about that, because I think they're very young, but I feel they're good for each other. They know how much it hurts to lose and how good it feels to win, and they can share the ups and downs.

PLAYBOY: Chris gets a lot of headlines, but not as many as Billie Jean King. How do you feel about being the number-one woman tennis player in terms of public recognition, when Margaret Court may have won more tournaments?

KING: You mean major titles? I have purposely not played in as many major title tournaments as Margaret. I've been much more active than she has in starting new things, taking risks. Margaret's always waited, always been one of the status-quo people. She's a great tennis player, but she doesn't like to think of new ideas. She doesn't like to change. And that's fine—for Margaret. Not for me. Now, I could have gone around and tried to play all the major tournaments every year, but I worked harder in other areas. She has won more titles. But what are titles? A lot of the titles we win have no depth. I've won a lot of titles, but I don't think they mean anything. It's *who* you beat that makes you get turned on.

PLAYBOY: You and Margaret have been competitors for a long time. In your book *Billie Jean*, you said you've been thinking a lot about going head to head with her in a 25-match series and settling things once and for all. How do you think such a series would turn out?

KING: It's hard to tell. I think right now, the score would probably be about 10 all, with five to go. I've become the kind of person who rises to big occasions, and I think I could handle that kind of series of matches better than Margaret, who is very different from me, more mechanical. She's taller and stronger physically, and I have to depend more on speed and skill and my ability to make more shots. She can't hit a top-spin backhand and doesn't have a lot of touch—but she doesn't need it with her height, whereas I have to depend on it.

PLAYBOY: We've heard a lot about you and about Margaret and about Chris. Are there any good new women players coming up?

KING: Oh, yes, lots. I sometimes wish the media would get off the Chris Evert, Evonne Goolagong, Billie Jean King, Margaret Court thing. I think we've been overexposed at times. Rosie Casals gets a lot of mileage, but not as much. Well, she hasn't earned it. In other sports, they're always talking about the rookies, the new players. We need more new faces. I think with a network TV contract, people will see more new faces, get more of a feeling of depth.

PLAYBOY: Is there any new player coming up whom you fear?

KING: I always fear all of them, because you never know what may come out of the woodwork. Martina Navratilova, the Czech player, has a lot of ability. She's very strong. She wants it.

PLAYBOY: You mean she's lean and hungry?

KING: She's pretty chunky. Says she's going to lose some weight. Sure, I know what you mean. She has talent, ability and, I think, desire.

PLAYBOY: Speaking of weight, you are forever swearing off your main food passion, ice cream, in order to shed a few pounds. Do you diet because of your looks or because of tennis?

KING: Tennis. I don't care what I look like as long as I feel good. I can move better when I'm thinner.

PLAYBOY: Who do you think is the *best* player in tennis today?

KING: Rod Laver is probably the best player ever, followed by John Newcombe, who is more consistent and has the best second serve of any player.

PLAYBOY: What do you think of Ilie Nastase?

KING: I think he's ridiculous, always trying to put his opponent off. He's a good enough player not to have to resort to tantrums and theatrics on court—childish gamesmanship. Off the court, however, I really like him as a person. Also, he has a great body. He and Roger Taylor are really gorgeous men.

PLAYBOY: What do you mean by a gorgeous man? What turns you on about men?

KING: I like to see guys' legs and their bahoolas, which is probably one reason I like to watch tennis. And I like to see something alive in a man's face and eyes. Mostly, though, even if I'm turned on physically, I want to know what a man is like as a human being.

PLAYBOY: Any other male tennis players you admire? What about Connors?

KING: Jimmy was golden at Wimbledon. He was nervous but contained, and he used that nervous energy properly. If you can do that, you'll play super tennis—and he did.

PLAYBOY: What do you think is the difference between a champion and a consistent runner-up?

KING: Champions try harder and longer. And on match point against him—at the moment when the whole match is on the line—a champion will suddenly get about three times tougher, while the ordinary good player will just keep on playing at the same pace.

PLAYBOY: With the exception of Arthur Ashe, there are no black tennis champions, despite the ability blacks have demonstrated in other sports. What's the reason for that? Is it racial bias?

KING: Well, in many people's minds, tennis is still a sport not only for the white but for the rich. That's beginning to change now, but you have to remember that it's only recently that we began opening the doors for all income levels. In five or 10 years, you're going to see a lot of top players who are black or members of other minority groups, but they're probably only 12 or 13 years old now. You don't develop champions overnight.

PLAYBOY: Why do you think Ashe hasn't made it to number one?

KING: Because he can't compromise. He hits every ball too hard. And I don't think he ever thinks for himself. He's pretty much a follower, not a leader. Nevertheless, he's done exceptionally well and has made it to the finals in a lot of World Championship Tennis tournaments. Personally, I always wanted Arthur to do better, because I like him. But I don't think he'll ever be number one.

PLAYBOY: How do you think you'd stand up against Ashe or some of the other top male players today?

KING: I wouldn't have a chance against them. For that matter, some of the senior players today—such as Pancho Gonzales, Pancho Segura and Tony Trabert—would kill me. I've always said that. First of all, they'd beat me on sheer strength; and they'd have a psychological edge.

PLAYBOY: How much of that is psychological edge? Why is a little Ken Rosewall faster and stronger than a big Margaret Court?

KING: I'm not sure that he's faster and stronger. What people don't realize is that there's a huge overlap, a physical overlap, between men and women, and between different men and different women. Margaret Court is much taller and stronger than I am. Stan Smith is much taller and stronger than Ken Rosewall. But we all play one another.

People always try to put women on one side of the fence and men on the other. You can't do that. You can't do that in brain power. You can't do it in physical power. There is an overlap. I may not be the number-one tennis player in the men's division, but that doesn't mean I couldn't hold my own somewhere in the men's division. Especially if I had conditioned myself for it for 20 years the way many of the men have. Women aren't going to catch up overnight, just like the blacks and other minorities aren't going to catch up overnight. It will take a while.

PLAYBOY: But it's been said that women are afraid to win against men. Is that true?

KING: Yes. I am. I don't like to win against men. It doesn't make me feel good at all, and I know it's because of my conditioning. There are young women on the staff of our interviews who say, "Oh, I love to beat my boyfriend, because he gets so upset." Well, now, that's got to be a switch! That's the other extreme.

PLAYBOY: When you play Larry, does he expect you to beat him?

KING: No, he gives me a go. He's getting better. Probably in five more years, he'll start beating me—and I'll get really ticked.

PLAYBOY: Why didn't Bobby Riggs do better against you?

KING: Because he wasn't in shape and he underestimated me after his match with Margaret Court. If Riggs were to play Gonzales, Pancho would tear him apart, because Bobby isn't even the best senior; he's just the best promoter. I think Riggs is a nice, amusing guy, though, and he's been good for tennis.

PLAYBOY: Do you think we'll ever see another man-versus-woman match in a different sport—and, if so, what?

KING: I'm sure there'll be other times. Golf, maybe.

PLAYBOY: What woman golfer is good enough to challenge Jack Nicklaus?

KING: I didn't challenge a John Newcombe. I beat an old man. What if Carol Mann and Doug Sanders played? They're both great golfers. But I'm not sure it would have the same kind of drama, because ours was the first. Bobby Riggs is an unusual personality. I think the combination is going to be difficult to find.

PLAYBOY: Just before the Riggs match, your husband went on TV and read a statement explaining why Gene Scott was doing the color instead of ex-champion Jack Kramer, who's head of the Association of Tennis Professionals. Larry made it clear that you don't like Kramer and didn't want him in the press box. When did the feud start?

KING: That goes back to the time in the Pacific Southwest Championships when he screwed us up. I walked off, I was so mad at him. He was the official referee and when we had a dispute over line calls, he couldn't be bothered to come down to the court to make the final decision. He was up in the TV box. He could have been down on that court in 20 seconds. I asked for him and asked for him and he wouldn't come down. I said, "That's it. I'm not playing." That just did it for me. Up yours, Jack. Why should I give him worldwide exposure? He doesn't like women's tennis, which is fine. But he won't admit it. He's two-faced. I don't like two-faced people. He really is. I don't think Jack cares about anybody but Jack. The male players work for him; he doesn't work for them.

PLAYBOY: Your share of the Riggs match combined with your income from TV commercials, advertisements, promotions and other enterprises related to tennis probably brought you an income of more than a million dollars in 1974. That's a tremendous amount of money for a tennis player to earn, especially a woman. Don't you agree?

KING: It's a lot of money for *anyone* to earn. Larry's the only one who can tell you exactly what my income last year was, because he handles the books. I have a question for you, though: Do female entertainers get paid less than male entertainers? No. Their pay depends on whether they draw at the box office. Entertainment value, getting people through the turnstiles, that's the name of the game. One of the things we're trying to do in World Team Tennis is to enhance the entertainment value of the sport.

PLAYBOY: Is that why WTT allows, even encourages, yelling and rooting during a match? The Hawaii Leis, whose name has inspired a series of bad jokes, passed out megaphones to their fans during a recent match. Pittsburgh has its rally girls, the Goola-gongs, and the Boston Lobsters have as their cheerleading mascot a guy dressed up in a red lobster suit with a racket in one claw and shocking-pink panty hose peeking out from under his tail. In Philadelphia, a huge replica of the Liberty Bell rings every time the Freedoms win a set. As a player, don't you find all this hoopla disconcerting?

KING: Not at all. I love partisan crowds, for me or against me. Part of being a good tennis player is being able to put up with that and keep your concentration. The point is that we want people to get *involved* with tennis the way they're involved with other sports. They don't sit on their hands when they're watching a football or basketball game, so why should they sit quietly to watch tennis?

PLAYBOY: The point scoring in each WTT game is one, two, three, four, rather than the traditional 15, 30, 40, game. And if a game goes to three-three, the player who scores the next point wins; there are no advantages or deuces. Do you think this new no-ad system will become popular in other tournaments?

KING: Yes, I do. It's much better, because it makes the game more crucial, and the more crucial points you have, the more involved the fans get—although it's much tougher on the players mentally, because they can't let up. And because the games don't go on endlessly, with advantages in and out, old-timers such as Roy Emerson, who's 39, Fred Stolle, 35, and Maria Bueno, 34, can keep up their careers and perhaps stay on as coaches. We've extended the playing life of the top pros, and that's all to the good.

PLAYBOY: Another unique feature of WTT is its format for play: one set each of women's singles, men's singles, women's doubles and men's doubles, with a 10-minute break before concluding with mixed doubles—although not always with the same players, which means that none of the players gets much of a workout. Do you like that format?

KING: Most of the men I've talked with agree that the traditional five-set match is ridiculous, because they all have such heavy schedules. I also think the audience gets bored with long matches. In WTT, we go to six all and then play a nine-point tie breaker, which makes every point more dramatic for the spectators. It's easier on the promoter, too, because he can schedule a lot of matches, which has got to be a plus from his point of view as well as the fans', who want to see a lot of tennis players in action. People don't want to see stamina; they want to see *skill*.

PLAYBOY: What part of the format do audiences seem to like most?

KING: Mixed doubles. I think mixed doubles is by far the most exciting form of tennis.

PLAYBOY: Why?

KING: Because there's immediate identification for everybody in the audience. A man looks at Smith and wonders, "Could I do that?" If it's a woman, she wonders if she could return that guy's serve.

We're still not making tennis fun enough for enough of the public, but we're getting there. I want the players to have better, more informative introductions on television, for example. I want to help other players learn how to express themselves better, because they're the future stars. It's like show business. The stars have to be personalities, not just great tennis players anymore.

PLAYBOY: Like movie stars?

KING: Court stars. It's the same thing.

PLAYBOY: Are you still in tennis because you love it—or are you in it for the money?

KING: Money doesn't make me try harder and never has. I just want to go out and do my best, and I firmly believe that's the way most athletes are. When I'm at a table, negotiating a contract, I try to get the most I can, but once the contract is signed, I don't think it makes any difference. Some individuals, and I'm one of them, are going to bust a gut day in and day out because that's the way they are as human beings. And the ones who won't bust a gut aren't going to make it.

Another thing that motivates me is fear of failing. On the way up, there's always that insidious, nagging fear that you're not quite going to make it, that in the crunch you're going to come up just a bit short. And once you reach the top, there's the absolute dread of the day when it's all going to end. You can never win enough titles, or money, or awards, because people always expect you to do it one more time and, of course, you come to expect it of yourself. Tennis may be pretty insignificant in the overall picture, but for those few hours during a match, it really is life or death.

PLAYBOY: Were you depressed after losing at Wimbledon in 1974?

KING: Of course I was. Winning is almost a relief, and you tend to forget a victory; but losing always hurts—and you always remember *that*. Olga Morozova played me to a T at Wimbledon, so I have no excuses—but I'm still upset about it. I was depressed and angry with myself for 24 hours and I didn't want to see people. But then I started working a lot harder. I had given up ice cream for five months and was the thinnest I've ever been and running every day, which, at 30 years of age, was a lot harder on me than it was a few years ago—and then to lose anyway! Man, that's not easy to handle. But I know that on any given day I may lose, because there are people today who can beat me. I think that's what makes an athlete humble. I've said it before and I'll say it again: Victory is fleeting, but losing is forever.

PLAYBOY: Was there a turning point in your life when you decided that you could be number one?

KING: Yes, and ironically, it was a defeat that told me I could become number one. The turning point came during the summer of 1965 at Forest Hills, when I lost to Margaret Court. I had beaten her once at Wimbledon, in 1962, but lost 14 consecutive matches to her after that. In the first eight games of the first set in '65, I played fantastically well and built a five-three lead but lost the set, eight-six. The same thing happened in the second set: I had a five-three lead and even got to 40-15, double set point, on my serve in the tenth game. But then Margaret picked herself up and I didn't. I played carefully and didn't cut loose. Certain players never develop this ability. They play brilliantly and steadily to the last point and then they choke, which is what I had been doing.

During the trophy presentation, I suddenly realized that I'd had the match in my hands and then didn't go for the kill. I knew then that I could beat Margaret—and anyone else in the world, too. It came to me just as clear as a bell: I really could be number one. The next time I played Margaret was in the finals of the South African Nationals in April 1966, and I beat her easily, six-three, six-two. Three months later, we played again in the semifinals at Wimbledon and again I won, easily. I finally had the right mental attitude.

PLAYBOY: What do you love most about the game?

KING: The perfect shot. I've made only a few, but I can still remember them. It's a beautiful feeling, just like an orgasm; thrills and chills all through your body. But once it's over, it's over, and after you get the check or the trophy, all you think of is the next match. You never linger. But I remember one of the most satisfying shots I've ever hit was during the 1972 Wimbledon final against Evonne Goolagong. Neither of us was outstanding that day and I was playing just to win the match as best I could and get off the court. I kept going down the line on my backhand all afternoon—that's the percentage shot—but there was just enough of a crosswind to hold the ball up in the air long enough for Evonne to run it down. So I waited and told myself that on match point I'd do just the opposite and bomb a cross-court shot. I served. She returned down the line to my backhand and I just snapped a short top-spin shot cross court, catching her off balance, prepared to cover down the line. My shot was a winner. I threw my racket into the air and thought, I did it! I hit a perfect shot!

PLAYBOY: Do you always play to win?

KING: Not always, and never in social tennis, when I just try to keep the ball in play so everyone has a good time. And I suppose I shouldn't say it, because most people will never believe it, but I have let up a couple of times in matches because I felt sorry for my opponent. But that's rare. I usually play my best.

PLAYBOY: Could you tell us whom you've let up on?

KING: I could, but I won't.

PLAYBOY: You've said in the past that you consider tennis an art form. In what way?

KING: When tennis is played properly, it's capable of getting an emotional, almost sensual, reaction from both players and audience—one similar to that you might feel when you hear a great piece of music. I always thought that way, even when I was a child learning to play. That's why, when I was 12 years old and our minister, Bob Richards, the Olympic pole-vault champion, asked me what I was going to do with my life, I said, "I know exactly what I'm going to do, Reverend. I'm going to be the best tennis player in the world."

PLAYBOY: Do you consider yourself a religious person?

KING: Not now. I was then. There was a time when I thought of being a missionary. I'd probably consider myself an agnostic now. I don't go to church. Stan Smith is really into religion, and I think that's great for him. He says the written word in the Bible tells you how to live your life. I think it's most important that *you* figure it out. I think it's pretty obvious how to live; you don't try to hurt others. I think the spirit of God or whatever is within . . . people. I almost said man; can you believe it? I'm conditioned.

PLAYBOY: In what ways other than in your attitude toward religion have you changed over the years?

KING: In the beginning of my career, when I was a chubby little prodigy from Long Beach, I wanted everybody to love Billie Jean King, and I was certain that when I became a champion, they'd love me even more. Now I know that it doesn't matter whether people love me. What matters is that I love *myself* and make myself happy; then I can give love and happiness to others, and it's not important that they return it to me. And I realize now that being number one isn't glamorous. It's more like being the fastest gun in the West. You can never let up, because you have to prove yourself against all comers.

PLAYBOY: At the moment, you're *not* number one—at least not as far as the U.S. Lawn Tennis Association is concerned. You've just been replaced by Chris Evert as the top-ranked woman tennis player on the USLTA list. How did that strike you, in view of the fact that you beat Chris two out of three times last year?

KING: Chris had a good year and she deserved what she got. Rankings don't bother me. In the beginning, I was naïve enough to think that being a champion would solve all my problems, but it often creates more than it solves.

PLAYBOY: How has your lifestyle changed in the past few years?

KING: Well, for about six years, Larry and I had an apartment with a bed, a fold-out couch, a stereo, a small desk and a huge painting heavy on the blacks and grays and blues, done by a friend of ours in 30 seconds with a spray gun. No furniture. It was really something out of *Future Shock*. Then, just recently, we moved to a new apartment in San Mateo near our magazine and offices. But I haven't seen it yet and I'm sure one of the secretaries did the furnishing, because I don't have the time and there are so many other things on my mind right now. I like things neat and organized—as long as I don't have to do them. And here in

Philadelphia, I have a three-story house on Society Hill that was built in 1730 and restored. It's a blast. I have somebody come in once a week to clean and pick up and I cook for myself. Dick Butera, who owns the Freedoms, found the house and organized the help. I wouldn't make it, with my lifestyle, unless everyone were very helpful.

PLAYBOY: Do you take things with you when you travel, to give you the feeling of being at home?

KING: I like being mobile, so I'm not big on that at all. I used to carry records with me, but then I had to stop doing it because of the weight and bulk. But now that I'm more or less based in Philadelphia, I've bought a great stereo and a tape recorder and I'm putting everything I like on tape—Gladys Knight and the Pips, Aretha Franklin, Bob Dylan, Roberta Flack, Helen Reddy, Cher. But I think Elton John is probably my favorite. I burn incense and listen to my records.

PLAYBOY: Have you ever smoked grass?

KING: Yes, I tried it, but I didn't like it. It's just not my trip. Generally speaking, I don't think people should smoke anything, because it's bad for them.

PLAYBOY: Isn't that something of a contradiction, when you've been so heavily involved in tournaments sponsored by a cigarette manufacturer?

KING: The Virginia Slims people have never encouraged us to smoke. They just try to get people who already smoke to switch to Virginia Slims. They get a lot out of the promotion—four years ago, they were number 50, and now they're in the top 20 brands—but so do we.

Anyway, about pot, I shouldn't put my own trip on everybody else. If people enjoy pot and they know about the harm it can do and they still want to use it, that's their business.

PLAYBOY: Do you feel the same way about pornography?

KING: To my way of thinking, pornography is in the eyes of the viewer. You and I can look at the same picture or read the same book and you might get turned on while I don't. So what may be pornographic for you isn't for me. Anyway, I don't know why people get hung up on such things, which I don't think hurt anybody.

PLAYBOY: Have you ever seen a porn film?

KING: Larry and I went together to see *Deep Throat* but left halfway through it. I wanted to see it all, but Larry wanted to leave.

PLAYBOY: Did you like it?

KING: It was OK, but too repetitious. I'd probably go to see more porn films if I had the time, because I'm curious. I guess I want to try everything once. Well, maybe not everything—so don't ask what I haven't tried yet.

PLAYBOY: In your recent autobiography, you wrote that Ayn Rand's *Atlas Shrugged* had done much to change your life. How?

KING: Sometime in the spring of 1972, a friend of mine rushed up to me with a copy of *Atlas Shrugged* and said, "You've got to read this. You're Dagney Taggart." During the next few months, I read the book and thought about it a lot and realized that she was right, that in a lot of ways I was like Dagney Taggart. That book told me a lot about why other people reacted to me, sometimes pretty strongly, the way they did. I can't summarize the book in a paragraph or two, but it seemed to me that the two main themes were right on target: how an intense love for something can be a source of strength as well as weakness, and how success can sometimes breed envy, resentment and even hate. The book really turned me around, because, at the time, I was going through a bad period in tennis and thinking about quitting. People were constantly calling me and making me feel rotten if I didn't play in their tournament or help them out. I realized then that people were beginning to use my strength as a weakness—that they were using me as a pawn to help their own ends and if I wasn't careful, I'd end up losing myself. So, like Dagney Taggart, I had to learn how to be selfish, although the word selfish has the wrong connotation. As I see it, being selfish is really doing your own thing. Now I know that if I can make myself happy, I can make other people happy—and if that's being selfish, so be it. That's what I am.

PLAYBOY: When you were growing up, who were some of your heroes and heroines?

KING: I didn't have any. I always thought it important to have your own thing. I wasn't up on the film stars of the time, because I didn't have money to go to the movies when I was young. So most of the people I admired were sports figures like Hank Aaron. It's funny how it all worked out for him. I always thought when he was a youngster that he was unappreciated. Great wrists. Love those wrists.

PLAYBOY: What kind of people—sports figures, movie stars, whoever— would you most like to spend your time with?

KING: The trouble with my life now is that I rarely have time to spend with anyone but the team, and it's a pretty narrow life. That's one of the reasons I'm cutting down on my schedule, so I can start spending time with other people and maybe get out in the world and learn a little. Everyone has something to offer. But, to answer your question, my best friend is my former secretary, Marilyn Barnett, and some of the tennis players, such as Fred Stolle and Vicki Berner, are fun to be with. I'd also like to see more of Marcos Carriedo, who introduced Larry and me at college. Dick Butera is a good friend and a riot; he's interested in the world around him. And Elton John has been super to us. I'd like to see more of him, too.

PLAYBOY: Why didn't you mention Rosemary Casals as a friend?

KING: Didn't I? Over the years that Rosie and I were friends and partners on the court, she often told me that she wanted to be number one. OK. But I think she envied my position so much that she came to hate me. She tried not to, but I felt she did and, although we're still friends, it's difficult for her, because we're in the same profession and the media keep her in my shadow. It's just not good for either of us. Another girl I used to be friendly with is Kristien Kemmer, a left-handed player. One day she said to me, "I can't be around you anymore, because I want to be the best, and when I'm with you, I see all the attention you get and it's just not good for me."

PLAYBOY: Doesn't that kind of honesty turn you off?

KING: No, it turns me on. The best thing about it is that Kristien and I are good enough friends to be honest and open. But Rosie wouldn't come out with it; I had to pull it out of her. Kristien was so open that there was no way I couldn't accept it. But it's sad, in a way, that I can't be friends with some of the people I like, because it means I end up being on my own a lot and more lonely.

PLAYBOY: Do you find it difficult to make friends?

KING: You have to understand that most of the people I meet are tennis players, and sometimes it's easy for me to be their friend but difficult for them to be mine. I figure I'll have a lot more friends after I phase out and I'm not in competition with them anymore. Most of the top male players in tennis are my friends. We all help one another, and that's as good a basis for friendship as you can find.

PLAYBOY: We've heard that among the male players, the Australians are legendary drinkers. Is that true?

KING: Definitely.

PLAYBOY: What about the women?

KING: No, women athletes drink a lot less than men. I suppose it's image again, the way we were brought up. But women athletes are also very serious about their sport, about keeping in shape. The men—Australian, American, anybody—drink a lot more than the women.

PLAYBOY: Do women tennis players engage in the kind of backslapping, locker-room repartee that men do?

KING: Oh, we talk about men all the time.

PLAYBOY: Yeah?

KING: Oh, yeah. Who's got the best body. We're very physically oriented, anyway.

PLAYBOY: Do you ever say things like, "Boy, would I like to have a roll in the hay with that guy"?

KING: Oh, yeah. Sure. The locker room is exactly like that. That's exactly how we talk. You got it!

I'll say one thing the women don't do that men do, though. They don't talk about it. Maybe to their best friend, but that would be it. Otherwise, they don't say, "Oh, this guy was really great in bed" or "That guy was lousy," or whatever. That's the big difference. Women don't feel they have to boast about it. For some reason, men have been convinced that they'd better be able to talk about it. I always wondered about their talk: whether they're talkers or doers.

PLAYBOY: We haven't talked much about another aspect of your career—your coaching. A recent article in *The New York Times* said you'd have to be considered, along with Don Shula of the Miami Dolphins and Fred Shero of the Philadelphia Flyers, as the coach of the year. Do you like being a coach?

KING: Yes. I enjoy being Big Momma, and it's gratifying to see the players improve. Julie Anthony has really come up this year. Brian Fairlie's serve has gotten better and Fred Stolle played better than at any time in the past five years. Fred was especially important to us, not only as team captain but as a good coach, too. I grew up in team sports, and that's the way the American psyche is conditioned. Everyone helps everyone else. The players develop more as human beings when they're part of a team. They remain individuals, but they're an integral part of the whole unit.

PLAYBOY: Will we ever see women coaches in other sports—pro football, for example?

KING: Of course. Someday a woman will be a coach in pro football or basketball or a manager in baseball. A woman can do anything if she studies and if she's qualified.

PLAYBOY: How long is that going to take? About 20 years?

KING: Try five.

PLAYBOY: Last November, when you turned 31, you said you were at a crossroads in your life. What did you mean?

KING: I meant I really don't know where I'm at right now. The next decade should be the best of my life, and while I'm physically healthy, I think I should take advantage of those years. I don't know if I want to settle down and have kids right away. I'm getting a lot of pressure to go into politics.

PLAYBOY: From whom?

KING: Friends, college kids, people who write to me and stop me on the street and say, "Billie Jean, we need help." Politics doesn't appeal to me, though. You have to glad-hand people for their votes 52 weeks a year to get into office and stay there, and all the precious time you spend glad-handing and ass kissing takes you away from the job you should be doing.

What I've said today may not be what I think tomorrow, because the whole process of learning and maturing is change. The one thing I'm positive about is that I want to see certain things happen in this country. I want to see more women—not necessarily me—in politics, and I want to see sports change. But I don't know what role I want to play in effecting these changes. I need time to think it all over in peace, to take a deep breath and maybe sit on the beach and watch the waves breaking for a while. See you when I get back—maybe with a few answers.

JOE NAMATH

A candid conversation with the superswinger quarterback

Last January's Super Bowl victory by the New York Jets over the Baltimore Colts was by far professional sports' most dramatic event since Bobby Thomson's ninth-inning home run won a pennant for the New York Giants 18 years ago. The Jet win was doubly meaningful: It not only proved that the American Football League had achieved parity with the older NFL; it also vindicated Jet quarterback Joe Namath, who boasted before the game that his 17-point underdog team would vanquish the supposedly invincible Colts. In an era when athletes are no longer averse to publicly assessing their chances of victory, it seems ludicrous that Namath's cockiness could have so outraged the sporting world and the public at large, but it did—and does. Namath scoffs at the selfless stoicism America demands from its athletes; his hedonistic, almost anarchic approach to life turns his fans on as sharply as it turns his detractors off. But at least one fact of Namath's life is beyond contention: He is easily the most flamboyant—and probably the premier—quarterback in football today.

He is also sports' most publicized figure; seldom has America been as interested in an athlete as it is in Joe Namath. Transmogrified from grid superstar into cult hero, he now finds himself cast as a kind of Belmondo with a jockstrap. And Namath's off-the-field activities—centering mostly on sexual conquests—have assumed the dimensions of modern myth; he is already rumored to have befriended and bedded more women than Casanova in his prime. Even his most irrelevant idiosyncrasies—growing a goatee, owning a black mink coat (which was stolen from him) or having a few drinks—have become causes célèbre in the popular press. That any young man should be the focal point of such approbation and abuse is remarkable; that it has happened to Joseph William Namath is truly extraordinary.

Certainly, nothing in Namath's background seems to have qualified him for the image he's acquired—and cheerfully accepted. Born on May 31, 1943, in Beaver Falls, Pennsylvania, a small steel town 30 miles west of Pittsburgh, Joe was the youngest of four sons in a Hungarian household that included an adopted daughter. His father was a steel-mill worker who, like many men in the area, wanted his boys to make it in the world through athletics. Joe's brothers, all of whom were athletes, studiously schooled their kid brother, until, by the time he was 18, Namath had become an outstanding basketball, baseball and football player. And an unforgettable local character, as well: Namath's flashy skintight attire was topped off by a black beret, sunglasses and a toothpick carried jauntily in the right side of his mouth. In his senior year—the only full season Joe played quarterback for Beaver Falls High School—he completed 85 of 146 passes for 1564 yards, led his team to a Conference championship and had virtually every major college scout in the country hanging around the family home.

After a long selection process, Namath finally enrolled at the University of Alabama, where he was coached by Paul W. (Bear) Bryant, who—by reputation, at least—makes the Washington Redskins' disciplinarian Vince Lombardi seem a veritable Brownie scoutmaster. In his sophomore season, Namath soon established himself as a quarterback par excellence by completing 76 of 146 passes and displaying the kind of deceptive ball-handling finesse that can be gained only through arduous practice. "On the field," recalls Namath, "the motto was kill or be killed. I worked for that man. I even played defense; would you believe it?" Anyone who knows Bryant, of course, would; on his office wall, there hangs a sign reading "Winning Is Not Everything, But It Sure Beats Anything That Comes In Second." Bryant remembers Namath as a socially unsure youngster who matured enormously at Alabama: "When Joe first came to our school, he was timid and shy. But he never lacked any confidence on the football field—and by the time he left here, he was a well-poised young man. I think Joe is the most talented player I've ever been around."

In his junior year, a maturing Namath showed he could think like a fox, run like a deer—and drink like a fish: With several teammates, he broke the squad temperance rule one night and was promptly suspended for the last two games of the season. "He made a mistake," Bryant said at the time, "but if he's the kind of person I think he is, Joe will prove worthy of another opportunity." Namath accepted the suspension without involving the others with whom he had been drinking. Even though Bryant didn't really appreciate Namath's first goatee (Joe sensed his displeasure and shaved it off) nor the fact that Namath once began a frug on the sidelines while a marching band performed on the field, the coach and his superstar grew steadily closer; and in his senior year, Namath went on to become an All-American—completing 64 percent of his passes on the gridiron and probably even more than that with Alabama's comely contingent of Southern belles. But Namath's continuing, whispered adventures as a lothario only added to the heroic stature he had achieved throughout the state.

Though injured in the fourth game of the season, Namath grittily kept playing, despite a torn cartilage in his right knee; he wasn't about to let an injury squeeze him out of a fat professional contract. In practice several days before Alabama's 1965 Orange Bowl date with the University of Texas, Namath's damaged knee suddenly collapsed, and he was slated to sit out the game; but he was called on to play when the team's substitute quarterback couldn't get the offense moving. Joe responded by connecting on 18 of 37 passes—and was named the Orange Bowl's Most Valuable Player.

With the last game of his college career behind him, Namath began weighing offers from the two teams that had drafted him—the AFL Jets and the NFL St. Louis Cardinals. At the time, the leagues were involved in a talent-buying contest and the younger league, with little prestige to recommend it, had to put its money where its ambitions were. Sonny Werblin, then head of the Jets, was searching for a quarterback with a personality fans could latch onto. Said show-business-oriented Werblin (formerly president of the Music Corporation of America): "I needed to build a franchise with somebody who could do more than just play. So we went down to Birmingham and the minute Joe walked into the room and lit it up, I knew he was our man." After much deliberation, Namath signed with New York for a reported $427,000.

He was rechristened Broadway Joe almost immediately, and comments about his unprecedented contract ranged from the caustic to the coy. (Said Bob Hope, "Joe Namath's the only quarterback in history who'll play in a business suit.") Before entering the Sunday wars, however, Namath first had to enter Manhattan's Lenox Hill Hospital for knee surgery. All the cartilage in Namath's right knee was removed, but the operation was a success. Soon afterward, he was found physically unfit for military service, and a huge public outcry erupted, with the result that Namath was reexamined—only to flunk the physical again. "How can I win, man?" he said later. "If I say I'm glad, I'm a traitor, and if I say I'm sorry, I'm a fool."

Since then, precious little about Namath's life has gone unreported: In 1965, Joe moved to Manhattan, where he installed himself in a luxurious East Side apartment. Decorated at a cost of $25,000, Namath's penthouse pad features such sybaritic touches as Siberian snow-leopard throw pillows, brown-suede sofas, an oval bed, a black-leather bar and the pièce de résistance, a wall-to-wall white llama rug. Namath instantly became the darling of New York's media—and of a significant segment of its most striking young women as well. And when autumn arrived, Joe showed he was worth every penny of his paycheck: In his first pro season, he threw 18 touchdown passes, was voted Rookie of the Year and the AFL All-Star game's Most Valuable Player. Jet receiver Don Maynard, an All-Pro in his own right, remarked during Namath's first year, "The big thing about him is his coolness under stress. I don't think you can do anything to make this guy lose his poise. He also knows his football."

Since 1965, Namath has steadily honed his gridiron skills to a fine edge and last year, in leading his team to the Eastern Division title, AFL championship and Super Bowl victory, proved beyond any doubt how accomplished a quarterback he is. Off the field, meanwhile, his activities have added spice to the mystique that already surrounds the 26-year-old superpro. In 1967, several months after another knee operation, Namath ducked out of training camp one night and allegedly (Namath says it didn't happen) got into a bar brawl with *Time* interviews sports editor Charles Parmiter; then he grew the only Fu Manchu mustache ever to become a national controversy, and finally shaved it off—for a fee of $10,000 from the Schick Electric Razor Company. And the girl talk escalated: He was supposedly cavorting with hordes of socialites and celebrities, from Kay Stevens (which he denies) to Mamie Van Doren (which he doesn't).

Then, in the midst of last season, Namath and former Alabama teammate Ray Abruzzese put up the cash for an East Side Manhattan cocktail lounge they called Bachelors III (partner number three was Joe Dellapina, who managed the bar). In the afterglow of the Jet Super Bowl championship, Namath held court almost nightly at his club, which quickly became Manhattan's toughest nightery to get into. All was copacetic for Namath, it seemed, until June 6, when he shocked the sporting world by announcing at a hastily organized press conference that football commissioner Pete Rozelle had ordered him to sell his interest in Bachelors III because mobsters were reportedly frequenting the bar; after weighing the facts, said Namath, he concluded that the allegations were untrue and he had, therefore, chosen to retire from football rather than sell out. Seven weeks later, after a series of meetings with Rozelle—and amid a rash of purple prose in the press, most of which agreed with Rozelle's charges—Namath came out of his short retirement, agreed to sell his half ownership in Bachelors III, again maintained that the bar was free of Mafia clientele and finally got down to the tough business of training for the current football season—his last, according to Joe, because of his worsening knees.

Playboy Associate Editor Lawrence Linderman, who conducted this exclusive interview with Namath, reports: "I met Joe a week after his retirement announcement—at midnight in Bachelors III. The bar was filled with couples; it's a pleasant, quiet spot to drink, and unremarkable in every way. A few minutes before 12, the pace of the place suddenly quickened. I turned in time to see Namath entering with a gorgeous blonde on his arm and a drink being placed in his free hand. He cuts one hell of a striking figure: Today's fashions are tailored for men of modest physique; Namath, at 6'2" and 185 pounds, has a boxer's build—slim at the waist, broad through the torso—and this night, in a white-lace body shirt and broadly striped bell-bottom slacks, he was Errol Flynn swashbuckling his way into the hearts of every girl in the club. They really come on with him, and vice versa.

"After a quick introduction, I was able to tear Joe away from friends and celebrity touchers, and we went downstairs to discuss the interview in his cramped office; on the way, we passed the men's room and Namath shouted in, 'I don't mind if you guys use the pay phones, but do me a favor, will ya? Call your bookie from somewhere else.' Much chortling from the urinals. We arranged to meet that Friday morning in Boston at the Sheraton.

"Namath arrived half an hour after I did; and that evening, the same blonde who'd been with Namath when I met him in New York flew up to spend the weekend with him. I had hoped to monopolize Namath's attention for the interview, but I was clearly overmatched. We spent the night dining and drinking at Gino Cappelletti's The Point After restaurant; and the next morning, retired Boston Patriot receiver Jim Colclough and his wife, Namath and his girl, along with me and my tape recorder—still unused—flew in a Lear jet to ocean-side Provincetown.

"After arriving at our hotel, we went into town and the first thing we did was buy a football; the second thing we did was buy two bottles of Johnnie Walker Red Label Scotch; the third thing we did was hit the beach, where we threw the football and drank the scotch. In the evening, Namath disinterestedly taped some background information for me while watching a televised college All-Star football game. We finally talked informally for an hour when we got back to the hotel, and then caught the jet back to Boston. But I still had no interview; so, several weeks later, after Namath had returned to football, I dropped in unannounced at Hofstra University in Hempstead, New York, where the Jets were holding their preseason training camp. It had been raining steadily for the better part of a week and he and I—at long last—were able to talk productively for many hours over the course of two days. Namath's return to the Jets was less than a week old at the time, and the Bachelors III controversy was still being played up in the press. Since the entire affair so obviously rankled him, it provided the logical opening for our interview."

PLAYBOY: Although you sold your half ownership in Bachelors III, your last word on the subject was that the Manhattan night spot was *not* a hangout for mobsters. Are you absolutely sure about that?

NAMATH: Damned right I am. There wasn't a single shred of fact in any of the charges made about Bachelors III. The reasons I sold had nothing to do with the bar itself—and everything to do with not disappointing a hell of a lot of people I know and the fact that I happen to love playing football. If you'd like to hear what really happened, I'll tell it to you.

PLAYBOY: We're listening.

NAMATH: I and Ray Abruzzese, my roommate in New York and a former teammate at Alabama, decided we wanted to buy a bar in Manhattan and use it as a place to hang out in—a place where we could meet our friends and feel comfortable. So we got a list of available bars from realtors and we walked around Manhattan for about six months, checking places out. We finally decided on the right place, called it Bachelors III and opened for business last November. We weren't looking to make money or lose money on it; once it opened, though, Bachelors III showed a profit—not a big profit, but we were more than satisfied with it. It was just extra gravy.

PLAYBOY: When did you first learn formally Bachelors III was being investigated?

NAMATH: The first word of any kind I received about the place came in February, when someone in the New York Jets office handed me a list of nine names and told me that the men on it were "unsavory characters" who were hanging out at Bachelors III and who could be a source of trouble for me. Well, the first name on that list was one of our managers and the second was one of our attorneys. Both of these men are straight-ace guys; and although I sure didn't think much of that list, I had it sent down to the district attorney's office. Detectives there promised to tell us if anything was happening—if mob guys were coming in. Well, they investigated and told us we had nothing to worry about, so we didn't. That was in February. Then, in June, at the Football Writers Association banquet in New York, a couple of guys from AFL-NFL security—after taking us to a private room—told coach Weeb Ewbank and me that Bachelors III was going to be raided and closed up the following day and that the league wanted me to sell out that night. I couldn't even answer them, man. I didn't know *what* to say—or think. I immediately called up my lawyers, Mike Bite and Jimmy Walsh, and they drove right over to talk about it with me. To tell you the truth, we didn't know what the hell to do. Then, right after the banquet, Pete Rozelle called me to say there was no need to sell that night, because the raid had been postponed, and to meet with him the following morning, a Wednesday. Jimmy Walsh and I met with Rozelle and two guys from league security, who told us that Bachelors III had been under surveillance almost since we bought it. The word from dependable sources was that Bachelors III was going to be closed down on Friday—and that I definitely had to sell by then.

PLAYBOY: What was your reaction to all this?

NAMATH: The news really caught me by surprise. I mean, we'd checked the thing out in February and didn't think anything more about it. Anyway, here it was, Wednesday, and I had to sell before the raid took place on Friday. Well, my lawyers and I got straight to the heart of the thing in a hurry. It wasn't right that I had to sell, we all agreed on that, but it was certainly the logical thing to do—logical in that if Bachelors III was to be closed down by the police, they must have reasons for it; and even if I felt that there were no reasons, they obviously had the inside track. But I couldn't come up with any indications from any of the local law-enforcement branches that Bachelors III was in trouble. So I asked a few guys for advice. One of the people I talked to was Tom Marshall, president of the Broadway Joe restaurant chain. Tom was really straight with me: "Listen," he said, "you have to do what you feel is right. I know it'll hurt the company some, it might hurt the stock; but, damn it, you have to live with yourself, not us, so don't get hung up about the company." That helped me out a lot. Anyway, by Friday, the day of the great raid, instead of selling, I retired.

PLAYBOY: And was Bachelors III raided?

NAMATH: Hell, no. Like I told you, there was never any reason for the place to be closed down, and it never was. Meanwhile, we kept checking with the law and nobody knew anything about a raid being planned for Bachelors III. If you'll excuse the expression, I run a clean joint.

PLAYBOY: What happened next?

NAMATH: What happened next is that I met with Rozelle and this time caught *him* by surprise. I found out—as I told Rozelle—that his information came from an AFL-NFL security guy, who told this story to several people: About four years ago, this guy supposedly came over to my table at a restaurant, pulled out his identification and told me the people I was with were mob guys, that I shouldn't be seen talking to them and that he didn't *want* me to talk to them. I supposedly told him, "Listen, when I'm not on a football field, I hang with whoever I want to hang with; and as long as it doesn't affect what I do on the field, you can just go fuck yourself." Since he supposedly was with a couple of people at the time, he took that badly and got very, very upset.

PLAYBOY: You say this confrontation "supposedly" took place. Did it or didn't it?

NAMATH: Maybe it did, maybe it didn't; I can't remember all the people I've talked to over the past four years and what I've said to 'em. Anyway, ever since then, this guy has carried a vendetta against me and was dumb enough to admit it to several of the Jets. He told them how I'd told him to go fuck himself, that I was bad for the game and that as long as I stayed in pro football, I'd be a thorn in his side. This man started everything. I'm not going to give you the names of the Jets he talked to; but when Rozelle came out to our training camp in June, he was told about this conversation. Johnny Sample, who isn't with the Jets anymore, asked Rozelle a very direct question: How can he allow a man to work in the security office when he admits to having a tremendous grudge against a ballplayer? Aren't the security guys supposed to help us, protect us, rather than going all out to screw us up?

After first springing all this on Rozelle, I asked him for about the 9000th time to document one single charge against Bachelors III. I told him if I was in the wrong—if Bachelors III was being frequented by mobsters—then I'd sell immediately, because I wouldn't want any part of it. I mean, I know where my number-one thing is at: That's football, and I don't want to put it in jeopardy. But damn, they couldn't show me *one* thing wrong. Just lots of talk about, "Well, I'm acting on reliable information." I asked Rozelle, "*What* reliable information? We have reliable information that your reliable information is unreliable." But Rozelle said he had different people in all the law branches telling him different things than they told me. It seemed like everybody was getting into the act, but there was no action taken against Bachelors III. Even so, Rozelle wasn't about to be budged.

PLAYBOY: Did you feel *he* was out to get you, too?

NAMATH: Definitely not, man. Our talks were very friendly and we got along well. But he felt he had to act on the information he received from his security people; it just happened to be the wrong information. Meanwhile, I was getting slaughtered by the press: *Life* magazine and *Sports Illustrated*, the bastards, wanted some juice to sell their magazines, so they started writing all kinds of shit about me. Well, Rozelle said the matter had now become so exposed to the public that it was all out of proportion. He felt that between the magazines and various screwy people, there had been about 25 charges brought up—things like somebody using our Bachelors III telephones to call in bets, "undesirable" guys coming up to hold crap games in my apartment, etc. "With all those accusations, if only one or two turn out to be right," he said, "then you've got to be in the wrong." "I agree with you," I said, "but none of them are true."

PLAYBOY: Could you elaborate on that *Sports Illustrated* story about crap games with mobsters in your apartment?

NAMATH: I think *Sports Illustrated* might check out their stories a little more closely before publishing them. If they had, they would have discovered that my next-door neighbors are three FBI agents sharing a pad. Somehow, I don't think it would be very wise for mobsters to hold big crap games in a location like that. Actually, when I first read the story, I thought, shit, this is kinda funny; but then I got properly pissed off. I mean, they're implying that old Joe is tied up with Mafia people. In an issue some weeks later, they implied it again—only this time they had it in parentheses that Namath himself was never in the apartment when the crap games were going on. I think they were simply trying to back off. Beats the hell out of me how they got the story, but the son of a bitch who wrote it ought to be working for Looney Tunes. We're deciding whether or not to go ahead with a lawsuit.

PLAYBOY: What finally made you decide to sell your interest in Bachelors III and go back to football?

NAMATH: Well, up until the day I did it, I really didn't think I would ever play again. Rozelle and I were meeting and he said that even though I might agree to sell the bar, from now on, I also had to *stay out* of Bachelors III. Well, I wouldn't give him my word on that, because some night I might just want to drop in, with a girl or solo. My friends were there and I just wasn't going to stay away permanently. And then he said, "You know, Joe, if you really want to, you can do it. You gave up smoking like that. When you put your mind to something, you do it." And I said, "What the hell is this all about? I don't want to sell—so I'm not selling." We'd been meeting for two and a half hours and, man, I knew what was right and I *put* my mind to it: Do what the hell you want to do and, if you haven't hurt anybody, then you're OK. Well, at that point, Mike Bite and Jimmy Walsh and Rozelle sat down to talk for an hour and when they came back, we talked for another hour, concessions were made and finally I said—ah, the hell with it. So I sold. But I wouldn't have sold if it were just me involved.

PLAYBOY: Wasn't it just you involved?

NAMATH: No. First of all, I had a whole lot of teammates to think of. One man doesn't even come close to being responsible for a football club's success, but quarterback's an important position and, if I stepped out on them, the Jets would be hurt—and there are a lot of guys on the team, myself included, who think we can win another Super Bowl. Secondly, there were other business partners who were getting hurt financially while this thing was going on: Stock in Broadway Joe's fell more than four points. My lawyers were nervous wrecks, all because of me. But mostly, it was my mother. She'd read all those damned lies in the press and got really upset, and as many times as I told her not to believe that stuff, I knew she was still thinking that if it wasn't true, how come it was there in black and white? When I retired, I did it because I felt one way about the whole thing: Fuck the money and everything else. I was *right*, man; there was nothing wrong with Bachelors III. But finally, with the concessions and all, the point just didn't seem all that important.

PLAYBOY: What kind of concessions?

NAMATH: First, let me tell you why there *had* to be concessions: I think Rozelle was right in the way he acted, in that it's his job to keep football above suspicion. That's why he's commissioner. When all the magazine stories were out, the public was wondering just what the hell was going to happen. Well, I realized then, as I do now, that to answer the public and keep any question about football's integrity from even being raised, getting me the hell out of Bachelors III was the only answer. So he was right in doing what he had to do—and I was right in doing what I had to do, which was to retire. But Rozelle didn't want me to quit football almost as much as I didn't want to quit, which is why we had meetings and why there were compromises on each side—with my main concession being to sell Bachelors III in New York. By selling and having pro football take me back, I think it indicates that I wasn't involved with any person or establishment or with any crap games and things like that. If his information had been factual, I think there's no doubt they would have told me to stay out of football or at least given me a year's suspension. Furthermore, Rozelle and I agreed that even though I'm selling the New York Bachelors III, I'm free to open up other Bachelors IIIs with the same management—which we've already done in Boston, and plan to do in L.A. and Miami. If Bachelors III was bad, they certainly wouldn't allow me to stay in business with the same people. Finally, I'm glad Rozelle helped me "unretire." Sports has done everything for me: It's been my life since high school and probably even before that.

PLAYBOY: Were you what sportswriters call a "high school phenom?"

NAMATH: I was—but not in football, at least not right away. Until my senior year, baseball and basketball were my best sports; and even when I was a senior, I still wanted to play baseball professionally. But the family wanted me to go to college and I guess I agreed with them or else I would have accepted some of the offers I got.

PLAYBOY: How many were there?

NAMATH: Four teams were interested in me. The St. Louis Cardinals wanted to sign me for $15,000 when I was a junior in high school. When my dad asked me what I planned to do with the money, I told him I'd seen this great-looking convertible; he didn't exactly think it would be such a great idea if that's all I wanted. Anyway, the Orioles and Kansas City A's wanted me, too; but the big offer I got was in my senior year, when the Chicago Cubs offered me $50,000.

PLAYBOY: What had you done to attract all this attention?

NAMATH: Nothing in particular; I was just a really outstanding, power-hitting outfielder. I could throw and I could hit. I have no idea what my batting average was in high school, but I know it wasn't below .450, and that's pretty good hitting where I come from.

PLAYBOY: Do you think you could have gotten as far in baseball as you have in football?

NAMATH: No. I think I could have become an outstanding professional baseball player, but I don't think I could have reached the heights that I have in football—being one of the very top players in the game, being a world champion. I might have been part of a team that won the World Series, I guess, but I don't think I would have gotten the acclaim that I've gotten so far in football.

PLAYBOY: Is that why you finally passed up the baseball offers?

NAMATH: No. Shoot, when I got those offers, I sure as hell wanted to take the money and run. But, like I said, my mom and dad wanted me to go to college: so did my three older brothers.

PLAYBOY: Were they athletes, too?

NAMATH: Yeah, and starting about the time I was six, they'd get out every day and work with me. My brother Bobby was a pretty good quarterback, but he never finished high school. He was three years behind my brother John in school and when John went into the Service, Bob had to quit in order to work and help Mom and Dad out. Bobby was never able to put the time in athletics that he needed to. My brother Frank did well in high school and got a football scholarship to Kentucky. When he went to Kentucky, though, Frank didn't know he'd had a baseball offer: My father had been contacted by a major-league team that wanted to sign Frank, but because he wanted Frank in college, he just didn't tell him about it. Frank later found out when he was in college, got very upset and ended up quitting school and working.

PLAYBOY: Did this cause a serious break between them?

NAMATH: Yes, but they've made up. Frank moved from Detroit to Beaver Falls a few months ago, has a nice family and is doing very well in the insurance business. Anyway, my father didn't want to go through something like that again, so he told me about my offers and left it up to me. Football only happened in my senior year; in my sophomore year, I was the smallest guy on the team and played two minutes during the season, on defense. In my junior season, I started the first two or three games at quarterback and must have caused around 93 fumbles. It was really ridiculous, man; I couldn't play worth a flip. But before my senior year, we practiced all summer; and in the fall, we beat everybody and won the western-Pennsylvania championship.

PLAYBOY: How good did you think you were by that time?

NAMATH: I rated myself best in the country, and that's the truth. I made all-state and I felt I could play better than anybody else in that position. And then, of course, I got all those college scholarship offers, which were proof to me that I knew what I was doing on a football field.

PLAYBOY: How many offers were there?

NAMATH: I usually say 52, but it was more than that. Athletes today get a hell of a lot more offers than that, because more colleges are offering more scholarships than they did in 1961, when I graduated from high school. But it was strange coming out of high school and having colleges offer me as much money as my father made in a year—and they did just that. This softened my disappointment on the baseball thing, because the schools were going to pay me.

PLAYBOY: Which schools made the biggest offers?

NAMATH: I'm not copping out, but I don't think it would be right for me to name them, because this stuff took place eight and a half years ago; and if I told you the schools, a lot of them could be under different systems now. Things could have changed and telling you would only be detrimental to them. I'm not saying things have changed, only that they *may* have changed. But I will tell you that the two schools I finally got serious about—Maryland and Alabama—were the only colleges that offered me a straight scholarship and the standard $15 a month for laundry. I got around the country a lot before I boiled it down, though: I visited Arizona State, Minnesota, Iowa, Miami, Indiana, Maryland and Notre Dame.

PLAYBOY: Why did you decide not to play for Notre Dame?

NAMATH: Two reasons: I talked with their coach, who at the time was Joe Kuharich, and I wasn't very impressed by him. More important was the fact that there were no girls at Notre Dame. Man, they told me they had a women's college right across the lake. What was I supposed to do—swim over to make a date? Anyway, when I finally decided where I wanted to go to school—the University of Maryland—I couldn't get in. My college-boards score was five points below their admission requirements.

PLAYBOY: And Alabama was your second choice?

NAMATH: No; at that point, I hadn't been in any contact with them at all. What happened was that Tom Nugent, Maryland's coach, got on the phone to Paul Bryant at Alabama to tell him that I was still loose and to come after me. I found out later that he called Alabama because Maryland never plays Alabama and Nugent didn't want me to wind up on a team he'd be facing someday. I guess the reason I finally chose Alabama was because my brother Frank had played under two of Alabama's coaches when they were at Kentucky and another of Alabama's coaches had been a senior at Kentucky when Frank had been a freshman there. He liked the guys and thought it was a good idea for me to go down there. By that time, I was so disgusted with the whole recruitment business that I just said screw it and agreed to go to Alabama. I hadn't even visited the campus.

PLAYBOY: How did you like it when you arrived?

NAMATH: It was hell, man. I was a Northerner and 99 percent of the guys were Southerners. It was really lonely for guys from up North. We had a kid from Cleveland, one from Silver Creek, New York, one from Dayton and one from Rhode Island; but in our freshman year, they all quit.

PLAYBOY: Why?

NAMATH: Partly because they couldn't cut it on the football field, partly because of scholastics, but mostly because they were just plain homesick. When I got to my sophomore year, only one other "Northerner" was on the team—and he was from Virginia. At that time, coming from the North and going to school in the South was rougher than it is today.

PLAYBOY: In what way?

NAMATH: The race thing. It was really out of sight, man. My family lived in a part of Beaver Falls that was called the Lower End, a low-income part of town. It was a predominately black neighborhood and the guys I hung out with were black. Like, in high school, I was the only white boy on the starting basketball team and the four other guys were black; they were all friends of mine from the neighborhood. The only time I'd ever run into any kind of race thing had been when I was little, when me and a black kid went into a pizza place and got thrown out. The lady who ran it just told us to get the hell out, so we both left. But when I got to the University of Alabama—wow! Coming from where I came from, I couldn't believe it. Water fountains for whites were painted white; there were different bathrooms for whites and blacks; blacks had to sit in the backs of buses and whites had to sit up front. I just couldn't understand it.

PLAYBOY: Were there any black students there at the time?

NAMATH: When I first got there, no. They integrated in my sophomore year, right after George Wallace, who was governor then, stood in the doorway and tried to keep them out.

PLAYBOY: Did you ever get into any arguments about race?

NAMATH: Nope. Not a *rough* argument, anyway. But I did get the nickname Nigger, and that, of course, had to do with race. In my freshman year, I was sitting in my room doing something and one of the fellas picked up a picture of the Beaver Falls High School football queen and her court. My girl at the time was the football queen and the crown bearer was a black girl. The guy asked, "Hey Joe, is this your girl?" and I answered yes, thinking he was pointing at the queen. But he was pointing at the black girl. He said, "Oh, yeah?" and ran out and told everybody he could find that I was dating a black girl; so they started calling me Nigger. I had a lot of bad times in the beginning, but it all changed. They got to respect the way I felt and I think I might even have turned some of them around on a few things. In my senior year, they voted me captain of the team; and when I think about it—about me mixed in with a bunch of guys from Alabama, Tennessee, Mississippi, Georgia, Florida—I consider it a very high honor.

PLAYBOY: By the time you left the University of Alabama in 1965, did you see any evidence that race attitudes had changed?

NAMATH: Oh, I think they're getting more liberal in the South, I guess because they're getting more educated. But I don't think the South will ever be completely integrated; in fact, we probably won't live to see complete integration anywhere in America. The problem is stronger in the South, because that's where it all originated, but I see plenty of segregation everywhere. Even in New York, there's a lot of restaurants that don't like to admit black people. It's going to take a long time before the race problem gets straightened out, but it's changed plenty since I first got to Alabama.

PLAYBOY: Why were you the only Northerner who didn't quit during that first year?

NAMATH: I wanted to quit about 15 times during my freshman year. I wanted to quit and play professional baseball. But I talked to a guy named Bubba Church, who used to pitch for the Philadelphia Phillies. He was living in Mobile at the time and coach Bryant knew what I was thinking and, since he didn't want me to quit, he asked Bubba to come up and talk to me. Bubba explained that I could still play baseball after college and that getting an education was something I'd never regret; whereas I might look back afterward and be sorry I hadn't stuck in school. But I told him I didn't care, I just wanted to go home. Well, right then and there, Bubba just pulled some money out of his wallet and said, "You fly home. You can stay there if you like, but I think it would be better for you to come back." Well, after I got home, I decided maybe Bubba was right, and I decided to stick it out.

PLAYBOY: How much did Bryant contribute to your development as a quarterback?

NAMATH: A hell of a lot. I guess most coaches know a good deal about the technical side of the game, but only a very few of them are able to demand and receive 110 percent effort from each of their players. This is true about coach Bryant. In the years I played for him, he taught me that on the football field, you play to win and to hate even the thought of losing. He's a man I totally respect. Coach Bryant also gave me good advice when I was drafted by both the American and National football leagues in my senior year.

PLAYBOY: What kind of advice?

NAMATH: Well, after the last game of my senior year, he came into our dressing room and said, "Joe, you know these pro-football people are going to be coming around to see you. Do you have any idea how much money you're going to ask for?" Shoot, I didn't know. He told me to ask for $200,000. "You might not get $200,000," he said, "but it's a good place to start from, and maybe you'll wind up with $150,000 or so." The first team I talked with was the NFL's St. Louis Cardinals; when they asked me what I wanted, I was embarrassed, but I told them—$200,000. They agreed to it.

PLAYBOY: Did that surprise you?

NAMATH: I almost had a coronary right there. But I hadn't yet talked to the Jets, so I decided to see their people, too. Actually, the final sums offered by both teams were about equal and the quarterback situations were about the same: The Jets needed a quarterback bad and so did the Cardinals, because their guy, Charley Johnson, had a two-year Service obligation to fulfill, although he didn't finally go into the Army until two years later. I signed with the Jets because of two people: Sonny Werblin, who was then head of the Jets, because he seemed genuinely interested in me and convinced me that the AFL was going to be better than the

NFL in a short time; and the Jets' coach, Weeb Ewbank. Mr. Bryant told me that over the years, Weeb had impressed the hell out of him, that his coaching records had been outstanding and that he was in every possible way a good football man. So I signed a Jets contract.

PLAYBOY: For how much?

NAMATH: It was $427,000, to be paid out over a three-year period, and it was broken down in various ways so that I could get the best tax breaks possible. Man, I didn't know what the hell to do with all that bread. In fact, that's about all I knew: that I wasn't capable of handling any big financial matters. So I had to get people who specialized in those things, whose advice could be trusted. I'm learning about business now, but it'll be a long time before I go into any heavy investments without checking on the opinions of associates. But at the time I signed, I really wasn't thinking about all those things. I was just happy.

PLAYBOY: Did you know that your contract was the biggest ever given to a football player up to then? Most veteran pros, in fact, reacted in much the same way as former Cleveland quarterback Frank Ryan, who said, "If Namath's worth $400,000, I'm worth a million."

NAMATH: Then all I can say is that I hope he got his million. Sure, there was hostility, but I hoped a lot of it wouldn't be directed at me. I sort of thought that other players could point to my salary to justify asking for raises of their own; after all, I wasn't taking any bread out of their mouths.

PLAYBOY: What was the reaction of your Jet teammates?

NAMATH: Well, some of the guys resented it; but I can understand that, too. That year, though, we had a couple of other high-paid draft choices: John Huarte of Notre Dame got $200,000 and Bob Schweickert of Virginia Tech got $150,000. Anyway, I felt that if I could do the job on the field, then nobody had any right to gripe about my salary, even if they paid me $2 million. But the publicity the contract caused didn't help me get settled in with my teammates.

PLAYBOY: Were they also upset about the fact that nearly every word being written about the Jets seemed to be about you?

NAMATH: Sure they were; and I can't really blame them for that, either. Shit, before I came to camp, it was football as usual; and then, all of a sudden, it became like a show-business thing, with all kinds of photographers and writers around. It wasn't all bad, though. One of the things rookies have to do is sing their team fight song in front of the rest of the guys; but when I got up, everybody started singing "There's No Business

Like Show Business" and it was a good gag. But I could see where it could be upsetting to them, like that Broadway Joe thing.

PLAYBOY: How did the nickname come about?

NAMATH: In 1965, *Sports Illustrated* ran a story about the Jets' highly paid rookies; as I said, I was only one of 'em, but *Sports Illustrated* ran a cover photo of me standing in the middle of Broadway—in uniform—at about 8:30 in the evening. We were in the locker room the day the interviews came out and offensive tackle Sherman Plunkett looked at it, kind of shook his head a little and said, "There goes Broadway Joe." And it stuck.

PLAYBOY: And grew to legendary proportions. What do you think of all the publicity that surrounds you?

NAMATH: Not much, believe me. I don't pick up a newspaper every day, because there have been so many dumb things written about me—by so many people who haven't even talked to me—that it's just ridiculous, man. As far as football writers go, I don't think one of them *really* knows what's happening on the field—why the team has to do one thing more than another at a particular point in the game. They simply don't spend enough time around the ball club to be well-educated about the technical side of the game, and football is very complicated. It's not going to happen, but teams should give football writers in their cities weekly clinics on what the hell the game is about, so that the press could be more than fairly well-informed spectators. Another thing that happens to almost every ballplayer is that quotes get jumbled up something fierce. Usually, even if reporters get the words right in a quote, they screw up the emphasis, and the next morning, you discover you've said something you just never said. In general, I think most sportswriters want to do a good job, and if they talk straight to me, I give them straight answers. But about the only writers I speak to regularly are all in New York—guys like Dave Anderson of *The New York Times*, Larry Merchant of the *Post* and Murray Janoff of *Newsday*. Mostly, I don't dig the press.

PLAYBOY: Because they're not football experts?

NAMATH: No, because the press doesn't care how much it hurts people like me, so long as there's a good headline. Look, I realize I wouldn't be where I am without the press, but after a while, you can't help getting annoyed over the bullshit papers print about you. I'm not going to go into what they were writing about me during the Bachelors III thing again, but another good example happened last year in Miami, when I was stopped for speeding. The front page of *The Miami Herald* ran something like "Namath Arrested in Car Chase," but the only chase that took place was in that headline and in a lot of headlines in papers all over the country. The whole thing was so stupid. I was tagged for going 15 miles above the speed limit; it was either 50 in a 35-mile zone or 55 in a 40-mile zone. The officer also tried to give me a reckless-driving charge, but all I did was swerve out of one lane—which had construction blocking it—into another. The officer said I was drunk and I called him a damn liar, and then he got pissed off and I got pissed off and I wound up taking a drunkometer test three times and passed it all three times. Well, they dropped that charge and the reckless-driving charge. But because the prick had to give me *something*, he gave me a speeding ticket—although he had no proof of that and I don't see how he could have, since he was about a half mile away when the speeding supposedly took place. So I wound up with a $50 fine, and after all the headlines about drunken and reckless driving, there was a little paragraph hidden in the Miami papers that said something like "Namath drunken-driving charge dropped." Period. No apology for all their crappy so-called reporting. I always think of it like the *Pueblo* thing—how innocent we were and what bad cats they were to capture our ship; but five months later, on the third page of *The New York Times*, about the sixth column over and four lines from the bottom, we find out that the *Pueblo* was spying on the North Koreans, just as they claimed. Well, shit, that's what papers are like, so why should you believe what they print? When I read about myself and know flat-out that they're writing nonsense, why should I take their word on anything else, particularly when they keep screwing up? Talk about credibility gaps, man; the American press has any politician beat by a long shot.

PLAYBOY: Is the Broadway Joe lifestyle simply a myth manufactured by the press?

NAMATH: Parts of it are, parts of it aren't. For instance, there are a lot of stories about me trying to be flamboyant by wearing white football shoes. When I was playing at Alabama, our football shoes felt too light on my feet, flimsy; and when I ran, they would turn out on me. So before every game, I taped them up for support, which made them heavier, until they felt like they were kind of part of me. Well, the one game I didn't tape them up was in my senior year against North Carolina State, when my knee collapsed. I wasn't hit on the play; my knee just went. So I've been taping them up ever since, including when I got to the Jets. But one day, when I got to Shea Stadium, a pair of white shoes was in my locker; I never asked for 'em, but there they were, so I started wearing them.

PLAYBOY: The Broadway Joe legend also pictures you as one of the great womanizers of our time. Do you think your reputation for amorous exploits is merited?

NAMATH: I think it's merited, in the sense that I'm young, single, I have some money, I'm in the press a lot, and so I do all right with the ladies.

PLAYBOY: What about the thousands of sexual conquests that have been attributed to you?

NAMATH: Oh, I wouldn't put the number *that* high.

PLAYBOY: How high would you put it?

NAMATH: A conservative estimate?

PLAYBOY: That would be fine.

NAMATH: I'd say at least 300—but that's a conservative estimate. Probably too conservative, because when I was in boring classes at Alabama, I used to start making out lists to see how well I was doing and I guess I was pretty close to 300 by the time I graduated.

PLAYBOY: You say that with a great big smile. Are those fond memories?

NAMATH: They sure are. And the older I get, the more I enjoy sex—and the more I learn about it. For instance, when I was younger, the aim of making love was simply to reach a climax, achieve your own satisfaction and not even worry about your partner's. Well, as you grow up, you start understanding that sex is a two-way street and that it's much better for both of you to be sexually satisfied. Once you realize this, you should really go all out and make a sincere effort to make 'em happy, because then sex becomes a very beautiful thing.

PLAYBOY: That sounds like the kind of pep talk Vince Lombardi would give if he were coaching a team in the Sexual Freedom League. There are thousands of guys—some of them fairly glamorous celebrities—who feel the same way about giving as well as getting sexual satisfaction. But they don't make out like you do. What's your secret?

NAMATH: I really like women. But I'm not a very forward guy. There are so many times when I see a girl I'd love to get to know, but I won't approach her. I usually don't feel like going over and introducing myself, because right after I say something like, "Hello, my name is Joe Namath, what's yours?," there are too many times when I get a quick stare that says, "So what?" I mean, a lot of girls get antagonistic, man. If expressions could talk, I'd be hearing things like, "You think you're such a big deal. You expect me to go to bed with you just because you're Joe Namath; but I won't, because I'm different!" Hell, I don't expect to go to bed with every good-looking girl I meet. I'd like it, but I don't *expect* it. All I want to do is get to know them and *hope* to get sexually involved with them.

PLAYBOY: What do you do when you meet a girl who's intent on putting you down?

NAMATH: I immediately drop back 15 yards and punt. Why waste my time and hers?

PLAYBOY: How do you like to spend your time with those who like you—aside from the traditional way?

NAMATH: Well, I don't like going out on a date unless I know the broad a little bit beforehand. By the way, broad to me is not a detrimental term for women; it's simply another word for female. Anyway, I don't really go out a whole lot, because there aren't many girls I like to take out and spend a whole evening with—at least not an evening in public. I enjoy staying in with a girl much more than going out. Mostly, I prefer just meeting a girl at a nice, quiet bar, where we can get to know each other. That's one of the reasons I guess I got into Bachelors III. It was a good way to meet girls, and it still is.

PLAYBOY: Are there any particular types of girls that especially attract you more than others?

NAMATH: I dig fairly tall, blonde-haired girls—I mean, they just flat turn me on. That's not saying I don't like brunettes; it's just that when I see a blonde, she doesn't have to be beautiful for me to look two or three times when she walks by. Also, I'm a leg man more than a chest man. I like a quiet girl, as opposed to a talkative, laughing, boisterous extrovert. I mean, I don't hold it against a girl if she talks a lot or if she laughs a lot, but I enjoy myself better, I feel more comfortable with a soft-spoken girl.

PLAYBOY: According to reputation, you've sampled girls from every region in America. Is there any area you prefer?

NAMATH: I like Southern girls. For some reason, they seem sweeter, gentler. They're not as hard as New York girls, simply because they're not confronted with the things that girls in Manhattan are confronted with every day: vulgar language in the streets and a toughness caused by fear of all the sex crimes that take place in New York. New York girls are more hardened than Southern girls, but as I said just after the Jets won the AFL championship, I want to thank the broads in New York for all they did for me last season. They really helped build my morale.

PLAYBOY: Do you get many propositions from female admirers?

NAMATH: Sure; I've received letters that were just out-and-out sexual invitations on several occasions. But I don't remember ever following any of them up.

PLAYBOY: Why not?

NAMATH: Well, I don't find it strange for a girl to *write* a letter like that, but it would certainly be strange if she expected me to answer her. I mean, if it's on her mind and it'll make her feel good to let me know, I appreciate it. I guess if I really dug a broad or felt like I did, I might send a letter to her to find out if we could get together; possibly, we *could* get together. But I don't like answering those requests, because you never know what's in back of them. It could be a practical joke or it could be a plan to get me into some kind of trouble. You don't know what it's goin' to be, man; it could end up in a bad deal, and I have enough trouble without having to go look for it. If I happen to run into a girl who feels that way about me, though, it can be a different story.

PLAYBOY: Does that kind of thing happen to you often?

NAMATH: I don't know how often it happens, but it happens. And most of the time, I don't even mind if they're interested in me just because I'm Joe Namath. If that's the way they come on and they can swing with it, I guess I can, too.

PLAYBOY: Do you think you're as good in bed as you are on a football field?

NAMATH: I can't honestly answer that question, because in football, there are comparisons you can make, but I don't think you can do the same with sex. First of all, you're only at your best with a girl who really turns you on. It's a total thing that has to do with how much feeling she has for you and how you feel about her, and that's more important than if she's beautiful or well-built. You certainly can't measure your performance by the number of climaxes you reach, because after the first few times, you just can't expect to keep having orgasms. I think the important thing is how *long* you're able to make love. With the right girl, a guy can go just about all night long. And there have been lots of times when I've done just that. I'm a great believer in sex.

PLAYBOY: We've noticed that. One of sports' great traditions decrees that the night before the big game, the athlete goes to bed early—and by himself. Do you?

NAMATH: No. I spent the nights before the Jets' two biggest games last year—for the AFL championship and the Super Bowl—with girls. But I don't consider that bad or foolish of me. Look, I'm a football player, and that's my number-one thing; I'm not about to take a chance on how I perform by breaking my own schedule. But I've been playing football for a long time, and by now, I know what I should do and shouldn't do to stay ready at all times. The night before a game, I prepare myself both mentally and physically for the next day. I think a ballplayer has to be relaxed to play well; and if that involves being with a girl that night, he should do it. If some ballplayers don't feel that way, they shouldn't do it. But *I* feel that way.

PLAYBOY: Do you make a *point* of going to bed with a girl on the eve of a game?

NAMATH: I try to; it depends on how I feel that night. Before one game last year, I just sat home by myself and watched television, drank a little tequila to relax and went to sleep fairly early. But most of the nights before games, I'll be with a girl. One of the Jets' team doctors, in fact, told me that it's a good idea to have sexual relations before a game, because it gets rid of the kind of nervous tension an athlete doesn't need.

PLAYBOY: Did the doctor relay this bit of medical advice to Weeb Ewbank?

NAMATH: No, he didn't; and if he ever does, I don't think Weeb will go out and hire 40 prostitutes to make sure the Jets are pro football's most relaxed team. Since a lot of the guys on the team are married, I want their wives to know that when we're on the road, the married fellas really mope around the hotel all day and all night. But I don't.

PLAYBOY: In line with your much-reported fondness for Johnnie Walker Red Label Scotch: Has drinking ever taken anything away from your performance on the field?

NAMATH: Excessive drinking could. But I don't drink too much. I know my drinking limits and I rarely take a third drink the night before a game.

PLAYBOY: Have you ever played high?

NAMATH: No, but I do remember the only game I wasn't prepared for. In 1966, we were playing Boston in the last game of the season, and it didn't matter at all whether we won or lost, as far as our place in the standings was concerned, but Boston needed to win to tie for the Eastern Division title. Well, the night before the game, I was up late, after clowning around and drinking a little more than I usually do. I had a hell of a headache in the first half, but I was feeling no pain after halftime: We won, 38 to 28. Last year, though, I decided to give up drinking entirely before the Buffalo game. It turned out to be our worst afternoon of the season; we lost, 37 to 35. A little later in the season, before we played Oakland, I told a couple of teammates that I was thinking of knocking off drinking again. Dave Herman, a guy I wouldn't want to mess with, came up and said, "If you don't want to drink, I'll grab you and pour it down your throat myself." So I haven't given up booze and I don't plan to.

PLAYBOY: Doesn't the league frown on ballplayers who drink in public?

NAMATH: Yes, but I think it's childish, in the sense that we're all at least three times seven, and if we didn't know by now how to handle our bodies, then we wouldn't be capable of playing—and if a guy can't do his job, he should be fired. The owners may worry about the public's reaction on seeing a player out drinking, but I sure as hell don't. Rules like that are really hypocritical and outdated. In a standard player contract, there are at least a half-dozen fool rules that the team doesn't even enforce. One rule, for instance: Players must at all times wear coats and ties while in a hotel lobby. Hell, that's not important at all. And then there's this whole insane reaction to a guy if he doesn't keep his hair cut short.

PLAYBOY: Whose reaction are you talking about?

NAMATH: People in professional sports and the majority of the public. Look, I've dedicated myself to football; I've played the game for a long time now and I am absolutely positive about one thing: My hair does not slow me down. But I've read so many times that you can't play football or baseball with hair that's the least bit long. Well, if coaches feel that way, their minds are getting away from the game. I think if they just concentrate on the sport and forget a guy's hairstyle or clothes, everybody will be better off, man. Too many times, we judge a person by the way he dresses or cuts his hair.

PLAYBOY: Has a lot of that kind of criticism been directed your way?

NAMATH: Last year, when I had a mustache, I got hundreds of letters, saying it's bad for the image or it's bad for children to see a ballplayer with sideburns and a mustache. Who tells the children it's bad? Parents—they're the ones at fault, because they tell their child that mustaches and long hair are only worn by freaks. Where else does a kid get the idea that mustaches shouldn't be worn and that a man can't have more than a crewcut? As soon as that child looks at our history books and sees all that hair on our forefathers, he's gonna wonder what the hell kind of history we've *had*.

PLAYBOY: Do you think of yourself as a rebel?

NAMATH: I've been reading things and hearing people say I'm a rebel, that I have a noninstitutional personality and such, but that's not true. If I don't believe in something, though, I'm not gonna go along with it; it has nothing to do with being anti-establishment or whatever; it's just that if it's not right for me, then I can't go along with it. I'm not trying to fight society—I'm just trying to be myself and do what I think is best. I don't bother anybody and I don't want anybody to bother me. And I don't think I do anything wrong—at least I try hard not to. Oh, sometimes, I might hurt someone's feelings by refusing an autograph; but even that doesn't happen often, if I'm in a place where there aren't going to be too many to sign. I just don't dig people who think I have to go along with things I don't want to do.

PLAYBOY: Is there anything you'd like to do that you don't or can't?

NAMATH: Yes. I'd like to be able to run the way I used to; but for that, I'd need new knees. When I was in college, I fitted right in with coach Paul Bryant's offense: Quarterbacks did a lot of running at Alabama, because our most effective play was usually the run-pass option. Before I was hurt in my senior year, I was able to cover 40 yards in 4.7 seconds, which is pretty fast for a quarterback in uniform. It's lucky for me that running isn't necessary for a pro quarterback today; the only time you run with the ball is to try to make a first down on a broken-pass play or, if it's the only thing you can do, move the ball out of bounds.

PLAYBOY: How seriously are your knees injured?

NAMATH: Pretty seriously. I've had two operations on the right knee, one on the left, and I have more coming up. But I'm not looking for any sympathy. I think that for a quarterback, I still have good mobility. I can drop back to throw a pass faster and deeper than most quarterbacks. But during a season, my knees hurt my effectiveness, because after a game, they swell up and get sore for a few days and I can't practice very much during the week. Practicing just puts too much pressure and strain on the knees. During a game, it's all pain; but except for running laterally, my movements aren't affected all that much, and that's the important thing. Of course, I have a definite weakness: If I were to get hit with a direct shot to the knee, then I would be out of the game for good. But anyone, even with good knees, can be in trouble if he gets hit that way.

PLAYBOY: Do your knees give you trouble off the field as well?

NAMATH: They sure do. Going up and down stairs is a problem for me, once the season is under way, and even walking bothers me. But it's something you just accept; shit, that's the way it is. You're lucky if you have legs at all, and if they hurt, they hurt. I know that by the time I'm 50, I'm really going to have problems walking; but there isn't anything I can do about it, so there's no sense in tying up my mind with shit like that.

PLAYBOY: How do you relieve the pain?

NAMATH: Fluid is always collecting on my knees, so when they hurt too much or the flexion is decreased, I get the fluid drained. Before a game, I usually get shots of cortisone and butazolidin, and afterward, I'll have a few stiff drinks; alcohol helps as a painkiller.

PLAYBOY: Do a lot of pros go through the same physical pain you do?

NAMATH: You just don't play football today without being injured. I know very few players who are really healthy, especially during the season. Many, many guys play even though they're hurt; and after the game, they hurt all the more. Lots of us couldn't play at all without various medications; I know I couldn't play at times without the shots.

PLAYBOY: Did you undergo the same kind of physical punishment in college?

NAMATH: No, because in college, you play about half as many games, if you count pro exhibition games, and you're younger and better able to recuperate from getting hit. And the guys who are hitting you aren't 275-pound linemen. Learning to put up with pain is part of becoming a pro; and if you don't have terribly serious injuries, it's a very easy part, compared with what you have to learn—and learn quickly—in order to stick with a pro team.

PLAYBOY: Is professional football really that difficult for a collegiate All-American to master?

NAMATH: It's difficult because in college, you can be the best ballplayer in the country; but when you come out, you're playing against professional guys with a hell of a lot more experience. And they're not going to make the errors you're going to make; they've been there that many times more. Also, pro defenses are so much more sophisticated, just as offenses are, than in the college game. For instance, a pro lineman today doesn't merely hit his man; he has to hit and move his opponent almost to the exact spot the coach points to. The precision involved in pro ball—where you have to be of All-American caliber just to sit on the bench—makes it much tougher than the college game.

PLAYBOY: What was the toughest part of breaking into the pros for you?

NAMATH: Learning how to read the other team's defenses and calling the proper audible—changing the play at the line of scrimmage. In college, we never ran any real audibles; me and two other guys on the team would exchange signals if the play was being changed, because coach Bryant felt that real audibles would provide too much chance for error on a college team—that one of the 11 guys on the field would miss the play or goof up.

PLAYBOY: Did you have any doubts when you joined the Jets that you'd become a good pro quarterback?

NAMATH: I guess so. At first, it didn't seem too hard, especially at the beginning of my rookie season: I wasn't starting and I wasn't playing. But when I finally did start playing—damn, it was really a tough job to figure out.

PLAYBOY: In what way?

NAMATH: In *every* way. I remember playing against Kansas City and having one strong impression—of bodies movin' all *over* the place. But the only way a quarterback learns is by playing. He can look at all the films he wants to off the field, and he can practice all day long out there on the field, but the only time he's going to be tested is when he gets into that live battle. When those guys are coming at you, they're going to do a *job* on you—if they get to you. And the other guys are playing a defense you're not familiar with. You can watch them all you want on film, but you still have to be out there to get the experience that counts.

PLAYBOY: What was the first time you proved to yourself that you could really make it in the pro ranks?

NAMATH: In my rookie year, we were playing against the Boston Patriots in a close game. Boston was using a stunt defense; a lot of the time, their linebackers and some of their linemen would shift around, making it necessary to change most of the plays at the line of scrimmage. They were only three points behind the Jets, with eight minutes and 40 seconds left; but we started an offensive drive and wound up holding the ball for that long—and scoring a touchdown to clinch the game. Well, when we controlled the ball against the Patriots that long, I was very pleased; the play calling, which had to do with figuring out their defenses and reacting to them on the spot, was good. After that game, I felt I was a real pro quarterback.

PLAYBOY: How long does it usually take a college star to become a good pro quarterback?

NAMATH: Well, I thought I was good in my first year, but I wasn't what you could call topflight, because I was only a damn rookie; I just didn't have the experience. Daryle Lamonica of the Oakland Raiders said a while back that it takes a good college quarterback five years to become good in the pros, but that's a bunch of shit. I was a good quarterback in my third year.

PLAYBOY: Who do you think is the best quarterback currently playing?

NAMATH: Naturally, I think I am. I could say someone else, to be polite, but no one else is better than me. You have to take into consideration, though, that I also feel every player should think he's the best man at his position.

PLAYBOY: Why do you think you're professional football's number-one quarterback?

NAMATH: A lot of things go into being a quarterback. The most important: You have to be able to throw. I think I can throw better than anybody else. After a couple of other abilities—like calling the right plays and reading defenses—the next most important asset of a quarterback is his attitude, and I think I have the right attitude and the right temperament.

PLAYBOY: What do you mean?

NAMATH: Knowing that you're going to win and getting it across to the rest of the players. When I say something about winning, I think the team is going to believe me—they do now, anyway. And that attitude spreads. When a guy like Winston Hill tells me he can block his man, I know he can block him; he won't tell me he can do something he can't. When a guy like Don Maynard tells me he can get open on a pass play, he can. And does. Pretty soon, nobody says they can do something just because of anxiety. That's a big part of a winning attitude.

PLAYBOY: Are there any outstanding football players who don't have this attitude?

NAMATH: If there are, I don't know them. Hell, I think how much you want to win has practically as much to do with playing as ability does. As long as you're in good physical condition, attitude is just about the biggest part of your game. Sometimes, people wonder why an underdog occasionally beats a heavily favored team, the way Denver and Buffalo beat us last year. Well, they had more desire to win than we did. The Jets went into those games half-assed and lackadaisical, and Denver and Buffalo didn't. They jumped on us with both feet; and in pro football, when you give *any* club a head start on you, they're hard to catch up to. So when your team is a 20-point favorite, you've got to watch out for a letdown.

PLAYBOY: Do you ever find yourself having to manufacture that all-out will to win in such a situation?

NAMATH: Yes, because sometimes, when you play a really weak team, you can't help playing a sloppy game. But in that situation, you tend to wake up as soon as you look at the scoreboard and see it's not the way it should be. The Buffalo and Denver games I mentioned were about the only two games I remember not being mentally ready for, and by that I mean not having the top anxiety and top enthusiasm about playing the game.

PLAYBOY: Is there an aspect to quarterbacking that you find you have to work on especially hard?

NAMATH: No, not anymore. I work on everything fairly hard, but there's not one phase of the game I think I have to stress over other things. I practice throwing every day, reading defenses, ball handling and footwork. I have no problem dropping back various ways, backpedaling, turning and going back.

PLAYBOY: Even though you've already quarterbacked a championship team, do you think you've yet to hit your peak as a pro?

NAMATH: I really don't know, because I'm a guy who believes young people are better. I'm 26 now; by the time I'm 27, I don't think I'll have the quickness that I have now. I don't know if, by the end of this season, I'll be as good as I was last year, because I don't know how my legs are going to hold up. The one phase of quarterbacking that I know I've improved on, though, is play calling. In fact, last year I began approaching the game differently.

PLAYBOY: In what way?

NAMATH: I suppose I began to get more conservative. In our loss to Buffalo last year, I did a very dumb thing: There was no reason for the Jets to be going out there and trying to score like crazy. Instead of passing as much as I did, we could have gone out there and run three plays and punted to Buffalo and let *them* make the mistakes, because they didn't have a quarterback; the starter and the backup passer had both been injured. They had no offense at all, so we should have let them commit the errors. But I kept getting us in trouble by having passes intercepted, and we kept getting out, and we finally ended up blowing the game, 37 to 35. After that, I got conservative to a certain extent: I knew our defense could hold the other team and that we could wait for their mistakes. You've got to do whatever it takes to win and after those two bad games, we did.

PLAYBOY: You went from 28 intercepted passes in 1967 to 17 in 1968. How did you manage that?

NAMATH: There are always reasons for interceptions. Out of the 17 last year, 10 came in two games. Some of them were just downright good defensive plays, some of them were downright stupid plays on my part and some of them were breaks of the game—a ball bounces up off a guy's hands and into an opponent's. Again, I think knowing that our defense was so tough stopped me from worrying about scoring early and often in a game. So if my first receiver was covered and if my second also hadn't gotten free, instead of going to the third or fourth and taking a big chance on having the pass intercepted, I'd just throw it away or keep it. A couple of years ago, I read that Johnny Unitas once said, "When you know what you're doing, you don't get intercepted." That year, he just about led the league in interceptions. I remember thinking that was a pretty stupid thing for him to say.

PLAYBOY: There's been a great deal written about your "quick release"— your ability to get rid of a pass quickly. Do you think it's a vital asset?

NAMATH: No question about it. The quicker you can get rid of the ball, the fewer times you're going to get caught with it—and the faster the ball gets to the receiver. I'd say I save at least two tenths of a second, and probably even more than that, on a pass play. That's worth a lot, when you consider that on a pass play, the quarterback would like to have four seconds from the time the ball is snapped until he throws it. You'd *like* to have four seconds, but you don't always get it. Pro football is a lot more complicated than most people think: In those few seconds, you have to pick from among four or five receivers, locating them and judging instantly how well they're covered.

PLAYBOY: At the same time, 280-pound defensive linemen are trying to get to you before you pass the ball. When your receivers aren't free for a pass and opponents are about to tackle you, how do you brace yourself?

NAMATH: I don't. You know you're going to get hit, but you can't do anything differently, because then you'll just screw up. By that I mean that you'll rush a pass, and that's usually when you get intercepted. So you have to ignore the guys coming in and if you get hit, well, you get back up again.

PLAYBOY: When was the hardest you ever got hit on a football field?

NAMATH: Well, I hate to give the bastards credit for anything, but when I was in college, Georgia Tech really creamed me in a game. I didn't know one of their guys was coming at me and he just about crunched every bone in my body; I mean, he really knocked the hell out of me. I was almost completely out.

PLAYBOY: How hard did Ben Davidson of the Oakland Raiders hit you when he broke your cheekbone?

NAMATH: Hard enough to break it but not hard enough to put me out of the game. The thing about getting hit—even like that—is that it doesn't bother you while you're still on the field. While you're moving around, the adrenaline is pumping. But it really gets bad after you cool off; that's when you feel the aches and pains and discover all the bruises. I don't think the game is too physically demanding, but it's really something else to see such big guys in such great shape coming at you. A lot of pro linemen are 6'6" and 6'7", run just as fast as the little guys, are very, very agile, weigh close to 300 pounds—and can really slam you.

PLAYBOY: As a key to the Jet offense, do you ever feel that opposing linemen would like to sideline you with an injury rather than simply tackle you before you get rid of the ball?

NAMATH: Of course. We want to get their quarterbacks out of action, too. You get the quarterback out and you got a good shot at winning the game.

PLAYBOY: How cleanly is this done?

NAMATH: Well, I know *our* guys don't do anything dirty—but they do try to kill the other quarterback. When there's an interception, for instance, our guys are still supposed to find the passer and hit him hard.

PLAYBOY: What do you do when *you* throw an interception?

NAMATH: Backtrack; I look around pretty good. But everybody knows the other guy is making a living and that if you play dirty, you get paid back—and so will your quarterback. Because the other team can hit just as hard and play it any way you want to play it. So if a guy starts taking cheap shots at someone, the other team is going to look him up in a hurry. That doesn't happen very often; it's about the ugliest part of the sport.

PLAYBOY: What do you consider—for you—the best part of the game?

NAMATH: Winning; that's the best thing about it. After that, it's feeling I'm the best of anybody at my job, and that's the most satisfying thought I have about football. And then putting it all together and being on the best team and becoming world champions. That's what you have to strive for: to be the best.

PLAYBOY: To the amazement of most football experts around the nation, the Jets proved they were just that by beating the Baltimore Colts in the 1969 Super Bowl. When did you first think your team could win the championship?

NAMATH: Well, certainly not in training camp; it's a long season, and the thing we were really trying to do was to win our division; and then, if we won the AFL championship, great, we'd be in the Super Bowl. But it was a long road to get there. I think it started happening right after we beat San Diego, in the 11th game of the season. The week before, we had lost to Oakland when they scored two touchdowns in the last nine seconds; but we recovered from that and beat San Diego pretty good. That's when I knew we had a good football team; I guess that's when we started thinking about going to the Super Bowl.

PLAYBOY: In the two Super Bowls prior to this year's, the Green Bay Packers twice soundly defeated AFL championship teams. Most people felt those victories were indicative of NFL supremacy. Did you?

NAMATH: No, I thought that was a stupid way to think. Hell, the Packers beat just about everybody they played that bad. I know they had a couple of tough games with the Dallas Cowboys, but they always beat them. All I thought about the two Packer Super Bowl victories was that Green Bay was just better than any other team in pro football—something they had shown all year long. But that didn't say anything to me about the strength of the two leagues. The thing everybody kept conveniently forgetting was that the AFL has been drafting its players from the same source as the NFL and getting top talent for a lot of years. In preseason games last year, AFL teams kicked the hell out of NFL teams and nobody wanted to believe it. It was there in front of them all the time. It kind of bothered me that not only were the teams in the AFL downgraded but so were the players.

PLAYBOY: Whom do you have in mind?

NAMATH: I have AFL quarterbacks in mind. Look, before the Super Bowl, a lot of people thought I was bum-rapping Earl Morrall of the Baltimore Colts when I said there were four guys in the AFL who were better than he is. Well, I wasn't putting him down. But when you talk about quarterbacks, you've got to put John Hadl of San Diego, Bob Griese of Miami, Daryle Lamonica and myself right up there. Sure, you can't take anything away from NFL quarterbacks like Sonny Jurgensen and Roman Gabriel and Bart Starr and Johnny Unitas. But the point is that no one wanted to recognize that the AFL has more than its share of topflight quarterbacks. A lot of people still don't want to, but because we won the Super Bowl last season, they *have* to.

PLAYBOY: In Miami, just a few days before the Super Bowl, you bragged, "The Jets will win Sunday. I guarantee it." Certainly, the Colts had to be among the strongest teams you faced all year; were you really that confident, or was that remark intended to boost your teammates' morale?

NAMATH: Well, it may have had that effect on some people, but a whole lot of Jets were almost as sure as I was that we were going to beat the Colts. You know, there were a lot of writers coming around and advising me not to say anything, because the Colts were going to read what I'd said and really get up for the game. Well, I knew—and I'm sure they did, too—that if they needed something like that to get them fired up for a ball game, then they were in big trouble. In a championship game, you don't need to build up incentive to want to win: The championship is enough. We had a lot of faith in ourselves, and if I seemed to have more faith than anybody else on the team, it was because of what I saw in the films of Colt games—and what I knew I could do to them if I was on my game.

PLAYBOY: What was it you saw?

NAMATH: That they used a lot of various safety blitzes. I was absolutely confident that if they tried that stuff against us—and they had to, because it was their game—we could move the ball on them, score on them. First of all, we have excellent blocking in the backfield along with the line; our line is one of the very best in pro football. George Sauer and Don Maynard and Pete Lammons and I, along with the backs, read defenses very well; so I felt that as soon as any of our guys detected a weakness, we would move with it. It was obvious to us early in the game that the Colts had to use double coverage on Don Maynard to protect against the long pass. Don had had a pulled muscle, and if I'd known it was still sore, I don't think I would have overthrown him when he shook free and was all alone for a touchdown. This left single coverage on George Sauer, and he's too good to be guarded by one man; George probably runs the best pass patterns in football today. Anyway, we knew before the game that we would figure out their weaknesses. We knew that guys like Winston Hill and Bob Talamini—I was sorry to see him retire this year—could be depended on to block their men. I was sure Matt Snell was going to have a fine game, and it didn't come as a surprise to me when he had a *great* game. So we thought we could pass on them, we thought we could run on them, but we didn't know what we'd be able to do best until the game actually started. The one thing we knew, though, was that we could get some points up on the board, enough points to win. Actually, I think we could have gotten more points. I threw only 28 passes against the Colts all day; hell, I've thrown more than that in a quarter. But I wasn't about to take any chances. We played to win—and we did. And by winning, we showed that the AFL doesn't have to take a back seat to the NFL and that we were and are the best team in pro football.

PLAYBOY: Do you think the Jets can do it again?

NAMATH: If everybody stays healthy, I *know* we can do it again. When you've won a championship, you have a lot of confidence going for you. You know you did it, did it as a heavy underdog and under pressure that was supposedly only on us, not on the Colts. This year, I think we should make fewer mistakes and so be that much better. The one thing that could stop us is this new damn AFL two-game playoff for the championship. If we finish first or second in our division, which we'll do, we'll still have to play two tough games back to back before we qualify for the Super Bowl. At the end of a season, a lot of guys are worn down physically; I know it's true for the other teams as well, but it still means that we won't be at the top of our game.

PLAYBOY: There are many fans and sportswriters who think that the Jets' Super Bowl victory was a fluke. How do you feel about it?

NAMATH: People can tell us we had a lucky year, but athletes know better. They can say our victory was a fluke, but the fact is that we did it. They can talk about Baltimore coming back and getting revenge by beating us in 1970. Well, they might come back and they might beat us, but last season's Super Bowl is going to be something they'll remember for the rest of their lives; they know they can't take that away from us. January 12, 1969, belonged to the Jets and Baltimore can't ever get even for it. They lost it; they got beat.

PLAYBOY: How many more seasons do you think you'll be able to play?

NAMATH: I honestly don't know. Sometimes, I think not more than another year, which is why I'm investing my money in different things and looking out for what's ahead.

PLAYBOY: Speaking of money, how much do you earn a year, all told?

NAMATH: Again, I honestly don't know. Conservatively, about $200,000 in ordinary income—salary and different phases of contracts. That's just a base; I also have a few percentage things going. The nice thing about having this kind of bread is that when I'm through with football—something I don't usually think about—I can take my time getting into something new.

PLAYBOY: Last summer, you appeared in *Norwood*, a film starring Glen Campbell. Are you planning to do what former Cleveland fullback Jim Brown has done—pursue an acting career after retirement?

NAMATH: I don't have any strong ambitions about it at this stage, because I don't know enough about acting yet. I don't know whether or not I really like it and what kind of talent I have. But until I make up my mind either way, I'm going to ride with it. Now, I know damned well that right now I'm no actor; I never even acted in grade school or high school. But a lot of people have been talking to me about more films, and there's a gas of a comedy that I've agreed to play the lead in, called *The Sidelong Glances of a Pigeon Kicker.*

PLAYBOY: What do you think of your acting in *Norwood?*

NAMATH: I saw rushes last summer, when I was in California for the film. I liked the way I photographed, but I felt like a fool watching myself talk. It didn't seem very natural to me. It's hard to know if I was good or lousy in the movie, because I'm not sure that the movie people I've talked to aren't saying nice things just to make me feel good. About the straightest thing I can go on is that they want me to do some more; if they're willing to bank money on me, it indicates that they're happy.

PLAYBOY: Is there any aspect of acting that you dislike?

NAMATH: Yes, the schedule: I don't like the idea of getting up at five or six in the morning and going out for a long day's work—which, in movies, means sitting around most of the time.

PLAYBOY: Did that timetable cut into your night-owl rounds during the filming of *Norwood?*

NAMATH: Absolutely not. I wouldn't let it. I'd hate to think about a future in which my work would cancel out seeing women.

PLAYBOY: Would you also hate to think about a future that might include marriage?

NAMATH: Not at all. I've been going out with a girl named Suzie Storm for a few years and I feel that someday I'm going to marry her. But I'm not ready to get married yet; I don't think I could be faithful. It's very idealistic and seldom true, but when you're married, I think you're supposed to be married and that's it—no clowning around. Now, I'm not saying that when I get married I'm going to be that way; but I'm going to try my best not to clown around, because, believe it or not, I really don't want to. If you're going to play those games, then you've got to expect your wife to do the same, and I don't think any man wants to put up with that. *I* sure don't. I'm not saying that when I get married, I won't ever see another girl for sexual reasons, but I'd try not to do that. And right now, I can't honestly say that I'm ready to be true to one girl. Suzie is very understanding about it. And I think that as far as the two of us are concerned, time is on her side.

PLAYBOY: And what do you see for yourself in time?

NAMATH: I've got a good thing going. I don't think I'll ever have to worry about being able to support a family. It's really nice having money, but only so that you don't have to think about it. I don't have any extravagant tastes; I don't have any expensive hobbies. I spend my dough on girls, clothes and good times, and I don't need more to enjoy myself. If I get hurt playing football tomorrow and I can't come back, it's good to feel that I won't have to change the way I live. I can look around until I find something to do with my life that turns me on. The bread and all the fame hasn't loused me up, and I don't think it ever will. I've always been my own man, always been *free*. I live my life according to one rule: As long as you don't hurt anybody and you don't hurt yourself, do what you want to do. That's just what I'm going to do.

 August 1996

SHAQUILLE O'NEAL

A candid conversation with the future of basketball about his lust for action, the miracles of wealth, his fears about the Olympics and why he still can't sink a free throw

Shaquille O'Neal was ascending into heaven. That's how it seemed to the fans reaching for him as he climbed the steps to the VIP lounge at the Embassy, an Orlando nightclub. It was supposed to be a small, private party, but a radio station had passed the word and half the town showed up. The line stretched nearly half a mile as thousands of people waited three hours for a glimpse. When he arrived, dressed like a titanic leprechaun in a bright green suit and matching derby, the crowd surged forward and tore off the club's glass doors.

The occasion: O'Neal's 24th birthday.

The phenomenon: Shaqmania, which he can't escape even on "quiet" nights on the town. Never one to shun the spotlight, O'Neal sports a tattoo of the Superman logo. He says the S is for Shaq. Another tattoo reads "The World Is Mine," and this summer, at least, it's no idle boast: The recent NBA season was O'Neal's most impressive in four All-Star years as the Orlando Magic's center of attention. With $17 million a year in endorsements and with a megamillion-dollar contract pending, he trails only Michael Jordan and Mike Tyson on the jock-wealth list. This month O'Neal will share the spotlight at the Olympics in Atlanta, where he is the pivot of Dream Team III. His fame is such that the Magic pays a security expert to deal with Shaqmania on road trips. O'Neal has been mobbed in Athens, Tokyo, Hong Kong and London. The hoopster–rap star (*Shaq Diesel* went platinum and his second CD, *Shaq-Fu*, went gold)–pitchman (Pepsi, Reebok, Taco Bell) is also an actor (*Blue Chips* with Nick Nolte) who has a new movie. He stars in *Kazaam* as a joking, rapping genie. In short, he's typecast. The film exemplifies O'Neal's style. It is a blend of seeming opposites, a joint effort by Disney and the rap conglomerate Interscope. But just as O'Neal makes his backboard-shattering dunks seem fun rather than fierce, he thinks he can make happy rap without losing the hip in hip-hop. It wouldn't be the first unlikely mix for the man who has been called "a cross between Bambi and the Terminator," just the latest installment in a goofy, all-American melodrama—his life. In the 1991-1992 season, the year before O'Neal hit the NBA, Otis Thorpe led the league with 162 dunks. Rookie Shaq nearly doubled the record. In 1993-1994 he set a new mark with an absurd 387 dunks. Hall of Famer Bill Walton called him "a combination of Wilt Chamberlain and Magic Johnson," an irresistible force with unstoppable charm. O'Neal seemed to have leaped out of nowhere direct to center stage. In fact, he had spent a troubled youth half a world away before making his mark. Shaquille Rashuan O'Neal, whose first and middle names are Islamic for "little warrior," was born in Newark, New Jersey on March 6, 1972. His father soon disappeared. His stepdad was an Army sergeant who moved the family to a U.S. Army base in West Germany when O'Neal was a sixth grader. That's where college coach Dale Brown taught a clinic, spotted young Shaq and asked, "How tall are you, soldier?" "I'm not a soldier, sir. I'm only 13."

After his stepdad was transferred to Texas, O'Neal led San Antonio's Cole High to the state title. He signed on with coach Brown at Louisiana State University and averaged 13.9 points per game as a freshman. By his junior year he was averaging 24.1 points, but opposing teams had adopted a strategy still seen in the pros: In the hack-a-Shaq defense, two or three or four defenders swarm O'Neal whenever he touches the ball. He skipped his senior year at LSU to join the NBA, where such tactics are technically illegal—which simply means more sophisticated. The number one pick in the 1992 pro draft was supposed to be the salvation of the pitiful Orlando Magic. Pepsi and Reebok committed $30 million in endorsement fees before O'Neal played his first NBA minute.

As a Magic rookie he tore down the rim on a ferocious dunk. And not just the rim. In a long, loud, nearly slow-motion process, the rim crumpled, followed by the backboard and finally by the steel-reinforced goal support. The NBA hired engineers to fortify goals around the league. More important, the woeful Magic improved from

21-61 to 41-41. That off-season the Rookie of the Year had a small part in the hoops film *Blue Chips*, starring Nick Nolte. O'Neal didn't make the first five in the credits, but his fame was jumping fast. Posters for the film read "Nolte-Shaq."

In 1993-1994, his second pro year, O'Neal averaged 29.3 points, second in the league to San Antonio's David Robinson. Orlando made the playoffs for the first time. A year later O'Neal again averaged 29.3, this time winning the scoring title. His 11.4 rebounds per game were the league's third best. He led Orlando to the NBA finals, where the Magic lost to Hakeem Olajuwon and the Houston Rockets. After that series Olajuwon called Shaq "the future of this league." As his basketball skills improve, O'Neal's fame grows. He's a natural force who never appears to work hard, yet last summer he sweated with fitness trainer Billy Blanks and got stronger than ever. His seemingly listless, earthbound playing style can shift instantly into mad spells of dunking, driving, shot-blocking genius. He is the sports world's top colossus, but like Wilt Chamberlain before him he can't master his game's simplest task: The guy can't hit a free throw. We sent Contributing Editor Kevin Cook to meet him at his home outside Orlando, just down the road from Disney World. Cook reports: "Casa Shaq is a 22,000-square-foot mansion jammed with fan mail, pinball machines, computer games and life-size figures of movie monsters. It's as if Tom Hanks' character in *Big* became an NBA All-Star. O'Neal's music studio and putting green are under construction. When Shaq is there, everything seems in perspective. After all, this is a man who wears a 22EEE shoe and a size 52 shirt (or XXXXL). His four dogs' names are all pop references: Thor, Shazam, Prince and Die-Hard. Since O'Neal is a starstruck superstar, one wall of his TV room is covered with the framed jerseys of dozens of other famous jocks, his heroes. Two of these mementos bear the number 32, which is also Shaq's number. One is Magic Johnson's Laker jersey, inscribed, 'To the most versatile big man ever. Keep rappin'.' Another 32 is a USC jersey, signed 'Peace,' from O.J. Simpson. Our most exciting moment took place about 3200 miles west of the Shaq Shack. One day in Long Beach, California, where he was working on a Taco Bell commercial, I waited three hours for the interview session he'd promised. But filming ran late, and Quincy Jones, Shaq's dinner date, was waiting for him in Beverly Hills, 45 minutes north. There was only one way we could talk: I would drive Shaq to

Beverly Hills. Unfortunately I had a midsize rental car. Fortunately Shaquille was game: He squashed his seven-foot frame into the car, his knees almost touching his forehead, and held my tape recorder to his lips so the car's noise wouldn't cover our talk. Then his agent Leonard Armato, whom we were to follow to Beverly Hills, took off like a comet in his black Mercedes-Benz, forcing me to hop curbs and run red lights to keep up. There was no time for seat belts. The car chase continued as Armato hit the freeway and zipped between speeding cars. A few times we were inches from a crack-up. I saw the next day's headline: Shaq Bruises Thumb—Unknown Man Dies. But we squeaked through, and Shaquille, who can be monosyllabic on an ordinary day but responds well to danger, talked openly about the unlikely transformation of a once clumsy boy into an athletic conglomerate."

PLAYBOY: We almost crashed on the freeway, but you never blinked.

O'NEAL: Nothing scares me. I'm an action guy. Scuba diving, bungee jumping, motorcycles—I'm there. I bungeed off a crane in Orlando and loved it. I'm getting a new motorcycle, too, a specially made, really big Harley.

PLAYBOY: Doesn't your contract forbid dangerous hobbies?

O'NEAL: Yes. I'm not allowed to skydive, ride motorcycles, stuff like that. But I like going fast. I wiped out on a moped in Hawaii, rubbed a bunch of skin off my leg. My Harley will be a lot faster than any moped, but I won't get hurt. And I am going to skydive.

PLAYBOY: So you've violated your $41 million contract with the Magic? What if you get hurt and they quit paying you?

O'NEAL: They could. I would still go skydiving.

PLAYBOY: What other stunts have you tried?

O'NEAL: Parasailing in Mexico. A boat pulls you almost 100 miles an hour and you go hundreds of feet up in the air. Then you come down and hit hard. You could break your leg. But I always approach things thinking, What's the worst thing that could happen here? With parasailing the worst thing is landing wrong, so I concentrate on turning at the last second, hitting the water with the side of my leg. One thing about me, whether I'm sailing or cycling or jumping my Sea-Doo like a crazy man: I know how to land.

PLAYBOY: And you'll bet $41 million on it.

O'NEAL: I'm not a worrier.

PLAYBOY: Now you've landed a starring role in the Olympics. Can you cover the 50-point spread against Lithuania?

O'NEAL: Dream Teams I and II set such high standards, people almost expect us to slip up. That's why I'm telling Lenny Wilkens I don't want to start. I want to be the sixth man. That way at least you get big applause when you go in.

PLAYBOY: Will you get emotional at the medals ceremony?

O'NEAL: Nah. The Olympics is a job. It's my job to kick some butt and bring back the gold. Maybe have some fun with the guys.

PLAYBOY: You outplayed Michael Jordan in this year's All-Star game, but he got the MVP award. Were you pissed?

O'NEAL: A little. With the game in San Antonio I figured David [Robinson] would play unbelievably and be the MVP. But he got off to a slow start and nobody took over the game, so I thought, Let me. I hit three fadeaways, got a big dunk late, thought I was a shoo-in. Then politics took over. But it's cool, it's over now. Me and Jordan, man, we're friends. He came to me after the game with the trophy under his arm. He said, "Here, take it. You deserved it." But I said no. I don't want to win MVP like that. I want the system to give it to me.

PLAYBOY: Why would the writers voting on the award want to slight you?

O'NEAL: Maybe it's my size. People think big guys have it easy, that we don't even have to try. But I just congratulated Jordan that day. The guy still amazes me. A few guys can surprise you—Magic, Charles—but Jordan, with his quickness, does stuff you can't practice, things you can't even dream of. My rookie year, the first time we played Chicago, the first play I ever faced him, he blocked my shot. I think he was actually flying.

PLAYBOY: You had another embarrassing moment last season when your pants came off. Nobody caught it on film and you wouldn't tell reporters who pantsed you.

O'NEAL: It was Jordan. I was going up, but he grabbed my shorts. I had to go change in a huddle. That stuff happens a lot. I get held, pushed. Guys like to lean on my arm, pin it to my side so I can't rebound. If you watch close you'll see it almost every play. I just don't usually lose my pants.

PLAYBOY: One NBA coach says you get hacked and smacked—"tormented"—more than any player in history.

O'NEAL: I won't take it forever. I'm stronger than ever now, and it's on my clock to stop the abuse. I won't give any warning, either. One night I'll just go crazy and start breaking up people.

PLAYBOY: This year?

O'NEAL: [Grins] If I tell you it won't be a surprise, will it?

PLAYBOY: We'll come back to hoops in a minute. Tell us about your new job in movies.

O'NEAL: *Kazaam.* I play a hip-hop rapping genie with an attitude. He's half human, half magic, so you never know what he'll do. I wanted to make a children's movie because my target audience is four to 14, and I'm still a child myself. I always say that deep down inside I'm 10 years younger than my actual age. So I really just turned 14.

PLAYBOY: Shaq hits puberty—could that cause earthquakes?

O'NEAL: I can feel it coming on.

PLAYBOY: Will you fret about reviews, or will you be as worry-free as an actor too?

O'NEAL: It's my first starring role, so I told everybody on the set, "If it's not right, tell me." I don't want Siskel and Ebert blasting me.

PLAYBOY: How did they like you as a college dunkster in *Blue Chips*?

O'NEAL: Thumbs up.

PLAYBOY: How many times have you seen *Blue Chips*?

O'NEAL: A million. I sat in my house and watched it over and over till I wore the tape out. Because it was cool, but also to study the movie and what I did in it. It's a basketball role, so I didn't have to act much, but I thought, The kid's OK.

PLAYBOY: What's your acting method? Do you try to feel your character's emotions?

O'NEAL: Nick Nolte, who played my coach in the movie, amazed me with how he could turn his emotions on and off. In one second he'd go from tears onscreen to joking around when the camera was off. Now I try to do that. I think about simple feelings: mad, sad, happy. To get pissed off I'll think about losing all my money. To be happy I'll think, I just won $800 million! To be sad I'll think my girlfriend dumped me.

PLAYBOY: Has that happened?

O'NEAL: Of course not.

PLAYBOY: Do you talk acting with your neighbor Wesley Snipes?

O'NEAL: I'm not a versatile actor like Wesley or Denzel Washington. Wesley could play a gangster, a cop, a lover, anything. I'll probably always be a basketball player or a silly comedian.

PLAYBOY: You sound wistful.

O'NEAL: I get a lot of scripts. There was a good one I turned down—they wanted to make me a gangster, a killer. But I'm a role model. Too many of my fans are little kids. Action films, though, they're different. My all-time favorite movies are *New Jack City* and the *Godfather* films. Seen 'em a hundred times. I want to make *Terminator 3*. I've told Arnold we'd be great beating each other up, tearing up the city.

PLAYBOY: Schwarzenegger looks huge to most of us. Does he seem puny to you?

O'NEAL: Just normal. But his muscles are big.

PLAYBOY: Do you ad-lib or stick to the script?

O'NEAL: It depends on the director. On *Blue Chips* Billy Friedkin was lenient. He said, "Have fun with it." I didn't do anything great. One line was, "Somebody owes me a hundred dollars," and I said, "Somebody owes my ass a hundred dollars."

PLAYBOY: You put your ass on the line.

O'NEAL: It added a little. My best ad-libs are in commercials, though. In my first one for Reebok, where I need a password to go in with the legends—Wilt, Walton, Kareem, Bill Russell—the line was no good: "Speak softly and carry a big stick." I made it, "Don't fake the funk on a nasty dunk." Now I tell all the companies I deal with to make the ads funny. I'm a comedian. For the Pepsi commercial where I want a drink but the little boy won't give me one, I remembered a Coke ad from when I was little, the one where Mean Joe Greene gave a kid his jersey. We kind of played off that but made it funny—the kid tells me, "Don't even think about it."

PLAYBOY: Unlike most jocks, you have equity in the companies you flack. That gives you more creative control. What ad ideas have you vetoed?

O'NEAL: Shaqzilla. I turned down a King Kong ad, too. I said no, I'm more versatile than King Kong. Ad agencies get paid a lot to create commercials, but I turn most of them down. The ad guys get mad, but they don't like to challenge me. They go to the Reebok or Pepsi people and complain.

PLAYBOY: Didn't you veto an NBA ad?

O'NEAL: When I was a rookie they wanted me to tell kids to stay in school. How could I do that when I left LSU a year early? So we compromised. They changed the line to, "Stay in high school."

PLAYBOY: What is it that makes a good commercial?

O'NEAL: Don't talk much. Make a funny face, then say a good one-liner. I'm always trying to think of great ones, like "Make my day." My Pepsi ad had a pretty good one-liner. I run through all the old-time TV shows and then say, "Who says there's nothing good on TV?"

PLAYBOY: You develop spin moves in workouts with Hakeem Olajuwon. Do you practice funny faces too?

O'NEAL: Sure. I work at everything. As a kid I thought I would be on TV someday, so I mocked commercials and watched myself in a mirror. I still try different faces and deliveries in the mirror.

PLAYBOY: Anything you won't endorse?

O'NEAL: I was offered a couple hot dog commercials, but then Jordan came out with his hot dog ad, so I said no. Didn't want to be a follower. I turned down the Shaqdanna, a head rag. One company wanted to bottle my sweat and sell it as cologne. They were going to call it EOS, Essence of Shaq. I'm no marketing genius, but I don't think millions of people want that.

PLAYBOY: Your candy bar, Mr. Big, keeps selling despite its close resemblance to a turd.

O'NEAL: Mr. Big is a cross between my favorite candy bars, Whatchamacallit and Milky Way. I must have taste-tested hundreds of them.

PLAYBOY: How many did you reject?

O'NEAL: None.

PLAYBOY: What do you think of the NBA's marketing?

O'NEAL: It works. If I were a kid I'd have the top guys up on my wall—Jordan, me, Charles. Telecommunications are so powerful now, we're known all over the world. I did a clinic in Greece one summer; there were supposed to be about 1500 people there but 34,000 showed up. I dunked and the crowd went crazy. I had to run and hide in the locker room. With me, some of it's the comedy. People like funny faces. Some of it's my size and even my name. Shaq is so easy a two-year-old can say it. As far as the NBA goes, I think Jason Kidd might be the next big name.

PLAYBOY: What about an older name? We take it you never had Bill Laimbeer's poster on your wall.

O'NEAL: He was a flopper. That's a guy who sees me coming 800 miles an hour and falls down, trying to get a foul. Guys who can't play, flop. Laimbeer was the worst.

PLAYBOY: He liked shooting free throws. That's not exactly your style—this year you're hitting fewer than half your free throws. Why?

O'NEAL: I don't concentrate. I practice them a lot and always hit them in practice, but in games I keep missing. I have to concentrate harder.

PLAYBOY: Rick Barry, one of the best foul shooters ever, shot them underhanded. He thinks you should too.

O'NEAL: That's a horrible suggestion. I would never shoot underhand.

PLAYBOY: It looks girlish, but aerodynamically it's the best way.

O'NEAL: Never.

PLAYBOY: How about the theory and practice of dunking?

O'NEAL: It's the best way to score. Sometimes I dunk so hard it hurts. Especially if a guy tries to block it. I'll think, Let's see if I can break his fingers on the rim. It can really hurt my hands, but with all the adrenaline I don't feel it till after the game, and by then it's OK. The points are on the scoreboard.

PLAYBOY: This year you hit your first three-pointer.

O'NEAL: That was great. I have an NBA video game at home where you can be Shaq or Scott Skiles, the guard who shoots the threes. I'm always Skiles. This time, real life, time was running out, I threw it up and I knew it was in. Knew it, felt it—it's mine.

PLAYBOY: Come on. It banked in.

O'NEAL: Yeah, but I called glass.

PLAYBOY: Do you have any friends on enemy teams?

O'NEAL: I started a group of us, the Knuckleheads. Kind of the NBA bad guys. Not just Orlando players like me and Dennis Scott, but Litterial Green, Rod Strickland, the unusual guys. We let Rodman in. He gets away with a lot—pushing and grabbing—that I'd get called for. He's cool, though. We'll see each other and say, "Get over here, knucklehead!" But I had to retire from the Knuckleheads because I'm a role model. So they have no leader now. I guess Rodman will have to take over.

PLAYBOY: What did you think when Magic Johnson rejoined the Lakers? Were you concerned about getting AIDS?

O'NEAL: I was. But when Magic came back the league sent a doctor around to all the teams. He told us the ways you can get AIDS. He told us to be careful. But you can't get it from sweat, and if you're bleeding and the other guy has a cut too, the odds are still that you won't get it. There were people with HIV who came with the doctor and told their stories. It's helpful, it makes you think. I mean, who can you trust? AIDS has definitely changed the way of life around the league. Guys are more careful. The thinking is, If you don't know someone, then maybe you shouldn't, you know? I always practice safe sex.

PLAYBOY: Every single time?

O'NEAL: Well, almost.

PLAYBOY: Is sex different for a man who's 7'1", 320 pounds?

O'NEAL: No. Women like big men. We can protect them.

PLAYBOY: Were you always so confident with women?

O'NEAL: Nope. I lost my virginity late. I was 17, in college already. I wasn't too awkward about it, but I wasn't a big sex man. One night I was out with the boys and I met a girl. She was older. She had an apartment in Baton Rouge. That's where it happened and it was OK, but just OK.

PLAYBOY: You've said that you sometimes intimidate women.

O'NEAL: Some are scared of my size. I can see it in their eyes. But they don't have to be. I won't bite.

PLAYBOY: Do you have any advice about women?

O'NEAL: Be nice to them. Don't BS them, because they're smart. Give them what they want.

PLAYBOY: Tell us about the two nude women who knocked on your hotel room door.

O'NEAL: That's a good rumor, but it never happened. Women do ask me to sign their panties, though. And one woman broke into my house when I was sleeping, came into the bedroom and started climbing me. I'm trying to wake up, spinning around, but she's hanging on my neck, saying, "Oh, you're so great!" Finally the police came.

PLAYBOY: Other than being climbed at dawn, what turns you off?

O'NEAL: Fast-talking women. Heavy makeup. And I don't like women approaching me. I like to do the choosing. A woman needs a sense of humor too. One girl I dated was beautiful, but she had no humor at all. I had to get out of there.

PLAYBOY: At your birthday party a woman looked at you and said, "A horny Shaq, that would be a force of nature." Reaction?

O'NEAL: It's reasonable. But I'm not looking around. I've had the same girlfriend for five years.

PLAYBOY: You're very secretive about her—the woman you call "my wife."

O'NEAL: Well, maybe we're secretly married. She was going to college in Texas, but she just graduated. Now she's chilling out with me at home.

PLAYBOY: Are you monogamous?

O'NEAL: I'm faithful. I can look at a roomful of women and it doesn't turn me on. But faithful depends on your situation. Ours is, "You be honest and so will I."

PLAYBOY: Ever break anyone's heart?

O'NEAL: I couldn't bring myself to hurt a girl's feelings. I'd do crazy things instead. Act silly, burp at the table, anything to irritate her so she'd break up with me.

PLAYBOY: You were more direct as an NBA matchmaker. Didn't you tell the Magic to trade for your brilliant teammate Penny Hardaway?

O'NEAL: He'd worked on *Blue Chips*, too. That's when I saw how good we could be together. I went to the front office and told them I had analyzed everything, that I wanted to win and this was how to do it. They listened. Certain guys have always had that kind of influence. Magic, Larry Bird. That was when I went up to that level.

PLAYBOY: Orlando traded the rights to Chris Webber, who has had a troubled career, for Hardaway, who's now an All-Star, and got three draft picks to boot.

O'NEAL: I look like a genius, don't I?

PLAYBOY: But you've made noises about leaving Orlando. You may be a free agent by the time this interview appears. Don't you feel any obligation to the Magic after helping shape the club's roster?

O'NEAL: Not really. I did the right thing at the time. If I go to another club, I'll feel I helped this one get better. And if I go, it won't be to another team that needs rebuilding. It'll be one like Orlando is now, one that's doing things right. Because I want to win. Soon.

PLAYBOY: Everyone suspects you're headed for the Lakers.

O'NEAL: [*Winks*] Los Angeles is a very nice town. I really like the climate. I'd never go where it's cold and snowy.

PLAYBOY: Bad news for Minnesota.

O'NEAL: Sorry, Timberwolves.

PLAYBOY: Is it true that your asking price is $140 million?

O'NEAL: I can't say. There's going to be a negotiation and I need to maximize my value. My agent may start out saying I want $600 million. The other side might say, "Oh, maybe $300 million," and we would come down.

PLAYBOY: It's an economic conundrum—finding the market value of a unique commodity.

O'NEAL: Right. See, I collect things—weird, one-of-a-kind things. I have a pair of mink-lined alligator boots and I don't even know what they cost. I didn't ask. Because a guy making mink-lined alligator boots in my size, 22EEE, can charge whatever he wants. He's the only one doing what he does. It's like the other night when I got to the hotel after the game and I was thirsty, but the stores were closed. This is Charlotte in the middle of the night, the middle of nowhere, but they're smart and they know they've got you. So the hotel charges $1.75 for a Pepsi. I mean, please! If there's a store open that night, another Pepsi anywhere, they'd bring the price down. But it's late and you're thirsty, so you pay it. That's economics.

PLAYBOY: If you got a $140 million contract, would you have enough money?

O'NEAL: Not really, because I wouldn't get it up front. It's paid over years and years, so it doesn't get me all that much closer to my goal.

PLAYBOY: Which is?

O'NEAL: To have $100 million clear by the age of 28.

PLAYBOY: That sounds realistic.

O'NEAL: If I can get to $500 million I plan to give each of my relatives half a mil.

PLAYBOY: Do they know that?

O'NEAL: They didn't until now. But I'm fairly generous with them. I'm always giving my sister money, so one time I made her work for it instead. I paid her $300 to make me a peanut butter and jelly sandwich.

PLAYBOY: What's a lot of money to you?

O'NEAL: Five hundred million. I may have to win the lottery.

PLAYBOY: You play the lottery?

O'NEAL: I play scratchers. I get five of my friends, I tell each one to buy 20 tickets, and if we win we'll split it up. So far our biggest win is one dollar. We don't even cash those in. I won't cash one in for less than $100.

PLAYBOY: How do you bet the financial markets?

O'NEAL: I don't gamble. That's how greedy people lose their money, by trying to make $2 million into $100 million. I don't need to make $100 million that fast. I earn it. Mostly with the government. The Treasury has most of my money.

PLAYBOY: So, do you read *The Wall Street Journal?*

O'NEAL: No, I get a monthly statement from my people. What I got, what I spent, what I saved. I'm doing well for a young millionaire in my age group, better than most of them. I don't like to speculate. The stock market is so up and down it scares me. I keep more than half my money in Treasury bills. That way I don't have to worry about interest rates; I just stay with my four, six percent. I don't get much back percentagewise, but it adds up.

PLAYBOY: As in four percent of $10 million is $400,000.

O'NEAL: So I got my money in the government with President Clinton, got my T-bills with Bill.

PLAYBOY: Who advises you on financial matters?

O'NEAL: The business side of my crew is six people. There's Leonard Armato, my agent, who handles the big stuff. Dennis Tracey, my personal assistant, takes care of the day-to-day. Lester Knispel, my tax genius, does most of my money. My mother does the fan mail. My cousins Joe and Ken, two guys I took out of the ghetto to teach them responsibility, they work in my businesses too. My crew is named TWISM. It stands for The World Is Mine. We all have matching tattoos.

PLAYBOY: Even Mom?

O'NEAL: Well, not Mom.

PLAYBOY: Your investments include Reebok, which provided a sheaf of stock options as a signing bonus, plus exclusive deals on candy, souvenirs and other Shaqabilia. What else?

O'NEAL: My Pepsi deal made me part owner of Pepsi South Africa. I have a third of it. Whitney Houston has another third. I'm not sure exactly what it's worth, but it's a lot and it could get huge.

PLAYBOY: Do you keep a lot of cash around? How do you pay, for example the pizza man?

O'NEAL: I pay my own bills, sign the checks myself. I keep my checking account filled to $100,000. That way I can keep up with the bills, maybe buy a car.

PLAYBOY: What's your current net worth?

O'NEAL: Don't know, don't want to look. It seems petty to look, to count your money all the time. Still, I don't think I'm overpaid. Firemen, cops, teachers, those people are underpaid. But I didn't make the salary structure. I just gave it a ride.

PLAYBOY: What's the last thing you didn't buy because of the price?

O'NEAL: A Rolls-Royce. They wanted $275,000, and I don't think you should pay more than about $60,000 for a car. Got six of them now. One has a plate that says Shaq-fu, one says "Dunkon-U" and one, the Van of Def, says "Shaq Attaq." All with good stereo systems, which I will spend money on. The system in my Suburban cost $60,000. The one in the Van of Def cost $150,000—a lot more than the van cost. That's my priorities.

PLAYBOY: Is wealth what you expected it to be?

O'NEAL: Pretty much. It means you don't have to wait to get your toys.

PLAYBOY: As a kid, what did you want to be when you grew up?

O'NEAL: A stuntman. I studied stunts on TV. I actually used to tape plastic bags over my hands, jump off roofs and try to fly. I'd land on stacks of cardboard boxes. I was always thinking about flying. Even on swings—you know how you swing real high and jump off at the top, and for a second you're flying? I could do that all day.

PLAYBOY: Were you always a jock?

O'NEAL: No, I was clumsy. Always flunked gym, right up to high school. Even now I can do only about 10 pushups. I had size but couldn't climb a rope or wrestle. Actually, I wasn't allowed to wrestle after the time I got mad, threw a boy down and broke his wrist.

PLAYBOY: How did he make you mad?

O'NEAL: He was winning.

PLAYBOY: You were clumsy and strong.

O'NEAL: It turned out I had Osgood-Schlatter's disease. That's a bone disorder where your body grows too fast. The joints in your legs can't catch up. My knees hurt all the time. And because I was different the other kids called me names. Bigfoot. Shaqueer. That made me a bully. I had to show how tough I was, knock people out. In sixth grade a boy told on me, so I waited for him after school. He tried to sneak out, but I caught him. Punched him in the face, almost killed him. He swallowed his tongue, went into convulsions. And I didn't try to help him. I just ran.

PLAYBOY: You were scared.

O'NEAL: I don't get scared. But things got worse—it turned out his father was an Army officer.

PLAYBOY: And you were an Army brat, weren't you?

O'NEAL: My dad was a drill sergeant, Sergeant Philip Harrison. I grew up in Newark, then we went to a base in Germany. I hated it there. I was clumsy, I stuttered. I stayed home and watched a lot of TV. Tom and Jerry, Spider-Man, *Good Times*, Bugs Bunny. One guy I liked was the Hulk, the guy who just got mad and went wild.

PLAYBOY: How wild were you?

O'NEAL: Not very. Mostly dumb shit. One time I pulled a fire alarm and got caught. My father had to come get me at the MP station and he gave me a beating right there. It hurt. After the boy swallowed his tongue, I lied to the Sergeant about it. I got beat for that. Sometimes for leaving my shirttail out, because he said you had to be neat. There were whuppings all the time.

PLAYBOY: Yet you kept acting up.

O'NEAL: I found out about a law on the base. If parents couldn't handle their kids they had to send them back to the States. I didn't want to grow up in Germany, so I did crazy stuff. But I never got sent back, and finally I thought I was letting my parents down. They both worked hard. My mom was a secretary. My dad drove a truck when he was off duty, and he even shined shoes. I didn't want them to think I was a disgrace, and I felt like they did think that. And I wanted them to love me. So I thought, How can I make them smile at me? And how can I get the stuff other kids have? I started studying, brought home Bs and Cs and my dad started being nice to me.

PLAYBOY: As you grew up, did you hate your father? Did you rebel?

O'NEAL: Never. Kids rebel because they don't respect their parents. I didn't like getting beat, but I respected him. And there was something else: He was never going to give up. Even when I was rowdy, doing everything wrong, I knew one of us eventually had to give up, and I knew my dad would never, ever give up.

PLAYBOY: Do you have any particularly warm memories?

O'NEAL: Yes. After I got a whupping, I had to go to my room for an hour. When I came out there would be cookies and ice cream on the table. He was telling me it was over. I caused the situation and deserved what I got, but it was OK now. It was over. That's how the Sarge taught me cause and effect.

PLAYBOY: Did you ever have a birds-and-the-bees talk with him?

O'NEAL: Sure did. I was about 11. He used to fall asleep on the couch watching Benny Hill, and I'd sneak out and look at the titties. One night he woke up and caught me. So pretty soon he gets out our *Encyclopaedia Britannica* and shows me the parts of the anatomy. I didn't know the words, only the bad ones. I'd never heard "penis" and "vagina." He came out with them sounding just like a drill sergeant. That's my dad.

PLAYBOY: Of course, he's really your stepdad. You paid him a tribute in a rap song on "Shaq-Fu, Biological Didn't Bother," saying you consider him your true father. How did you find out the truth?

O'NEAL: My mother told me about my biological father when I was five. I said, "Where is he?" She said, "He was no good. So I left, and I met the Sarge." I thought about that for a while, then I said, "That's cool." I've never met my biological father. He tried to meet me. The team was in Chicago when a guy told me he saw my father on TV. I asked Mom why the Sarge was on TV and she said, "No, it was your biological father." He wanted to contact me. I think he wants money. I mean, he could have called from the time I was zero to 20. He lives in New Jersey where all my relatives are; he could have met me if he'd wanted to.

PLAYBOY: Ever feel a genetic debt to him? The Sergeant's a big man, but he's no giant.

O'NEAL: My size is from my mother's side. My great-grandfather Johnny was a farmer in Dublin, Georgia, and he was 6'10". I have a grandma who's 6'4". My mother's brother is 6'7". Tall people.

PLAYBOY: Is your biological father a big man?

O'NEAL: Don't know. I've never seen him.

PLAYBOY: Not even during his media blitz? You see everything else on TV.

O'NEAL: I didn't see it!

PLAYBOY: All right, we'll get back to the game. When did you find basketball?

O'NEAL: Eighth grade. My knees got better. I started watching games on TV, wanting to be Dr. J. While everybody else was getting in trouble I started sleeping with my basketball, dribbling the sidewalks doing my Dr. J. moves. In the winter I'd walk to the gym in the snow. This gym was only 10 minutes away, but when it snowed hard you could barely get there. I'd get up, put on my dad's gloves and his Army boots and walk an hour to get there.

PLAYBOY: And you were an instant star.

O'NEAL: I was lousy. The soldiers I played with were a lot older and they'd be yelling, "You're 6'7" and you're horrible! You'll never play. You might as well join the Army." But I kept playing. Finally I stopped being clumsy when I was 15. That's the first time I got my name in the paper. We won the U.S. Army European tournament, and people said, "He might be pretty good."

PLAYBOY: The base was an American island in Germany. Did you get used to that?

O'NEAL: It was strange. Some of the people didn't want us there. They would sneak on the base and paint all the vehicles blue as a protest. Once I took an Army bus to a base in Czechoslovakia, and they were waiting, throwing eggs and bottles and sticks. It wasn't racial because I saw blacks in the crowd—half-blacks, anyway, from the times black soldiers would sneak off the base and party. I didn't get it—they didn't want us, but we were protecting them.

PLAYBOY: After your stepfather was transferred to San Antonio, you led Cole High School to a 68-1 record over two years. We hate to quibble, but what happened on your bad night?

O'NEAL: I got four fouls in the first two minutes. When I came back in at the end, we were down by one. I shot two free throws with five seconds left in the game. Missed them both. That's the only time I ever cried.

PLAYBOY: During the game the white players from Liberty Hills High School yelled racist taunts at you.

O'NEAL: No. Who says?

PLAYBOY: It's true, isn't it?

O'NEAL: Well, yes, a lot of racist comments. "Go back to Africa." The N word. But losing hurt more.

PLAYBOY: You seem cautious about your choice of words. Why would you avoid talking about racism?

O'NEAL: It doesn't do any good.

PLAYBOY: How about corruption? What offers did you get from college basketball recruiters?

O'NEAL: None. They had heard about the Sarge. They knew I would tell him and they would be in trouble. And anyway, that's like selling a piece of your soul. I worked in the summer for eight dollars an hour and had a Pell grant for about $1400 a year, so I was OK. I went to college all by myself, you know. June 16, 1989, my first day at LSU—that was the day I grew up.

PLAYBOY: There was a tornado in Baton Rouge that day.

O'NEAL: I was riding my bicycle when it hit. At first I thought it was just high winds. Then I saw the tornado coming down, right for me. I wasn't scared. It seemed like fun. I ran and ducked for cover and actually saw the tube of it going by—whoosh. That was the day I took a job at an industrial construction company. There wasn't anything going on, so I went up on the boss' roof—about 25 feet high—and jumped off.

PLAYBOY: You leaped off a two-story building? What did you land on?

O'NEAL: My feet.

PLAYBOY: Twenty-five feet is an exaggeration, isn't it?

O'NEAL: No, it's a house.

PLAYBOY: You could have died.

O'NEAL: You get hurt only if you think you'll get hurt. I landed right. It's easy—you just hit soft, drop and roll.

PLAYBOY: You said that you grew up at LSU—

O'NEAL: I lost my virginity there. I had my last fight. A football player and a basketball player were fighting over a girl, and I went to break it up. The football guy thought he was bad so he hit me. I hit him and then we had 100 football players against us 12, the basketball team, and we did all right. I came out markless. I'm no martial artist yet, but I'm so big and powerful—let's just say I can punch a hole in a wall. With ease.

PLAYBOY: Any other college highlights?

O'NEAL: One day I wake up, I'm rubbing sleep out of my eyes, and there's Dr. J. standing over my bed. He was at LSU to give a talk. He took me to breakfast. He didn't have a lot of advice or anything, and I wasn't asking a bunch of questions. It was just that he was there, he wanted to see me. I'll never forget that.

PLAYBOY: Last winter you met some other heroes. Weren't you snowed in at a hotel with the cast of *Sesame Street Live*?

O'NEAL: Chillin' and singing in the hotel bar with Grover, Big Bird and Oscar. They were stuck there, too. I started singing "Sun-ny day . . ." and they joined in. Pretty soon we had the whole bar singing.

PLAYBOY: Grover was probably looped, but you don't drink, do you?

O'NEAL: Nah. I've seen what it does to people. Slobbering, falling down. I don't want to do that to my body. And you can party longer without it. Jordan's the same way—if you're out till two A.M. but you're not getting drunk, you won't be messed up the next day. On Christmas, New Year's and my birthday I'll have a glass of wine, but that's it. You want to know what my habit is? Miniature golf. We put in a real grass course in front of my house, but the grass died, so we're doing it over in Astroturf. My crew and I play for dinner or movie tickets. I generally win. You can tell Chi Chi Rodriguez or any of them to come to my house for goofy golf. I'm ready.

PLAYBOY: The president is a golfer. Maybe you two could bet Treasury bills.

O'NEAL: I met Bill. He has a good, firm handshake. I met Bush, too. Those guys have it hard because nobody's on their side. It's all criticism.

PLAYBOY: You met another heavyweight while he was in prison.

O'NEAL: I went to see Mike Tyson. Not to be political. I admire him as a fighter. I got into the prison and the guys looked so young. Some of them were younger than me. Tyson was bigger from doing pushups. They wouldn't let him lift weights, so he was doing a whole lot of push-ups. He looked strong. We sat at a table and had a couple minutes of privacy. All he really told me was not to get in a place like that. "Stay out of trouble," he said.

PLAYBOY: You're uneasy talking about race. How has it affected you since the Liberty Hills game?

O'NEAL: It hasn't, not personally. But I saw what happened to Rodney King. I saw the policemen who beat him get acquitted and I couldn't figure it. I thought about a basketball saying: "The tape don't lie."

PLAYBOY: You had an encounter of your own with the LAPD.

O'NEAL: I was just driving in downtown L.A. about midnight. My stereo's loud but not that loud, and nobody's out there anyway. But I got pulled over. I guess they thought I was a hoodlum type—hat on backward, driving a nice Benz. So the cop starts yelling at me. "Where'd you get the car? Is it stolen?" I said, "No, I bought it in Beverly Hills. I paid $80,000 cash." He checked and since it was my car, all he could do was give me a ticket for my loud stereo.

PLAYBOY: LAPD racism again?

O'NEAL: The cop was black. I was surprised because I always expect people to be nice if I'm nice and respectful to them, but at the same time I knew where he was coming from. My uncle's a police officer. I know what he goes through on the job. There's a typical thing that happens: If you pull over 10 guys today and eight of them are bad guys, acting crazy and maybe planning to shoot you, you expect the next guy to be crazy too. If I had that job I'd probably be yelling at everybody.

PLAYBOY: What if it had been a white cop? Would you still be so understanding?

O'NEAL: I hope. I always try to think about all the consequences in anything that happens. You can't always do it. For instance, I slipped the other day. I did a Taco Bell ad—"I'm on fire"—with fire coming off me as I dunk. And I didn't think about burn victims. Now I'm hearing from them. This guy who represents burn victims says, "How could you?" I guess I screwed up. The special effects were so good I forgot everything else. Another time I messed up was when I bought a fur coat. I didn't think about animal rights groups. "Animal killer!" they called me.

PLAYBOY: Did they throw any red paint on you?

O'NEAL: They wouldn't do that. We'd be fighting all day.

PLAYBOY: Speaking of fighting, would you go to war for your country? Would you fight in Bosnia?

O'NEAL: No. And the reason is the same one Muhammad Ali had. Those people never called me Negro. And I also think it's a bad idea to fight on somebody else's turf. I've seen those Vietnam shows on TV, and that stuff is deadly. You're walking in the jungle, they got people in underground tunnels just waiting to reach out and pow!, you're dead. No thanks, it's not for me. Somebody wants to go to war, he can come to my house. I'll pop up from behind a couch and knock him right out.

PLAYBOY: Ali was more outspoken than you—he actually used the word nigger. He also went to jail to avoid military service. Would you?

O'NEAL: I won't go to war.

PLAYBOY: What would the Sarge think of that?

O'NEAL: Not much. The Sarge, oh yeah, he's war, war, war. He'd probably want me to fight, but I'm not a war man. I'm a lover, not a fighter.

PLAYBOY: Has he mellowed as he's gotten older and you've gotten famous?

O'NEAL: He has. But he knows what I know—good things came to me when I started listening to him. We don't talk about it, but he knows.

PLAYBOY: Do you say "I love you" to each other?

O'NEAL: Yeah. That's something we had to develop. He was the first to say it. It wasn't planned, it just happened one day. He came out with it. Now we can both say it.

PLAYBOY: What about kids of your own? Will you spank them?

O'NEAL: I'm definitely going to have kids. And they'll get a good old-fashioned butt-whupping when they deserve it. I might be even harder than the Sarge. But not on a little girl if I have one, because they can do that thing to you. They cry and you just fall over and give them whatever they want.

PLAYBOY: What's your proudest moment?

O'NEAL: When my mother and father call me and tell me they love me.

PLAYBOY: You're both simpler and more complex than you appear. You're a reformed JD turned faithful son turned worldwide celeb, a Disney genie who won't be 25 till next spring. What's your secret?

O'NEAL: Playing possum. I like people to think I can't do something. That's when I'll sit back and chill. And observe. You shouldn't give away all your secrets, not all at once, but I think I could be almost anything. I could play pro baseball, no question. I can hit and I throw real hard. I'd be like Randy Johnson, the Big Unit. Maybe I'd be the Bigger Unit. As far as basketball goes I may sign the next contract, play it out and that could be it for the NBA. I'd still have acting. I'd have the business world. I might want to just chill with my children when I have them. I'm just trying to be intelligent. In a few years it'll be somebody else everybody wants to see and talk with, not me. Even the sun don't stay hot forever, you know? That's why I'm doing all I can while I'm hot, so later I can sit back and watch somebody else do it.

PLAYBOY: You're nobody's shrinking violet.

O'NEAL: You know what it is? I don't like waking up on an off day and having nothing to do. It makes me uncomfortable. That's why I tell my agent, "Keep it coming. I'll tell you when I'm tired."

PLAYBOY: Ever want to be alone?

O'NEAL: Someday I'll take a vacation. But it won't be alone. I'll take my boys with me, because it's not safe if you don't. You've got to be careful. There are people out there who aren't right in the head. There are stalkers. I don't want to get shot by somebody who hates me because he's crazy.

PLAYBOY: When you're roaming around in your mansion late at night, when everyone else is asleep, what are you thinking?

O'NEAL: I thank God for blessing me. For helping me to not give up when people said I should just join the Army. Because I knew. I knew my hard work would pay off. And I'm still working. I raise my game every year. Last summer I worked on a hook shot and a turnaround. I took karate lessons, lifted weights to build my strength, because you need strength when guys are hanging on you, pinning down your arms. You have to be strong. And not scared.

PLAYBOY: You're still trying to fly.

O'NEAL: Remember that three-story building we passed? No way would I jump off it, because there was a concrete sidewalk below. But I thought about it. If there were water down there, a swimming pool, I'd go do it right now. Yeah, easily. No joke. I promise you I'd do it.

PLAYBOY: Why?

O'NEAL: For fun.

PLAYBOY: What does scare you? Death? Referees?

O'NEAL: Nothing.

PLAYBOY: Fess up.

O'NEAL: I told you I don't get scared.

PLAYBOY: Never?

O'NEAL: OK. When I was little I thought our house was haunted. I'd go to bed with the closet door open, and the clothes looked like they were making faces at me. But to beat fear you gotta face fear. I knew that even then. So one night I jumped out of bed, ran over and punched them. Then I slammed the door.

PLAYBOY: You weren't fearless after all.

O'NEAL: I was scared of frogs, too. I would watch this really big frog outside our house, and he scared me. The son of a bitch was just too slimy. Till one day I grabbed him, picked him up, squeezed him, just grossed myself out. Then I threw him back down.

PLAYBOY: A rough day for the frog. Did he survive?

O'NEAL: Yeah, he did. We both did.

PETE ROSE

A candid conversation with baseball's "Charlie Hustle" about managers, fans, hitting, sliding, money, drugs and sex—and his own overall terrificness

Twenty-some years ago, Peter Edward Rose was just another tough kid growing up in the river wards of Cincinnati. He was a tough kid who liked girls and fast and fancy cars and baseball. Today, at the age of 38, not much has changed about Pete Rose. The girls have turned to women and fast cars are getting more expensive. But Rose, who makes his living—and a very good one, at that—playing baseball, is still tough. And he is still very much a kid.

Rose may play with different toys now—a $4000 fur coat, an $8000 gold-and-diamond watch and a $44,000 car that goes 130 miles an hour—but he hasn't really changed. Baseball has. The game has become big business and he has grabbed more than his share of the big bucks that go along with it. At an age when the major decision facing most players is whether to become a car salesman or to open a taproom, Rose was faced with the enviable task of choosing from among a slew of major-league teams offering him millions of dollars for starters. And Rose, who had never played a home baseball game outside Cincinnati, picked the Philadelphia Phillies, who would pay him at least $3,200,000 over four years.

But how, many asked, could Rose be worth the money? Well, he packs ballparks. And while, as a technician, he really can't be ranked up there with the Dave Parkers, the Rod Carews and the Jim Rices, Rose has one very important thing going for him. He has become perhaps the most famous white sports star in the world.

Just last year, a world far beyond baseball watched as Rose took on the seemingly unbreakable record of Yankee great Joe DiMaggio—who hit safely in 56 straight games. In a streak that started in mid-June, Rose scratched, clawed, hustled and bunted his way to one plateau after another. On July 31, 1978, he set a National League mark of 44 straight games. The streak would stop there, but Pete Rose would go on to a White House visit with Jimmy Carter, a highly heralded tour of Japan and commercial deals that would make him millions. And while Cincinnati's Riverfront Stadium was only a line drive away from his boyhood home, Rose had come a long way.

Rose is the son of a bank employee. His father's passion for sports rubbed off easily on him. Too small to make it as a football player, he concentrated on baseball. He played hard and tough, but he never had a great deal of natural talent. Luckily, he knew somebody in the business. His uncle was a minor-league scout for his hometown team, the Reds. He talked them into giving the kid a tryout. Rose was impressive enough to be signed to a minor-league contract. He spent three years riding the battered buses of the farm teams. The Reds finally called him up in 1963.

That's when baseball people really started to take notice of this hard-nosed kid who ran to first on a base on balls, the hustling hot-shot who, instead of sliding, dove headfirst into bases. They noticed him enough to vote him Rookie of the Year.

It was the beginning of a notable career. Along the way, he would lead the league in batting, runs scored, hits and doubles. Rose would become the perennial All-Star and consummate team player, switching positions, moving to wherever he was needed most.

In 1976, Rose, who broke in making less than $15,000, led his team to a world-series sweep over the Yankees. He had become the major drawing card for the 2,600,000 fans who came to Riverfront Stadium that year. He had become the strongest driving force on a team that was called the Big Red Machine. And Rose decided it was high time his wallet got oiled. He decided he was worth $400,000 a year. That, he said, was what the Reds would have to pay him to retain his services.

That contract ended with last season, one that had Rose spending much of his time in the sports headlines. When the Reds' management refused to talk to him about a bigger money package, he decided to test his value in the open market. He became a free agent, negotiating with any team that would have him. And many would. They saw Rose as a team leader and a great drawing card. He traveled all over, eventually narrowing his choice to five cities—St. Louis, Atlanta, Kansas City, Pittsburgh and Philadelphia. He presented his case and sat back and listened to the offers. In addition to tremendous amounts of money, they included everything from a beer distributorship to racehorses.

The team that was offering the least financially was Philadelphia. Why go with the lowest price? Well, Rose had some friends there. But mostly it was because the team was a winner. And if there was one thing Rose hated more than anything else, it was losing.

He had survived some rocky times in his marriage, a relationship that yielded him a 14-year-old daughter, a carbon-copy 10-year-old son and, last summer, a troubled separation from his wife, Karolyn. And just when things were back together and looking good again, Rose was slapped with a paternity suit by a young woman from Tampa who had spent a good deal of time in his company.

With the pressures of the season, the suit and the big money hanging over him, Rose has been reluctant to talk about much more than baseball clichés. To get the real story behind this curious American folk hero, *Playboy* sent Maury Z. Levy and Samantha Stevenson, who had teamed up recently to write *The Secret Life of Baseball* (*Playboy*, July 1983), to talk with Rose. Levy is editorial director of *Philadelphia* magazine and Stevenson is a seasoned sports freelancer who made headlines when she successfully sued to get into the Phillies' locker room.

They followed Rose halfway across the country, starting in Philadelphia, following him home to Cincinnati, and then on the road to St. Louis and New York, to talk with him. Levy's report:

"Rose thought this was going to be just another interview. And he'd been through so damned many of them, he had his act down pat. We spent the first couple of hours in his hotel room in Philadelphia. It was all very patterned. He had answers to questions that weren't asked. He was running through his basic Pete Rose interview, the one he had done on national TV with Phil Donahue and others and the one that had appeared in almost every newspaper in the country. He had it down so well he didn't even bother looking at me through most of it. Instead, he lay in bed, his eyes fixed on the television set that he insisted on leaving on. He was watching *Days of Our Lives*.

"It was clear through all the cliches, though, that Rose was not just another dumb athlete. He's not much of an elegant speaker, but you learn quickly to look beyond that. He has a street sense that is very sharp. It was OK for him to be talking about baseball in generalities, but when it came to money, he was specific to the penny. He rattled off profit margin from projected business deals like a Wall Street wizard.

"'I see you're wearin' one of them Cartier watches,' he said to me. 'See this baby,' he said, pointing to a very large Corum gold-and-diamond Rolls-Royce watch on his own wrist, 'this baby cost me 8000 bucks. That could buy a lot of Cartiers, couldn't it?'

"Rose had easily convinced me that he could buy and sell me. He had also proved that he had the attention span of an eight-year-old. He couldn't sit still for more than a few minutes. His mind would wander and then his body. 'Ain't you asked enough questions yet?' he would constantly want to know. 'You're all business, man. Don't you ever have any fun?'

"Rose's idea of fun was driving me around Cincinnati at 90 miles an hour while he blasted Rod Stewart tapes on his stereo. I kept expecting him to pull into a hamburger joint, grease back his hair and try to pick up some girls. When I told him about my own hot-rodding experiences, he was finally convinced that I was all right.

"'But why are you carrying that excess baggage around with you?' he asked when we were alone. He was referring to Samantha. He just couldn't see her as one of the guys."

Says Stevenson:

"Rose never thought of me as a journalist. I was just window dressing to him. He thinks a woman's place is in the kitchen and the bedroom. And when he looked at me, I felt he was thinking exactly that.

"And I wasn't the only one. During one session, we watched a golf tournament together. Nancy Lopez was playing. Rose kept commenting on how pretty she was and he kept asking me if I didn't think her breasts had gotten bigger.

"He just couldn't understand why I wanted to know the answer to all those sports questions. Why would a girl be so interested in all that? He kept referring to my suit against the Phillies that finally won me equal rights in the locker room.

"'Tell me,' he said, 'how does it feel to have all those cocks staring you in the face? Doesn't it make you embarrassed? Do you like it?'

"'All those cocks,' as Rose called them, finally got to him. He realized that some of the other players didn't think it was too cool for him to be seen talking with me in the locker room. And Rose is the kind of guy who never wants to look like he's not cool. So he gave into the peer pressure. He stopped talking to me. He made the last hours of the interview like a wild-goose chase, setting up appointments with me and then standing me up, going to the track with the guys instead. He was stonewalling me, but I wasn't so sure whether it was just because I was a woman or because I stopped asking the baseball questions and started getting into his personal life. That's when he ducked me the most. And that's when he really started to lose his cool."

PLAYBOY: Who's the best player in major-league baseball?

ROSE: I am.

PLAYBOY: How do you figure that? Are you a better hitter than Rod Carew? A better slugger than Dave Parker? A better all-around player than Cesar Cedeno?

ROSE: It's not that simple. If you're talking about everything included—selling the game of baseball, public relations, popularity off the field as well as on the field, versatility playing more than one position, hitting the baseball from both sides—I'm number one. That's why I make the most money.

PLAYBOY: A lot of people would dispute that. There are other players who make more—

ROSE: You can take my word for it, there will be no ballplayer or no athlete. I don't think there will be any athlete anywhere that will make more money than me this year.

PLAYBOY: What about Carew's salary and Parker's?

ROSE: Yeah, you can read this stuff about Dave Parker and you can start saying—well, you can get $100,000 if he is a Most Valuable Player and $50,000 if he is second. So he will be a millionaire if he does all these things he has to do, including helping the parks that draw 1,500,000 people. So there is a lot of stipulations in his contract.

PLAYBOY: And there aren't any stipulations in *your* contract?

ROSE: That is my salary. I don't have to get 200 hits or draw 2,000,000 people or anything like that.

PLAYBOY: You sound pretty sure of yourself.

ROSE: Look, I've been here 16 years and I still do it all. I got the fan appeal. I play harder than anybody. I've played against Willie Mays, Stan Musial, Henry Aaron, Roberto Clemente. It's hard to become number one when you've got guys like that around. But I done it.

PLAYBOY: Does that make you a superstar?

ROSE: Yeah, I think so. I think I'm consistent, adjust to situations, handle people. I think I do all those things. A superstar don't necessarily mean you have got to hit 40 home runs. It don't mean you have to get 234 hits or 235 hits every year. I mean, a superstar does a little bit of each. A little bit of everything. Now, Frank Sinatra is a superstar in what he does. He's consistent over a period of time. He can handle situations. That is why he is a superstar. Just like me.

PLAYBOY: So you feel you're some kind of legend?

ROSE: I don't even know what a legend is. A legend is old times. A legend to me is something like a Jesse James or Bat Masterson or somebody like that. Jesse James. Babe Ruth is a legend. I guess I have a lot better chance of being a legend if I get Stan Musial's record [for most hits in the National League]. You know, I will become the number-one hitter in the history of our league. That is really something to work for. How many guys in the history of this league do you think have a chance to do that?

PLAYBOY: Is that how you feel you became a legend?

ROSE: Well, you know a legend—there aren't too many guys who can look at you and say I have got a little girl 14 years old. I only failed to hit .300 one time since she was born. Fourteen years old she is.

PLAYBOY: If you're not a legend yet, how *would* you describe yourself?

ROSE: How would I describe me? Well, I have fun. I play the game with enthusiasm. I play unorthodox. I'm not graceful. You know, most guys are graceful. But I'm not one of those guys that everything's got to look smooth. I swing good. But I'm not smooth when I catch a ball. I'm not smooth when I run. But I just play like a roughneck. I play baseball like a football player would play it. I'm hard and I'm tough.

PLAYBOY: And you're pretty cocky.

ROSE: Well, some people will call me cocky and arrogant, but I'm not arrogant. I'm just confident. And I just learned a long time ago that I have to have confidence and believe in myself, because there's going to be people who doubt you out there. There's going to be people who don't like you out there. I mean, a lot of people thought that I was arrogant when I made the statement that I felt I should be the highest-paid player in baseball. A lot of people don't realize that I'm not the same as the other ballplayers in baseball. There's a little difference with me, because the other ballplayers in the game, they're not as well known as I am everywhere. That's the truth. There may be a couple close. But other than Muhammad Ali, who is the most recognizable athlete in this country?

PLAYBOY: O.J. Simpson, maybe.

ROSE: And me. So I'm the only white one, right?

PLAYBOY: If you say so.

ROSE: No contest.

PLAYBOY: And you didn't exactly get to the top in your game on grace and finesse, did you?

ROSE: Naw, like I said, I was a roughneck. I wasn't scared of nothin'. And I didn't give a shit about anything. I still don't worry about anything. I'm not a worrier. If something's going to go wrong with your business or your marriage or things like that—the best way to make the problems easier is to have a good year. You create more problems if you hit .220. You create less problems if you hit .310 every year. You'll have less problems than anybody. That's the best way to go about your job, just have a good year and everything will fall into place. It'll take care of itself. You'll get the commercials. You'll get the raise in pay and everything.

PLAYBOY: That's if it's all going right. What if it's not?

ROSE: Everything goes wrong when you have a bad year if you're an athlete.

PLAYBOY: And as you get older, isn't it easier for things to go wrong?

ROSE: Well, I didn't shrink last year. It was one of the most at-bat seasons I ever had in my career, 700, and I struck out 30 times, the all-time low. So what that says is, the more experience you get, the smarter you get and the more you learn. I'm smart enough to know it's going to come to an end someday. But I've been fortunate to be able to prolong it.

PLAYBOY: Why do you say fortunate? Don't you have the reputation for taking good care of yourself?

ROSE: I like to think I play every game like it's the last one. That's a good way to play the game. But maybe it's just something that's interlocked inside your mind, that this might be your last year or next year might be your last year. So I don't think about what's going to happen tomorrow. I worry about what's going to happen today.

I play like a machine. I don't get tired. I just keep coming back and coming at you. I'm the type of guy, if I was in a fight, the other guy would knock me down and I would get back up and he would knock me down and I would get back up. I would be like Rocky.

PLAYBOY: Is that how you'd like to be remembered?

ROSE: Well, I don't want them to forget me as a man out of baseball. I don't want them to forget me. I mean, I just want people to say there is a guy that worked the hardest and the longest to become a switch-hitter, the best switch-hitter that ever lived, plus the guy who no matter where he played, he was a winner.

PLAYBOY: You mentioned being the most popular guy in the game—but you do have a lot of people who dislike you. Why is that?

ROSE: There's people who would dislike me if I'd signed for the Reds for $300,000, or if I had said I'll play for the Reds for $100,000 and to hell with the money. There's still somebody who'd say, well, he still makes too much. You know, there are so many people in the world. There's idiots everywhere. Just downright stupid people. They have no values of money or no values of talent or nothing. They're just stupid people.

PLAYBOY: What do you think makes the fans so angry with you?

ROSE: There's a lot of things that make them mad about me. Maybe the way I talk on TV. There are some people who don't like me the way I play, because I prove to people if you work hard at something, you can accomplish it without super talent. And, see, I make the lazy guy look into the mirror and be mad at himself. I show up lazy people because I play hard and play every day. Because they could do it if they worked hard themselves, and they know they've messed up.

PLAYBOY: And so they resent you?

ROSE: Sure. They resent it because they're saying, "There's no ballplayer worth that." I mean, was I supposed to say I don't want it? I'm not worth it? You know, I don't understand people.

PLAYBOY: Maybe the fans forget that you are being paid to entertain.

ROSE: Yeah, but they don't get mad if Rod Stewart makes millions of dollars for his concerts. They don't say nothing. I never hear anybody say anything about Wayne Newton making $5,000,000 a year in Vegas. You know, I'm not saying he's not worth it. He's the best entertainer out there. Frank Sinatra gets $250,000 a week out there. Ann-Margret makes $200,000 a week. But they're worth it, because they get up and they do two shows a night.

PLAYBOY: And Sinatra doesn't get booed if he misses a note. How does it feel, getting booed?

ROSE: Booing's something you learn to live with. But sometimes the fans go nuts. Like, a guy threw a whiskey bottle at Bake McBride in St. Louis. You know, that kind of shit, that ain't part of the game. And I've had that happen to me. I've had to be taken off two or three fields. L.A., New York and Chicago. I had to be taken off the field because garbage was being thrown at me. I don't agree with people who think that's part of the game.

PLAYBOY: Were you in danger at any of those times?

ROSE: Well, a whiskey bottle just missed my head. I got shot on my neck with a paper clip and it bled for three innings. What if the guy had put my eye out? What's the guy gonna get, a $25 misdemeanor fine? And my career is over? Guys threw bottles, chicken bones, garbage. A guy threw a crutch at me once in left field in Chicago.

PLAYBOY: That sounds as though it could have hurt.

ROSE: See, you're just like the fans. Whaddaya mean, that *coulda* hurt? When a crutch hits you, you get hurt. I don't classify them idiots as fans. Most fans who go to the ballpark are good fans. There's always a couple. You know, you get a 40,000 crowd, there's got to be an idiot in the crowd. I mean, there's got to be some people who just don't have any sense. They're just there to make a scene.

Look, I go watch *Rocky*, Sylvester Stallone ain't gonna give me an autograph. He's not gonna give me a boxing glove. He's not gonna talk to me. If people go to the ballpark, they think they're supposed to get an autograph. You're supposed to give them a bat. They think all that's part of the four-dollar ticket. I mean, they forget about the entertainment of the nine-inning game.

PLAYBOY: Maybe there are some people who still don't think *you're* worth it.

ROSE: I don't give a shit what people think. I used to really worry about that, too. I really did. When I used to hold out for more money every year, I used to worry about that, because I always wanted to make everybody like me. Playing hard, being nice, signing autographs. I used to give in to the Reds a lot, because I didn't want to hold out. But when you start getting letters like I get and phone calls and stuff like that, and people being idiots, I say the hell with them. I'm not going to worry about anybody.

PLAYBOY: What kind of letters do you get?

ROSE: Oh, you know . . . racial letters and shit like that. I say the hell with them. I mean, some guy is sitting behind me when I'm getting in my car one night. He's getting in his truck and he's got his load of people with him and he's gotta yell at me. He's gotta tell me, "Got all your money in your suitcase?" I say, "I can't get it all in there, asshole." And he just shut up. I mean, why don't he just get in his car and move on?

PLAYBOY: Fans can be fanatics.

ROSE: Oh, yeah. They always want a piece of you. I was at a place the other day; I'm sitting upstairs with [Larry] Bowa and Schmitty [Mike Schmidt], we're having breakfast and I come in and I go to the john. So I'm sitting there, going to the john, and all of a sudden I hear this guy come in. Now, I haven't said nothing to Bowa and Schmitty. And this guy, I guess he's taking a leak or something, and this other guy walks in and he asks him how he's doing. He says, "Oh, I'm doing fine." He says, "I just been upstairs and had breakfast with Pete Rose and I been talking to him." And he don't know I'm sitting in there. You know, I'm sitting there, saying, "You're a goddamn liar." That's why when I go in a bar, I don't drink and I never let anybody buy me a drink, never. Because people go to work next day and say, "I was out drinking with Pete Rose till four in the morning"—only I left at 10:30.

PLAYBOY: Are you hassled by fans at home?

ROSE: Oh, I can go home, where I can listen to prank telephone calls. Shit, I get my phone number changed every three months. It's the idiots that just sit and think of reasons why they should call. That's the way people are. I just laugh at them. That shit don't really bother me. Nothing bothers me except these people that start calling me disloyal and stuff like this. I abandoned Cincinnati? I put in a lot of endless hours of hard work for that city, both on and off the field. And I'm not looking for anything for it. That's why I ain't gonna try to satisfy everyone. Just like the time the Reds' management told me not to drive my Rolls-Royce to the ballpark, because it makes the fans mad.

PLAYBOY: And, naturally, you didn't agree with their way of thinking.

ROSE: I told them to go to hell. I worked hard for that car. They didn't tell [Joe] Morgan and those guys not to drive their $20,000 Corvettes and Cadillacs to the ballpark.

PLAYBOY: Those sound like the problems of a rich and successful athlete. Were you always a winner? How about when you were growing up?

ROSE: No, I was a loser with the books. I was too busy playing ball and getting into trouble.

PLAYBOY: Did you ever get into any real trouble in school?

ROSE: No, just punk stuff, like throwing rocks at windows and putting shit in a bag and setting it on fire. Knocking on somebody's door. Let them open the bag.

PLAYBOY: What about chasing girls?

ROSE: I had my share when I was a kid. I think I got the pretty girls. I don't know if they got the good-looking guy, but they got the guy everybody knew.

PLAYBOY: When did you first get involved with girls?

ROSE: What are you asking, when did I get my first piece of ass? Is that what you are asking?

PLAYBOY: Not exactly, but that's a good start.

ROSE: I don't remember specifically what day it was or how old I was. I'm no different than any other kid.

PLAYBOY: Well, were you a teenager?

ROSE: Probably. No, I don't think I was a teenager yet, I don't remember.

PLAYBOY: Since we brought up the subject, let's talk about sex. Should an athlete have sex before a game?

ROSE: No.

PLAYBOY: Why?

ROSE: It makes you tired.

PLAYBOY: You believe that old wives' tale?

ROSE: Well, let me ask you a question. If you make love for a half hour or 45 minutes or an hour on the day of a game, are you tired? How are you going to go to the ball game and perform at the utmost of your ability if you are mellow? If you have got to go to the ballpark hyper?

PLAYBOY: But you've had other things to take your mind off the game. You and your wife, Karolyn, separated last summer. Wasn't she ready to file for a divorce?

ROSE: Well, I don't think it is anybody's business. I don't know what the accounts were. But I don't think she was going to file for a divorce. It was better to separate when I did, because, like I just said, one of the secrets of playing baseball is not going to the ballpark and being worried or being mad about something. So if I was going to be mad living at home, the separation was my fault, it wasn't her fault. So it proved that I had some weaknesses. I mean, I am not the only guy in the world who ever separated from his wife for a couple of months. So it ain't that big a deal to me. It ain't nobody's problem in Philadelphia and no one's problem is the same as mine. And I handled it. I handled it in my own way. Other guys would have handled it differently. I handled it my own way.

PLAYBOY: Did it work?

ROSE: Yeah, well, obviously.

PLAYBOY: Still, aren't there women everywhere who turn your head?

ROSE: Once in a while they turn my head. As long as I don't touch.

PLAYBOY: What kind of women do you like?

ROSE: Just, I guess, I like class. I don't mean rings and cars and clothes. I mean just people who you can just tell have class by looking at them. You know, just the way they handle themselves and the way they walk. I like people with personality.

PLAYBOY: Do you like pretty women around you?

ROSE: Oh, yeah. I like women with pretty legs. Pretty legs and pretty mouths.

PLAYBOY: What is it about mouths?

ROSE: I just think because that is what you look at. You don't talk to somebody and look at their navel or at their shoulder. People with pretty mouths are pretty. And most people with pretty legs are built good. So those two qualities usually make a complete girl.

PLAYBOY: You don't like breasts?

ROSE: I can only speak for mine. I don't like mine. I mean, to be kissed. I don't know. I can't stand it. It bugs the shit out of me. It makes me feel like someone's taking their fingers to a screen door.

PLAYBOY: What's your fantasy life like?

ROSE: What's a fantasy?

PLAYBOY: Imagination. Illusion. You can have sexual fantasies.

ROSE: What is the sense of having a fantasy about going to bed with somebody that is supposed to be the prettiest girl in the world? If I can't do it, why should I waste my time even wondering about it? Sitting here right now, I am fantasizing about playing in the World Series with the Phillies. I would like that to happen. Yeah. That is the utmost thing on my mind right now.

PLAYBOY: OK, back to baseball. You mentioned earlier that you get "racial" letters from baseball fans. What did you mean?

ROSE: It goes back a long way. I was actually called into the office in 1963 for hanging with the black players too much.

PLAYBOY: Why?

ROSE: The white players didn't want to associate with me. See, in 1961, the Reds won the pennant and they had a guy named Don Balsingame on second base. In 1962, he had his best year ever. He hit .281. So because of those reasons, in 1963, they all thought that he could help them win their pennant again. Fred Hutchinson, the manager, stuck me at second base, and they all resented that. They didn't want a rookie on second base, because they had veterans in all the other positions. And the only guys that treated me with any dignity and decency were Frank Robinson and Vada Pinson, the black guys. It was a very cliquish team in those days. That's why they didn't win.

The black players were just like me when I was a kid. No car, no money, no suit of clothes. All they had to do was play sports. If you ride downtown Manhattan, every time you go by a basketball court or a handball court, they're all blacks out there playing. How else are they going to get an education? How else are they going to make a good living? So the blacks do it because they don't have the things.

PLAYBOY: Had you always been a second baseman?

ROSE: I was a catcher all the way up to high school. That's why I was never a polished fielder. When I made the big leagues, I was only second baseman for three years. One year of high school and two years of the minors. And you don't become a good fielder if you don't practice day in and day out.

PLAYBOY: Why do you think that fans started coming back to baseball?

ROSE: Because we brought them back. Me and the Reds, after that '75 World Series with Boston. That was the greatest World Series in the history of baseball, action-wise. Five out of seven of the games were one-run games. That's what started people coming back. Baseball was exciting again. And then there was my hitting streak . . . What that did, what the 44 streak did, what that did to me is, a lot of people were rooting for me that didn't even know me, that didn't know anything about me. Because that got a lot of national attention—or publicity. You know, 'cause people started following that every day. Every day that I hit, they had it on TV. So that really helped me out in that respect. It brought a lot of fans back, too.

PLAYBOY: What was the most memorable thing to you about the '75 series?

ROSE: I was Most Valuable Player.

PLAYBOY: Anything else?

ROSE: Well, getting some key hits, making some key plays and winning. There's a big difference in winning a world series or just losing one. Most guys are just happy to get there and they don't even concentrate on winning. Not me. I don't get nowhere to lose.

PLAYBOY: How do you find Philadelphia? Is it as straitlaced a town as Cincinnati?

ROSE: We had too many rules in Cincinnati. I guess it was because it was such a conservative town. No long hair, no mustaches—things like that. I guess in Philly, I can really let my hair down.

PLAYBOY: And you don't like to follow rules?

ROSE: Well, if a guy sets rules, yeah, I'll follow them. In Philadelphia, you have the type of players who don't need a lot of rules. Danny Ozark don't have to stand there with a gun and make sure I get my ground balls. He's got guys that are professional enough that they go about their job in the right way. What Danny does is tell you what he wants done and lets you go about it. He lets you be your own man.

PLAYBOY: Is one of your goals to become a team leader to the Phillies?

ROSE: No. That's not my goal. I probably coulda had a better impact on the team as far as leadership if I had a good spring training as far as getting a lot of hits. But I hit .194. You know. But I think the guys on the Phillies know that I work hard and I do my job and I'm just gonna play hard every day. You know, it takes some time to earn the respect of your teammates. You just don't walk in and say, "I hit in 44 in a row, I got 3000 hits, I'm your leader." I mean, you just can't do it.

PLAYBOY: But you would *like* to be the leader of the team, wouldn't you?

ROSE: Oh, sure. I think it took a long time for me to become a leader in Cincinnati, even though you got a guy like Johnny Bench. He hits all them great home runs, makes all them All-Star teams and is a great player. Great, but that don't qualify you as a team leader. A team leader has to come from a guy respected from the way you play day in and day out. Consistency. You don't have to be the best player to be a team leader. No, you have to be a certain type player. Johnny Bench is good, but he just ain't the type.

PLAYBOY: When do you think you became the leader of the Reds?

ROSE: I think probably after the '73 play-offs with the trouble with New York. The fight I had with Bud Harrelson. I just knocked the Mideast war off the cover of the New York *Daily News.*

PLAYBOY: And *that's* when the Reds noticed you?

ROSE: Yeah: "Look at this guy. He's incredible. He don't care about nothin'. All he wants to do is win." I was playing the whole city of Manhattan.

PLAYBOY: You were certainly swinging away then. Would you categorize the Phillies as a swinging team?

ROSE: I don't know what you mean by swingers. I don't drink, so I never been out with any of them. I don't know what they do off the field. In order to have that image, you have to hang in bars. I mean, because girls don't hang in supermarkets. I just don't like to go to bars and stuff—and I'm not a prude or anything—I just haven't been able to convince myself that drinking is gonna do anything for me. That don't make them guys bad guys and me a good guy. Some guys like to go have a beer after the game and just relax. It's good for you in that respect. I'd rather go home and watch TV and get room service and that way no one bothers me. I take my phone off the hook at 11 o'clock, and I'll be a son of a bitch if some guy didn't call me at 20 after two and wanted to get an autograph. In the hotel. I don't know how he got through. They say it's the price you gotta pay, but if I go someplace to eat, all I do is sign autographs.

PLAYBOY: Is that bad?

ROSE: It's getting worse. I don't have no time of my own. Somebody always wants somethin' from me.

PLAYBOY: So you just stay in your room and hide?

ROSE: No, I go out some. I go into bars, but I don't drink. Yet, there will be people who say they saw me in there drinking. People have a tendency to think you're drinkin' if they see you there in a bar. If they see me go into a room with a girl, they think we're in there screwin'. That's what people want. They think what they want to think. It's the truth. Regardless of what happens, people are always going to think the negative things. That's just the way the world is.

PLAYBOY: How about on the field? How is the atmosphere in the Phillies' dugout?

ROSE: Good. Wide-awake. Well, you're rooting for each other and if you make a good play, they're always patting each other on the back. You know, keepin' in the game—bein' involved in the game. The players should be out there rootin' for each other. They shouldn't be up in the clubhouse during a game, drinkin' coffee or playin' cards during a game.

PLAYBOY: What do players talk about in the dugout?

ROSE: The game. The situation of the game. Always. You don't talk about where you're going to eat and shit like that. You may do that if you're ahead 12-1 or something. A laugher. But in a close ball game, there's strict attention to what's going on.

PLAYBOY: Do you give advice or offer help to players?

ROSE: I always do. Every time I come back, I always tell the guys what the pitcher is throwing. If they're smart, they listen to me.

PLAYBOY: Who's the most eccentric player you know?

ROSE: The guy that's craziest, is that what you mean? On the field?

PLAYBOY: Yes.

ROSE: Probably the most eccentric guy I ever played with was Pedro Borbon. He'll pitch his ass off any time they ask him and if there's a fight, he'll be the first one there. He's the type of guy if he gets in a fight, you just have to kill him to stop him. He don't give a shit about nothin'.

Just a nice, even-tempered guy, but if you push him the wrong way, he's got that Latin temper and he can get his dander up real good.

PLAYBOY: What are your feelings now about being on first base?

ROSE: There's a lot of action there. Boy, it's fun. I'm getting more and more used to it every day. I like the communication there. The action part of it is nice. Hell, you talk to the runners, the coach, the umpires, the pitcher. You're talking to everybody there.

PLAYBOY: Do you psych guys out when they get on first base?

ROSE: No, you can't psych major-league ballplayers out.

PLAYBOY: What do you say on first base to your visitors?

ROSE: I just tell them nice hitting. What kind of pitch was it? You want that one back you fouled? Stuff like that. Kidding. Having fun. I might ask them about their family, 'cause a lot of guys ask me that—

PLAYBOY: Such as "How's Karolyn"?

ROSE: No, like how my little boy is. They just talk about my boy, they don't talk about how my *wife* is.

PLAYBOY: Do you have it a lot easier now in the field, playing first base?

ROSE: Hey, the people who say first base is easy are full of it. It's the most involved position I've ever played. You make put-outs, you hold the runners on base, you work real close with the pitcher. You don't have to have a ball even hit to you and you get an easy 15 chances a game. You never handle that many chances at third base. Plus, you've gotta bust your butt hustling over to be the cutoff man. But it's fun.

PLAYBOY: What's the hardest thing you've ever done in baseball? Was it your hitting streak?

ROSE: No, the hardest thing I ever had to do was keep my edge during the 1975 World Series against Boston. We were rained out . . . what . . . three straight days? I guess that was good for the league, 'cause they got all that extra ink, but it was tough on the players. I'll never forget a bus ride out to Tufts University for those practices. There we were, a major-league baseball team in full uniform, sitting on a Greyhound bus, stopping at a gas station to ask directions to the school.

PLAYBOY: Doesn't it all get to you after a while, playing baseball every day without rest?

ROSE: When you don't play games, you lose your sharpness. You gotta play a week, 10 days straight to really find your groove. When you play a game, then sit around for two or three days, it slows you down. If I set up the schedule, I'd have all the Eastern clubs play on the West Coast the first month. There's a lot of things they could do to improve the schedule.

They could eliminate off days. That way, they could start the season two weeks later and end it two weeks earlier. Weather wouldn't be as big a factor. We don't need off days. I didn't have an off day last year. Every day we didn't have a game, I worked out. What's the difference?

PLAYBOY: After a game, your locker looks like a delicatessen on a Saturday morning. All those people waiting to talk to you. Does that get to you?

ROSE: It's been quite a challenge to get my work done and still be cooperative with the media. I could have been a bad guy about it, but I'm not that way. I try to cooperate with everybody, but it's hard to find peace. The games are the easiest part. So you can get away from all the questions. I wish they'd stop asking me about my salary. That's all anybody ever talks about—money. In St. Louis the other day, a group of fans said they expected me to catch a ball that was 10 rows in the stands because I was making $800,000 a year. It's just not fair. I didn't ask for anything. I turned down twice that amount.

PLAYBOY: What really makes the Phillies your kind of team?

ROSE: Well, this team will entertain you more ways than any team in baseball. We have speed, long-ball power, great defense, guys who are capable of pitching no-hitters, a great bullpen. And, sure, I think we're gonna win, but what's more important, I think we're gonna have fun. The old Reds team, we used to have fun. Everybody was loose, cutting up. Did you see the Reds when we played them this spring? I stood around the batting cage. I couldn't believe how quiet it was. Nobody said a word. That's not like the Reds. Morgan and those guys were always yapping. There's just something missing now.

PLAYBOY: Have you analyzed the Phillies' problems? The team seems to fold during playoff games. What do you think?

ROSE: I don't know, they just ran into bad breaks. They don't play with the same aggressiveness in the playoffs that they do in the season, it seems like. Why? I don't know. It's just experience. If we get in the Series this year, things will be all right.

PLAYBOY: And what if you don't make it to the world series?

ROSE: Well, I can't do everything.

PLAYBOY: One of your trademarks is the headfirst slide into first base. Have you always done it that way?

ROSE: Yeah, always did it that way. I used to practice that. I used to practice in the swimming pool all the time, used to always dive in the swimming pool like that. Exactly like you're playing baseball. That's about the only place you can practice that without getting hurt.

PLAYBOY: Why do you do that? Some people think it's just to showboat.

ROSE: Showboat, shit. It's just the easy way to slide and the fastest. And the safest, I think.

PLAYBOY: Is that how you got the nickname Charlie Hustle?

ROSE: No, that came in 1963, in spring training. Mickey Mantle and Whitey Ford gave it to me because I ran to first every time I got a walk.

PLAYBOY: What made you start that?

ROSE: Oh, my father brought that to my attention one night. He just said that's the way to play the game of baseball. You play it hard. Always run. Have fun and be happy.

PLAYBOY: That was the Hustle. When did the Charlie come in?

ROSE: Back in those days, any time you did anything, you know, you put Charlie in front of it. Hot-dog Charlie. Hollywood Charlie. Charlie Tuna. Anything.

PLAYBOY: Do you like that name?

ROSE: Yeah, that name's all right. The image is OK, because it's not a phony image. It's not something that I started doing when I became a big-league baseball player. I can honestly say that the reason that I run to first on a base on balls is just that it's a habit. It's something I've been doing ever since I was nine years old. I run to first if I'm 0 for 15 or if I'm 15 for 15. I still run to first on base on balls.

PLAYBOY: How about running to your position? You've stopped doing that.

ROSE: I know how to conserve my energy. I don't walk to my position. But I don't sprint. I get out there and I look good on the way.

PLAYBOY: Why do you think you are such a consistent hitter?

ROSE: Well, there's a lot of reasons. I'm a switch-hitter. I don't strike out. I know how to hit. I hit the ball to all fields. There's a lot of reasons why I'm a good hitter. But when I give a hitting clinic, the less you can talk about, the better off you are. There's just three or four different things you talk about—you don't want to get a kid thinking about 15 different things. I just think if you've got good eyes and strong hands, you can be a good hitter if you practice.

PLAYBOY: OK, so a kid is up there ready to learn how to hit. Tell us what you would tell him.

ROSE: Well, aggressiveness. Swing and get the bat out front, lift from the top. Don't worry about your shoe, or your feet or your knees or hip. Don't worry about anything. Your ribs, your shoulders. Don't worry about how you look. Just go and hit the ball. Because it's immaterial how you look. The whole secret to hitting is being comfortable.

Then you just put the basics of getting the bat out in front and being aggressive and being quick. You can't tell a guy to swing at strikes only. Because there's some guys if they swung at strikes only, they wouldn't be aggressive. Roberto Clemente, if he swung at strikes only, he'd have been a .230 hitter. But he was super-, superaggressive. Yogi Berra was another one. Bad-ball hitter. But a good one. Joe Morgan swings at nothing but strikes, and he's been successful that way. So, you know, whatever you're successful at, that's what you should do.

PLAYBOY: Is choking a mental thing?

ROSE: Yeah, 75 percent. There's 15,000 different things that can go wrong as you hit the baseball, and when you're hitting the baseball, everybody knows what you're doing wrong. All the experts know. I do six things when I go in a slump. I move back in the box, up in the box, further away from the plate, closer to the plate. Heavier or lighter bat. I can tell what I'm doing wrong by the flight of the ball. If I'm batting left-handed and everything I'm hitting is over the third-base dugout, I know it's swinging late. If I'm fouling everything down here, I'm swinging too early. That's why before every game, I clean my bat off. After I bat the first time, I go back and look at my bat. I can see where I'm going wrong, where I'm hitting the ball. I make adjustments when I'm not at the plate hitting. Other guys don't do that.

PLAYBOY: Are baseball players an unintelligent group of men? Are they dumber than other groups of athletes?

ROSE: Oh, I don't know. I think baseball players are some of the smarter guys. Because, you know, a lot of the football and basketball players, when they have college education, all their college education is, is physical education. And baseball players get the education of hard knocks, going through the minor leagues and becoming street smart like me. You know, they may not talk like it, put their words together right. Just like me. I don't talk good, but you understand everything I'm saying. I think I have a vocabulary and tone for getting things people understand. Kids understand me. I can get across to kids because I talk just like them. I've listened to football players and basketball players on interviews and I don't know what the hell they're saying. That don't mean they're stupid. I can get up in front of a bunch of people and I can have them laughing for a half hour. But I have to—because I can get $5000 for starters to do it.

PLAYBOY: You don't seem to be stupid when it comes to making money.

ROSE: Well, nowadays you have to be more conscious about what you are going to have and what you are going to do after you get out of baseball. You know, 20 years ago, 30 years ago, the old-time ballplayers, they didn't worry about saving money. They didn't worry about what they were going to do when they got out of baseball. But today, with the prices the way they are and what is expected of you today, to be in a baseball park, you have to be taught about what is going to take place when your baseball-playing days are over. You don't want to play baseball your whole life and at the age of 35, you have to pick up and get a new job and don't have any money to start in that job. So I think we are more thinking about what is going to happen when you are through playing.

PLAYBOY: Do you realize that you are only playing a *game?*

ROSE: I realize it's a game, but the odds of the game are the win. You know, you learn that in professional sports, you get in trouble sometimes, when you say that around kids, but winning is everything.

PLAYBOY: What kids are told is that winning or losing isn't important; it's playing the game that counts.

ROSE: It all depends on what kind of person you are. I mean, there are some guys that just fall in the trend that they're used to losing. Other guys—some guys can't stand the pressure of playing on a winning team. They can't. I mean, that's what I was reading the other day. I didn't say it, but somebody was saying the other day that they wondered how Carew's reaction would be if he played with the Yankees, a winning team. I don't know. There are some guys who can't play—because there are some guys who feel the pressures of being on a winner every day, day in and day out. Anybody can play on a last-place team.

Winning and losing is everything. I think you learn the differences in professional sports. I think you should teach it to kids, because winning and losing is important in life or in sports or in schoolwork or anything. I mean, if you had to worry about winning and losing in school, you wouldn't worry about passing or flunking. I mean, winning or losing is passing or flunking, isn't it? So when parents say that it is not important to my kid to worry about winning and losing, it's just not true.

PLAYBOY: But the bottom line today, past who wins or loses, is how much money you're paid to win, right?

ROSE: Well, I'm not in it to make everything I can as fast as I can, just to make a fast buck. The guys in Atlanta offered me $7,000,000 for four years—with some conditions attached. That's pretty serious. So I didn't get into this game to try to become independently wealthy overnight.

A lot of people seem to think that. The Philly deal is a great deal. All the deals were great deals. I couldn't have gone wrong with any deal. And when you start talking about friends on other teams and personnel on other teams and fans and ballparks, the Phillies lack nothing. Everything I looked at, the Phillies were right at the top. Fans, fan appeal, ball club, personnel on the ball club, the ballpark, the ownership. Everything I looked at for the Phillies was positive. Now, Pittsburgh is a good ball club, good ownership, good management. No fans. No fan appeal. Nobody goes to the ballpark.

PLAYBOY: Having all those people bid so highly on you must have swelled your head a little.

ROSE: I don't know why that should be. The only difference between this year and last year, or the only difference today as compared with when I was nine years old, I get just as dirty today playing ball as I did when I was nine years old. The only difference today, I make better money. I wasn't a poor guy last year. I made almost $400,000. That's not exactly suffering. But I gotta play to make it. My philosophy is, I gotta prove to Philly I deserve it. That's the funny thing about this game. No matter how old you are or how good you are, you can hit .300 for 15 years and you get 38 years old and you gotta prove to people that you're not old. By hitting .300 this year, I've got to prove to them next year that I'm not going downhill. Because there's some people who are just sitting there, waiting for me to go downhill, so they can start yelling at me.

PLAYBOY: What is your net worth? With all the deals and endorsements you've got going, do you really know how much money you've got?

ROSE: I get a statement every three months. But I'm not going to tell you how much. It's not good to do that, because you get idiots who're kidnappers sitting out there, waiting for that kind of stuff. But unless it's totally necessary, I don't see the importance of putting a specific figure in the paper. I mean, so I'm a millionaire ballplayer. OK. I mean, everybody knows that. So what's the difference if I got $2,200,000 or $1,600,000?

PLAYBOY: It's a big difference from last year, isn't it?

ROSE: Oh, I made good money last year. Well, I knew all that hard work and all that busting my ass and everything was going to pay off. I mean, the one reason, besides pride, I guess, that I worked so damned hard to get it is so I won't have to worry about where I get my next meal from. I've seen many, many of my friends and guys I've played with, and they don't even have a job. They're looking for a job and their home is in hock and their family is hungry. Once I sign the contract, I forget about the money. Money's not that important. It goes to my financial advisor, anyway. I never see a check.

PLAYBOY: How has your lifestyle changed?

ROSE: None. Hasn't changed at all.

PLAYBOY: Nothing? Still buy the same clothes?

ROSE: My wife still shops at Kmart.

PLAYBOY: You have a Rolls-Royce.

ROSE: Well, you know, I don't try and be a big shot because my wife drives a Rolls-Royce. I think it's smart to buy a Rolls-Royce rather than buying a Lincoln or something—or a Cadillac every year and losing $3000, $4000 on it. Get a Rolls-Royce, you ain't going to lose no money.

PLAYBOY: How did you manage to become an international media celebrity out of Cincinnati, Ohio?

ROSE: The reason for that is that I've been very fortunate to have a lot of things exciting happen to me on national TV. The fight with Harrelson started the All-Star thing with Ray Fosse. The World Series, the hitting streak, you know, all the magazine articles, covers of *Sport*, *Sports Illustrated*. You know that I've been on the cover of every magazine. I mean, I've been on the cover of *Ebony*!

PLAYBOY: You've become a highly marketable commodity, in other words?

ROSE: Other ballplayers don't understand that that's why I got that big contract. Because I'm recognizable, I'm marketable. You know, Parker, [Jim] Rice, Carew, those guys are tremendous ballplayers, but I mean, do you think they deserve the money that I do? Because you have to put more things in perspective than just hitting the baseball. I mean, Ted Turner, in Atlanta, wanted me to play for his team so he could sell his TV station. You know, the guy from Pittsburgh wanted me to play with their Pirates so they could turn their attendance around. The Phillies wanted to sign me to a contract and surpass their all-time record of season tickets by 5000. That proves something to me, that somebody thinks I'm marketable.

PLAYBOY: Is there a point where you begin worrying that you might be over-commercializing yourself?

ROSE: No, because if the stuff is credible and it's class, you can't be overexposed. If you get attached to a nice bank or a good supermarket, a good automobile agency, oil company, you don't have to worry about it. But baseball players as a rule don't make a lot of money in commercials. I mean, I do commercials for Aqua Velva and I get paid pretty good. But, hell, if I told you some of the salaries Bob Hope and those guys get. . . .

Because there's only one Bob Hope. If they don't want Pete Rose, if he says no to Aqua Velva, they can get Larry Bowa. If he says no, they'll go to Dave Parker. There's so many guys they can get.

PLAYBOY: But one of the reasons you are considered so marketable is that you're a white athlete, wouldn't you agree?

ROSE: It has *something* to do with it. Look, if you owned Swanson's Pizza, would you want a black guy to do the commercial on TV for you? Would you like the black guy to pick up the pizza and bite into it? Try to sell it? I mean, would you want Dave Parker selling your pizza to America for you? Or would you want Pete Rose?

PLAYBOY: Doesn't all that show business interfere with your game?

ROSE: Oh, I don't do that shit during the summer. No, once baseball starts, I don't fool with it. I don't do no autograph signings, no charitable work, none of that stuff when the season starts. I'm not going to mess up the hand that feeds the mouth. I just play baseball in the summertime.

PLAYBOY: But off season, you seem to be everywhere. What's next, the movies?

ROSE: I could have went into that last year. I just didn't feel like it. What they wanted me to do, it just seemed like a lot of time and hard work for what they were going to pay me.

PLAYBOY: What movie were you going to be in?

ROSE: I was going to be a copilot in an airplane cockpit. Something to do with the government. I didn't get all the details, because I didn't want to do it. I don't need them. I didn't need that film publicity.

PLAYBOY: How about the new candy bar you've come out with? Supercharg'r?

ROSE: Not candy. Don't put candy down there. It's all natural. It don't have no sugar.

PLAYBOY: Just lots of royalties.

ROSE: Yes, that could be the best royalty I've ever got. I've had other bars—energy bars. When you took a bite out of them, you almost needed a glass of water to wash it down. But you can substitute them for a meal, too. They sell half of what the projection is, I'll make one and a half times more than I do with the Phillies.

PLAYBOY: Do you have a ballpark idea of how many you think you will sell?

ROSE: Some of the competitors sell 57,000,000 and they don't taste good. If I sold 300,000,000 of those bars, I would make $4,500,000 myself, just me. There's no question about it. I can't wait.

PLAYBOY: So you're a pretty good money man. That must have helped you in your negotiations with other teams.

ROSE: Yeah, I guess you could say I really had my pick.

PLAYBOY: What were some of the other deals like, the ones you didn't take? We've heard some outrageous stories.

ROSE: That ain't so outrageous. Ted Turner, he's a real character. He wanted to pay me 1,000,000 bucks a season for the years I could play and then $100,000 a year for as long as I live. See, he owns the TV station down there that carries the Braves games. He figured he'd make up the money easy in what they'd bring in on bigger ratings.

PLAYBOY: Sounds good. Why didn't you go for it?

ROSE: I'm telling you, I really wasn't in it for the money. What could I have done for the Braves? Make them a contender, maybe. There's not much more one man could do for that club. It was more important to me to play with a team that could win the pennant, a team that could take the world series.

PLAYBOY: But turning down $1,000,000 a year?

ROSE: And that wasn't the only one. John Galbreath, the Pirates' owner, wanted to make me a millionaire, too. He owns Darby Dan Farm, too. He was going to give me racehorses. Brood mares. He knows what a horse-race nut I am. He was going to give me some mares to breed with a couple of the best studs in the world. You know what that would be worth? You can't even put a price on that. And the guy was going to pay me $400,000 a year besides that.

PLAYBOY: That must have been hard to turn down.

ROSE: Yeah, and there was others, too. Kansas City was offering me over $1,000,000 a year. And Augie Busch in St. Louis was going to throw in a big beer distributorship with his money. I really coulda had my pick.

PLAYBOY: And you picked Philadelphia for less money?

ROSE: Well, the money wasn't *that* much less. And I got lots of friends on the Phils. This team's got a first-class front office. That meant a lot to me after what happened in Cincinnati.

PLAYBOY: What exactly *did* happen?

ROSE: Well, I'll tell you, my problem over all these years with contracts in Cincinnati was that I am always too fair. See, some guys, if they want $100,000, they ask for $500,000. If they want $50,000, they ask for $80,000. You know, one year, I wanted $100,000, I got $92,000. Another year, I wanted $85,000 I got $75,000. I asked for $50,000 and I got

$36,000. I never went over my head and then compromised. That's the way it should've been done.

PLAYBOY: The president of the Cincinnati Reds, Dick Wagner, seems to have been a thorn in your side during negotiations with the Reds. If he had come through, would you still be a Red?

ROSE: I looked at Dick Wagner last year and I said, "Dick, what do you negotiate a contract on?" "All right," he said, "it's consistency. Years of experience. Popularity and statistics." And I said, "What the hell do I lack in? On those four categories, what do I lack in as far as being number one in America? Who's been more consistent over a 16-year period than me? Don't say Rod Carew, because he's only been there 12 years. And stats. Who's got the stats? Now, if you say stats and a guy looks at me and says, well, you've only got 150 home runs. That's more than anybody in the history of the National League for a switch-hitter."

PLAYBOY: What did Wagner say to that?

ROSE: He didn't say nothing. What could he say?

PLAYBOY: Does he have something against you?

ROSE: Evidently. Maybe it's the flamboyant style I have off the field. But he should realize that all that does is sell tickets.

PLAYBOY: Let us play the devil's advocate for a moment.

ROSE: All right. You give me what you think he's saying and I'll answer it.

PLAYBOY: He's got you under contract. He's paying you $400,000 and you're busting your ass and he knows it. You're the big draw. Let's say 40,000 people come to a game. Now, if he doubles your salary, you're not going to double attendance for him.

ROSE: That's probably right.

PLAYBOY: You might not even add 10,000 more people a game.

ROSE: Well, look at it like this. Just like the Phillies said. They sold 5000 more seats in tickets per game this year.

PLAYBOY: But the Phillies didn't have you.

ROSE: No, you're misleading yourself. Because the Reds were not going to take me from $400,000 to $800,000. The Reds could've had me for $450,000. Four-five-oh for the rest of my career. They would not do it. Not $550,000 not $650,000, not $750,000—$450,000.

PLAYBOY: And you would have been happy with that figure?

ROSE: When I got my 3000th hit on May fifth, the Reds decided to have a Pete Rose Day, and my attorney, Reuven Katz, said, "Mr. Wagner, why don't you give Pete—for the fans on Pete Rose Day—a career, nonguaranteed contract of $450,000 a year?" Career nonguaranteed contract.

Wagner said, "Well, we don't want to negotiate during the season." But a week before, he was negotiating with Mike Lumm and his attorney and he had a meeting set up for two weeks after that. Which was later canceled because we found out about it. So those are the double standards I'm telling you about.

PLAYBOY: When was your next meeting with Wagner?

ROSE: After the season was over, we go in to see him and he says, "Well, that's just a little bit too much." I said, "Well, OK, if that's the way you feel, there's no reason why I shouldn't just go through the free-agent draft to see what other teams think I'm worth." Then we went to Japan for exhibition games and the draft took place. At no time in Japan did the Reds ever try to negotiate with me. So, finally, two days before Wagner leaves to come back to the United States, he says he'd like to have a meeting with me when he gets back. I said, "Don't worry about it. I will never sign another contract before I talk to the Cincinnati Reds." We get back and we go down and have a meeting with him. Now, this is almost two months after the season is over, right? And we go in there and we sit down, and he has an idea what these other teams have offered. We say, "Well, Dick, have you come up with anything? What do you think?" You know what he says? He says, "I haven't had time to think about it." Been two months. It's a Friday. He says he'll get back to us Sunday. He gets back to us Sunday. He calls me and says, "I don't think we have any common ground to negotiate with." And that was it. He's still on the $400,000 figure. Which is less money than he's paying a couple other players on the team. Now, is there any way possible you can see it to be fair for me to be the third-highest-paid player on Cincinnati's team? They even had polls on TV in Cincy. Should Pete Rose be the highest-paid player on the Reds? You know, should he make the most money? More than any other player on the Reds? I mean, that's a stupid question for anybody to ask anybody.

PLAYBOY: Did Wagner realize he could have gotten you for $50,000 more?

ROSE: Well, what happened, Wagner knew that he could've had me for $430,000, $440,000 of $450,000 way back in June. And he probably told his bosses that. Now, all of a sudden, it's up to $650,000. What's he gonna do, tell his people he can get me for $650,000? Well, they'll say, "Hey, you could've gotten him for $450,000 three months ago. What the hell happened?" It makes him look bad. So he just said, "The hell with it. Take a chance." Wagner took the chance that I wouldn't have a good year. Do you think he knew I was going to go on a 44-game hitting streak? He took a chance and he lost.

PLAYBOY: How did that make you feel? Hurt, pissed off?

ROSE: No, I can't be hurt because one guy didn't like me. How can I be hurt?

PLAYBOY: Because he prevented you from having what could have been a continuous career—hometown boy, sticking with one uniform. . . .

ROSE: Well, that's another thing that was awful peculiar, as far as I'm concerned. Here's a guy, Wagner, that's an outsider. I'm 16 years a Cincinnati Red. Louis Nippert is a grand gentleman who owns the Cincinnati Reds, 89 percent, or something like that. I negotiate with all these guys I'm just telling you about. They pick me up at the airport, they drive me to their house, they negotiate and they drive me back to the airport. Mr. Busch, I negotiated with him four hours in the hospital where he was in for a hernia operation. So, finally, I asked Mr. Wagner, I said, "Mr. Wagner, why don't you let me sit down and talk to Mr. Nippert? He owns the team. He's from Cincinnati." You know what he says? "You can talk to him but not about money." Then doesn't it seem strange here that at no time did I ever get to talk to the Cincinnati Reds' owner? I spent 16 years, starting headfirst and playing anywhere they wanted me to play.

PLAYBOY: Did Nippert try to contact you?

ROSE: Mr. Nippert made a quote in the paper that no one ever asked him if I could talk to him. I never once got to negotiate about my contract. And I used to sit with him on the bus in Japan on the way to the ballpark and talk to him. Nice fellow, great. But that just goes to show you that in Cincinnati, Mr. Nippert has nothing to do with what goes on with the ball club. It's all Mr. Wagner.

PLAYBOY: Did you really want to finish out your career in Cincinnati?

ROSE: Sure. I used to think, especially when I went to St. Louis, I used to walk to the ballpark there. I used to dream about having a statue like they've got of Stan Musial down at the Reds' stadium. I probably screwed that up now.

PLAYBOY: How has all the fuss affected your wife? What is Karolyn like?

ROSE: Crazy. Funny personality. She's got a better personality than I got. She gets along better with people than anybody I've ever seen. Very outgoing. She'll go to a banquet, a baseball banquet, and before we leave, she'll have already kissed 10 guys goodbye. I mean, nice to see you again and you know. She's like a Jewish person. You know, all they do is kiss and shake hands.

PLAYBOY: Is that right?

ROSE: Yeah, you know it's true.

PLAYBOY: How do you keep your marriage together? Obviously, there have been rocky times.

ROSE: I don't worry about it. Nothing bothers me. If I'm home in bed, I sleep. If I'm at the ballpark, I play baseball. If I'm on my way to the ballpark, I worry about how I'm going to drive. Just whatever is going on, that's what I do. I don't worry about a bunch of things.

PLAYBOY: Is Karolyn a good baseball wife?

ROSE: She's a perfect baseball player's wife. Yeah. She went to a Cincinnati wrestling match and refereed the match between the Sheik and Bobo Brazil, and she came home, I swear to God—she had a sweat suit on, and she had, on one side, all the way down one side, nothing but blood on her pants. I mean, real blood.

PLAYBOY: She really got into it?

ROSE: Oh, man, they threw a chair and it just missed her. She had blood all over the damn place. She had fun.

Karolyn is understanding. She knows I go on road trips. She knows I am going to be away from home half the time. And she is a great mother, great housekeeper. She has got her own personality. She is outgoing, with a great personality. I guess marriagewise, her best enemies are her friends.

PLAYBOY: Why? Do they tattle on you?

ROSE: Because a lot of people have a tendency to think they know everything that goes on about me. They don't know nothing. So a lot of people always talk about hearsay. And they can't wait to tell her about hearsay. And hearsay can start more trouble than anything.

PLAYBOY: Karolyn told us that she has called you on the road and not been able to find you; she said she presumes you are screwing around. She seems to make a joke out of it.

ROSE: Well, she wouldn't make a joke about it. But she will take it. She won't say nothin'. She knows what I like for her to say or not to say.

PLAYBOY: Doesn't sound like much of an example as far as equality goes. What about kids? Do you think much about the example you set for them?

ROSE: You mean in baseball?

PLAYBOY: Not necessarily. How about other areas—such as drugs?

ROSE: I have never been on drugs.

PLAYBOY: No one ever passed a joint at a party?

ROSE: I have been around where there has been, but I never did. I always worry too much if I do, something like that and some guy with a camera takes my picture or they arrest me. I have got too much to lose for something like that.

PLAYBOY: Cocaine has become the playtime drug of the major leagues, according to a *Playboy* poll. What do you think about your teammates' using it?

ROSE: It is OK with me. You know all of my teammates don't do it. I hope the guys who I play against do it. I don't give a shit. It is just going to make my job easier.

PLAYBOY: What if you found out that particular teammates were doing it?

ROSE: I'd try to straighten them out. And I would try to make them see the light. I mean, I am no Elmer Gantry. Even though I don't hang in bars and drink or nothin'. I mean, I'd try to make them see the light. In everything you do, there is a right way to do something and a wrong way to do something. And just explain it to them the right way without . . . I forgot the word . . . you know I'm not—I don't disagree with every thing—I am not a pure person.

I guess I heard some of the guys I used to play with did cocaine or marijuana and I tried to talk to them, but, you know, I can think of a couple of guys that should have listened to me. 'Cause they are under 30 and they are out, they are gone now, looking for jobs.

PLAYBOY: A lot of guys say they need an amphetamine, or two or three before a game. What do you think?

ROSE: Well, a lot of guys might think that there are certain days you might need a greenie, an upper.

PLAYBOY: Would you take one?

ROSE: I might. I have taken stuff before.

PLAYBOY: What stuff?

ROSE: A painkiller when I had a bad arm. You know, just, it's not against the law to do that.

PLAYBOY: No. We mean something to pick you up.

ROSE: Well, that would get you up.

PLAYBOY: Have you taken greenies?

ROSE: Well, I might have taken a greenie last week. I mean, if you want to call it a greenie. I mean, if a doctor gives me a prescription of 30 diet pills, because I want to curb my appetite, so I can lose five pounds before I go to spring training, I mean, is that bad? I mean, a doctor is not going to write a prescription that is going to be harmful to my body.

PLAYBOY: It depends on your body.

ROSE: So a greenie can be a diet pill. That's all a greenie is, is a diet pill. Am

I right or wrong? I know I am right. An upper is nothing but a diet pill.

PLAYBOY: But would you use them for anything other than dieting?

ROSE: There might be some day when you played a doubleheader the night before and you go to the ballpark for a Sunday game and you just want to take a diet pill, just to mentally think you are up. You won't be up, but mentally you might think you are up.

PLAYBOY: Does that help your game?

ROSE: It won't help the game, but it will help you mentally. When you help yourself mentally, it might help your game.

PLAYBOY: You keep saying you *might* take a greenie. *Would* you? Have you?

ROSE: Yeah, I'd do it. I've done it.

PLAYBOY: Have you ever found homosexuality among baseball players?

ROSE: I have never heard anything mentioned about any homosexual in baseball. Either on my team or on the opposing team. So I know nothing about it. I read about it on football teams, but I don't know.

PLAYBOY: Psychologists have claimed that there are homosexual tendencies in everything athletes do—patting and hugging. Do you agree?

ROSE: I disagree with it. When the shot is from under the butt, it is just a good place to slap because of the way your hand is. Your hand is right there, I mean. In hockey, they do that, too. They also hit each other on the head. Well, most guys pat guys on the butt because they already passed them. We always hit each other on the hand. But you can't hit a guy on the hand if he has already walked by you, so the only place to hit—there is only one place to hit him. I disagree with that stuff. They want me to *be* that way, that is why they say that. You can't tell me. Because I hit more guys on the butt than anybody. They're going to say that I have homosexual ways. I just scream at them. I just say that is stupid.

PLAYBOY: There's just one more topic to talk about, and that's the paternity suit filed against you by Terryl Rubio, the young woman in Florida who says she had your baby.

ROSE: I ain't gonna say nothin' about that. You're wastin' your time even askin' me.

PLAYBOY: Why won't you talk about it?

ROSE: It's nobody's business. It's private.

PLAYBOY: Private? It's been on national television and in every newspaper in the country. And there are a lot of people in baseball who've told us that you spent much of last season traveling around with the girl while she was pregnant. You didn't seem to be hiding it then. How can it be so private? Do you deny the allegation now?

ROSE: Look, you can say anything you want, 'cause you ain't gonna get nothin' from me.

PLAYBOY: Then let's go on and finish the interview. There are still a couple of things we'd like to clear up.

ROSE: What the hell more do you need? I've already talked to you for weeks.

PLAYBOY: We know that; we made that clear to you from the outset. You're the one who has canceled appointments and stood us up.

ROSE: Well, it's finished. I don't want to talk to fuckin' reporters anymore.

PLAYBOY: Why? You made such a point of how you always cooperate with the press.

ROSE: Look, I know what you're gonna ask me and I ain't gonna talk about that shit. So why bother me? That's personal shit, man.

PLAYBOY: So the interview's over?

ROSE: Fuckin' right it is.

 May 2000

A candid conversation with Charlie Hustle about the gambling controversy that won't die, where baseball's gone wrong and why Hillary Clinton is one sexy babe

Pete Rose was a linedrive–hitting, headfirst-sliding Cincinnati Reds rookie in 1963, when the team's veterans hung the derisive nickname Charlie Hustle on his cocky crewcut head. He has been pissing off people ever since. Every fan knows Rose's claim to fame: 4256 base hits, 67 more than Ty Cobb had. But even nonfans know his claim to shame: the charge that he bet on baseball games while managing the Reds. That's what keeps Rose out of the Hall of Fame and keeps him hustling to defend his name even as he sells it to anybody willing to ante up and get in line: Get your red-hot autographed bats, balls, cards, caps, jerseys and posters!

Rose's enemies include baseball commissioner Bud Selig, former commissioner Fay Vincent and baseball inquisitors John Dowd (the lawyer whose report on Rose's gambling helped get the Hit King exiled in 1989) and Jim Gray, whose World Series Rose-grilling made headlines 10 years later. But if his shit list is long, it's a Post-it note compared with the roster of Rose fans who flock to his autograph signings or add their names to the cyberscroll at Sportcut.com, the website that set an Internet record for hits for a sports site on the day Rose's Hall of Fame petition appeared there. "One thing about Pete," says an old National League rival who once duked it out with him, "he's overcome his shyness."

The son of a bank clerk who played semi-pro football, Rose won the 1963 National League Rookie of the Year award and went on to win back-to-back batting titles in 1968 and 1969. In 1973 he hit .338 and was the league's most valuable player. Next came World Series titles for Cincinnati's Big Red Machine in 1975 (when Rose was Series MVP) and 1976. Through it all, baseball's player of the decade for the 1970s tooted his horn like Miles Davis. You don't have to look up Rose's numbers—just ask him and he'll spew: 16-time All-Star who set an NL record with a 44-game hitting streak in 1978, signed the next year with Philadelphia for $800,000, the highest salary in the game, and hit .331. He retired in 1986 with a .303 career average, 2165 runs scored (fourth-highest in baseball history), 746 doubles (second) and 11 major league batting records, including hits, games and, tellingly, most games in which his team won.

There are no official records for bets placed, expletives uttered or Baseball Annies nailed.

Vulgar? Fifty-nine-year-old Rose favors gold chains and sweatpants with mesh pockets, the better to show off the fist-sized wad of bills he carries around. Before a radio appearance with Howard Stern (a man he calls a "fucking genius"), he sat in Stern's waiting room and mused about "all the tits that have been in here." You can call Rose crass or an ass and you'll get little argument from the lords of baseball, who cringe at publicity stunts like his annual autograph-hustling event at Cooperstown on Hall of Fame weekend. But, vulgar or not, you're talking about one of the toughest, winningest SOBs in sports, an overgrown Little Leaguer who parlayed sharp eyes, steel-cable wrists and the sheer cussedness of 10 mean drunks into a record that may stand forever. Last winter, when stats guru Bill James crunched the numbers and estimated all active Players' chances to catch Rose, every major leaguer wound up with the same chance—zero—except the Yankees' Derek Jeter, who James figures has a one percent shot at surpassing the Hit King.

Number 14 was a showboat, but he was also baseball's number one gamer. When he bowled over Indians catcher Ray Fosse in the 1970 All-Star game, effectively ending Fosse's career and leaving him with arm and shoulder pain that has dogged him for 30 years, there was one good reason. It won the game. After signing with the underachieving Phillies in 1979, he helped lead them to the World Series. Never was Rose's nose for the spotlight more evident than in the last game of that 1980 Series, when Phils catcher Bob Boone let a pop foul frog-hop out of his mitt, only to watch first baseman Rose snatch it and squeeze it, killing the Royals.

Such men can't retire. They need action, competition. From 1984 to 1989 Rose managed the Reds, and he gambled. On football, he says. On baseball, lawyer Dowd and commissioner Bart Giamatti said. In 1989 Rose signed his own death warrant, a lifetime suspension that states, "Nothing in this agreement shall be deemed either an admission or a denial by Peter Edward Rose of the allegation that he bet on any major league baseball game." He remained eligible for the Hall of Fame, but in 1991—the year before he would be eligible for induction—the Hall's directors passed a new rule: Suspended players were no longer allowed. Rose felt double-crossed, and he charges baseball with "brainwashing" the public about him. "Admit I bet on baseball?" he says. "Forget it."

The fans are on his side. They voted Rose onto baseball's All-Century Team, giving him the last outfield spot over Roberto Clemente and giving Selig a PR headache. That led to Jim Gray's televised grilling of Rose, which backfired on Gray and made Rose more popular than ever. Even Bill Clinton called on baseball to let Pete back in, saying, "I'd like to see it worked out. God knows he's paid a price." Soon Rose, class act that he is, lamented that he and the president had both suffered horribly in recent years—along with O.J. Simpson. Selig was unmoved, announcing in February that "there is not a scintilla of give" in baseball's hardline position.

Who is Pete Rose? As his lawyers huddled with baseball's lawyers to hash out his fate, we sent writer Mark Ribowsky to meet the Hit King in New York and Florida. Ribowsky's report follows:

"Rose opened the door to his hotel room, clad in a natty gray sports jacket and tan slacks, a little piece of toilet paper stuck to a shaving cut on his chin. His agent, Warren Greene, a man who looks both cuddly and beleaguered, tended to the cut before we piled into a limousine for the short drive to Michael Jordan's restaurant in Grand Central Station, where Rose met with investors of Sportcut.com.

"In the limo he wondered about the point spread in that day's Monday Night Football game. Later, after two hours of mingling with businessmen, his mind was on the models who had been hired to stand around in polo shirts and tight pants. 'I liked the one with the big Jewish ass,' he said.

"What makes him tick? Pride, anger, sex, self-righteousness, money, money and money. We began with a topic I was sure he'd enjoy."

PLAYBOY: The long, loud ovation you got when you were introduced as a member of the All-Century Team—was that as good as sex?

ROSE: Playing baseball is as good as sex. The sixth game of the 1975 World Series against Boston was like sex. It don't get better than that. But this was close—getting a bigger ovation than Hank Aaron in Atlanta is like outdoing God in heaven. When Hank told me, "Hey, you got a bigger hand than me," I said, "Hank, you throw out the first ball here once a month. They're tired of seeing you." Imagine what it would have been like if that game was in Cincinnati. They would have clapped for 15 minutes.

PLAYBOY: Did Commissioner Bud Selig say anything to you that night?

ROSE: I thanked him for letting me be part of the celebration, and he said, "It's a great pleasure to have you with us." He told my son Tyler that he was always a fan of Pete Rose. So there's nothing personal there. I don't dislike Bud Selig. I didn't dislike Bart Giamatti. I got along with Giamatti, and I think that if Bart was still around I'd be reinstated, because he was a fair man.

PLAYBOY: Are you still mad at NBC's Jim Gray for his interview that night?

ROSE: Jim Gray is a liar. He told Mike Schmidt to tell me that if I did that interview, it would get me into the Hall of Fame. So Mike tells me, "He says he has inside information from the commissioner's office that will help you."

PLAYBOY: But all Gray did was press you to admit you had bet on baseball.

ROSE: It's not like I haven't been asked those questions hundreds of times, but he was too persistent about it. It's been 10 years, Jim, let it go. Let a guy enjoy the All-Century Team. But he attacked, and to make it worse, the next day he told the press I knew he was going to talk about gambling. That's a lie, and when he said I wasn't mad at him when it was over, that's another fucking lie, and he knows it. After the interview I looked at him and said, "You fucking treat a friend like that? How in the fuck can you say I'm a friend?" and walked away. He was stunned by that. Then Craig Sager, the other on-field reporter for NBC, comes over and he has tears in his eyes. He says, "Pete, I've got to apologize for my profession. That was the worst thing I've ever heard, and I couldn't work the rest of the night if I didn't get this off my chest."

PLAYBOY: Sager denies saying any such thing.

ROSE: Maybe he's scared for his job. That makes me think, Craig, why can't you be a man about it? I mean, nobody's going to fire Craig Sager because he knew Jim Gray was a disgrace.

PLAYBOY: Any advice for Gray?

ROSE: Forget the goddamn attitude and just do the job.

PLAYBOY: Suppose Selig continues your suspension but offers to make you eligible for the Hall of Fame. Would you agree to that?

ROSE: Baseball would be committing suicide to do that. Going into the Hall of Fame is not going to let me make a living. I'm not knocking the Hall of Fame—my kids would think that's the greatest thing in the world, because after 10 years they'd see their daddy for what he was, a great ballplayer. All they've heard their whole lives is what a louse I am. But is having a plaque on a wall in Cooperstown going to make me a couple of million dollars a year? I'm a baseball person, a baseball teacher. I want to get back on the field. I'm the best ambassador baseball has, and I can't step on a big-league field.

PLAYBOY: But you clear more than $1 million a year from memorabilia shows and the like. How can you moan about money?

ROSE: I'm not moaning. I can't moan and whine and be bitter and say baseball fucked me and created all my problems, because I'm the one who called the bookmakers and made the bets. I wrote the checks to the bookmakers. But the fact that I make good now is irrelevant. I never see my family. I'm always on an airplane going somewhere.

PLAYBOY: Still hustling. You make frequent appearances at casinos. Given that you were suspended for gambling, isn't that inappropriate?

ROSE: Are you telling me to starve? Why should I stay away from casinos? Bart Giamatti told me to go and "reconfigure" my life, and I've done that. I don't hang around with them sleazeballs no more. Yes, I still go to the track. I enjoy it and it's legal. I go to casinos, but I don't gamble in them. Hell, even if I did play blackjack or roulette, which I don't, I wasn't suspended for playing blackjack, was I? I can see where people would be disturbed if I walked into a sports book in a Las Vegas casino and started making bets. But do I do that? Never. Last October I went to Atlantic City to be in a show with all the living players who have 3000 hits, and people said, "How can you do a show in Atlantic City?" What the hell was I supposed to do, stiff Hank Aaron and Willie Mays and all the guys in the 3000-hit club who were there? How can you have a fucking 3000-hit show if the Hit King ain't there?

Why are people alarmed if I go to Atlantic City? Because it looks bad? Tell me this: Did it look bad that a couple of the 3000-hit guys were drunk and playing blackjack the night before that show? Nobody ever sees me loaded. I don't drink or smoke. And if I look bad going to casinos, why do major league ballparks have casino signs all over the place? But I'll make you a deal: If baseball doesn't want me in that environment, give me a fucking job in baseball. Until then, I have a family to support.

PLAYBOY: Pure baseball question: Which team would win a Series between the 1975-1976 Red Machine and the 1998-1999 Yankees?

ROSE: How many guys on the Yankees are going to the Hall of Fame? Bernie Williams, Derek Jeter? Who else? Nobody. How many are in the Hall of Fame from the Big Red Machine? Morgan, Perez, Bench. I belong. And if guys like Pee Wee Reese start making it at shortstop, what about Dave Concepcion? If you gave our team the Yankees' pitching staff, we'd have won 135 games a year. But then, give the Yankees our starting lineup and they'd win 135. The real difference is in the competition. The game's good now, but it's weaker. The pitching is terrible. Most teams have a good stopper because you only have to develop one guy. But where are the middle relievers? Look closely and you'll see that it's the middle innings when most of the runs are scored. How many teams have a good guy leading up to the stopper? Not even the Yankees. It's because pitchers aren't pitchers anymore; they're $35 million investments.

These days, if a pitcher gets a kink in his elbow, they're not going to let him throw a fucking pitch until they find out what it is. So nobody throws hard anymore. We used to go into Houston and see Larry Dierker, Don Wilson, Jim Ray and Dick Farrell, and all of them threw 92 or 93 miles an hour. We'd go to Los Angeles and face Koufax, Drysdale, Bill Singer, Don Sutton. In San Francisco it was Billy Pierce, Gaylord Perry, Jack Sanford, Bob Bolin. All blowers. Now there's maybe two hard throwers on a staff. The rest throw screwballs or palmballs or forkballs. I could take a bat up there today and rock them guys. I could have rocked the old-timers, too. They say Walter Johnson and Christy Mathewson pitched both ends of doubleheaders. Well, I used to excel in the seventh or eighth inning, when the pitcher was tired. That's why you can't compare me to Ty Cobb. Would Cobb have had a .367 lifetime batting average if he came up in 1963 and played till 1986? That guy never faced a relief pitcher.

PLAYBOY: Do you get all the credit you deserve?

ROSE: I played more games than anybody and got more hits. Yet all I hear is that Rickey Henderson is the greatest leadoff hitter ever. Why? Because he hits home runs? I got over 1300 RBI. Check Rickey Henderson's RBI, see how many he's got. [Editor's note: The answer is 1020 through 1999.]

How could I not be in the top 50 of ESPN's Greatest Athletes of the Century? Mark Spitz? That guy worked two weeks! I worked 24 years. They say I was just a singles hitter, but I'm sixth in history for total bases.

PLAYBOY: Quick—describe the Eric Show pitch you hit to set the record.

ROSE: Fastball, down and in.

PLAYBOY: Who was the best pitcher you faced?

ROSE: Juan Marichal. Bob Gibson was the toughest competitor. Koufax was the hardest thrower. Think of all the Hall of Famers I faced. I got 77 hits off Phil Niekro and 30 against his brother Joe—I got one forty-second of all my hits against one family! I had a five-for-five against Warren Spahn, a five-for-five off Phil Niekro and a five-for-five off Gaylord Perry. That's 15-for-15 off three Hall of Famers.

PLAYBOY: Did Perry load it up on you?

ROSE: Sure. Four out of my five hits in that game were off spitballs. There's a guy who cheated for 20 years, and he's in the Hall. Other guys loaded it up, too. Sutton cut the ball, and I'll tell you, when I watch Greg Maddux' ball move, that's not normal. Kevin Brown's ball movement isn't normal. It looks like they're doing something to the ball, but I'm not saying they're cheaters. I never say someone's cheating unless I know it. Their balls have so much movement that it's abnormal. On the other hand, take Pedro Martinez. This guy is a freak. He has six pitches he throws for strikes from about six different angles. Tony Gwynn, the best hitter in baseball today, is overmatched against Martinez. I think I'd be overmatched against Martinez. I really don't think I could hit him, and I've never said that about a pitcher.

PLAYBOY: What's the biggest misconception about Pete Rose?

ROSE: That I was suspended for betting on baseball. Under baseball's Rule 21 you can be banned for three things: bribing an umpire, betting on baseball [specifically, on one's own team; betting on baseball in general carries a one-year suspension] and associating with undesirables. In the agreement I signed, it says there's no finding that Pete Rose bet on baseball. What is so hard to understand about that? Ask any fifth grader what "no finding" means. It means I didn't do it. When Bart Giamatti and Peter Ueberroth, who was the outgoing commissioner, summoned me to New York that spring, I admitted to them that I had bet $2000 on the San Francisco 49ers against the Cincinnati Bengals in the last Super Bowl. They said, "We could care less about that." Then they told me to lie. I'm getting ready to leave and I say, "Gentlemen, I left spring training to come here, and when a manager leaves spring training for a day, people want to know where the fuck he went. What do I tell 'em?" They say, "Tell the press the new commissioner wanted to talk to you about things in the best interest of baseball." Now to me, that means I went to New York to help the new commissioner get off on the right foot. From the beginning, they were lying about the case.

PLAYBOY: Your old teammate Johnny Bench has said he doubts your side of the story. He said, "If Pete didn't do it, why doesn't he say he didn't do it?"

ROSE: Because I couldn't! I was under a gag order—I'd agreed not to talk about it. It hurt when Bench said that, because I took Johnny under my wing when he came up to the Reds. But it became a jealousy situation. Johnny Bench is jealous that I was more popular than he was. He's jealous that they named a street outside Cinergy Field Pete Rose Way, not Johnny Bench Way. Johnny has a big ego, and he's kind of pissed off that people like me. The next time Johnny Bench does a radio or TV show, someone should ask him, "Did you ever make an illegal bet on a football game?" See what he says.

PLAYBOY: Is gambling a danger to society and to baseball?

ROSE: I don't think it should be a crime. I've got a 15-year-old son, Tyler, and a 10-year-old daughter, Cara Chea, and if they were going to do one of the following things—be an alcoholic, be a drug offender, beat their wife or their husband, or gamble—I hope they would gamble. Ty Cobb and Tris Speaker are in the Hall of Fame and they were known gamblers. Leo Durocher associated with known gamblers and he's in the Hall. Guys in other sports have been suspended for a year for gambling—look at Paul Hornung and Alex Karras in football. If Bart Giamatti were smart, he would have fined me on the day I was called to New York. People would have accepted that. I would have accepted it, and the whole thing would have ended.

PLAYBOY: Do you think Giamatti was biased against you?

ROSE: Look at who Bart Giamatti was. When he was president of Yale, he was kind of a powermonger. He wrote papers saying that absolute power ain't so bad. So here's a guy with that mentality taking over as commissioner of baseball, and who was the number one guy in the game? You're looking at him. But baseball didn't need me. I wasn't a player anymore, I was a manager. Do you think I'd have been suspended if I was a player? No fucking way. Look at Albert Belle. He wrote $40,000 in money orders to bookmakers during the season, and what did baseball do? Nothing.

With me, it was easy for baseball to say, Let's take the household name and straighten his ass up. Funny how they never say that to a guy doing drugs. If I had been busted for drugs instead of gambling, I'd still be managing the Reds and baseball would be paying for my rehab.

PLAYBOY: You call baseball's Dowd report a biased "prosecutor's brief," but Dowd didn't invent the 29 checks that wound up with bookmakers, or the fingerprints on betting slips.

ROSE: I'm not going to tell you I didn't bet. I did—I bet on football. Just look when those checks were mailed. They went out in the winter. I was making my payoffs for football games. The betting slips they got are football betting slips.

PLAYBOY: One that was dated April 9, 1987 features baseball games. One of the games is listed as Cin at Mont—Reds at Expos—with a W after Montreal.

ROSE: Was there a circle? The team you bet on would have a circle around it.

PLAYBOY: Isn't that what that W means, that you'd be betting on Cincinnati?

ROSE: No. How can that be? Who's the favorite? Who's the underdog? That's not a real betting slip. They also said I bet the same amount on every game, $2000. But you can't bet two dimes on baseball games because every game, from what I'm told, is different. Depending on who's pitching, sometimes you have to put up more than two grand to win two grand. That's how the odds work in baseball.

PLAYBOY: The fingerprints on the betting slips?

ROSE: The piece of paper they're telling you about, with those games they say I bet on—they say it has one thumbprint of mine. One print. But would a betting slip that I did a lot of writing on have one fucking thumbprint on it? Anyway, my handwriting experts say all those betting slips are so faded and discolored, they wouldn't stand up in court. I'm not saying they were forged. I'll leave that to my experts. I am saying I didn't write them. Who did? Someone who has no knowledge of baseball. Just look at the date of that Reds-Expos game and you'll see it was Montreal at Cincinnati, not Cincinnati at Montreal. You think I'd bet on a game and I don't know who the fucking home team is?

PLAYBOY: Dowd believed he caught you in a lie over a $34,000 check written in March 1987. He said you claimed it was to cover losses on the 1987 Super Bowl and NCAA basketball championships, but the NCAA tournament began the same day as the date on the check.

ROSE: What's his point? That I was making payoffs on baseball? It was March—was I betting on spring training games? Is John Dowd so dumb he can't figure out that I was betting on college basketball all winter? Does he think I only bet the NCAA tournament? He didn't catch me in no lie.

PLAYBOY: Then why did you sign the agreement with Giamatti and not fight on in court?

ROSE: My lawyers and I were preparing to go to federal court when baseball called us. They wanted to suspend me, and they wanted me to wait 22 years before I could apply for reinstatement. We said, "You're crazy." So the next morning they came back and said 11 years. Again we said no way. That afternoon they said "OK, make it one year." I could still have gone to court, but I would have also had to spend another half a million dollars in legal fees. I was happy to get the fucking thing over with, because for six fucking months every time I left my house there was a camera in my face. I'm surprised I didn't get radiation burn. So we said OK, a year. I signed the agreement with no finding that I bet on baseball—the same finding I would have gotten in court. As far as its being a lifetime suspension, maybe I misread that. Maybe I misconstrued it. I never saw it as permanent. I looked at it as a chance to come back in one year. A lot of people go to prison for life, but then they apply for parole and get out, right?

PLAYBOY: Are you a compulsive gambler?

ROSE: Ten years ago I asked myself, Could I have a problem? I went to Gamblers Anonymous. I went to see a doctor. Then I went on *The Phil Donahue Show* and said I had a problem, which is what that doctor told me. I didn't believe it, and it was a big mistake. From then on, if I was anywhere near a racetrack or a casino someone would see me and go, "Uh-oh, what's he doing here?"

But I knew I wasn't a compulsive gambler. I told that doctor, "I've never taken my gas or phone or electric bill money or my house payment to the track." You may think I'm a fucking genius in baseball, but I'm like everybody else who bets on sports. Nobody wins. You bet for enjoyment, for pleasure, for entertainment, but not to make money.

You know why I go to the track? Because I used to go with the only person I've ever idolized, my dad. He would take me to the track on Saturday mornings when I was a kid. My dad wasn't a compulsive gambler, he was a recreational gambler. So am I.

PLAYBOY: You had trouble with the commissioner in 1988—a 30-day suspension and a $10,000 fine—for bumping umpire Dave Pallone during a rhubarb. Did you know at the time that Pallone was gay?

ROSE: Yeah, I knew. We all knew. Something like that gets around, just like you know if somebody in baseball has HIV. But I didn't care that he was gay. I cared that he made a horseshit call at first base that cost me a goddamn ball game, and when I was arguing with him he scratched me with his fingernail and cut my face. That's when I pushed him. I should have killed the son of a bitch. Dave Pallone—that was another fight baseball didn't want. After that, he got into trouble. [Accused in a sex scandal, Pallone was cleared but forced to leave the game.] Giamatti gave him six figures to retire because he didn't want to fire a gay umpire and take on the gay activists.

PLAYBOY: Let's say Selig reinstates you. Do you call Reds general manager Jim Bowden and ask for your old managing job back?

ROSE: I'm not gonna call nobody. I'll wait and see. But there are a couple teams right where I live that need somebody like me in the worst way, because they have bad attitudes. I'm talking about the Dodgers and the Angels. Those teams have too much talent to be as bad as they've been, and I'm a hell of an attitude changer.

PLAYBOY: You had a good quote about the Cubs' losing ways.

ROSE: God told the Cubs, "Don't do anything until I get back." They're a good example of the attitude I'm talking about. The Cubs have great fans, but I think the fans are partly responsible for that team's demise. Cubs fans go to see the Cubs play. Reds fans go to see the Reds win. Cubs fans have been through losing so long that they go to the game to have fun, sit in the bleachers, take their shirts off and look at the ivy. When you don't get pissed off about losing, you get in a rut, and the Cubs have been in that rut for a long time. I loved it when Don Baylor took over as manager and said it's great to be part of such a great tradition. What tradition?

PLAYBOY: Could you step in and manage a team tomorrow?

ROSE: I've already picked out my coaching staff: Doug Flynn, Tony Perez, Dave Parker and Wally Horsman [who operates the Bucky Dent Baseball School].

PLAYBOY: Why didn't the Reds give your son Pete Jr. a longer look?

ROSE: That is a mystery to me and to Petey. He was called up from the minors for two weeks at the end of the 1997 season. He started one game, on Labor Day, which was heavily promoted. The Reds had sold 12,000 season tickets that year. They had 34,000 for that game. Petey got a base hit and made two good plays at third base. Now, wouldn't you think he made enough money for the Reds that day, and showed enough promise, to be invited to spring training the next year? But he wasn't. My son is 6'2", 240 pounds, solid as a rock, a gamer, a guy everybody loves, a guy who hits .300 every year.

A writer from Dayton told me that after Pete made an error in another game, Jack McKeon, the manager, said, "That's all I need to see of this Rose kid." Petey thinks it wasn't because of any error but because he got to the ballpark earlier than McKeon did, and McKeon thought he was making him look bad, being in the clubhouse before the manager.

PLAYBOY: You have problems with McKeon? He was the National League manager of the year.

ROSE: The problem McKeon may have with me is that Jim Bowden said he'd love to hire me as the manager if I was eligible. Maybe McKeon sees me as a threat. I hope he's not so shallow that he held that against my son.

PLAYBOY: Do you still talk to Pete Jr.'s mom, your first wife, Karolyn?

ROSE: Not since I had to get a court order to take Petey to the 1980 World Series. We were going through a divorce, which Karolyn didn't want, and that was her way of getting back at me. She thought that I was sleeping around.

PLAYBOY: You mean you weren't?

ROSE: When I was 22, 23, 24 years old, I made mistakes with my family life. But to do everything people said I did, I would have needed three dicks. I was never the type to go out looking for pussy in every town. If I liked somebody in the town I was in, I would take her to the next town so I didn't have to go out looking. It's better to know who you're sleeping with. You won't catch a disease. One time a girl sued me for paternity. Not the one in Tampa—that was legitimate. This one was in Franklin, Ohio, and I didn't even fuck this girl! How can you knock up a girl you don't even fuck?

PLAYBOY: You once noted nastily that Karolyn had gone from a size two to a size 20.

ROSE: All I was saying is that someone who wants to stay married to me should care about her appearance. That's a matter of self-respect and respect for me. Look at me. I could still play. I'm not sexist, and what I like most in a woman isn't physical. It's the way she carries herself. That's how you tell if she's confident, bright, intelligent. I think Hillary Clinton is sexy. She gets better and better. She'd make a hell of a president. Same thing goes for Dole's wife. I like [Texas Senator] Kay Bailey Hutchison. I like Barbara Walters.

PLAYBOY: Barbara Walters is sexy?

ROSE: I find all kinds of women sexy. I'm not queer, so why wouldn't I?

PLAYBOY: There's a story that you went to a strip joint in Mexico, jumped onstage and had sex with one of the strippers.

ROSE: My first year with the Reds, we went to Mexico City during spring training. It wasn't a strip club. I've never been in a strip club. It was a bar. I was 22. I was there with some of my teammates, and in the next room was the manager, Fred Hutchinson, a real tough son of a bitch. He saw me and said, "What the fuck are you doing here, kid?" I was scared to death of the man, but I said, "What the fuck are you doing here?" And from that night on, he liked my style. That's why he started me as a rookie. But public sex? Shit, no.

PLAYBOY: The Reds' veterans weren't too crazy about you.

ROSE: They had Don Blasingame at second, a guy they really liked. All of a sudden Hutchinson puts this young, brash rookie in the lineup. I'd already gotten a reputation—in spring training we played the Yankees, and Mickey Mantle and Whitey Ford called me Charlie Hustle. The name got in all the papers and it stuck. So these guys didn't want to associate with me. The only guys that would were the black players, guys like Frank Robinson and Vada Pinson. I was actually called into the Reds' front office and told to stop hanging around with the blacks. This came from Mr. William O. DeWitt Sr., the owner, and Mr. Phil Seghi, the assistant general manager. I thought that was stupid. You win and lose as a team; what does a guy's skin color have to do with it?

PLAYBOY: Yet you're still friendly with former Reds owner Marge Schott, who referred to her "million-dollar niggers" after she bought the Reds in 1985.

ROSE: I don't think Marge Schott is a racist. I think Marge don't like anybody. She thinks everyone's against her. Is Marge a Nazi because someone was at her house and found a swastika in a dresser drawer? Because the person who found it is Jewish, he said, "What's up with this?" Marge said a veteran had given it to her as a souvenir, but the press made it sound like there were swastikas all over her damn house.

PLAYBOY: What about her saying, "Hitler was OK at the beginning. He just went too far"?

ROSE: That's just Marge. Hitler was too extreme, we all know that, but Marge is harmless.

PLAYBOY: OK, Marge Schott's not a racist. How about John Rocker, who, during his infamous *Sports Illustrated* tirade against foreigners, single mothers and "queers with AIDS," called one of his Braves teammates a "fat monkey"?

ROSE: I don't know John Rocker. But from watching his teammates talk about him, and from guys who knew him in the minor leagues, I don't think he's a racist. Nobody ever said he was a racist. I mean, are you a racist part-time? Here is a young kid who made some stupid statements he probably regrets, but he didn't expect the writer to put them in the article. I don't know if what the writer did to him is fair or not, but he may have done a lot of harm. I don't know if Rocker can weather what happened. I hope he can. But he didn't pitch all that good after taking on the people in New York in the playoffs. You really have to be a special type of person, mentally, to go through that and keep your cool. I know, because the same thing happened to me in 1973 when the Reds played the Mets in the playoffs. I took the entire brunt of New York in that series, especially after I had that fight with Bud Harrelson, which started after I slid hard into him to break up a double play and he called me a cocksucker. I told him, "I don't go that way." They wanted to kill me in New York. But I hit a home run in the 12th inning to win the next game, and I think I was the only guy alive who could have done that, to play the whole city of New York and beat them. That could really fuck up his head.

PLAYBOY: Who's going to win it all this season?

ROSE: The Mets. Most improved of anyone. They were good last year, and getting Mike Hampton, a real good lefthanded pitcher, will put them over the top. Even though they signed Todd Zeile to play first base, I think Mike Piazza is going to play there eventually, because it'll save wear and tear on his body. He was all beaten up last year. Obviously, you have to consider the Yankees, because they've really earned that respect. And now that they signed a new contract with Madison Square Garden, the money from that will allow them to fill in any needs. The teams that played good last year will be good again. The Braves will be good. The Indians will be good. But the Red Sox aren't any better than they were at the end of last season, and they had a lot of guys that had career years. And even though the Astros lost Hampton to the Mets, it ain't gonna be a lock for the Reds. Don't forget they lost Juan Guzman. If anything, the Cardinals will be better because they picked up some needed pitching. They brought Andy Benes back. I just want to see Mark McGwire get a shot at a World Series. He and Sammy Sosa are guys we need to see in October. The game needs to see that.

PLAYBOY: How would you rate yourself as a parent? Your first wife has said you found it extremely hard to show emotion.

ROSE: But my kids knew I loved them. Maybe I missed Petey's Little League games when I was on the road, but I can't think of any ballplayer who was as close to his son. When the team was at home, Petey went to the ballpark every fucking night. He was there a lot more than Ken Griffey Jr. was. Looking back, I think there's only one person I ever cheated: my daughter Fawn. And I wouldn't have cheated her if she'd been a boy. I couldn't take her to the ballpark. A girl couldn't go into the clubhouse, and how could I leave her sitting alone in the stands? What if somebody kidnapped her? But I didn't miss my little girl's graduation from college. I flew in on a private plane from St. Louis for it, and now Fawn is going to work for me in my restaurant in Los Angeles. I'm a better dad now—hugging and kissing my kids, telling them I love them. I never used to do that. A man has to be tough to survive, but he needs a gentle streak in him, too, or he'll end up miserable.

PLAYBOY: Ever cry?

ROSE: Twice. Once in 1970, when my father died. The other time was when I got my record-setting hit and was standing on first base, drinking in that nine-minute ovation, thinking about what my dad would have thought.

PLAYBOY: You've wept only twice in your 59 years?

ROSE: Actually, it was twice for a long time. Now I can get teary watching my daughter act. [Cara Chea, 10, has acted under the name Chea Courtney on *Melrose Place* and the daytime soap *Passions*.] God, her concentration and work ethic are just like mine were. Or I'll cry watching Tyler play basketball—he's 5'7" and can palm the ball. I cry at movies. I was so pissed off when the girl died in *Patch Adams*! I'm mellowing in age.

PLAYBOY: You once introduced your current wife to reporters by saying, "You would probably call her 'Wow,' but I call her Carol." Aside from the obvious, what attracted you to Carol?

ROSE: Her personality. She's built like an athlete, too, and she's a great mother.

PLAYBOY: People might be surprised that your marriage has lasted 15 years if they remember Roger Kahn's 1991 *Playboy* article, in which Carol said that she was "lonely" and had "ambivalent sexual feelings" toward you. When Kahn said she could always leave you, Carol said, "Pete would kill me."

ROSE: Bullshit. I have a great marriage. Roger Kahn never talked to my wife. Next time you see Roger Kahn, ask him why he stiffed me for $25,000. He wrote a book with me called *Pete Rose: My Story*, a bullshit title because it was more his story than mine. The publisher paid the advance for the book but sent too much by mistake, and took the difference from what I got. So we went to Roger to get what he owed me, and he had pissed it all away. [Editor's note: Through his attorney, Kahn declined to discuss his relationship to Rose.]

Roger Kahn is yesterday's news. He's lived his whole life on one thing, *The Boys of Summer*, and he's got nothing else. Me and another writer, Peter Golenbock, were the only two guys at his son's wake.

PLAYBOY: Speaking of sportswriters, what do you think of women reporters in the locker room?

ROSE: I don't care if you wear a skirt or pants if you're a good journalist. It never bothered me if a woman was there to do a job. What bothered me was if she didn't care about writing sports but just wanted to be the first woman in there. Don't come in looking for trouble, trying to make guys feel uncomfortable. I think that's what happened with Samantha Stevenson, who sued baseball to be let into our locker room when I was with the Phillies. That girl had a mission. She even wrote an article about the size of basketball players' cocks. Is that all she had to do, stand around and look at cocks all day?

PLAYBOY: Stevenson had a few choice words about you after she interviewed you for *Playboy* in 1979. She said it was you who seemed fixated on cocks, asking her, "How does it feel to have all those cocks staring you in the face? Doesn't it make you embarrassed? Do you like it?"

ROSE: Samantha Stevenson's credibility went out the window because of what she did to Julius Erving. She trapped him, didn't she? She had his baby [now tennis pro Alexandra Stevenson]. Does that speak well of her?

PLAYBOY: Your defender Bill Clinton was almost brought down by Monica Lewinsky. Was he wrong to lie about what they did in the White House?

ROSE: It's not acceptable to lie, but the press went too far. It wasn't anybody's business. There are very few people without skeletons in their closets. The only difference between me and President Clinton on one hand, and everybody else on the other, is that our skeletons are all out. So unless you're a saint about sex, or gambling, you'd better keep your fucking mouth shut.

PLAYBOY: You haven't been a saint, but plenty of baseball fans adore you. Has it been hell to be out of the game?

ROSE: No. I love baseball, but when I took the spikes off, the game was over for me. There was always more to my life. I'll tell you a story: It was 1967 and I was going to Vietnam, me and Joe DiMaggio. The only reason I agreed to the trip was to meet DiMaggio. We went to visit American military advisors in the Mekong Delta. So there we were, me and Joe DiMaggio, in the middle of the jungle, with the fucking war going on around us. I looked up and saw tracer bullets being fired out of helicopters, rat-a-tat-tat. Then the copters landed and they began loading bags, big black bags. They were body bags, with dead Marines inside. The bags were piled up in the street; I counted 21 of them. You see something like that and the importance of baseball disappears in a hurry.

PLAYBOY: Is that why you've sold so many of your awards, trophies and mementos? Don't they mean anything to you?

ROSE: Go take a look around my restaurant in Florida, the Pete Rose Ballpark Café. What do you see? World Series rings, silver bats—it's all there. I love taking sportswriters there and saying, "Want to look at all the stuff I sold to pay my gambling debts?" I keep things that have special meaning: my first Gold Glove, my first batting championship trophy. The rest, I could care less. When I set the hits record, the story went around that I wore nine different uniforms that night and sold them all. You've heard that, haven't you?

PLAYBOY: We heard it and believed it.

ROSE: I wore three uniforms. One went to the Hall of Fame, one went to Marge Schott and the other I kept. The real story is never as bad as the writers want it to be.

O.J. SIMPSON

A candid conversation with the best-liked, best-paid football player ever

Only a few weeks before we went to press, the national guessing game surrounding O.J. Simpson's football future had at last been resolved. Simpson, who last June announced he'd retire if he weren't traded from the Buffalo Bills to a west coast team, changed his mind at the last moment. With the pro-season opener a day away—and with the Bills having failed to trade him—Simpson signed the most lucrative player contract in the history of U.S. football. For him, it meant he'd receive a reported $2,500,000 if he completes three more seasons of autumnal glory; for the Bills and the National Football League, it meant that football's most spectacular performer—and leading gate attraction—would continue to dazzle the sporting public.

Quite simply, football has never before seen the likes of Orenthal James Simpson. Combining the speed and deerlike grace of a Gale Sayers and the durability and determination of a Jim Brown, Simpson has by now solidly established himself as the premier running back of his time—and perhaps of all time. Says Howard Cosell, "Certainly, O.J. has every skill a truly great running back needs. He's got the most spontaneous reflexes of anyone I've ever seen, he has an uncanny ability to lead his blockers and find that extra inch that will allow him to knife through, he seems to have instant acceleration and he also has the strength to break tackles. I wouldn't venture to call anyone the greatest running back of all time, because there are too many intangibles involved, but I'll say this much about O.J. Simpson: I've never seen any man come to the position with greater gifts."

O.J.'s career credentials back up that assessment. Born in San Francisco in 1947, he became an all-American during both of his varsity seasons at the University of Southern California and set a number of NCAA running records to close out his undergraduate days by sweeping the Heisman Trophy and every other major college-football award. Following O.J.'s senior year, his coach at USC, John McKay—who this year took over the NFL's new Tampa Bay Buccaneers—said, "Simpson was not only the greatest player I ever had—he was the greatest player anyone ever had." USC's football adversaries didn't necessarily find such praise excessive. After watching Simpson zigzag his way for 150 yards through a vaunted Fighting Irish defensive wall, a Notre Dame sports publicist lamented, "His nickname shouldn't be Orange Juice. The O.J. should stand for Oh, Jesus—as in 'Oh, Jesus, there he goes again!'"

O.J. has made a similar impression in the pro ranks. His NFL records include most rushing yards gained in one season (2003), most rushing yards gained in a single game (250) and most touchdowns scored in a season (23). Currently fourth on the NFL's list of all-time ground gainers, he has 8123 rushing yards to his credit in seven seasons and he'll move up to third place and possibly second by the end of this year. Although it's doubtful that he'll ever eclipse Jim Brown's career rushing mark of 12,312 yards, O.J. has come reasonably close, despite being used sparingly during the first three of his seven NFL campaigns.

Aside from his consummate artistry at running with a football, Simpson has also emerged as the best-liked athlete in American sports. He rarely turns away autograph seekers, shows up at more than his share of charity functions and keeps himself especially accessible to youngsters. He is no less in favor among his peers. At Buffalo, he has repeatedly focused attention on his blockers and, as a result, such previously unsung players as Reggie McKenzie, Joe DeLamielleure, Mike Montler, Dave Foley and Donnie Green have been able to win stardom (and significant salary increases) on their own as The Electric Company—an aggressive aggregation whose duty is "to turn on the Juice." Simpson's appreciation of his blockers' efforts hasn't been restricted to flattering references in the press; following the 1973 season, he presented members of the Bills' offense and coaching staff with gold bracelets, a gesture that reportedly cost him more than $20,000.

Simpson could afford such largess, for in addition to the mere $300,000 salary he was supposedly then earning with the Bills, he was hauling down a bundle in other careers—as a sports commentator for ABC-TV, as a commercial pitchman for several companies and as an actor. He has already appeared in five films and has several movie commitments for the coming year. Does he have any talent? Says Lee Strasberg of the Actors Studio, "Simpson is already an actor, an excellent one. A natural one."

But, above all, O.J. Simpson remains a superlative football player; and to interview the superstar of Rent-a-Car, the silver screen and the NFL, we sent freelancer Lawrence Linderman to meet with him in Southern California. (We also had interviewer Fred Robbins ask O.J. some questions about his acting career while Simpson was in Rome earlier this year.) Linderman reports:

"In June, O.J. and I arranged to tape the *Playboy Interview* while he was in Palm Springs filming a series of Hertz commercials, but the timing couldn't have been worse. A few hours before we sat down to talk, he had informed Bills head coach Lou Saban that he wouldn't be returning to Buffalo in the fall, and what had previously been an informed rumor suddenly became the nation's hottest sports story. Simpson's decision had left him depressed and by late afternoon, reporters from all over the country were telephoning every few minutes to confirm his decision. We did precious little taping during the next several days.

"But the following week in Los Angeles was a different story. An hour after I arrived in town, a buoyant O.J. picked me up in a Rolls-Royce and drove me to his home. As we headed north on the San Diego Freeway in 65-mph bumper-to-bumper traffic, cars zoomed abreast of us, motorists honked and smiled, O.J. waved and I mostly cringed.

"O.J. cuts an imposing figure. Slightly better-looking than he photographs, at 6'1" and 212 pounds, he keeps himself in supershape by running and playing tennis and basketball. He is very achievement-oriented; and since he admits that about the only thing he can't do well is sing, he's working on that aspect of his game with the help of a friend, Bill Withers. O.J. has a distinctive sound, but who wants to hear a foghorn try to warble ballads?

"Luckily, Simpson can do other things. For instance, he can walk into a room and suddenly everyone in it is smiling and feeling amiable. True, celebrities always cause a crowd's pulse to quicken, but O.J. seems to make people glow as opposed to, say, Warren Beatty, who immediately gets people wondering if their sex lives are all they should be. People who know O.J. rave about his easy, up-front good humor, and I certainly didn't detect any chinks in the armor.

"Simpson and I stayed in touch throughout the summer, and he was plainly surprised when the Rams and the Bills didn't quickly conclude a trade for him. As the NFL exhibition season came and went, his surprise turned to well-disguised anguish. A few days before the start of the regular season, the NFL's interconference trading deadline also came and went, which effectively ruled out any possibility of Simpson's being dealt to either the Rams or the 49ers—and at that point, the only team with a chance of landing him seemed to be the Oakland Raiders. On Friday, September 10th, Bills owner Ralph C. Wilson, Jr., flew to Los Angeles to talk with O.J.—and their meetings provided the opening subject for our conversation."

PLAYBOY: How did Ralph Wilson convince you to return to the Buffalo Bills? Did he simply make you an offer you couldn't refuse?

SIMPSON: I can't say that money wasn't a big factor, but it wasn't the *major* factor. Actually, I knew Ralph was going to try to sign me when, a few days before the season started, he called to say he was flying out to see me; I told him not to come, but he insisted. I was still totally against going back to Buffalo so I thought his trip was going to be pointless.

Well, Ralph got to Los Angeles on a Friday and he, my wife, Marguerite, and I spent a good four hours talking at our house. His main point was that he had tried his best to make a trade for me but that it just hadn't worked out. He said he felt it was the wrong time for me to retire from football and that the Bills would like to have me back.

PLAYBOY: Just how close do you think you came to being traded?

SIMPSON: It's hard for me to say. Ralph told me he had tried his best, and I have to take him at his word. On the other hand, Carroll Rosenbloom, the owner of the Rams, told me about midway during their negotiations—right after the Olympics—that the Rams wanted me bad but that he didn't think the trade would be made, because he didn't want to destroy his own team in the process. He was concerned about the defensive players Ralph asked the Rams to give up—Mike Fanning, who'll take over at tackle when Merlin Olsen retires, and end Jack Young-blood—because next year the Rams could be in the same situation the Bills are in this year: a lot of offense and no defense. They were also being asked to give up running back Lawrence McCutcheon and two first-round draft picks. Rosenbloom felt Ralph was asking too much, so the Rams announced the trade talks had fallen through.

I have to admit that, at that point, I was very upset. I'd gotten it into my head that I'd be going to work every day and coming back at night and seeing my wife and kids all season long. Don't get me wrong: Aside from L.A., I'd rather play in Buffalo than anywhere else in the NFL, because I really like my teammates. But I *live* in L.A., and I don't know a guy in pro football who doesn't want to play for his hometown team.

I was also upset because I didn't see why I couldn't be traded. I was just being told. "OK, we couldn't trade you, so you either play in Buffalo or you don't play." But other guys who've gone other routes—publicly criticized the management and coaches of their teams, things like that—have had no trouble getting traded. Players who have gotten into fistfights with teammates and demanded to be traded have been traded. There are players who have gotten into trouble with the law, and *they've* been able to get traded. So I was walking around, thinking. "Hey, here I am, leveling with the Bills, doing it the right way, yet I might have to leave the game just because I want to play in my home-town." Right about then, I started wondering if it's true that nice guys really *do* finish last.

PLAYBOY: Is that when you considered suing?

SIMPSON: I did seek legal help. I got a lawyer and found out that I have some *solid* legal rights. But that only put me through heavier mental trips, because I sure as hell didn't want to end my career with a lawsuit against the NFL.

PLAYBOY: By playing the game, in both senses of the phrase, you no doubt picked up a fat contract for this year. Is the $2,500,000 figure quoted by Larry Merchant on NBC-TV accurate?

SIMPSON: Merchant doesn't know what he's talking about. But if I may anticipate your next question, I'm not going to get into the terms of my contract, except to say that I'm very happy and satisfied with it and that I guarantee you that as long as I play football, I won't ask for another raise.

PLAYBOY: You still haven't told us exactly how Wilson convinced you to return.

SIMPSON: Well, as I said, we talked a long time. He told us what kind of money the Bills were willing to pay, and when we had finished talking, I drove him back to his hotel. I still had no intention of playing for the Bills, but late that night, I changed my mind.

PLAYBOY: What did the trick?

SIMPSON: Things my wife told me. Marquerite said I had been a grouch for about a week and that maybe my pride was getting in my way. Pride can be a funny thing, because sometimes it can keep you from doing what you really want to do—and she thought that what I really wanted to do was play football. I was still being stubborn about it, but we finally decided that if Ralph cleared up some contractual things the next day, which was Saturday, I'd leave for Buffalo on Sunday. Well, Ralph cleared those things up at breakfast the next morning, so on Sunday, I caught the first flight out to Buffalo. Ralph thought it would take me a couple of weeks to get ready, but I said, "Hey, Ralph, I'm going to play Monday night!" And I did.

PLAYBOY: Did those things that were cleared up somehow negate your original objections to returning to Buffalo?

SIMPSON: No; the major problem is that I'm separated from my family. The kids are in school and Marquerite doesn't want to be moving them in and out of schools in Los Angeles and Buffalo, and I can't argue with that. So she and our two children stay in L.A.—they visit me, of course, but for the most part, we're separated for five months. That's not easy on me and it sure isn't easy on them.

PLAYBOY: But aren't you home much of the remaining seven months?

SIMPSON: No, I'm not. When football is over for the year, it seems like I'm always on the road, making appearances for the companies I work for and, in the past couple of years, acting in movies. I gotta do that, because football is gonna be part of my past pretty soon and I have to think about my future—which means finding another career. But all that keeps me on the road and has led to a lot of trouble for us. Marquerite and I were apart more than we were together and a marriage can't work when you're separated so much of the time. I had to make a decision, which to me seemed really to boil down to a question of my family versus playing football away from home again.

PLAYBOY: Was it just a matter of mileage, or did the city of Buffalo itself play a part in your decision?

SIMPSON: A *big* part. Marquerite wasn't happy in Buffalo; she just didn't have much to do. And I'm an outdoor person, but unless you're into snow, Buffalo is not the place to be—and I'm not into snow. My biggest problem, I guess, is that I like to do a lot of different things, and in Buffalo, whatever we do one night is pretty much what we do the next night, 'cause it just doesn't have the variety of people and occupations that you find in a city like L.A. There's only one word to describe the negative side of Buffalo: tedium.

PLAYBOY: Is there a positive side of the city for you?

SIMPSON: Absolutely. Buffalo has allowed me to get in touch with myself. In that environment, it's hard to get lost in the party scene the way people do in Hollywood. In Buffalo, you tend to discover what you really need out of life; the frills aren't there, so you get down to basics, and in that respect, I think, the town has been good for me. I'll tell you something else: I never had a friend come visit me in Buffalo who didn't have a ball. Anyway, that business about leaving Buffalo is all behind me now. I intend to finish out my career with the Bills. But I'll tell you this: I think the Bills would have been better off if they'd made a trade for me.

PLAYBOY: What leads you to that conclusion?

SIMPSON: To start with, I may retire after this season, and if I do, the Bills will wind up with nothing for me. During the summer, they could have made a trade that would have ensured them of being a top-caliber team for many years. One thing last season proved was that I couldn't make them a champion. The Bills were the best offensive team in football and we broke an all-time NFL record for first downs—but we were eliminated from the playoffs with two games left in the season.

Obviously, what the team needs is defensive ball players; they have an excellent offense, even without me. I try to do everything from a positive point of view and, looking at it positively, the trade was gonna be better for the Bills, better for the fans in Buffalo—'cause the team would win more games—and it would certainly be better for me, because I could end my career at home on the west coast with a team that is a potential Super Bowl champion.

PLAYBOY: Do you think you were being realistic about the Bills' prospects minus O.J. Simpson?

SIMPSON: I think I was. Listen, our highlights film last year was called *They Sure Were Exciting*, and there's no getting around that fact: The Bills in '75 had fans jumping out of their seats. Now, you can win and be a dull team, and the Rams are frequently accused of that. But even though the Bills played some damned wild games last year, the team's lack of defense kept it out of the playoffs. Essentially, Buffalo would've had a fine offense even if it had come up with a merely adequate runner in my place—and Lawrence McCutcheon, the guy Wilson wanted from the Rams, is much more than an adequate runner. The better the runner, the better the offense; but in any case, it had to be a good offense. The defensive players the Bills could have received would have been the key to the trade.

PLAYBOY: Can't they acquire such players without losing you?

SIMPSON: Honestly? Yes, they can get a couple of guys who can help without getting rid of me. You have to go back to that old football cliché about paying the price. George Allen sees guys who might help him get to the Super Bowl today, and all of a sudden John Riggins, Calvin Hill, Jean Fugett, Jake Scott and Pat Sullivan are Washington Redskins. Allen pays whatever price he has to and doesn't worry about later on, because his philosophy is very simple: The future is now.

PLAYBOY: Judging from the boos that greeted you the night of the Bills' nationally televised season opener, didn't your near defection lose you some of your popularity with the Buffalo fans?

SIMPSON: I took that with a grain of salt, because after I had carried the ball a few times, most of the boos turned to cheers, probably because the fans in Buffalo know that I'm there to play football and I don't give them anything but my very best. What booing there was, well, you gotta remember that Buffalo has the most vocal fans in the NFL and they take the game very personally. When you're winning, they really let you know how proud they are of you.

Of course, early in my career, when we looked like a bunch of bums out on the field, they took *that* personally, too. Except for my first three years in the league, the people in Buffalo have treated me really well. But those three years were rough, because I'd always been cheered—and for the first time in my life, I was being booed.

PLAYBOY: Why were the fans on your case?

SIMPSON: Because we weren't winning. When I got to Buffalo, I was supposed to be the kid from California who was gonna instantly turn things around for the Bills, but there was no way that could happen.

PLAYBOY: Why not?

SIMPSON: That had to do with our head coach at the time, John Rauch. Rauch has a tremendous amount of pride, and I mean he's stubborn as *hell*. He's a guy who, once he says something, will stick with it no matter what—which I think worked against him in Buffalo and which I know worked against *me*. He and I never hit it off, starting from the time I reported to Buffalo, when he tried to make me a receiver instead of a runner. I was a rookie, so I had to go along with all that, but Rauch and I really started having run-ins during my second year. By then, it was clear to me that the offense wasn't working and I thought we should try something else. Rauch was trying to impress the players with his system and he was determined to stay with it, no matter what our record was or what it was costing the players.

PLAYBOY: How hot did it get between you and Rauch?

SIMPSON: About as hot as it *could* get. I still take pride in the fact that I never asked to be traded during those years, but believe me, there were times I just wanted to scream and get out of there.

PLAYBOY: Why didn't you?

SIMPSON: Two reasons: The first was Jack Horrigan, a great dude who was the Bills' public-relations man at the time. Jack was dying of leukemia, but at moments when I was ready to bail out, he'd come around and comfort *me*. "Juice," he'd say, "there are times in your life when stuff like this is gonna happen, and you just have to ride it out. Things'll get better." When things *did* get better, Jack unfortunately passed away.

The second reason I didn't leave involved hurting my left knee during my second season. In our eighth game of the year, I got hit pretty good returning a kickoff against Cincinnati, and I was through for the season. On the day I returned to camp the following summer, Rauch was fired—and was replaced by Harvey Johnson, a great guy but certainly not a man qualified to be a head coach, in my opinion. We won one game that year. By then, I was about as disillusioned with the Bills as I could be. A pro football team is a $17,000,000 business, but the Bills' operation wasn't run as well as my high school football program. And coming out of USC, where everything we did was first-class, I found the Bills to be rinky-dink.

PLAYBOY: As in tacky?

SIMPSON: Right. The facilities were incredibly bad. War Memorial Stadium had to be seen to be believed, but when I first saw it I *didn't* believe it. I guess I was naïve. In college, I'd played at the L.A. Coliseum, which you can see from a half mile away. In Buffalo, you'd be walking through a black neighborhood and suddenly, 60 feet in front of you, you'd see this old, rundown stadium. I'm an optimist, so I figured, Hey, it doesn't matter, 'cause I'm gonna be on the field, not in the stands. But that should have let me know what I was in for. Check *this* out: Our locker room for practices was located in a public ice rink—and we shared it with kids getting dressed for hockey games. Team meetings were conducted in the hallway of the ice rink, but not exactly in privacy: We had to put a sheet up over a wire so that the mothers and kids wouldn't barge in. We held our meetings right around the ice rink's refreshment machines, so while we'd be going over game plans, kids would come through to get ice cream and sodas. That seemed a little strange.

PLAYBOY: When did things get better for the Bills?

SIMPSON: My fourth year. Lou Saban was rehired as head coach and brought stability and organization to the franchise—and, by then, Buffalo had started building a new stadium. Lou made us a running football team, but even more important to the players, he treated us like men. Under Rauch, we'd stay over in Niagara Falls the night before home games—without our wives of course. We had an 11 o'clock curfew—which the Bills still have—but Rauch would come to our room and there'd be trouble if we weren't actually in *bed*. Three hours before a game, he would give us a written test and we'd have to answer questions like, "Who are we playing today?" It was as if the players were in the third grade, and it alienated us. We even had hair and dress codes, which prohibited us from wearing things like flared pants. When Lou came in, all that shit went right out the window. I'm like a lot of older NFL players in that I think back on those days and wonder how I ever put up with that crap.

PLAYBOY: You said earlier you wouldn't discuss the exact terms of your contract, but we may assume that you're earning well over $500,000. Do you think you're worth that kind of salary?

SIMPSON: I think a person is worth what he gets. And I also think you can't bellyache about bad breaks, because what happens to you is what you *allow* to happen to you. When I was a rookie, Ralph offered me $50,000 and I thought I was worth much, much more. I'd been the Heisman Trophy winner; I'd gotten a lot of publicity in college and, when they drafted me, the Bills also got a lot of publicity. But I never said Ralph didn't offer me what I *deserved*. I just went to him and fought for more money.

PLAYBOY: Did you win?

SIMPSON: Nope, and I'm kind of thankful I didn't. At the time, I'd placed myself in the hands of some financial people who wanted Wilson to give me a $500,000 loan, which I'd invest on Wall Street. Ralph wouldn't go for it, but they finally got him to set up a loan for $100,000, which we immediately invested—and which immediately went down the tubes. That's one reason I'm handling myself today. I'd be willing to bet that about 40 percent of the deals that agents get athletes into don't do better than break even, and the rest of the time, the guys get hurt.

Anyway, when I couldn't budge Ralph to go above $50,000, I became the NFL's longest holdout in my rookie year. I might *still* be a holdout, but there were pressures on me to play. I'd signed a three-year contract with Chevrolet that guaranteed me $180,000; I had one with RC Cola for $37,500 a year, and I'd also signed with ABC Sports. All those things were tied to my football career, which is why I always tell Ralph that he got me cheap. I finally agreed to play for $50,000.

PLAYBOY: Sports commentators often charge that doing product endorsements detracts from an athlete's concentration, hence from his performance. Do you disagree?

SIMPSON: Sure I do. I've done my share of endorsements and I think my record as a football player speaks for itself. You hear sportswriters say that crap about how endorsements and doing TV distract a player, but, hey, that stuff is gonna sustain me *long* after my football career is over. Don't misunderstand me; football made it all possible, but I think I've given back to the game whatever I've gotten out of it. I repay the game with everything I have every time I walk onto the field.

I also know that the game goes on and that while you may be the greatest today, no one will know where you are tomorrow. When your playing days are over, the roar of the crowd becomes just a loud echo. Players today know *exactly* what football can do for them: put money in the bank.

PLAYBOY: Isn't that a bit cynical?

SIMPSON: I'm not being cynical, just realistic. There are only two reasons guys become pro football players—to make money and because they enjoy playing the game. Pro football can give you things like pride and discipline, but the only *tangible* reward it offers is money. People never hear what happens to most players after their careers—which average only about five and a half years—are over. When all that adulation is withdrawn, it's *traumatic*, Jack. I doubt if figures exist on this, but believe me, the divorce rate among retired pro football players is just staggering. The press, management—they don't talk about stuff like that. Instead, you hear things from them about *loyalty*, which is what I heard when I said I wouldn't return to Buffalo. But over the years, I've learned that loyalty in pro sports goes hand in hand with finance, and it's not black and white, it's black and red: The minute an owner starts losing money, his loyalty to a player or a city completely changes. Players don't talk about loyalty; that stuff comes strictly from upstairs. And the players recognize that kind of double-talk for what it is: bullshit.

PLAYBOY: Do you agree with the owners' predictions that if players are made free agents, rich teams will outbid poor teams for talent—with the result that NFL franchises in smaller cities like Buffalo and Green Bay will soon go bankrupt?

SIMPSON: You know, it's funny how team owners always talk about competition having made America great, but *they* sure don't want no competition. Instead, you hear how rich franchises would outbid poor franchises for players on the open market—but meanwhile, which NFL franchise is poor? Green Bay, Wisconsin, is the smallest town in the NFL, but how can the Packers be poor when they damn near sell out every game? And how can any team afford to offer players more money than the Bills, when Buffalo continues to outdraw every other club in the NFL? Ralph Wilson has done *very* well in Buffalo; he's got the most profitable franchise in pro football.

The truth is that *no* club has enough money to buy itself a team of All-Pros. Right now, I don't even think any team could afford to sign both me *and* Joe Namath. And I don't see how any team could *ever* wind up with an O.J. Simpson, a Mercury Morris and a Chuck Foreman, because none of us would want to be benchwarmers. As far as I'm concerned, all that talk about possible bidding wars is there to help owners smoke-screen the college draft—which was finally ruled illegal in court this fall.

PLAYBOY: Why do you take issue with the NFL's system of drafting college players?

SIMPSON: Well, I've always had a very simple question concerning the draft: What's bigger, the NFL's bylaws or the U.S. Constitution? The Constitution says we're all free to choose how and where we want to earn a living. Hey, when I came out of college, I was told that if I wanted to play pro football in America, I'd have to go to Buffalo. I had no choice in the matter. Owners justified the college draft by saying they needed it to maintain the league's "competitive balance," but they've used that argument to take advantage of the players.

Listen, I think the NFL *does* need some kind of college-draft system, but it's never tried to come up with an alternative that takes the player into consideration. For instance, why shouldn't a player have a choice of signing with at least a *couple* of teams? By way of an answer, the NFL—which means the team owners—says that pro football can survive only by following the rules, but they make *up* the rules. Well, the Constitution is there to give everybody an equal shot, and if football can't survive within constitutional limits, maybe we'd better sit down and talk about it—and change it. Which is what's happening: A lot of NFL rules—like the Rozelle Rule—have been thrown out, and a lot more are *gonna* be thrown out.

PLAYBOY: Do you think pro football could be destroyed in the process?

SIMPSON: It's possible, because as the players gain more control, they might put through changes that could weaken the sport. The one thing I'm sure of is that in the past eight years, pro football has become a better sport for the players and less than the greatest investment for businessmen who want to be team owners. Chris Hemmeter, the last president of the World Football League, got a jump on what's happening. He introduced a plan that didn't have a chance to work out, because people didn't go to WFL games, but it was a sound idea and I guarantee you that the NFL will eventually adopt something like it. The Hemmeter Plan was simple: It gave the players a certain percentage of the money that a franchise makes. Let's say the team gets 43 percent; the average player might sign a contract for one percent and a superstar might get two or three, depending on what the other stockholders—his teammates—have to say. What it finally boils down to is that as the rewards of pro football get greater, the players are gonna have to step in and take some of the financial risk.

Obviously, team owners are eventually going to be eliminated, because football is a game that can survive without them. Granted, it hasn't so far; there's that old saying about how players come and go, but the owners stay. But in the future, players are going to get more control, and if pro football lasts for another 50 years, the players will own all the teams.

PLAYBOY: If something akin to the Hemmeter Plan were in effect, do you think your teammates would vote to pay you as much as you're making now?

SIMPSON: No way; so in one way, I guess I'm lucky that I'll be long gone by the time all that takes place.

PLAYBOY: Which brings us to the subject of your imminent retirement: How firm *are* you about your announced intention to leave pro football after this season?

SIMPSON: Pretty firm. I'll be 30 before the start of next season, and about the only runners I can think of who played well at that age were journeymen backs like Bill Brown, Tom Woodeshick and Tom Matte. But I can't think of any of *my* kind of runner who played well once they turned 30. At that age, you start to lose one step in terms of speed, and most people don't realize it, but all that separates the better backs from the journeymen is that one step. Leroy Kelley of the Browns was still good at 31, but he'd lost an awful lot by then. Kelley was amazing in that he knew just where the holes would open up. He played his last two years on his knowledge of the game and I think I could, too. But I don't *want* to. I don't ever want to be out on the field and remember a move and think, I can't do that anymore.

The thing is, I want to leave the game like Jim Brown—who quit while he was still the best—and not like Johnny Unitas. Johnny Unitas was one of the greatest quarterbacks who ever played the game, but young guys who saw him at the end of his career saw a guy who wasn't anywhere *near* the great player he'd been. It's like something I once read about Willie Mays. A guy took his son to see Willie play and he gave the kid a big build-up about Willie, but by then, he was with the Mets and what the kid saw was almost a caricature of Mays: He was thick with age, his hat didn't fall off when he ran and he couldn't hit or run the way he used to. The kid finally walked out of the stadium doubting that Mays had *ever* been great, and I don't want that to happen to me.

But, having said all that, I also gotta say that I'm still as fast as when I came into the league. If I trained for track, I think I could run the 100-yard dash in 9.4 seconds. In fact, I'm sure of it; last year, I ran the 100 in 9.6 in tennis shoes and on asphalt for ABC's *Superstars* show. So while I think this is my last season, I'm sure I could play next year at the same level I played at in '75.

PLAYBOY: What are the chances that you will?

SIMPSON: I'll tell you who really has the say-so on that: Dino De Laurentiis and Milos Forman—De Laurentiis' director on *Ragtime*. They haven't cast the movie yet, but if I get the part of Coalhouse Walker Jr., and they shoot it next fall, then that's it for me and pro football. But in the meantime, I don't have the part—or even an inside track on it.

PLAYBOY: Why are you so ready to quit football for *Ragtime*? Aren't you being offered other movie roles?

SIMPSON: Yes, but there are certain parts that can build a movie career very quickly—and I think that Coalhouse Walker is one of those parts.

They don't come around that often, either. This might not be the best example, but I remember that Robert Redford was hangin' in for a lotta years before he made *Butch Cassidy and the Sundance Kid*, which is when his career *really* took off.

PLAYBOY: How serious *are* you about becoming an actor?

SIMPSON: Very serious, because it's what I want to do with my life when I'm through with football. I've been acting since my rookie year in the NFL, when I did an episode of *Medical Center*. I played a top college football player who was sick but who was trying to convince everybody he wasn't so he could be drafted by the pros and get that big bonus for his momma. It was supposed to be the sixth show of the series, but the producers liked it so much that they used it for the series' premiere. People in the industry who saw it said, "Hey, this kid can *act*," and for almost two years after that, I was told to follow it up with something. Between football, working for Chevrolet and RC Cola and going to sports banquets. I didn't really have time. But after my third year in the NFL, a friend named Jack Gilardi, who was senior vice-president at Creative Management Associates, arranged for me to be in a film called *Why?* The whole movie was improvised; it was about a bunch of kids going through a marathon group-encounter session. We'd just sit there eight hours a day with the cameras grinding, and it was like being paid to take acting lessons, which is why it didn't matter to me that the movie was never shown in theaters. A year later, some guy talked to me about *The Klansman*, and all of a sudden, I had a part in it. It was a hell of a surprise, because being in a movie with actors like Lee Marvin and Richard Burton couldn't do me anything but good.

PLAYBOY: When *The Klansman* was on location in Oroville, California, it was reported that you were usually the only sober actor on the set. Was that accurate?

SIMPSON: Oh, there was some vodka *absorbed*, Jack. Like cases and *cases* of it. I learned that in the acting industry, the heavy drinkers all go for vodka, because it doesn't smell. Lee Marvin amazed me with his stamina, 'cause he'd go through an entire bottle and still do his lines without a hitch. Same thing with Richard Burton. And sometimes, when he was inebriated, Richard would start ramblin' on in that booming voice of his, maybe recitin' from *Camelot* or something, just to get your attention. We'd play a game in which we'd all try to ignore him, but we couldn't. And I've never seen a cat, tipsy or not, who could charm a lady more than Richard could. I spent about six weeks working on *The Klansman*, and even though critics destroyed the movie, I got reviews saying that the only redeeming thing about it was my performance. After that, I got a part in *The Towering Inferno* as a security guard, and that led to a couple of other movies, *Killer Force* and *The Cassandra Crossing*, which has people in it like Sophia Loren, Ava Gardner, Richard Harris and Burt Lancaster. So it seems to be happening, you know?

PLAYBOY: Have you set any goals for yourself as an actor?

SIMPSON: I'll settle for becoming what producers call bankable—having enough of a following to know that people will go to see movies I'm in. But I don't want to just play action parts where I do a lot of runnin' around. The guys I want to be like are character actors. I'd *really* like to be a cat like Dustin Hoffman, who I think is probably the greatest actor in the world. Another guy I dig is Martin Balsam, and I'll go to watch him—like in *The Anderson Tapes*, where he played a fag—just to see what kind of trip he's into. I'm also not lookin' for parts that necessarily call for a black cat; the role I played in *The Cassandra Crossing* was written for James Coburn, but when he got tied up in another movie, they got me. I play a priest in it.

PLAYBOY: A priest? How did you prepare for that kind of role?

SIMPSON: Well, I sort of surprised my wife for the last two months before I went to Rome to make the film by going to church with her every Sunday. She's Catholic. And after church, I would speak to some of the priests. I also knew a few priests in San Francisco who used to work with the baseball teams that I was on; so when I went back to the city, I made it a point to look them up, just to be around them, to pick up maybe a few of their mannerisms, how they said things and how they kind of carried themselves. I watched them and I thought, if I were a priest, how would I act? That's pretty much my approach to all the roles I've gotten into; it's worked for me.

PLAYBOY: What was it like working with people like Sophia Loren and Richard Harris? Did they accept you, a comparative newcomer to acting?

SIMPSON: They made it very easy for me. The first time I met Richard Harris, even before I saw him, I heard somebody yelling "Juice, Juice" and describing a play, "Second and ten, and clock's running out; Fergy drops back, hits Juice going down the middle 64 yards, he scores! Buffalo wins, 24-23." I looked around and it was Richard Harris. He was describing one of the big plays of the past season, so I knew he was a fan. He came up and made me feel at ease. Sophia Loren, the first day I was on the set, noticed me watching her when she had a little break. She said, "Come over and sit down," and she started helping me with a little Italian. Later, she became my gin partner. Whenever we were on the set, we were playing gin. She's a great poker player, too.

PLAYBOY: Did your wife and your children go with you to Rome?

SIMPSON: No, but if I had to do it over again, I'd take them with me. All my life, I'd always visualized myself as a father, with kids, but I never really thought about being a husband, and there are certain responsibilities you have as a husband. That's hard for a free spirit like me. But, fortunately, I've got a good lady and she's made adjustments for it.

PLAYBOY: Are you referring to the fact that a guy in your position is constantly surrounded by groupies?

SIMPSON: Well, I haven't run into a plethora of groupies; but it all comes down to the two of us, how much we trust each other and how much we love each other. We've had our problems, like any other couple, probably a few more of them, because of my lack of privacy. Of course, we married young—I was 19 and my wife was 18—so we had a lot of growing up to do.

PLAYBOY: Early marriage isn't as popular as it used to be. How do you feel about it today?

SIMPSON: I wouldn't advise it for everybody, but for me it was probably the best thing. I was pretty extroverted and I did a lot of messing around, and marriage sort of gave me some responsibility at an age when I needed it. I stayed home nights with my wife—she was working, so she was usually too tired to go out—and did my homework. If I hadn't been married and had her to go home to, I think I could have been moving a little too fast for myself.

PLAYBOY: There's no subtle way to ask this question, so let's just bulldoze into it: Have you ever found yourself in a situation that was ugly purely because of its racial overtones?

SIMPSON: I've been in places in the South—and also in the North—where some dude started making race remarks. But when loudmouths say those kinds of things, I just make 'em disappear: To me, they're not even there. Of course, you can only take it so far and then you gotta let a guy know he's out of line. I've heard guys in bars yell, "C'mere, boy. Hey, *boy*, come over here." I ignore them until they try to pull me over to where they are. That's when Hertz comes in.

PLAYBOY: Hertz?

SIMPSON: Right, baby. I give 'em a hard little jab in the chest and say, "Hertz, *don't* it? Not Avis—Hertz." Politely, you let 'em know they're startin' to walk on thin ice. I've been fortunate in that I haven't run into too many racial situations; but when they've come up, I've been able to handle them in some places and avoid them in others. I think that when you find guys beatin' up on dudes because of race remarks, it's generally because of some insecurities. But, hey, I know who I am: I'm the Juice. I'm black—and that's cool with me, baby, and just another *reason* why I'm the Juice. If you came up to me and called me a nigger, I'd probably look you in the eye and say, "Oh, is *that* what I am?" But if you're *gonna* call me a nigger, you best not touch me or give me any legal reason to hit ya, Jack. 'Cause, believe me, I *will*.

PLAYBOY: Somehow, that doesn't jibe with the Mr. Clean image you project in your Hertz commercials. Is there a real difference between your media image and your private personality and, if so, does it bother you?

SIMPSON: At times it worries me, because I don't quite understand the reasons for it. It might be because I have a lot of friends, and a friend often tends to make you seem like a good guy. Another reason, I suppose, is that I always try to be as direct and honest as I can be, maybe because I don't have to deal with who I am, especially in terms of race. I'm black and that's it. I can't change it and I wouldn't *want* to change it, as much as I couldn't and wouldn't want to change what's in the damn sky. I'm happy with being black and I don't trip about it.

PLAYBOY: Have you ever gotten racial putdowns from blacks?

SIMPSON: Only when I was in college. When I was at USC, black athletes across the nation were looking for an identity and we all did things like grow our hair long. At some colleges, half the football team would be suspended for doing that, but on our campus, there was no resistance, because coach John McKay made any adjustments he needed to make without a hassle. Most of the cats on our team were cool, anyway, so it was never a big deal. But a lot of the middle- and upper-class black students were having a tough time discovering who in the hell they were. I remember that all of a sudden, USC had a black student union and then—bingo!—the black student union was talking about who was *black enough*. Students from affluent black communities like Baldwin Hills were coming up to guys like me who came from lower-class areas and tellin' us we weren't *black* enough. I'd tell those cats, "Hey, I don't have to go through any changes to prove that I'm *black* enough; I am *black*. I grew *up* black. I knew it the day I was born, I knew it when I went to school—I knew it *all* the time. You're just finding it out, but that's *your* problem, not mine, so deal with it the best you can. But don't judge my trip by yours—and don't tell me about who's doing more for whom, or what. That ain't *my* trip, Jack."

PLAYBOY: Is there any particular reason why it isn't?

SIMPSON: Yeah, and it goes back to something that happened when I was about 15 years old. I'd been sent to the Youth Guidance Center in San Francisco for about a week—it had to do with a fight I had had—and a couple of hours after I got back home, somebody knocked on the door and said there was a guy downstairs who wanted to see me. So I went outside and there, sittin' in his car, was my boyhood hero—Willie Mays. I was the most loyal Giants fan you ever saw, and every day after school when the Giants were in town, me and my friends would sneak into Seals Stadium—that was before they built Candlestick Park—just to see Willie play. And there was Willie Mays, waitin' for *me*! I found out afterward that a neighbor had told him I was in trouble and had brought Mays around to talk to me. But Willie didn't give me no discipline rap; we drove over to his place and spent the afternoon talking sports. He lived in a great big house in Forest Hill and he was exactly the easygoing, friendly guy I'd always pictured him to be. It was a fantastic day for me. Well, a short time after that, Jackie Robinson took a shot at Mays by saying he didn't do enough for his people. That hurt me; I took it like he'd said it about me, 'cause it was like *I* was Willie Mays back then. I'd always admired Robinson, but I never really saw him play and, besides, Mays was my *man*. Willie always put out good vibes, and even after I got to college, I knew that he had done more for me than anybody else. I was well aware of what Jackie Robinson had done and I appreciated it, just like I appreciate what George Washington and Thomas Jefferson and Thomas Edison did. But I don't think he should have gotten on Mays. For myself, if I reach a lot of people and have a positive influence on them, that's great. I got that from Willie Mays; he was there to help a kid who was in trouble.

PLAYBOY: How much trouble *did* you get into when you were young?

SIMPSON: Oh, I wasn't *bad*, just mischievous. Some of that had to do with growing up in the Potrero Hill district of San Francisco, which to me was the greatest place in the world. My mother worked—my father didn't live with us—and me, my brother and my two sisters always had a terrific time. Blacks talk about other blacks bein' your brothers and sisters, and that applies even more in the projects, where everybody's momma is your momma and three or four nights a week you'll be eatin' over at somebody else's house. It's like living in a federally funded commune.

On a real level, Potrero Hill was an area where 70 percent of the people were on welfare, and it's bullshit to think they sat on their asses waiting for government checks, because the fathers were always out looking for jobs, but there wasn't any work for them. I wasn't aware of all that, of course. To me, Potrero Hill was America the Beautiful, and I think most of the people who lived there felt the same way. I remember that at World Series time, everybody would crowd around a radio to listen to the games, and when the national anthem was played, the whole room would stand up. *Everybody*—mothers, fathers, kids—would be on their feet, and this was in the projects. Mostly, I remember all the adventures we had. There was a polliwog pond, railroad tracks, a lumberyard and lots of factories nearby, and in the summer, when there wasn't anything to do, somebody would say, "Hey, let's go hit the *pie* factory." So we'd go down there, sneak around the fence and set up what looked like a little bucket brigade, and we'd steal maybe 30 pies. My favorite was blackberry; man, that was *good*. Or we'd hit the Hostess Bakery or the milk factory. We had a good group of dudes and my best friends then are still just about my best friends now. We also had the toughest gang on Potrero Hill; couldn't nobody whup us on the Hill.

PLAYBOY: Was it dangerous to belong to a gang?

SIMPSON: I think it was more dangerous *not* to. There was never any blame attached to it, and if you weren't in one, you had to be kind of goofy or else just plain out of it. When I was 13, I joined my first gang, the Gladiators, and I was the president; me and all my little cronies got these great burgundy-satin jackets that I later learned were baseball windbreakers. There were about 14 of us and we stayed on Potrero Hill and never dealt with any gang outside the district, because we were too young.

I joined my first *fighting* gang when I got to junior high and got with the Persian Warriors. There were about 25 guys in the club and I think I was the only one who didn't live in the Fillmore District. And, of course, we had our ladies' auxiliary; the Persian Parettes were the best female club in San Francisco. I was 14 when the Parettes came into my life and, man, they gave me an *education*. We did a pretty good amount of fighting and the big showdowns would usually take place on holidays, when everybody would get on down to Market Street. You'd hear cats sayin', "You gonna be at the Golden Gate Theater tomorrow? The Roman Gents are gonna fight the Sheiks!" I joined a club called the Superiors when I got to high school, and that's when we started steppin' out of all that rowdy shit and started giving dances instead. I think the IRS would've been interested to find out about them, because we made us some bucks. One year, we rented a hall in the Sheraton-Palace Hotel and gave a Halloween party that hundreds of kids came to. We cleared about $3300 for the night, which, to us, was almost unbelievable.

PLAYBOY: What did you do with all that money?

SIMPSON: We put it in our kitty and then put on a picnic that the whole city was invited to. The Superiors finally broke up when about four of the guys went to jail and a few others joined the Army. All of a sudden, there were only about four active members left, and the club had $2800, so we did what we thought was best for everyone concerned: We voted to split up the treasury. All *right!*

PLAYBOY: Had you ever scored like that before?

SIMPSON: No, but as a kid, I always managed to keep myself in lunch money, especially during football season. We'd go down to the 49ers games and sneak in, and then afterward, when the game was over, the management would give you a nickel for every seat cushion you turned in. Me and my friends would grab all the cushions we could, and sometimes we'd also grab all the cushions *other* little dudes had picked up. It was like a *dogfight*.

But the way to make real money at 49ers games was to hustle tickets. To do that, you needed a little dough up front to work with. If my momma would lend me a few bucks, I was over like a fat rat, but most of the time I'd have to get the money together by myself. So on Fridays, I'd go fishing down at the pier and then sell my catch in the projects. On Saturdays, I'd hustle bottles for the deposit money, and by game time on Sunday, I'd have $3.50 for a reserved-seat ticket. That wasn't to get in, 'cause we'd *sneak* in; that was money to work with. I'd go up to people outside the stadium and ask if they had extra tickets. Lots of times, cats would be waiting for friends who didn't show, and if I thought a guy could be talked out of a ticket, I'd kinda whimper and say, "Oh, I just *got* to see old Hugh McElhenny." Some people would give you the ticket, but the average cat would want something for it and he'd say, "Nope, I won't *give* it to you, but how much money you got?" You'd tell him $1.50 or two bucks, he'd sell it to you, and then you'd go sell it to somebody else for the $3.50. Sometimes you'd catch a seat on the 50-yard line and you could scalp those for four or five bucks. By game time, I'd pick up about $40—and this was a little dude whose momma gave him a quarter a day for lunch.

PLAYBOY: You weren't exactly shy and naïve as a child, then?

SIMPSON: Hey, I was *aggressive*. I've always had lots of energy, which is why my teammates on the Bills started calling me Juice. That didn't have anything to do with orange juice, only with the kind of guy I am—always juiced up, always movin' around. A lot of guys probably think I'm *too* active and *too* loud, but that's the way I am and that's the way I was as a kid. But I wasn't called O.J. or Juice when I was little. As a kid, I was called Headquarters and Waterhead, because my head was about the same size then as it is now, and I was very sensitive about that. I was also sensitive about my legs. When I was, oh, maybe two years old, I came down with rickets—a lack of calcium in the bones—and the disease made my legs skinny and left me bowlegged and pigeon-toed. I needed braces to correct both of those things, but my mom couldn't afford them, so I wore a pair of shoes connected by an iron bar. I'd get into that contraption a few hours everyday and until I was almost five, I'd be shufflin' around the house. But then my legs improved and I got to be a very rowdy character.

PLAYBOY: *How* rowdy?

SIMPSON: Well, at dances, I'd wear this long white hat down over my eyes, and if I saw a girl who looked good, I'd go right up to her and start rappin', even if she was with a guy. I didn't care *what* the dude said, 'cause I'd tell him, "Hey, I'm talkin' to her, not *you*, man. If she don't *want* me to talk to her, she'll *tell* me she don't want me to talk to her." It rarely got into punches, because most of the dudes didn't want to fight me.

PLAYBOY: Why not? Were you such a tough kid?

SIMPSON: Oh, I could handle myself, but you also gotta realize that San Francisco isn't a big town and it ain't that hard to develop a reputation. I got most of mine from a fight I had with a guy named Winky. He belonged to the toughest club in the city, the Roman Gents, and when we fought, he must've been about 20 and I was maybe 15. That was one fight I sure didn't start: One night, I was at a dance in the Booker T. Washington Community Center when, all of a sudden, this *loud* little sucker—an older O.J.—comes up to me and says, "What did you say about my sister?" I'd heard of Winky—just about everyone had—but I didn't know that was who this was, so I just said, "Hey, man, I don't know your sister. I don't even know *you*." It wasn't cool to fight in the community center, so the guy started walking away, but he was still talkin' crap to me and I yelled back, "Fuck you, too, man!"

Well, a few minutes later, I see a whole bunch of Roman Gents trying to get this cat to be cool, but nope, he's comin' over to me and he shouts, "Motherfucker, I'm gonna kick your ass!!" And then—bingo!—the music stops and I hear everybody whisperin', "Winky's gettin' ready to fight." *Winky!* Damn, I didn't want to fight *him.* So as he walks up to me, I say, "Hey, man, I really didn't say *anything* about your sister." But before I can say anything else, Winky's on me, and swingin'. Well, I beat his ass—I just cleaned up on the cat—and as I'm givin' it to him, I see this girl Paula, who I just loved, so I start getting loud. And as I'm punchin', I'm also shouting: "*Muthafuckah! You gonna fuck with me?!*"

Well, the head of the community center finally pulled me off, but Winky and his friends waited for me outside and I had to sneak home. For the next few weeks, wherever I'd show up, it wouldn't be too long before somebody would come up to me and say, "Hey, man, Winky and his boys are on their way over here to get you."

It really got *hot* for me—no jokin' around—so that summer, I moved in with an uncle in Las Vegas. When I went back, I was sure things had cooled off, but one night I'm comin' out of a party and who do I bump into? Right, Winky and his boys. But instead of fightin' with me, he says, "Hey, little dude, you got a lot of guts. Come on in and have a drink with us." I was leery as hell, but there wasn't much I could do—I was surrounded by all these *big* mothers—so I went back inside and Winky told everybody, "This is our little dude. From now on, anybody fucks with him gotta fuck with *us.*" And so, throughout my high school years, most of the guys around San Francisco knew who I was.

PLAYBOY: Did you ever take advantage of your notoriety?

SIMPSON: Nope, I never infringed on people. I was just like Clint Eastwood: I only beat up dudes who deserved it.

PLAYBOY: And how often would *that* be?

SIMPSON: At least once a week, usually on Friday or Saturday night. If there wasn't no fight, it wasn't no weekend.

PLAYBOY: Did it ever get beyond fists?

SIMPSON: Not with me, it didn't. I was in *gang* fights where a couple of guys got croaked, and you could be at the YMCA with 600 people when a mini-riot would break out and, the next day, you'd read about some cat gettin' stabbed. But, basically, me and my buddies were all into sports. And even then, sports was lucky for me: If I hadn't been on the high school football team, there's no question but that I would've been sent to jail for three years.

PLAYBOY: Why?

SIMPSON: When I was in the 10th grade at Galileo High—I think it was 1962—the whole Haight-Ashbury thing had already started. San Francisco always used to have beatniks, but now all these weirdos were coming in from all over the country and the only thing they talked about was *margarine* or *marinara*; I finally found out it was called marijuana. Up till then, me and my friends thought dope was something you only put in your arm, so we decided to make it over to Haight-Ashbury and see what was happening. We'd go down Page and Stanyan streets and walk into parties and see bald-headed Japanese cats praying and all *kinds* of characters smokin' that shit, and to us, it was just *weird*.

Naturally, the boys had to check out marijuana, and one day at school, we got hold of a joint; but when they passed it around, I just pretended to take a hit. I was a diehard athlete, and besides that, I didn't want to get *deranged*, right? I finally tried it one day and didn't get high—but I ran all the way home from school, breathing real hard *to get it out of my system*. I believed every horror story I'd heard about grass, and while I was runnin', I remember thinking, Goddamn, why did I do *that*? I'm gonna get *addicted*!

Anyway, during football season, a friend of mine named Joe Bell came up to me and my buddy Al Cowlings and showed us these two joints he had. Joe told us that a teacher wanted to buy them for a dollar apiece. Me and Al had football practice—Joe had been kicked off the football team—so we couldn't go with him to sell them. It turned out that the teacher was a narc. Joe wasn't a pusher, but for sellin' two joints to a narc, he spent three years in the big house. When Joe got out, he went to the University of Washington on a football scholarship, got his master's and is now working on his doctorate—he's into prison reform. Me and Al just happened to have football practice that afternoon, or else we'd have been sent up, too. That's the kind of life it was for us. We were just kids like any other kids, but we weren't growing up in Beverly Hills.

PLAYBOY: Earlier, you alluded to having spent time in the Youth Guidance Center. What kinds of things did the police arrest you for?

SIMPSON: Fighting, and once for stealing, which I didn't do. I don't want to make myself sound good, but one time our club was giving a dance and instead of buying the wine, the guys decided to rip it off. I kept tellin' 'em we had the money to buy the stuff, but no, they wanted to steal it. I didn't even go into the liquor store with 'em. I waited outside and when they came out, we walked around the corner—and right into the hands of the police. We'd planned that dance for months, had sent out hundreds of invitations, had done all *kinds* of advance work—we were calling it The Affair of the Year—and there we were, up against the wall, and then in jail. It was the worst. But we're only talking about the hairy moments now, and they were a real small part of growing up. Mostly, we had *super* times. And the majority of 'em had to do with bein' in the park from the time school was out until it got dark. We'd get out of school at three o'clock and we'd have a game goin' by 3:20.

PLAYBOY: What kind of game?

SIMPSON: Baseball. Everybody thought I'd become a major-league catcher and I probably would have if I hadn't kept busting up my right hand. The first time it happened was on a play at home plate during a high school baseball game. When I couldn't play baseball anymore that spring, I started running track—and I discovered that, while no one came to the baseball games, all the pretty girls showed up for track meets. At Galileo High, I ran in the 880 relays and we set a city record. The same kind of thing happened when I got to junior college: I broke my hand during baseball season, so I joined the track team, ran in the 880 relays and we set a national collegiate record.

PLAYBOY: How did you injure your hand a second time?

SIMPSON: You ever hear of an actress named Vonetta McGee? I broke my hand hittin' her brother Donald in the head. That *hurt*, Jack. It also convinced me to cool it on the fighting.

PLAYBOY: When did you begin playing football?

SIMPSON: Oh, I'd always played it, and I was on the team all through high school. But I never thought about playing *college* ball until the latter part of my senior year. Up until then, we'd always been easy to beat; in fact, in my junior year, we didn't win a game. In my senior year, though, we started winning and I made All-City. But I was overshadowed by the runners on the two top high school teams. I was the third back; and when the All-City team got written up, the papers said, "And O.J. Simpson rounds out the backfield." When I graduated, I didn't get a single scholarship offer.

PLAYBOY: In retrospect, that seems hard to believe. Why not?

SIMPSON: One reason was my grades: They were lousy. My only interest in school was in gettin' out, so I took courses like home economics and didn't exactly kill myself studying. I was gonna join the Marines and fight in Vietnam, but before I graduated, a friend came back from Vietnam missing a leg, and I thought I had to be *crazy* to go there. The football coach at Arizona State had shown some interest in me, but he took one look at my grades and told me he'd be in touch when I got out of junior college. So I enrolled at City College of San Francisco and in my two years there, I broke all the national junior college rushing records. That time around, I got a *lot* of scholarship offers.

PLAYBOY: Isn't it true that major football colleges staged a virtual bidding war for your services?

SIMPSON: Right: A whole bunch of 'em were offering all kinds of under-the-table shit. In addition to a regular scholarship, most of the schools were talking about $400 or $500 a month and stuff like a car. One school was gonna arrange for my mother to clean up an office for $1000 a month; another was gonna get my mother a house. A lot of stupid Watergate-type recruiting shit went on in those days, but in recent years, it's changed for the better, because the NCAA has cracked down pretty hard on a lot of schools. Even then, the NCAA was tryin', because they let it be known they were gonna investigate *whatever* school I picked.

PLAYBOY: Did USC offer you anything under the table?

SIMPSON: No, and it was probably the only school that *didn't*. It was also the only school I'd ever wanted to play for. When I was in the tenth grade and had just finished my first season of high school football, USC was playing Wisconsin in the Rose Bowl and I watched the game on TV. Early in the game, USC scored a touchdown and all at once, a beautiful white horse was galloping around the field. Right then and there, I thought, "That's the school *I* want to go to!"

Well, at the end of my first year in junior college, we played in a bowl game—the *Prune* Bowl, can you dig it? We were playing Long Beach, the defending national champion, and after being behind 20-0 in the first half, we came back and destroyed 'em, 40-20. I scored three touchdowns in the second half and was voted Most Valuable Player, and as I was walking off the field, a guy came up to me and said, "O.J. Simpson, that was a great game. My name is Jim Stangland and I'm a coach at USC. How would you like to be a Trojan?"

The man had just said the magic word. Inside my head, *bugles* were blowin' and that white horse was *gallopin'*! But I had a problem: Because of my high school record, USC couldn't get me in after just one year of junior college. I really didn't want to stay in junior college for another year, but USC assistant coach Marv Goux convinced me I should. So I did.

PLAYBOY: How did he get you to change your mind?

SIMPSON: He guaranteed me that if I went to USC and played the kind of football he thought I was capable of playing, I'd get more money out of pro football than anybody else ever got—much, much more than any other *school* could offer me. And the reason I love USC so much is that's exactly what happened. I was in the right place at the right time: We were good football players and in the two years I was there, our team was on television 17 times. The L.A. media are very powerful, and all that exposure during my first year helped me get voted UPI's player of the year. The second year, I won the Heisman Trophy.

I had the time of my life at USC, probably because that's where I started getting recognition—and when you're raised in a poor area, that's what you want more than anything else. It's the same thing Rocky Graziano felt when he was a kid: I am *somebody*. Recognition is more of a motivating force than money, because it's really hard to sit home and dream about *dollars*. You can think about what money will buy you, but recognition is really what you want. It was certainly the thing I wanted.

PLAYBOY: Few football experts, if any, would dispute the notion that you've been the most successful running back of your time. What do you think enabled you to become unique as a runner?

SIMPSON: That's hard to say. I never consciously tried to develop a running style or to imitate anybody else's, because any time you do that, you ain't gettin' into nothing but trouble. When they hand you the ball, you don't think, because you don't have *time* to think. You just run. And you *react*. You gotta be able to recognize certain things that are happening out there and react without thinking. To do that, you have to daydream about running. I can watch a million game films, but I do myself more good driving down the freeway, daydreaming about runs against various teams. Last season, you wouldn't *believe* how much I daydreamed about running 90 yards against Pittsburgh, which is one reason I was able to do it. When you're really into it, incredible things can happen. I've had teammates come up to me and ask, "How did you fake *that* cat? You never even saw him!" And I'll look at game films and it's true—I *have* put moves on guys I didn't see, but the thing is, when you're running, you can sometimes *feel* when a guy's almost on you. What you have to do is react as if he's already there, 'cause you may not even have the time to *look*. Some of the guys call that transcendental meditation, but to me, it's just putting yourself out there beforehand and imagining everything that's supposed to happen on every play. You got to be *very* receptive to that during a game, but that's not always easy. It calls for deep concentration.

PLAYBOY: At what point during a game does all this concentration become something like pleasure?

SIMPSON: When I'm doing my thing, man: The rush part of a game for me is running, and the biggest rush is in settin' a cat down. When you're running with the ball and you put an unbelievable move on a guy, just about every fan watching the game feels the same thing you do. It's a rush and the whole stadium shares it with you.

PLAYBOY: Is that what separates the superstar from his colleagues—the ability to make inspired moves?

SIMPSON: I think so. In basketball, you can cheer for a solid player like Lou Hudson, who can stand out there and pop for 25 points every night, but then you have to look at the difference between him and Earl Monroe. Well, Hudson comes down and hits his shots and he's methodical and he's great, but the Pearl will show you stuff you ain't never *seen* before, and suddenly you're on your feet, 'cause he's just too *much!*

In football, you watch good journeymen running backs like Ed Podolak and Jim Kiick, and they can put that shoulder down and follow their blocking and maybe get a little dippy, but when they make a move, it's usually a move that you saw coming. Then you look at Mercury Morris and just when you think he's trapped in the backfield, he'll do something you never saw before and everybody in the stadium is shouting, "Did you see *that?!*" And your friend's coming up the aisle with beers and you're yelling, "Man, you *missed* it! Mercury just done some shit you wouldn't *believe!*"

I call that *crazy* running and guys who do it are cats like Mercury, Chuck Foreman, Greg Pruitt, Otis Armstrong and Johnny Rodgers, who's playing up in Montreal. They all make insane moves that don't seem to have any logic, but somehow it turns out brilliant. And the crowds really dig it; lots of times I've gotten up after gaining maybe all of eight yards and the entire stadium is on its feet. More times than not, even the guy who was tryin' to tackle you is standing there starin', 'cause he knows he's lookin' stupid—and *you* know you just blew his *mind.*

PLAYBOY: How much are you going to miss all that—or are you?

SIMPSON: Oh, I can't say I'm not gonna miss football; I'll *miss* it, Jack. But the cold fact of the matter is that I'm gonna *have* to miss it, because I have no choice in the matter. If I couldn't have played this season, it would've been tougher to take, but eventually, you reach a point where you just *can't* play anymore. Once an athlete reaches that point of no return—and I'm not far from it—he realizes he's gonna have to retire. So I've tried to prepare myself for it. I've been watching other guys who've left the game and I've tried to evaluate where they are now. I've also thought about whether I could ever reach the same level in another profession that I've reached in football, and that's a tough one to answer. But whatever happens, I think I'll be able to handle it, even though you never know how you'll react to *anything* until it happens. I guess the only thing I can finally do is look back on what I did and be happy for it. And I am. I always enjoyed football and I think the guys I played with and against will remember me as a pretty good dude. In terms of being remembered as a player, I really think that if the game endures, then I'll endure. Hey, I'm *more* than willing to settle for that.

 October 2003 ───────────────────────────

A candid talk with the world's most notorious ex-athlete about his kids, his women, his brushes with the police and why he doesn't feel like a pariah

Few Americans, living or dead, carry the notoriety of Orenthal James Simpson. And few celebrities have ever divided the public so decisively. How one views O.J. Simpson—and the verdict in his 1995 criminal trial for double murder—has become a litmus test for all matters of race, injustice, police power and celebrity in the U.S. In a tale filled with strange twists and turns, this may be the strangest: The former All-Pro running back and B-list actor stands as one of the most intriguing—and most despised—figures of the late 20th century.

Forget Scott Peterson and Robert Blake. No accused murderer, and no crime, has captivated the nation quite like the murders of Simpson's ex-wife Nicole Brown and her friend Ronald Goldman. From the first news reports of the near decapitation and multiple stabbings to the bizarre Ford Bronco chase broadcast live on TV to the subsequent trial of the century, which found Simpson not guilty, America was riveted. Some considered the verdict an appalling miscarriage of justice; others saw it as vindication for a man who had been framed by a racist police force. Next year is the 10th anniversary of the 1994 murders, and the controversy has yet to diminish.

Despite his acquittal in the criminal trial, Simpson was found responsible for the murders in a 1997 civil suit brought by the victims' families, who were awarded $33.5 million in damages. Nicole's parents also sued Simpson for custody of their grandchildren Sydney and Justin.

After the court awarded him custody of his own children, Simpson moved his family from Los Angeles to southern Florida, but controversy dogged him there, too. In December 2000 he was charged with battery related to an alleged road-rage incident (he was acquitted). Later that year, federal agents searched his home for ecstasy and other drugs. No charges were filed. Several reports allege violent incidents involving Simpson and his current girlfriend, Christie Prody. Earlier this year, Sydney, who was 17, called 911 while fighting with her father. Child protective services investigated, but once again, no charges were filed. In addition to appearing in police blotters, Simpson is constantly in the tabloids. Recent reports claim that he received millions of dollars to star in a porno video and that buckets of golf balls were being dropped on his home at night, allegedly by police who were annoyed by being called so often.

Despite owing millions of dollars in legal fees, Simpson lives comfortably, albeit without the lavish perks of his former life. His primary income is his NFL pension, which, according to published accounts, totals $300,000 a year. Simpson may be a perpetual subject of the press, which reports on his comings and goings from courthouses, restaurants and golf courses, but since his move to Florida he has rarely granted interviews. Recently, Simpson agreed to sit down for his most in-depth and candid interview since the murder trial. To face off with him, *Playboy* sent Contributing Editor David Sheff to Miami. Simpson was accompanied throughout the interview, as well as in a subsequent follow-up session, by Yale Galanter, his attorney.

PLAYBOY: Nearly a decade after the murders of Nicole Brown and Ron Goldman, do you still maintain your innocence?

SIMPSON: I do. I had nothing to do with it. I am totally innocent.

PLAYBOY: And yet you remain one of the most hated men in America, someone most people think got away with murder.

SIMPSON: Maybe according to the media, but that's not my experience. Most people are supportive.

PLAYBOY: Most people we talk to are still angry about your acquittal.

SIMPSON: Early on, a few times somebody would get up and leave a restaurant when I sat down, though not much. Somebody broke the antenna on my car, someone spit on my car. I read stories about how I was kicked out of all these places or they wouldn't serve me, but it's bullshit. The truth is, I have trouble paying for my meals when I go out. People are always picking up the tab. Maybe somewhere people are saying other things, but I don't hear about it, except on television.

PLAYBOY: Are you resentful that your acquittal wasn't enough to exonerate you in the minds of most Americans?

SIMPSON: If the trial hadn't been on TV, most people would feel differently. If this had happened in Canada, where they don't let the media go on and on during a trial, it would be different. I was tried by the media before I was tried in court. Look at Scott Peterson. Ask anyone in America about him. They'll say the guy is guilty. But [at the time of this interview] we haven't heard one shred of evidence.

PLAYBOY: But Americans heard evidence in your case.

SIMPSON: They watched the media coverage. Most people don't know what was a rumor, what was true. There's a lot of money to be made by continuing the O.J. story. The other day I was trying on a pair of golf gloves, and the next day it's in the papers. The guy in the store sold the story. Negative stories sell. It's just like the reactions from people on the street. They have never been as bad as the media have made them out to be. The media want me to be this pariah, and I'm not.

PLAYBOY: That depends on who you talk to.

SIMPSON: No matter how they approach me, most people's reactions come down to this: "You went to court, and the jury says you didn't do it." Many people say, "You got screwed." Some say, "We don't know if you did it or not, but please take care of those kids."

PLAYBOY: Though you were acquitted in the criminal trial, you were held responsible for the murders in the civil trial.

SIMPSON: The civil trial was just a money thing. I don't think anybody can put the two in the same category. The chairman of a tobacco company gets sued because he allegedly knew that his company was killing people. But I'm willing to bet he's still in the same country clubs, he goes to the same restaurants. He paid his fine, and that's that. That's the way civil trials generally work. In my life, the important trial was the criminal trial. I was convicted by the media, not by the jury. The media blame everyone for the fact that I was found not guilty. They blame Judge Lance Ito, even though he consistently ruled for the prosecution. They blame Marcia Clark, the district attorney. They blame everything except the fact that I was innocent.

PLAYBOY: But most people don't believe in your innocence.

SIMPSON: The jury did. They came back with their decision quickly. If there was any reasonable doubt, they would not have come back so quickly. The majority felt I was jobbed. Unfortunately, the media didn't let that be the story. The show went on. Many people blame jury nullification, the fact that the jury was loaded with blacks. That's the biggest pile of crap I've ever heard. Go into the jury room in almost any major city. The vast majority of jurors, no matter how many blacks live in the city, are black. I've seen the jurors talk about my case. The older Caucasian lady said something like, "Look, when you see nothing there one day, and then three weeks later it's there—"

PLAYBOY: You're referring to the charge that the police planted evidence.

SIMPSON: Yes, and even people who believe I'm guilty believe that the police planted evidence. Early in my trial, after [LAPD detectives] Philip Vannatter, Tom Lange and Mark Fuhrman testified, one of the deputies in the jail told me, "I don't know if you did it or not, but those guys are liars and the jury knows they're lying. You're going home." When the jury knows that the cops are lying, they never convict.

PLAYBOY: Were you as confident?

SIMPSON: I was, because of my faith. From the start, I thought they were going to let me out of jail any day. I got a little disappointed as time went on, because I never thought it would go that far. I didn't understand the impact of the media, though. In a high-profile case, if you ask the public at the beginning of a trial and again after the verdict if they think someone is guilty, there's not much difference.

PLAYBOY: Are there parallels in your opinion between your case and the Scott Peterson case?

SIMPSON: I heard that Scott Peterson had $10,000 on him when he was arrested. Well, they said that I had $10,000 when I was arrested, but I had $3 or something. You never hear about it when it proves untrue. The first report on CNN about the Peterson case said that he had changed his look and was 30 miles from the Mexican border. It gave the impression that they caught him fleeing the country. They didn't say that's where he lives. They didn't say that he may have changed his looks so he could go out without everybody recognizing him—so he could go out on the golf course. They created the impression that he was fleeing, so he's guilty. I'm not saying that he isn't, but I don't pretend to know. I will say that at least 50 percent of my new friends thought I was guilty before they met me. They've changed their minds now that they've hung out with me, met my friends and met Nicole's real friends—not the Faye Resnicks and the wannabes, those party people the media focused on. Now, when they see the tabloid stories about me, they get madder than I do. I have to calm them down. Someone puts out that I did a porno movie. It starts in some tabloid, then the mainstream media pick it up.

YALE GALANTER: The *Globe* or *The National Enquirer* came out with a headline: "O.J. Simpson Gets Paid $10 Million To Do Porno Film." I can assure you that if anybody offered O.J. Simpson $10 million to be in front of a camera, with or without clothes on, we would take the money.

SIMPSON: I would have done it in the middle of Bayshore Boulevard. Before the article came out, the person who tried to set me up admitted the truth, but the paper still wrote the story as if it were a fact.

PLAYBOY: Who tried to set you up?

SIMPSON: Some guy. He tried to set me up with these girls: "Come in the room. Have a drink." They had cameras, thinking they were going to catch me doing someone. I guess the guy sort of felt guilty. He warned me—not that I was going to do anything anyway. Another time, in Las Vegas, I went to a room with a guy who had half a million dollars and these two girls who were in the porn business. He said, "After sex, we'll put a million and a half dollars wherever you want." I wasn't interested, though I might have been with one of the girls. All my friends thought I was crazy. They would have gone for it. I'm a bachelor—I can do what I want. But my mother was still alive at the time. I have two young children. I have turned down millions of dollars. That's the truth, but no one is interested in that story.

PLAYBOY: How does the media scrutiny affect your day-to-day life?

SIMPSON: I am calcified by it all.

PLAYBOY: Does it make you angry?

SIMPSON: It's one thing to target me, but don't try to put these inferences on my kids. I think the average person would agree that my kids have gone through a lot. It's not too much for me to ask that they be left alone. They are terrific kids. The president's daughters have gotten into trouble. Governor Jeb Bush's daughters have had troubles. Nobody calls President Bush or Governor Bush bad parents. If my son and daughter had committed any of those indiscretions, the reaction would be, "Oh, those poor kids. What would you expect?" Nobody wants to give me credit that, as a single parent, I've done something right, because I have two exceptionally well-adjusted kids.

PLAYBOY: Yet Sydney recently called 911, reportedly after a fight with you.

SIMPSON: I keep asking her why she called. She says, "Well, I just wanted to ask them a question," and she did: "Is it abuse if he tells me I'm a pain in the ass?" It wasn't even an argument. She was on the wrong side of something with her brother, and I told her to look in the mirror. She's kind of driving everybody crazy around here. It's just a teenage-daughter thing. The media make it a hundred times more than that. Nobody was in danger, nobody was threatened, and the police let it go. It was a nonincident.

PLAYBOY: How many teenagers call 911 just because their parents reprimanded them?

SIMPSON: Evidently it happens quite often. When the police came, they knew immediately what it was, and yet it became a media event because someone sold the story. I have learned that you can't believe what you read or hear. I don't know if Robert Blake or Scott Peterson is guilty. I have my opinion, but I would never say it publicly. Until these guys are proven guilty, they are innocent.

PLAYBOY: Which of your children had the hardest time losing their mother and then surviving the trial and custody battle?

SIMPSON: My daughter had more time with her mother. She was just a teenage girl. My son, Justin, is probably more easygoing. Sydney's a little more serious. From day one she has been more protective of me. She's heard people, relatives or otherwise, say things about me, and it took her a while to forgive them. Anytime she perceives that somebody has slighted me, she tenses.

PLAYBOY: It was recently reported that someone, possibly the police, has been pelting your house with buckets of golf balls, dropping them from a helicopter.

with no visible means of support for years leading up to Nicole's death. Just look at her tax returns. She was on welfare. She helped bankrupt Orange County. Her only income in the past 15 years has been since Nicole's death.

PLAYBOY: We read that Denise is running for Senate.

SIMPSON: She never would. She would have to open up her books and her past. Trust me, I know her past. There are bodies buried. And I mean literally.

PLAYBOY: Literally?

SIMPSON: Everybody knows she had a lot of problems. She has a boyfriend who was murdered.

PLAYBOY: Are you saying that she was involved?

SIMPSON: No, I'm not suggesting she had anything to do with it. I'm not saying she killed anybody, but I'm just appalled at what she has done.

PLAYBOY: Back to the changes in your life. What's it like playing public golf courses after playing only private country clubs?

SIMPSON: People think I was kicked out of all these private golf courses, but it's bullshit. I chose to resign. I just didn't think it was right for me to come there bringing all that baggage. I've played a lot of private country clubs since then with no problems, though. It's ironic when I do get shit, because I ain't been convicted of nothing. The vice president has two DUIs. The president has one, doesn't he? I don't even have drunk driving on my record.

PLAYBOY: Still, you were charged, and acquitted, in a road-rage incident. It was reported that you cut off some guy, got in his face, screamed at him and yanked off his glasses. What happened?

SIMPSON: I was driving my kids home. We were all fine, and all of a sudden this guy's on my tail. I stopped, got out and looked to see if something was wrong with my car. He got out and said, "You cut me off!" I said, "Man, you chased me down." He was in my face and I said, "Man, look—fuck you." I got in the car laughing. I said to my daughter, "Now, that guy needs decaf." Then they tried to prosecute me. They said that I took a guy's glasses off his face? Allegedly, that's my crime. For that, they asked for the maximum sentence of 17 years. It was the most amazing thing I ever heard. If the kids hadn't been in the car I would have made a deal. I would have taken anger management. I wouldn't have run the risk of going to jail. But because I've preached to them, "You've got to stand up; you can't let people run over you," I had to go to court and fight this. I wasn't nervous the day they read the verdict in the criminal trial, but I was nervous as hell when they were about to read this verdict. Everything I've ever believed in wouldn't matter if I was found guilty in any of these trials, or if I didn't get my kids in the custody trial. The only trial I lost was the civil trial, and for that the only thing I lost was some money. I didn't have much anyway by that time. Every other significant trial, I won.

PLAYBOY: Do you acknowledge that you lost more than money in the civil trial? It confirmed what most people suspected, and you lost your reputation.

SIMPSON: That's the only reason I kept fighting. A lot of friends told me that I couldn't win that trial. They had it all set up—the way they picked the jury. The hardest part afterward was adjusting to having two kids and not having unlimited funds. When we first moved here I had no credit cards. I had to get a car, buy a house. I had no cash to put down, so I was hustling. In many ways, though, my life is better now. My budget ain't what it was, that's all. I don't have the Ferrari, the Rolls-Royce. I always used to drive my Bronco anyway. I'm fine as long as I can get to and from the golf course.

PLAYBOY: How often do you play?

SIMPSON: Pretty much every day.

PLAYBOY: What do you get from golf?

SIMPSON: [When they found Laci Peterson's body] Scott Peterson was out playing golf, and people were saying, "What kind of guy is this? These may be his wife's remains, and he's going to play golf." Well, when I got home from Chicago the week Nicole was murdered, I wanted to get on a golf course. I wanted to get away from all the shit—all the hurt, all the pain. It's the only place I can go to get away from everything. I didn't go, but I had that feeling. I know that far more executives would be in therapy if it weren't for golf. A few of his friends helped Vitas Gerulaitis get off drugs, and then his addiction became golf. I used to play with him every day.

PLAYBOY: Is golf an addiction for you?

SIMPSON: It is. Next to sex, it is the single most addictive thing I've ever been into.

PLAYBOY: Some reports hold that you were on drugs before the murders, back in 1994. Were you using drugs?

SIMPSON: No, and I was tested about a hundred times.

PLAYBOY: What drugs have you used?

SIMPSON: I remember the first time I took a puff of pot. I was a kid, and I was going after a girl. I got so weirded out, I ran all the way home, virtually across town, trying to get it out of my lungs, thinking I would never play professional ball. Around 1972, there was a lot of pot around the NFL. Late in the season, when it was snowing in Buffalo and you couldn't go out, a lot of guys smoked pot. You could sit around and play cards, smoke a doobie and fall asleep, then go to practice the next day. I don't consider myself a pot smoker now, but I think it should be legal.

PLAYBOY: How about cocaine?

SIMPSON: When I retired from football, everybody was doing cocaine. If anybody in Hollywood tells you they weren't, they're lying their ass off. I was like everybody else, right? My house at the time of the murder was searched more than any house in America has ever been searched. If drugs were there, they would have found them.

PLAYBOY: There were in fact stories that you were using cocaine around the time of the murders.

SIMPSON: Faye Resnick said, "I was with him at a party once, and he went under the table." It was total bullshit.

PLAYBOY: Do you use any drugs now, even occasionally?

SIMPSON: I drink some scotch. My drug of choice now is Vioxx. When I got out of jail, I kind of appreciated pot more than I ever had in my life. I didn't have my kids at first. I couldn't go nowhere. They used to call me Two Puffs: Two puffs, I'm home. I watch TV. Then I'd sleep like a baby.

PLAYBOY: How about ecstasy?

SIMPSON: In 1993, one rather famous young lady brought ecstasy to a party. About 20 people took it. I never felt the high. I'm not a pill guy. Pills are not my thing, except glucosamine.

PLAYBOY: It was reported that your home was recently searched in relation to an international ecstasy ring.

SIMPSON: We can't discuss this, because it relates to an ongoing case.

PLAYBOY: According to a report in the media, police allegedly found four bags of marijuana, cocaine residue, two drug pipes and a can with marijuana residue.

GALANTER: [*To Simpson*] Don't say anything. The police did not find any drugs, any illegal materials at all, and Mr. Simpson has never been charged. If you read it somewhere, it's bad journalism.

PLAYBOY: Do you take sleeping pills?

SIMPSON: I took them the whole time I was in jail, but not now.

PLAYBOY: Do you ever have nightmares about Nicole or her murder?

SIMPSON: I used to a lot. At first I wasn't able to sleep at all, which is why I took sleeping pills. Now I hardly ever dream about it.

PLAYBOY: As an athlete, you probably wondered if women were interested in you or in your celebrity. Did the murders bring you a different type of attention?

SIMPSON: Strange thing is that it's actually easier now. Celebrity and notoriety are an attraction device. I never thought I was handsome. When interviewers asked about it, I said, "What good looks?" I said I was fit but never felt I was handsome. Now everybody is fit and I'm not. I can pretty much tell girls who hit on me just for me. Hell, after the criminal trial, two or three of my first affairs were with people I met at the front gate at my house. The tourists would stop in the driveway, and I got to know them and would have a little fling with them.

PLAYBOY: Did some of that attention surprise you? We read that women threw panties over your gate.

SIMPSON: They threw them over the wall. The media wrote that I was bragging about it. No, I wasn't bragging about it. I was perplexed by it. I've always got over with women as a good guy—a nice-guy athlete—but when I became an infamous guy, it was almost like I had some kind of Spanish fly emanating from my body. Really. Somebody needs to study this phenomenon.

PLAYBOY: How did life change when you moved to Florida?

SIMPSON: There is a little more international flavor here. It's a very Latin community. And it ain't like I've dated a lot of girls. I'm 55 years old. I've always had this reputation of dating a bunch of girls, but it's not true. Most of my relationships, even my illicit ones, were longterm relationships. One of my pet peeves is the tabloids saying I'm always into blondes. My first wife wasn't blonde. Nicole was, but Paula Barbieri wasn't a blonde. Christie Prody, when I first met her, was a brunette. She lightened her hair like a lot of women do. And let me tell you something: A man has no say what a woman is doing to her hair.

PLAYBOY: It was said that Christie dyed her hair to look more like Nicole, that she was a Nicole look-alike. To many people, that seemed creepy.

SIMPSON: She is by far not the first girl they said was a Nicole look-alike. But with Christie the papers airbrushed her and they took the cleft out of her chin. You know what they can do with photos. Truth is, they don't look alike. I see some of these people on these shows: "It's eerie. She looks so much like Nicole." Well, if I saw a girl who looked like Nicole, I would be totally turned on by her. I always loved the way Nicole looked. I've seen guys marry carbon copies of the lady they divorced. What is so eerie about this?

PLAYBOY: Are you still going out with Christie Prody?

SIMPSON: Yes. We have dated on and off a few times. We got back together not long ago. She went off to do what she had to do, and I'm seeing her now.

PLAYBOY: Are your children critical of the women you date?

SIMPSON: There is no doubt about it. Any teenage daughter is going to be critical of anything her father does or says. Boys are a little more understanding of what single dads do than daughters are.

PLAYBOY: Would you run any prospective girlfriends by her?

SIMPSON: I don't have to, because she is always giving me her opinion, like it or not. Lately, all we've been talking about is college. That's been the big focus with her and me.

PLAYBOY: Do you have to approve Sydney's boyfriends?

SIMPSON: With kids, you have no say. I have tried to raise these kids to be independent. I've probably given them more room than I should have and spoiled them a little bit. My daughter drives a Lexus. But I spoil everybody in my life. In addition, my kids have had to endure more than most people's kids. For whatever reason, they have come out of it in pretty good shape. More than not, they still give me fatherly respect.

PLAYBOY: How cautious are you when you meet new people?

SIMPSON: I can't live in fear.

PLAYBOY: Are you suspicious?

SIMPSON: Most of my friends and my daughter have been on me, because they say I am still too trusting. If somebody wants to get you, they're gonna get you. This is me. You like me or you don't. I don't care what your opinion is. What's amazing to me now is that some people can't let me go—Bill O'Reilly, Geraldo Rivera. In a way, it's almost flattery. Ten years later, and they can't let me go. So many things have happened in this country, but they just can't let me go.

PLAYBOY: Are some charges more offensive than others?

SIMPSON: The worst is the abuse. That bothers me as much as anything.

PLAYBOY: Do you admit that you did get physically violent with Nicole?

SIMPSON: There was the one incident that everyone knows about. Her mother and her best friend said publicly, "Nicole came in the room and attacked him." I never made any bones that I reacted wrongly. They investigated, went to every girlfriend I've ever had, and my girlfriends stood up for me. How many guys in this country can go back their whole lives, and their exes all have nothing but good things to say about them? Yet I'm this poster boy for abuse. That bothers me. As an adult I've never had a fight with anybody. Sometimes you have to check a guy who gets a little out of line, but you don't hit him.

PLAYBOY: How do you explain the series of visits from the police related to rows with Christie Prody?

SIMPSON: I was living in a hotel when I moved here. Christie got a flat tire about a mile away. She walked to the hotel. I wasn't registered in my name, and apparently she gave the desk a hard time. They called me, and I told them to send her up. They sent her to the wrong room. I heard something down the hall. I looked out and saw her, and I said, "I'm down here." She was walking toward me, just beside herself. A lady behind her, who was already pissed at her for whatever had taken place downstairs, called the police.

PLAYBOY: The woman reported that Prody hit you.

SIMPSON: She never hit me. It was nothing, and yet the next day, media trucks were everywhere. People like Bill O'Reilly refer to it as the knock-down, drag-out fight at the hotel. It's part of O.J.'s legacy. Another time, I went to her house to drop something off. When I drove up, I saw a neighbor staring. The guy sprints into his house. Five minutes later, I leave. I'm driving home, and I get a call from Christie: "O.J., you won't believe this. The cops just came and asked me if I was all right." I didn't think anything about it, but the next day the papers reported that she and I had a fight so loud that the neighbors called the police. I was pissed. We asked the neighbors. It was just one guy. Two weeks later, they released the 911 call. The guy didn't even call to report a fight. He thought there was some type of court order against me being within 100 yards of her. It was a total mistake.

PLAYBOY: Another time, you apparently called 911 regarding a woman who was high on drugs. The media reported that it was Prody.

SIMPSON: It wasn't. Some friends were trying to do an intervention on a girl with a drug problem. She went into hysterics and got in a car. I did exactly what everybody tells their kids to do: Don't let a friend drive under the influence. She wasn't my friend, but I called 911. I just wanted the cops to stop her. I just didn't want this girl to kill herself or somebody else. Suddenly it's a fight between me and my girlfriend. Drugs were involved. I'm the big news.

PLAYBOY: It sounds like you think it's an accident that you are involved in so many incidents with the police. Most people make it through their lives without the police being called at all.

SIMPSON: It's because I'm big news and people make money on it. It all becomes part of the O.J. story.

PLAYBOY: Throughout this interview, you have seemed incredulous that people still think you are guilty.

SIMPSON: No, it doesn't surprise me, because every day something was in the media—the shovel, the plastic bag. They never talked about the explanations. After the trial I spoke at Oxford and a couple colleges in L.A., and I put it to a vote: Who thinks I'm guilty? Eighty percent did. Why would I do it? Jealousy. Show me one shred of evidence that they presented in the court that goes with the jealousy theory. To this day you hear people say it was about jealousy and control. Yes, she had the thing with Marcus Allen, but that happened years before. They made it like it just happened. On *20/20*, Barbara Walters said, "We found out that O.J. had some financial strains. His Hertz deal was up, and they weren't going to rehire him. His NBC deal was up. He's paying in the neighborhood of $50,000 to $55,000 a month in alimony and support." Hugh Downs said, "A lot of people say that might give a person a reason to do something drastic." Then they go off the air. They've left the American public with a motive. But NBC had just extended my contract and given me a raise. Hertz, two or three months earlier, had extended my contract and given me a big raise. I didn't pay any alimony. This is supposedly an investigative journalism show, and they just flat-out lied. They could easily have called Hertz, NBC or any lawyer involved in the divorce. They could have called Nicole's parents. They would have known that every facet of this story was a lie. I was so pissed off, I got Barbara Walters on the phone, and she gave me some hullabaloo: "Well, O.J., that really wasn't my story. They just put it on the Teleprompter. I didn't have time to check it. I will look into this." Has she ever gone public and said that story was absolutely false?

PLAYBOY: The infamous Bronco ride didn't help. Why, if you weren't guilty, were you trying to get away?

SIMPSON: Don't you find it curious that in not one of the trials did the prosecution bring up the Bronco ride? The perception was better than the facts.

PLAYBOY: Which were?

SIMPSON: I wasn't trying to get away. And I wasn't even driving.

PLAYBOY: That's not relevant. Your friend could have been trying to help you flee.

SIMPSON: We called the police. They knew where we were going. We were going to my house from the cemetery.

GALANTER: One of the first things they teach you in law school is that evidence of flight can be used as evidence of guilt. It's not flight if someone calls the police and says, "This is where we're going, if you want to meet us."

PLAYBOY: Many Americans watched the chase on TV. You sure looked like someone who was guilty.

SIMPSON: Looked like? Maybe, but you have to know the facts. I was going home, and the police knew it.

GALANTER: It wasn't a flight situation. If it were, the prosecution would have used it.

PLAYBOY: If the police knew where you were heading, why were they after you?

SIMPSON: Ask them! Police from every jurisdiction were there.

GALANTER: It was because it was an event. It was on the national news. They preempted everything else on television.

PLAYBOY: How do you respond to the theory that you committed the crime but don't know that you did—that you blacked out or have blocked it out?

SIMPSON: How ridiculous is that? I don't think I've ever come across as some flighty kind of guy. I've always been outspoken and loud. That's some pseudointellectual analysis. Listen, I know I was a very well-liked guy before. I'm an easy target. If everything people like Bill O'Reilly say about my trial were real facts, I wouldn't be here talking to you. I realize that O'Reilly's show is about him being a dick sometimes. But it amazes me that our society has reached a point where the nastier you are, the more popular you are. The other reason my story wouldn't go away is that it helped so many careers, and these people keep it going. They refer to it all the time.

PLAYBOY: Does it bother you that many people have made careers off you?

SIMPSON: To be honest, I don't begrudge anybody. I don't begrudge Marcia Clark getting $4 million for her book. I don't have any feelings one way or the other.

PLAYBOY: How about the others?

SIMPSON: I have a little sore spot with Robert Kardashian and Larry Schiller, because they didn't have to lie and use everybody, from me to Lee Bailey to Johnnie Cochran. What they did was dishonest. Bob needed the money, and we all agreed to help him with his book. As a lawyer, though, some privileged things couldn't be in the book. To get around that in the end, because they wanted dirt, they made it Schiller's book, with Bob as an advisor. That was wrong. It was bullshit.

PLAYBOY: Did any journalists give you a fair shake?

SIMPSON: Linda Deutsch, Greta Van Susteren—those are people I have respect for. Greta doesn't try to belittle people. I'm a big Greta fan. But if I start talking about the ones I think were just totally dishonest, the list would be way too long. Barbara Walters and I had finally almost made up and I was going to do her show. At the last minute they wouldn't do it because I wanted it live. I'm not gonna tape it so you can make it whatever way you want. So she told everyone that she didn't want me. I'll be damned if she didn't call me. Barbara Walters can kiss my ass. That lady has no integrity as far as I'm concerned. Larry King kind of came and went with me. We were going to have a debate between my camp and Fuhrman's. We were told that Fuhrman wouldn't go on with my guy, so they canceled him. Larry King told the audience that they wanted somebody from the O.J. camp but we declined to send anybody. I lost my respect for him, though I've gotten some of it back.

PLAYBOY: Many people feel that your dream team of defense lawyers are the ones responsible for a murderer—you—walking around free. The verdict infuriated many people who thought you got off because you were rich and famous, and money in America is what matters.

SIMPSON: Well, I didn't commit the crime. That is why I got off. I feel in my heart that I got off because I was innocent, but I don't know if I could have proven my innocence if I didn't have the money. And that's a shame. Yes, it is a shame that in this country it costs so much to get good representation.

PLAYBOY: If a friend of yours were in a similar situation and could afford the dream team, would you recommend the same configuration, or would you revise it?

SIMPSON: The problem I had, and this became a full-time job, was ego, headed by the feud between Shapiro and Lee Bailey. Knowing what I know now, I wouldn't make changes. How can you change success? Obviously, there were too many lawyers, too many cooks, but everybody did a great job.

PLAYBOY: Recent reports claim that you will be doing a reality TV show.

SIMPSON: I saw a poll the other day that said 93 percent of people would watch a reality show of mine. That's a hell of a number for anybody. People have been talking to me about doing one, but I expect it will get bogged down somewhere. The average person on the street would love to hear me comment on Robert Blake or Scott Peterson. I have a unique insight on what they're going through.

PLAYBOY: Do you know Blake?

SIMPSON: We used to work out at the same gym back in the 1970s. I understood when he wanted to speak to the public. I fought Johnnie Cochran on that, too. I felt I had to take the stand. Marcia and them would say all these things in argument and in their opening and closing statements, and I wanted to address them. I never could.

PLAYBOY: You once said that your mission now is to convince the public of your innocence. Do you still think you can?

SIMPSON: I still think that I might be able to. The last thing a couple of people would want is for me to find out I've got six months to live. Then I think I would get to the truth real quick.

PLAYBOY: What are you implying?

SIMPSON: Why don't we just leave it at that? I always thought that if they had put pressure on Faye Resnick in the beginning, especially when they found out she'd lied to me, they may have learned the truth about who killed Nicole.

PLAYBOY: Are you saying Resnick knows?

SIMPSON: Not that she killed Nicole, but they never investigated those people around her, the circle. Maybe it was people she hung out with in that crowd. I'm not saying that Faye was involved directly, but she may know more than she has said. I can't dwell on that. I have my life, my children.

PLAYBOY: Do you go to church?

SIMPSON: I do. I take my children to a Catholic church. They are Catholic because of their mother. I go to a Baptist church, too. In jail, I read the Koran as well as the Bible. I still read both.

PLAYBOY: Do you believe in heaven and hell?

SIMPSON: I do.

PLAYBOY: Where will you be heading?

SIMPSON: Heaven. I'll be seeing my mother there.

PLAYBOY: What's the best O.J. Simpson joke you've heard?

SIMPSON: I was in the Bronco and when I realized where we were heading, I said to A.C., "I said Costa Rica, motherfucker, not Costa Mesa."

PLAYBOY: What one thing would you like to say to those of us who are convinced you're guilty of murder?

SIMPSON: Worry about your own soul. I'll worry about mine. Worry about your own soul.

MIKE TYSON

A candid conversation with the angriest man in boxing about the violence and rage that have dogged his life and the demons that still haunt him

When Mike Tyson enters the lobby of the Trump International Hotel in New York, he makes it clear he's none too happy. And when the meanest boxer who has ever lived is in a bad mood, it's a sight to behold. He is scheduled to finish the second lengthy session of the *Playboy Interview* in his hotel suite, but his mood, and the rules, have changed. He demands that this phase of the interview take place in Central Park, where the sun and humidity will cause his bodyguard to fetch a towel so Tyson can mop his sweat.

The weather isn't the only thing that's hot. Tyson's temper continues to boil as well. He flares at questions that he considers negative and slips into either brooding silence or manic free association. He is an athlete as famous for his troubled personal life as for his sports achievements, and on this sweltering New York afternoon, it's easy to see why. Of course, he has reason to be upset. In a few days, Tyson's lawyers will begin proceedings to help him regain his boxing license, first in New Jersey, then in Nevada. He lost his license—in spectacular fashion—in June 1997 in Las Vegas when, during his second bout with Evander Holyfield (Mike had lost the first), Tyson became so enraged that he bit off part of his opponent's ear. The Nevada State Athletic Commission hit him with a $3 million fine and revoked his license for a minimum of one year.

As he sits in the park, Tyson doesn't know if he'll be allowed to fight again. He feels that the sport needs him—no boxer since Muhammad Ali has captured the public's imagination the way Tyson has, and no other fighter can command the multimillion-dollar deals that make everyone in boxing happy. At the same time, no other athlete has been demonized the way Tyson has, though he has brought on much of the flack himself. The 32-year-old has been in frequent trouble with the law, including a highly publicized rape conviction for which he served a three-year prison term. Even his suspension has been marred by controversy—more problems with the police and a dramatic split from his promoter Don King, who Tyson claims has bilked him out of millions of dollars. No wonder he's angry. He's been angry his entire life.

Tyson was born on June 30, 1966 and grew up the youngest of three children in the Brownsville section of Brooklyn. He became a pickpocket on public buses, rolling drunks and relieving old ladies of their purses. By the time he was 13, he had been arrested 38 times and was eventually held in a "bad cottage" in the Tryon School for Boys detention facility in upstate New York.

It was there that Tyson learned to box. Bobby Stewart, one of the counselors and a former boxer himself, sensed Tyson's potential and took him under his wing. Stewart introduced the teenager to legendary trainer Cus D'Amato, a man considered odd even by boxing standards. D'Amato believed he had ESP and had a lecture for every human weakness. Over the years he had produced two champions—Floyd Patterson and Jose Torres. D'Amato was a suspicious man, generally had no use for society and was a socialist. By the time he got Tyson, he was viewed as a cranky recluse who ran a gym in Catskill, New York.

Aging and desperate for another champion, D'Amato became obsessed with the young Tyson. He channeled Tyson's physical strength and rage, and set about chiseling his masterpiece, a kid who he predicted would be a champion by the age of 19.

Tyson's brief amateur career showed promise, but it wasn't until he turned pro in March 1985 that he began to fulfill that promise. By the end of that year, he had 15 victories, all by knockouts, and no defeats. *Sports Illustrated* called him "the most devastating puncher in boxing, a remorseless attacker." After 27 consecutive victories, he fought Trevor Berbick for the World Boxing Council heavyweight title in November 1986. The match took less than six minutes, and when it was over, Mike Tyson was the youngest heavyweight champ ever at the age of 20—missing D'Amato's prediction by only one year.

D'Amato didn't live to see his protègè get the belt—he died of pneumonia in November 1985. That left Tyson's career in the hands of co-managers Jimmy Jacobs and Bill Cayton, who had worked with D'Amato. But when Jacobs died in 1988, Tyson felt he had lost his family. His career continued to thrive, however. He unified the heavyweight division, winning the title from all three boxing associations, and became the first undisputed heavyweight champ since Ali 10 years earlier. Even more impressive were the purses: $20 million for fighting Michael Spinks in 1988; $30 million for a bout with Frank Bruno in 1996. The ill-fated incident with Holyfield broke records with 1.8 million viewers on pay-per-view, bringing in $90 million in revenues.

Tyson couldn't have done this alone. At his side (or inside his head, depending on whom you want to believe) was the colorful Don King, the most powerful promoter in boxing.

What drew Tyson to King was the fact that King too was an ex-con, and in Tyson's mind, he had the èlan of a gangster. Tyson's view of King wavered between awe and disrespect. The latter surfaced whenever the press hinted that King was running him. Rumors circulated that Tyson had slapped King on several occasions and berated him at whim. Earlier this year Tyson fired King, though time remains on the promoter's contract. A long and bitter legal fight is under way.

This kind of fight will be nothing new to Tyson. He has spent more time in court than he has in the ring. In all, Tyson has fought fewer than 200 rounds during his professional career and has gone the full 12 rounds only three times—giving him a 45-3 record, with 39 knockouts.

In 1988, he married actor Robin Givens—a relationship that was marred by Givens' accusations (made during the couple's televised interview with Barbara Walters) that Tyson abused her. He had a couple of highly publicized car crashes (after running his Rolls-Royce into a parked car, Tyson told the cops to keep the $180,000 automobile, saying, "I've had nothing but bad luck with this car") and a few miscellaneous run-ins with police. He's been accused of assaulting various photographers and parking lot attendants, and has seen his share of brawling outside the ring.

In 1990, his fight with Alex Stewart was postponed when Tyson supposedly got a sparring cut. Not so, reported *New York Newsday*. Trump Plaza staffers said that a woman hit him over the head with a champagne bottle in one of the hotel rooms. Security guards found the woman "not in great shape," with a bleeding Tyson yelling, "The bitch deserved it!"

Events took a more serious turn on July 20, 1991 when Desiree Washington, then 18, filed rape charges against Tyson in Indianapolis, where she was competing in the Miss Black America Pageant. On February 10, 1992, he was convicted of rape and two counts of criminal deviate conduct. Although sentenced to six years, Tyson steadfastly denies the rape, saying he and Washington had had consensual sex. He was released after three years from the Indiana Youth Center minimum-security prison, during which time he converted to Islam.

After prison Tyson seemed to settle down, and he punched his way through a group of "unfits" toward Holyfield. In April 1997 he married his current wife, Monica Turner, a pediatrician (the mother of two of his children). They live in a sizable house that borders the Congressional Country Club in Bethesda, Maryland, just outside Washington. He also has large homes in Las Vegas and Ohio, and an estate in Connecticut. Recently, he considered selling the Connecticut house to shore up his dwindling finances. He changed his mind and earned extra cash appearing at a wrestling pay-per-view event and accepting an acting job.

It wasn't until this past winter that he found trouble again with the law. Tyson was at a Georgetown restaurant in D.C. in the early morning when he reportedly got into an altercation with two women who claimed he verbally and physically abused them. A lawsuit is pending.

Playboy sent freelance writer Mark Kram, who has interviewed such heavyweights as Sonny Liston and Muhammad Ali, to check in with Tyson at this crossroads in his life and career. Kram reports: "It took half a year to get Tyson to sit down and talk. His new management company in California kept saying that Mike was eager to get together, but he broke one engagement after another. The first interview took place in his Bethesda home. Present was his wife, Monica, a pleasant and charming woman who sat with us the entire time, remaining silent except to request that the name of a psychiatrist be expunged.

"We arranged to meet again three weeks later at the Trump International Hotel in Manhattan, just off Central Park. It wasn't a good day. I had to switch the tape recorder off whenever Tyson sulked, then we would talk quietly as I tried to bring him around. At one point he said, 'The interview is over,' yet he kept sitting there. I just let the silence surround him until he agreed to talk more.

"He was in a foul mood. He answered some questions in a crazed stream of consciousness. He kept slapping me on the thigh with his finger for emphasis. He frequently digressed from the subject without returning to it. Mike Tyson is the darkest figure in sports I've ever encountered. I left thinking that I had never before met a 32-year-old man so eaten up by rage, so hostile, despondent and absolutely convinced of his irredeemability."

PLAYBOY: A lot of fans, foes and boxing commentators are asking the same question: Is it over for Tyson?

TYSON: They said the same thing about Ali after his losses. No. It's not over. Not over at all.

PLAYBOY: Still, particularly after Holyfield, some people say you've lost the crown for good. How do you respond?

TYSON: Hit you upside your head, maybe. How's that?

PLAYBOY: We understand you're upset. Has it been particularly difficult for you to have fallen so far—prison, the suspension from boxing—after being the champion?

TYSON: I don't see myself as a superstar or icon. Other people might, but I don't. My record is not hype. It stands on its own. What do you want from me?

PLAYBOY: We want to learn about you. Are you looking forward to getting in the ring again?

TYSON: I don't give a fuck. The people don't give a fuck about me. There will be others after me.

PLAYBOY: While waiting to be allowed to fight again, you refereed a pay-per-view wrestling event. Why?

TYSON: It was cool.

PLAYBOY: You didn't consider it to be undignified?

TYSON: You remember Joe Louis?

PLAYBOY: Louis refereed after his boxing career was over. But wrestling isn't boxing; it's phony.

TYSON: The checks aren't phony.

PLAYBOY: Aren't you worried about your image?

TYSON: What image do I need to worry about? I've been in prison. I've been convicted of rape. I've had problems in and out of court. Are you kidding me? I do what I want. I'm not going to dance to nobody's tune.

PLAYBOY: But after being the heavyweight champion of the world—

TYSON: Which I deserved. What can I do? What I really want now is to hang out and deal with the problems in my life. Real life. Send the kids to school, go to PTA meetings and all that stuff. These are the things I'm trying to grasp now.

PLAYBOY: How hard have you been training?

TYSON: Me and a friend are just working out. Getting in shape. I've been cautious. I have tried to make better decisions. I consult my wife about everything. She was mad that I fought too soon after I got out of prison. I got out in March and fought in August.

PLAYBOY: Do you agree with your wife—that you fought too soon after leaving prison?

TYSON: I don't know.

PLAYBOY: Was prison worse than you thought it would be?

TYSON: It's something you get accustomed to. You can't wait to get home. I was just happy to make it through the day without being written up. Those were successful days. If you made it to the next day, the last count, boom! Another day you didn't get written up.

PLAYBOY: Were you ever attacked in prison?

TYSON: People will try you. They'll try the strongest. You have to be a man. They'll try anybody. They start by saying something funny, something sarcastic, to see how far they can go. But you nip it in the bud. You don't let anyone get away with saying anything funny or sarcastic. You have to demonstrate who you are right on the spot. That's what I do. That's who I am. I'm a settler. I'm in my glory in a place like that. Chaos all over. Yeah, they tried me a few times.

PLAYBOY: Did anyone pull a knife on you?

TYSON: They had them, but they didn't have anything I didn't have.

PLAYBOY: Did you see instances of sexual assault?

TYSON: All over the place. I didn't intervene. It wasn't my business. If I was getting fucked or raped, you think somebody would intervene? No. My job was to do my time, no one else's.

PLAYBOY: You spent time in solitary confinement. Was it particularly difficult?

TYSON: The hole was cool.

PLAYBOY: You didn't mind the isolation?

TYSON: No. The box was my savior.

PLAYBOY: It's been speculated that you were driven sort of crazy in the hole—and that's why you bit off Holyfield's ear.

TYSON: No. The hole could never drive you crazy. I like to be alone. That's who I am. I need to be into myself, in order to deal with the issues that are happening around me.

PLAYBOY: Let's get back to the infamous night when you bit Holyfield. Why did you do it?

TYSON: It was the second Holyfield fight. I was angry more than anything else. I snapped. I was an undisciplined soldier. I wanted to hurt him. I never thought about what I was doing.

PLAYBOY: What were you angry about?

TYSON: Just angry. Just mad. Just thinking about life and about the first fight, the people harassing me. I never take a fight personally.

PLAYBOY: Were you thinking about the earlier loss against Holyfield?

TYSON: I was angry. He was butting me with his head. I was hurt in the first and second rounds. No one believed me until they saw the film. I blacked out. Then the second fight: Whoa, I had that feeling again. And then it clicked. I saw him looking at my eyes, and I said, "This motherfucker." George Foreman said Holyfield is the dirtiest fighter he's ever seen. That first fight I didn't know what happened. I wasn't even feeling the punches. You could see them, you could hear them, but I didn't feel them. I was numb. I was getting hit and didn't feel them and couldn't do anything. He did the head butting intentionally. He knows he did and the ref knows he did. He did it intentionally.

PLAYBOY: Did you bite him out of anger or revenge?

TYSON: I wanted to kill him, bite him. I was just enraged and angry.

PLAYBOY: How did you feel afterward?

TYSON: I felt all messed up afterward. I didn't feel too cool about it. But it was over and I had to deal with it. I was upset that I did it. I never allowed myself to be angry in a fight before that. Never. I know I might appear to be angry, but I was never angry before in a fight. So I was embarrassed. I was shocked, scared. I didn't want to do that to him. I'd rather have him beat me.

PLAYBOY: How did you feel about Holyfield's reaction?

TYSON: He's a fighter. He's no fool. He understands what happens in our business. It happens.

PLAYBOY: How did the two Holyfield fights affect your place in boxing history? Where will you be ranked?

TYSON: Not too high. I have so many enemies. They control all that stuff. You know people don't give a damn about that stuff. They try to discredit me as much as possible. Fuck 'em. I know I fucked up my chance to be in the Hall of Fame, to be the kind of guy I always dreamed of being, but fuck 'em, fuck 'em, fuck 'em. The critics may use the Holyfield fights to deny me. But Ali lost fights. I don't give a fuck. My life is doomed the way it is. I have no future. I just live my life.

PLAYBOY: Doomed? Do you really feel that way?

TYSON: Oh, I'm going to make a lot of money, win titles. Good things are going to happen, but my social standing? Zero. I really feel bad about my outlook, how I feel about people and society, and that I'll never be part of society the way I should. After all my ordeals, I look at myself and people totally different.

PLAYBOY: Are you worried about the physical toll boxing has taken on you?

TYSON: No one else really cares, so why should I care? You should go down to Brooklyn, or Brownsville, or South Central, or Compton, and talk to those kids. "What do you think about being hit? Getting shot? Getting hit in the head?" They'll tell you, "I'm not going to get hurt. I'm going to kill me some motherfuckers." That's how I think. No one's going to hurt me, but I'm going to hurt some people.

PLAYBOY: Haven't you learned that you can be hurt?

TYSON: I've got kids to feed, and a wife. You think I care about my risks? I don't think about my risks.

PLAYBOY: Does your wife worry?

TYSON: I have to do what I have to do, she has to do what she has to do. I'm sure she worries, but she knew the route she chose when she married me. She knew what I did for a living. She knew her life was going to be different when she married me.

PLAYBOY: Do you think you will again be a great fighter? Have you lost the drive that made you great?

TYSON: I've lost my desire for certain people in the fight business, but not my desire to fight.

PLAYBOY: Who in the fight business have you lost your desire for?

TYSON: People in Don King's posse. He is more visible than anybody else, but he's not the worst. He's not the worst, trust me.

PLAYBOY: Trainers? Managers?

TYSON: They're scum. They should stand on their mothers' shoulders and kiss my ass. They say I have no character. You don't accomplish what I've accomplished without character.

PLAYBOY: How would you now describe your relationship with King?

TYSON: Don King isn't the worst person who's fucked me. He probably fucked me more royally.

PLAYBOY: How about Bill Cayton, who helped handle your career after Cus D'Amato died?

TYSON: Listen, I have opinions about these guys, but I want to say it to their faces, not behind their backs. And I don't want any sympathy from anybody. All I get is more bombardment. Fuck 'em! I'm ready to fight anybody. Not physically, just whatever is necessary. I just want to fight someone. That's who I am. Fuck 'em! That's why I'm assertive and aggressive and take no shit. I'm ready to go any time.

PLAYBOY: To the ring?

TYSON: Wherever. Hell. Heaven.

PLAYBOY: Has it been hell?

TYSON: Yeah, because they're faggots, bitches, wimps, weak, and they're not the man I am. Can't they live their lives? What fucking lives do they have? They don't know who the fuck they are. They'd give anything in the world to be me. They would be like me if they had the fucking nerve.

PLAYBOY: Do you believe Don King ruined you?

TYSON: Who knows if he ruined me. Please. I'm going to be champ again. Are you kidding?

PLAYBOY: Do you blame King for much of what you've been through?

TYSON: I'm my own person. Mike does what Mike wants to do. That's why I sometimes get in trouble, because I just want to do what I want to do. I don't trust people enough to take most of their advice.

PLAYBOY: Do you trust anyone?

TYSON: My best friends, my family—anyone else, to hell with them.

PLAYBOY: Did you trust King?

TYSON: Let's move on.

PLAYBOY: What type of contract did you have with King?

TYSON: I'm sorry. I can't tell you.

PLAYBOY: You've been harshly criticized by your former trainer Teddy Atlas. What do you think of him?

TYSON: I love him anyway.

PLAYBOY: Even though Atlas is critical of you?

TYSON: You know why? Because he wishes he was with me. If he's such a great trainer, why didn't he make someone else like me? None of his fighters ever beat me. Why didn't he put any of his fighters in there with me? He had Michael Moorer. Let me tell you something. These guys don't like me because they wish they were with me. I don't care how many fights their guys win, they ain't Mike Tyson.

PLAYBOY: Atlas is the one who says you have no character.

TYSON: I did three years in prison, I was denied workouts, training, doing anything, and came back and still won a title. That's no character? Am I not one of the rare flowers that blossom in adversity? And I don't have no character? I bet if I was with him he'd say how great I am, because I'm one of the greatest fighters that ever lived. What is he going to say about me when I'm dead? All of them will say, "He fucked it up, but he was the greatest." Listen, you can't find Atlas's name in the paper unless he's talking about me. You can't find any of those guys in the paper. The only thing he's got to contribute to what he does in life is to talk about me, someone who redesigned boxing.

PLAYBOY: How did you redesign boxing?

TYSON: I took it back to its raw form. Kill or be killed. The winner gets it all. That's what people want. I gave everybody what they want. And they paid me for it. People are afraid I'm going to unmask them for what they are. Hypocrites. What do I do to offend people? I go to a restaurant and get into a skirmish with someone, and 30 people write petitions that say I was justified in what I did. Yet I'm the bad guy.

PLAYBOY: Were you frustrated when you were barred from boxing?

TYSON: People discourage me. I'm engulfed by a whole bunch of emotional stuff right now.

PLAYBOY: Such as?

TYSON: Just a lot of personal endeavors, nothing I can't handle.

PLAYBOY: Legal matters?

TYSON: That and other matters.

PLAYBOY: Is it distracting?

TYSON: I'm working my way out of it.

PLAYBOY: How do you respond to the critics who say you were overrated from the beginning?

TYSON: That's their opinion. The quickest way to fail is to try to please everyone. Make everyone happy. I can't do that. I accomplished a lot as a fighter at a young age. I plan to accomplish more. I just got to be happy. All about me as a fighter is being happy.

PLAYBOY: Are you plagued by self-doubt?

TYSON: I don't know if it plagues me. What produces the self-doubt is boredom and idleness, when you're alone, when you're with your thoughts. In the midst of action I never have self-doubt.

PLAYBOY: It has been written that you suffer from depression. Do you?

TYSON: Sometimes. That's the way I've been all my life.

PLAYBOY: Has your behavior ever been diagnosed as manic-depressive?

TYSON: I don't think I'm manic, just depressed sometimes.

PLAYBOY: Do you take medicine?

TYSON: I don't take medicine. Probably one day in the future.

PLAYBOY: Have you been in therapy?

TYSON: I talk to a doctor now.

PLAYBOY: Does it help?

TYSON: Yeah, it helps. I'm a little apprehensive about expressing my thoughts to a middle-aged Jewish man. But I like him. I had such a need to do it.

PLAYBOY: When did you go into therapy?

TYSON: I've been in therapy for a while, since I left prison. I had one guy that was a quack. What a problem. He was seeing dollar signs. He wanted to be a member of my boxing team more than he wanted to be my therapist.

PLAYBOY: How often do you see your therapist?

TYSON: It's nobody's business how often I go.

PLAYBOY: What do you take away from it?

TYSON: I get shit off my chest, whatever it may be. It feels a lot better than just exploding.

PLAYBOY: A lot better?

TYSON: Yeah. Listen, I don't know if I need therapy or if I want therapy. I know I have to go to therapy. It's cool. When people think of Mike Tyson in therapy, they think of the extreme psycho, the walking time bomb. I say to those people, "You don't know me. Fuck you! You can't define me. I know who I am and what I am." They have no idea who I am or what I am. They just go by what they see in the paper, what people say. What I am you can't see in statistics. Because you have to look inside my soul. They don't care. They don't really care enough about me as a person to see who I am and what I am.

PLAYBOY: What would you like people to see?

TYSON: I'm not looking for someone to tell me that I'm great. I'm just living my life the way I want to. I'm not hurting anybody.

PLAYBOY: Many people can't get past the Desiree Washington rape trial when they think of you.

TYSON: The fact is, nobody gives a fuck about Mike Tyson. It's easy to hate Mike Tyson, to do something to Mike Tyson and get away with it. Mike Tyson is just that kind of person. Even if he didn't do it, he's capable of it, right? People don't get arrested and convicted because of what they actually do. They get arrested for what they're capable of doing.

PLAYBOY: What's your version of what happened?

TYSON: She comes to my room, and takes off her panty shield, ready to fuck. I fuck her, suck her on her ass, suck all over her. I perform fellatio [sic] on her. Then you're going to tell me [whispering] I took some ass? I'm holding you down, sucking your ass? I don't care if you believe it or not. Look at the common sense behind it. Now, of course, I'm a scumbag. I'm used to being that. But the fact that I took somebody's ass, that's a real riot.

PLAYBOY: So you claim there was never a rape.

TYSON: A lot of young women don't know what they're getting themselves into. Then they find, Hey, I'm above my head in this shit. A lot of them think it's fun, a game, and they don't understand what they're getting into when they're with men. All they know is what they read. But they truly don't know what they're into when they lock themselves in a room and engage in sex with a man who knows how to handle a woman.

PLAYBOY: And Washington?

TYSON: I don't know. I think she's mean and vindictive. She had it planned from the beginning. That's what I think.

PLAYBOY: What are your feelings about women in general? How do you feel about NOW protesting your reinstatement based on the rape conviction?

TYSON: I don't give a fuck about them. I've never done anything to those people. If I gave them some money, they'd say, "He should be reinstated, he's a great guy." Don't tell me about no fucking women's lib. How can a bunch of pussy-whipped men let their women parade around in a crusade saying, "All men are pigs. Us against them." Fuck you! I've done nothing to them. I've had problems with particular women who they might not like either if they knew them. Tell them I said fuck you. What about me? I got three daughters. What are they saying? That I'm fucked up, so my daughters are fucked up, too? That I don't care about women? That I'm going to abuse my daughters? I'm just a scoundrel? If I see a woman in a vulnerable situation, I'm going to take advantage of it, right? Is that what they're saying? Fuck you again. You don't know me. I've done nothing to no one. Just because I got accused of it, it all looks my way. Ask any woman on the street, an experienced woman, about my situation, what she's read, what she's seen, she can't understand it. How can you understand that?

PLAYBOY: Do you expect other people to believe you're innocent?

TYSON: I expect the worst to happen to me in my life. I expect people to fuck me and treat me bad. That's just what I expect. I fight it. I try to do something about it. I'm not going to let anybody walk over me. I expect that one day somebody, probably black, will blow my fucking brains out over some fucking bullshit, that his fucking wife or girlfriend might like me, and I don't even know she exists. Some bullshit will happen. I expect that to happen in my life. No one gives a fuck about Mike Tyson. If someone accuses Mike Tyson of a horrible crime, they say, "Yeah, he's capable of that, Mike probably did it." Nobody's fighting a crusade for my black ass.

PLAYBOY: Were you surprised by the trial and your sentence?

TYSON: What can I say? They fucked me. I been fucked most of my life. What the fuck can I do? I paid the money. Big fucking deal! What the fuck can you do if it happens to you? Am I the only person? What the fuck can I do?

PLAYBOY: You're obviously very angry.

TYSON: Please, sir, I'm not personally mad at you. That's just the way I talk. I put my life in someone else's hands, what can I do? I don't know anything about law. So they put a grim reality on my life. But I was born in a den of iniquity. I was born in guck, mud. Humiliation. I used to be tortured, brutalized. Any bit of hope was destroyed. That's where I come from. A guy may get on the honor roll. Fuck him! He's a fucking mark! He's a sucker. If he ain't out there getting money at age 12, he doesn't have a couple thousand in his pocket, not wearing the finest clothes of the day, well fuck him! Fuck him! I don't give a fuck if he dies! That's where we come from. Every now and then you run into some good people who ain't gonna let somebody kill some white boys who are asking for directions and are grabbed, pulled out of the car, robbed and beaten. Some good people come out, get on these motherfuckers' asses and say, "Motherfuckers, these are people! You let these people go their way." Then again, there are people who say, "Kill 'em. Kill them white motherfuckers. Kill 'em. I hope they fucking die! They kill and beat us every day." You see, these people are hurt and bitter in their hearts. But they're good people. Their pain and bitterness overfuckingwhelms them. Then when it's over they feel bad because somebody was hurt. The first thing they see is that we were killed like animals, like in Canarsie in the late seventies. We had no rights. Motherfuckers kill us, get only five, maybe ten years.

PLAYBOY: You said you were born in a den of iniquity. Is that how you characterize your childhood in Brownsville?

TYSON: We all have hard lives. It's the way the wind blows. You go into the heart of Brownsville, looks like World War II hit it. The buildings aren't stable. Here, they'd put up a new one. In Brownsville they leave it, then it falls and kills people. Who gives a fuck? No one gives a fuck.

PLAYBOY: What was it like at home?

TYSON: Apartment. Very small. Four, five people sometimes, sometimes more. Other people would stay over till they got situated. It was hard. Paying the bills: water bills, light bills. Light goes off, heat goes off, water goes off. Have to pay somebody to go down there to handle the mechanics.

PLAYBOY: Was there always food on the table?

TYSON: We got home so tired we didn't care if we ate or not. They had a free lunch program at school and we'd stand in line for it: sandwich, an orange, banana or pear, and juice and milk.

PLAYBOY: What do you remember about your father?

TYSON: He always had Cadillacs. Who knows what he was doing back then. He was a gambler probably. Always a hip guy. Everybody knew him and talked about him. No responsibility. He was just a cool guy. All the women loved him.

PLAYBOY: Some reports claim that he was a pimp.

TYSON: I don't know what he did. He was very handy with women. Back in 1991, 1992, me and him started talking to one another.

PLAYBOY: What did you talk about?

TYSON: He was always trying to explain what happened between him and my mother, but I wasn't interested. By that time I'd been through a relationship and had children and realized that people just don't get along sometimes. And sometimes kids suffer. It just happens. I always loved my father. I never held anything against him.

PLAYBOY: What did your mother think of your father?

TYSON: Never said much about him, because she knew I loved my dad. He died when I was in prison.

PLAYBOY: Your mother raised you and your brother and sister, right?

TYSON: Yeah.

PLAYBOY: Did you miss having your father around?

TYSON: All the time. A woman can't teach a man how to be a man. You need a man to do that.

PLAYBOY: Is that partly why you got in trouble as a youth?

TYSON: It's rare in that neighborhood to see a guy who gets straight A's in school, who goes to school every day. Instead, you see a guy like me—in trouble all his life. Everybody says, "He'll be in prison for the rest of his life."

PLAYBOY: You obliged them.

TYSON: Yeah, but I didn't turn out the way they thought. They didn't think I'd make it to 16.

PLAYBOY: At what age were you more or less on your own on the street?

TYSON: About 10.

PLAYBOY: You have a high voice. Did kids make fun of you?

TYSON: The objective of man is to be tough. If anyone insults you, you got to fight. That's just the law of the street. Some people would make fun of me. I'd fight 'em.

PLAYBOY: Were you in many fights?

TYSON: Many. If somebody gets beat up real bad they don't want to use the system anymore. They get their knife, their gun, they want to fight. They want to hurt somebody. We have the animal instinct to survive. I got hit with bats, sticks, bottles across my face.

PLAYBOY: You've said that you are sometimes depressed. Were you depressed as a child?

TYSON: I don't remember. It wasn't depression back then. You know, you're poor, you don't have good doctors. You have poor doctors who say, "He's hyperactive" or "He's a special ed student. We'll put him somewhere else so he won't disrupt the other students."

PLAYBOY: Were you ever labeled violent or antisocial?

TYSON: Not really.

PLAYBOY: You were once described as borderline retarded, a term that is no longer used. Did the labeling affect you?

TYSON: I appeared to be retarded. I never thought I was, though.

PLAYBOY: When you look at yourself then, is it the same person you see now, only younger?

TYSON: Two different people. They wouldn't even hang out together. They'd never like each other, just feel contempt for each other.

PLAYBOY: Were you on welfare as a child?

TYSON: Yeah. And I hated it. It's humiliating, embarrassing.

PLAYBOY: Did you do lots of drugs?

TYSON: I did a lot when I was a kid. But it wasn't my thing. I never got hooked. If you get hooked on drugs, you must not have a thing to do in your life. You know how boring drugs are? Being high all the time? You know how fucking boring that is? I want motherfucking action. I need action.

PLAYBOY: You raise pigeons. What do they mean to you?

TYSON: It's something I've done all my life. Something like racing horses or gambling. Just something I do.

PLAYBOY: Weren't you once nearly hanged for stealing pigeons? The story goes that a noose was around your neck and you were going to be dropped off a building, but someone saved you.

TYSON: When I was younger that's what people did. What does that have to do with this interview?

PLAYBOY: It's your life.

TYSON: I don't like to talk about that.

PLAYBOY: You don't like to talk about your childhood?

TYSON: Every time you talk about Brownsville it sounds negative. It was happy, too. Nothing big, just going to the pool. Gambling without anybody getting killed or robbed over a dice game. Laughing. Cooking food outside and music. That was fun. May not be fun to you. It was fun to us.

PLAYBOY: Is it true you went back to Brownsville after you were a successful fighter, put on a ski mask and begged for coins on the street?

TYSON: I've done quite a few things in my life. Most of them I'm not proud of, some just happened.

PLAYBOY: You wound up at Tryon, a reformatory, when you were 13. What was it like?

TYSON: Just a bunch of bad kids no one cared about in a square box.

PLAYBOY: Do you remember those as terrible times?

TYSON: The best and worst times.

PLAYBOY: Is that where Cus D'Amato found you?

TYSON: He didn't find me. Someone, an ex-boxer, introduced me to him. Cus taught me how to fight. You have to understand: When I went there I had a bad reputation. I did some things I wasn't proud of when I was a kid. I was young, like 11. I was big and strong and all I had at the time was my power. If there was any kind of altercation at Tryon, there was no, like, "Let's talk about it." When you start your life out bad, it perpetuates so much you just can't be any worse. So they shipped me to this other institution, where you are basically locked up most of the time. And that's where I learned to box. I wanted to be the best; I wanted to be somebody.

PLAYBOY: Was D'Amato an important teacher?

TYSON: Basically, he knew I was a raw kid and he tried to cultivate me. Do the right thing, say the right thing. That's not who I am. My biggest problem in life is that I never learned to play the game. There are people who want to live in the sunshine 24 hours a day every day of the week, but that's not realistic. You have to deal with some rain. You have to suffer to know what the sun's going to feel like.

PLAYBOY: D'Amato took you to Jimmy Jacobs. Is that how you wound up in your first professional fight?

TYSON: Somebody saw me train and he told Jimmy about me. That was a good man, Jimmy Jacobs.

PLAYBOY: Did you—

TYSON: I don't understand. I'm no fucking animal. Don't interview me like I'm some maniac that might explode at any minute. I think you've got the wrong impression.

PLAYBOY: What makes you think we've got the wrong impression?

TYSON: Maybe it's me, because I'm real bitter and defensive. Maybe it's not you at all. I'm just always ready to attack. I know how pervasive the idea of me is out there. Please, sir, don't take it personally. I'm a very hateful motherfucker right now, a hateful individual. I'm really pissed off at the world. [*Pause*] I'm always trying to be cool, take care of my children, not kill nobody, not say anything anymore. I always do my best to be cool. I know I'm going to blow one day.

PLAYBOY: Blow in what way?

TYSON: I know I'm going to blow one day. But I'm going to make sure that when I blow, my kids are fine. There's not much more of this shit I can take. I'm going to blow one day. I try very hard, I'm doing a very good job, sir. I'm doing a very good job. I'm just really angry these days. Really, really angry. This whole year has been a total retrospect of my life.

PLAYBOY: How much did prison contribute to these feelings?

TYSON: Fuck everybody. Fuck going back to prison.

PLAYBOY: Is this interview upsetting you?

TYSON: I'm just living my life. I have kids who are going to be great artists, big stars one day. I'm producing them on my label, Mike Tyson

Records. That's an awesome project. But I want to fight. That's what I was born to do. I get carried away sometimes. I get mad, I lose fucking fights now and then. I'm just a nut like that. But that is truly what I do.

PLAYBOY: Is your mood getting worse these days?

TYSON: It gets worse and worse. When I'm by myself, I'm deep in retrospection. When I'm with my wife, she's so bright, she keeps me up, keeps me from thinking. I don't have time to think about getting angry. Like right now, I'm calming. We're sitting here in the park. This is incredible. No one's coming by. I like looking at people. You know what I like looking at more than anything? Young kids in love. Of course, I never want to see my daughter hugging and kissing a guy in public. But if I was objective, I'd say it was a great scene. I never had that when I was young. I was never involved with girls. See those two young kids, holding hands? They don't know anything about love, but there's still that feeling. I just like to watch it because it's innocent.

PLAYBOY: Did you feel that way with Robin Givens?

TYSON: I could have. I don't know. I may have felt that way.

PLAYBOY: Do you ever think about that marriage?

TYSON: I wonder how she's doing, is she OK. I have no wish to meet her. But I know how it feels to get fucked over, and I don't want anybody feeling like that. Listen, I wasn't the best husband in the world. I'm no fucking angel. I was a boy then, 20 years old, when you have two young kids who shouldn't be married in the first place. The whole world's looking at you. Every time something happens in your life it's on the front page or the television. You're a young boy—and you think you can handle that?

PLAYBOY: Are you tough to live with?

TYSON: Oh, yeah. I don't see how my wife does it. I'm a difficult person to live with.

PLAYBOY: Do you get any easier to live with as you get older?

TYSON: It gets more intense. I have no one to blame but myself. Even though many people contribute to it, I have to carry the weight of the fool alone.

PLAYBOY: Has your fame made it harder or easier?

TYSON: I don't know anything about fucking fame.

PLAYBOY: How about money?

TYSON: Money's just a false sense of security. Money's just to help your family and loved ones. I don't trip about no fucking money.

PLAYBOY: Is it true that you used to slip diamonds under Robin Givens's pillow?

TYSON: I don't know. I'm capable of doing that shit.

PLAYBOY: We read that you bought her a Porsche when you went out for a bottle of milk.

TYSON: Yeah, when somebody's with me, they're with me. I want to make them feel complete. When I'm not around, I want them to feel OK. My wife, you see, wants to understand boxing, but I don't want her to get infected by that bug. See, she doesn't need to get involved in my life, because that's not cool. She doesn't need to be infected by the people I associate with. I attract scumbags. They may be sophisticated, good at what they do, but they're still scumbags, because there's big money involved. They want that money and will do anything to get it. I don't care how they may appear.

PLAYBOY: How interested in politics are you?

TYSON: All black people are into politics whether they like it or not. People in control say, "We're going to give them welfare. Take away welfare. How hard are we going to work these blacks? How much will they take?" They know how much we'll take, how many people they can kill before we retaliate. Nothing changes. They kill us. Abuse us. And we burn our neighborhoods down! Show our rage by taking it out on one another. Why are we killing each other? Because we're mad at what you did to us. We burn down the store that gives us credit. Now we can't get credit from nobody. Guy gives us credit for 10, 15 years. Now we got nothing. We're deeper in the hole. I don't like Newt Gingrich. I think he's a racist and an intellectual bigot. But as a man I respect him. I guess I'm more a socialist than anything else. I'm not about taking from anybody, or giving to anybody who doesn't deserve it. To be sincere and honest, welfare is worse than crack can ever be. Welfare had a worse effect on us than dope ever did. It made us dependent. You want to see a rebellion? Take away welfare, tell people they have to work. You know how easy it is to get a freebie? You don't have to do anything but lie on your fat fucking ass and have children, just get screwed by different men. That's how you lose your moral and ethic and work values. That's what it does to you.

PLAYBOY: Black athletes can play an important role in the lives of black kids in the ghetto—by showing those kids a way out. Did you ever feel you had that responsibility?

TYSON: Black athletes make a lot of money, but we don't know what to do with it. I don't care how many congressmen, how many bankers, lawyers, astronauts or great fighters we've become. We never broke the cycle, because we detest what we are. We're not smart.

PLAYBOY: Do you include such great athletes as Michael Jordan and—

TYSON: Why can't Michael Jordan do something about having some black ownership in the NBA? Why does David Stern have to own everything? Why are there no black owners?

PLAYBOY: Stern is the commissioner, not the owner of an NBA team.

TYSON: But David Stern is the boss. He's so despotic and so supreme. He appears as though he is the boss of the entire league. People turn to ice cubes if he's angry at them.

PLAYBOY: Why do you think there's no black ownership?

TYSON: Because there's not enough protest for it.

PLAYBOY: Has Dennis Rodman helped or hurt basketball?

TYSON: I like Dennis, he's OK. I met him a couple times. I never thought of him as a fag or freak or nothing like that. He's cool.

PLAYBOY: Does it bother you that he separates himself from the team, doesn't show up for practices, doesn't sit on the bench and walks out on games?

TYSON: Does that interfere with him getting 15 rebounds? He's doing his job. As long as it doesn't interfere with him doing his job, cool.

PLAYBOY: What did you think when he posed in a wedding dress?

TYSON: That was cool too. He wasn't hurting anybody.

PLAYBOY: Do you like his hair?

TYSON: He's not bothering anybody.

PLAYBOY: For all his bad press, Rodman seems to have a sense of humor and seems to be enjoying his success. Throughout this interview, you have sounded down, even self-destructive. Are you?

TYSON: Nothing's going to happen to Mike Tyson. People want it to happen. They want me to rot away, to say, "He was great, but he rotted away." People love to see that. What did Scott Fitzgerald say? Show me a hero and I'll show you a tragedy? People want tragic stories. Because they are jealous. Like when people talk about Princess Di. And Jackie Onassis. They're jealous. It kills their fucking hearts. People hate the fact that these people are considered perfect. They want to prove otherwise. Perfection's not granted to me. Fuckers like you will make sure I'm far from perfect. Reporters, that is. Nothing personal, sir.

PLAYBOY: OK. Let's talk about boxing. Do you agree that the sport is in trouble, particularly the heavyweight division?

TYSON: I can't help it if the game's in bad shape. The people pick somebody; they can make a superstar of anyone. Then once they make someone a star, they don't like him no more. They think he's too big for his britches. The reason I am who I am is because of you. It's not all about being the best fighter and beating everybody; it's about being the people's choice and the people's champion. The belt symbolizes what you are, but the people define what you are.

PLAYBOY: Obviously the people gravitated toward you when you began.

TYSON: Like I said, I've never seen myself as a superstar or a major star. It's other people who say it.

PLAYBOY: Who are your favorite boxers from the past?

TYSON: I like Joe Louis, Joe Frazier, Rocky Marciano, I love them all. They all have something. I love Sonny Liston! Liston's orgasmic. Oh man. It's incredible to watch him, to watch him train. Listen, I'm an ultra, ultra, ultra heterosexual man. But Liston is orgasmic. He's somebody who physically destroys you. Oh man. Liston is just a monster to watch. Ali is better, but the performance is not like watching Sonny Liston. I would love to watch Liston rip a man apart, then watch Ali subdue and humiliate him. Sonny Liston ripped your soul apart.

PLAYBOY: Didn't you once visit Liston's grave and place flowers there?

TYSON: Yeah, I did that. I put flowers on Joe Louis's grave, on old Joe Gans's grave in Baltimore. That's an old slave cemetery there. Got on my knees, cleaned the gravesite up. Over 100 years old, that site. Used Ajax. Cleaned the whole thing up. He had a lion headstone. I put orchids on Sonny's grave. When you look at Sonny, you know he was a tough motherfucker. You know he was a man. I don't know if the Mob had him, but if he worked for the Mob, you can bet your ass he got paid. Because he was Liston. I know him just as a fighter. He had a great jab, put your teeth in back of your head. You know Al Capone was a fighter too, right? A heavyweight, had about six knockouts. Those gangsters had balls of steel.

PLAYBOY: What do your diehard fans, the ones who are still with you, see in you?

TYSON: Rebelliousness. I don't really believe I'm a rebellious individual, but that's what they see.

PLAYBOY: You're not rebellious?

TYSON: I just express myself. Maybe it seems I'm rebellious.

PLAYBOY: Are you misunderstood?

TYSON: Yeah. But the truth is, I'm pretty simple. People think I'm some big, glamorous star, that I walk into clubs and leave with five girls at my side. No. I'm just a normal guy. I'm not a superstar, no megastar. Not the icon like they think. On one hand they hold me up as some superstar. On the other, they think I'm barely civilized. But I am. They expect me to be a wild man, uncontrollable. I'm sure you were warned before you came to talk to me: "Be careful when you go over there, he might flip or something." They want you to believe that. I know who I am. I'm not a villain. I don't take much shit from people and probably I'm quick to curse somebody and be belligerent on television or in public. So that perception is out there. But it's not that I'm not good. I may misbehave, but I'm good. I have good intentions. The fact is, people don't like me. But if you're telling me, "Mike, you're a crazy motherfucker, you're an animal," I'll crack you in your fucking face.

PLAYBOY: Is that how you're taking these questions?

TYSON: I'm not pointing directly to you, I'm just saying people in general. They could say this or write that, but they will never say it to my face. The press enjoys my misfortunes.

PLAYBOY: You said you're not a villain.

TYSON: I'm a different kind of villain, if you're going to call me a villain. I'm just like John L. Sullivan. He was a villain, but he was a villainous hero. People associate villains with bad guys. But a guy like Sullivan is a villain and doesn't like anybody—the good guys or the bad guys. Would you believe that Rocky Marciano wasn't a popular champion when he was fighting? People thought he was a fake, that he fought bums. But when he died they made him a superhero.

PLAYBOY: After all this, do you blame the press?

TYSON: I don't care what they do as long as they respect me. The only people I want to love me are my wife and my family.

PLAYBOY: Do they respect you?

TYSON: They have to. I demand that. I demand that. Do you see any other reporters around? You're here because you've done nothing wrong, and you've done nothing to disrespect me. Do you see [New York Post columnist] Wally Matthews in my house? He better not come close to my house.

PLAYBOY: Do you have a personal problem with him? He has written some tough things about you.

TYSON: I don't have a problem with nobody personally. Unless they violate me personally.

PLAYBOY: You mean physically?

TYSON: That too. I haven't killed nobody. I haven't done anything to nobody. They treat me so bad that they make me feel horrible sometimes. I know who I am. I don't have to define who Mike Tyson is. I'm a father. I'm a brother, I'm a son, I'm many things. I've been many things. I've been a convict. I've been a street hustler. So what is it that they think I am?

PLAYBOY: You didn't mention the label "rapist." That still brands you.

TYSON: Yeah. People really hate me because of where I come from. Also, they see me in my cars and feel I'm rich. And I'm a fairly decent-looking guy, I'm all right. I have a beautiful wife. Smart wife, a doctor. That irritates people. I can't help it if she's a doctor and I love her and she loves me. I mean, everybody strives for something in life. You know what I mean? Everybody strives to better themselves in life. People hate me because I want to better myself.

PLAYBOY: Ali was famous for an enormous entourage that traveled with him. You seem to have fewer people around than you used to.

TYSON: I don't have as much money as I used to. I'm not in the mix, maybe that's the word. I'm not in the spotlight as much anymore. Matthews called me a "rapist recluse." I'm not a recluse. My fans see me. They see I'm in the community. They see me in stores, they see me around. I hang out with my family.

PLAYBOY: Do you still hang out in clubs?

TYSON: No, no. I have a small record label. And to really get in the mix you should go to clubs, but I don't go.

PLAYBOY: You've been involved in the rap music scene for some time. Apparently you were good friends with Tupac Shakur. What do you remember most about him?

TYSON: Misplaced loyalty. He was around people who were into drugs, but that wasn't who he was. He was a good person. He got a lot of bad rap—I've never seen a good rapper with a good image. They're good guys, though.

PLAYBOY: Did you and Tupac have serious talks?

TYSON: Yeah, we spoke. I was older than him and I was always telling him to be cool, be mellow. I'm thinking I'm trying to be the cool guy, trying to chill him out. But in reality, I never listened to what the man had to say.

PLAYBOY: What exactly were you trying to tell him?

TYSON: Just about being a man. We talked about people hurting him, not treating him good. He couldn't understand why, when he was doing bad, somebody couldn't help him.

PLAYBOY: Did Shakur seem violent?

TYSON: I don't know nothing about that. He shot somebody. He got shot too. So I don't know if he's violent or if it was self-defense. Who knows?

PLAYBOY: Who are the artists on Mike Tyson Records?

TYSON: I have Protege from Baltimore, R&B. We're in negotiations for a woman named Donnie, a sensational singer. I have a singer named Turane Howard who is going to be splendid. I have a rap group.

PLAYBOY: Is your record label designed to provide an income when you no longer fight?

TYSON: It's fun. I just want to take some kids and help them, make them singing sensations. It's hard work, but it's got to be done.

PLAYBOY: What else interests you?

TYSON: I just want to get more associated with my family. My wife is going to open a little clinic. I got a couple of houses.

PLAYBOY: In Las Vegas. Ohio. Bethesda. It's been reported that your house in Connecticut is worth $22 million. If you needed the money, would you sell it?

TYSON: I don't think so. I'm going to give it to my kids. I was there the other day and I was thinking, God, maybe I should give this house to my kids. They've all stayed there with their friends. My first two are eight and nine now, and 10 years from now they'll be in college somewhere and they'll probably stay at that house during the summer.

PLAYBOY: Do you worry about losing the house and the rest of the things you've accumulated?

TYSON: The press writes that I'm broke, and it's their best day ever. The reality is, I'm not going to be broke in my life. I'm Mike Tyson. How long you think it would take me to make $100 million?

PLAYBOY: So it's other things that worry you.

TYSON: My life.

PLAYBOY: Have you ever been suicidal?

TYSON: No.

PLAYBOY: What about the car accidents, the motorcycle accidents?

TYSON: You think I'm going to kill myself on a motorcycle? If I wanted to kill myself, I'd take a motorcycle at 160 miles an hour and run into a Mack truck. I don't want to die.

PLAYBOY: You could have died in one of those accidents.

TYSON: At 20 miles an hour? If I had wanted to kill myself, I would have killed myself 10 minutes before, when I was doing 130 miles an hour.

PLAYBOY: Were you ever badly hurt in an accident?

TYSON: I hurt my leg and my ribs. A rib cracked and punctured my lung.

PLAYBOY: You once drove your Rolls-Royce into a tree.

TYSON: See, the road was gravelly, and the car spun out. And I hit the tree. I lost control and hit the tree. If I wanted to kill myself, trust me, there's easier ways to do it. Especially in the rural Catskills, in New York. If I wanted to do it, I would go in the woods and do it and never be found. Some of those places have probably never been explored. But you don't read about me killing myself or doing something bizarre like that.

PLAYBOY: We'll never read that?

TYSON: You'll never read that, because it's not my fault I'm this way. Write a letter to God. "God, why did you bring this black convict into the world? Why did you do that, God?" He's the reason I am what I am. Blame the big boy. Blame God.

PLAYBOY: We read that a hawk once killed 98 of your pigeons. How did you feel?

TYSON: You can't imagine what was in my head, what I was going to do to that hawk. I waited for him a long, long time. Finally I trapped him. I had him, right there in the trap, but I just stared at him. He was huge and powerful and intimidating and ominous-looking. I didn't have enough nerve to do anything. I couldn't kill him. I opened the gate, let him out, watched him fly away.

INDEX